GOTHIC

TERRIFYING GHOSTS SHORT STORIES

ANTHOLOGY OF NEW & CLASSIC TALES

Foreword by Clare Frances Elliott

FLAME TREE PUBLISHING

FANTASY

This is a FLAME TREE Book

Publisher & Creative Director: Nick Wells
Project Editor: Gillian Whitaker
Editorial Board: Josie Karani, Taylor Bentley, Catherine Taylor

Publisher's Note: Due to the historical nature of the classic text, we're aware that there may be some language used which has the potential to cause offence to the modern reader. However, wishing overall to preserve the integrity of the text, rather than imposing contemporary sensibilities, we have left it unaltered.

FLAME TREE PUBLISHING
6 Melbray Mews, Fulham,
London SW6 3NS, United Kingdom
www.flametreepublishing.com

First published 2021

23 25 24 22
3 5 7 9 10 8 6 4

ISBN: 978-1-83964-481-8
Special ISBN: 978-1-83964-713-0

The cover image is created by Flame Tree Studio based on artwork by Slava Gerj and Gabor Ruszkai.

A copy of the CIP data for this book is available from the British Library.

Printed and bound in China

GOTHIC

TERRIFYING GHOSTS

SHORT STORIES

ANTHOLOGY OF NEW & CLASSIC TALES

Foreword by Clare Frances Elliott

FLAME TREE PUBLISHING

FANTASY

Contents

Foreword: Terrifying Ghosts Short Stories

IN DAVID LOWERY'S strange film *A Ghost Story* (2017), Casey Affleck plays a man who wears a white bedsheet with eye-hole cut-outs as he haunts the home where his young wife grieves. The film is not really frightening at all, but rather appears to be a meditation on grief in response to the writer's own fears about climate change and the state of the world in the early twenty-first century. Like Lowery's film, ghost stories have long enthralled listeners, readers and viewers, while often tackling grief as much as engineering abject fear. Ghosts in literature illustrate the point. In Shakespeare's tragedy *Hamlet* (1603), the supernatural return of King Hamlet is perturbing for the grief-stricken son, though hardly terrifying; modern performances of the play have treated the ghost of Hamlet's father as an illusion springing from the protagonist's own mental turmoil, usually influenced by Sigmund Freud's identification of Hamlet's oedipal desires. Later, the idea of a ghost returning to haunt the grief-stricken was a common trope in folklore and ballads of the sixteenth and seventeenth centuries. These ghosts, imaginative resurrections of lost loved-ones, testified to the processing of grief.

But ghosts started to feature in tales of pure terror in the Romantic period, when gothic fiction popularized an interest not merely in the lost homely figure to be mourned, but also in its opposite: what Freud would later term the *unheimlich* (the uncanny, or literally the unhomely). Eighteenth-century novels by Ann Radcliffe, Monk Lewis and Horace Walpole created a frenzy for uncanny plots and settings that excited feelings of terror. Yet the ghost story as a genre in its own right emerged at the point when Romantic gothic novels were declining in popularity. When we encounter ghostly or monstrous figures in nineteenth-century fiction, such as in Mary Shelley and Charles Dickens, the emphasis seems to fall once again on loss and longing rather than on chilling gothic supernaturalism. True, the ghosts in *A Christmas Carol* (1843) create a certain frisson or unanticipated otherness, but Dickens's celebrated festive story can be summarized as being about missed opportunities in life and starting over, and its ghosts provide a way into something much more ordinary: the acknowledgement of life's mistakes and disappointments. Likewise, *Frankenstein* (1818) is a novel filled with sadness, remorse, loss, and longing – and very few scares, despite its interest in uncanny doubles. If the novel makes it clear from the start that we ought to have sympathy for the devil, it is equally concerned with human limitations and our capacity to hurt and alienate one another.

Look out for those same themes in this collection of stories, which marries classic ghost fiction with more recent writing. You'll find stories that share an interest in the sorrowful and the macabre and frightful. The Irish writer Sheridan Le Fanu, for example, revived the gothic genre in his famous stories of the 1870s and '80s, and his novella *Carmilla* (1872) is one of the earliest examples of a vampire story in English literature. In his 'Schalken the Painter' (1851), reprinted here, Rose Velderkaust, the only love of the painter of the title, is pursued by an 'unnatural' and 'unhuman' predatory stalker. This figure, the uncannily unblinking (and seemingly unbreathing) Wilken Vanderhausen, may be the preternatural animation of the statue of Saint Anthony that the painter curses earlier in the story. Saint Anthony is the patron saint of lost things, and Rose herself becomes lost to his creeping shadow in a way that anticipates the iconic German horror film *Nosferatu* (1922). Like the original ghost stories of lore, Le Fanu's story has very few terrifying moments and in fact it leaves the reader to reflect on lost connections and a love torn apart by powerful forces of wealth and patriarchal control, as the grieving Schalken and Rose are destined to be apart for all eternity. It is a reminder that ghost stories have frequently been about grief, above all. When our own cultural moment seems to be awash with news about pandemics and the anticipated death of the planet, arguably we need ghost stories more than ever to teach us about loss. It is possible to enjoy the thrilling terrors in this collection, but look out, too, for the mournful: after all, the bedsheet ghost moans, not really to scare, but because it is missed.

Clare Frances Elliott

Publisher's Note

There's nothing quite like a good ghost story told amongst friends. It is with this in mind that we've collated some of the creepiest tales we could find, in a fascinating tour from the genre's early beginnings to modern stories inspired by the world today. Amongst the classic fiction, we have sought to include some well known and some not so well known – from the fantastically creepy *The Turn of the Screw* to 'The Portent of the Shadow', or 'The Phantom Coach', set in the atmospheric snowy moors of northern England. We're also pleased to be able to reprint two stories from Lafcadio Hearn's 1904 *Kwaidan* collection, offering different types of unsettling ghosts from Japanese folklore. All this in addition to the sinister apparitions brought into being by such masters as E.F. Benson, Edith Wharton and M.R. James.

In response to our call for new and recent stories, we received nearly a thousand submissions. As usual, the task of honing these down has been both challenging and rewarding, as we tried to choose stories that sit comfortably alongside the older works while providing the settings, views and voices of our era. Often across the tales in this book it is not simply the ghosts themselves that can be frightening, but the power their presence has on the living: whether the hauntings are an outright vengeful menace or cause more of a subtle devastation. At the heart of them all though, is a tantalizing ambiguity, where any firm line between living and dead, real and unreal, sanity and madness, is repeatedly at threat. We hope that in the final combined selection, the reader can enjoy all the thrills and chills of an enduring genre, whose phantoms may have evolved for the times, but whose ability to intrigue and entertain has remained constant through the generations.

GOTHIC

TERRIFYING GHOSTS

SHORT STORIES

ANTHOLOGY OF NEW & CLASSIC TALES

Foreword by Clare Frances Elliott

FLAME TREE PUBLISHING

FANTASY

A Dead Finger

S. Baring-Gould

Chapter I

WHY the National Gallery should not attract so many visitors as, say, the British Museum, I cannot explain. The latter does not contain much that, one would suppose, appeals to the interest of the ordinary sightseer. What knows such of prehistoric flints and scratched bones? Of Assyrian sculpture? Of Egyptian hieroglyphics? The Greek and Roman statuary is cold and dead. The paintings in the National Gallery glow with colour, and are instinct with life. Yet, somehow, a few listless wanderers saunter yawning through the National Gallery, whereas swarms pour through the halls of the British Museum, and talk and pass remarks about the objects there exposed, of the date and meaning of which they have not the faintest conception.

I was thinking of this problem, and endeavouring to unravel it, one morning whilst sitting in the room for English masters at the great collection in Trafalgar Square. At the same time another thought forced itself upon me. I had been through the rooms devoted to foreign schools, and had then come into that given over to Reynolds, Morland, Gainsborough, Constable, and Hogarth. The morning had been for a while propitious, but towards noon a dense umber-tinted fog had come on, making it all but impossible to see the pictures, and quite impossible to do them justice. I was tired, and so seated myself on one of the chairs, and fell into the consideration first of all of why the National Gallery is not as popular as it should be; and secondly, how it was that the British School had no beginnings, like those of Italy and the Netherlands. We can see the art of the painter from its first initiation in the Italian peninsula, and among the Flemings. It starts on its progress like a child, and we can trace every stage of its growth. Not so with English art. It springs to life in full and splendid maturity. Who were there before Reynolds and Gainsborough and Hogarth? The great names of those portrait and subject painters who have left their canvases upon the walls of our country houses were those of foreigners – Holbein, Kneller, Van Dyck, and Lely for portraits, and Monnoyer for flower and fruit pieces. Landscapes, figure subjects were all importations, none home-grown. How came that about? Was there no limner that was native? Was it that fashion trampled on home-grown pictorial beginnings as it flouted and spurned native music?

Here was food for contemplation. Dreaming in the brown fog, looking through it without seeing its beauties, at Hogarth's painting of Lavinia Fenton as Polly Peachum, without wondering how so indifferent a beauty could have captivated the Duke of Bolton and held him for thirty years, I was recalled to myself and my surroundings by the strange conduct of a lady who had seated herself on a chair near me, also discouraged by the fog, and awaiting its dispersion.

I had not noticed her particularly. At the present moment I do not remember particularly what she was like. So far as I can recollect she was middle-aged, and was quietly yet well dressed. It was not her face nor her dress that attracted my attention and disturbed the current of my thoughts; the effect I speak of was produced by her strange movements and behaviour.

She had been sitting listless, probably thinking of nothing at all, or nothing in particular, when, in turning her eyes round, and finding that she could see nothing of the paintings, she began to study me. This did concern me greatly. A cat may look at the king; but to be contemplated by a lady is a compliment sufficient to please any gentleman. It was not gratified vanity that troubled my thoughts, but the consciousness that my appearance produced – first of all a startled surprise, then undisguised alarm, and, finally, indescribable horror.

Now a man can sit quietly leaning on the head of his umbrella, and glow internally, warmed and illumined by the consciousness that he is being surveyed with admiration by a lovely woman, even when he is middle-aged and not fashionably dressed; but no man can maintain his composure when he discovers himself to be an object of aversion and terror.

What was it? I passed my hand over my chin and upper lip, thinking it not impossible that I might have forgotten to shave that morning, and in my confusion not considering that the fog would prevent the lady from discovering neglect in this particular, had it occurred, which it had not. I am a little careless, perhaps, about shaving when in the country; but when in town, never.

The next idea that occurred to me was – a smut. Had a London black, curdled in that dense pea-soup atmosphere, descended on my nose and blackened it? I hastily drew my silk handkerchief from my pocket, moistened it, and passed it over my nose, and then each cheek. I then turned my eyes into the corners and looked at the lady, to see whether by this means I had got rid of what was objectionable in my personal appearance.

Then I saw that her eyes, dilated with horror, were riveted, not on my face, but on my leg.

My leg! What on earth could that harmless member have in it so terrifying? The morning had been dull; there had been rain in the night, and I admit that on leaving my hotel I had turned up the bottoms of my trousers. That is a proceeding not so uncommon, not so outrageous as to account for the stony stare of this woman's eyes.

If that were all I would turn my trousers down.

Then I saw her shrink from the chair on which she sat to one further removed from me, but still with her eyes fixed on my leg – about the level of my knee. She had let fall her umbrella, and was grasping the seat of her chair with both hands, as she backed from me.

I need hardly say that I was greatly disturbed in mind and feelings, and forgot all about the origin of the English schools of painters, and the question why the British Museum is more popular than the National Gallery.

Thinking that I might have been spattered by a hansom whilst crossing Oxford Street, I passed my hand down my side hastily, with a sense of annoyance, and all at once touched something cold, clammy, that sent a thrill to my heart, and made me start and take a step forward. At the same moment, the lady, with a cry of horror, sprang to her feet, and with raised hands fled from the room, leaving her umbrella where it had fallen.

There were other visitors to the Picture Gallery besides ourselves, who had been passing through the saloon, and they turned at her cry, and looked in surprise after her.

The policeman stationed in the room came to me and asked what had happened. I was in such agitation that I hardly knew what to answer. I told him that I could explain what had occurred little better than himself. I had noticed that the lady had worn an odd expression, and had behaved in most extraordinary fashion, and that he had best take charge of her umbrella, and wait for her return to claim it.

This questioning by the official was vexing, as it prevented me from at once and on the spot investigating the cause of her alarm and mine – hers at something she must have seen on my leg, and mine at something I had distinctly felt creeping up my leg.

The numbing and sickening effect on me of the touch of the object I had not seen was not to be shaken off at once. Indeed, I felt as though my hand were contaminated, and that I could have no rest till I had thoroughly washed the hand, and, if possible, washed away the feeling that had been produced.

I looked on the floor, I examined my leg, but saw nothing. As I wore my overcoat, it was probable that in rising from my seat the skirt had fallen over my trousers and hidden the thing, whatever it was. I therefore hastily removed my overcoat and shook it, then I looked at my trousers. There was nothing whatever on my leg, and nothing fell from my overcoat when shaken.

Accordingly I reinvested myself, and hastily left the Gallery; then took my way as speedily as I could, without actually running, to Charing Cross Station and down the narrow way leading to the Metropolitan, where I went into Faulkner's bath and hairdressing establishment, and asked for hot water to thoroughly wash my hand and well soap it. I bathed my hand in water as hot as I could endure it, employed carbolic soap, and then, after having a good brush down, especially on my left side where my hand had encountered the object that had so affected me, I left. I had entertained the intention of going to the Princess's Theatre that evening, and of securing a ticket in the morning; but all thought of theatre-going was gone from me. I could not free my heart from the sense of nausea and cold that had been produced by the touch. I went into Gatti's to have lunch, and ordered something, I forget what, but, when served, I found that my appetite was gone. I could eat nothing; the food inspired me with disgust. I thrust it from me untasted, and, after drinking a couple of glasses of claret, left the restaurant, and returned to my hotel.

Feeling sick and faint, I threw my overcoat over the sofa-back, and cast myself on my bed.

I do not know that there was any particular reason for my doing so, but as I lay my eyes were on my great-coat.

The density of the fog had passed away, and there was light again, not of first quality, but sufficient for a Londoner to swear by, so that I could see everything in my room, though through a veil, darkly.

I do not think my mind was occupied in any way. About the only occasions on which, to my knowledge, my mind is actually passive or inert is when crossing the Channel in *The Foam* from Dover to Calais, when I am always, in every weather, abjectly seasick – and thoughtless. But as I now lay on my bed, uncomfortable, squeamish, without knowing why – I was in the same inactive mental condition. But not for long.

I saw something that startled me.

First, it appeared to me as if the lappet of my overcoat pocket were in movement, being raised. I did not pay much attention to this, as I supposed that the garment was sliding down on to the seat of the sofa, from the back, and that this displacement of gravity caused the movement I observed. But this I soon saw was not the case. That which moved the lappet was something in the pocket that was struggling to get out. I could see now that it was working its way up the inside, and that when it reached the opening it lost balance and fell down again. I could make this out by the projections and indentations in the cloth; these moved as the creature, or whatever it was, worked its way up the lining.

"A mouse," I said, and forgot my seediness; I was interested. "The little rascal! However did he contrive to seat himself in my pocket? And I have worn that overcoat all the morning!" But no – it was not a mouse. I saw something white poke its way out from under the lappet; and in another moment an object was revealed that, though revealed, I could not understand, nor could I distinguish what it was.

Now roused by curiosity, I raised myself on my elbow. In doing this I made some noise, the bed creaked. Instantly the something dropped on the floor, lay outstretched for a moment, to recover itself, and then began, with the motions of a maggot, to run along the floor.

There is a caterpillar called 'The Measurer', because, when it advances, it draws its tail up to where its head is and then throws forward its full length, and again draws up its extremity, forming at each time a loop; and with each step measuring its total length. The object I now saw on the floor was advancing precisely like the measuring caterpillar. It had the colour of a cheese-maggot, and in length was about three and a half inches. It was not, however, like a caterpillar, which is flexible throughout its entire length, but this was, as it seemed to me, jointed in two places, one joint being more conspicuous than the other. For some moments I was so completely paralysed by astonishment that I remained motionless, looking at the thing as it crawled along the carpet – a dull green carpet with darker green, almost black, flowers in it.

It had, as it seemed to me, a glossy head, distinctly marked; but, as the light was not brilliant, I could not make out very clearly, and, moreover, the rapid movements prevented close scrutiny.

Presently, with a shock still more startling than that produced by its apparition at the opening of the pocket of my great-coat, I became convinced that what I saw was a finger, a human forefinger, and that the glossy head was no other than the nail.

The finger did not seem to have been amputated. There was no sign of blood or laceration where the knuckle should be, but the extremity of the finger, or root rather, faded away to indistinctness, and I was unable to make out the root of the finger.

I could see no hand, no body behind this finger, nothing whatever except a finger that had little token of warm life in it, no coloration as though blood circulated in it; and this finger was in active motion creeping along the carpet towards a wardrobe that stood against the wall by the fireplace.

I sprang off the bed and pursued it.

Evidently the finger was alarmed, for it redoubled its pace, reached the wardrobe, and went under it. By the time I had arrived at the article of furniture it had disappeared. I lit a vesta match and held it beneath the wardrobe, that was raised above the carpet by about two inches, on turned feet, but I could see nothing more of the finger.

I got my umbrella and thrust it beneath, and raked forwards and backwards, right and left, and raked out flue, and nothing more solid.

Chapter II

I PACKED my portmanteau next day and returned to my home in the country. All desire for amusement in town was gone, and the faculty to transact business had departed as well.

A languor and qualms had come over me, and my head was in a maze. I was unable to fix my thoughts on anything. At times I was disposed to believe that my wits were deserting me, at others that I was on the verge of a severe illness. Anyhow, whether likely to go off my head or not, or take to my bed, home was the only place for me, and homeward I sped, accordingly. On reaching my country habitation, my servant, as usual, took my portmanteau to my bedroom, unstrapped it, but did not unpack it. I object to his throwing out the contents of my Gladstone bag; not that there is anything in it he may not see, but that he puts my things where I cannot find them again. My clothes – he is welcome to place them where he likes and where they belong, and this latter he knows better than I do; but, then, I carry about with me other things than a dress suit, and changes of linen and flannel. There are letters, papers, books – and the proper destinations of these are known only to myself. A servant has a singular and evil knack of putting away literary matter and odd volumes in such places that it takes the owner half a day to find them again. Although I was uncomfortable, and my head in a whirl, I opened and unpacked my own portmanteau. As I was thus engaged I saw something curled up in my collar-box, the lid of which had got broken in by a boot-heel impinging on it. I had pulled off the damaged cover to see if my collars had been spoiled, when something curled up inside suddenly rose on end and leapt, just like a cheese-jumper, out of the box, over the edge of the Gladstone bag, and scurried away across the floor in a manner already familiar to me.

I could not doubt for a moment what it was – here was the finger again. It had come with me from London to the country.

Whither it went in its run over the floor I do not know, I was too bewildered to observe.

Somewhat later, towards evening, I seated myself in my easy-chair, took up a book, and tried to read. I was tired with the journey, with the knocking about in town, and the discomfort and alarm produced by the apparition of the finger. I felt worn out. I was unable to give my attention to what I read, and before I was aware was asleep. Roused for an instant by the fall of the book from my hands, I speedily relapsed into unconsciousness. I am not sure that a doze in an armchair ever does good. It usually leaves me in a semi-stupid condition and with a headache. Five minutes in a horizontal position on my bed is worth thirty in a chair. That is my experience. In sleeping in a sedentary position the head is a difficulty; it drops forward or lolls on one side or the other, and has to be brought back into a position in which the line to the centre of gravity runs through the trunk, otherwise the head carries the body over in a sort of general capsize out of the chair on to the floor.

I slept, on the occasion of which I am speaking, pretty healthily, because deadly weary; but I was brought to waking, not by my head falling over the arm of the chair, and my trunk tumbling after it, but by a feeling of cold extending from my throat to my heart. When I awoke I was in a diagonal position, with my right ear resting on my right shoulder, and exposing the left side of my throat, and it was here – where the jugular vein throbs – that I felt the greatest intensity of cold. At once I shrugged my left shoulder, rubbing my neck with the collar of my coat in so doing. Immediately something fell off, upon the floor, and I again saw the finger.

My disgust – horror, were intensified when I perceived that it was dragging something after it, which might have been an old stocking, and which I took at first glance for something of the sort.

The evening sun shone in through my window, in a brilliant golden ray that lighted the object as it scrambled along. With this illumination I was able to distinguish what the object was. It is not easy to describe it, but I will make the attempt.

The finger I saw was solid and material; what it drew after it was neither, or was in a nebulous, protoplasmic condition. The finger was attached to a hand that was curdling into matter and in process of acquiring solidity; attached to the hand was an arm in a very filmy condition, and this arm belonged to a human body in a still more vaporous, immaterial condition. This was being dragged along the floor by the finger, just as a silkworm might pull after it the tangle of its web. I could see legs and arms, and head, and coat-tail tumbling about and interlacing and disentangling again in a promiscuous manner. There were no bone, no muscle, no substance in the figure; the members were attached to the trunk, which was spineless, but they had evidently no functions, and were wholly dependent on the finger which pulled them along in a jumble of parts as it advanced.

In such confusion did the whole vaporous matter seem, that I think – I cannot say for certain it was so, but the impression left on my mind was – that one of the eyeballs was looking out at a nostril, and the tongue lolling out of one of the ears.

It was, however, only for a moment that I saw this germ-body; I cannot call by another name that which had not more substance than smoke. I saw it only so long as it was being dragged athwart the ray of sunlight. The moment it was pulled jerkily out of the beam into the shadow beyond, I could see nothing of it, only the crawling finger.

I had not sufficient moral energy or physical force in me to rise, pursue, and stamp on the finger, and grind it with my heel into the floor. Both seemed drained out of me. What became of the finger, whither it went, how it managed to secrete itself, I do not know. I had lost the power to inquire. I sat in my chair, chilled, staring before me into space.

"Please, sir," a voice said, "there's Mr. Square below, electrical engineer."

"Eh?" I looked dreamily round.

My valet was at the door.

"Please, sir, the gentleman would be glad to be allowed to go over the house and see that all the electrical apparatus is in order."

"Oh, indeed! Yes – show him up."

Chapter III

I HAD RECENTLY placed the lighting of my house in the hands of an electrical engineer, a very intelligent man, Mr. Square, for whom I had contracted a sincere friendship.

He had built a shed with a dynamo out of sight, and had entrusted the laying of the wires to subordinates, as he had been busy with other orders and could not personally watch every detail. But he was not the man to let anything pass unobserved, and he knew that electricity was not a force to be played with. Bad or careless workmen will often insufficiently protect the wires, or neglect the insertion of the lead which serves as a safety-valve in the event of the current being too strong. Houses may be set on fire, human beings fatally shocked, by the neglect of a bad or slovenly workman.

The apparatus for my mansion was but just completed, and Mr. Square had come to inspect it and make sure that all was right.

He was an enthusiast in the matter of electricity, and saw for it a vast perspective, the limits of which could not be predicted.

"All forces," said he, "are correlated. When you have force in one form, you may just turn it into this or that, as you like. In one form it is motive power, in another it is light, in another heat. Now we have electricity for illumination. We employ it, but not as freely as in the States, for propelling vehicles. Why should we have horses drawing our buses? We should use only electric trams. Why do we burn coal to warm our shins? There is electricity, which throws out no filthy smoke as does coal. Why should we let the tides waste their energies in the Thames? in other estuaries? There we have Nature supplying us – free, gratis, and for nothing – with all the force we want for propelling, for heating, for lighting. I will tell you something more, my dear sir," said Mr. Square. "I have mentioned but three modes of force, and have instanced but a limited number of uses to which electricity may be turned. How is it with photography? Is not electric light becoming an artistic agent? I bet you," said he, "before long it will become a therapeutic agent as well."

"Oh, yes; I have heard of certain impostors with their life-belts."

Mr. Square did not relish this little dig I gave him. He winced, but returned to the charge. "We don't know how to direct it aright, that is all," said he. "I haven't taken the matter up, but others will, I bet; and we shall have electricity used as freely as now we use powders and pills. I don't believe in doctors' stuffs myself. I hold that disease lays hold of a man because he lacks physical force to resist it. Now, is it not obvious that you are beginning at the wrong end when you attack the disease? What you want is to supply force, make up for the lack of physical power, and force is force wherever you find it – here motive, there illuminating, and so on. I don't see why a physician should not utilise the tide rushing out under London Bridge for restoring the feeble vigour of all who are languid and a prey to disorder in the Metropolis. It will come to that, I bet, and that is not all. Force is force, everywhere. Political, moral force, physical force, dynamic force, heat, light, tidal waves, and so on – all are one, all is one. In time we shall know how to galvanise into aptitude and moral energy all the limp and crooked consciences and wills that need taking in hand, and such there always will be in modern civilisation. I don't know how to do it. I don't know how it will be done, but in the future the priest as well as the doctor will turn electricity on as his principal, nay, his only agent. And he can get his force anywhere, out of the running stream, out of the wind, out of the tidal wave.

"I'll give you an instance," continued Mr. Square, chuckling and rubbing his hands, "to show you the great possibilities in electricity, used in a crude fashion. In a certain great city away far west in the States, a go-ahead place, too, more so than New York, they had electric trams all up and down and along the roads to everywhere. The union men working for the company demanded that the non-unionists should be turned off. But the company didn't see it. Instead, it turned off the union men. It had up its sleeve a sufficiency of the others, and filled all places at once. Union men didn't like it, and passed word that at a given hour on a certain day every wire was to be cut. The company knew this by means of its spies, and turned on, ready for them, three times the power into all the wires. At the fixed moment, up the poles went the strikers to cut the cables, and down they came a dozen times quicker than they went up, I bet. Then there came wires to the hospitals from all quarters for stretchers to carry off the disabled men, some with broken legs, arms, ribs; two or three had their necks broken. I reckon the company was wonderfully merciful – it didn't put on sufficient force to make cinders of them then and there; possibly opinion might not have liked it. Stopped the strike, did that. Great moral effect – all done by electricity."

In this manner Mr. Square was wont to rattle on. He interested me, and I came to think that there might be something in what he said – that his suggestions were not mere nonsense. I was glad to see Mr. Square enter my room, shown in by my man. I did not rise from my chair to shake his hand, for I had not sufficient energy to do so. In a languid tone I welcomed him and signed to him to take a seat. Mr. Square looked at me with some surprise.

"Why, what's the matter?" he said. "You seem unwell. Not got the 'flue, have you?"

"I beg your pardon?"

"The influenza. Every third person is crying out that he has it, and the sale of eucalyptus is enormous, not that eucalyptus is any good. Influenza microbes indeed! What care they for eucalyptus? You've gone down some steps of the ladder of life since I saw you last, squire. How do you account for that?"

I hesitated about mentioning the extraordinary circumstances that had occurred; but Square was a man who would not allow any beating about the bush. He was downright and straight, and in ten minutes had got the entire story out of me.

"Rather boisterous for your nerves that – a crawling finger," said he. "It's a queer story taken on end."

Then he was silent, considering.

After a few minutes he rose, and said: "I'll go and look at the fittings, and then I'll turn this little matter of yours over again, and see if I can't knock the bottom out of it, I'm kinder fond of these sort of things."

Mr. Square was not a Yankee, but he had lived for some time in America, and affected to speak like an American. He used expressions, terms of speech common in the States, but had none of the Transatlantic twang. He was a man absolutely without affectation in every other particular; this was his sole weakness, and it was harmless.

The man was so thorough in all he did that I did not expect his return immediately. He was certain to examine every portion of the dynamo engine, and all the connections and burners. This would necessarily engage him for some hours. As the day was nearly done, I knew he could not accomplish what he wanted that evening, and accordingly gave orders that a room should be prepared for him. Then, as my head was full of pain, and my skin was burning, I told my servant to apologise for my absence from dinner, and tell Mr. Square that I was really forced to return to my bed by sickness, and that I believed I was about to be prostrated by an attack of influenza.

The valet – a worthy fellow, who has been with me for six years – was concerned at my appearance, and urged me to allow him to send for a doctor. I had no confidence in the local practitioner, and if I sent for another from the nearest town I should offend him, and a row would perhaps ensue, so I declined. If I were really in for an influenza attack, I knew about as much as any doctor how to deal with it. Quinine, quinine – that was all. I bade my man light a small lamp, lower it, so as to give sufficient illumination to enable me to find some lime-juice at my bed head, and my pocket-handkerchief, and to be able to read my watch. When he had done this, I bade him leave me.

I lay in bed, burning, racked with pain in my head, and with my eyeballs on fire.

Whether I fell asleep or went off my head for a while I cannot tell. I may have fainted. I have no recollection of anything after having gone to bed and taken a sip of lime-juice that tasted to me like soap – till I was roused by a sense of pain in my ribs – a slow, gnawing, torturing pain, waxing momentarily more intense. In half-consciousness I was partly dreaming and partly aware of actual suffering. The pain was real; but in my fancy I thought that a great maggot was working its way into my side between my ribs. I seemed to see it. It twisted itself half round, then reverted to its former position, and again twisted itself, moving like a bradawl, not like a gimlet, which latter forms a complete revolution.

This, obviously, must have been a dream, hallucination only, as I was lying on my back and my eyes were directed towards the bottom of the bed, and the coverlet and blankets and sheet intervened between my eyes and my side. But in fever one sees without eyes, and in every direction, and through all obstructions.

Roused thoroughly by an excruciating twinge, I tried to cry out, and succeeded in throwing myself over on my right side, that which was in pain. At once I felt the thing withdrawn that was awling – if I may use the word – in between my ribs.

And now I saw, standing beside the bed, a figure that had its arm under the bedclothes, and was slowly removing it. The hand was leisurely drawn from under the coverings and rested on the eider-down coverlet, with the forefinger extended.

The figure was that of a man, in shabby clothes, with a sallow, mean face, a retreating forehead, with hair cut after the French fashion, and a moustache, dark. The jaws and chin were covered with a bristly growth, as if shaving had been neglected for a fortnight. The figure did not appear to be thoroughly solid, but to be of the consistency of curd, and the face was of the complexion of curd. As I looked at this object it withdrew, sliding backward in an odd sort of manner, and as though overweighted by the hand, which was the most substantial, indeed the only substantial portion of it. Though the figure retreated stooping, yet it was no longer huddled along by the finger, as if it had no material existence. If the same, it had acquired a consistency and a solidity which it did not possess before.

How it vanished I do not know, nor whither it went. The door opened, and Square came in.

"What!" he exclaimed with cheery voice; "Influenza is it?"

"I don't know – I think it's that finger again."

Chapter IV

"NOW, look here," said Square, "I'm not going to have that cuss at its pranks any more. Tell me all about it."

I was now so exhausted, so feeble, that I was not able to give a connected account of what had taken place, but Square put to me just a few pointed questions and elicited the main facts. He pieced them together in his own orderly mind, so as to form a connected whole. "There is a feature in the case," said he, "that strikes me as remarkable and important. At first – a finger only, then a hand, then a nebulous figure attached to the hand, without backbone, without consistency. Lastly, a complete form, with consistency and with backbone, but the latter in a gelatinous condition, and the entire figure overweighted by the hand, just as hand and figure were previously overweighted by the finger. Simultaneously with this compacting and consolidating of the figure, came your degeneration and loss of vital force and, in a word, of health. What you lose, that object acquires, and what it acquires, it gains by contact with you. That's clear enough, is it not?"

"I dare say. I don't know. I can't think."

"I suppose not; the faculty of thought is drained out of you. Very well, I must think for you, and I will. Force is force, and see if I can't deal with your visitant in such a way as will prove just as truly a moral dissuasive as that employed on the union men on strike in – never mind where it was. That's not to the point."

"Will you kindly give me some lime-juice?" I entreated.

I sipped the acid draught, but without relief. I listened to Square, but without hope. I wanted to be left alone. I was weary of my pain, weary of everything, even of life. It was a matter of indifference to me whether I recovered or slipped out of existence.

"It will be here again shortly," said the engineer. "As the French say, *l'appetit vient en mangeant*. It has been at you thrice, it won't be content without another peck. And if it does get another, I guess it will pretty well about finish you."

Mr. Square rubbed his chin, and then put his hands into his trouser pockets. That also was a trick acquired in the States, an inelegant one. His hands, when not actively occupied, went into his pockets, inevitably they gravitated thither. Ladies did not like Square; they said he was not a gentleman. But it was not that he said or did anything 'off colour', only he spoke to them, looked at them, walked with them, always with his hands in his pockets. I have seen a lady turn her back on him deliberately because of this trick.

Standing now with his hands in his pockets, he studied my bed, and said contemptuously: "Old-fashioned and bad, fourposter. Oughtn't to be allowed, I guess; unwholesome all the way round."

I was not in a condition to dispute this. I like a fourposter with curtains at head and feet; not that I ever draw them, but it gives a sense of privacy that is wanting in one of your half-tester beds.

If there is a window at one's feet, one can lie in bed without the glare in one's eyes, and yet without darkening the room by drawing the blinds. There is much to be said for a fourposter, but this is not the place in which to say it.

Mr. Square pulled his hands out of his pockets and began fiddling with the electric point near the head of my bed, attached a wire, swept it in a semicircle along the floor, and then thrust the knob at the end into my hand in the bed.

"Keep your eye open," said he, "and your hand shut and covered. If that finger comes again tickling your ribs, try it with the point. I'll manage the switch, from behind the curtain."

Then he disappeared.

I was too indifferent in my misery to turn my head and observe where he was. I remained inert, with the knob in my hand, and my eyes closed, suffering and thinking of nothing but the shooting pains through my head and the aches in my loins and back and legs.

Some time probably elapsed before I felt the finger again at work at my ribs; it groped, but no longer bored. I now felt the entire hand, not a single finger, and the hand was substantial, cold, and clammy. I was aware, how, I know not, that if the finger-point reached the region of my heart, on the left side, the hand would, so to speak, sit down on it, with the cold palm over it, and that then immediately my heart would cease to beat, and it would be, as Square might express it, 'gone coon' with me.

In self-preservation I brought up the knob of the electric wire against the hand – against one of the ringers, I think – and at once was aware of a rapping, squealing noise. I turned my head languidly, and saw the form, now more substantial than before, capering in an ecstasy of pain, endeavouring fruitlessly to withdraw its arm from under the bedclothes, and the hand from the electric point.

At the same moment Square stepped from behind the curtain, with a dry laugh, and said: "I thought we should fix him. He has the coil about him, and can't escape. Now let us drop to particulars. But I shan't let you off till I know all about you."

The last sentence was addressed, not to me, but to the apparition.

Thereupon he bade me take the point away from the hand of the figure – being – whatever it was, but to be ready with it at a moment's notice. He then proceeded to catechise my visitor, who moved restlessly within the circle of wire, but could not escape from it. It replied in a thin, squealing voice that sounded as if it came from a distance, and had a querulous tone in it. I do not pretend to give all that was said. I cannot recollect everything that passed. My memory was affected by my illness, as well as my body. Yet I prefer giving the scraps that I recollect to what Square told me he had heard.

"Yes – I was unsuccessful, always was. Nothing answered with me. The world was against me. Society was. I hate Society. I don't like work neither, never did. But I like agitating against what is established. I hate the Royal Family, the landed interest, the parsons, everything that is, except the people – that is, the unemployed. I always did. I couldn't get work as suited me. When I died they buried me in a cheap coffin, dirt cheap, and gave me a nasty grave, cheap, and a service rattled away cheap, and no monument. Didn't want none. Oh! there are lots of us. All discontented. Discontent! That's a passion, it is – it gets into the veins, it fills the brain, it occupies the heart; it's a sort of divine cancer that takes possession of the entire man, and makes him dissatisfied with everything, and hate everybody. But we must have our share of happiness at some time. We all crave for it in one way or other. Some think there's a future state of blessedness and so have hope, and look to attain to it, for hope is a cable and anchor that attaches to what is real. But when you have no hope of that sort, don't believe in any future state, you must look for happiness in life here. We didn't get it when we were alive, so we seek to procure it after we are dead. We can do it, if we can get out of our cheap and nasty coffins. But not till the greater part of us is mouldered away. If a finger or two remains, that can work its way up to the surface, those cheap deal coffins go to pieces quick enough. Then the only solid part of us left can pull the rest of us that has gone to nothing after it. Then we grope about after the living. The well-to-do if we can get at them – the honest working poor if we can't – we hate them too, because they are content and happy. If we reach any of these, and can touch them, then we can draw their vital force out of them into ourselves, and recuperate at their expense. That was about what I was going to do with you. Getting on famous. Nearly solidified into a new man; and given another chance in life. But I've missed it this time. Just like my luck. Miss everything. Always have, except misery and disappointment. Get plenty of that."

"What are you all?" asked Square. "Anarchists out of employ?"

"Some of us go by that name, some by other designations, but we are all one, and own allegiance to but one monarch – Sovereign discontent. We are bred to have a distaste for manual work; and we grow up loafers, grumbling at everything and quarrelling with Society that is around us and the Providence that is above us."

"And what do you call yourselves now?"

"Call ourselves? Nothing; we are the same, in another condition, that is all. Folk called us once Anarchists, Nihilists, Socialists, Levellers, now they call us the Influenza. The learned talk of microbes, and bacilli, and bacteria. Microbes, bacilli, and bacteria be blowed! We are the Influenza; we the social failures, the generally discontented, coming up out of our cheap and nasty graves in the form of physical disease. We are the Influenza."

"There you are, I guess!" exclaimed Square triumphantly. "Did I not say that all forces were correlated? If so, then all negations, deficiencies of force are one in their several manifestations. Talk of Divine discontent as a force impelling to progress! Rubbish, it is a paralysis of energy. It turns all it absorbs to acid, to envy, spite, gall. It inspires nothing, but rots the whole moral system. Here you have it – moral, social, political discontent in another form, nay aspect – that is all. What Anarchism is in the body Politic, that Influenza is in the body Physical. Do you see that?"

"Ye-e-s-e-s," I believe I answered, and dropped away into the land of dreams.

I recovered. What Square did with the Thing I know not, but believe that he reduced it again to its former negative and self-decomposing condition.

Out of the Sea

A.C. Benson

IT WAS about ten of the clock on a November morning in the little village of Blea-on-the-Sands. The hamlet was made up of some thirty houses, which clustered together on a low rising ground. The place was very poor, but some old merchant of bygone days had built in a pious mood a large church, which was now too great for the needs of the place; the nave had been unroofed in a heavy gale, and there was no money to repair it, so that it had fallen to decay, and the tower was joined to the choir by roofless walls. This was a sore trial to the old priest, Father Thomas, who had grown grey there; but he had no art in gathering money, which he asked for in a shamefaced way; and the vicarage was a poor one, hardly enough for the old man's needs. So the church lay desolate.

The village stood on what must once have been an island; the little river Reddy, which runs down to the sea, there forking into two channels on the landward side; towards the sea the ground was bare, full of sand-hills covered with a short grass. Towards the land was a small wood of gnarled trees, the boughs of which were all brushed smooth by the gales; looking landward there was the green flat, in which the river ran, rising into low hills; hardly a house was visible save one or two lonely farms; two or three church towers rose above the hills at a long distance away. Indeed Blea was much cut off from the world; there was a bridge over the stream on the west side, but over the other channel was no bridge, so that to fare eastward it was requisite to go in a boat. To seaward there were wide sands, when the tide was out; when it was in, it came up nearly to the end of the village street. The people were mostly fishermen, but there were a few farmers and labourers; the boats of the fishermen lay to the east side of the village, near the river channel which gave some draught of water; and the channel was marked out by big black stakes and posts that straggled out over the sands, like awkward leaning figures, to the sea's brim.

Father Thomas lived in a small and ancient brick house near the church, with a little garden of herbs attached. He was a kindly man, much worn by age and weather, with a wise heart, and he loved the quiet life with his small flock. This morning he had come out of his house to look abroad, before he settled down to the making of his sermon. He looked out to sea, and saw with a shadow of sadness the black outline of a wreck that had come ashore a week before, and over which the white waves were now breaking. The wind blew steadily from the north-east, and had a bitter poisonous chill in it, which it doubtless drew from the fields of the upper ice. The day was dark and overhung, not with cloud, but with a kind of dreary vapour that shut out the sun. Father Thomas shuddered at the wind, and drew his patched cloak round him. As he did so, he saw three figures come up to the vicarage gate. It was not a common thing for him to have visitors in the morning, and he saw with surprise that they were old Master John Grimston, the richest man in the place, half farmer and half fisherman, a dark surly old man; his wife, Bridget, a timid and frightened woman, who found life with her harsh husband a difficult business, in spite of their wealth, which, for a place like Blea, was great; and their son Henry, a silly shambling man of forty, who was his father's butt. The three walked silently and heavily, as though they came on a sad errand.

Father Thomas went briskly down to meet them, and greeted them with his accustomed cheerfulness. "And what may I do for you?" he said. Old Master Grimston made a sort of gesture with his head as though his wife should speak; and she said in a low and somewhat husky voice, with a rapid utterance, "We have a matter, Father, we would ask you about – are you at leisure?" Father Thomas said, "Ay, I am ashamed to be not more busy! Let us go within the house." They did so; and even in the little distance to the door, the Father thought that his visitors behaved themselves very strangely. They peered round from left to right, and once or twice Master Grimston looked sharply behind them, as though they were followed. They said nothing but "Ay" and "No" to the Father's talk, and bore themselves like people with a sore fear on their backs. Father Thomas made up his mind that it was some question of money, for nothing else was wont to move Master Grimston's mind. So he had them into his parlour and gave them seats, and then there was a silence, while the two men continued to look furtively about them, and the goodwife sate with her eyes upon the priest's face. Father Thomas knew not what to make of this, till Master Grimston said harshly, "Come, wife, tell the tale and make an end; we must not take up the Father's time."

"I hardly know how to say it, Father," said Bridget, "but a strange and evil thing has befallen us; there is something come to our house, and we know not what it is – but it brings a fear with it." A sudden paleness came over her face, and she stopped, and the three exchanged a glance in which terror was visibly written. Master Grimston looked over his shoulder swiftly, and made as though to speak, yet only swallowed in his throat; but Henry said suddenly, in a loud and woeful voice: "It is an evil beast out of the sea." And then there followed a dreadful silence, while Father Thomas felt a sudden fear leap up in his heart, at the contagion of the fear that he saw written on the faces round him. But he said with all the cheerfulness he could muster, "Come, friends, let us not begin to talk of sea-beasts; we must have the whole tale. Mistress Grimston, I must hear the story – be content – nothing can touch us here." The three seemed to draw a faint content from his words, and Bridget began:

"It was the day of the wreck, Father. John was up betimes, before the dawn; he walked out early to the sands, and Henry with him – and they were the first to see the wreck – was not that it?" At these words the father and son seemed to exchange a very swift and secret look, and both grew pale. "John told me there was a wreck ashore, and they went presently and roused the rest of the village; and all that day they were out, saving what could be saved. Two sailors were found, both dead and pitifully battered by the sea, and they were buried, as you know, Father, in the churchyard next day; John came back about dusk and Henry with him, and we sate down to our supper. John was telling me about the wreck, as we sate beside the fire, when Henry, who was sitting apart, rose up and cried out suddenly, 'What is that?'"

She paused for a moment, and Henry, who sate with face blanched, staring at his mother, said, "Ay, did I – it ran past me suddenly."

"Yes, but what was it?" said Father Thomas trying to smile; "a dog or cat, methinks."

"It was a beast," said Henry slowly, in a trembling voice – "a beast about the bigness of a goat. I never saw the like – yet I did not see it clear; I but felt the air blow, and caught a whiff of it – it was salt like the sea, but with a kind of dead smell behind."

"Was that all you saw?" said Father Thomas; "belike you were tired and faint, and the air swam round you suddenly – I have known the like myself when weary."

"Nay, nay," said Henry, "this was not like that – it was a beast, sure enough."

"Ay, and we have seen it since," said Bridget. "At least I have not seen it clearly yet, but I have smelt its odour, and it turns me sick – but John and Henry have seen it often – sometimes it lies and seems to sleep, but it watches us; and again it is merry, and will leap in a corner – and John saw it skip upon the sands near the wreck – did you not, John?" At these words the two men again exchanged a glance, and then old Master Grimston, with a dreadful look in his face, in which great anger seemed to strive with fear, said "Nay, silly woman, it was not near the wreck, it was out to the east."

"It matters little," said Father Thomas, who saw well enough this was no light matter. "I never heard the like of it. I will myself come down to your house with a holy book, and see if the thing will meet me. I know not what this is," he went on, "whether it is a vain terror that hath hold of you; but there be spirits of evil in the world, though much fettered by Christ and His Saints – we read of such in Holy Writ – and the sea, too, doubtless hath its monsters; and it may be that one hath wandered out of the waves, like a dog that hath strayed from his home. I dare not say, till I have met it face to face. But God gives no power to such things to hurt those who have a fair conscience." And here he made a stop, and looked at the three; Bridget sate regarding him with a hope in her face; but the other two sate peering upon the ground; and the priest divined in some secret way that all was not well with them. "But I will come at once," he said rising, "and I will see if I can cast out or bind the thing, whatever it be – for I am in this place as a soldier of the Lord, to fight with works of darkness." He took a clasped book from a table, and lifted up his hat, saying, "Let us set forth." Then he said as they left the room, "Hath it appeared today?"

"Yes, indeed," said Henry, "and it was ill content. It followed us as though it were angered."

"Come," said Father Thomas turning upon him, "you speak thus of a thing, as you might speak of a dog – what is it like?"

"Nay," said Henry, "I know not; I can never see it clearly; it is like a speck in the eye – it is never there when you look upon it – it glides away very secretly; it is most like a goat, I think. It seems to be horned, and hairy; but I have seen its eyes, and they were yellow, like a flame."

As he said these words Master Grimston went in haste to the door, and pulled it open as though to breathe the air. The others followed him and went out; but Master Grimston drew the priest aside, and said like a man in a mortal fear, "Look you, Father, all this is true – the thing is a devil – and why it abides with us I know not; but I cannot live so; and unless it be cast out it will slay me – but if money be of avail, I have it in abundance."

"Nay," said Father Thomas, "let there be no talk of money – perchance if I can aid you, you may give of your gratitude to God."

"Ay, ay," said the old man hurriedly, "that was what I meant – there is money in abundance for God, if he will but set me free."

So they walked very sadly together through the street. There were few folk about; the men and the children were all abroad – a woman or two came to the house doors, and wondered a little to see them pass so solemnly, as though they followed a body to the grave.

Master Grimston's house was the largest in the place. It had a walled garden before it, with a strong door set in the wall. The house stood back from the road, a dark front of brick with gables; behind it the garden sloped nearly to the sands, with wooden barns and warehouses. Master Grimston unlocked the door, and then it seemed that his terrors came over him, for he would have the priest enter first. Father Thomas, with a certain apprehension of which he was ashamed, walked quickly in, and looked about him. The herbage of the garden had mostly died down in the winter, and a tangle of sodden stalks lay over the beds. A flagged path edged with box led up to the house, which seemed to stare at them out of its dark windows with a sort of steady gaze. Master Grimston fastened the door behind them, and they went all together, keeping close one to another, up to the house, the door of which opened upon a big parlour or kitchen, sparely furnished, but very clean and comfortable. Some vessels of metal glittered on a rack. There were chairs, ranged round the open fireplace. There was no sound except that the wind buffeted in the chimney. It looked a quiet and homely place, and Father Thomas grew ashamed of his fears. "Now," said he in his firm voice, "though I am your guest here, I will appoint what shall be done.

We will sit here together, and talk as cheerfully as we may, till we have dined. Then, if nothing appears to us," – and he crossed himself – "I will go round the house, into every room, and see if we can track the thing to its lair: then I will abide with you till evensong; and then I will soon return, and lie here tonight. Even if the thing be wary, and dares not to meet the power of the Church in the daytime, perhaps it will venture out at night; and I will even try a fall with it. So come, good people, and be comforted."

So they sate together; and Father Thomas talked of many things, and told some old legends of saints; and they dined, though without much cheer; and still nothing appeared. Then, after dinner, Father Thomas would view the house. So he took his book up, and they went from room to room. On the ground floor there were several chambers not used, which they entered in turn, but saw nothing; on the upper floor was a large room where Master Grimston and his wife slept; and a further room for Henry, and a guest-chamber in which the priest was to sleep if need was; and a room where a servant-maid slept. And now the day began to darken and to turn to evening, and Father Thomas felt a shadow grow in his mind. There came into his head a verse of Scripture about a spirit which found a house 'empty, swept and garnished', and called his fellows to enter in.

At the end of the passage was a locked door; and Father Thomas said: "This is the last room – let us enter."

"Nay, there is no need to do that," said Master Grimston in a kind of haste; "it leads nowhither – it is but a room of stores."

"It were a pity to leave it unvisited," said the Father – and as he said the word, there came a kind of stirring from within. "A rat, doubtless," said the Father, striving with a sudden sense of fear; but the pale faces round him told another tale. "Come, Master Grimston, let us be done with this," said Father Thomas decisively; "the hour of vespers draws nigh." So Master Grimston slowly drew out a key and unlocked the door, and Father Thomas marched in. It was a simple place enough. There were shelves on which various household matters lay, boxes and jars, with twine and cordage. On the ground stood chests. There were some clothes hanging on pegs, and in a corner was a heap of garments, piled up. On one of the chests stood a box of rough deal, and from the corner of it dripped water, which lay in a little pool on the floor. Master Grimston went hurriedly to the box and pushed it further to the wall. As he did so, a kind of sound came from Henry's lips. Father Thomas turned and looked at him; he stood pale and strength-less, his eyes fixed on the corner – at the same moment something dark and shapeless seemed to slip past the group, and there came to the nostrils of Father Thomas a strange sharp smell, as of the sea, only that there was a taint within it, like the smell of corruption.

They all turned and looked at Father Thomas together, as though seeking a comfort from his presence. He, hardly knowing what he did, and in the grasp of a terrible fear, fumbled with his book; and opening it, read the first words that his eye fell upon, which was the place where the Blessed Lord, beset with enemies, said that if He did but pray to His Father, He should send Him forthwith legions of angels to encompass Him. And the verse seemed to the priest so like a message sent instantly from heaven that he was not a little comforted.

But the thing, whatever the reason was, appeared to them no more at that time. Yet the thought of it lay very heavy on Father Thomas's heart. In truth he had not in the bottom of his mind believed that he would see it, but had trusted in his honest life and his sacred calling to protect him. He could hardly speak for some minutes – moreover the horror of the thing was very great – and seeing him so grave, their terrors were increased, though there was a kind of miserable joy in their minds that someone, and he a man of high repute, should suffer with them.

Then Father Thomas, after a pause – they were now in the parlour – said, speaking very slowly, that they were in a sore affliction of Satan, and that they must withstand him with a good courage – "and look you," he added, turning with a great sternness to the three, "if there be any mortal sin upon your hearts, see that you confess it and be shriven speedily – for while such a thing lies upon the heart, so long hath Satan power to hurt – otherwise have no fear at all."

Then Father Thomas slipped out to the garden, and hearing the bell pulled for vespers, he went to the church, and the three would go with him, because they would not be left alone. So they went together; by this time the street was fuller, and the servant-maid had told tales, so that there was much talk in the place about what was going forward. None spoke with them as they went, but at every corner you might see one check another in talk, and a silence fall upon a group, so that they knew that their terrors were on every tongue. There was but a handful of worshippers in the church, which was dark, save for the light on Father Thomas' book. He read the holy service swiftly and courageously, but his face was very pale and grave in the light of the candle. When the vespers were over, and he had put off his robe, he said that he would go back to his house, and gather what he needed for the night, and that they should wait for him at the churchyard gate. So he strode off to his vicarage. But as he shut to the door, he saw a dark figure come running up the garden; he waited with a fear in his mind, but in a moment he saw that it was Henry, who came up breathless, and said that he must speak with the Father alone. Father Thomas knew that somewhat dark was to be told him. So he led Henry into the parlour and seated himself, and said, "Now, my son, speak boldly." So there was an instant's silence, and Henry slipped on to his knees.

Then in a moment Henry with a sob began to tell his tale. He said that on the day of the wreck his father had roused him very early in the dawn, and had told him to put on his clothes and come silently, for he thought there was a wreck ashore. His father carried a spade in his hand, he knew not then why. They went down to the tide, which was moving out very fast, and left but an inch or two of water on the sands. There was but a little light, but, when they had walked a little, they saw the black hull of a ship before them, on the edge of the deeper water, the waves driving over it; and then all at once they came upon the body of a man lying on his face on the sand. There was no sign of life in him, but he clasped a bag in his hand that was heavy, and the pocket of his coat was full to bulging; and there lay, moreover, some glittering things about him that seemed to be coins. They lifted the body up, and his father stripped the coat off from the man, and then bade Henry dig a hole in the sand, which he presently did, though the sand and water oozed fast into it. Then his father, who had been stooping down, gathering somewhat up from the sand, raised the body up, and laid it in the hole, and bade Henry cover it with the sand. And so he did till it was nearly hidden. Then came a horrible thing; the sand in the hole began to move and stir, and presently a hand was put out with clutching fingers; and Henry had dropped the spade, and said, "There is life in him," but his father seized the spade, and shovelled the sand into the hole with a kind of silent fury, and trampled it over and smoothed it down – and then he gathered up the coat and the bag, and handed Henry the spade. By this time the town was astir, and they saw, very faintly, a man run along the shore eastward; so, making a long circuit to the west, they returned; his father had put the spade away and taken the coat upstairs; and then he went out with Henry, and told all he could find that there was a wreck ashore.

The priest heard the story with a fierce shame and anger, and turning to Henry he said, "But why did you not resist your father, and save the poor sailor?"

"I dared not," said Henry shuddering, "though I would have done so if I could; but my father has a power over me, and I am used to obey him." Then said the priest, "This is a dark matter. But you have told the story bravely, and now will I shrive you, my son." So he gave him shrift. Then he said to Henry, "And have you seen aught that would connect the beast that visits you with this thing?"

"Ay, that I have," said Henry, "for I watched it with my father skip and leap in the water over the place where the man lies buried." Then the priest said, "Your father must tell me the tale too, and he must make submission to the law."

"He will not," said Henry. "Then will I compel him," said the priest. "Not out of my mouth," said Henry, "or he will slay me too." And then the priest said that he was in a strait place, for he could not use the words of confession of one man to convict another of his sin. So he gathered his things in haste, and walked back to the church; but Henry went another way, saying "I made excuse to come away, and said I went elsewhere; but I fear my father much – he sees very deep; and I would not have him suspect me of having made confession."

Then the Father met the other two at the church gate; and they went down to the house in silence, the Father pondering heavily; and at the door Henry joined them, and it seemed to the Father that old Master Grimston regarded him not. So they entered the house in silence, and ate in silence, listening earnestly for any sound. And the Father looked oft on Master Grimston, who ate and drank and said nothing, never raising his eyes. But once the Father saw him laugh secretly to himself, so that the blood came cold in the Father's veins, and he could hardly contain himself from accusing him. Then the Father had them to prayers, and prayed earnestly against the evil, and that they should open their hearts to God, if he would show them why this misery came upon them.

Then they went to bed; and Henry asked that he might lie in the priest's room, which he willingly granted. And so the house was dark, and they made as though they would sleep; but the Father could not sleep, and he heard Henry weeping silently to himself like a little child.

But at last the Father slept – how long he knew not – and suddenly brake out of his sleep with a horror of darkness all about him, and knew that there was some evil thing abroad. So he looked upon the room. He heard Henry mutter heavily in his sleep as though there was a dark terror upon him; and then, in the light of the dying embers, the Father saw a thing rise upon the hearth, as though it had slept there, and woke to stretch itself. And then in the half-light it seemed softly to gambol and play; but whereas when an innocent beast does this in the simple joy of its heart, and seems a fond and pretty sight, the Father thought he had never seen so ugly a sight as the beast gambolling all by itself, as if it could not contain its own dreadful joy; it looked viler and more wicked every moment; then, too, there spread in the room the sharp scent of the sea, with the foul smell underneath it, that gave the Father a deadly sickness; he tried to pray, but no words would come, and he felt indeed that the evil was too strong for him. Presently the beast desisted from its play, and looking wickedly about it, came near to the Father's bed, and seemed to put up its hairy forelegs upon it; he could see its narrow and obscene eyes, which burned with a dull yellow light, and were fixed upon him. And now the Father thought that his end was near, for he could stir neither hand nor foot, and the sweat rained down his brow; but he made a mighty effort, and in a voice which shocked himself, so dry and husky and withal of so loud and screaming a tone it was, he said three holy words. The beast gave a great quiver of rage, but it dropped down on the floor, and in a moment was gone. Then Henry woke, and raising himself on his arm, said somewhat; but there broke out in the house a great outcry and the stamping of feet, which seemed very fearful in the silence of the night. The priest leapt out of his bed all dizzy, and made a light, and ran to the door, and went out, crying whatever words came to his head. The door of Master Grimston's room was open, and a strange and strangling sound came forth; the Father made his way in, and found Master Grimston lying upon the floor, his wife bending over him; he lay still, breathing pitifully, and every now and then a shudder ran through him. In the room there seemed a strange and shadowy tumult going forward; but the Father saw that no time could be lost, and kneeling down beside Master Grimston, he prayed with all his might.

Presently Master Grimston ceased to struggle and lay still, like a man who had come out of a sore conflict. Then he opened his eyes, and the Father stopped his prayers, and looking very hard at him he said, "My son, the time is very short – give God the glory." Then Master Grimston, rolling his haggard eyes upon the group, twice strove to speak and could not; but the third time the Father, bending down his head, heard him say in a thin voice, that seemed to float from a long way off, "I slew him … my sin." Then the Father swiftly gave him shrift, and as he said the last word, Master Grimston's head fell over on the side, and the Father said, "He is gone." And Bridget broke out into a terrible cry, and fell upon Henry's neck, who had entered unseen.

Then the Father bade him lead her away, and put the poor body on the bed; as he did so he noticed that the face of the dead man was strangely bruised and battered, as though it had been stamped upon by the hoofs of some beast. Then Father Thomas knelt, and prayed until the light came filtering in through the shutters; and the cocks crowed in the village, and presently it was day. But that night the Father learnt strange secrets, and something of the dark purposes of God was revealed to him.

In the morning there came one to find the priest, and told him that another body had been thrown up on the shore, which was strangely smeared with sand, as though it had been rolled over and over in it; and the Father took order for its burial.

Then the priest had long talk with Bridget and Henry. He found them sitting together, and she held her son's hand and smoothed his hair, as though he had been a little child; and Henry sobbed and wept, but Bridget was very calm. "He hath told me all," she said, "and we have decided that he shall do whatever you bid him; must he be given to justice?" and she looked at the priest very pitifully. "Nay, nay," said the priest. "I hold not Henry to account for the death of the man; it was his father's sin, who hath made heavy atonement – the secret shall be buried in our hearts."

Then Bridget told him how she had waked suddenly out of her sleep, and heard her husband cry out; and that then followed a dreadful kind of struggling, with the scent of the sea over all; and then he had all at once fallen to the ground and she had gone to him – and that then the priest had come.

Then Father Thomas said with tears that God had shown them deep things and visited them very strangely; and they would henceforth live humbly in his sight, showing mercy.

Then lastly he went with Henry to the store-room; and there, in the box that had dripped with water, lay the coat of the dead man, full of money, and the bag of money too; and Henry would have cast it back into the sea, but the priest said that this might not be, but that it should be bestowed plentifully upon shipwrecked mariners unless the heirs should be found. But the ship appeared to be a foreign ship, and no search ever revealed whence the money had come, save that it seemed to have been violently come by.

Master Grimston was found to have left much wealth. But Bridget would sell the house and the land, and it mostly went to rebuild the church to God's glory. Then Bridget and Henry removed to the vicarage and served Father Thomas faithfully, and they guarded their secret. And beside the nave is a little high turret built, where burns a lamp in a lantern at the top, to give light to those at sea.

Now the beast troubled those of whom I write no more; but it is easier to raise up evil than to lay it; and there are those that say that to this day a man or a woman with an evil thought in their hearts may see on a certain evening in November, at the ebb of the tide, a goatlike thing wade in the water, snuffing at the sand, as though it sought but found not. But of this I know nothing.

The Face

E.F. Benson

HESTER WARD, sitting by the open window on this hot afternoon in June, began seriously to argue with herself about the cloud of foreboding and depression which had encompassed her all day, and, very sensibly, she enumerated to herself the manifold causes for happiness in the fortunate circumstances of her life. She was young, she was extremely good-looking, she was well-off, she enjoyed excellent health, and above all, she had an adorable husband and two small, adorable children. There was no break, indeed, anywhere in the circle of prosperity which surrounded her, and had the wishing-cap been handed to her that moment by some beneficent fairy, she would have hesitated to put it on her head, for there was positively nothing that she could think of which would have been worthy of such solemnity. Moreover, she could not accuse herself of a want of appreciation of her blessings; she appreciated enormously, she enjoyed enormously, and she thoroughly wanted all those who so munificently contributed to her happiness to share in it.

She made a very deliberate review of these things, for she was really anxious, more anxious, indeed, than she admitted to herself, to find anything tangible which could possibly warrant this ominous feeling of approaching disaster. Then there was the weather to consider; for the last week London had been stiflingly hot, but if that was the cause, why had she not felt it before? Perhaps the effect of these broiling, airless days had been cumulative. That was an idea, but, frankly, it did not seem a very good one, for, as a matter of fact, she loved the heat; Dick, who hated it, said that it was odd he should have fallen in love with a salamander.

She shifted her position, sitting up straight in this low window-seat, for she was intending to make a call on her courage. She had known from the moment she awoke this morning what it was that lay so heavy on her, and now, having done her best to shift the reason of her depression on to anything else, and having completely failed, she meant to look the thing in the face. She was ashamed of doing so, for the cause of this leaden mood of fear which held her in its grip, was so trivial, so fantastic, so excessively silly.

"Yes, there never was anything so silly," she said to herself. "I must look at it straight, and convince myself how silly it is." She paused a moment, clenching her hands.

"Now for it," she said.

She had had a dream the previous night, which, years ago, used to be familiar to her, for again and again when she was a child she had dreamed it. In itself the dream was nothing, but in those childish days, whenever she had this dream which had visited her last night, it was followed on the next night by another, which contained the source and the core of the horror, and she would awake screaming and struggling in the grip of overwhelming nightmare. For some ten years now she had not experienced it, and would have said that, though she remembered it, it had become dim and distant to her. But last night she had had that warning dream, which used to herald the visitation of the nightmare, and now that whole store-house of memory crammed as it was with bright things and beautiful contained nothing so vivid.

The warning dream, the curtain that was drawn up on the succeeding night, and disclosed the vision she dreaded, was simple and harmless enough in itself. She seemed to be walking on a high sandy cliff covered with short down-grass; twenty yards to the left came the edge of this cliff, which sloped steeply down to the sea that lay at its foot. The path she followed led through fields bounded by low hedges, and mounted gradually upwards. She went through some half-dozen of these, climbing over the wooden stiles that gave communication; sheep grazed there, but she never saw another human being, and always it was dusk, as if evening was falling, and she had to hurry on, because someone (she knew not whom) was waiting for her, and had been waiting not a few minutes only, but for many years. Presently, as she mounted this slope, she saw in front of her a copse of stunted trees, growing crookedly under the continual pressure of the wind that blew from the sea, and when she saw those she knew her journey was nearly done, and that the nameless one, who had been waiting for her so long was somewhere close at hand. The path she followed was cut through this wood, and the slanting boughs of the trees on the sea-ward side almost roofed it in; it was like walking through a tunnel. Soon the trees in front began to grow thin, and she saw through them the grey tower of a lonely church. It stood in a graveyard, apparently long disused, and the body of the church, which lay between the tower and the edge of the cliff, was in ruins, roofless, and with gaping windows, round which ivy grew thickly.

At that point this prefatory dream always stopped. It was a troubled, uneasy dream, for there was over it the sense of dusk and of the man who had been waiting for her so long, but it was not of the order of nightmare. Many times in childhood had she experienced it, and perhaps it was the subconscious knowledge of the night that so surely followed it, which gave it its disquiet. And now last night it had come again, identical in every particular but one. For last night it seemed to her that in the course of these ten years which had intervened since last it had visited her, the glimpse of the church and churchyard was changed. The edge of the cliff had come nearer to the tower, so that it now was within a yard or two of it, and the ruined body of the church, but for one broken arch that remained, had vanished. The sea had encroached, and for ten years had been busily eating at the cliff.

Hester knew well that it was this dream and this alone which had darkened the day for her, by reason of the nightmares that used to follow it, and, like a sensible woman, having looked it once in the face, she refused to admit into her mind any conscious calling-up of the sequel. If she let herself contemplate that, as likely or not the very thinking about it would be sufficient to ensure its return, and of one thing she was very certain, namely, that she didn't at all want it to do so. It was not like the confused jumble and jangle of ordinary nightmare, it was very simple, and she felt it concerned the nameless one who waited for her...But she must not think of it; her whole will and intention was set on not thinking of it, and to aid her resolution, there was the rattle of Dick's latch-key in the front-door, and his voice calling her.

She went out into the little square front hall; there he was, strong and large, and wonderfully undreamlike.

"This heat's a scandal, it's an outrage, it's an abomination of desolation," he cried, vigorously mopping. "What have we done that Providence should place us in this frying-pan? Let us thwart him, Hester! Let us drive out of this inferno and have our dinner at – I'll whisper it so that he shan't overhear – at Hampton Court!"

She laughed: this plan suited her excellently. They would return late, after the distraction of a fresh scene; and dining out at night was both delicious and stupefying.

"The very thing," she said, "and I'm sure Providence didn't hear. Let's start now!"

"Rather. Any letters for me?"

He walked to the table where there were a few rather uninteresting-looking envelopes with half penny stamps.

"Ah, receipted bill," he said. "Just a reminder of one's folly in paying it. Circular ... unasked advice to invest in German marks... Circular begging letter, beginning 'Dear Sir or Madam'. Such impertinence to ask one to subscribe to something without ascertaining one's sex... Private view, portraits at the Walton Gallery... Can't go: business meetings all day. You might like to have a look in, Hester. Someone told me there were some fine Vandycks. That's all: let's be off."

Hester spent a thoroughly reassuring evening, and though she thought of telling Dick about the dream that had so deeply imprinted itself on her consciousness all day, in order to hear the great laugh he would have given her for being such a goose, she refrained from doing so, since nothing that he could say would be so tonic to these fantastic fears as his general robustness. Besides, she would have to account for its disturbing effect, tell him that it was once familiar to her, and recount the sequel of the nightmares that followed. She would neither think of them, nor mention them: it was wiser by far just to soak herself in his extraordinary sanity, and wrap herself in his affection... They dined out-of-doors at a river-side restaurant and strolled about afterwards, and it was very nearly midnight when, soothed with coolness and fresh air, and the vigour of his strong companionship, she let herself into the house, while he took the car back to the garage. And now she marvelled at the mood which had beset her all day, so distant and unreal had it become. She felt as if she had dreamed of shipwreck, and had awoke to find herself in some secure and sheltered garden where no tempest raged nor waves beat. But was there, ever so remotely, ever so dimly, the noise of far-off breakers somewhere?

He slept in the dressing-room which communicated with her bedroom, the door of which was left open for the sake of air and coolness, and she fell asleep almost as soon as her light was out, and while his was still burning. And immediately she began to dream.

She was standing on the seashore; the tide was out, for level sands strewn with stranded jetsam glimmered in a dusk that was deepening into night. Though she had never seen the place it was awfully familiar to her. At the head of the beach there was a steep cliff of sand, and perched on the edge of it was a grey church tower. The sea must have encroached and undermined the body of the church, for tumbled blocks of masonry lay close to her at the bottom of the cliff, and there were gravestones there, while others still in place were silhouetted whitely against the sky. To the right of the church tower there was a wood of stunted trees, combed sideways by the prevalent sea-wind, and she knew that along the top of the cliff a few yards inland there lay a path through fields, with wooden stiles to climb, which led through a tunnel of trees and so out into the churchyard. All this she saw in a glance, and waited, looking at the sand-cliff crowned by the church tower, for the terror that was going to reveal itself. Already she knew what it was, and, as so many times before, she tried to run away. But the catalepsy of nightmare was already on her; frantically she strove to move, but her utmost endeavour could not raise a foot from the sand. Frantically she tried to look away from the sand-cliffs close in front of her, where in a moment now the horror would be manifested...

It came. There formed a pale oval light, the size of a man's face, dimly luminous in front of her and a few inches above the level of her eyes. It outlined itself, short reddish hair grew low on the forehead, below were two grey eyes, set very close together, which steadily and fixedly regarded her. On each side the ears stood noticeably away from the head, and the lines of the jaw met in a short pointed chin. The nose was straight and rather long, below it came a hairless lip, and last of all the mouth took shape and colour, and there lay the crowning terror. One side of it, soft-curved and beautiful, trembled into a smile, the other side, thick and gathered together as by some physical deformity, sneered and lusted.

The whole face, dim at first, gradually focused itself into clear outline: it was pale and rather lean, the face of a young man. And then the lower lip dropped a little, showing the glint of teeth, and there was the sound of speech. "I shall soon come for you now," it said, and on the words it drew a little nearer to her, and the smile broadened. At that the full hot blast of nightmare poured in upon her. Again she tried to run, again she tried to scream, and now she could feel the breath of that terrible mouth upon her. Then with a crash and a rending like the tearing asunder of soul and body she broke the spell, and heard her own voice yelling, and felt with her fingers for the switch of her light. And then she saw that the room was not dark, for Dick's door was open, and the next moment, not yet undressed, he was with her.

"My darling, what is it?" he said. "What's the matter?"

She clung desperately to him, still distraught with terror.

"Ah, he has been here again," she cried. "He says he will soon come to me. Keep him away, Dick."

For one moment her fear infected him, and he found himself glancing round the room.

"But what do you mean?" he said. "No one has been here."

She raised her head from his shoulder.

"No, it was just a dream," she said. "But it was the old dream, and I was terrified. Why, you've not undressed yet. What time is it?"

"You haven't been in bed ten minutes, dear," he said. "You had hardly put out your light when I heard you screaming."

She shuddered.

"Ah, it's awful," she said. "And he will come again…"

He sat down by her.

"Now tell me all about it," he said.

She shook her head.

"No, it will never do to talk about it," she said, "it will only make it more real. I suppose the children are all right, are they?"

"Of course they are. I looked in on my way upstairs."

"That's good. But I'm better now, Dick. A dream hasn't anything real about it, has it? It doesn't mean anything?"

He was quite reassuring on this point, and soon she quieted down. Before he went to bed he looked in again on her, and she was asleep.

Hester had a stern interview with herself when Dick had gone down to his office next morning. She told herself that what she was afraid of was nothing more than her own fear. How many times had that ill-omened face come to her in dreams, and what significance had it ever proved to possess? Absolutely none at all, except to make her afraid. She was afraid where no fear was: she was guarded, sheltered, prosperous, and what if a nightmare of childhood returned? It had no more meaning now than it had then, and all those visitations of her childhood had passed away without trace… And then, despite herself, she began thinking over that vision again. It was grimly identical with all its previous occurrences, except… And then, with a sudden shrinking of the heart, she remembered that in earlier years those terrible lips had said: "I shall come for you when you are older," and last night they had said: "I shall soon come for you now." She remembered, too, that in the warning dream the sea had encroached, and it had now demolished the body of the church. There was an awful consistency about these two changes in the otherwise identical visions. The years had brought their change to them, for in the one the encroaching sea had brought down the body of the church, in the other the time was now near…

It was no use to scold or reprimand herself, for to bring her mind to the contemplation of the vision meant merely that the grip of terror closed on her again; it was far wiser to occupy herself, and starve her fear out by refusing to bring it the sustenance of thought. So she went about her household duties, she took the children out for their airing in the park, and then, determined to leave no moment unoccupied, set off with the card of invitation to see the pictures in the private view at the Walton Gallery. After that her day was full enough, she was lunching out, and going on to a matinée, and by the time she got home Dick would have returned, and they would drive down to his little house at Rye for the week-end. All Saturday and Sunday she would be playing golf, and she felt that fresh air and physical fatigue would exorcise the dread of these dreaming fantasies.

The gallery was crowded when she got there; there were friends among the sightseers, and the inspection of the pictures was diversified by cheerful conversation. There were two or three fine Raeburns, a couple of Sir Joshuas, but the gems, so she gathered, were three Vandycks that hung in a small room by themselves. Presently she strolled in there, looking at her catalogue. The first of them, she saw, was a portrait of Sir Roger Wyburn. Still chatting to her friend she raised her eye and saw it…

Her heart hammered in her throat, and then seemed to stand still altogether. A qualm, as of some mental sickness of the soul overcame her, for there in front of her was he who would soon come for her. There was the reddish hair, the projecting ears, the greedy eyes set close together, and the mouth smiling on one side, and on the other gathered up into the sneering menace that she knew so well. It might have been her own nightmare rather than a living model which had sat to the painter for that face.

"Ah, what a portrait, and what a brute!" said her companion. "Look, Hester, isn't that marvellous?"

She recovered herself with an effort. To give way to this ever-mastering dread would have been to allow nightmare to invade her waking life, and there, for sure, madness lay. She forced herself to look at it again, but there were the steady and eager eyes regarding her; she could almost fancy the mouth began to move. All round her the crowd bustled and chattered, but to her own sense she was alone there with Roger Wyburn.

And yet, so she reasoned with herself, this picture of him – for it was he and no other – should have reassured her. Roger Wyburn, to have been painted by Vandyck, must have been dead near on two hundred years; how could he be a menace to her? Had she seen that portrait by some chance as a child; had it made some dreadful impression on her, since overscored by other memories, but still alive in the mysterious subconsciousness, which flows eternally, like some dark underground river, beneath the surface of human life? Psychologists taught that these early impressions fester or poison the mind like some hidden abscess. That might account for this dread of one, nameless no longer, who waited for her.

That night down at Rye there came again to her the prefatory dream, followed by the nightmare, and clinging to her husband as the terror began to subside, she told him what she had resolved to keep to herself. Just to tell it brought a measure of comfort, for it was so outrageously fantastic, and his robust common sense upheld her. But when on their return to London there was a recurrence of these visions, he made short work of her demur and took her straight to her doctor.

"Tell him all, darling," he said. "Unless you promise to do that, I will. I can't have you worried like this. It's all nonsense, you know, and doctors are wonderful people for curing nonsense."

She turned to him.

"Dick, you're frightened," she said quietly.

He laughed.

"I'm nothing of the kind," he said, "but I don't like being awakened by your screaming. Not my idea of a peaceful night. Here we are."

The medical report was decisive and peremptory. There was nothing whatever to be alarmed about; in brain and body she was perfectly healthy, but she was run down. These disturbing dreams were, as likely as not, an effect, a symptom of her condition, rather than the cause of it, and Dr. Baring unhesitatingly recommended a complete change to some bracing place. The wise thing would be to send her out of this stuffy furnace to some quiet place to where she had never been. Complete change; quite so. For the same reason her husband had better not go with her;

he must pack her off to, let us say, the East coast. Sea-air and coolness and complete idleness. No long walks; no long bathings; a dip, and a deck-chair on the sands. A lazy, soporific life. How about Rushton? He had no doubt that Rushton would set her up again. After a week or so, perhaps, her husband might go down and see her. Plenty of sleep – never mind the nightmares – plenty of fresh air.

Hester, rather to her husband's surprise, fell in with this suggestion at once, and the following evening saw her installed in solitude and tranquillity. The little hotel was still almost empty, for the rush of summer tourists had not yet begun, and all day she sat out on the beach with the sense of a struggle over. She need not fight the terror any more; dimly it seemed to her that its malignancy had been relaxed. Had she in some way yielded to it and done its secret bidding? At any rate no return of its nightly visitations had occurred, and she slept long and dreamlessly, and woke to another day of quiet. Every morning there was a line for her from Dick, with good news of himself and the children, but he and they alike seemed somehow remote, like memories of a very distant time. Something had driven in between her and them, and she saw them as if through glass. But equally did the memory of the face of Roger Wyburn, as seen on the master's canvas or hanging close in front of her against the crumbling sand-cliff, become blurred and indistinct, and no return of her nightly terrors visited her. This truce from all emotion reacted not on her mind alone, lulling her with a sense of soothed security, but on her body also, and she began to weary of this day-long inactivity.

The village lay on the lip of a stretch of land reclaimed from the sea. To the north the level marsh, now beginning to glow with the pale bloom of the sea-lavender, stretched away featureless till it lost itself in distance, but to the south a spur of hill came down to the shore ending in a wooded promontory. Gradually, as her physical health increased, she began to wonder what lay beyond this ridge which cut short the view, and one afternoon she walked across the intervening level and strolled up its wooded slopes. The day was close and windless, the invigorating sea-breeze which till now had spiced the heat with freshness had died, and she looked forward to finding a current of air stirring when she had topped the hill. To the south a mass of dark cloud lay along the horizon, but there was no imminent threat of storm. The slope was easily surmounted, and presently she stood at the top and found herself on the edge of a tableland of wooded pasture, and following the path, which ran not far from the edge of the cliff, she came out into more open country. Empty fields, where a few sheep were grazing, mounted gradually upwards. Wooden stiles made a communication in the hedges that bounded them. And there, not a mile in front of her, she saw a wood, with trees growing slantingly away from the push of the prevalent sea winds, crowning the upward slope, and over the top of it peered a grey church tower.

For the moment, as the awful and familiar scene identified itself, Hester's heart stood still: the next a wave of courage and resolution poured in upon her. Here, at last was the scene of that prefatory dream, and here was she presented with the opportunity of fathoming and dispelling it. Instantly her mind was made up, and under the strange twilight of the shrouded sky, she walked swiftly on through the fields she had so often traversed in sleep, and up to the wood, beyond which he was waiting for her. She closed her ears against the clanging bell of terror, which now she could silence for ever, and unfalteringly entered that dark tunnel of wood. Soon in front of her the trees began to thin, and through them, now close at hand, she saw the church tower. In a few yards farther she came out of the belt of trees, and round her were the monuments of a graveyard long disused. The cliff was broken off close to the church tower: between it and the edge there was no more of the body of the church than a broken arch, thick hung with ivy. Round this she passed and saw below the ruin of fallen masonry, and the level sands strewn with headstones and disjected rubble, and at the edge of the cliff were graves already cracked and toppling. But there was no one here, none waited for her, and the churchyard where she had so often pictured him was as empty as the fields she had just traversed.

* * *

A huge elation filled her; her courage had been rewarded, and all the terrors of the past became to her meaningless phantoms. But there was no time to linger, for now the storm threatened, and on the horizon a blink of lightning was followed by a crackling peal. Just as she turned to go her eye fell on a tombstone that was balanced on the very edge of the cliff, and she read on it that here lay the body of Roger Wyburn.

Fear, the catalepsy of nightmare, rooted her for the moment to the spot; she stared in stricken amazement at the moss-grown letters; almost she expected to see that fell terror of a face rise and hover over his resting-place. Then the fear which had frozen her lent her wings, and with hurrying feet she sped through the arched pathway in the wood and out into the fields. Not one backward glance did she give till she had come to the edge of the ridge above the village, and, turning, saw the pastures she had traversed empty of any living presence. None had followed; but the sheep, apprehensive of the coming storm, had ceased to feed, and were huddling under shelter of the stunted hedges.

Her first idea, in the panic of her mind, was to leave the place at once, but the last train for London had left an hour before, and besides, where was the use of flight if it was the spirit of a man long dead from which she fled? The distance from the place where his bones lay did not afford her safety; that must be sought for within. But she longed for Dick's sheltering and confident presence; he was arriving in any case tomorrow, but there were long dark hours before tomorrow, and who could say what the perils and dangers of the coming night might be? If he started this evening instead of tomorrow morning, he could motor down here in four hours, and would be with her by ten o'clock or eleven. She wrote an urgent telegram: "Come at once," she said. "Don't delay."

The storm which had flickered on the south now came quickly up, and soon after it burst in appalling violence. For preface there were but a few large drops that splashed and dried on the roadway as she came back from the post-office, and just as she reached the hotel again the roar of the approaching rain sounded, and the sluices of heaven were opened. Through the deluge flared the fire of the lightning, the thunder crashed and echoed overhead, and presently the street of the village was a torrent of sandy turbulent water, and sitting there in the dark one picture leapt floating before her eyes, that of the tombstone of Roger Wyburn, already tottering to its fall at the edge of the cliff of the church tower. In such rains as these, acres of the cliffs were loosened; she seemed to hear the whisper of the sliding sand that would precipitate those perished sepulchres and what lay within to the beach below.

By eight o'clock the storm was subsiding, and as she dined she was handed a telegram from Dick, saying that he had already started and sent this off *en route*. By half-past ten, therefore, if all was well, he would be here, and somehow he would stand between her and her fear. Strange how a few days ago both it and the thought of him had become distant and dim to her; now the one was as vivid as the other, and she counted the minutes to his arrival. Soon the rain ceased altogether, and looking out of the curtained window of her sitting-room where she sat watching the slow circle of the hands of the clock, she saw a tawny moon rising over the sea. Before it had climbed to the zenith, before her clock had twice told the hour again, Dick would be with her.

It had just struck ten when there came a knock at her door, and the page-boy entered with the message that a gentleman had come for her. Her heart leaped at the news; she had not expected Dick for half an hour yet, and now the lonely vigil was over. She ran downstairs, and there was the figure standing on the step outside. His face was turned away from her; no doubt he was giving some order to his chauffeur. He was outlined against the white moonlight, and in contrast with that, the gas-jet in the entrance just above his head gave his hair a warm, reddish tinge.

She ran across the hall to him.

"Ah, my darling, you've come," she said. "It was good of you. How quick you've been!" Just as she laid her hand on his shoulder he turned. His arm was thrown out round her, and she looked into a face with eyes close-set, and a mouth smiling on one side, the other, thick and gathered together as by some physical deformity, sneered and lusted.

The nightmare was on her; she could neither run nor scream, and supporting her dragging steps, he went forth with her into the night.

* * *

Half an hour later Dick arrived. To his amazement he heard that a man had called for his wife not long before, and that she had gone out with him. He seemed to be a stranger here, for the boy who had taken his message to her had never seen him before, and presently surprise began to deepen into alarm; enquiries were made outside the hotel, and it appeared that a witness or two had seen the lady whom they knew to be staying there walking, hatless, along the top of the beach with a man whose arm was linked in hers. Neither of them knew him, but one had seen his face and could describe it.

The direction of the search thus became narrowed down, and though with a lantern to supplement the moonlight they came upon footprints which might have been hers, there were no marks of any who walked beside her. But they followed these until they came to an end, a mile away, in a great landslide of sand, which had fallen from the old churchyard on the cliff, and had brought down with it half the tower and a gravestone, with the body that had lain below.

The gravestone was that of Roger Wyburn, and his body lay by it, untouched by corruption or decay, though two hundred years had elapsed since it was interred there. For a week afterwards the work of searching the landslide went on, assisted by the high tides that gradually washed it away. But no further discovery was made.

The Step

E.F. Benson

JOHN CRESSWELL was returning home one night from the Britannia Club at Alexandria, where, as was his custom three or four times in the week, he had dined very solidly and fluidly, and played bridge afterwards as long as a table could be formed. It had been rather an expensive evening, for all his skill at cards had been unable to cope with such a continuous series of ill-favoured hands as had been his. But he had consoled himself with reasonable doses of whisky, and now he stepped homewards in very cheerful spirits, for his business affairs were going most prosperously and a loss of twenty-five or thirty pounds tonight would be amply compensated for in the morning. Besides, his bridge-account for the year showed a credit which proved that cards were a very profitable pleasure.

It was a hot night of October, and, being a big plethoric man, he strolled at a very leisurely pace across the square and up the long street at the far end of which was his house. There were no taxis on the rank, or he would have taken one and saved himself this walk of nearly a mile; but he had no quarrel with that, for the night air with a breeze from the sea was refreshing after so long a session in a smoke-laden atmosphere. Above, a moon near to its full cast a very clear white light on his road. There was a narrow strip of sharp-cut shadow beneath the houses on his right, but the rest of the street and the pavement on the left of it, where he walked, were in bright illumination.

At first his way lay between rows of shops, European for the most part, with here and there a café where a few customers still lingered. Pleasant thoughts beguiled his progress; the Egyptian sugar-crop, in which he was much interested, had turned out very well and he saw a big profit on his options. Not less satisfactory were other businesses in which he did not figure so openly. He lent money, for instance, on a large scale, to the native population, and these operations extended far up the Nile. Only last week he had been at Luxor, where he had concluded a transaction of a very remunerative sort. He had made a loan some months ago to a small merchant there and now the appropriate interest on this was in default: in consequence the harvest of a very fruitful acreage of sugar-cane was his. A similar and even richer windfall had just come his way in Alexandria, for he had advanced money a year ago to a Levantine tobacco merchant on the security of his freehold store. This had brought him in very handsome interest, but a day or two ago the unfortunate fellow had failed, and Cresswell owned a most desirable freehold. The whole affair had been very creditable to his enterprise and sagacity, for he had privately heard that the municipality was intending to lay out the neighbourhood, a slum at present, where this store was situated, in houses of flats, and make it a residential quarter, and his newly acquired freehold would thus become a valuable property.

At present the tobacco merchant lived with his family in holes and corners of the store, and they must be evicted tomorrow morning. John Cresswell had already arranged for this, and had told the man that he would have to quit: he would go round there in the forenoon and see that they and their sticks of furniture were duly bundled out into the street. He would see personally that this was done, and looked forward to doing so. The old couple were beastly creatures, the woman a perfect witch who eyed him and muttered, but there was a daughter who was not ill-looking, and someone of the beggared family would be obliged to earn bread. He did not dwell on this, but the thought just flitted through his brain… Then doors would be locked and windows barred in the store that was now his, and he would lunch at the club afterwards. He was popular there; he had a jovial geniality about him, and a habit of offering drinks before they could be offered to him. That, too, was good for business.

Ten minutes' strolling brought him to the end of the shops and cafés that formed the street, and now the road ran between residential houses, each detached and with a space of garden surrounding it, where dry-leaved palms rattled in this wind from the sea. He was approaching the flamboyant Roman Catholic church, to which was attached a monastic establishment, a big white barrack-looking house where the Brothers of Poverty or some such order lived. Something to do with St. Mark, he vaguely remembered, who by tradition had brought Christianity to Egypt nearly nineteen hundred years ago. Often he met one of these odd sandal-footed creatures with his brown habit, his rosary and his cowled head going in or out of their gate, or toiling in their garden. He did not like them: lousy fellows he would have called them. Sometimes in their mendicant errands they came to his door asking alms for the indigent Copts. Not long ago he had found one actually ringing the bell of his front door, instead of going humbly round to the back, as befitted his quality, and Cresswell told him that he would loose his bulldog on the next of their breed who ventured within his garden gate. How the fellow had skipped off when he heard talk of the dog! He dropped one of his sandals in his haste to be gone, and not sparing the time to adjust it again, had hopped and hobbled over the sharp gravel to gain the street. Cresswell had laughed aloud to see his precipitancy, and the best of the joke was that he had not got any sort of dog on his premises at all. At the remembrance of that humorous incident he grinned to himself as he passed the porch of the church.

He paused a moment to mop his forehead and to light a cigarette, looking about him in great good humour. Before him and behind the road was quite empty: lights gleamed behind venetian shutters from a few upper windows of the houses, but all the world was in bed or on its way there. There were still three or four hundred yards to go before he came to his house, and as he turned his face homewards again and walked a little more briskly, he heard a step behind him, sharp and distinct, not far in his rear. He paid no heed: someone, late like himself, was going home, walking in the same direction, for the step followed him.

His cigarette was ill-lit; a little core of burning stuff fell from it on to the pavement and he stopped to rekindle it. Possibly some subconscious region of his mind was occupied with the step which had sprung up so oddly behind him in the empty street, for while he was getting his cigarette to burn again he noticed that the step had ceased. It was hardly worth while to turn round (so little the matter interested him), but a casual glance showed him that the wayfarer must have turned into one of the houses he had just passed, for the whole street, brightly moonlit, was as empty as when he surveyed it a few minutes before. Soon he came to his own gate and clanged it behind him.

The eviction of the Levantine merchant took place in the morning, and Cresswell watched his porters carrying out the tawdry furniture – a few tables, a few chairs, a sofa covered in tattered crimson plush, a couple of iron bedsteads, a bundle of dirty sheets and blankets. He was not certain in his own mind whether these paltry articles did not by rights belong to him, but they were fit for nothing except the dust-heap, and he had no use for them. There they stood in the clean bright sunshine, rubbish and no more, blocking the pavement, and a policeman told their owner that he had best clear them away at once unless he wanted trouble. There was the usual scene to which he was quite accustomed: the man's wife snivelling and slovenly, witch-like and early old, knelt and kissed his hand, and wheezingly besought his compassion. She called him

"Excellency", she promised him her prayers, which he desired as little as her pots and pans. She invoked blessings on his head, for she knew that out of his pity he would give them a little more time. They had nowhere to go nor any roof to shelter them: her husband had money owing to him, and he would collect these debts and pay his default as sure as there was a God in heaven. This was a changed note from her mutterings of yesterday, but of course Cresswell had a deaf ear for this oily rigmarole, and presently he went into the store to see that everything had been removed.

It was in a filthy, dirty state; floors were rotten and the paint peeling, but the whole place would soon be broken up and he was not going to spend a piastre on it, so long as the ground on which it stood was his. Then he saw to the barring of the windows and the doors, and he gave the policeman quite a handsome tip to keep an eye on the place and take care that these folk did not get ingress again. When he came out, he found that the old man had procured a handcart, and he and his son were loading it up, so of course they had somewhere to go: it was all a pack of lies about their being homeless. The old hag was squatting against the house wall, but now there were no more prayers and blessings for him, and she had taken to her mutterings again. As for the daughter, seen in the broad daylight, she had a handsome face, but she was sullen and dirty and forbidding, and he gave no further thought to her. He hailed a taxi and went off to the club for lunch.

Though Cresswell, in common parlance, 'did himself well', taking his fill of food and drink and tobacco, he was also careful of that great strong body of his, and the occasions were few when he omitted, at the end of the day's work, to walk out in the direction of Ramleh for a brisk hour or two, or, during the hotter months, to have a good swim in the sea and a bask in the sun. On the day following this eviction he took a tramp along the firm sands of the coast, and then, turning inland, struck the road that would bring him back to his own house. This stood quite at the end of the rows of detached houses past which he had walked two evenings before: beyond, the road ran between tumbled sand-dunes and scrub-covered flats. Here and there in sheltered hollows a few Arab goatherds and such had made themselves nomadic tentlike habitations of a primitive sort: half a dozen posts set in the sand supported a roof of rugs and blankets stitched together. If they encroached too near the outskirts of the town the authorities periodically made a clearance of them, for they were apt to be light-fingered, pilfering folk, whose close vicinity was not desirable.

Today as he returned from his walk, Cresswell saw that a tent of this kind had newly been set up within twenty yards of his own garden wall. That would not do at all, that must be seen to, and he determined as soon as he had had his bath and his change of clothes to ring up his very good friend the chief inspector of police and request its removal. As he got nearer to it he saw that it was not quite of the usual type. The roof was clearly an outworn European carpet, and standing outside it on the sand were chairs and a sofa. Somehow these seemed familiar to him, though he could not localise the association. Then out of the tent came that old Levantine hag who had kissed his hand and knelt to him yesterday, invoking on him all sorts of blessings and prosperities, if only he would have compassion. She saw him, for now not more than a few dozen yards separated them, and then, suddenly pointing at him, she broke out into a gabble and yell of curses. That made him smile.

"So you've changed your tune again, have you?" he thought, "for that doesn't sound much like good wishes. Curse away, old woman, if it relieves your mind, for it doesn't hurt me. But you'll have to be shifting once more, for I'm not going to have you and your like squatting there."

Cresswell rang up his friend the chief inspector of police, and was most politely told that matter should be seen to in the morning. Sure enough when he set out to go to his office next day, he saw that it was being attended to, for the European carpet which had served for a roof was already down, and the handcart was being laden with the stuff. He noticed, quite casually, that the two women and the boy were employed in lading it; the Levantine was lying on the sand and taking no part in the work. Two days later he had occasion to pass the pauper cemetery of Alexandria, where the poorest kind of funeral was going on. The coffin was being pushed to the side of the shallow grave on a handcart: a boy and two women followed it. He could see who they were.

He dined that night at the club in rare good-humour with the affairs of life. Already the municipality had offered him for his newly acquired freehold a sum that was double the debt for which it had been security, and though possibly he might get more if he stuck out for a higher price he had accepted it, and the money had been paid into his bank that day. To get a hundred per cent in a week was very satisfactory business, and who knew but that some new scheme of improvement might cause them to change their plans, leaving him with a ramshackle building on his hands for which he had no manner of use? He enjoyed his dinner and his wine, and particularly did he enjoy the rubber of bridge that followed. All went well with his finesses; he doubled his adversaries two or three times with the happiest results, they doubled him and were sorry for having spoken, and there would be a very pleasant item to enter in his card-account that evening.

It was later than usual when he quitted the club. Just outside there was a beggar-woman squatting at the edge of the pavement, who held her palm towards him and whined out blessings. Good-naturedly he fumbled in his pocket for a couple of piastres, and the blessings poured out in greater shrillness and copiousness as she pushed back the black veil that half shrouded her face to thank him for his beneficence to the needy widow. Next moment she threw his alms on the pavement, she spat at him, and like a moth she flitted away into the shadows.

Cresswell recognised her even as she had recognised him and picked up his piastres. It was amusing to think that the old hag so hated him that even his alms were abhorrent to her. "I'll drop them into that collecting-box outside the church," he thought to himself.

Tonight, late though it was, there were many folk about in the square, natives for the most part, padding softly along, and there were still a few taxis on the rank. But he preferred to walk home, for he had been so busy all day that he had given his firm fat body no sort of exercise. So crossing the square he went up the street which led to his house. Here the cafés were already closed, and soon the pavements grew empty. The waning moon had risen, and though the lights of the street grew more sparse as he emerged into the residential quarter, his way lay bright before him. In his hand he still held the two piastres which had been flung back at him ready for the collection-box. He walked briskly, for the night was cool, and it was no exercise to saunter. Not a breath of wind stirred the air, and the clatter of the dry palm-leaves was dumb.

He was now approaching the Roman Catholic church, when a step suddenly sounded out crisp and distinct behind him. He remembered then for the first time what had happened some nights ago and halted and listened: not a sound broke the stillness. He whisked round, but the street seemed empty. On he went again, now more slowly, and there was the following step again, neither gaining on him nor falling behind; to judge by the loudness of it, it could not be more than a dozen paces in his rear. Then a very obvious explanation occurred to him: no doubt this was some echo of his own footsteps. He went more quickly, and the steps behind him quickened; he stopped and they stopped. The whole thing was clear enough, and not a shadow of uneasiness, or anything approaching it, was in his mind. He slipped his ironical alms into the collecting-box outside the church, and was amused to hear that they evoked no tinkle from within. "Quite a little windfall for those brown-gowned fellows; they'll buy another rosary," he said to himself, and soon, with the echo of his own steps following, he turned in at his gate. Once inside, he slipped behind a myrtle bush that stood at the edge of the gravel walk, to see if by chance anyone passed on the road outside. But nothing happened, and his theory of the echo, though it was odd that he should never have noticed it till so lately, seemed quite confirmed.

From that night onwards he made it a practice, if he dined at the club, to walk home. Sometimes the step followed him, but not always, and this was an objection to that sensible echo theory. But the matter was no sort of worry to him except sometimes when he woke in the night, and found that his brain, still drowsy and not in complete control, was brooding over it with an ever-increasing preoccupation. Often that misgiving faded away and he dropped off to dreamless sleep again; sometimes it was sufficiently disquieting to bring him broad awake, and then with all his senses about him, it vanished. But there was this condition, halfway between waking and sleeping, when in the twilight chamber of his brain something listened, something feared. When fully awake he no more thought of it than he thought of that frowsy Levantine tobacco merchant whom he had evicted and whose funeral he chanced to have seen.

Early in December his cousin and partner in the sugar-business came down from Cairo to spend a week with him. Bill Cresswell may be succinctly described as 'a hot lot', and often after dinner at the club he left his cousin to his cronies and the sedater pleasures of bridge, and went out with a duplicate latchkey in his pocket on livelier private affairs. One night, the last of Bill's sojourn here, there was 'nothing doing' and the two set forth together homewards from the club.

"Nice night, let's walk," said John. "Nothing like a walk when there's liquid on board. Clears the brain for you and I must have a final powwow tonight, if you're off tomorrow. There are some bits of things still to go through."

Bill acquiesced. The cafés were all closed, there was nothing very promising.

"Night life here ain't a patch on Cairo," he observed. "Everyone seems to go to bed here just about when we begin to get going. Not but what I haven't enjoyed my stay with you. Capital good fellows at your club and brandy to match."

He stopped and ruefully scanned the quiet and emptiness of the street.

"Not a soul anywhere," he said. "Shutters up, all gone to bed. Nothing for it but a powwow, I guess."

They walked on in silence for a while. Then behind them, firm and distinct to John's ears, there sprang up the sound of the footsteps, for which now he knew that he waited and listened. He wheeled round.

"What's up?" asked Bill.

"Curious thing," said John. "Night after night now, though not every night, when I walk home, I hear a step following me. I heard it then."

Bill gave a vinous giggle.

"No such luck for me," he said. "I like to hear a step following me about one of a morning. Something agreeable may come of it. Wish I could hear it."

They walked on, and again, clearer than before, John heard what was inaudible to the other. He told himself, as he often did now, that it was an echo. But it was odd that the echo only repeated the footfalls of one of them. As he recognised this, he felt for the first time, when he was fully awake, some sudden chill of fear. It was as if a cold hand closed for a moment on his heart, just pressing it softly, almost tenderly. But they were now close to his own gate, and presently it clanged behind them.

Bill returned next day to the gladder life of Cairo. John Cresswell saw him off at the station and was passing out into the street again through the crowd of loungers and porters and passengers when there defined itself to his ear the sound of that footstep which he now knew so well. How he recognised it and isolated it from the tread of so many other feet he had no idea: simply his brain told him that it was following him again. He took a taxi to his office, and as he mounted the white stone stairs once more it was on his track. Once more the gentle pressure of cold fingers seemed to assure him of the presence that, though invisible, was very close to him, and now it was as if those fingers were pressed on some bell-push in his brain, and there sounded out a shrill tingle of fear. So hard-headed and sensible a man, of course, had nothing but scorn for all the clap-trap bogy tales of spirits and ghosts and hauntings, and he would have welcomed any sort of apparition in which the step manifested itself, in order to have the pleasure of laughing in its face. He would have liked to see a skeleton or some shrouded figure stand close to him; he would have slashed at it with his stick and convinced himself that there was nothing there. Whatever his own eyes appeared to see could not be so unnerving as these tokens of the invisible.

A stiff drink pulled him together again, and for the rest of the day there occurred no repetition of that tapping step which had begun to sprout with terror for him. In any case he was determined to fight it, for he realised that it was chiefly his own fear that troubled him. No doubt he was suffering from some small nervous derangement; he had been working very hard, and after Christmas, if the thing continued to worry him, probably he would see a doctor, who would prescribe him some tonic or some sedative which would send the step into the limbo from which it had come. But it was more probable that his cure was in his own hands: his own resistance was all the medicine he needed.

It was in pursuance of this very sane policy that he set out that night after an evening at the club to walk home: he faced it just because he knew that some black well was digging itself into his soul. To yield, to take a taxi, was to retreat, and if he did that, if he gave way an inch, he guessed that he might be soon flying in panic before an invading and imaginary host of phantoms. He had no use for phantoms; the solid satisfactions of life were enough occupation. Once more, as he drew near the church, the step sprang up, and now he sought no longer to tell himself it was an echo. Instead he fixed his mind on it, saying to himself, "There it is and it can't hurt me. Let it walk all day and night behind me if it chooses. It's got a fancy for me." Then his garden gate shut behind him, and with a sigh of relief he knew that he had passed out of its beat, for when once he was within, it never came farther.

He stood for a moment on his threshold, after he had opened his door, pleased with himself for having faced it. The bright light shone full on to the straight gravel walk he had just traversed. It was quite empty, and nothing was looking in through his gate. Then he heard from close at hand the crunch of the gravel underneath the heel of some invisible wayfarer. Now was the time to assert himself again, to look his fear in the eyes and mock at it.

"Come along, whoever you are," he called, "and have a drink before you get back to hell. Something cooling. Drop of cold water, isn't it?"

Thick sweat had broken out on his forehead, and his hand on the doorknob shook as with ague as he stood there looking out on to the bright empty path. But he did not flinch from the lesson he was teaching himself. The seconds ticked away: he could count them from the pulse that hammered in his throat. "I'll give it a hundred beats," he said to himself, "and then I'll say goodnight to Mr. Nothing-at-all."

He counted his hundred, he gave ten beats more for good luck. "Goodnight, you old fraud," he said, and went in and secured the door.

It seemed indeed for the week that followed that he had rightly gauged the nature of the hallucination which had threatened to establish its awful dominion over him. Never once, whether by day or night, did there come to his ears that footfall which he feared and listened for, nor, if in the dead hours of the darkness he lay for a while between sleep and waking, did he quake with a sense that something unseen and aware was watching him. A little courage, a flat denial of his fears had been sufficient not only to scotch them, but to snuff out the manifestation which had caused them. He kept his thoughts well in hand, he would not even conjecture what had been the cause of that visitation. Occasionally, while it still vexed him, he had cast about for the origin of it, he had wondered whether that shrill Levantine hag calling curses on him could somehow have found root in his mind. But now it was past and done with: he would have a few days' remission from work, if it was overwork that had been at the bottom of it, at Christmas, and perhaps it would be prudent not to be quite so free with the club brandy.

On Christmas Eve he and his friends sat at their bridge till close on midnight, then lingered over a drink, wished each other seasonable greetings and dispersed. Cresswell hesitated as to whether he should not take a taxi home, for the object with which he had trudged back there so often seemed to be gained, and he no longer feared the recurrence of the step. But he thought he would just set the seal on his victory and went on foot.

He had come to the point in his walk where he had first heard the step. Tonight, as usual, there was none, and he stopped a moment looking round him securely and serenely. It was a bright night, luminous with a moon a little after the full, and it amazed him to think that he had ever fashioned a terror to himself in this quiet, orderly street. From not far ahead there came the sound of the bells of the church saluting Christmas morning. They would have been holding their midnight Mass there. He breathed the night air with content, and throwing the butt of his spent cigar into the roadway, he walked on again.

With a sudden sinking of his heart, he heard behind him the step which he thought he had silenced for ever. It was faint at first, but tonight, instead of keeping at a uniform distance behind him, it was approaching. Louder and more crisp it sounded, until it was close to him. On and on it came, still gaining on him, and now there brushed by him, though not quite touching him, the figure of a man in European dress, with his head wrapped in a shawl.

"Hullo, you there," called Cresswell. "You're the skunk who's been following me, are you, and slipping out of sight again? No more of your damned conjuring tricks. Let's have a look at you."

The figure, now some two or three yards ahead of him, stopped at the sound of his voice and turned round. The shawl covered its face, but for a narrow chink between the edges.

"So you understand English," said Cresswell. "Now I'll thank you to take that shawl off your face, and let me see who it is that's been dogging me."

The man raised his hands and threw back the shawl. The moonlight shone on his face, and that face was just a slab of smooth yellowish flesh extending from ear to ear, empty as the oval of an egg without eyes or nose or mouth. From the upper edge of the shawl where it crossed the forehead there depended a few wisps of grey hair.

Cresswell looked, and a wave of panic fear submerged his very soul. He gave a little thin squeal and started to run, listening the while in an agony of terror to hear if the steps of that nameless, faceless, creature were following. He must run, he must run, to get away from that thing out of hell which had manifested itself.

Then close at hand he saw the lights of the church, and there perhaps he could find sanctuary from it. The door was open, and he sprang up the steps. Close by there were lights burning on the altar of a side chapel, and he flung himself on his knees. Not for years had he attempted to pray, and now in the agony of his soul he could but say in a gabbling whisper, "O my God: O my God." Over and over he said it.

By degrees some sort of self-control came back to him. There were holy images, there was a sacred picture above the altar, a smell of hallowing incense was in the air. Surely there was protection here, a power that would intervene between him and the terror of that face. A sort of tranquillity overscored his panic, and he began to look round.

The church was darker than it had been when he entered, and he saw that some of those cowled brown-habited men of the order were moving quietly about, quenching the lights. Those at the altar in front of which he knelt were still bright, and now he saw one of these cowled figures move up close to him, as if waiting for him to finish his devotions. He was calm now, his panic had quite passed, and he rose from his knees.

"I've had a terrible fright, Father," he said to the monk. "I saw something just now out in the street which must have come out of hell."

The figure turned a little towards him: the cowl concealed its face altogether, and the voice came muffled.

"Indeed, my son," he said. "Tell me what it is that frightened you."

Cresswell felt some backwash of his panic returning.

"A man passed me as I was going back to my house," he said, "and I told him to stop and let me have a look at him. He wore a shawl over his head and he threw it back. Oh, my God, that face!"

The monk quietly raised his hands and grasped the edges of his cowl. Then with a quick movement he threw it back.

"That sort of face?" he said.

The Secret of Macarger's Gulch

Ambrose Bierce

NORTHWESTWARDLY from Indian Hill, about nine miles as the crow flies, is Macarger's Gulch. It is not much of a gulch – a mere depression between two wooded ridges of inconsiderable height. From its mouth up to its head – for gulches, like rivers, have an anatomy of their own – the distance does not exceed two miles, and the width at bottom is at only one place more than a dozen yards; for most of the distance on either side of the little brook which drains it in winter, and goes dry in the early spring, there is no level ground at all; the steep slopes of the hills, covered with an almost impenetrable growth of manzanita and chemisal, are parted by nothing but the width of the water course. No one but an occasional enterprising hunter of the vicinity ever goes into Macarger's Gulch, and five miles away it is unknown, even by name. Within that distance in any direction are far more conspicuous topographical features without names, and one might try in vain to ascertain by local inquiry the origin of the name of this one.

About midway between the head and the mouth of Macarger's Gulch, the hill on the right as you ascend is cloven by another gulch, a short dry one, and at the junction of the two is a level space of two or three acres, and there a few years ago stood an old board house containing one small room. How the component parts of the house, few and simple as they were, had been assembled at that almost inaccessible point is a problem in the solution of which there would be greater satisfaction than advantage. Possibly the creek bed is a reformed road. It is certain that the gulch was at one time pretty thoroughly prospected by miners, who must have had some means of getting in with at least pack animals carrying tools and supplies; their profits, apparently, were not such as would have justified any considerable outlay to connect Macarger's Gulch with any center of civilization enjoying the distinction of a sawmill. The house, however, was there, most of it. It lacked a door and a window frame, and the chimney of mud and stones had fallen into an unlovely heap, overgrown with rank weeds. Such humble furniture as there may once have been and much of the lower weatherboarding, had served as fuel in the camp fires of hunters; as had also, probably, the curbing of an old well, which at the time I write of existed in the form of a rather wide but not very deep depression near by.

One afternoon in the summer of 1874, I passed up Macarger's Gulch from the narrow valley into which it opens, by following the dry bed of the brook. I was quail-shooting and had made a bag of about a dozen birds by the time I had reached the house described, of whose existence I was until then unaware. After rather carelessly inspecting the ruin I resumed my sport, and having fairly good success prolonged it until near sunset, when it occurred to me that I was a long way from any human habitation – too far to reach one by nightfall. But in my game bag was food, and the old house would afford shelter, if shelter were needed on a warm and dewless night in the foothills of the Sierra Nevada, where one may sleep in comfort on the pine needles, without covering. I am fond of solitude and love the night, so my resolution to 'camp out' was soon taken, and by the time that it was dark I had made my bed of boughs and grasses in a corner of the room and was roasting a quail at a fire that I had kindled on the hearth. The smoke escaped out of the ruined chimney, the light illuminated the room with a kindly glow, and as I ate my simple meal of plain bird and drank the remains of a bottle of red wine which had served me all the afternoon in place of the water, which the region did not supply, I experienced a sense of comfort which better fare and accommodations do not always give.

Nevertheless, there was something lacking. I had a sense of comfort, but not of security. I detected myself staring more frequently at the open doorway and blank window than I could find warrant for doing. Outside these apertures all was black, and I was unable to repress a certain feeling of apprehension as my fancy pictured the outer world and filled it with unfriendly entities, natural and supernatural – chief among which, in their respective classes, were the grizzly bear, which I knew was occasionally still seen in that region, and the ghost, which I had reason to think was not. Unfortunately, our feelings do not always respect the law of probabilities, and to me that evening, the possible and the impossible were equally disquieting.

Everyone who has had experience in the matter must have observed that one confronts the actual and imaginary perils of the night with far less apprehension in the open air than in a house with an open doorway. I felt this now as I lay on my leafy couch in a corner of the room next to the chimney and permitted my fire to die out. So strong became my sense of the presence of something malign and menacing in the place, that I found myself almost unable to withdraw my eyes from the opening, as in the deepening darkness it became more and more indistinct. And when the last little flame flickered and went out I grasped the shotgun which I had laid at my side and actually turned the muzzle in the direction of the now invisible entrance, my thumb on one of the hammers, ready to cock the piece, my breath suspended, my muscles rigid and tense. But later I laid down the weapon with a sense of shame and mortification. What did I fear, and why? – I, to whom the night had been

a more familiar face
Than that of man –

I, in whom that element of hereditary superstition from which none of us is altogether free had given to solitude and darkness and silence only a more alluring interest and charm! I was unable to comprehend my folly, and losing in the conjecture the thing conjectured of, I fell asleep. And then I dreamed.

I was in a great city in a foreign land – a city whose people were of my own race, with minor differences of speech and costume; yet precisely what these were I could not say; my sense of them was indistinct. The city was dominated by a great castle upon an overlooking height whose name I knew, but could not speak. I walked through many streets, some broad and straight with high, modern buildings, some narrow, gloomy, and tortuous, between the gables of quaint old houses whose overhanging stories, elaborately ornamented with carvings in wood and stone, almost met above my head.

I sought someone whom I had never seen, yet knew that I should recognize when found. My quest was not aimless and fortuitous; it had a definite method. I turned from one street into another without hesitation and threaded a maze of intricate passages, devoid of the fear of losing my way.

Presently I stopped before a low door in a plain stone house which might have been the dwelling of an artisan of the better sort, and without announcing myself, entered. The room, rather sparely furnished, and lighted by a single window with small diamond-shaped panes, had but two occupants; a man and a woman. They took no notice of my intrusion, a circumstance which, in the manner of dreams, appeared entirely natural. They were not conversing; they sat apart, unoccupied and sullen.

The woman was young and rather stout, with fine large eyes and a certain grave beauty; my memory of her expression is exceedingly vivid, but in dreams one does not observe the details of faces. About her shoulders was a plaid shawl. The man was older, dark, with an evil face made more forbidding by a long scar extending from near the left temple diagonally downward into the black moustache; though in my dreams it seemed rather to haunt the face as a thing apart – I can express it no otherwise – than to belong to it. The moment that I found the man and woman I knew them to be husband and wife.

What followed, I remember indistinctly; all was confused and inconsistent – made so, I think, by gleams of consciousness. It was as if two pictures, the scene of my dream, and my actual surroundings, had been blended, one overlying the other, until the former, gradually fading, disappeared, and I was broad awake in the deserted cabin, entirely and tranquilly conscious of my situation.

My foolish fear was gone, and opening my eyes I saw that my fire, not altogether burned out, had revived by the falling of a stick and was again lighting the room. I had probably slept only a few minutes, but my commonplace dream had somehow so strongly impressed me that I was no longer drowsy; and after a little while I rose, pushed the embers of my fire together, and lighting my pipe proceeded in a rather ludicrously methodical way to meditate upon my vision.

It would have puzzled me then to say in what respect it was worth attention. In the first moment of serious thought that I gave to the matter I recognized the city of my dream as Edinburgh, where I had never been; so if the dream was a memory it was a memory of pictures and description. The recognition somehow deeply impressed me; it was as if something in my mind insisted rebelliously against will and reason on the importance of all this. And that faculty, whatever it was, asserted also a control of my speech. "Surely," I said aloud, quite involuntarily, "the MacGregors must have come here from Edinburgh."

At the moment, neither the substance of this remark nor the fact of my making it, surprised me in the least; it seemed entirely natural that I should know the name of my dreamfolk and something of their history. But the absurdity of it all soon dawned upon me: I laughed aloud, knocked the ashes from my pipe and again stretched myself upon my bed of boughs and grass, where I lay staring absently into my failing fire, with no further thought of either my dream or my surroundings. Suddenly the single remaining flame crouched for a moment, then, springing upward, lifted itself clear of its embers and expired in air. The darkness was absolute.

At that instant – almost, it seemed, before the gleam of the blaze had faded from my eyes – there was a dull, dead sound, as of some heavy body falling upon the floor, which shook beneath me as I lay. I sprang to a sitting posture and groped at my side for my gun; my notion was that some wild beast had leaped in through the open window. While the flimsy structure was still shaking from the impact I heard the sound of blows, the scuffling of feet upon the floor, and then – it seemed to come from almost within reach of my hand, the sharp shrieking of a woman in mortal agony. So horrible a cry I had never heard nor conceived; it utterly unnerved me; I was conscious for a moment of nothing but my own terror! Fortunately my hand now found the weapon of which it was in search, and the familiar touch somewhat restored me. I leaped to my feet, straining my eyes to pierce the darkness. The violent sounds had ceased, but more terrible than these, I heard, at what seemed long intervals, the faint intermittent gasping of some living, dying thing!

As my eyes grew accustomed to the dim light of the coals in the fireplace, I saw first the shapes of the door and window, looking blacker than the black of the walls. Next, the distinction between wall and floor became discernible, and at last I was sensible to the form and full expanse of the floor from end to end and side to side. Nothing was visible and the silence was unbroken.

With a hand that shook a little, the other still grasping my gun, I restored my fire and made a critical examination of the place. There was nowhere any sign that the cabin had been entered. My own tracks were visible in the dust covering the floor, but there were no others. I relit my pipe, provided fresh fuel by ripping a thin board or two from the inside of the house – I did not care to go into the darkness out of doors – and passed the rest of the night smoking and thinking, and feeding my fire; not for added years of life would I have permitted that little flame to expire again.

* * *

Some years afterward I met in Sacramento a man named Morgan, to whom I had a note of introduction from a friend in San Francisco. Dining with him one evening at his home I observed various 'trophies' upon the wall, indicating that he was fond of shooting. It turned out that he was, and in relating some of his feats he mentioned having been in the region of my adventure.

"Mr. Morgan," I asked abruptly, "do you know a place up there called Macarger's Gulch?"

"I have good reason to," he replied; "it was I who gave to the newspapers, last year, the accounts of the finding of the skeleton there."

I had not heard of it; the accounts had been published, it appeared, while I was absent in the East.

"By the way," said Morgan, "the name of the gulch is a corruption; it should have been called 'MacGregor's'. My dear," he added, speaking to his wife, "Mr. Elderson has upset his wine."

That was hardly accurate – I had simply dropped it, glass and all.

"There was an old shanty once in the gulch," Morgan resumed when the ruin wrought by my awkwardness had been repaired, "but just previously to my visit it had been blown down, or rather blown away, for its *débris* was scattered all about, the very floor being parted, plank from plank. Between two of the sleepers still in position I and my companion observed the remnant of a plaid shawl, and examining it found that it was wrapped about the shoulders of the body of a woman, of which but little remained besides the bones, partly covered with fragments of clothing, and brown dry skin. But we will spare Mrs. Morgan," he added with a smile. The lady had indeed exhibited signs of disgust rather than sympathy.

"It is necessary to say, however," he went on, "that the skull was fractured in several places, as by blows of some blunt instrument; and that instrument itself – a pick-handle, still stained with blood – lay under the boards nearby."

Mr. Morgan turned to his wife. "Pardon me, my dear," he said with affected solemnity, "for mentioning these disagreeable particulars, the natural though regrettable incidents of a conjugal quarrel – resulting, doubtless, from the luckless wife's insubordination."

"I ought to be able to overlook it," the lady replied with composure; "you have so many times asked me to in those very words."

I thought he seemed rather glad to go on with his story.

"From these and other circumstances," he said, "the coroner's jury found that the deceased, Janet MacGregor, came to her death from blows inflicted by some person to the jury unknown; but it was added that the evidence pointed strongly to her husband, Thomas MacGregor, as the guilty person. But Thomas MacGregor has never been found nor heard of. It was learned that the couple came from Edinburgh, but not – my dear, do you not observe that Mr. Elderson's boneplate has water in it?"

I had deposited a chicken bone in my finger bowl.

"In a little cupboard I found a photograph of MacGregor, but it did not lead to his capture."

"Will you let me see it?" I said.

The picture showed a dark man with an evil face made more forbidding by a long scar extending from near the temple diagonally downward into the black mustache.

"By the way, Mr. Elderson," said my affable host, "may I know why you asked about 'Macarger's Gulch'?"

"I lost a mule near there once," I replied, "and the mischance has – has quite – upset me."

"My dear," said Mr. Morgan, with the mechanical intonation of an interpreter translating, "the loss of Mr. Elderson's mule has peppered his coffee."

Of Water

Die Booth

"ARE THERE dead people down there, Nain?"

Elain looks down at him, Leo grinning mischief back, his little hand hot in hers. The sun beats down across the lake, casting a mirage shimmer on the copper-green turrets of the Straining Tower. Turning it all fairy-tale, above water-level.

"Now, whyever would you ask that?"

"Because it's a *body* of water!"

She chuckles, more at how pleased with himself he is, than at the joke. "Very clever, young man. Too clever by half."

"Too right, too," Harry pipes up, beside her.

Elain rolls her eyes. "Don't you start." But knows as she says it that he's already started.

"Do you know what this lake is called, Leo?" Harry crouches down to look Leo in the eye: Elain hears the creak of his knees.

"Llyn Morwyn," Leo says. He shades his eyes with one hand to squint up into Harry's face.

"Aye, that's its *official* name, but do you know its *other* name?"

Leo shakes his head. Elain says, "You're as bad as one another." Looking between them, it's hard to see sixty years separating them, so similar are their bright expressions of almost vindictive curiosity.

"Do you know there's a village down there, under the lake?" Leo nods. Oh, he knows. All the children love that tale: the one that starts out with Queen Victoria's Authorities flooding a Welsh valley to make a reservoir to service the English, with little regard of the community they relocated to do it. It becomes, in the retelling, an eerie little Atlantis. "That was the original Pont Y Forwen, before they built the new Pont Y Forwen where your nain lives. Maiden's Bridge, that means, and they named the lake after it – Maiden's Lake. But what we call the lake round here is Llyn Ysbryd. Know what that means, lad?"

"Nope."

Elain looks out, across the calm expanse of water. It reflects the clouds so clearly, that if she blurs her eyes behind her spectacles, it's easy to forget which way is up and which is down. The trees that crawl the slope of every bank are golden green. On the horizon, the hills are hazy blue as the sky…

"*Ghost* lake," Harry announces, drama-laden.

Leo's face dawns a smile of sheer delight. "It's *haunted*? Did the people drown?"

"Nobody drowned," Elain says. "They moved all the families out into the new houses they'd built for them long before they flooded the valley."

"But Harry said there's bodies!"

"How on earth did you get so morbid?" His little face is so eager. "Well, when they had everybody move house, they didn't move the graveyard, so all of the bodies stayed buried down there when it was all flooded. The people from the village weren't happy about it." Leo frowns. He looks puzzled, as if he can't understand why anyone would be upset about such a thing. Elain sighs. "So… I suppose that the lake *might* be haunted, then."

The frown smooths, at that, like rippled water calming. "Coooool!" Elain pats his close-cropped curls, her smile coming in spite of herself.

"And did your nain ever tell you, sometimes in the summer, when the water level gets really low, you can still see the church steeple sticking out of the water? And when it's a really dark night, you can hear the church bell tolling, ding, ding, ding, still calling the people to prayer through the deep?"

"Don't say that, Harry, you'll scare the boy!"

Leo grins. "I'm not scared."

No, thinks Elain. *No, you're not.*

* * *

That night, the church bells stir her in her dreams, sounding a longing bidding, but when she wakes fully, the night is silent except for the wind, and the creaks, and the ever-present drip of the house. When she goes to look out across the moonlit expanse of water, silver and flat as the mirror by the window, it's there again.

She saw it first by the Straining Tower, distant across the silent depths. At first she'd thought it was some strangeness of the process – the tower backwashing water out – and then, perhaps some trick of the moonlight. Nobody has ever lived in that tower. It was built, in all of its gothic splendour, to filter the contents of the reservoir before it went on its way via aqueduct to supply Coverdale with tap-water, and it was never manned. Still, Elain dreams often that she lives there. That her place is switched with it, and the world she sees from the window replaces her own, mirrored. That whatever she sees, night after night, drawing closer across the shimmering lake, is beneath her window, lapping at the stones, seeking entry.

* * *

"Nain, why don't we dissolve in water?"

"Because we're people, not aspirin."

The sun still glares, turning the landscape to glass and powder, but the shadows are longer now. Elain adjusts the brim of her hat as Leo skips ahead, along the wide dam bridge with its scalloped balustrades.

"But if we're made of seventy per cent water, why doesn't it leak out?"

"Because it's not just sitting there in our bellies. It's inside our cells and flesh and our blood. Blood's liquid, but it doesn't just leak out of us willy-nilly, does it?"

As soon as she says it, Elain feels a little strange and wishes she hadn't, but Leo just laughs and says, "No." And the anticipated gory speculation doesn't come. Then, "Sometimes we leak, though. Tears."

"Yes, I suppose so. Sometimes."

She watches him run ahead, spreading his arms wide, his shadow leaping around his feet. When she leans against the balustrade of the dam, the stone is warm, rough beneath her elbows. She bends her head. The water beckons. Down there, in the serene darkness, soft weeds blanket a sleeping village, populated now only by darting trout.

This time, when she sees it, she's almost expecting it. It's closer now, groping at the water's edge, where the weeds fringe the soaked earth. Lapping water, greenish-clear as old glass, agitated as if churned up by a boat's oars. Coalescing into something more. It looks like a pair of arms, butterfly-stroke flapping up onto the shore from the shallows like a beached fish, smashing itself to droplets on the mud and running back into the water, before starting again. Elain watches, feeling the push of the sun against her back. She should feel something. Some dread, as it reaches out to her. As it illuminates a long-locked hollow inside her heart.

"Nain?" Leo's voice tugs her from her thoughts; a jerked mooring rope.

She blinks as she turns to him. "Yes, love?"

"Is the Lady of the Lake in there?"

Glancing back at the shore below, Elain expects to see the water calmed, whatever trick of the currents it was to be over. But it's still there, a stray mermaid striving for land. "She might be," Elain says.

* * *

Autumn trails the rain along. It stays. Maiden's Lake loses its summer sparkle, and turns slate-grey and pensive. The house shivers. There's a chronic problem with damp, rivulets of water invading through every crack. The window panes ripple with it. The paint curls. Elain keeps the heating turned up on constant, else the carpets and cushions get so chilled they feel clammy.

In these days of misting rain, when the hills hide themselves in cloaks of fog and the banks of the lake turn treacherous with a slick of orange leaves, rotting to black, Leo plays indoors. His visits have a different texture. Biscuits and hot chocolate replace ice cream and pop, and Harry drops by with films on DVD that he borrows from his niece.

Something noisy is happening on-screen, but it seems far away to Elain. She's sitting by the window with her embroidery, making the most of the failing daylight. Across the lake, the verdigris turrets of the Straining Tower become a place where princesses are imprisoned by jealous law; the long pulley chain sways ominously against the pale curve of stonework. Elain is trapped. Gazing out through the condensation to the grey rain.

Plummeting droplets smash on the path slabs. It's heavy fall. Already the little lawn is waterlogged, pools pocking the trodden grass. The curtain of rain is so thick, almost a solid thing, that Elain imagines she can see shapes forming from it. It's almost as if she expects to see it. *Wants* to see it. The Lady of the Lake. Leaning closer, her breath adds opacity to the condensed window glass. One shape, shivering and indistinct, coalescing from the drops, reaching through the spaces in between… Elain wipes the fogged pane briskly with the corner of her sleeve. It's gone. It's… she squints, closer and yet more indistinct. The water has collected in the dip before the front doorstep. It pushes up from the puddle, groping for shape, raising up a shuddering head and shoulders, before collapsing back under its own weight like a burst water balloon. As she watches, Elain sees reaching fingers, breaking – tentative but determined – the surface of the pool.

"Nain!" She doesn't look at him. Can't pull her gaze away from the uninvited guest at her front door. Leo's voice grows impatient. "You're not watching properly!"

"Sorry, love." The room is warm with yellow light, the flash and clamour of superheroes on-screen. Its cosy hold feels less real than the cold outside. With effort, she turns her attention towards the television. The now. "Tell me again. Who's that, there, then?"

She can hear Leo answering, explaining, excited, but she doesn't know what he's saying. The falling water is watching. Quickly, she draws the curtains.

* * *

The weather persists into winter. Elain buys a new lamp for the living room, and angles the mirror more towards the window, hoping to reflect more light; but all it really reflects is the flicker of falling rain.

"It's so dark so early these days." She lets the curtain fall back in place, the words out before she realises what she's saying. "I'm sick of shadows."

"It's OK, Nain. You've got me here."

"I do. I do." When she closes her eyes, the water curls behind them, stirred with shadow like two colours of ink marbled together.

"Nain… are you going to marry Harry?"

In her mind's eye the water swirls, takes on the shape of flowing robes. A woman twirling. She opens her eyes and smiles at Leo. "No, love. Harry's just your nain's friend."

* * *

When the rain won't quit, Leo skips his next visit. Elain watches the rising waters reflected in the mirror, and does not have him there. Swirling water covers the front step and the damp runs down the walls like waterfalls. Everything feels cold to the touch. She drags sandbags to the doors, and goes upstairs to bed, and sleeps the dreamless sleep of the dead.

At first light, she's shaken awake by a crash. The winter world is underwater blue and when she goes downstairs she's met at the foot by the flood. The world is leaking. She wades. Her dressing gown floats around her like robes of old. In the living room, familiar things turned foreign bob on the tide. The mirror by the window, dislodged by the wash and fallen, lies cracked side to side. Perhaps the dam cracked too, and the Ghost Lake is taking new Pont Y Forwen down, to drown alongside the old. Or maybe the water just wanted to come in. Inside. The lake has come inside. Elain's strides swish. She searches for her.

"Come out."

It's deep enough, now.

She stretches out a hand and the flood reaches out to take it. "I knew you'd come for me."

The lady is the lake. She stands from it, of it, a fountain in the form of figure, limbs rippling with the purl of water. Clear as glass is her streaming cloak. Her eyes are made of joyful tears. Lit from within. She is glorious. And Elain recognises, now, her face.

Eveline's Visitant

Mary Elizabeth Braddon

IT WAS AT a masked ball at the Palais Royal that my fatal quarrel with my first cousin André de Brissac began. The quarrel was about a woman. The women who followed the footsteps of Philip of Orleans were the causes of many such disputes; and there was scarcely one fair head in all that glittering throng which, to a man versed in social histories and mysteries, might not have seemed bedabbled with blood.

I shall not record the name of her for love of whom André de Brissac and I crossed one of the bridges, in the dim August dawn on our way to the waste ground beyond the church of Saint-Germain des Prés.

There were many beautiful vipers in those days, and she was one of them. I can feel the chill breath of that August morning blowing in my face, as I sit in my dismal chamber at my château of Puy Verdun tonight, alone in the stillness, writing the strange story of my life. I can see the white mist rising from the river, the grim outline of the Châtelet, and the square towers of Notre Dame black against the pale-grey sky. Even more vividly can I recall André's fair young face, as he stood opposite to me with his two friends – scoundrels both, and alike eager for that unnatural fray. We were a strange group to be seen in a summer sunrise, all of us fresh from the heat and clamour of the Regent's saloons – André in a quaint hunting-dress copied from a family portrait at Puy Verdun, I costumed as one of Law's Mississippi Indians; the other men in like garish frippery, adorned with broideries and jewels that looked wan in the pale light of dawn.

Our quarrel had been a fierce one – a quarrel which could have but one result, and that the direst. I had struck him; and the welt raised by my open hand was crimson upon his fair womanish face as he stood opposite to me. The eastern sun shone on the face presently, and dyed the cruel mark with a deeper red; but the sting of my own wrongs was fresh, and I had not yet learned to despise myself for that brutal outrage.

To André de Brissac such an insult was most terrible. He was the favourite of Fortune, the favourite of women; and I was nothing – a rough soldier who had done my country good service, but in the boudoir of a Parabère a mannerless boor.

We fought, and I wounded him mortally. Life had been very sweet for him; and I think that a frenzy of despair took possession of him when he felt the life-blood ebbing away. He beckoned me to him as he lay on the ground. I went, and knelt at his side.

"Forgive me, André!" I murmured.

He took no more heed of my words than if that piteous entreaty had been the idle ripple of the river near at hand.

"Listen to me, Hector de Brissac," he said. "I am not one who believes that a man has done with earth because his eyes glaze and his jaw stiffens. They will bury me in the old vault at Puy Verdun; and you will be master of the château. Ah, I know how lightly they take things in these days, and how Dubois will laugh when he hears that Ça has been killed in a duel. They will bury me, and sing masses for my soul; but you and I have not finished our affair yet, my cousin. I will be with you when you least look to see me – I, with this ugly scar upon the face that women have praised and loved. I will come to you when your life seems brightest. I will come between you and all that you hold fairest and dearest. My ghostly hand shall drop a poison in your cup of joy. My shadowy form shall shut the sunlight from your life. Men with such iron will as mine can do what they please, Hector de Brissac. It is my will to haunt you when I am dead."

All this in short broken sentences he whispered into my ear. I had need to bend my ear close to his dying lips; but the iron will of André de Brissac was strong enough to do battle with Death, and I believe he said all he wished to say before his head fell back upon the velvet cloak they had spread beneath him, never to be lifted again.

As he lay there, you would have fancied him a fragile stripling, too fair and frail for the struggle called life; but there are those who remember the brief manhood of André de Brissac, and who can bear witness to the terrible force of that proud nature.

I stood looking down at the young face with that foul mark upon it, and God knows I was sorry for what I had done.

Of those blasphemous threats which he had whispered in my ear I took no heed. I was a soldier, and a believer. There was nothing absolutely dreadful to me in the thought that I had killed this man. I had killed many men on the battlefield; and this one had done me cruel wrong.

My friends would have had me cross the frontier to escape the consequences of my act; but I was ready to face those consequences, and I remained in France. I kept aloof from the court, and received a hint that I had best confine myself to my own province. Many masses were chanted in the little chapel of Puy Verdun, for the soul of my dead cousin, and his coffin filled a niche in the vault of our ancestors.

His death had made me a rich man; and the thought that it was so made my newly acquired wealth very hateful to me. I lived a lonely existence in the old château, where I rarely held converse with any but the servants of the household, all of whom had served my cousin, and none of whom liked me.

It was a hard and bitter life. It galled me, when I rode through the village, to see the peasant-children shrink away from me. I have seen old women cross themselves stealthily as I passed them by. Strange reports had gone forth about me; and there were those who whispered that I had given my soul to the Evil One as the price of my cousin's heritage. From my boyhood I had been dark of visage and stern of manner; and hence, perhaps, no woman's love had ever been mine. I remembered my mother's face in all its changes of expression; but I can remember no look of affection that ever shone on me. That other woman, beneath whose feet I laid my heart, was pleased to accept my homage, but she never loved me; and the end was treachery.

I had grown hateful to myself, and had well-nigh begun to hate my fellow-creatures, when a feverish desire seized upon me, and I pined to be back in the press and throng of the busy world once again. I went back to Paris, where I kept myself aloof from the court, and where an angel took compassion upon me.

She was the daughter of an old comrade, a man whose merits had been neglected, whose achievements had been ignored, and who sulked in his shabby lodging like a rat in a hole, while all Paris went mad with the Scotch Financier, and gentlemen and lacqueys were trampling one another to death in the Rue Quin-campoix. The only child of this little cross-grained old captain of dragoons was an incarnate sunbeam, whose mortal name was Eveline Duchalet.

She loved me. The richest blessings of our lives are often those which cost us least. I wasted the best years of my youth in the worship of a wicked woman, who jilted and cheated me at last.

I gave this meek angel but a few courteous words – a little fraternal tenderness – and lo, she loved me. The life which had been so dark and desolate grew bright beneath her influence; and I went back to Puy Verdun with a fair young bride for my companion.

Ah, how sweet a change there was in my life and in my home! The village children no longer shrank appalled as the dark horseman rode by, the village crones no longer crossed themselves; for a woman rode by his side – a woman whose charities had won the love of all those ignorant creatures, and whose companionship had transformed the gloomy lord of the chateau into a loving husband and a gentle master. The old retainers forgot the untimely fate of my cousin, and served me with cordial willingness, for love of their young mistress.

There are no words which can tell the pure and perfect happiness of that time. I felt like a traveller who had traversed the frozen seas of an arctic region, remote from human love or human companionship, to find himself on a sudden in the bosom of a verdant valley, in the sweet atmosphere of home. The change seemed too bright to be real; and I strove in vain to put away from my mind the vague suspicion that my new life was but some fantastic dream.

So brief were those halcyon hours, that, looking back on them now, it is scarcely strange if I am still half inclined to fancy the first days of my married life could have been no more than a dream.

Neither in my days of gloom nor in my days of happiness had I been troubled by the recollection of André's blasphemous oath.

The words which with his last breath he had whispered in my ear were vain and meaningless to me. He had vented his rage in those idle threats, as he might have vented it in idle execrations.

That he will haunt the footsteps of his enemy after death is the one revenge which a dying man can promise himself; and if men had power thus to avenge themselves, the earth would be peopled with phantoms.

I had lived for three years at Puy Verdun; sitting alone in the solemn midnight by the hearth where he had sat, pacing the corridors that had echoed his footfall; and in all that time my fancy had never so played me false as to shape the shadow of the dead. Is it strange, then, if I had forgotten Andre's horrible promise? There was no portrait of my cousin at Puy Verdun. It was the age of boudoir art, and a miniature set in the lid of a gold bonbonnière, or hidden artfully in a massive bracelet, was more fashionable than a clumsy life-size image, fit only to hang on the gloomy walls of a provincial chateau rarely visited by its owner. My cousin's fair face had adorned more than one bonbonnière, and had been concealed in more than one bracelet; but it was not among the faces that looked down from the panelled walls of Puy Verdun.

In the library I found a picture which awoke painful associations. It was the portrait of a De Brissac, who had flourished in the time of Francis the First; and it was from this picture that my cousin Andre had copied the quaint hunting-dress he wore at the Regent's ball. The library was a room in which I spent a good deal of my life; and I ordered a curtain to be hung before this picture.

We had been married three months, when Eveline one day asked, "Who is the lord of the château nearest to this?"

I looked with her in astonishment.

"My dearest," I answered, "do you not know that there is no other chateau within forty miles of Puy Verdun?"

"Indeed!" she said; "that is strange."

I asked her why the fact seemed strange to her; and after much entreaty I obtained from her the reason of her surprise.

In her walks about the park and woods during the last month, she had met a man who, by his dress and bearing, was obviously of noble rank. She had imagined that he occupied some château near at hand, and that his estate adjoined ours. I was at a loss to imagine who this stranger could be; for my estate of Puy Verdun lay in the heart of a desolate region, and unless when some traveller's coach went lumbering and jingling through the village, one had little more chance of encountering a gentleman than of meeting a demigod.

"Have you seen this man often, Eveline?" I asked.

She answered, in a tone which had a touch of sadness, "I see him every day."

"Where, dearest?"

"Sometimes in the park, sometimes in the wood. You know the little cascade, Hector, where there is some old neglected rock-work that forms a kind of cavern. I have taken a fancy to that spot, and have spent many mornings there reading. Of late I have seen the stranger there every morning."

"He has never dared to address you?"

"Never. I have looked up from my book, and have seen him standing at a little distance, watching me silently. I have continued reading; and when I have raised my eyes again I have found him gone. He must approach and depart with a stealthy tread, for I never hear his footfall. Sometimes I have almost wished that he would speak to me. It is so terrible to see him standing silently there."

"He is some insolent peasant who seeks to frighten you."

My wife shook her head.

"He is no peasant," she answered. "It is not by his dress alone I judge, for that is strange to me. He has an air of nobility which it is impossible to mistake."

"Is he young or old?"

"He is young and handsome."

I was much disturbed by the idea of this stranger's intrusion on my wife's solitude; and I went straight to the village to inquire if any stranger had been seen there. I could hear of no one. I questioned the servants closely, but without result. Then I determined to accompany my wife in her walks, and to judge for myself of the rank of the stranger.

For a week I devoted all my mornings to rustic rambles with Eveline in the park and woods; and in all that week we saw no one but an occasional peasant in sabots, or one of our own household returning from a neighbouring farm.

I was a man of studious habits, and those summer rambles disturbed the even current of my life. My wife perceived this, and entreated me to trouble myself no further.

"I will spend my mornings in the pleasaunce, Hector," she said; "the stranger cannot intrude upon me there."

"I begin to think the stranger is only a phantasm of your own romantic brain," I replied, smiling at the earnest face lifted to mine. "A châtelaine who is always reading romances may well meet handsome cavaliers in the woodlands. I daresay I have Mdlle. Scuderi to thank for this noble stranger, and that he is only the great Cyrus in modern costume."

"Ah, that is the point which mystifies me, Hector," she said. "The stranger's costume is not modern. He looks as an old picture might look if it could descend from its frame."

Her words pained me, for they reminded me of that hidden picture in the library, and the quaint hunting costume of orange and purple, which André de Brissac wore at the Regent's ball.

After this my wife confined her walks to the pleasaunce; and for many weeks I heard no more of the nameless stranger. I dismissed all thought of him from my mind, for a graver and heavier care had come upon me. My wife's health began to droop. The change in her was so gradual as to be almost imperceptible to those who watched her day by day. It was only when she put on a rich gala dress which she had not worn for months that I saw how wasted the form must be on which the embroidered bodice hung so loosely, and how wan and dim were the eyes which had once been brilliant as the jewels she wore in her hair.

I sent a messenger to Paris to summon one of the court physicians; but I knew that many days must needs elapse before he could arrive at Puy Verdun.

In the interval I watched my wife with unutterable fear.

It was not her health only that had declined. The change was more painful to behold than any physical alteration. The bright and sunny spirit had vanished, and in the place of my joyous young bride I beheld a woman weighed down by rooted melancholy. In vain I sought to fathom the cause of my darling's sadness. She assured me that she had no reason for sorrow or discontent, and that if she seemed sad without a motive, I must forgive her sadness, and consider it as a misfortune rather than a fault.

I told her that the court physician would speedily find some cure for her despondency, which must needs arise from physical causes, since she had no real ground for sorrow. But although she said nothing, I could see she had no hope or belief in the healing powers of medicine.

One day, when I wished to beguile her from that pensive silence in which she was wont to sit an hour at a time, I told her, laughing, that she appeared to have forgotten her mysterious cavalier of the wood, and it seemed also as if he had forgotten her.

To my wonderment, her pale face became of a sudden crimson; and from crimson changed to pale again in a breath.

"You have never seen him since you deserted your woodland grotto?" I said.

She turned to me with a heart-rending look.

"Hector," she cried, "I see him every day; and it is that which is killing me."

She burst into a passion of tears when she had said this. I took her in my arms as if she had been a frightened child, and tried to comfort her.

"My darling, this is madness," I said. "You know that no stranger can come to you in the pleasaunce. The moat is ten feet wide and always full of water, and the gates are kept locked day and night by old Massou. The châtelaine of a mediaeval fortress need fear no intruder in her antique garden."

My wife shook her head sadly.

"I see him every day," she said.

On this I believed that my wife was mad. I shrank from questioning her more closely concerning her mysterious visitant. It would be ill, I thought, to give a form and substance to the shadow that tormented her by too close inquiry about its look and manner, its coming and going.

I took care to assure myself that no stranger to the household could by any possibility penetrate to the pleasaunce. Having done this, I was fain to await the coming of the physician.

He came at last. I revealed to him the conviction which was my misery. I told him that I believed my wife to be mad. He saw her – spent an hour alone with her, and then came to me. To my un-speakable relief he assured me of her sanity.

"It is just possible that she may be affected by one delusion," he said; "but she is so reasonable upon all other points, that I can scarcely bring myself to believe her the subject of a monomania. I am rather inclined to think that she really sees the person of whom she speaks. She described him to me with a perfect minuteness. The descriptions of scenes or individuals given by patients afflicted with monomania are always more or less disjointed; but your wife spoke to me as clearly and calmly as I am now speaking to you. Are you sure there is no one who can approach her in that garden where she walks?"

"I am quite sure."

"Is there any kinsman of your steward, or hanger-on of your household – a young man with a fair womanish face, very pale and rendered remarkable by a crimson scar, which looks like the mark of a blow?"

"My God!" I cried, as the light broke in upon me all at once. "And the dress – the strange old-fashioned dress?"

"The man wears a hunting costume of purple and orange," answered the doctor.

I knew then that André de Brissac had kept his word, and that in the hour when my life was brightest his shadow had come between me and happiness.

I showed my wife the picture in the library, for I would fain assure myself that there was some error in my fancy about my cousin. She shook like a leaf when she beheld it, and clung to me convulsively.

"This is witchcraft, Hector," she said. "The dress in that picture is the dress of the man I see in the pleasaunce; but the face is not his."

Then she described to me the face of the stranger; and it was my cousin's face line for line – André de Brissac, whom she had never seen in the flesh. Most vividly of all did she describe the cruel mark upon his face, the trace of a fierce blow from an open hand.

After this I carried my wife away from Puy Verdun. We wandered far – through the southern provinces, and into the very heart of Switzerland. I thought to distance the ghastly phantom, and I fondly hoped that change of scene would bring peace to my wife.

It was not so. Go where we would, the ghost of André de Brissac followed us. To my eyes that fatal shadow never revealed itself. That would have been too poor a vengeance. It was my wife's innocent heart which Andre made the instrument of his revenge. The unholy presence destroyed her life. My constant companionship could not shield her from the horrible intruder. In vain did I watch her; in vain did I strive to comfort her.

"He will not let me be at peace," she said; "he comes between us, Hector. He is standing between us now. I can see his face with the red mark upon it plainer that I see yours."

One fair moonlight night, when we were together in a mountain village in the Tyrol, my wife cast herself at my feet, and told me she was the worst and vilest of women. "I have confessed all to my director," she said; "from the first I have not hidden my sin from Heaven. But I feel that death is near me; and before I die I would fain reveal my sin to you."

"What sin, my sweet one?"

"When first the stranger came to me in the forest, his presence bewildered and distressed me, and I shrank from him as from something strange and terrible. He came again and again; by and by I found myself thinking of him, and watching for his coming. His image haunted me perpetually; I strove in vain to shut his face out of my mind. Then followed an interval in which I did not see him; and, to my shame and anguish, I found that life seemed dreary and desolate without him. After that came the time in which he haunted the pleasaunce; and – O, Hector, kill me if you will, for I deserve no mercy at your hands! – I grew in those days to count the hours that must elapse before his coming, to take no pleasure save in the sight of that pale face with the red brand upon it. He plucked all old familiar joys out of my heart, and left in it but one weird unholy pleasure – the delight of his presence. For a year I have lived but to see him. And now curse me, Hector; for this is my sin. Whether it comes of the baseness of my own heart, or is the work of witchcraft, I know not; but I know that I have striven against this wickedness in vain."

I took my wife to my breast, and forgave her. In sooth, what had I to forgive? Was the fatality that overshadowed us any work of hers? On the next night she died, with her hand in mine; and at the very last she told me, sobbing and affrighted, that he was by her side.

The Rebus

Nancy Brewka-Clark

"COME HERE, child. Come, come, I don't bite, you know."

Margaret took a tentative step forward, her hand over her mouth and nose. The lady smelled sweetish but nasty, like flower stems left too long in stagnant water.

"Ah, now then, let me have a look at you. A proper look."

A shiver ran down Margaret's spine as the manicured hand, rosy nails gleaming, plucked her own fingers away from her face.

"Oh, my, yes, the same eyes, the same winged brows, the same flawless skin, pink and sweet as a pippin's."

Margaret was beginning to be sorry, very sorry, that she'd slipped away from the little group out in the garden of the big brick house. Although the gloomy October day sensibly called for being indoors, it had appeared that her parents were going to stand there talking endlessly with the skinny blonde woman named Ms. Langley. Nobody even noticed when she'd darted around the corner to peer through the French doors. When they opened onto a vast, empty room that still held a trace of lost glamor with its gold and blue flocked wallpaper, she'd entered without a qualm.

Margaret tried to smile as the heavily powdered face drew even closer. It was like being inspected by a sea turtle, one whose breath reflected a diet of sea creatures not quite properly digested.

"You're a fine little girl. Yes, you're as fair and fine as my own dear Bonnie. A bit more meat on your bones, but that's to be expected these days with all those emporia for fatty treats scattered about."

Hearing about meat and bones when it concerned herself disturbed Margaret mightily, but she decided if the lady was truly a witch it would be foolish to show it. The lady was probably some sort of caretaker, although why she'd be wearing a dressing gown of faded rose-colored velvet with matching slippers as if she were ready for bed was a mystery. But then most things that adults did were mysteries, like her parents' penchant for attending Open Houses in places that possessed what her dad called an 'aristocratic pedigree'. He'd assured her time and again that they had absolutely no intention of moving from their flat in a tall cement and glass building on a side street far across town. But dreaming of better things, he'd said with a grin, was perfectly acceptable.

"What is your name, child?"

The question brought an anxious flush to Margaret's smooth cheeks. She'd been told a thousand times never to talk to strangers.

Just as the silence was becoming awkward, her mother called, "Margaret? Margaret, you little terror, where have you gone?"

"Ah," the woman said again, her plum-colored eyelids blinking heavily. "So, your name is Margaret. That's a lovely name. Poets think so. Did you know that?"

"Excuse me. I have to go."

"Yes, I suppose you must. Wait just a moment. Take this, Margaret. Bonnie won't mind."

Margaret stared at the small, glowing glass ball lying in the yellowish palm. It was a deep shade of blue with a ribbon of gold running through it.

"Go on, child." When Margaret turned away to look anxiously at the door, the woman said sadly, "Don't you want it? Bonnie loved marbles. This was her favorite."

"Margaret? For heaven's sake, where on earth did you go?"

"Here." When the woman leaned forward, Margaret could see light through her elaborate hairdo. The frosty pile reminded her of the spun-sugar cones Mum would never buy for her at the local church fete. "It's quite lovely when the sun catches it. Like a little world unto itself."

While Margaret was still debating whether or not to take the proffered gift, the lady bent her finger into a crook, hooked open the pocket on Margaret's pink sweater and plopped in the marble. Having no choice, Margaret mumbled, "Thank you," and ran to the door without looking back.

"Well, finally. There you are." Mum was crunching through the unraked leaves with a smile on her face, but Margaret knew from the tone of her voice that she was in trouble. "Don't tell me you went into that house all by yourself?"

Did that mean she should tell her, or not? Expressions like this were always popping out of Mum. Dad, on the other hand, just made jokes about everything, and that was equally confusing.

"Carol, let's continue our adventure." Dad was dangling an old-fashioned key chain bristling with keys. "No harm in looking."

"No, Samuel," Mum said quietly but with great force, locking eyes with him. "Absolutely not."

Dad said, "I understand the owner is exceedingly anxious to sell." His glance slid toward the estate agent. "It's begging for a new lady of the manor."

"Lady of a tumbledown tip," Mum corrected.

With pink cheeks, Ms. Langley said, "All it needs is some TLC."

"Tender loving care is my specialty," Dad said softly, gazing at the ground.

"Well," Mum began, but let the word hang tantalizingly in the air before adding, "I guess I should at least look at the interior before making up my mind."

"This way," the agent said eagerly.

Margaret slipped her hand into her pocket and clutched the marble. Mum and Dad now had big smiles on their faces. When they looked at her, Margaret smiled, too.

* * *

"Good evening, child."

Margaret's eyes flew open. The June twilight lasted well past her eight o'clock bedtime and the room was still filled with shadows. Deep within them stood the lady. Margaret wanted desperately to pull the sheets up over her face, but her arms wouldn't obey her. Fixing up the interior of the house to at least be inhabitable, as Mum put it, had taken all fall and winter. By the time they moved in, she'd almost forgotten about her first encounter with the elderly stranger in the drawing room.

"My Bonnie always asked me to read her a bedtime story." When the lady sank down next to her, Margaret saw that she was holding a small book with a worn brown cloth cover. "Would you like that?"

"What's your name?" Margaret whispered.

"You may call me Nana."

"I already have a Nana." Margaret almost forgot what she was saying as the lady opened the book. Even though it was the old-fashioned proper kind, the pages were emitting a soft glow like a computer screen. "Actually, two of them."

"Now you have three." False Nana tapped the open page. "Tell me what you see."

With an inward sigh of surrender, Margaret said, "Some letters and some pictures."

"Very good."

The brackish odor Margaret remembered from her first encounter was still present. Perhaps it was coming from that velvet dressing gown, surely the same one the lady been wearing the last time. Edging away, she said, "I'm supposed to be asleep."

"In due time. Margaret, look at the page. Good. Now, give me a word for this picture."

Margaret frowned at the little drawing. "I don't know what that thing is."

"It's a very famous landmark," False Nana said. "In Paris."

This time Margaret sighed aloud. "What's Paris?"

"Oh, please." The lidded eyes glimmered for a moment. "You're more than old enough to have heard of Paris, France."

Margaret hung her head sullenly. "No, I'm not."

"Very well. I'll help you, then." The finger, dusted with some sort of pinkish powder, traced the filigreed lines. "This is the Eiffel Tower. Can you remember that?"

Margaret shrugged.

"Not very convincing," False Nana said drily. "But it will have to do. Now, what did I just say the name of this tower is?"

Margaret pretended to think.

"Come, come, I haven't got all night. What is the name of this tower, Margaret?"

Hoping the lady would go away if she said it, Margaret mumbled, "Eiffel."

"Excellent." False Nana closed the book. "That's enough for tonight." The bed springs made no noise as she stood up, the covers undisturbed where she'd sat. "But, there is one more thing, my dear."

"What?" Margaret asked, squinting into the darkness. Without the glow from the book, she couldn't see False Nana at all.

"Oh, never mind," the voice said from a great distance. "It will keep."

* * *

"Listen to me, Sam. I have no choice. Do you understand?"

Margaret crouched against the bannister, her icy hands clenching the rails.

"No, I don't," Dad said. "When you took that job, nobody said anything about travel."

"Well, actually, they did." Mum's voice grew louder. "I knew better than to bring it up because you'd grouse. Just as you're doing now, may I point out."

"Is there more money in it?"

"Of course. Not that it will be enough to make this mausoleum livable. Bills, bills, and more bills, all because of this crazy old pile of a house. Georgian, my foot. It's been trashed to the point where the mad king himself wouldn't recognize it."

"Oh, right, blame the house." Margaret heard something slam. "You're the one who wanted the best."

"I wanted to stay in that flat, Sam, until something suitable came up. I never wanted to move to this money pit and you well know it."

"You can't go on business trips like you were footloose and fancy free. You have a child, remember?"

"It's the twenty-first century, Sam. We're equal partners. I go, you stay and take care of the kid. People do it every day."

Margaret rested her cheek against the railing. In two weeks, school would start. Would Mum be back by then? She didn't mind staying behind with Dad, but he wasn't anywhere near as good at picking out clothes and backpacks and school supplies as she was. Maybe she and Mum could go shopping before Mum left.

"And, remember, she's here because of you. You, Sam. Your choice. Your decision. I acquiesced, but I often wonder if I should have."

"Margaret's a great little kid. How can you even suggest—"

"What I'm doing is asserting myself. Besides, I should think you'd love having me out of the way so you can lavish all that proclaimed TLC on your pet projects. Sam? Did you hear me?"

"Loud and clear. No worries, my love. Things will be fine."

Margaret padded back up the staircase, being careful not to make a sound. When she entered her bedroom, she looked around the way she always did, but False Nana wasn't there. She hadn't seen her since the night of the picture-book. If she ever came back, Margaret would surprise her by saying "Eiffel" before she said anything else.

* * *

"Eiffel."

"My goodness, what an excellent memory you have, Margaret."

Even seeing False Nana was a bit of a help, because Dad had become just about invisible, saying he had work to do and enclosing himself in his home office. Last evening Margaret had stood outside the door, not daring to disturb him but desperately wanting company, when she heard him say, "Well, my lovely Ms. Langley, I'm formally inviting you over so we can play house." It almost made her laugh, until she heard smacking noises and little grunts and realized Dad must be kissing the phone. "Oh, yes, *droit du seigneur* and all that, you saucy wench."

"Now," False Nana said, opening the book, "here's the next clue."

Margaret knew what a clue was, but was surprised they were actually doing more of the same puzzle. "Is Eiffel a clue, too?"

"Of course. This puzzle is called a rebus. Didn't I say that before?" When Margaret shook her head solemnly, False Nana pointed to the glowing picture on the page. "What do you suppose this is?"

"It's an eyeball. It looks like my marble."

"You are a clever girl, just like my Bonnie. Very perceptive, indeed. But what else can you tell me about this eyeball, Margaret?"

Margaret studied the picture. "It's blue."

"Yes. But what is it doing?"

Margaret shook her head. "I don't know."

"Well, child, which way is it looking?" The varnished nail tapped the page. "You see, just there? That's the pupil. Which way is it looking?"

The white part and the black dot of the pupil were at the bottom of the eyeball instead of in the middle. "Down?"

"Yes. Excellent." False Nana turned the page. Another eyeball, this one peering right out at them, seemed to be floating in the center of the page.

Margaret shuddered. "It's staring straight at us."

"You are brilliant." For a moment Margaret feared that False Nana was going to kiss her. That plummy lipstick would be hard to rub off her cheek, although probably Dad wouldn't even notice. "If you had to make a sentence using these pictures, including the one of the tower, what would it say?"

"Eiffel," Margaret said, and stopped.

"Yes," False Nana whispered.

Margaret reached out and touched the book. When False Nana didn't say anything, she turned the page back. "Down." Her heart leaped. "I fell down."

"Where?" False Nana hissed.

"I fell downstairs," Margaret crowed and then clapped her hand over her mouth so Dad wouldn't hear.

"Yes." False Nana flipped the page. "Now that you understand, what does this say?"

Margaret stared at the items on the page until nothing but a glow remained in her head.

"Just read them one by one."

The first one was a tied ribbon. "Bow," Margaret whispered.

The next showed a bent leg with an arrow pointing to the joint. "Knee."

Margaret studied the next drawing of a little pin with a round plastic handle until her eyes felt like they were popping out of her skull. "I don't know."

The lady thrust out both arms at her, palms outward. "Don't push me," Margaret cried and then drew back in bewilderment when False Nana asked, "Don't what?"

"Push—"

"Yes!" False Nana exulted.

Margaret studied the single letter on the page. When she couldn't think of anything else to say about it, she said, "T?"

"Yes, you clever child." The lady pointed at herself. "Don't push—?"

"Me."

"Say the words all together now."

"Bow knee push T me."

"And so she did." False Nana raised her chin. "My own daughter pushed me down those stairs, child."

"Why?" Margaret gasped.

"She came home from school a bit early and saw me kissing a man goodbye. When she asked who the man was, I decided to tell her the truth. I said he would be her new daddy because her father and I were getting a divorce. She threw a tantrum."

"Dear me," Margaret broke in, excited and upset at the same time. "She does sound a bit wicked. Did you punish her?"

"I told her to go to her room until she got control of herself. She called me several horrible names, heaven knows where she'd learned them, and ran up the staircase. I chased her, threatening to send her away to a home for wicked girls. At the top of the stairs, she turned and – well, now you know my secret."

Margaret felt a rush of sympathy. "I have a secret, too. My Dad pretends to be kissing Ms. Langley."

"Does he."

Margaret nodded. "I believe he must like her a lot because he invited her over to play house."

False Nana stared down at the page of drawings. "Do you think your mother would like that?"

Margaret thought about it. "I don't know."

"Well, when she comes home, you must tell her." False Nana closed the book with an authoritative little pop. "And then you'll have the answer to another puzzle."

* * *

Margaret thrust her gloved hand deeper into her coat pocket. There was still nothing there except a hole. What a bad day this was turning out to be. Not only had she lost the blue marble, but

Ms. Langley's black Mini was in clear view. Usually she got home just in time to see her driving off, but sometimes the skinny blonde lady would be running just a little bit late. Those times, she'd burst through the front door while Margaret shivered out of sight on the rusted settee.

This time, Margaret didn't hear the front door close first. Instead she heard a car door slam. Curious, she peeped around the corner of the house. "Mummy!"

There she was getting out of a taxicab, home a full two days early.

Margaret was still clinging to her in a great, proper hug when Mum stood erect. "Is that Ms. Langley's car?"

Feeling important, Margaret said, "Dad asks her over." Before she could say why, Mum was already striding up the walk.

"Mummy," Margaret called, and ran after her. "Wait."

But she was already through the door and dashing up the staircase.

Margaret stood undecided at the foot of the stairs as Mum disappeared down the hall. The crash of the bedroom door flying open was drowned out by Mum's voice, harsh and wild, screaming words Margaret had never heard before.

Ms. Langley appeared in the hallway, her navy blazer's gold buttons in the wrong holes, her hair a bit mussed like pale feathers, her cheeks a bright pink.

Behind her came Mum.

"Get out," Mum screamed.

"Gladly," Ms. Langley screamed back. One foot in its silly high heel came forward, hovering for an instant above a small blue flash bright as a beacon.

Ms. Langley came at Margaret with wild eyes and an open, screaming mouth that banged shut as her chin hit the wood. Down, down, down, she came, bumping and going all topsy-turvy, arms flying one way, legs cutting airy wedges as she kicked to gain purchase, looming nearer and nearer, fingers hooked into claws ripping wood and air as she twisted faster.

"Bonnie, oh, my God, Bonnie."

And there came Dad, shoving Mum out of the way at the top of the stairs, thumping down after her in his stockinged feet and crying out the name of False Nana's bad daughter, until, whoop, down he went. Tumbling over and sideways, he slammed head-first into the stately old newel post.

Knocked out of its resting place, the smeared marble bounced at Margaret's feet. She stooped to pick it up. When she stood, the shadows in the hallway were rippling behind Mum to coalesce into False Nana, her arms outstretched, her eyes bright and brimming with vengeful malice.

Margaret threw the marble as hard as she could.

With a shriek Mum fell forward, clutching her eye.

Up, up the staircase dashed Margaret, fast as her legs would carry her, to catch the full weight of her. Warm and breathing and sobbing and bleeding, entangled as they never had been, Margaret held onto her Mum for dear life as the two of them tumbled and banged. They thudded to a halt against Dad, who was still except for a trickle of blood from his ear.

"Horrible child," Mum sobbed. "I will never forgive you."

"No, Mummy, no," Margaret whimpered.

But already she knew it was true.

Passing Through Peacehaven

Ramsey Campbell

"WAIT," Marsden shouted as he floundered off his seat. His vision was so overcast with sleep that it was little better than opaque, but so far as he could see through the carriages the entire train was deserted. "Terminate" was the only word he retained from the announcement that had wakened him. He blundered to the nearest door and leaned on the window to slide it further open while he groped beyond it for the handle. The door swung wide so readily that he almost sprawled on the platform. In staggering dangerously backwards to compensate he slammed the door, which seemed to be the driver's cue. The train was heading into the night before Marsden realised he had never seen the station in his life.

"Wait," he cried, but it was mostly a cough as the smell of some October fire caught in his throat. His eyes felt blackened by smoke and stung when he blinked, so that he could barely see where he was going as he lurched after the train. He succeeded in clearing his vision just in time to glimpse distance or a bend in the track extinguish the last light of the train like an ember. He panted coughing to a halt and stared red-eyed around him.

Two signs named the station Peacehaven. The grudging glow of half a dozen lamps that put him in mind of streetlights in an old photograph illuminated stretches of both platforms but seemed shy of the interior of the enclosed bridge that led across the pair of tracks. A brick wall twice his height extended into the dark beyond the ends of the platform he was on. The exit from the station was on the far side of the tracks, through a passage where he could just distinguish a pay phone in the gloom. Above the wall of that platform, and at some distance, towered an object that he wasted seconds in identifying as a factory chimney. He should be looking for the times of any trains to Manchester, but the timetable among the vintage posters alongside the platform was blackened by more than the dark. As he squinted at it, someone spoke behind him.

It was the voice that had wakened him. Apart from an apology for a delay, the message was a blur. "I can't hear much at the best of times," Marsden grumbled. At least the station hadn't closed for the night, and a timetable on the other platform was beside a lamp. He made for the bridge and climbed the wooden stairs to the elevated corridor, where narrow grimy windows above head height and criss-crossed by wire mesh admitted virtually no illumination. He needn't shuffle through the dark; his mobile phone could light the way. He reached in his overcoat pocket, and dug deeper to find extra emptiness.

Marjorie wouldn't have approved of the words that escaped his lips. He wasn't fond of them himself, especially when he heard them from children in the street. He and Marjorie would have done their best to keep their grandchildren innocent of such language and of a good deal else that was in vogue, but they would need to have had a son or daughter first. He ran out of curses as he trudged back across the bridge, which felt narrowed by darkness piled against the walls. The platform was utterly bare. Did he remember hearing or perhaps only feeling the faintest thump as he'd left his seat? There was no doubt that he'd left the mobile on the train.

He was repeating himself when he wondered if he could be heard. His outburst helped the passage to muffle the announcer's unctuous voice, which apparently had information about a signal failure. Marsden wasn't going to feel like one. He marched out of darkness into dimness, which lightened somewhat as he reached the platform.

Had vandals tried to set fire to the timetable? A blackened corner was peeling away from the bricks. Marsden pushed his watch higher on his wizened wrist until the strap took hold. Theoretically the last train – for Bury and Oldham and Manchester – was due in less than twenty minutes. "What's the hold-up again? Say it clearly this time," Marsden invited not quite at the top of his voice. When there was no response he made for the phone on the wall.

Was it opposite some kind of memorial? No, the plaque was a ticket window boarded up behind cracked glass. Surely the gap beneath the window couldn't be occupied by a cobweb, since the place was staffed. He stood with his back to the exit from the station and fumbled coins into the slot beside the receiver before groping for the dial that he could barely see in the glimmer from the platform.

"Ray and Marjorie Marsden must be engaged elsewhere. Please don't let us wonder who you were or when you tried to contact us or where we can return the compliment..." His answering message had amused them when he recorded it – at least, Marjorie had made the face that meant she appreciated his wit – but now it left him feeling more alone than he liked. "Are you there?" he asked the tape. "You'll have gone up, will you? You'll have gone up, of course. Just to let you know I'm stranded by an unexpected change of trains. If you play me back don't worry, I'll be home as soon as practicable. Oh, and the specialist couldn't find anything wrong. I know, you'll say it shows I can hear when I want to. Not true, and shall I tell you why? I'd give a lot to hear you at this very moment. Never mind. I will soon."

Even saying so much in so many words earned him no response, and yet he didn't feel unheard. His audience could be the station announcer, who was presumably beyond one of the doors that faced each other across the corridor, although neither betrayed the faintest trace of light. "I nearly didn't say I love you," he added in a murmur that sounded trapped inside his skull. "Mind you, you'll know that, won't you? If you don't after all these years you never will. I suppose that had better be it for now as long as you're fast asleep."

He still felt overheard. Once he'd hung up he yielded to a ridiculous urge to poke his head out of the corridor. The platforms were deserted, and the tracks led to unrelieved darkness. He might as well learn where he'd ended up while there was no sign of a train. "Just stepping outside," he informed anyone who should know.

The corridor didn't seem long enough to contain so much blackness. He only just managed to refrain from rubbing his eyes as he emerged onto an unpromising road. The front of the station gave it no light, but the pavements on either side of the cracked weedy tarmac were visibly uneven. Beyond high railings across the road the grounds of the factory bristled with tall grass, which appeared to shift, although he couldn't feel a wind. Here and there a flagstone showed pale through the vegetation. A sign beside the open gates had to do with motors or motor components, and Marsden was considering a closer look to pass the time when the announcer spoke again. "Going to attract effect" might have been part of the proclamation, and all that Marsden was able to catch.

Some delay must be owing to a track defect, of course. Much of the voice had ended up as echoes beyond the railings or simply dissipated in the night, but he also blamed its tone for confusing him. It had grown so oily that it sounded more like a parody of a priest than any kind of railway official. Marsden tramped into the passage and knocked on the door beside the ticket window. "Will you repeat that, please?"

If this sounded like an invitation to an argument, it wasn't taken up. He found the doorknob, which felt flaky with age, but the door refused to budge. He rubbed his finger and thumb together as he crossed to the other door, which tottered open at his knock, revealing only a storeroom. It was scattered with brushes and mops, or rather their remains, just distinguishable in the meagre light through a window so nearly opaque that on the platform he'd mistaken it for an empty poster frame. Vandals must have been in the room; the dimness smelled as ashen as it looked, while the tangles of sticks that would once have been handles seemed blackened by more than the dark. That was all he managed to discern before the voice spoke to him.

Was the fellow too close to the microphone? If he was trying to be clearer, it achieved the opposite. Of course nobody was next to alive; a train was the next to arrive. "Speak clearly, not up," Marsden shouted as he slammed the door and hurried to the bridge, where he did his best to maintain his pace by keeping to the middle of the passage. If an object or objects were being dragged somewhere behind him, he wanted to see what was happening. He clumped breathlessly down the stairs and limped onto the platform. How could he have thought the windows were poster frames? There was one on either side of the exit, and although both rooms were unlit, a figure was peering through the window of the office.

Or was it a shadow? It was thin and black enough. There was no light inside the room to cast it, and yet it must be a shadow, since it had nothing for a face. Marsden was still trying to identify its source when he noticed that the door he'd slammed was wide open. It had felt unsteady on its hinges, and at least he had an explanation for the dragging sound he'd heard. He set about laughing at his own unease, and then the laugh snagged in his throat like another cough. The silhouette was no longer pressed against the window.

Had it left traces of its shape on the discoloured glass? As he paced back and forth, trying either to confirm or shake off the impression, he felt like an animal trapped in a cage and watched by spectators. He'd met with no success by the time the voice that might belong to the owner of the shadow had more to say. "Where's the party?" Marsden was provoked to mutter. "What's departing?" he demanded several times as loud. "It's supposed to arrive first," he pointed out, glaring along the tracks at the unrelieved night. The few words he'd managed to recognise or at least to guess had sounded oilier than ever, close to a joke. Why couldn't the fellow simply come and tell him what to expect? Was he amusing himself by spying on the solitary passenger? "Yes, you've got a customer," Marsden declared. "He's the chap who has to stand out here in the cold because you can't be bothered to provide a waiting-room."

The complaint left him more aware of the storeroom, so that he could have imagined he was being observed from there too. He would much rather fancy his return home to the bed that he hoped Marjorie was keeping warm for him. As he hugged himself to fend off the late October chill he wasn't too far from experiencing how her arms would feel when she turned in her sleep to embrace him. He couldn't help wishing that the tape had brought him her voice.

The only one he was likely to hear was the announcer's, and he needed to ensure he did. He lowered himself onto a bench opposite the exit and planted his hands on his knees. Though the seat felt unwelcomingly moist if not actually rotten, he concentrated on staying alert for the next message. His ears were throbbing with the strain, and his skin felt as if his sense of being watched were gathering on it, by the time his attention was rewarded.

Was someone clinking glasses? Had the staff found an excuse to celebrate? Marsden had begun to wonder if they were deriding his predicament when he identified the noise of bricks knocking together. The factory was more dilapidated than he'd been able to make out, then, and there was movement in the rubble. Perhaps an animal was at large – more than one, by the sound of it – or else people were up to no good. Suppose they were the vandals who'd tried to set fire to the station? Would the announcer deign to emerge from hiding if they or others like them trespassed on railway property, or was he capable of leaving his solitary customer to deal with them? Marsden could hear nothing now except his own heart, amplified by his concentration if not pumped up by stress. He wasn't sure if he glimpsed surreptitious movement at the exit, where he could easily imagine that the dark was growing crowded; indeed, the passage was so nearly lightless that any number of intruders might sneak into it unseen. He was gripping his knees and crouching forward like a competitor at the start of some pensioners' event while he strained to see whether anyone was sidling through the gloom when his heart jumped, and he did.

The voice was louder than ever, and its meaning more blurred. Even the odd relatively clear phrase amid the magnified mumbling left much to be desired. Marsden could have thought he was being warned about some further decay and informed that he had a hearing problem. The latter comment must refer to engineering, but wasn't this unreasonable too? How many hindrances was the train going to encounter? The reports of its progress were beginning to seem little better than jokes. But here was a final one, however inefficiently pronounced. It meant that the train was imminent, not that anything would shortly be alive.

Perhaps the man was slurring his words from drunkenness, and the clinking had indeed been glass, unless the contrivance of equality had reached such a pitch that the station was obliged to employ an announcer with a speech impediment. On that basis Marsden might seek a job as a telephone operator, but he and Marjorie were resigned to leaving the world to the young and aggressive. He peered along the railway, where the view stayed as black as the depths of the corridor opposite. All that his strained senses brought him besides a charred smell and a crawling of the skin was, eventually, another message.

"You won't be burying this old man," he retorted under his clogged breath. While the announcement must have referred to the train to Bury and Oldham, the voice had resembled a priest's more than ever. "And where's this train that's supposed to be arriving?" he demanded loud enough to rouse an echo in the exit corridor.

The next message was no answer. Presumably he was being told that unattended luggage would be removed without warning, but since he had no luggage, what was the point? Couldn't the fellow see him? Perhaps some legislation allowed him to be blind as well as largely incomprehensible. Still, here were another few words Marsden understood, even if he couldn't grasp where passengers were being told to change. "What was that?" he shouted, but the announcer hadn't finished. His tone was so ecclesiastical that for the space of an exaggerated heartbeat Marsden fancied he was being offered some kind of service, and then he recognised the phrase. It was "out of service".

He sucked in a breath that he had to replace once he'd finished coughing. "What's out?" he spluttered. "Where's my train?"

The only reply was an echo, all the more derisive for sounding more like "Where's my Ray?" He levered himself to his feet, muttering an impolite word at having somehow blackened the knee of his trousers, and hobbled to the bridge. An arthritic pang set him staggering like an old drunk, but he succeeded in gaining the top of the stairs without recourse to the banisters. He preferred to keep to the middle of the bridge, especially along the passage over the tracks. It was too easy to imagine that the darkness beneath the obscured windows was peopled with supine figures. Surely the humped mounds consisted simply of litter, despite the marks on a window about halfway along, five elongated trails that might have been left by a sooty hand as its owner tried to haul his body up. That afternoon Marsden had given a few coins to a woman lying in a railway underpass, but he hoped not to encounter anyone of the kind just now. He faltered and then stumbled fast to the end of the passage, mumbling "No change" as he clattered down to the platform.

"Here's your customer," he said at several times the volume, "and what are you going to do about it?" The question trailed away, however, and not only because the office was so thoroughly unlit from within. The imprint on the window had silenced him. He might still have taken it for a shadow if it weren't so incomplete. Just the top half of a face with holes for eyes was recognisable, and the bones of a pair of hands.

Some grimy vandal must have been trying to see into the room. Of course the marks weren't on the inside of the glass, or if they were, that was no reason to think that the figure at the window had stood in the same place. Nevertheless Marsden wasn't anxious to look closer, although he'd managed to distinguish nothing in the office. He made for the door with all the confidence he could summon up.

The storeroom distracted him. Even if his stinging eyes had adjusted to the dimness, he couldn't understand how he'd failed to see that the room was more than untidy. It was full of burned sticks and bits of stick, some of which were thin as twigs. One charred tangle that, to judge by the blackened lump at the nearer end, consisted partly of a mop or brush came close to blocking the door. When he lurched to shut away the sight the edge of the door caught the object, and he glimpsed it crumbling into restless fragments before the slam resounded through the passage. He limped to the office door and, having rapped on a scaly panel, shouted "Will you come and tell me to my face what's happening?"

As far as he could determine, silence was the answer. He could have fancied that the station and its surroundings were eager for his next outburst. "You're meant to make yourself plain," he yelled. "I couldn't understand half of what you said."

If he was hoping to provoke a response, it didn't work. Had he offended the man? "I need to know where I'm going," he insisted. "I don't think that's unreasonable, do you?"

Perhaps the fellow thought he could behave as he liked while he was in charge. Perhaps he felt too important to descend to meeting the public, an attitude that would explain his tone of voice. Or might he not be on the premises? If he was beyond the door, what could he expect to gain by lying low? Surely not even the worst employee would act that way – and then Marsden wondered if he'd strayed on the truth. Suppose it wasn't a railway employee who was skulking in the office?

The kind of person who'd tried to set fire to the station would certainly be amused by Marsden's plight and think it even more of a joke to confuse him. Perhaps the indistinctness of the announcements was the result of suppressed mirth. Marsden shouldn't waste any more time if the information was false. He hurried to the phone and glared at the dim wall, which didn't bear a single notice.

No doubt vandals had removed any advertisements for taxis. At least the phone wasn't disabled. He fumbled the receiver off its hook and leaned almost close enough to kiss the blackened dial as he clawed at an enquiry number. He could have thought his hearing had improved when the bell began to ring; it sounded close as the next room. The voice it roused was keeping its distance, however. "Can you speak up?" Marsden urged.

"Where are you calling, please?"

This was sharp enough for a warning. Presumably the speaker was ensuring he was heard. "Peacehaven," Marsden said. "Taxis."

"Where is that, please?"

"Peacehaven," Marsden pronounced loud enough for it to grow blurred against his ear before he realised that he wasn't being asked to repeat the name. "Somewhere near Manchester."

In the pause that ensued he might have heard movement outside the passage. His hectic pulse obscured the noise, which must have been the tall grass scraping in a wind, even if he couldn't feel it. He was relieved when the voice returned until he grasped its message. "Not listed," it said.

"Forgive me, I wasn't asking for Peacehaven Taxis. Any cab firm here will do."

"There is no listing."

Was the fellow pleased to say so? He sounded as smug as the worst sort of priest. "The nearest one, then," Marsden persisted. "I think that might be— "

"There are no listings for Peacehaven."

"No, that can't be right. I'm in it. I'm at the railway station. You must have a number for that at least."

"There is none."

Marsden was aware of the dark all around him and how many unheard lurkers it could hide. "Is there anything more I can do for you?" the voice said.

It sounded so fulsome that Marsden was convinced he was being mocked. "You've done quite enough," he blurted and slammed the receiver on its hook.

He could try another enquiry number, or might he call the police? What could he say that would bring them to his aid yet avoid seeming as pathetic as he was determined not to feel? There was one voice he yearned to hear in the midst of all the darkness, but the chance of this at so late an hour seemed little better than infinitesimal. Nevertheless he was groping for change and for the receiver. He scrabbled at the slot with coins and dragged the indistinct holes around the dial. The bell measured the seconds and at last made way for a human voice. It was his own. "Ray and Marjorie Marsden must be engaged elsewhere..."

"I am. I wish you weren't," he murmured and felt all the more helpless for failing to interrupt his mechanical self. Then his distant muffled voice fell silent, and Marjorie said "Who is it?"

"It's me, love."

"Is that Ray?" She sounded sleepy enough not to know. "I can hardly hear you," she protested. "Where have you gone?"

"You'd wonder." He was straining to hear another sound besides her voice – a noise that might have been the shuffling of feet in rubble. "I'm stuck somewhere," he said. "I'll be late. I can't say how late."

"Did you call before?"

"That was me. Didn't you get me?"

"The tape must be stuck like you. I'll need to get a new one."

"Not a new husband, I hope." He wouldn't have minded being rewarded with the laugh he'd lived with for the best part of fifty years, even though the joke felt as old as him, but perhaps she was wearied by the hour. "Anyway," he said, "if you didn't hear me last time I'll sign off the same way, which as if you didn't know—"

"What was that?"

For too many seconds he wasn't sure. He'd been talking over it, and then she had. Surely it had said that a train was about to arrive; indeed, wasn't the noise he'd mistaken for thin footsteps the distant clicking of wheels? "It's here now," he tried to tell her through a fit of coughing. By the time he would be able to speak clearer, the train might have pulled in. Dropping the receiver on the hook, he dashed for the platform. He hadn't reached it when he heard a scraping behind him.

The storeroom was open again, but that wasn't enough in itself to delay him. His eyes had grown all too equal to the gloom in the passage, so that he was just able to discern marks on the floor, leading from outside the station to the room. Could someone not be bothered to pick up their dirty feet? The trails looked as if several objects had been dragged into the room. He didn't believe they had just been left; that wasn't why they made him uneasy. He had to squint to see that they were blurred by more than the dark. Whatever had left them – not anybody shuffling along, he hoped, since their feet would have been worse than thin – had crumbled in transit, scattering fragments along the route. He thought he could smell the charred evidence, and swallowed in order not to recommence coughing, suddenly fearful of being heard. What was he afraid of? Was he growing senile? Thank heaven Marjorie wasn't there to see him. The only reason for haste was that he had a train to catch. He tramped out of the passage and might have maintained his defiant pace all the way to the bridge if a shape hadn't reared up at the window of the storeroom.

Was the object that surmounted it the misshapen head of a mop? He couldn't distinguish much through the grimy pane, but the idea was almost reassuring until he acknowledged that somebody would still have had to lift up the scrawny excuse for a figure. It hadn't simply risen or been raised, however. A process that the grime couldn't entirely obscure was continuing to take place. The silhouette – the blackened form, rather – was taking on more substance, though it remained alarmingly emaciated. It was putting itself back together.

The spectacle was so nightmarishly fascinating that Marsden might have been unable to stir except for the clatter of wheels along the tracks. He staggered around to see dim lights a few hundred yards short of the station. "Stop," he coughed, terrified that the driver mightn't notice him and speed straight through. Waving his arms wildly, he sprinted for the bridge.

He'd panted up the stairs and was blundering along the middle of the wooden corridor when he thought he heard a noise besides the approach of the train. Was he desperate to hear it or afraid to? He might have tried to persist in mistaking it for wind in the grass if it weren't so close. He did his utmost to fix his shaky gaze on the far end of the corridor as he fled past shadow after crouching shadow. He almost plunged headlong down the further stairs, and only a grab at the slippery discoloured banister saved him. As he dashed onto the platform he saw that both doors in the passage out of the station were open. The sight brought him even closer to panic, and he began to wave his shivering arms once more as he tottered to the edge of the platform. "Don't leave me here," he cried.

The squeal of brakes seemed to slice through the dark. The engine blotted out the view across the tracks, and then a carriage sped past him. Another followed, but the third was slower. Its last door halted almost in front of him. Though the train was by no means the newest he'd ridden that day, and far from the cleanest, it seemed the next thing to paradise. He clutched the rusty handle and heaved the door open and clambered aboard. "You can go now. Go," he pleaded.

Who was the driver waiting for? Did he think the noises on the bridge were promising more passengers? There was such a volume of eager shuffling and scraping that Marsden almost wished his ears would fail him. He hauled at the door, which some obstruction had wedged open. He was practically deaf with his frantic heartbeat by the time the door gave, slamming with such force that it seemed to be echoed in another carriage. At once the train jerked forward, flinging him onto the nearest musty seat. He was attempting to recover his breath when the announcer spoke.

Was a window open in the carriage? The voice sounded close enough to be on the train, yet no more comprehensible. It was no longer simply unctuous; it could have been mocking a priest out of distaste for the vocation. Its only recognisable words were "train now departing", except that the first one was more like Ray – perhaps not just on this occasion, Marsden thought he recalled. He craned towards the window and was able to glimpse that both doors in the exit corridor were shut. Before he had time to ponder any of this, if indeed he wanted to, the train veered off the main line.

"Where are you taking me?" he blurted, but all too soon he knew. The train was heading for the property behind the station, a turn of events celebrated by a short announcement. There was no question that the speaker was on board, though the blurring of the words left Marsden unsure if they were "Ray is shortly alive." The swerve of the train had thrown open the doors between the carriages, allowing him to hear a chorused hiss that might have signified resentment or have been an enthusiastic "Yes" or, possibly even worse, the collapse of many burned objects into the ash he could smell. As the train sped through a gateway in the railings, he read the name on the sign: not

Peacehaven Motors at all, or anything to do with cars. Perhaps the route was only a diversion, he tried to think, or a short tour. Perhaps whoever was on the train just wanted somebody to visit the neglected memorials and the crematorium.

William Tyrwhitt's 'Copy'

Bernard Capes

THIS is the story of William Tyrwhitt, who went to King's Cobb for rest and change, and, with the latter, at least, was so far accommodated as for a time to get beyond himself and into regions foreign to his experiences or his desires. And for this condition of his I hold myself something responsible, inasmuch as it was my inquisitiveness was the means of inducing him to an exploration, of which the result, with its measure of weirdness, was for him alone. But, it seems, I was appointed an agent of the unexplainable without my knowledge, and it was simply my misfortune to find my first unwitting commission in the selling of a friend.

I was for a few days, about the end of a particular July, lodged in that little old seaboard town of Dorset that is called King's Cobb. Thither there came to me one morning a letter from William Tyrwhitt, the polemical journalist (a queer fish, like the cuttle, with an ink-bag for the confusion of enemies), complaining that he was fagged and used up, and desiring me to say that nowhere could complete rest be obtained as in King's Cobb.

I wrote and assured him on this point. The town, I said, lay wrapped in the hills as in blankets, its head only, winking a sleepy eye, projecting from the top of the broad steep gully in which it was stretched at ease. Thither few came to the droning coast; and such as did, looked up at the High Street baking in the sun, and, thinking of Jacob's ladder, composed them to slumber upon the sand and left the climbing to the angels. Here, I said, the air and the sea were so still that one could hear the oysters snoring in their beds; and the little frizzle of surf on the beach was like to the sound to dreaming ears of bacon frying in the kitchens of the blest.

William Tyrwhitt came, and I met him at the station, six or seven miles away. He was all strained and springless, like a broken child's toy – "not like that William who, with lance in rest, shot through the lists in Fleet Street." A disputative galley-puller could have triumphed over him morally; a child physically.

The drive in the inn brake, by undulating roads and scented valleys, shamed his cheek to a little flush of self-assertion.

"I will sleep under the vines," he said, "and the grapes shall drop into my mouth."

"Beware," I answered, "lest in King's Cobb your repose should be everlasting. The air of that hamlet has matured like old port in the bin of its hills, till to drink of it is to swoon."

We alighted at the crown of the High Street, purposing to descend on foot the remaining distance to the shore.

"Behold," I exclaimed, "how the gulls float in the shimmer, like ashes tossed aloft by the white draught of a fire! Behold these ancient buildings nodding to the everlasting lullaby of the bay waters! The cliffs are black with the heat apoplexy; the lobster is drawn scarlet to the surface. You shall be like an addled egg put into an incubator."

"So," he said, "I shall rest and not hatch. The very thought is like sweet oil on a burn."

He stayed with me a week, and his body waxed wondrous round and rosy, while his eye acquired a foolish and vacant expression. So it was with me. We rolled together, by shore and by road of this sluggard place, like spent billiard balls; and if by chance we cannoned, we swerved sleepily apart, until, perhaps, one would fall into a pocket of the sand, and the other bring up against a cushion of sea-wall.

Yet, for all its enervating atmosphere, King's Cobb has its fine traditions of a sturdy independence, and a slashing history withal; and its aspect is as picturesque as that of an opera bouffe fishing-harbour. Then, too, its High Street, as well as its meandering rivulets of low streets, is rich in buildings, venerable and antique.

We took an irresponsible, smiling pleasure in noting these advantages – particularly after lunch; and sometimes, where an old house was empty, we would go over it, and stare at beams and chimney-pieces and hear the haunted tale of its fortunes, with a faint half-memory in our breasts of that one-time bugbear we had known as 'copy'. But though more than once a flaccid instinct would move us to have out our pencils, we would only end by bunging our foolish mouths with them, as if they were cigarettes, and then vaguely wondering at them for that, being pencils, they would not draw.

By then we were so sinewless and demoralised that we could hear in the distant strains of the European Concert nothing but an orchestra of sweet sounds, and would have given ourselves away in any situation with a pound of tea. Therefore, perhaps, it was well for us that, a peremptory summons to town reaching me after seven days of comradeship with William, I must make shift to collect my faculties with my effects, and return to the more bracing climate of Fleet Street.

And here, you will note, begins the story of William Tyrwhitt, who would linger yet a few days in that hanging garden of the south coast, and who would pull himself together and collect matter for 'copy'.

He found a very good subject that first evening of his solitude.

I was to leave in the afternoon, and the morning we spent in aimlessly rambling about the town. Towards midday, a slight shower drove us to shelter under the green verandah of a house, standing up from the lower fall of the High Street, that we had often observed in our wanderings. This house – or rather houses, for it was a block of two – was very tall and odd-looking, being all built of clean squares of a whitish granite; and the double porch in the middle base – led up to by side-going steps behind thin iron railings – roofed with green-painted zinc. In some of the windows were jalousies, but the general aspect of the exterior was gaunt and rigid; and the whole block bore a dismal, deserted look, as if it had not been lived in for years.

Now we had taken refuge in the porch of that half that lay uppermost on the slope; and here we noticed that, at a late date, the building was seemingly in process of repair, painters' pots and brushes lying on a window sill, and a pair of steps showing within through the glass.

"They have gone to dinner," said I. "Supposing we seize the opportunity to explore?"

We pushed at the door; it yielded. We entered, shut ourselves in, and paused to the sound of our own footsteps echoing and laughing from corners and high places. On the ground floor were two or three good-sized rooms with modern grates, but cornices, chimney-pieces, embrasures finely Jacobean. There were innumerable under-stair and over-head cupboards, too, and pantries, and closets, and passages going off darkly into the unknown.

We clomb the stairway – to the first floor – to the second. Here was all pure Jacobean; but the walls were crumbling, the paper peeling, the windows dim and foul with dirt.

I have never known a place with such echoes. They shook from a footstep like nuts rattling out of a bag; a mouse behind the skirting led a whole camp-following of them; to ask a question was, as in that other House, to awaken the derisive shouts of an Opposition. Yet, in the intervals of silence, there fell a deadliness of quiet that was quite appalling by force of contrast.

"Let us go down," I said. "I am feeling creepy."

"Pooh!" said William Tyrwhitt; "I could take up my abode here with a feather bed."

We descended, nevertheless. Arrived at the ground floor, "I am going to the back," said William.

I followed him – a little reluctantly, I confess. Gloom and shadow had fallen upon the town, and this old deserted hulk of an abode was ghostly to a degree. There was no film of dust on its every shelf or sill that did not seem to me to bear the impress of some phantom finger feeling its way along. A glint of stealthy eyes would look from dark uncertain corners; a thin evil vapour appear to rise through the cracks of the boards from the unvisited cellars in the basement.

And here, too, we came suddenly upon an eccentricity of out-building that wrought upon our souls with wonder. For, penetrating to the rear through what might have been a cloak-closet or butler's pantry, we found a supplementary wing, or rather tail of rooms, loosely knocked together, to proceed from the back, forming a sort of skilling to the main building. These rooms led direct into one another, and, consisting of little more than timber and plaster, were in a woeful state of dilapidation. Everywhere the laths grinned through torn gaps in the ceilings and walls; everywhere the latter were blotched and mildewed with damp, and the floorboards rotting in their tracks. Fallen mortar, rusty tins, yellow teeth of glass, whitened soot – all the decay and rubbish of a generation of neglect littered the place and filled it with an acrid odour. From one of the rooms we looked forth through a little discoloured window upon a patch of forlorn weedy garden, where the very cats glowered in a depression that no surfeit of mice could assuage.

We went on, our nervous feet apologetic to the grit they crunched; and, when we were come to near the end of this dreary annexe, turned off to the left into a short gloom of passage that led to a closed door.

Pushing this open, we found a drop of some half-dozen steps, and, going gingerly down these, stopped with a common exclamation of surprise on our lips.

Perhaps our wonder was justified, for we were in the stern cabin of an ancient West Indiaman.

Some twenty feet long by twelve wide – there it all was, from the deck transoms above, to the side lockers and great curved window, sloping outwards to the floor and glazed with little panes in galleries, that filled the whole end of the room. Thereout we looked, over the degraded garden, to the lower quarters of the town – as if, indeed, we were perched high up on waves – and even to a segment of the broad bay that swept by them.

But the room itself! What phantasy of old sea-dog or master-mariner had conceived it? What palsied spirit, condemned to rust in inactivity, had found solace in this burlesque of shipcraft? To renew the past in such a fixture, to work oneself up to the old glow of flight and action, and then, while one stamped and rocked maniacally, to feel the refusal of so much as a timber to respond to one's fervour of animation! It was a grotesque picture.

Now, this cherished chamber had shared the fate of the rest. The paint and gilding were all cracked and blistered away; much of the glass of the stern-frame was gone or hung loose in its sashes; the elaborately carved lockers mouldered on the walls.

These were but dummies when we came to examine them – mere slabs attached to the brickwork, and decaying with it.

"There should be a case-bottle and rummers in one, at least," said William Tyrwhitt.

"There are, sir, at your service," said a voice behind us.

We started and turned.

It had been such a little strained voice that it was with something like astonishment I looked upon the speaker. Whence he had issued I could not guess; but there he stood behind us, nodding and smiling – a squab, thick-set old fellow with a great bald head, and, for all the hair on his face, a tuft like a teasel sprouting from his under lip.

He was in his shirt-sleeves, without coat or vest; and I noticed that his dirty lawn was oddly plaited in front, and that about his ample paunch was buckled a broad belt of leather. Greased hip-boots encased his lower limbs, and the heels of these were drawn together as he bowed.

William Tyrwhitt – a master of nervous English – muttered "Great Scott!" under his breath.

"Permit me," said the stranger – and he held out to us a tin pannikin (produced from Heaven knows where) that swam with fragrance.

I shook my head. William Tyrwhitt, that fated man, did otherwise. He accepted the vessel and drained it.

"It smacks of all Castille," he said, handing it back with a sigh of ecstasy. "Who the devil are you, sir?"

The stranger gave a little crow.

"Peregrine Iron, sir, at your service – Captain Penegrine Iron, of the *Raven* sloop amongst others. You are very welcome to the run of my poor abode."

"Yours?" I murmured in confusion. "We owe you a thousand apologies."

"Not at all," he said, addressing all his courtesy to William. Me, since my rejection of his beaker, he took pains to ignore.

"Not at all," he said. "Your intrusion was quite natural under the circumstances. I take a pleasure in being your cicerone. This cabin (he waved his hand pompously) – a fancy of mine, sir, a fancy of mine. The actual material of the latest of my commands brought hither and adapted to the exigencies of shore life. It enables me to live eternally in the past – a most satisfying illusion. Come tonight and have a pipe and a glass with me."

I thought William Tyrwhitt mad.

"I will come, by all means," he said.

The stranger bowed us out of the room.

"That is right," he exclaimed. "You will find me here. Goodbye for the present."

As we plunged like dazed men into the street, now grown sunny, I turned on my friend.

"William," I said, "did you happen to look back as we left the cabin?"

"No."

"I did."

"Well?"

"There was no stranger there at all. The place was empty."

"Well?"

"You will not go tonight?"

"You bet I do."

I shrugged my shoulders. We walked on a little way in silence. Suddenly my companion turned on me, a most truculent expression on his face.

"For an independent thinker," he said, "you are rather a pusillanimous jackass. A man of your convictions to shy at a shadow! Fie, sir, fie! What if the room *were* empty? The place was full enough of traps to permit of Captain Iron's immediate withdrawal."

Much may be expressed in a sniff. I sniffed.

That afternoon I went back to town, and left the offensive William to his fate.

It found him at once.

The very day following that of my retreat, I was polishing phrases by gaslight in the dull sitting-room of my lodgings in the Lambeth Road, when he staggered in upon me. His face was like a sheep's, white and vacant; his hands had caught a trick of groping blindly along the backs of chairs.

"You have obtained your 'copy'?" I said.

I made him out to murmur "yes" in a shaking under-voice. He was so patently nervous that I put him in a chair and poured him out a wine-glassful of London brandy. This generally is a powerful emetic, but it had no more effect upon him than water. Then I was about to lower the gas, to save his eyes, but he stopped me with a thin shriek.

"Light, light!" he whispered. "It cannot be too light for me!"

"Now, William Tyrwhitt," I said, by-and-by, watchful of him, and marking a faint effusion of colour soak to his cheek, "you would not accept my warning, and you were extremely rude to me. Therefore you have had an experience—"

"An awful one," he murmured.

"An awful one, no doubt; and to obtain surcease of the haunting memory of it, you must confide its processes to me. But, first, I must put it to you, which is the more pusillanimous – to refuse to submit one's manliness to the tyranny of the unlawful, or to rush into situations you have not the nerve to adapt yourself to?"

"I could not foresee, I could not foresee."

"Neither could I. And that was my very reason for declining the invitation. Now proceed."

It was long before he could. But presently he essayed, and gathered voice with the advance of his narrative, and even unconsciously threw it into something the form of 'copy'. And here it is as he murmured it, but with a gasp for every full-stop.

"I confess I was so far moved by the tone of your protest as, after your departure, to make some cautious inquiries about the house we had visited. I could discover nothing to satisfy my curiosity. It was known to have been untenanted for a great number of years; but as to who was the landlord, whether Captain Iron or another, no one could inform me; and the agent for the property was of the adjacent town where you met me. I was not fortunate, indeed, in finding that anyone even knew of the oddly appointed room; but considering that, owing to the time the house had remained vacant, the existence of this eccentricity could be a tradition only with some casual few, my failure did not strike me as being at all bodeful. On the contrary, it only whetted my desire to investigate further in person, and penetrate to the heart of a very captivating little mystery. But probably, I thought, it is quite simple of solution, and the fact of the repairers and the landlord being in evidence at one time, a natural coincidence.

"I dined well, and sallied forth about nine o'clock. It was a night pregnant with possibilities. The lower strata of air were calm, but overhead the wind went down the sea with a noise of baggage-wagons, and there was an ominous hurrying and gathering together of forces under the bellying standards of the clouds.

"As I went up the steps of the lonely building, the High Street seemed to turn all its staring eyes of lamps in my direction. 'What a droll fellow!' they appeared to be saying; 'and how will he look when he reissues?'

"'There ain't nubbudy in that house,' croaked a small boy, who had paused below, squinting up at me.

"'How do you know?' said I. 'Move on, my little man.'

"He went; and at once it occurred to me that, as no notice was taken of my repeated knockings, I might as well try the handle. I did, found the door unlatched, as it had been in the morning, pushed it open, entered, and swung it to behind me.

"I found myself in the most profound darkness – that darkness, if I may use the paradox, of a peopled desolation that men of but little nerve or resolution find insupportable. To me, trained to a serenity of stoicism, it could make no demoralising appeal. I had out my matchbox, opened it at leisure, and, while the whole vaulting blackness seemed to tick and rustle with secret movement, took a half-dozen vestas into my hand, struck one alight, and, by its dim radiance, made my way through the building by the passages we had penetrated in the morning. If at all I shrank or perspired on my spectral journey, I swear I was not conscious of doing so.

"I came to the door of the cabin. All was black and silent.

"'Ah!' I thought, 'The rogue has played me false.'

"Not to subscribe to an uncertainty, I pushed at the door, saw only swimming dead vacancy before me, and tripping at the instant on the sill, stumbled crashing into the room below and slid my length on the floor.

"Now, I must tell you, it was here my heart gave its first somersault. I had fallen, as I say, into a black vault of emptiness; yet, as I rose, bruised and dazed, to my feet, there was the cabin all alight from a great lanthorn that swung from the ceiling, and our friend of the morning seated at a table, with a case-bottle of rum and glasses before him.

"I stared incredulous. Yes, there could be no doubt it was he, and pretty flushed with drink, too, by his appearance.

"'Incandescent light in a West Indiaman!' I muttered; for not otherwise could I account for the sudden illumination. 'What the deuce!'

"'Belay that!' he growled. He seemed to observe me for the first time.

"'A handsome manner of boarding a craft you've got, sir,' said he, glooming at me.

"I was hastening to apologise, but he stopped me coarsely.

"'Oh, curse the long jaw of him! Fill your cheek with that, you Barbary ape, and wag your tail if you can, but burn your tongue.'

"He pointed to the case-bottle with a forefinger that was like a dirty parsnip. What induced me to swallow the insult, and even some of the pungent liquor of his rude offering? The itch for 'copy' was, no doubt, at the bottom of it.

"I sat down opposite my host, filled and drained a bumper. The fire ran to my brain, so that the whole room seemed to pitch and courtesy.

"'This is an odd fancy of yours,' I said.

"'What is?' said he.

"'This,' I answered, waving my hand around – 'this freak of turning a back room into a cabin.'

"He stared at me, and then burst into a malevolent laugh.

"'Back room, by thunder!' said he. 'Why, of course – just a step into the garden where the roses and the buttercupses be agrowing.'

"Now I pricked my ears.

"'Has the night turned foul?' I muttered. 'What a noise the rain makes beating on the window!'

"'It's like to be a foul one for you, at least,' said he. 'But, as for the rain, it's blazing moonlight.'

"I turned to the broad casement in astonishment. My God! What did I see? Oh, my friend, my friend! Will you believe me? By the melancholy glow that spread therethrough I saw that the whole room was rising and sinking in rhythmical motion; that the lights of King's Cobb had disappeared, and that in their place was revealed a world of pale and tossing water, the pursuing waves of which leapt and clutched at the glass with innocuous fingers.

"I started to my feet, mad in an instant.

"'Look, look!' I shrieked. 'They follow us – they struggle to get at you, you bloody murderer!'

"They came rising on the crests of the billows; they hurried fast in our wake, tumbling and swaying, their stretched, drowned faces now lifted to the moonlight, now over-washed in the long trenches of water. They were rolled against the galleries of glass, on which their hair slapped like ribbons of seaweed – a score of ghastly white corpses, with strained black eyes and pointed stiff elbows crooked up in vain for air.

"I was mad, but I knew it all now. This was no house, but the good, ill-fated vessel *Rayo*, once bound for Jamaica, but on the voyage fallen into the hands of the bloody buccaneer, Paul Hardman, and her crew made to walk the plank, and most of her passengers. I knew that the dark scoundrel had boarded and mastered her, and – having first fired and sunk his own sloop – had steered her straight for the Cuban coast, making disposition of what remained of the passengers on the way, and I knew that my great-grandfather had been one of these doomed survivors, and that he had been shot and murdered under orders of the ruffian that now sat before me. All this, as retailed by one who sailed for a season under Hardman to save his skin, is matter of old private history; and of common report was it that the monster buccaneer, after years of successful trading in the ship he had stolen, went into secret and prosperous retirement under an assumed name, and was never heard of more on the high seas. But, it seemed, it was for the great-grandson of one of his victims to play yet a sympathetic part in the grey old tragedy.

"How did this come to me in a moment – or, rather, what was that dream buzzing in my brain of 'proof' and 'copy' and all the tame stagnation of a long delirium of order? I had nothing in common with the latter. In some telepathic way – influenced by these past-dated surroundings – dropped into the very den of this Procrustes of the seas, I was there to re-enact the fearful scene that had found its climax in the brain of my ancestor.

"I rushed to the window, thence back to within a yard of the glowering buccaneer, before whom I stood, with tossed arms, wild and menacing.

"'They follow you!' I screamed. 'Passive, relentless, and deadly, they follow in your wake and will not be denied. The strong, the helpless, the coarse and the beautiful – all you have killed and mutilated in your wanton devilry – they are on your heels like a pack of spectre-hounds, and sooner or later they will have you in their cold arms and hale you down to the secret places of terror. Look at Beston, who leads, with a fearful smile on his mouth! Look at that pale girl you tortured, whose hair writhes and lengthens – a swarm of snakes nosing the hull for some open port-hole to enter by! Dog and devil, you are betrayed by your own hideous cruelty!'

"He rose and struck at me blindly; staggered, and found his filthy voice in a shriek of rage.

"'Jorinder! Make hell of the galley-fire! Heat some irons red and fetch out a bucket of pitch. We'll learn this dandy galloot his manners!'

"Wrought to the snapping-point of desperation, I sprang at and closed with him; and we went down on the floor together with a heavy crash. I was weaponless, but I would choke and strangle him with my hands. I had him under, my fingers crooked in his throat. His eyeballs slipped forward, like banana ends squeezed from their skins; he could not speak or cry, but he put up one feeble hand and flapped it aimlessly. At that, in the midst of my fury, I glanced above me, and saw a press of dim faces crowding a dusk hatch; and from them a shadowy arm came through, pointing a weapon; and all my soul reeled sick, and I only longed to be left time to destroy the venomous horror beneath me before I passed.

"It was not to be. Something, a physical sensation like the jerk of a hiccup, shook my frame; and immediately the waters of being seemed to burst their dam and flow out peaceably into a valley of rest."

William Tyrwhitt paused, and "Well?" said I.

"You see me here," he said. "I woke this morning, and found myself lying on the floor of that shattered and battered closet, and a starved demon of a cat licking up something from the boards. When I drove her away, there was a patch there like ancient dried blood."

"And how about your head?"

"My head? Why, the bullet seemed stuck in it between the temples; and there I am afraid it is still."

"Just so. Now, William Tyrwhitt, you must take a Turkish, bath and some cooling salts, and then come and tell me all about it again."

"Ah! You don't believe me, I see. I never supposed you would. Goodnight!"

But, when he was gone, I sat ruminating.

"That Captain Iron," I thought, "walked over the great rent in the floor without falling through. Well, well!"

Ones and Zeros

Dan Coxon

STANDING in the porch she swears she can feel the building leaning, a camber to its moss-shrouded bricks that doesn't quite follow the lie of the land. The bay windows at the front of the cottage lean the other way, doubling the effect. She feels slightly queasy. Her fingers find the key in her handbag and she slides it into the lock. She traces the cast-iron numbers screwed into the oak door – '10' – then she turns it, feels the rusted tumblers fall into place and settle once again.

"Hello? Alan?"

She knows he's here somewhere, his Volvo is sitting on the drive, shaming her scraped, rusted Cortina, but there's no answer. The cottage squats in silence. For a moment she imagines something has happened to him, some horrific accident, but with an effort she pushes the thought away. It's a technique the therapist taught her – the third one, the goatee man – this visualisation of rejecting a fear, taking it in her hands and thrusting it away from her. Sometimes it works; other times, the fear is stronger than the visualisation.

"Alan? Are you there? Hello?"

The floorboards overhead let out a creak and she half expects him to come thumping down the stairs, grinning as always, full of life. Only more silence follows. Then a shout from the kitchen at the far end of the corridor.

"I'm down here, Sis. Come give me a hand, will you? Damned tap's leaking."

She staggers as she walks down the corridor, seasick on dry land, and she reaches out a hand to steady herself. The wallpaper is cool and slightly damp beneath her fingertips. Without thinking she wipes her fingers on her cardigan.

He's standing at the sink, the tap dismantled on the work surface beside him, doing something with a spanner. A toolbox sits open on the other side of the room, under the boiler.

"Grab me a wrench, will you? That's the one… no, that one… yes. Thanks, Sis. I'll get this fixed for you then leave you to it. The movers have dumped your boxes in the front two rooms, for whatever reason. You'll find them easy enough. You get down here alright?"

When she doesn't answer he looks up at her, his receding hairline glowing in the sunlight from the window.

"You okay?"

"Does the cottage seem straight to you?" She doesn't know why she says it, it just comes out. This happens sometimes, when she isn't paying attention. She tells herself to get a tighter grip. "I mean, it isn't leaning is it? It felt like it was leaning, when I was outside, and I've read about subsidence online. Clay shrinkage. There's a crack I thought I saw…"

Alan lets the spanner fall with a clatter into the sink and he takes her hand in his, leads her over to a wooden chair. It wobbles as she sits. Now that it's nestled within his, she feels her own hand shaking.

"We got all the surveys done, remember? All and then some. The place is solid, it's stood for close to three hundred years. It's just different is all. You're not in the city now, Sis. Just give it a bit of time. It's bound to feel strange."

She knows he's right. Of course he is. Good old dependable Alan; not at all like his younger sister.

"You just sit there. I'll fix you a cup of tea, as soon as I can find the box with the kettle in. It'll all be fine, you'll see."

* * *

She doesn't have to start work at once. The mortgage payments are half what she was paying back in the city and her accounts are looking healthier than they have in months. The therapist had suggested it might be good for her, though, and she has clients waiting. Some tweaks to a website, a batch job for a startup in Leeds. It's better than sitting and worrying about the cottage, she knows that. An active mind is a healthy mind.

Once her laptop is unpacked she sets up a workspace on the kitchen table, makes a pot of tea, opens a packet of Hobnobs. It's a comfort to settle back into the dev work again, to lose herself in the lines of code, the binary world that she prefers. There's an order to it – when programs go wrong, they obey rules, they follow reason. There's an explanation for everything.

She loses three hours to the website job, the teapot stone cold by the time she finishes. She's almost unaware of where she is until she logs out and turns off. Then she stares around the room, takes in its low ceiling, the stained oak of the window frames. It's almost dark outside, the light thick and brown. Her eyes find a crack in the corner of the room, follow it across the ceiling – no thicker than a thread, but a crack nonetheless. What was it Alan had said? The surveys were fine, all fine. No reason to worry. Push it away.

It's as she clears the biscuit crumbs from the tabletop that she hears it. A bang, but muffled, like a car door outside, or a cupboard slamming shut elsewhere in the house. She stops, rooted. Silence now. Only her own breath, the thudding of her heart. She waits a minute or more before she calls out.

"Alan? Hello?"

There's no one there. Nobody answers. He wouldn't be here, of course – he has something with the kids tonight, a parents' evening, some such responsibility. Still, she waits another minute. There's a creaking somewhere, like feet moving softly over boards. It stops, then starts again, the cottage shifting in its sleep.

"Hello?"

She stands at the table until the light fails, then she flicks the switch and sets about making her supper.

* * *

"I heard something, I swear I did. I'm not imagining this. There's either someone here, or something moving in the house, or the house itself… I don't know. But there were sounds, yesterday and today. I don't know what to do."

She can hear his sigh at the other end of the line. When he speaks it's in his slow, gentle voice, the one he always uses to talk her back from the edge.

"We've been through this, Sis. There's no one there. It's just an old place, remember? Buildings shift a little in their old age, make all sorts of noises. It's just the cottage settling."

"But you said it was fine. The surveys—"

"The surveys are all good, the noises are perfectly natural. It's just old. Listen, do you need me to come over? Shelley's at work still, but once she gets back she can have the boys. I could be there, maybe eightish?"

She stares at the wall. She knows he's been so kind already, so helpful, but she can hear that patience starting to fray. When she made the decision to move out of the city, to relocate to the country, twenty miles from her brother, it was with the understanding that he could help her if she needed him. If things started to unravel again. But she knows that there will come a point when he stops answering the phone.

"It's okay. I'm okay. You're right, I'm probably imagining things. Blood sugar's probably low. I'll make dinner, put some music on, maybe unpack some more boxes."

"You know I'm here if you need me? It's just a strange place. Somewhere new. You'll get used to it. The house isn't moving, there isn't anyone there. Until I turned up no one had set foot in it for months. You should have seen the dust bunnies I rounded up. Just give it time."

She wants to ask him about that, too. Not the dust, but the fact it was empty. There had been a woman in the cottage before, middle-aged, single. It was the estate agent who gave them all the details, his mouth running and running as if the more words he said, the more tightly it sealed the deal. Her uncle was selling the place because she'd disappeared. Done a runner, they thought; half her clothes gone, the house left abandoned. Something about irregularities at the bank where she worked. The estate agent had made a joke about her sunning herself on the Costa Brava. She wasn't sure how the uncle had been given power of attorney, but he had, and it meant there was no chain, an easy sale. Sitting in her flat in Islington, four thin walls packed tight about her, it had all made sense.

She doesn't ask him, though. She knows he will only sigh again, start wondering if he should be calling the men in white coats. It's unlike him not have asked her about the pills.

"Thanks Alan," she says, keeping her voice as level as she can. "I'm just nervous I guess. Give Shelley my love."

After she hangs up she tips the contents of her pill bottle out onto the kitchen table, a Morse code of little dots and dashes. She singles one out, pushes it around with her finger, then snatches at it and swallows it dry. She sits for a while and listens to the floorboards groaning overhead, and tries not to imagine a woman's feet pacing up and down.

* * *

That night she hears a baby crying, the noise waking her from a restless sleep. It seems a part of her dream at first, but then she's awake and it's real, the wailing cries rising in pitch as if it's in pain. Her first thought is that it's the woman's baby, but there has never been any mention of a child. And the woman isn't here, she reminds herself. There is nobody here.

The closest house is almost a mile away but the cries continue, until she convinces herself that someone has left a baby outside her door, an infant in a cardboard box, abandoned, scared. She never queries why someone would do this, whose child it is – she simply accepts it as fact. Bustling into her dressing gown she runs downstairs, turns the key in the lock and tugs at the door. It sticks in the frame for a moment and she has to pull even harder, the wood eventually coming unstuck without warning, the door banging against the wall.

There's a flash of russet as a pair of foxes bolt away, their fur a copper blur in the light from the porch. There is no box, no baby. She stands and stares at the dark, half expecting something – someone – to step out of it. Behind her the house moans like a ship settling against the storm.

As she closes the door she runs her fingers over the cool metal of the numbers again, the one and the zero. That is how life should be, in her head: binary; on or off; real or not. Something is or it isn't. There are no shades of grey. Life should be like one of her programs, obeying rules that she can learn, its problems fixed with a new line of code. She knows that isn't the case, but only because she has been told so time and time again by her therapists, her brother. In her heart it still feels true.

It takes her almost three hours to fall back to sleep. When the sun is starting to blush on the horizon she swings her legs over the side of the mattress, twists the cap from the pill bottle. She isn't sure how many she tumbles into her hand, how many little zeros. Ten, perhaps. Maybe more. They're tough to swallow all together, and she crunches them between her teeth, their powder dry and bitter.

At the point where she is tumbling into unconsciousness she thinks she feels the cottage shift beneath her, a beast settling its bulk. In her sleep she grips the sheets to keep from falling out.

* * *

When she wakes it is almost lunchtime and she's starving. Her stomach grumbles as she pulls her clothes on, and she thinks she hears the cottage murmur a growl in response, sharing her hunger. Staggering down the stairs they feel uneven and she almost trips.

The front door is wide open. She's certain she closed it last night. Didn't she? It can't have swung open by itself, the door is too tight in the frame. There's a scattering of leaves on the hall floor, though, so it must have been open for a while. She pushes it closed, the wood shrieking against the frame as she leans her weight against it. This time she waits to hear the latch click.

"Alan?"

The hole in her stomach has become something else now. She worries she might be sick. It's more than just emptiness; more like a whirlpool inside her, sucking everything down. Her head is fuzzy, and she braces herself against the wall.

The corridor looks wrong, the angles skewed as if it hasn't quite been put together right and the walls don't meet the floor, the ceiling pressing down towards her. There's a creaking like she hasn't heard before, louder and deeper, something rending in the foundations, and then the right-hand wall slides away beneath her hand. One moment it's there, the next it isn't. It's fallen back and to the side, opening a black doorway where once there was brick and mortar, the wallpaper shredded, fluttering in a musty breeze blowing in from who knows where. She blinks and stares, a scream drying up and withering in her throat.

Now she is sick, the paltry contents of her stomach erupting from between her lips, spattering onto the floor. She tries to calm her breathing, pull some air into her dusty lungs. Her skin feels clammy and tight. Somewhere nearby there is the sound of footsteps, quiet but firm on bare floorboards, and without warning five cold fingers interlace with hers. The hand leads her towards the black doorway and, after a moment's pause, she follows without looking back.

* * *

Alan drops by the cottage after work, Shelley having begrudgingly agreed to pick the boys up from rugby. He hasn't heard from his sister in almost three weeks. It's been worrying him for at least half that time, but he's been reluctant to insert himself into her life, to take on the burden. Shelley has told him enough times that he's too soft on her, that she needs to learn to look after herself. But he knows his sister's not well, and he has to check, so he incurs her scorn and makes the drive out to the cottage all the same.

The grass at the front is almost knee-high, he notes as he pulls into the drive, but that's no surprise. She never was that great at looking after herself. It looks like foxes have been at it on the lawn, the grass flattened in rough circles, what appears to be a lamb bone chewed and discarded to one side. He makes a mental note to have a word with her about weighing down the bin lids.

The door is closed but the latch isn't on, and it opens easily beneath his touch. There are leaves strewn across the hall floor. The air smells stale, blocked up drains and sour milk, and for the first time he's truly worried.

"Sis? You there? Anyone home?"

The house creaks but otherwise there is silence. As he steps back outside and starts thumbing the buttons on his mobile, he notices that the number one is missing from the front door. The zero hangs there alone, an open mouth caught in a silent scream.

In Kropfsberg Keep

Ralph Adams Cram

TO THE traveller from Innsbrück to Munich, up the lovely valley of the silver Inn, many castles appear, one after another, each on its beetling cliff or gentle hill – appear and disappear, melting into the dark fir trees that grow so thickly on every side – Laneck, Lichtwer, Ratholtz, Tratzberg, Matzen, Kropfsberg, gathering close around the entrance to the dark and wonderful Zillerthal.

But to us – Tom Rendel and myself – there are two castles only: not the gorgeous and princely Ambras, nor the noble old Tratzberg, with its crowded treasures of solemn and splendid mediaevalism; but little Matzen, where eager hospitality forms the new life of a never-dead chivalry, and Kropfsberg, ruined, tottering, blasted by fire and smitten with grievous years – a dead thing, and haunted – full of strange legends, and eloquent of mystery and tragedy.

We were visiting the von C—s at Matzen, and gaining our first wondering knowledge of the courtly, cordial castle life in the Tyrol – of the gentle and delicate hospitality of noble Austrians. Brixleg had ceased to be but a mark on a map, and had become a place of rest and delight, a home for homeless wanderers on the face of Europe, while Schloss Matzen was a synonym for all that was gracious and kindly and beautiful in life. The days moved on in a golden round of riding and driving and shooting: down to Landl and Thiersee for chamois, across the river to the magic Achensee, up the Zillerthal, across the Schmerner Joch, even to the railway station at Steinach. And in the evenings after the late dinners in the upper hall where the sleepy hounds leaned against our chairs looking at us with suppliant eyes, in the evenings when the fire was dying away in the hooded fireplace in the library, stories. Stories, and legends, and fairy tales, while the stiff old portraits changed countenance constantly under the flickering firelight, and the sound of the drifting Inn came softly across the meadows far below.

If ever I tell the Story of Schloss Matzen, then will be the time to paint the too inadequate picture of this fair oasis in the desert of travel and tourists and hotels; but just now it is Kropfsberg the Silent that is of greater importance, for it was only in Matzen that the story was told by Fräulein E—, the gold-haired niece of Frau von C—, one hot evening in July, when we were sitting in the great west window of the drawing room after a long ride up the Stallenthal. All the windows were open to catch the faint wind, and we had sat for a long time watching the Otzethaler Alps turn rose-color over distant Innsbrück, then deepen to violet as the sun went down and the white mists rose slowly until Lichtwer and Laneck and Kropfsberg rose like craggy islands in a silver sea.

And this is the story as Fräulein E— told it to us – the Story of Kropfsberg Keep.

* * *

A great many years ago, soon after my grandfather died, and Matzen came to us, when I was a little girl, and so young that I remember nothing of the affair except as something dreadful that frightened me very much, two young men who had studied painting with my grandfather came down to Brixleg from Munich, partly to paint, and partly to amuse themselves – 'ghost hunting' as they said, for they were very sensible young men and prided themselves on it, laughing at all kinds of 'superstition', and particularly at that form which believed in ghosts and feared them. They had never seen a real ghost, you know, and they belonged to a certain set of people who believed nothing they had not seen themselves – which always seemed to me *very* conceited. Well, they knew that we had lots of beautiful castles here in the 'lower valley', and they assumed, and rightly, that every castle has at least *one* ghost story connected with it, so they chose this as their hunting ground, only the game they sought was ghosts, not chamois. Their plan was to visit every place that was supposed to be haunted, and to meet every reputed ghost, and prove that it really was no ghost at all.

There was a little inn down in the village then, kept by an old man named Peter Rosskopf, and the two young men made this their headquarters. The very first night they began to draw from the old innkeeper all that he knew of legends and ghost stories connected with Brixleg and its castles, and as he was a most garrulous old gentleman he filled them with the wildest delight by his stories of the ghosts of the castles about the mouth of the Zillerthal. Of course the old man believed every word he said, and you can imagine his horror and amazement when, after telling his guests the particularly blood-curdling story of Kropfsberg and its haunted keep, the elder of the two boys, whose surname I have forgotten, but whose Christian name was Rupert, calmly said, "Your story is most satisfactory: we will sleep in Kropfsberg Keep tomorrow night, and you must provide us with all that we may need to make ourselves comfortable."

The old man nearly fell into the fire. "What for a blockhead are you?" he cried, with big eyes. "The keep is haunted by Count Albert's ghost, I tell you!"

"That is why we are going there tomorrow night; we wish to make the acquaintance of Count Albert."

"But there was a man stayed there once, and in the morning he was dead."

"Very silly of him; there are two of us, and we carry revolvers."

"But it's a *ghost*, I tell you," almost screamed the innkeeper; "are ghosts afraid of firearms?"

"Whether they are or not, we are *not* afraid of *them*."

Here the younger boy broke in – he was named Otto von Kleist. I remember the name, for I had a music teacher once by that name. He abused the poor old man shamefully; told him that they were going to spend the night in Kropfsberg in spite of Count Albert and Peter Rosskopf, and that he might as well make the most of it and earn his money with cheerfulness.

In a word, they finally bullied the old fellow into submission, and when the morning came he set about preparing for the suicide, as he considered it, with sighs and mutterings and ominous shakings of the head.

You know the condition of the castle now – nothing but scorched walls and crumbling piles of fallen masonry. Well, at the time I tell you of, the keep was still partially preserved. It was finally burned out only a few years ago by some wicked boys who came over from Jenbach to have a good time. But when the ghost hunters came, though the two lower floors had fallen into the crypt, the third floor remained. The peasants said it *could* not fall, but that it would stay until the Day of Judgment, because it was in the room above that the wicked Count Albert sat watching the flames destroy the great castle and his imprisoned guests, and where he finally hung himself in a suit of armor that had belonged to his mediaeval ancestor, the first Count Kropfsberg.

No one dared touch him, and so he hung there for twelve years, and all the time venturesome boys and daring men used to creep up the turret steps and stare awfully through the chinks in the door at that ghostly mass of steel that held within itself the body of a murderer and suicide, slowly returning to the dust from which it was made. Finally it disappeared, none knew whither, and for another dozen years the room stood empty but for the old furniture and the rotting hangings.

So, when the two men climbed the stairway to the haunted room, they found a very different state of things from what exists now. The room was absolutely as it was left the night Count Albert burned the castle, except that all trace of the suspended suit of armor and its ghastly contents had vanished.

No one had dared to cross the threshold, and I suppose that for forty years no living thing had entered that dreadful room.

On one side stood a vast canopied bed of black wood, the damask hangings of which were covered with mould and mildew. All the clothing of the bed was in perfect order, and on it lay a book, open, and face downward. The only other furniture in the room consisted of several old chairs, a carved oak chest, and a big inlaid table covered with books and papers, and on one corner two or three bottles with dark solid sediment at the bottom, and a glass, also dark with the dregs of wine that had been poured out almost half a century before. The tapestry on the walls was green with mould, but hardly torn or otherwise defaced, for although the heavy dust of forty years lay on everything the room had been preserved from further harm. No spiderweb was to be seen, no trace of nibbling mice, not even a dead moth or fly on the sills of the diamond-paned windows; life seemed to have shunned the room utterly and finally.

The men looked at the room curiously, and, I am sure, not without some feelings of awe and unacknowledged fear; but, whatever they may have felt of instinctive shrinking, they said nothing, and quickly set to work to make the room passably inhabitable. They decided to touch nothing that had not absolutely to be changed, and therefore they made for themselves a bed in one corner with the mattress and linen from the inn. In the great fireplace they piled a lot of wood on the caked ashes of a fire dead for forty years, turned the old chest into a table, and laid out on it all their arrangements for the evening's amusement: food, two or three bottles of wine, pipes and tobacco, and the chessboard that was their inseparable travelling companion.

All this they did themselves: the innkeeper would not even come within the walls of the outer court; he insisted that he had washed his hands of the whole affair, the silly dunderheads might go to their death their own way. *He* would not aid and abet them. One of the stable boys brought the basket of food and the wood and the bed up the winding stone stairs, to be sure, but neither money nor prayers nor threats would bring him within the walls of the accursed place, and he stared fearfully at the hare-brained boys as they worked around the dead old room preparing for the night that was coming so fast.

At length everything was in readiness, and after a final visit to the inn for dinner Rupert and Otto started at sunset for the Keep. Half the village went with them, for Peter Rosskopf had babbled the whole story to an open-mouthed crowd of wondering men and women, and as to an execution the awe-struck crowd followed the two boys dumbly, curious to see if they surely would put their plan into execution. But none went farther than the outer doorway of the stairs, for it was already growing twilight. In absolute silence they watched the two foolhardy youths with their lives in their hands enter the terrible Keep, standing like a tower in the midst of the piles of stones that had once formed walls joining it with the mass of the castle beyond. When a moment later a light showed itself in the high windows above, they sighed resignedly and went their ways, to wait stolidly until morning should come and prove the truth of their fears and warnings.

In the meantime the ghost hunters built a huge fire, lighted their many candles, and sat down to await developments. Rupert afterwards told my uncle that they really felt no fear whatever, only a contemptuous curiosity, and they ate their supper with good appetite and an unusual relish. It was a long evening. They played many games of chess, waiting for midnight. Hour passed after hour, and nothing occurred to interrupt the monotony of the evening. Ten, eleven, came and went – it was almost midnight. They piled more wood in the fireplace, lighted new candles, looked to their pistols – and waited. The clocks in the village struck twelve; the sound coming muffled through the high, deep-embrasured windows. Nothing happened, nothing to break the heavy silence; and with a feeling of disappointed relief they looked at each other and acknowledged that they had met another rebuff.

Finally they decided that there was no use in sitting up and boring themselves any longer, they had much better rest; so Otto threw himself down on the mattress, falling almost immediately asleep. Rupert sat a little longer, smoking, and watching the stars creep along behind the shattered glass and the bent leads of the lofty windows; watching the fire fall together, and the strange shadows move mysteriously on the mouldering walls. The iron hook in the oak beam, that crossed the ceiling midway, fascinated him, not with fear, but morbidly. So, it was from that hook that for twelve years, twelve long years of changing summer and winter, the body of Count Albert, murderer and suicide, hung in its strange casing of mediaeval steel; moving a little at first, and turning gently while the fire died out on the hearth, while the ruins of the castle grew cold, and horrified peasants sought for the bodies of the score of gay, reckless, wicked guests whom Count Albert had gathered in Kropfsberg for a last debauch, gathered to their terrible and untimely death. What a strange and fiendish idea it was, the young, handsome noble who had ruined himself and his family in the society of the splendid debauchees, gathering them all together, men and women who had known only love and pleasure, for a glorious and awful riot of luxury, and then, when they were all dancing in the great ballroom, locking the doors and burning the whole castle about them, the while he sat in the great keep listening to their screams of agonized fear, watching the fire sweep from wing to wing until the whole mighty mass was one enormous and awful pyre, and then, clothing himself in his great-great-grandfather's armor, hanging himself in the midst of the ruins of what had been a proud and noble castle. So ended a great family, a great house.

But that was forty years ago.

He was growing drowsy; the light flickered and flared in the fireplace; one by one the candles went out; the shadows grew thick in the room. Why did that great iron hook stand out so plainly? Why did that dark shadow dance and quiver so mockingly behind it? Why – but he ceased to wonder at anything. He was asleep.

It seemed to him that he woke almost immediately; the fire still burned, though low and fitfully on the hearth. Otto was sleeping, breathing quietly and regularly; the shadows had gathered close around him, thick and murky; with every passing moment the light died in the fireplace; he felt stiff with cold. In the utter silence he heard the clock in the village strike two. He shivered with a sudden and irresistible feeling of fear, and abruptly turned and looked towards the hook in the ceiling.

Yes, It was there. He knew that It would be. It seemed quite natural, he would have been disappointed had he seen nothing; but now he knew that the story was true, knew that he was wrong, and that the dead *do* sometimes return to earth, for there, in the fast-deepening shadow, hung the black mass of wrought steel, turning a little now and then, with the light flickering on the tarnished and rusty metal. He watched it quietly; he hardly felt afraid; it was rather a sentiment of sadness and fatality that filled him, of gloomy forebodings of something unknown, unimaginable. He sat and watched the thing disappear in the gathering dark, his hand on his pistol as it lay by him on the great chest. There was no sound but the regular breathing of the sleeping boy on the mattress.

It had grown absolutely dark; a bat fluttered against the broken glass of the window. He wondered if he was growing mad, for – he hesitated to acknowledge it to himself – he heard music; far, curious music, a strange and luxurious dance, very faint, very vague, but unmistakable.

Like a flash of lightning came a jagged line of fire down the blank wall opposite him, a line that remained, that grew wider, that let a pale cold light into the room, showing him now all its details, – the empty fireplace, where a thin smoke rose in a spiral from a bit of charred wood, the mass of the great bed, and, in the very middle, black against the curious brightness, the armored man, or ghost, or devil, standing, not suspended, beneath the rusty hook. And with the rending of the wall the music grew more distinct, though sounding still very, very far away.

Count Albert raised his mailed hand and beckoned to him; then turned, and stood in the riven wall.

Without a word, Rupert rose and followed him, his pistol in hand. Count Albert passed through the mighty wall and disappeared in the unearthly light. Rupert followed mechanically. He felt the crushing of the mortar beneath his feet, the roughness of the jagged wall where he rested his hand to steady himself.

The keep rose absolutely isolated among the ruins, yet on passing through the wall Rupert found himself in a long, uneven corridor, the floor of which was warped and sagging, while the walls were covered on one side with big faded portraits of an inferior quality, like those in the corridor that connects the Pitti and Uffizzi in Florence. Before him moved the figure of Count Albert – a black silhouette in the ever-increasing light. And always the music grew stronger and stranger, a mad, evil, seductive dance that bewitched even while it disgusted.

In a final blaze of vivid, intolerable light, in a burst of hellish music that might have come from Bedlam, Rupert stepped from the corridor into a vast and curious room where at first he saw nothing, distinguished nothing but a mad, seething whirl of sweeping figures, white, in a white room, under white light, Count Albert standing before him, the only dark object to be seen. As his eyes grew accustomed to the fearful brightness, he knew that he was looking on a dance such as the damned might see in hell, but such as no living man had ever seen before.

Around the long, narrow hall, under the fearful light that came from nowhere, but was omnipresent, swept a rushing stream of unspeakable horrors, dancing insanely, laughing, gibbering hideously; the dead of forty years. White, polished skeletons, bare of flesh and vesture, skeletons clothed in the dreadful rags of dried and rattling sinews, the tags of tattering grave-clothes flaunting behind them. These were the dead of many years ago. Then the dead of more recent times, with yellow bones showing only here and there, the long and insecure hair of their hideous heads writhing in the beating air. Then green and gray horrors, bloated and shapeless, stained with earth or dripping with spattering water; and here and there white, beautiful things, like chiselled ivory, the dead of yesterday, locked it may be, in the mummy arms of rattling skeletons.

Round and round the cursed room, a swaying, swirling maelstrom of death, while the air grew thick with miasma, the floor foul with shreds of shrouds, and yellow parchment, clattering bones, and wisps of tangled hair.

And in the very midst of this ring of death, a sight not for words nor for thought, a sight to blast forever the mind of the man who looked upon it: a leaping, writhing dance of Count Albert's victims, the score of beautiful women and reckless men who danced to their awful death while the castle burned around them, charred and shapeless now, a living charnel-house of nameless horror.

Count Albert, who had stood silent and gloomy, watching the dance of the damned, turned to Rupert, and for the first time spoke.

"We are ready for you now; dance!"

A prancing horror, dead some dozen years, perhaps, flaunted from the rushing river of the dead, and leered at Rupert with eyeless skull.

"Dance!"

Rupert stood frozen, motionless.

"Dance!"

His hard lips moved. "Not if the devil came from hell to make me."

Count Albert swept his vast two-handed sword into the fetid air while the tide of corruption paused in its swirling, and swept down on Rupert with gibbering grins.

The room, and the howling dead, and the black portent before him circled dizzily around, as with a last effort of departing consciousness he drew his pistol and fired full in the face of Count Albert.

* * *

Perfect silence, perfect darkness; not a breath, not a sound: the dead stillness of a long-sealed tomb. Rupert lay on his back, stunned, helpless, his pistol clenched in his frozen hand, a smell of powder in the black air. Where was he? Dead? In hell? He reached his hand out cautiously; it fell on dusty boards. Outside, far away, a clock struck three. Had he dreamed? Of course; but how ghastly a dream! With chattering teeth he called softly –

"Otto!"

There was no reply, and none when he called again and again. He staggered weakly to his feet, groping for matches and candles. A panic of abject terror came on him; the matches were gone! He turned towards the fireplace: a single coal glowed in the white ashes. He swept a mass of papers and dusty books from the table, and with trembling hands cowered over the embers, until he succeeded in lighting the dry tinder. Then he piled the old books on the blaze, and looked fearfully around.

No: It was gone – thank God for that; the hook was empty.

But why did Otto sleep so soundly; why did he not awake?

He stepped unsteadily across the room in the flaring light of the burning books, and knelt by the mattress.

* * *

So they found him in the morning, when no one came to the inn from Kropfsberg Keep, and the quaking Peter Rosskopf arranged a relief party – found him kneeling beside the mattress where Otto lay, shot in the throat and quite dead.

The Corpse Light

Dick Donovan

MY NAME is John Patmore Lindsay. By profession I am a medical man, and a Fellow of the Royal College of Surgeons, and Member of the Royal College of Physicians, London. I am also the author of numerous medical works, the best known, perhaps, being *How to Keep in Good Health and Live Long*. I was educated at one of the large public schools, and took my degree at Oxford. I have generally been regarded as 'a hard-headed man', and sceptical about all phenomena that were not capable of being explained by rational and known laws. Mysticism, occultism, spiritualism, and the like only served to excite my ridicule; and I entertained anything but a flattering opinion of those people who professed belief in such things. I was pleased to think it argued a weakness of mind.

I have referred to the few foregoing facts about myself because I wish to make it clear that I do not belong to that class of nervous and excitable people who fall a prey to their own fancies; conjure up shapes and scenes out of their imaginings, and then vow and declare that they have been confronted with stern realities. What I am about to relate is so marvellous, so weird and startling, that I am fain to begin my story in a half apologetic way; and even now, as I dwell upon it all, I wonder why I of all men should have been subjected to the unnatural and unearthly influence. But so it is, and though in a sense I am only half convinced, I no longer scoff when somebody reminds me that there is more in heaven and earth than is dreamt of in our philosophy.

But to my story, and when it is told the reader can judge for himself how powerful must have been the effect of what I witnessed, when it could induce a man of my mental fibre to commit to paper so astounding a narrative as the one I now pen. It is about twenty years ago that I took up a practice in the old-fashioned and picturesque little town of Brinton-on-sea. At that time there was no railway into Brinton, the nearest station being some seven or eight miles away. The result was, the town still retained a delightful old-time air, while the people were as primitive and old-fashioned as their town. Nevertheless, Brinton was far ahead of its neighbours, and, though in a purely agricultural district, was enterprising and business-like, while its weekly Tuesday market brought an enormous influx of the population of the district for miles around, and very large sums of money changed hands. Being the chief town of the parish, and boasting of a very curious and ancient church, and a still more ancient market cross, to say nothing of several delightful old hostelries, and a small though excellent museum of local curiosities, consisting principally of Roman remains and fossils, for which the district was renowned, it attracted not only the antiquary and the gourmand, but artists, tourists, and lovers of the picturesque, as well as those in search of quietude and repose. The nearest village was High Lea, about three miles away. Between the two places was a wide sweep of magnificent rolling down, delightful at all times, but especially so in the summer. Many an ancient farmhouse was dotted about, with here and there a windmill. The down on the seaside terminated in a high headland, from which a splendid lighthouse sent forth its warning beams over the fierce North Sea. Second only in conspicuousness to this lighthouse was an old and half ruined windmill, known all over the country side as 'The Haunted Mill'.

When I first went to live in Brinton this mill early attracted my attention, for it was one of the most picturesque old places of its kind I had ever seen; and as I had some artistic instincts, and could sketch with, as my too flattering friends said, 'no mean ability', the haunted mill appealed to me. It stood on rising ground, close to the high-road that ran between Brinton and High Lea. I gathered that there had been some dispute about the ownership, and, as is usually the case, the suckers of the harpies of the law had fastened upon it, so to speak, and drained all its vitality away after the manner of lawyers generally. The old-fashioned, legal luminaries of the country were a slow-going set, and for over a quarter of a century that disputed claim had remained unsettled; and during that long period the old mill had been gradually falling into ruin. The foundations had from some cause sunk, throwing the main building out of the perpendicular. Part of the roof had fallen in, and the fierce gales of a quarter of a century had battered the sails pretty well to matchwood. A long flight of wooden steps led up to the principal door, but these steps had rotted away in places, and the door itself had partly fallen inwards. Needless to say, this mill had become the home of bats and owls, and, according to the yokels, of something more fearsome than either. It was a forlorn and mournful-looking place, anyway, even in the full blaze of sunshine; but seen in moonlight its appearance was singularly weird, and well calculated to beget in the rustic mind a feeling of horror, and to produce a creepy and uncanny sensation in anyone susceptible to the influence of *outre* appearances. To me it did not appeal in any of these aspects. I saw in it only subject matter for an exceedingly effective picture, and yet I am bound to confess that even when transferred to board or canvas there was a certain grim suggestiveness of things uncanny, and I easily understood how the superstitious and unreasoning rustic mind was awed into a belief that this mouldering old mill was haunted by something more creepy and harrowing than bats and owls. Anyway, I heard wonderful tales, at which I laughed, and when I learned that the country people generally gave the mill a wide berth at night, blamed them for their stupidity. But it was a fact that worthy, and in other respects intelligent, farmers and market folk coming or going between Brinton and High Lea after dark preferred the much longer and dangerous route by the sea cliffs, even in the wildest weather.

I have dwelt thus long on the 'Haunted Mill' because it bulks largely in my story, as will presently be seen, and I came in time to regard it with scarcely less awe than the rustics did.

It was during the second year of my residence in Brinton that a young man named Charles Royce came home after having been absent at sea for three years. Royce's people occupied Gorse Hill Farm, about two miles to the south of Brinton. Young Charley, a fine, handsome, but rather wild youngster, had, it appears, fallen desperately in love with Hannah Trowzell, who was a domestic in the employ of the Rector of the parish. But Charley's people did not approve of his choice, and, thinking to cure him, packed him off to sea, and after an absence of three years and a month the young fellow, bronzed, hearty, more rollicking and handsome than ever, returned to his native village. I had known nothing of Charles Royce or his history up to the day of his return; but it chanced on that very day I had to pay a professional visit to the Rectory, and the Rector pressed me to lunch with him. Greatly interested in all his parishioners, and knowing something of the private history of most of the families in his district, the rev. gentleman very naturally fell to talking about young Royce, and he told me the story, adding, "Hannah is a good girl, and I think it's rather a pity Charley's people objected to his courting her. I believe she would have made him a capital wife."

"Has she given him up entirely?" I asked.

"Oh, yes, and is engaged to Silas Hartrop, whose father owns the fishing smack the 'North Sea Beauty'. I've never had a very high opinion of Silas. I'm afraid he is a little too fond of skittles and beer. However, Hannah seems determined to have him in spite of anything I can say, so she must take her course. But I hope she will be able to reform him, and that the marriage will be a happy one. I really shouldn't be a bit surprised, however, if the girl took up with her old lover again, for

I have reason to know she was much attached to him, and I fancy Charley, if he were so minded, could easily influence her to throw Silas overboard."

This little story of love and disappointment naturally interested me, for in a country town the affairs of one's neighbours are matter of greater moment than is the case in a big city.

So it came to pass that a few weeks after Charley's return it was pretty generally known that, even as the Rector had suggested it might be, young Royce and pretty Hannah Trowzell were spooning again, and Silas had virtually been told to go about his business. It was further known that Silas had taken his dismissal so much to heart that he had been seeking consolation in the beer-pot. Of course, folk talked a good deal, and most of them sympathised with Silas, and blamed Hannah. Very soon it began to be bruited about that Royce's people no longer opposed any objections to the wooing, and that in consequence Hannah and Charley were to become husband and wife at Christmas, that was in about seven weeks' time. A month of the time had passed, and the 'askings' were up in the parish church, when one day there went forth a rumour that Charles Royce was missing. Rumour took a more definite shape a few hours later when it was positively stated that two nights previously Charles had left his father's house in high spirits and the best of health to visit Hannah, and walk with her, as she was going into the town to make some purchases. On his way he called at the 'Two Waggoners', a wayside inn, where he had a pint of beer and purchased an ounce of tobacco. From the time he left the inn, all trace of him was lost, and he was seen no more. Hannah waited his coming until long past the appointed hour, and when he failed to put in an appearance, she became angry and went off to the town by herself. Next day her anger gave place to anxiety when she learnt that he had left his home to visit her, and had not since returned; and anxiety became alarm when two and three days slipped by without bringing any tidings of the truant. On the night that he left his home, the weather was very tempestuous, and it had been wild and stormy since. It was therefore suggested that on leaving the 'Two Waggoners' he might have got confused when he reached the common, which he had to cross to get to the Rectory; and as there were several pools and treacherous hollows on the common, it was thought he had come to grief, but the most diligent search failed to justify the surmise.

Such an event as this was well calculated to cause a sensation, not only in Brinton and its neighbourhood, but throughout the county. Indeed, for many days it was a common topic of conversation, and at the Brinton weekly market the farmers and the rustics dwelt upon it to the exclusion of other things; and, of course, everybody, or nearly everybody, had some wonderful theory of his or her own to account for the missing man's disappearance. One old lady, who every week for twenty years had trudged in from a village five miles off with poultry and eggs for the Brinton market, declared her belief that young Royce had been spirited away, and she recommended an appeal to a wondrous wise woman, locally known as 'Cracked Moll', but whose reputation for solving mysteries and discovering lost persons and things was very great. Ultimately Royce's people did call in the services of this ancient fraud, but without any result. And despite of wide publicity and every effort on the part of the rural and county police, to say nothing of a hundred and one amateur detectives, the mystery remained unsolved. Charles Royce had apparently disappeared from off the face of the earth, leaving not a trace behind.

In the process of time the nine days' wonder gave place to something else, and excepting by those directly interested in him, Charles Royce was forgotten. Hannah took the matter very seriously to heart, and for a while lay dangerously ill. Silas Hartrop, who was much affected by his disappointment with regard to Hannah, went to the dogs, as the saying is, and drank so heavily that it ended in an attack of delirium tremens. I was called in to attend him, and had hard work to pull him through. On his recovery his father sent him to an uncle at Yarmouth, who was in the fishing trade, and soon afterwards news came that young Hartrop had been drowned at sea. He was out in the North Sea in his uncle's fishing smack, and, though nobody saw him go, it was supposed that he fell overboard in the night. This set the local tongues wagging again for a time, but even the affairs of Brinton could not stand still because the ne'er-do-well Silas Hartrop was drowned. So sympathy was expressed with his people, and then the affair was dismissed.

About two years later I received an urgent message late one afternoon to hasten with all speed to High Lea, to attend to the Squire there, who had been taken suddenly and, as report said, seriously ill. I had had rather a heavy day of it, as there had been a good deal of sickness about for some time past, and it had taken me several hours to get through my list of patients. I had just refreshed myself with a cup of tea and was about to enjoy a cigar when the messenger came. Telling him to ride back as quickly as possible and say that I was coming, I busied myself with a few important matters which had to be attended to, as I might be absent for some hours, and then I ordered my favourite mare, Princess, to be saddled.

I set off from Brinton soon after seven. It was a November night, bitterly cold, dark as Erebus, while every now and then violent squalls swept the land from seaward. Princess knew the road well, so I gave the mare her head, and she went splendidly until we reached the ruined mill, when suddenly she wheeled round with such abruptness that, though I was a good horseman, I was nearly pitched from the saddle. At the same moment I was struck in the face by something that seemed cold and clammy. I thought at first it was a bat, but remembered that bats do not fly in November; an owl, but an owl would not have felt cold and clammy. However, I had little time for thought, as my attention had to be given to the mare. She seemed disposed to bolt, and was trembling with fear. Then, to my intense astonishment, I noticed what seemed to be a large luminous body lying on the roadway. It had the appearance of a corpse illuminated in some wonderful and mysterious manner. Had it not been for the fright of my mare I should have thought I was the victim of some optical delusion; but Princess evidently saw the weird object, and refused to pass it. So impressed was I with the idea that a real and substantial body was lying on the road, notwithstanding the strange unearthly light, that I slipped from the saddle, intending to investigate the matter, when suddenly it disappeared, and the cold and clammy *something* again struck me in the face.

I confess that for the first time in my life I felt a strange, nervous, unaccountable fear. I say 'unaccountable', because it would have been difficult for me to have given any explanation of my fear. Why and of what was I afraid? Now, whatever the phenomenon was, there was the hard, stern fact to face that my horse had seen what I had seen, and was terrified. There was something strangely uncanny about the whole business, and when a terrific squall, bringing with it sleet and rain, came howling from the sea, it seemed to emphasise the uncanniness, and the ruined mill, looming gaunt and grim in the darkness, caused me to shake with an involuntary shudder. The next moment I was trying to laugh myself out of my nervousness. "Princess and I," I mentally argued, "have been the victims of some atmospheric delusion." That was all very well, but the *something* cold and clammy that struck me in the face, and which *may* have struck the mare in the face also, was no atmospheric delusion. With an alacrity I did not often display, I sprang into the saddle, spoke some encouraging words to the mare, for she was still trembling, and when she bounded forward, and the haunted mill was behind me, I experienced a positive sense or relief.

I found my patient at High Lea in a very bad way. He was suffering from an attack of apoplexy, and though I used all my skill on his behalf he passed away towards midnight. His wife very kindly offered me a bed for the night, but as I had important matters to attend to early in the morning I declined the hospitality, though I was thankful for a glass or two of generous port wine and some sandwiches. It was half-past twelve when I left the house on my return journey. The incident by the haunted mill had been put out of my head by the case I had been called upon to attend, but as I mounted my mare the groom, who had brought her round from the stable, said, "It be a bad night, doctor, for riding; the kind o' night when dead things come out o' their graves."

I laughed, and replied: "Tom, lad, I am surprised to hear you talk such rubbish. I thought you had more sense than that."

"Well, I tell 'ee what, doctor; if I had to ride to Brinton tonight I'd go by the cliffs and chance being drowned, rather than pass yon old mill." These words for the moment unnerved me, and I honestly confess that I resolved to go by the cliffs, dangerous as the road was in the dark. Nevertheless, I laughed at Tom's fears, and ridiculed him, though when I left the squire's grounds I turned the mare's head towards the cliffs. In a few minutes I was ridiculing myself.

"John Patmore Lindsay," I mentally exclaimed, "you are a fool. All your life you have been ridiculing stories of the supernatural, and now, at your time of life, are you going to allow yourself to be frightened by a bogey? Shame on you."

I bucked up, grew bold, and thereupon altered my course, and got into the high road again.

There had been a slight improvement in the weather. It had ceased to rain, but the wind had settled down into a steady gale, and screeched and screamed over the moorland with a demoniacal fury. The darkness, however, was not so intense as it was, and a star here and there was visible through the torn clouds. But it was an eerie sort of night, and I was strangely impressed with a sense of my loneliness. It was absolutely unusual for me to feel like this, and I suggested to myself that my nerves were a little unstrung by overwork and the anxiety the squire's illness had caused me. And so I rode on, bowing my head to the storm, while the mare stepped out well, and I anticipated that in little more than half an hour I should be snug in bed. As we got abreast of the haunted mill the mare once more gibbed, and all but threw me, and again I was struck in the face by the cold clammy *something*.

I have generally prided myself on being a bold man, but my boldness had evaporated now, and I almost think my hair rose on end as I observed that the illuminated corpse was lying in the roadway again; but now it appeared to be surrounded by a lake of blood. It was the most horrible, weird, marrow-curdling sight that ever human eyes looked upon. I tried to urge Princess forward, but she was stricken with terror, and, wheeling right round, was setting off towards High Lea again. But once more I was struck in the face by the invisible *something*, and its coldness and clamminess made me shudder, while there in front of us lay the corpse in the pool of blood. The mare reared and plunged, but I got her head round, determining to make a wild gallop for Brinton and leave the horrors of the haunted mill behind. But the corpse was again in front of us, and I shrank back almost appalled as the *something* once more touched my face.

I cannot hope to describe what my feelings were at this supreme moment. I don't believe anything human could have daunted me; but I was confronted by a supernatural mystery that not only terrified me but the mare I was riding. Whichever way I turned, that awful, ghastly object confronted me, and the blow in the face was repeated again and again.

How long I endured the unutterable horrors of the situation I really don't know. Possibly the time was measured by brief minutes. It seemed to me hours. At last my presence of mind returned. I dismounted, and reasoned with myself that, whatever the apparition was, it had some import. I soothed the mare by patting her neck and talking to her, and I determined then to try and find a solution of the mystery. But now a more wonderful thing happened. The corpse, which was still made visible by the unearthly light, rose straight up, and as it did so the blood seemed to flow away from it in great, gurgling streams, for I solemnly declare that I distinctly heard gurgling sounds. The figure glided past me, and a sense of extraordinary coldness made me shiver. Slowly and gracefully the shining corpse glided up the rotting steps of the old mill, and disappeared through the doorway. No sooner had it gone than the mill itself seemed to glow with phosphorescent light, and to become transparent, and I beheld a sight that took my breath away. I am disposed to think that for some moments my brain became so numbed that insensibility ensued, for I am conscious of a blank. When the power of thought returned, I was still holding the bridle of the mare, and she was cropping the grass at her feet. The mill loomed blackly against the night sky. It had resumed its normal appearance again. The wind shrieked about it. The ragged scud raced through the heavens, and the air was filled with the sounds of the raging wind. At first I was inclined to doubt the evidence of my own senses. I tried to reason myself into a belief that my imagination had played me a trick; but I didn't succeed, although the mystery was too profound for my fathoming. So I mounted the mare, urged her to her fastest pace, galloped into Brinton, and entered my house with a feeling of intense relief.

Thoroughly exhausted by the prolonged physical and mental strain I had endured, I speedily sank into a deep though troubled slumber as soon as I got into bed. I was unusually late in rising the next day. I found that I had no appetite for breakfast. Indeed, I felt ill and out or sorts; and, though I busied myself with my professional duties, I was haunted by the strange incidents of the preceding night. Never before in the whole course of my career had I been so impressed, so unnerved, and so dispirited. I wanted to believe that I was still as sceptical as ever, but it was no use. What I had seen might have been unearthly; but I *had seen it*, and it was no use trying to argue myself out of that fact. The result was, in the course of the afternoon I called on my old friend, Mr. Goodyear, who was chief of the county constabulary. He was a strong-minded man, and, like myself, a hardened sceptic about all things that smacked of the supernatural.

"Goodyear," I said, "I'm out of sorts, and I want you to humour a strange fancy I have. Bring one of your best men, and come with me to the haunted mill. But first let me exact from you a pledge of honour that, if our journey should result in nothing, you will keep the matter secret, as I am very sensitive to ridicule."

He looked at me in amazement, and then, as he burst into a hearty laugh, exclaimed:

"I say, my friend, you are over-working yourself. It's time you got a *locum tenens*, and took a holiday."

I told him that I agreed with him; nevertheless, I begged him to humour me, and accompany me to the mill. At last he reluctantly consented to do so, and an hour later we drove out of the town in my dog-cart. There were four of us, as I took Peter, my groom, with me. We had provided ourselves with lanterns, but Goodyear's man and Peter knew nothing of the object of our journey.

When we got abreast of the mill I drew up, and giving the reins to Peter, I alighted, and Goodyear did the same. Taking him on one side, I said, "I have had a vision, and unless I am the victim of incipient madness we shall find a dead body in the mill."

The light of the dog-cart was shining full on his face, and I saw the expression of alarm that my words brought.

"Look here, old chap," he said in a cheery, kindly way, as he put his arm through mine, "you are not going into that mill, but straight home again. Come, now, get into the cart, and don't let's have any more of this nonsense."

I felt disposed to yield to him, and had actually placed my foot on the step to mount, when I staggered back and exclaimed:

"My God! Am I going mad, or is this a reality?"

Once again I had been struck in the face by the cold clammy *something*; and I saw Goodyear suddenly clap his hand to his face as he cried out – "Hullo, what the deuce is that?"

"Aha," I exclaimed exultantly, for I no longer thought my brain was giving way, "you have felt it too?"

"Well, something cold and nasty-like struck me in the face. A bat, I expect. Confound 'em."

"Bats don't fly at this time of the year," I replied. "By Jove, no more they do." I approached him, and said in a low tone – "Goodyear, this is a mystery beyond our solving. I am resolved to go into that mill." He was a brave man, though for a moment or two he hesitated; but on my insisting he consented to humour me, and so we lit the lantern, and leaving the groom in charge of the horse and trap, I, Goodyear, and his man made our way with difficulty up the rotting steps, which were slimy and sodden with wet. As we entered the mill an extraordinary scene of desolation and ruin met our gaze as we flashed the light of the lantern about. In places the floor had broken away, leaving yawning chasms of blackness. From the mouldering rafters huge festoons of cobwebs hung. The accumulated dust and dampness of years had given them the appearance of cords. And oh, how the wind moaned eerily through the rifts and crannies and broken windows! If ever there was a place on this earth where evil spirits might dwell it was surely that ghoul-haunted old mill. The startling aspect of the place impressed us all, perhaps me more than the other two. We advanced gingerly, for the floor was so rotten we were afraid it would crumble beneath our feet.

My companions were a little bewildered, I think, and were evidently at a loss to know what we had come there for. But some strange feeling impelled me to seek for something; though if I had been asked to define that something, for the life of me I could not have done it. Forward I went, however, taking the lead, and holding the lantern above my head so that its rays might fall afar. But they revealed nothing save the rotting floor and slimy walls. A ladder led to the upper storey, and I expressed my intention of mounting it. Goodyear tried to dissuade me, but I was resolute, and led the way. The ladder was so creaky and fragile that it was not safe for more than one to be on it at a time. When I reached the second floor and drew myself up through the trap, I am absolutely certain I heard a sigh. You may say it was the wind. I swear it was not. The wind was moaning drearily enough, but the sigh was a distinctive note, and unmistakable. As I turned the lantern round so that its light might sweep every hole and corner of the place, I noticed what seemed to be a sack full of something lying in a corner. I approached and touched it with my foot, and drew back in alarm, for touch and sound told me it contained neither corn nor chaff. I waited until my companions had joined me. Then I said to Goodyear, "Unless I am mistaken there is something dreadful in that sack."

He stooped and placed his hand on the sack, and I saw him start back. In another moment he recovered himself, and whipping out his knife cut the string which fastened up the mouth of the sack, and revealed a human skull with the hair and shrivelled mummified flesh still adhering to it.

"Great heavens!" he exclaimed, "Here is a human body."

We held a hurried conversation, and decided to leave the ghastly thing undisturbed until the morrow. So we scuttled down as fast as we could, and went home. I did not return to the mill again myself. My part had been played. Investigation made it absolutely certain that the mouldering remains were those of poor Charley Royce, and it was no less absolutely certain that he had been foully murdered. For not only was there a bullet-hole in the skull, and a bullet inside, but his throat had been cut. It was murder horrible and damnable. The verdict of the coroner's jury pronounced it murder, but there was no evidence to prove who had done the deed. Circumstances, however, pointed to Charley's rival, Silas Hartrop. Was it a guilty conscience that drove him to drink? And did the Furies who avenge such deeds impel him on that dark and stormy night in the North Sea to end the torture of his accursed earthly life? Who can tell? The sea holds its secrets, and not a scrap of legal evidence could be obtained. But though the law declined the responsibility of fixing the guilt of the dark deed on Silas, there was a consensus of opinion that he was the guilty party. It was a mystery, but the greatest mystery of all was that I, the sceptic, should have been selected by some supernatural power to be the instrument for bringing the foul crime to light. For myself, I attempt no explanation. I have told a true story. Let those who can explain it. I admit now that 'there are more things in heaven and earth than are dreamt of in our philosophy.'

The Captain of the Polestar

Arthur Conan Doyle

[Being an extract from the singular journal of JOHN M'ALISTER RAY, student of medicine.]

September 11th.

LAT. 81 DEGREES 40' N.; LONG. 2 DEGREES E.

Still lying-to amid enormous ice fields. The one which stretches away to the north of us, and to which our ice-anchor is attached, cannot be smaller than an English county. To the right and left unbroken sheets extend to the horizon. This morning the mate reported that there were signs of pack ice to the southward. Should this form of sufficient thickness to bar our return, we shall be in a position of danger, as the food, I hear, is already running somewhat short. It is late in the season, and the nights are beginning to reappear.

This morning I saw a star twinkling just over the fore-yard, the first since the beginning of May. There is considerable discontent among the crew, many of whom are anxious to get back home to be in time for the herring season, when labour always commands a high price upon the Scotch coast. As yet their displeasure is only signified by sullen countenances and black looks, but I heard from the second mate this afternoon that they contemplated sending a deputation to the Captain to explain their grievance. I much doubt how he will receive it, as he is a man of fierce temper, and very sensitive about anything approaching to an infringement of his rights. I shall venture after dinner to say a few words to him upon the subject. I have always found that he will tolerate from me what he would resent from any other member of the crew. Amsterdam Island, at the north-west corner of Spitzbergen, is visible upon our starboard quarter – a rugged line of volcanic rocks, intersected by white seams, which represent glaciers. It is curious to think that at the present moment there is probably no human being nearer to us than the Danish settlements in the south of Greenland – a good nine hundred miles as the crow flies. A captain takes a great responsibility upon himself when he risks his vessel under such circumstances. No whaler has ever remained in these latitudes till so advanced a period of the year.

9 p.m.

I have spoken to Captain Craigie, and though the result has been hardly satisfactory, I am bound to say that he listened to what I had to say very quietly and even deferentially. When I had finished he put on that air of iron determination which I have frequently observed upon his face, and paced rapidly backwards and forwards across the narrow cabin for some minutes. At first I feared that I had seriously offended him, but he dispelled the idea by sitting down again, and putting his hand upon my arm with a gesture which almost amounted to a caress. There was a depth of tenderness too in his wild dark eyes which surprised me considerably. "Look here, Doctor," he said, "I'm sorry I ever took you – I am indeed – and I would give fifty pounds this minute to see you standing safe upon the Dundee quay. It's hit or miss with me this time. There are fish to the north of us. How dare you shake your head, sir, when I tell you I saw them blowing from the masthead?" – this in a sudden burst of fury, though I was not conscious of having shown any signs of doubt.

"Two-and-twenty fish in as many minutes as I am a living man, and not one under ten foot.[1] Now, Doctor, do you think I can leave the country when there is only one infernal strip of ice between me and my fortune? If it came on to blow from the north tomorrow we could fill the ship and be away before the frost could catch us. If it came on to blow from the south – well, I suppose the men are paid for risking their lives, and as for myself it matters but little to me, for I have more to bind me to the other world than to this one. I confess that I am sorry for you, though. I wish I had old Angus Tait who was with me last voyage, for he was a man that would never be missed, and you – you said once that you were engaged, did you not?"

"Yes," I answered, snapping the spring of the locket which hung from my watch-chain, and holding up the little vignette of Flora.

"Curse you!" he yelled, springing out of his seat, with his very beard bristling with passion. "What is your happiness to me? What have I to do with her that you must dangle her photograph before my eyes?" I almost thought that he was about to strike me in the frenzy of his rage, but with another imprecation he dashed open the door of the cabin and rushed out upon deck, leaving me considerably astonished at his extraordinary violence. It is the first time that he has ever shown me anything but courtesy and kindness. I can hear him pacing excitedly up and down overhead as I write these lines.

I should like to give a sketch of the character of this man, but it seems presumptuous to attempt such a thing upon paper, when the idea in my own mind is at best a vague and uncertain one. Several times I have thought that I grasped the clue which might explain it, but only to be disappointed by his presenting himself in some new light which would upset all my conclusions. It may be that no human eye but my own shall ever rest upon these lines, yet as a psychological study I shall attempt to leave some record of Captain Nicholas Craigie.

A man's outer case generally gives some indication of the soul within. The Captain is tall and well-formed, with dark, handsome face, and a curious way of twitching his limbs, which may arise from nervousness, or be simply an outcome of his excessive energy. His jaw and whole cast of countenance is manly and resolute, but the eyes are the distinctive feature of his face. They are of the very darkest hazel, bright and eager, with a singular mixture of recklessness in their expression, and of something else which I have sometimes thought was more allied with horror than any other emotion. Generally the former predominated, but on occasions, and more particularly when he was thoughtfully inclined, the look of fear would spread and deepen until it imparted a new character to his whole countenance. It is at these times that he is most subject to tempestuous fits of anger, and he seems to be aware of it, for I have known him lock himself up so that no one might approach him until his dark hour was passed. He sleeps badly, and I have heard him shouting during the night, but his cabin is some little distance from mine, and I could never distinguish the words which he said.

This is one phase of his character, and the most disagreeable one. It is only through my close association with him, thrown together as we are day after day, that I have observed it. Otherwise he is an agreeable companion, well-read and entertaining, and as gallant a seaman as ever trod a deck. I shall not easily forget the way in which he handled the ship when we were caught by a gale among the loose ice at the beginning of April. I have never seen him so cheerful, and even hilarious, as he was that night, as he paced backwards and forwards upon the bridge amid the flashing of the lightning and the howling of the wind. He has told me several times that the thought of death was a pleasant one to him, which is a sad thing for a young man to say; he cannot be much more than thirty, though his hair and moustache are already slightly grizzled. Some great sorrow must have overtaken him and blighted his whole life. Perhaps I should be the same if I lost my Flora – God knows! I think if it were not for her that I should care very little whether the wind blew from the north or the south tomorrow.

There, I hear him come down the companion, and he has locked himself up in his room, which shows that he is still in an unamiable mood. And so to bed, as old Pepys would say, for the candle is burning down (we have to use them now since the nights are closing in), and the steward has turned in, so there are no hopes of another one.

September 12th.

Calm, clear day, and still lying in the same position. What wind there is comes from the south-east, but it is very slight. Captain is in a better humour, and apologised to me at breakfast for his rudeness. He still looks somewhat distrait, however, and retains that wild look in his eyes which in a Highlander would mean that he was 'fey' – at least so our chief engineer remarked to me, and he has some reputation among the Celtic portion of our crew as a seer and expounder of omens.

It is strange that superstition should have obtained such mastery over this hard-headed and practical race. I could not have believed to what an extent it is carried had I not observed it for myself. We have had a perfect epidemic of it this voyage, until I have felt inclined to serve out rations of sedatives and nerve-tonics with the Saturday allowance of grog. The first symptom of it was that shortly after leaving Shetland the men at the wheel used to complain that they heard plaintive cries and screams in the wake of the ship, as if something were following it and were unable to overtake it. This fiction has been kept up during the whole voyage, and on dark nights at the beginning of the seal-fishing it was only with great difficulty that men could be induced to do their spell. No doubt what they heard was either the creaking of the rudder-chains, or the cry of some passing sea-bird. I have been fetched out of bed several times to listen to it, but I need hardly say that I was never able to distinguish anything unnatural.

The men, however, are so absurdly positive upon the subject that it is hopeless to argue with them. I mentioned the matter to the Captain once, but to my surprise he took it very gravely, and indeed appeared to be considerably disturbed by what I told him. I should have thought that he at least would have been above such vulgar delusions.

All this disquisition upon superstition leads me up to the fact that Mr. Manson, our second mate, saw a ghost last night – or, at least, says that he did, which of course is the same thing. It is quite refreshing to have some new topic of conversation after the eternal routine of bears and whales which has served us for so many months. Manson swears the ship is haunted, and that he would not stay in her a day if he had any other place to go to. Indeed the fellow is honestly frightened, and I had to give him some chloral and bromide of potassium this morning to steady him down. He seemed quite indignant when I suggested that he had been having an extra glass the night before, and I was obliged to pacify him by keeping as grave a countenance as possible during his story, which he certainly narrated in a very straight-forward and matter-of-fact way.

"I was on the bridge," he said, "about four bells in the middle watch, just when the night was at its darkest. There was a bit of a moon, but the clouds were blowing across it so that you couldn't see far from the ship. John M'Leod, the harpooner, came aft from the fo'c's'le-head and reported a strange noise on the starboard bow.

"I went forrard and we both heard it, sometimes like a bairn crying and sometimes like a wench in pain. I've been seventeen years to the country and I never heard seal, old or young, make a sound like that. As we were standing there on the fo'c's'le-head the moon came out from behind a cloud, and we both saw a sort of white figure moving across the ice field in the same direction that we had heard the cries. We lost sight of it for a while, but it came back on the port bow, and we could just make it out like a shadow on the ice. I sent a hand aft for the rifles, and M'Leod and I went down on to the pack, thinking that maybe it might be a bear. When we got on the ice I lost sight of M'Leod, but I pushed on in the direction where I could still hear the cries. I followed them for a mile or maybe more, and then running round a hummock I came right on to the top of it standing and waiting for me seemingly. I don't know what it was. It wasn't a bear anyway. It was tall and white and straight, and if it wasn't a man nor a woman, I'll stake my davy it was something worse. I made for the ship as hard as I could run, and precious glad I was to find myself aboard. I signed articles to do my duty by the ship, and on the ship I'll stay, but you don't catch me on the ice again after sundown."

That is his story, given as far as I can in his own words. I fancy what he saw must, in spite of his denial, have been a young bear erect upon its hind legs, an attitude which they often assume when alarmed. In the uncertain light this would bear a resemblance to a human figure, especially to a man whose nerves were already somewhat shaken. Whatever it may have been, the occurrence is unfortunate, for it has produced a most unpleasant effect upon the crew. Their looks are more sullen than before, and their discontent more open. The double grievance of being debarred from the herring fishing and of being detained in what they choose to call a haunted vessel, may lead them to do something rash. Even the harpooners, who are the oldest and steadiest among them, are joining in the general agitation.

Apart from this absurd outbreak of superstition, things are looking rather more cheerful. The pack which was forming to the south of us has partly cleared away, and the water is so warm as to lead me to believe that we are lying in one of those branches of the gulf-stream which run up between Greenland and Spitzbergen. There are numerous small Medusae and sealemons about the ship, with abundance of shrimps, so that there is every possibility of 'fish' being sighted. Indeed one was seen blowing about dinner-time, but in such a position that it was impossible for the boats to follow it.

September 13th.

Had an interesting conversation with the chief mate, Mr. Milne, upon the bridge. It seems that our Captain is as great an enigma to the seamen, and even to the owners of the vessel, as he has been to me. Mr. Milne tells me that when the ship is paid off, upon returning from a voyage, Captain Craigie disappears, and is not seen again until the approach of another season, when he walks quietly into the office of the company, and asks whether his services will be required. He has no friend in Dundee, nor does anyone pretend to be acquainted with his early history. His position depends entirely upon his skill as a seaman, and the name for courage and coolness which he had earned in the capacity of mate, before being entrusted with a separate command. The unanimous opinion seems to be that he is not a Scotchman, and that his name is an assumed one. Mr. Milne thinks that he has devoted himself to whaling simply for the reason that it is the most dangerous occupation which he could select, and that he courts death in every possible manner. He mentioned several instances of this, one of which is rather curious, if true. It seems that on one occasion he did not put in an appearance at the office, and a substitute had to be selected in his place. That was at the time of the last Russian and Turkish war. When he turned up again next spring he had a puckered wound in the side of his neck which he used to endeavour to conceal with his cravat. Whether the mate's inference that he had been engaged in the war is true or not I cannot say. It was certainly a strange coincidence.

The wind is veering round in an easterly direction, but is still very slight. I think the ice is lying closer than it did yesterday. As far as the eye can reach on every side there is one wide expanse of spotless white, only broken by an occasional rift or the dark shadow of a hummock. To the south there is the narrow lane of blue water which is our sole means of escape, and which is closing up every day. The Captain is taking a heavy responsibility upon himself. I hear that the tank of potatoes has been finished, and even the biscuits are running short, but he preserves the same impassible countenance, and spends the greater part of the day at the crow's nest, sweeping the horizon with his glass. His manner is very variable, and he seems to avoid my society, but there has been no repetition of the violence which he showed the other night.

7:30 p.m.
My deliberate opinion is that we are commanded by a madman. Nothing else can account for the extraordinary vagaries of Captain Craigie. It is fortunate that I have kept this journal of our voyage, as it will serve to justify us in case we have to put him under any sort of restraint, a step which I should only consent to as a last resource. Curiously enough it was he himself who suggested lunacy and not mere eccentricity as the secret of his strange conduct. He was standing upon the bridge about an hour ago, peering as usual through his glass, while I was walking up and down the quarterdeck. The majority of the men were below at their tea, for the watches have not been regularly kept of late. Tired of walking, I leaned against the bulwarks, and admired the mellow glow cast by the sinking sun upon the great ice fields which surround us. I was suddenly aroused from the reverie into which I had fallen by a hoarse voice at my elbow, and starting round I found that the Captain had descended and was standing by my side. He was staring out over the ice with an expression in which horror, surprise, and something approaching to joy were contending for the mastery. In spite of the cold, great drops of perspiration were coursing down his forehead, and he was evidently fearfully excited.

His limbs twitched like those of a man upon the verge of an epileptic fit, and the lines about his mouth were drawn and hard.

"Look!" he gasped, seizing me by the wrist, but still keeping his eyes upon the distant ice, and moving his head slowly in a horizontal direction, as if following some object which was moving across the field of vision. "Look! There, man, there! Between the hummocks! Now coming out from behind the far one! You see her – you *must* see her! There still! Flying from me, by God, flying from me – and gone!"

He uttered the last two words in a whisper of concentrated agony which shall never fade from my remembrance. Clinging to the ratlines he endeavoured to climb up upon the top of the bulwarks as if in the hope of obtaining a last glance at the departing object. His strength was not equal to the attempt, however, and he staggered back against the saloon skylights, where he leaned panting and exhausted. His face was so livid that I expected him to become unconscious, so lost no time in leading him down the companion, and stretching him upon one of the sofas in the cabin. I then poured him out some brandy, which I held to his lips, and which had a wonderful effect upon him, bringing the blood back into his white face and steadying his poor shaking limbs. He raised himself up upon his elbow, and looking round to see that we were alone, he beckoned to me to come and sit beside him.

"You saw it, didn't you?" he asked, still in the same subdued awesome tone so foreign to the nature of the man.

"No, I saw nothing."

His head sank back again upon the cushions. "No, he wouldn't without the glass," he murmured. "He couldn't. It was the glass that showed her to me, and then the eyes of love – the eyes of love. I say, Doc, don't let the steward in! He'll think I'm mad. Just bolt the door, will you!"

I rose and did what he had commanded.

He lay quiet for a while, lost in thought apparently, and then raised himself up upon his elbow again, and asked for some more brandy.

"You don't think I am, do you, Doc?" he asked, as I was putting the bottle back into the after-locker. "Tell me now, as man to man, do you think that I am mad?"

"I think you have something on your mind," I answered, "which is exciting you and doing you a good deal of harm."

"Right there, lad!" he cried, his eyes sparkling from the effects of the brandy. "Plenty on my mind – plenty! But I can work out the latitude and the longitude, and I can handle my sextant and manage my logarithms. You couldn't prove me mad in a court of law, could you, now?" It was curious to hear the man lying back and coolly arguing out the question of his own sanity.

"Perhaps not," I said; "but still I think you would be wise to get home as soon as you can, and settle down to a quiet life for a while."

"Get home, eh?" he muttered, with a sneer upon his face. "One word for me and two for yourself, lad. Settle down with Flora – pretty little Flora. Are bad dreams signs of madness?"

"Sometimes," I answered.

"What else? What would be the first symptoms?"

"Pains in the head, noises in the ears flashes before the eyes, delusions—"

"Ah! what about them?" he interrupted. "What would you call a delusion?"

"Seeing a thing which is not there is a delusion."

"But she *was* there!" he groaned to himself. "She *was* there!" and rising, he unbolted the door and walked with slow and uncertain steps to his own cabin, where I have no doubt that he will remain until tomorrow morning. His system seems to have received a terrible shock, whatever it may have been that he imagined himself to have seen. The man becomes a greater mystery every day, though I fear that the solution which he has himself suggested is the correct one, and that his reason is affected. I do not think that a guilty conscience has anything to do with his behaviour. The idea is a popular one among the officers, and, I believe, the crew; but I have seen nothing to support it. He has not the air of a guilty man, but of one who has had terrible usage at the hands of fortune, and who should be regarded as a martyr rather than a criminal.

The wind is veering round to the south tonight. God help us if it blocks that narrow pass which is our only road to safety! Situated as we are on the edge of the main Arctic pack, or the 'barrier' as it is called by the whalers, any wind from the north has the effect of shredding out the ice around us and allowing our escape, while a wind from the south blows up all the loose ice behind us and hems us in between two packs. God help us, I say again!

September 14th.

Sunday, and a day of rest. My fears have been confirmed, and the thin strip of blue water has disappeared from the southward. Nothing but the great motionless ice fields around us, with their weird hummocks and fantastic pinnacles. There is a deathly silence over their wide expanse which is horrible. No lapping of the waves now, no cries of seagulls or straining of sails, but one deep universal silence in which the murmurs of the seamen, and the creak of their boots upon the white shining deck, seem discordant and out of place. Our only visitor was an Arctic fox, a rare animal upon the pack, though common enough upon the land. He did not come near the ship, however, but after surveying us from a distance fled rapidly across the ice. This was curious conduct, as they generally know nothing of man, and being of an inquisitive nature, become so familiar that they are easily captured. Incredible as it may seem, even this little incident produced a bad effect upon the crew. "Yon puir beastie kens mair, ay, an' sees mair nor you nor me!" was the comment of one of the leading harpooners, and the others nodded their acquiescence. It is vain to attempt to argue against such puerile superstition. They have made up their minds that there is a curse upon the ship, and nothing will ever persuade them to the contrary.

The Captain remained in seclusion all day except for about half an hour in the afternoon, when he came out upon the quarterdeck. I observed that he kept his eye fixed upon the spot where the vision of yesterday had appeared, and was quite prepared for another outburst, but none such came. He did not seem to see me although I was standing close beside him. Divine service was read as usual by the chief engineer. It is a curious thing that in whaling vessels the Church of England Prayer-book is always employed, although there is never a member of that Church among either officers or crew. Our men are all Roman Catholics or Presbyterians, the former predominating. Since a ritual is used which is foreign to both, neither can complain that the other is preferred to them, and they listen with all attention and devotion, so that the system has something to recommend it.

A glorious sunset, which made the great fields of ice look like a lake of blood. I have never seen a finer and at the same time more weird effect. Wind is veering round. If it will blow twenty-four hours from the north all will yet be well.

September 15th.

Today is Flora's birthday. Dear lass! It is well that she cannot see her boy, as she used to call me, shut up among the ice fields with a crazy captain and a few weeks' provisions. No doubt she scans the shipping list in the Scotsman every morning to see if we are reported from Shetland. I have to set an example to the men and look cheery and unconcerned; but God knows, my heart is very heavy at times.

The thermometer is at nineteen Fahrenheit today. There is but little wind, and what there is comes from an unfavourable quarter. Captain is in an excellent humour; I think he imagines he has seen some other omen or vision, poor fellow, during the night, for he came into my room early in the morning, and stooping down over my bunk, whispered, "It wasn't a delusion, Doc; it's all right!" After breakfast he asked me to find out how much food was left, which the second mate and I proceeded to do. It is even less than we had expected. Forward they have half a tank full of biscuits, three barrels of salt meat, and a very limited supply of coffee beans and sugar. In the after-hold and lockers there are a good many luxuries, such as tinned salmon, soups, haricot mutton, &c., but they will go a very short way among a crew of fifty men. There are two barrels of flour in the store-room, and an unlimited supply of tobacco. Altogether there is about enough to keep the men on half rations for eighteen or twenty days – certainly not more. When we reported the state of things to the Captain, he ordered all hands to be piped, and addressed them from the quarterdeck. I never saw him to better advantage. With his tall, well-knit figure, and dark animated face, he seemed a man born to command, and he discussed the situation in a cool sailor-like way which showed that while appreciating the danger he had an eye for every loophole of escape.

"My lads," he said, "no doubt you think I brought you into this fix, if it is a fix, and maybe some of you feel bitter against me on account of it. But you must remember that for many a season no ship that comes to the country has brought in as much oil-money as the old Polestar, and every one of you has had his share of it. You can leave your wives behind you in comfort while other poor fellows come back to find their lasses on the parish. If you have to thank me for the one you have to thank me for the other, and we may call it quits. We've tried a bold venture before this and succeeded, so now that we've tried one and failed we've no cause to cry out about it. If the worst comes to the worst, we can make the land across the ice, and lay in a stock of seals which will keep us alive until the spring. It won't come to that, though, for you'll see the Scotch coast again before three weeks are out. At present every man must go on half rations, share and share alike, and no favour to any. Keep up your hearts and you'll pull through this as you've pulled through many a danger before." These few simple words of his had a wonderful effect upon the crew. His former unpopularity was forgotten, and the old harpooner whom I have already mentioned for his superstition, led off three cheers, which were heartily joined in by all hands.

September 16th.

The wind has veered round to the north during the night, and the ice shows some symptoms of opening out. The men are in a good humour in spite of the short allowance upon which they have been placed. Steam is kept up in the engine-room, that there may be no delay should an opportunity for escape present itself. The Captain is in exuberant spirits, though he still retains that wild 'fey' expression which I have already remarked upon. This burst of cheerfulness puzzles me more than his former gloom. I cannot understand it. I think I mentioned in an early part of this journal that one of his oddities is that he never permits any person to enter his cabin, but insists upon making his own bed, such as it is, and performing every other office for himself. To my surprise he handed me the key today and requested me to go down there and take the time by his chronometer while he measured the altitude of the sun at noon. It is a bare little room, containing a washing-stand and a few books, but little else in the way of luxury, except some pictures upon the walls. The majority of these are small cheap oleographs, but there was one watercolour sketch of the head of a young lady which arrested my attention. It was evidently a portrait, and not one of those fancy types of female beauty which sailors particularly affect. No artist could have evolved from his own mind such a curious mixture of character and weakness. The languid, dreamy eyes, with their drooping lashes, and the broad, low brow, unruffled by thought or care, were in strong contrast with the clean-cut, prominent jaw, and the resolute set of the lower lip. Underneath it in one of the corners was written, 'M.B., aet. 19'. That anyone in the short space of nineteen years of existence could develop such strength of will as was stamped upon her face seemed to me at the time to be well-nigh incredible. She must have been an extraordinary woman. Her features have thrown such a glamour over me that, though I had but a fleeting glance at them, I could, were I a draughtsman, reproduce them line for line upon this page of the journal. I wonder what part she has played in our Captain's life. He has hung her picture at the end of his berth, so that his eyes continually rest upon it. Were he a less reserved man I should make some remark upon the subject. Of the other things in his cabin there was nothing worthy of mention – uniform coats, a camp-stool, small looking-glass, tobacco-box, and numerous pipes, including an oriental hookah – which, by-the-bye, gives some colour to Mr. Milne's story about his participation in the war, though the connection may seem rather a distant one.

11:20 p.m.

Captain just gone to bed after a long and interesting conversation on general topics. When he chooses he can be a most fascinating companion, being remarkably well-read, and having the power of expressing his opinion forcibly without appearing to be dogmatic. I hate to have my intellectual toes trod upon. He spoke about the nature of the soul, and sketched out the views of Aristotle and Plato upon the subject in a masterly manner. He seems to have a leaning for metempsychosis and the doctrines of Pythagoras. In discussing them we touched upon modern spiritualism, and I made some joking allusion to the impostures of Slade, upon which, to my surprise, he warned me most impressively against confusing the innocent with the guilty, and argued that it would be as logical to brand Christianity as an error because Judas, who professed that religion, was a villain. He shortly afterwards bade me goodnight and retired to his room.

The wind is freshening up, and blows steadily from the north. The nights are as dark now as they are in England. I hope tomorrow may set us free from our frozen fetters.

September 17th.

The Bogie again. Thank Heaven that I have strong nerves! The superstition of these poor fellows, and the circumstantial accounts which they give, with the utmost earnestness and self-conviction, would horrify any man not accustomed to their ways. There are many versions of the matter, but the sum-total of them all is that something uncanny has been flitting round the ship all night, and that Sandie M'Donald of Peterhead and 'lang' Peter Williamson of Shetland saw it, as also did Mr. Milne on the bridge – so, having three witnesses, they can make a better case of it than the second mate did. I spoke to Milne after breakfast, and told him that he should be above such nonsense, and that as an officer he ought to set the men a better example. He shook his weather-beaten head ominously, but answered with characteristic caution, "Mebbe aye, mebbe na, Doctor," he said; "I didna ca' it a ghaist. I canna' say I preen my faith in sea-bogles an' the like, though there's a mony as claims to ha' seen a' that and waur. I'm no easy feared, but maybe your ain bluid would run a bit cauld, mun, if instead o' speerin' aboot it in daylicht ye were wi' me last night, an' seed an awfu' like shape, white an' gruesome, whiles here, whiles there, an' it greetin' and ca'ing in the darkness like a bit lambie that hae lost its mither. Ye would na' be sae ready to put it a' doon to auld wives' clavers then, I'm thinkin'." I saw it was hopeless to reason with him, so contented myself with begging him as a personal favour to call me up the next time the spectre appeared – a request to which he acceded with many ejaculations expressive of his hopes that such an opportunity might never arise.

As I had hoped, the white desert behind us has become broken by many thin streaks of water which intersect it in all directions. Our latitude today was 80 degrees 52' N., which shows that there is a strong southerly drift upon the pack. Should the wind continue favourable it will break up as rapidly as it formed. At present we can do nothing but smoke and wait and hope for the best. I am rapidly becoming a fatalist. When dealing with such uncertain factors as wind and ice a man can be nothing else. Perhaps it was the wind and sand of the Arabian deserts which gave the minds of the original followers of Mahomet their tendency to bow to kismet.

These spectral alarms have a very bad effect upon the Captain. I feared that it might excite his sensitive mind, and endeavoured to conceal the absurd story from him, but unfortunately he overheard one of the men making an allusion to it, and insisted upon being informed about it. As I had expected, it brought out all his latent lunacy in an exaggerated form. I can hardly believe that this is the same man who discoursed philosophy last night with the most critical acumen and coolest judgment. He is pacing backwards and forwards upon the quarterdeck like a caged tiger, stopping now and again to throw out his hands with a yearning gesture, and stare impatiently out over the ice. He keeps up a continual mutter to himself, and once he called out, "But a little time, love – but a little time!" Poor fellow, it is sad to see a gallant seaman and accomplished gentleman reduced to such a pass, and to think that imagination and delusion can cow a mind to which real danger was but the salt of life. Was ever a man in such a position as I, between a demented captain and a ghost-seeing mate? I sometimes think I am the only really sane man aboard the vessel – except perhaps the second engineer, who is a kind of ruminant, and would care nothing for all the fiends in the Red Sea so long as they would leave him alone and not disarrange his tools.

The ice is still opening rapidly, and there is every probability of our being able to make a start tomorrow morning. They will think I am inventing when I tell them at home all the strange things that have befallen me.

12 p.m.

I have been a good deal startled, though I feel steadier now, thanks to a stiff glass of brandy. I am hardly myself yet, however, as this handwriting will testify. The fact is, that I have gone through a very strange experience, and am beginning to doubt whether I was justified in branding everyone on board as madmen because they professed to have seen things which did not seem reasonable to my understanding. Pshaw! I am a fool to let such a trifle unnerve me; and yet, coming as it does after all these alarms, it has an additional significance, for I cannot doubt either Mr. Manson's story or that of the mate, now that I have experienced that which I used formerly to scoff at.

After all it was nothing very alarming – a mere sound, and that was all. I cannot expect that anyone reading this, if anyone ever should read it, will sympathise with my feelings, or realise the effect which it produced upon me at the time. Supper was over, and I had gone on deck to have a quiet pipe before turning in. The night was very dark – so dark that, standing under the quarter-boat, I was unable to see the officer upon the bridge. I think I have already mentioned the extraordinary silence which prevails in these frozen seas. In other parts of the world, be they ever so barren, there is some slight vibration of the air – some faint hum, be it from the distant haunts of men, or from the leaves of the trees, or the wings of the birds, or even the faint rustle of the grass that covers the ground. One may not actively perceive the sound, and yet if it were withdrawn it would be missed. It is only here in these Arctic seas that stark, unfathomable stillness obtrudes itself upon you in all its gruesome reality. You find your tympanum straining to catch some little murmur, and dwelling eagerly upon every accidental sound within the vessel. In this state I was leaning against the bulwarks when there arose from the ice almost directly underneath me a cry, sharp and shrill, upon the silent air of the night, beginning, as it seemed to me, at a note such as prima donna never reached, and mounting from that ever higher and higher until it culminated in a long wail of agony, which might have been the last cry of a lost soul. The ghastly scream is still ringing in my ears. Grief, unutterable grief, seemed to be expressed in it, and a great longing, and yet through it all there was an occasional wild note of exultation. It shrilled out from close beside me, and yet as I glared into the darkness I could discern nothing. I waited some little time, but without hearing any repetition of the sound, so I came below, more shaken than I have ever been in my life before. As I came down the companion I met Mr. Milne coming up to relieve the watch. "Weel, Doctor," he said, "maybe that's auld wives' clavers tae? Did ye no hear it skirling? Maybe that's a supersteetion? What d'ye think o't noo?" I was obliged to apologise to the honest fellow, and acknowledge that I was as puzzled by it as he was. Perhaps tomorrow things may look different. At present I dare hardly write all that I think. Reading it again in days to come, when I have shaken off all these associations, I should despise myself for having been so weak.

September 18th.

Passed a restless and uneasy night, still haunted by that strange sound. The Captain does not look as if he had had much repose either, for his face is haggard and his eyes bloodshot. I have not told him of my adventure of last night, nor shall I. He is already restless and excited, standing up, sitting down, and apparently utterly unable to keep still.

A fine lead appeared in the pack this morning, as I had expected, and we were able to cast off our ice-anchor, and steam about twelve miles in a west-sou'-westerly direction. We were then brought to a halt by a great floe as massive as any which we have left behind us. It bars our progress completely, so we can do nothing but anchor again and wait until it breaks up, which it will probably do within twenty-four hours, if the wind holds. Several bladder-nosed seals were seen swimming in the water, and one was shot, an immense creature more than eleven feet long. They are fierce, pugnacious animals, and are said to be more than a match for a bear. Fortunately they are slow and clumsy in their movements, so that there is little danger in attacking them upon the ice.

The Captain evidently does not think we have seen the last of our troubles, though why he should take a gloomy view of the situation is more than I can fathom, since everyone else on board considers that we have had a miraculous escape, and are sure now to reach the open sea.

"I suppose you think it's all right now, Doctor?" he said, as we sat together after dinner.

"I hope so," I answered.

"We mustn't be too sure – and yet no doubt you are right. We'll all be in the arms of our own true loves before long, lad, won't we? But we mustn't be too sure – we mustn't be too sure."

He sat silent a little, swinging his leg thoughtfully backwards and forwards. "Look here," he continued; "it's a dangerous place this, even at its best – a treacherous, dangerous place. I have known men cut off very suddenly in a land like this. A slip would do it sometimes – a single slip, and down you go through a crack, and only a bubble on the green water to show where it was that you sank. It's a queer thing," he continued with a nervous laugh, "but all the years I've been in this country I never once thought of making a will – not that I have anything to leave in particular, but still when a man is exposed to danger he should have everything arranged and ready – don't you think so?"

"Certainly," I answered, wondering what on earth he was driving at.

"He feels better for knowing it's all settled," he went on. "Now if anything should ever befall me, I hope that you will look after things for me. There is very little in the cabin, but such as it is I should like it to be sold, and the money divided in the same proportion as the oil-money among the crew. The chronometer I wish you to keep yourself as some slight remembrance of our voyage. Of course all this is a mere precaution, but I thought I would take the opportunity of speaking to you about it. I suppose I might rely upon you if there were any necessity?"

"Most assuredly," I answered; "and since you are taking this step, I may as well—"

"You! You!" he interrupted. "*You're* all right. What the devil is the matter with *you*? There, I didn't mean to be peppery, but I don't like to hear a young fellow, that has hardly began life, speculating about death. Go up on deck and get some fresh air into your lungs instead of talking nonsense in the cabin, and encouraging me to do the same."

The more I think of this conversation of ours the less do I like it. Why should the man be settling his affairs at the very time when we seem to be emerging from all danger? There must be some method in his madness. Can it be that he contemplates suicide? I remember that upon one occasion he spoke in a deeply reverent manner of the heinousness of the crime of self-destruction. I shall keep my eye upon him, however, and though I cannot obtrude upon the privacy of his cabin, I shall at least make a point of remaining on deck as long as he stays up.

Mr. Milne pooh-poohs my fears, and says it is only the "skipper's little way". He himself takes a very rosy view of the situation. According to him we shall be out of the ice by the day after tomorrow, pass Jan Meyen two days after that, and sight Shetland in little more than a week. I hope he may not be too sanguine. His opinion may be fairly balanced against the gloomy precautions of the Captain, for he is an old and experienced seaman, and weighs his words well before uttering them.

* * *

The long-impending catastrophe has come at last. I hardly know what to write about it. The Captain is gone. He may come back to us again alive, but I fear me – I fear me. It is now seven o'clock of the morning of the 19th of September. I have spent the whole night traversing the great ice-floe in front of us with a party of seamen in the hope of coming upon some trace of him, but in vain. I shall try to give some account of the circumstances which attended upon his disappearance. Should anyone ever chance to read the words which I put down, I trust they will remember that I do not write from conjecture or from hearsay, but that I, a sane and educated man, am describing accurately what actually occurred before my very eyes. My inferences are my own, but I shall be answerable for the facts.

The Captain remained in excellent spirits after the conversation which I have recorded. He appeared to be nervous and impatient, however, frequently changing his position, and moving his limbs in an aimless choreic way which is characteristic of him at times. In a quarter of an hour he went upon deck seven times, only to descend after a few hurried paces. I followed him each time, for there was something about his face which confirmed my resolution of not letting him out of my sight. He seemed to observe the effect which his movements had produced, for he endeavoured by an over-done hilarity, laughing boisterously at the very smallest of jokes, to quiet my apprehensions.

After supper he went on to the poop once more, and I with him. The night was dark and very still, save for the melancholy soughing of the wind among the spars. A thick cloud was coming up from the north-west, and the ragged tentacles which it threw out in front of it were drifting across the face of the moon, which only shone now and again through a rift in the wrack. The Captain paced rapidly backwards and forwards, and then seeing me still dogging him, he came across and hinted that he thought I should be better below – which, I need hardly say, had the effect of strengthening my resolution to remain on deck.

I think he forgot about my presence after this, for he stood silently leaning over the taffrail, and peering out across the great desert of snow, part of which lay in shadow, while part glittered mistily in the moonlight. Several times I could see by his movements that he was referring to his watch, and once he muttered a short sentence, of which I could only catch the one word "ready". I confess to having felt an eerie feeling creeping over me as I watched the loom of his tall figure through the darkness, and noted how completely he fulfilled the idea of a man who is keeping a tryst. A tryst with whom? Some vague perception began to dawn upon me as I pieced one fact with another, but I was utterly unprepared for the sequel.

By the sudden intensity of his attitude I felt that he saw something. I crept up behind him. He was staring with an eager questioning gaze at what seemed to be a wreath of mist, blown swiftly in a line with the ship. It was a dim, nebulous body, devoid of shape, sometimes more, sometimes less apparent, as the light fell on it. The moon was dimmed in its brilliancy at the moment by a canopy of thinnest cloud, like the coating of an anemone.

"Coming, lass, coming," cried the skipper, in a voice of unfathomable tenderness and compassion, like one who soothes a beloved one by some favour long looked for, and as pleasant to bestow as to receive.

What followed happened in an instant. I had no power to interfere.

He gave one spring to the top of the bulwarks, and another which took him on to the ice, almost to the feet of the pale misty figure. He held out his hands as if to clasp it, and so ran into the darkness with outstretched arms and loving words. I still stood rigid and motionless, straining my eyes after his retreating form, until his voice died away in the distance. I never thought to see him again, but at that moment the moon shone out brilliantly through a chink in the cloudy heaven, and illuminated the great field of ice. Then I saw his dark figure already a very long way off, running with prodigious speed across the frozen plain. That was the last glimpse which we caught of him – perhaps the last we ever shall. A party was organised to follow him, and I accompanied them, but the men's hearts were not in the work, and nothing was found. Another will be formed within a few hours. I can hardly believe I have not been dreaming, or suffering from some hideous nightmare, as I write these things down.

7:30 p.m.

Just returned dead-beat and utterly tired out from a second unsuccessful search for the Captain. The floe is of enormous extent, for though we have traversed at least twenty miles of its surface, there has been no sign of its coming to an end. The frost has been so severe of late that the overlying snow is frozen as hard as granite, otherwise we might have had the footsteps to guide us. The crew are anxious that we should cast off and steam round the floe and so to the southward, for the ice has opened up during the night, and the sea is visible upon the horizon. They argue that Captain Craigie is certainly dead, and that we are all risking our lives to no purpose by remaining when we have an opportunity of escape. Mr. Milne and I have had the greatest difficulty in persuading them to wait until tomorrow night, and have been compelled to promise that we will not under any circumstances delay our departure longer than that. We propose therefore to take a few hours' sleep, and then to start upon a final search.

September 20th, evening.
I crossed the ice this morning with a party of men exploring the southern part of the floe, while Mr. Milne went off in a northerly direction. We pushed on for ten or twelve miles without seeing a trace of any living thing except a single bird, which fluttered a great way over our heads, and which by its flight I should judge to have been a falcon. The southern extremity of the ice field tapered away into a long narrow spit which projected out into the sea. When we came to the base of this promontory, the men halted, but I begged them to continue to the extreme end of it, that we might have the satisfaction of knowing that no possible chance had been neglected.

We had hardly gone a hundred yards before M'Donald of Peterhead cried out that he saw something in front of us, and began to run. We all got a glimpse of it and ran too. At first it was only a vague darkness against the white ice, but as we raced along together it took the shape of a man, and eventually of the man of whom we were in search. He was lying face downwards upon a frozen bank. Many little crystals of ice and feathers of snow had drifted on to him as he lay, and sparkled upon his dark seaman's jacket. As we came up some wandering puff of wind caught these tiny flakes in its vortex, and they whirled up into the air, partially descended again, and then, caught once more in the current, sped rapidly away in the direction of the sea. To my eyes it seemed but a snow-drift, but many of my companions averred that it started up in the shape of a woman, stooped over the corpse and kissed it, and then hurried away across the floe. I have learned never to ridicule any man's opinion, however strange it may seem. Sure it is that Captain Nicholas Craigie had met with no painful end, for there was a bright smile upon his blue pinched features, and his hands were still outstretched as though grasping at the strange visitor which had summoned him away into the dim world that lies beyond the grave.

We buried him the same afternoon with the ship's ensign around him, and a thirty-two pound shot at his feet. I read the burial service, while the rough sailors wept like children, for there were many who owed much to his kind heart, and who showed now the affection which his strange ways had repelled during his lifetime. He went off the grating with a dull, sullen splash, and as I looked into the green water I saw him go down, down, down until he was but a little flickering patch of white hanging upon the outskirts of eternal darkness. Then even that faded away, and he was gone. There he shall lie, with his secret and his sorrows and his mystery all still buried in his breast, until that great day when the sea shall give up its dead, and Nicholas Craigie come out from among the ice with the smile upon his face, and his stiffened arms outstretched in greeting. I pray that his lot may be a happier one in that life than it has been in this.

I shall not continue my journal. Our road to home lies plain and clear before us, and the great ice field will soon be but a remembrance of the past. It will be some time before I get over the shock produced by recent events. When I began this record of our voyage I little thought of how I should be compelled to finish it. I am writing these final words in the lonely cabin, still starting at times and fancying I hear the quick nervous step of the dead man upon the deck above me. I entered his cabin tonight, as was my duty, to make a list of his effects in order that they might be entered in the official log. All was as it had been upon my previous visit, save that the picture which I have described as having hung at the end of his bed had been cut out of its frame, as with a knife, and was gone. With this last link in a strange chain of evidence I close my diary of the voyage of the Polestar.

[NOTE by Dr. John M'Alister Ray, senior. – I have read over the strange events connected with the death of the Captain of the Polestar, as narrated in the journal of my son. That everything occurred exactly as he describes it I have the fullest confidence, and, indeed, the most positive certainty, for I know him to be a strong-nerved and unimaginative man, with the strictest regard for veracity. Still, the story is, on the face of it, so vague and so improbable, that I was long opposed to its publication. Within the last few days, however, I have had independent testimony upon the subject which throws a new light upon it. I had run down to Edinburgh to attend a meeting of the British Medical Association, when I chanced to come across Dr. P—, an old college chum of mine, now practising at Saltash, in Devonshire. Upon my telling him of this experience of my son's, he declared to me that he was familiar with the man, and proceeded, to my no small surprise, to give me a description of him, which tallied remarkably well with that given in the journal, except that he depicted him as a younger man. According to his account, he had been engaged to a young lady of singular beauty residing upon the Cornish coast. During his absence at sea his betrothed had died under circumstances of peculiar horror.]

Footnotes for *The Captain of the Polestar*

1. A whale is measured among whalers not by the length of its body, but by the length of its whalebone.

The Phantom Coach

Amelia B. Edwards

THE CIRCUMSTANCES I am about to relate to you have truth to recommend them. They happened to myself, and my recollection of them is as vivid as if they had taken place only yesterday. Twenty years, however, have gone by since that night. During those twenty years I have told the story to but one other person. I tell it now with a reluctance which I find it difficult to overcome. All I entreat, meanwhile, is that you will abstain from forcing your own conclusions upon me. I want nothing explained away. I desire no arguments. My mind on this subject is quite made up, and, having the testimony of my own senses to rely upon, I prefer to abide by it.

Well! It was just twenty years ago, and within a day or two of the end of the grouse season. I had been out all day with my gun, and had had no sport to speak of. The wind was due east; the month, December; the place, a bleak wide moor in the far north of England. And I had lost my way. It was not a pleasant place in which to lose one's way, with the first feathery flakes of a coming snowstorm just fluttering down upon the heather, and the leaden evening closing in all around. I shaded my eyes with my hand, and stared anxiously into the gathering darkness, where the purple moorland melted into a range of low hills, some ten or twelve miles distant. Not the faintest smoke-wreath, not the tiniest cultivated patch, or fence, or sheep-track, met my eyes in any direction. There was nothing for it but to walk on, and take my chance of finding what shelter I could, by the way. So I shouldered my gun again, and pushed wearily forward; for I had been on foot since an hour after daybreak, and had eaten nothing since breakfast.

Meanwhile, the snow began to come down with ominous steadiness, and the wind fell. After this, the cold became more intense, and the night came rapidly up. As for me, my prospects darkened with the darkening sky, and my heart grew heavy as I thought how my young wife was already watching for me through the window of our little inn parlour, and thought of all the suffering in store for her throughout this weary night. We had been married four months, and, having spent our autumn in the Highlands, were now lodging in a remote little village situated just on the verge of the great English moorlands. We were very much in love, and, of course, very happy. This morning, when we parted, she had implored me to return before dusk, and I had promised her that I would. What would I not have given to have kept my word!

Even now, weary as I was, I felt that with a supper, an hour's rest, and a guide, I might still get back to her before midnight, if only guide and shelter could be found.

And all this time, the snow fell and the night thickened. I stopped and shouted every now and then, but my shouts seemed only to make the silence deeper. Then a vague sense of uneasiness came upon me, and I began to remember stories of travellers who had walked on and on in the falling snow until, wearied out, they were fain to lie down and sleep their lives away. Would it be possible, I asked myself, to keep on thus through all the long dark night? Would there not come a time when my limbs must fail, and my resolution give way? When I, too, must sleep the sleep of death. Death! I shuddered. How hard to die just now, when life lay all so bright before me! How hard for my darling, whose whole loving heart but that thought was not to be borne! To banish it, I shouted again, louder and longer, and then listened eagerly. Was my shout answered, or did I only fancy that I heard a far-off cry? I halloed again, and again the echo followed. Then a wavering speck of light came suddenly out of the dark, shifting, disappearing, growing momentarily nearer and brighter. Running towards it at full speed, I found myself, to my great joy, face to face with an old man and a lantern.

"Thank God!" was the exclamation that burst involuntarily from my lips. Blinking and frowning, he lifted his lantern and peered into my face. "What for?" growled he, sulkily.

"Well – for you. I began to fear I should be lost in the snow."

"Eh, then, folks do get cast away hereabouts fra' time to time, an' what's to hinder you from bein' cast away likewise, if the Lord's so minded?"

"If the Lord is so minded that you and I shall be lost together, friend, we must submit," I replied; "but I don't mean to be lost without you. How far am I now from Dwolding?"

"A gude twenty mile, more or less."

"And the nearest village?"

"The nearest village is Wyke, an' that's twelve mile t'other side."

"Where do you live, then?"

"Out yonder," said he, with a vague jerk of the lantern.

"You're going home, I presume?"

"Maybe I am."

"Then I'm going with you."

The old man shook his head, and rubbed his nose reflectively with the handle of the lantern.

"It ain't o' no use," growled he. "He 'ont let you in – not he."

"We'll see about that," I replied, briskly. "Who is He?"

"The master."

"Who is the master?"

"That's nowt to you," was the unceremonious reply.

"Well, well; you lead the way, and I'll engage that the master shall give me shelter and a supper tonight."

"Eh, you can try him!" muttered my reluctant guide; and, still shaking his head, he hobbled, gnome-like, away through the falling snow. A large mass loomed up presently out of the darkness, and a huge dog rushed out, barking furiously.

"Is this the house?" I asked.

"Ay, it's the house. Down, Bey!" And he fumbled in his pocket for the key.

I drew up close behind him, prepared to lose no chance of entrance, and saw in the little circle of light shed by the lantern that the door was heavily studded with iron nails, like the door of a prison. In another minute he had turned the key and I had pushed past him into the house.

Once inside, I looked round with curiosity, and found myself in a great raftered hall, which served, apparently, a variety of uses. One end was piled to the roof with corn, like a barn. The other was stored with flour-sacks, agricultural implements, casks, and all kinds of miscellaneous lumber; while from the beams overhead hung rows of hams, flitches, and bunches of dried herbs for winter use. In the centre of the floor stood some huge object gauntly dressed in a dingy wrapping-cloth, and reaching halfway to the rafters. Lifting a corner of this cloth, I saw, to my surprise, a telescope of very considerable size, mounted on a rude movable platform, with four small wheels. The tube was made of painted wood, bound round with bands of metal rudely fashioned; the speculum, so far as I could estimate its size in the dim light, measured at least fifteen inches in diameter. While I was yet examining the instrument, and asking myself whether it was not the work of some self-taught optician, a bell rang sharply.

"That's for you," said my guide, with a malicious grin. "Yonder's his room."

He pointed to a low black door at the opposite side of the hall. I crossed over, rapped somewhat loudly, and went in, without waiting for an invitation. A huge, white-haired old man rose from a table covered with books and papers, and confronted me sternly.

"Who are you?" said he. "How came you here? What do you want?"

"James Murray, barrister-at-law. On foot across the moor. Meat, drink, and sleep."

He bent his bushy brows into a portentous frown.

"Mine is not a house of entertainment," he said, haughtily. "Jacob, how dared you admit this stranger?"

"I didn't admit him," grumbled the old man. "He followed me over the muir, and shouldered his way in before me. I'm no match for six foot two."

"And pray, sir, by what right have you forced an entrance into my house?"

"The same by which I should have clung to your boat, if I were drowning. The right of self-preservation."

"Self-preservation?"

"There's an inch of snow on the ground already," I replied, briefly; "and it would be deep enough to cover my body before daybreak."

He strode to the window, pulled aside a heavy black curtain, and looked out.

"It is true," he said. "You can stay, if you choose, till morning. Jacob, serve the supper."

With this he waved me to a seat, resumed his own, and became at once absorbed in the studies from which I had disturbed him.

I placed my gun in a corner, drew a chair to the hearth, and examined my quarters at leisure. Smaller and less incongruous in its arrangements than the hall, this room contained, nevertheless, much to awaken my curiosity. The floor was carpetless. The whitewashed walls were in parts scrawled over with strange diagrams, and in others covered with shelves crowded with philosophical instruments, the uses of many of which were unknown to me. On one side of the fireplace stood a bookcase filled with dingy folios; on the other, a small organ, fantastically decorated with painted carvings of medieval saints and devils. Through the half-opened door of a cupboard at the further end of the room, I saw a long array of geological specimens, surgical preparations, crucibles, retorts, and jars of chemicals; while on the mantelshelf beside me, amid a number of small objects, stood a model of the solar system, a small galvanic battery, and a microscope. Every chair had its burden. Every corner was heaped high with books. The very floor was littered over with maps, casts, papers, tracings, and learned lumber of all conceivable kinds.

I stared about me with an amazement increased by every fresh object upon which my eyes chanced to rest. So strange a room I had never seen; yet seemed it stranger still, to find such a room in a lone farmhouse amid those wild and solitary moors! Over and over again, I looked from my host to his surroundings, and from his surroundings back to my host, asking myself who and what he could be? His head was singularly fine; but it was more the head of a poet than of a philosopher. Broad in the temples, prominent over the eyes, and clothed with a rough profusion of perfectly white hair, it had all the ideality and much of the ruggedness that characterises the head of Ludwig van Beethoven. There were the same deep lines about the mouth, and the same stern furrows in the brow. There was the same concentration of expression. While I was yet observing him, the door opened, and Jacob brought in the supper. His master then closed his book, rose, and with more courtesy of manner than he had yet shown, invited me to the table. A dish of ham and eggs, a loaf of brown bread, and a bottle of admirable sherry, were placed before me. "I have but the homeliest farmhouse fare to offer you, sir," said my entertainer. "Your appetite, I trust, will make up for the deficiencies of our larder." I had already fallen upon the viands, and now protested, with the enthusiasm of a starving sportsman, that I had never eaten anything so delicious.

He bowed stiffly, and sat down to his own supper, which consisted, primitively, of a jug of milk and a basin of porridge. We ate in silence, and, when we had done, Jacob removed the tray. I then drew my chair back to the fireside. My host, somewhat to my surprise, did the same, and turning abruptly towards me, said:

"Sir, I have lived here in strict retirement for three-and-twenty years. During that time, I have not seen as many strange faces, and I have not read a single newspaper. You are the first stranger who has crossed my threshold for more than four years. Will you favour me with a few words of information respecting that outer world from which I have parted company so long?"

"Pray interrogate me," I replied. "I am heartily at your service."

He bent his head in acknowledgment; leaned forward, with his elbows resting on his knees and his chin supported in the palms of his hands; stared fixedly into the fire; and proceeded to question me. His inquiries related chiefly to scientific matters, with the later progress of which, as applied to the practical purposes of life, he was almost wholly unacquainted. No student of science myself, I replied as well as my slight information permitted; but the task was far from easy, and I was much relieved when, passing from interrogation to discussion, he began pouring forth his own conclusions upon the facts which I had been attempting to place before him. He talked, and I listened spellbound. He talked till I believe he almost forgot my presence, and only thought aloud. I had never heard anything like it then; I have never heard anything like it since.

Familiar with all systems of all philosophies, subtle in analysis, bold in generalisation, he poured forth his thoughts in an uninterrupted stream, and, still leaning forward in the same moody attitude with his eyes fixed upon the fire, wandered from topic to topic, from speculation to speculation, like an inspired dreamer. From practical science to mental philosophy; from electricity in the wire to electricity in the nerve; from Watts to Mesmer, from Mesmer to Reichenbach, from Reichenbach to Swedenborg, Spinoza, Condillac, Descartes, Berkeley, Aristotle, Plato, and the Magi and mystics of the East, were transitions which, however bewildering in their variety and scope, seemed easy and harmonious upon his lips as sequences in music.

By-and-by – I forget now by what link of conjecture or illustration – he passed on to that field which lies beyond the boundary line of even conjectural philosophy, and reaches no man knows whither. He spoke of the soul and its aspirations; of the spirit and its powers; of second sight; of prophecy; of those phenomena which, under the names of ghosts, spectres, and supernatural appearances, have been denied by the sceptics and attested by the credulous, of all ages.

"The world," he said, "grows hourly more and more sceptical of all that lies beyond its own narrow radius; and our men of science foster the fatal tendency. They condemn as fable all that resists experiment. They reject as false all that cannot be brought to the test of the laboratory or the dissecting-room. Against what superstition have they waged so long and obstinate a war, as against the belief in apparitions? And yet what superstition has maintained its hold upon the minds of men so long and so firmly? Show me any fact in physics, in history, in archaeology, which is supported by testimony so wide and so various. Attested by all races of men, in all ages, and in all climates, by the soberest sages of antiquity, by the rudest savage of today, by the Christian, the Pagan, the Pantheist, the Materialist, this phenomenon is treated as a nursery tale by the philosophers of our century. Circumstantial evidence weighs with them as a feather in the balance. The comparison of causes with effects, however valuable in physical science, is put aside as worthless and unreliable. The evidence of competent witnesses, however conclusive in a court of justice, counts for nothing. He who pauses before he pronounces, is condemned as a trifler. He who believes, is a dreamer or a fool."

He spoke with bitterness, and, having said thus, relapsed for some minutes into silence. Presently he raised his head from his hands, and added, with an altered voice and manner, "I, sir, paused, investigated, believed, and was not ashamed to state my convictions to the world. I, too, was branded as a visionary, held up to ridicule by my contemporaries, and hooted from that field of science in which I had laboured with honour during all the best years of my life. These things happened just three-and-twenty years ago. Since then, I have lived as you see me living now, and the world has forgotten me, as I have forgotten the world. You have my history."

"It is a very sad one," I murmured, scarcely knowing what to answer.

"It is a very common one," he replied. "I have only suffered for the truth, as many a better and wiser man has suffered before me."

He rose, as if desirous of ending the conversation, and went over to the window. "It has ceased snowing," he observed, as he dropped the curtain, and came back to the fireside.

"Ceased!" I exclaimed, starting eagerly to my feet. "Oh, if it were only possible – but no! it is hopeless. Even if I could find my way across the moor, I could not walk twenty miles tonight."

"Walk twenty miles tonight!" repeated my host. "What are you thinking of?"

"Of my wife," I replied, impatiently. "Of my young wife, who does not know that I have lost my way, and who is at this moment breaking her heart with suspense and terror."

"Where is she?"

"At Dwolding, twenty miles away."

"At Dwolding," he echoed, thoughtfully. "Yes, the distance, it is true, is twenty miles; but – are you so very anxious to save the next six or eight hours?"

"So very, very anxious, that I would give ten guineas at this moment for a guide and a horse."

"Your wish can be gratified at a less costly rate," said he, smiling. "The night mail from the north, which changes horses at Dwolding, passes within five miles of this spot, and will be due at a certain crossroad in about an hour and a quarter. If Jacob were to go with you across the moor, and put you into the old coach-road, you could find your way, I suppose, to where it joins the new one?"

"Easily – gladly."

He smiled again, rang the bell, gave the old servant his directions, and, taking a bottle of whisky and a wineglass from the cupboard in which he kept his chemicals, said:

"The snow lies deep, and it will be difficult walking tonight on the moor. A glass of usquebaugh before you start?"

I would have declined the spirit, but he pressed it on me, and I drank it. It went down my throat like liquid flame, and almost took my breath away.

"It is strong," he said; "but it will help to keep out the cold. And now you have no moments to spare. Goodnight!"

I thanked him for his hospitality, and would have shaken hands, but that he had turned away before I could finish my sentence. In another minute I had traversed the hall, Jacob had locked the outer door behind me, and we were out on the wide white moor.

Although the wind had fallen, it was still bitterly cold. Not a star glimmered in the black vault overhead. Not a sound, save the rapid crunching of the snow beneath our feet, disturbed the heavy stillness of the night. Jacob, not too well pleased with his mission, shambled on before in sullen silence, his lantern in his hand, and his shadow at his feet. I followed, with my gun over my shoulder, as little inclined for conversation as himself. My thoughts were full of my late host. His voice yet rang in my ears. His eloquence yet held my imagination captive. I remember to this day, with surprise, how my over-excited brain retained whole sentences and parts of sentences, troops of brilliant images, and fragments of splendid reasoning, in the very words in which he had uttered them. Musing thus over what I had heard, and striving to recall a lost link here and there, I strode on at the heels of my guide, absorbed and unobservant. Presently – at the end, as it seemed to me, of only a few minutes – he came to a sudden halt, and said:

"Yon's your road. Keep the stone fence to your right hand, and you can't fail of the way."

"This, then, is the old coach-road?"

"Ay, 'tis the old coach-road."

"And how far do I go, before I reach the crossroads?"

"Nigh upon three mile."

I pulled out my purse, and he became more communicative.

"The road's a fair road enough," said he, "for foot passengers; but 'twas over steep and narrow for the northern traffic. You'll mind where the parapet's broken away, close again the sign-post. It's never been mended since the accident."

"What accident?"

"Eh, the night mail pitched right over into the valley below – a gude fifty feet an' more – just at the worst bit o' road in the whole county."

"Horrible! Were many lives lost?"

"All. Four were found dead, and t'other two died next morning."

"How long is it since this happened?"

"Just nine year."

"Near the sign-post, you say? I will bear it in mind. Goodnight."

"Gude night, sir, and thankee." Jacob pocketed his half-crown, made a faint pretence of touching his hat, and trudged back by the way he had come.

I watched the light of his lantern till it quite disappeared, and then turned to pursue my way alone. This was no longer matter of the slightest difficulty, for, despite the dead darkness overhead, the line of stone fence showed distinctly enough against the pale gleam of the snow. How silent it seemed now, with only my footsteps to listen to; how silent and how solitary! A strange disagreeable sense of loneliness stole over me. I walked faster. I hummed a fragment of a tune. I cast up enormous sums in my head, and accumulated them at compound interest. I did my best, in short, to forget the startling speculations to which I had but just been listening, and, to some extent, I succeeded.

Meanwhile the night air seemed to become colder and colder, and though I walked fast I found it impossible to keep myself warm. My feet were like ice. I lost sensation in my hands, and grasped my gun mechanically. I even breathed with difficulty, as though, instead of traversing a quiet north country highway, I were scaling the uppermost heights of some gigantic Alp. This last symptom became presently so distressing, that I was forced to stop for a few minutes, and lean against the stone fence. As I did so, I chanced to look back up the road, and there, to my infinite relief, I saw a distant point of light, like the gleam of an approaching lantern. I at first concluded that Jacob had retraced his steps and followed me; but even as the conjecture presented itself, a second light flashed into sight – a light evidently parallel with the first, and approaching at the same rate of motion. It needed no second thought to show me that these must be the carriage-lamps of some private vehicle, though it seemed strange that any private vehicle should take a road professedly disused and dangerous.

There could be no doubt, however, of the fact, for the lamps grew larger and brighter every moment, and I even fancied I could already see the dark outline of the carriage between them. It was coming up very fast, and quite noiselessly, the snow being nearly a foot deep under the wheels. And now the body of the vehicle became distinctly visible behind the lamps. It looked strangely lofty. A sudden suspicion flashed upon me. Was it possible that I had passed the crossroads in the dark without observing the sign-post, and could this be the very coach which I had come to meet?

No need to ask myself that question a second time, for here it came round the bend of the road, guard and driver, one outside passenger, and four steaming greys, all wrapped in a soft haze of light, through which the lamps blazed out, like a pair of fiery meteors.

I jumped forward, waved my hat, and shouted. The mail came down at full speed, and passed me. For a moment I feared that I had not been seen or heard, but it was only for a moment. The coachman pulled up; the guard, muffled to the eyes in capes and comforters, and apparently sound asleep in the rumble, neither answered my hail nor made the slightest effort to dismount; the outside passenger did not even turn his head. I opened the door for myself, and looked in. There were but three travellers inside, so I stepped in, shut the door, slipped into the vacant corner, and congratulated myself on my good fortune. The atmosphere of the coach seemed, if possible, colder than that of the outer air, and was pervaded by a singularly damp and disagreeable smell. I looked round at my fellow-passengers. They were all three, men, and all silent. They did not seem to be asleep, but each leaned back in his corner of the vehicle, as if absorbed in his own reflections. I attempted to open a conversation.

"How intensely cold it is tonight," I said, addressing my opposite neighbour.

He lifted his head, looked at me, but made no reply.

"The winter," I added, "seems to have begun in earnest."

Although the corner in which he sat was so dim that I could distinguish none of his features very clearly, I saw that his eyes were still turned full upon me. And yet he answered never a word.

At any other time I should have felt, and perhaps expressed, some annoyance, but at the moment I felt too ill to do either. The icy coldness of the night air had struck a chill to my very marrow, and the strange smell inside the coach was affecting me with an intolerable nausea. I shivered from head to foot, and, turning to my left-hand neighbour, asked if he had any objection to an open window? He neither spoke nor stirred.

I repeated the question somewhat more loudly, but with the same result. Then I lost patience, and let the sash down. As I did so, the leather strap broke in my hand, and I observed that the glass was covered with a thick coat of mildew, the accumulation, apparently, of years. My attention being thus drawn to the condition of the coach, I examined it more narrowly, and saw by the uncertain light of the outer lamps that it was in the last stage of dilapidation. Every part of it was not only out of repair, but in a condition of decay. The sashes splintered at a touch. The leather fittings were crusted over with mould, and literally rotting from the woodwork. The floor was almost breaking away beneath my feet. The whole machine, in short, was foul with damp, and had evidently been dragged from some outhouse in which it had been mouldering away for years, to do another day or two of duty on the road. I turned to the third passenger, whom I had not yet addressed, and hazarded one more remark.

"This coach," I said, "is in a deplorable condition. The regular mail, I suppose, is under repair?"

He moved his head slowly, and looked me in the face, without speaking a word. I shall never forget that look while I live. I turned cold at heart under it. I turn cold at heart even now when I recall it. His eyes glowed with a fiery unnatural lustre. His face was livid as the face of a corpse. His bloodless lips were drawn back as if in the agony of death, and showed the gleaming teeth between.

The words that I was about to utter died upon my lips, and a strange horror – a dreadful horror – came upon me. My sight had by this time become used to the gloom of the coach, and I could see with tolerable distinctness. I turned to my opposite neighbour. He, too, was looking at me, with the same startling pallor in his face, and the same stony glitter in his eyes. I passed my hand across my brow. I turned to the passenger on the seat beside my own, and saw – oh Heaven! how shall I describe what I saw? I saw that he was no living man – that none of them were living men, like myself! A pale phosphorescent light – the light of putrefaction – played upon their awful faces;

upon their hair, dank with the dews of the grave; upon their clothes, earth-stained and dropping to pieces; upon their hands, which were as the hands of corpses long buried. Only their eyes, their terrible eyes, were living; and those eyes were all turned menacingly upon me! A shriek of terror, a wild unintelligible cry for help and mercy; burst from my lips as I flung myself against the door, and strove in vain to open it.

In that single instant, brief and vivid as a landscape beheld in the flash of summer lightning, I saw the moon shining down through a rift of stormy cloud – the ghastly sign-post rearing its warning finger by the wayside – the broken parapet – the plunging horses – the black gulf below. Then, the coach reeled like a ship at sea. Then, came a mighty crash – a sense of crushing pain – and then, darkness.

It seemed as if years had gone by when I awoke one morning from a deep sleep, and found my wife watching by my bedside I will pass over the scene that ensued, and give you, in half a dozen words, the tale she told me with tears of thanksgiving. I had fallen over a precipice, close against the junction of the old coach-road and the new, and had only been saved from certain death by lighting upon a deep snowdrift that had accumulated at the foot of the rock beneath. In this snowdrift I was discovered at daybreak, by a couple of shepherds, who carried me to the nearest shelter, and brought a surgeon to my aid. The surgeon found me in a state of raving delirium, with a broken arm and a compound fracture of the skull. The letters in my pocket-book showed my name and address; my wife was summoned to nurse me; and, thanks to youth and a fine constitution, I came out of danger at last.

The place of my fall, I need scarcely say, was precisely that at which a frightful accident had happened to the north mail nine years before. I never told my wife the fearful events which I have just related to you. I told the surgeon who attended me; but he treated the whole adventure as a mere dream born of the fever in my brain. We discussed the question over and over again, until we found that we could discuss it with temper no longer, and then we dropped it. Others may form what conclusions they please – I know that twenty years ago I was the fourth inside passenger in that Phantom Coach.

Flannery House

Felix Flynn

"HONEST! It's all real!

"My cousin's friend lived next to the Steward place. Said Devin Steward's Mom went missing up at the old Flannery house. Annie Steward was her name. You woulda heard the grownups talking about it back when it happened if you were old enough. I was six then. Four years since it happened?

"I don't know. Anyway, Mrs. Steward up and walked out of her house in the middle of the night. Left the door wide open. Her son – Devin, my cousin's friend – said he was up getting a glass of water. He heard her footsteps on the stairs, light as a feather. He sometimes had nightmares and for a minute he thought he was still caught half in sleep when he heard something moving and breathing real hard in the dark.

"He heard one of the steps creak, the one he said his Dad replaced a few weeks before 'cause it'd rotted through from water or something.

"So, he peeks his head out of the kitchen and she is just a shadow, weaving and wobbling, lit up from behind because of the moonlight that came in from the upstairs hallway window. Kinda like it is now. Look at the window over by the door. How you can see the old elm in the front yard with its branches all skinny and naked, plain as day because the moon is so full. Like that."

Tabitha pointed, making her little brother, Adam, turn his gaze to it. They'd set up a tent of sheets in the living room and snuggled down in the dark with no light except the flashlight and the blue glow from the window that Adam only noticed when Tabby pointed it out.

He wished she hadn't noted the tree. It was the same one she'd dared him to climb last spring and he'd fallen out of it only to wind up screaming on the ground with a broken arm. After he'd gotten the cast, she'd signed it with DUMMY in big red letters.

"You shouldn'ta been climbing it anyway," she'd said while capping the marker she'd dragged across the cast's surface.

Since then, he hadn't liked how that tree looked. It watched him sometimes, like it knew how he'd hurt and it liked when he screamed. Now its long fingers stretched towards him to nearly tap the glass, beckoning him out, daring him to climb it again like Tabby had.

"Yer lyin'." He accused, swallowing hard and looking back at her. His eyes were wide, trying to drink in the glow of the flashlight as if that'd help illuminate more of the room and not just Tabby's face. Shadows cast sharp cuts across her expression. The beam made her already wide grin wider and warped her face.

She was having fun. He knew it, knew she was messing with him like she always did. Still, there was a tingle at the nape of his neck. He was too old to let scary stories bother him. Back when he was still a baby, not grown up like he was now, he and Tabby watched *Night of the Living Dead* with out-of-focus shambling black and white zombies. He'd had nightmares for weeks.

That's probably why the Devin in Tabby's story had nightmares. She was putting bits of him into her tale, trying to shake him up. Mom and Dad had gone to bed warning Tabby not to tell him scary things. She liked to. Horror movies were already her favorite and she'd laugh when he'd hide his face behind his favorite stuffed bear when monsters showed up on the screen.

She told them she wouldn't. Crossed her heart and everything. When Dad started snoring through their open bedroom door, the sign that Mom and Dad were definitely asleep, she'd looked at him and said, "Wanna hear something scary?"

He did. He always did.

Even when he spent sleepless nights sitting up, his heart pounding fast as he watched shadows move about his room, he always wanted to hear her scary stories.

"Am not," she shot back.

They fell into silence and she dropped the flashlight, making the beam fall across the floor, illuminating a path along dingy tan carpet that abruptly turned into the checker-tiled kitchen.

"Well?"

"Well, what?" She turned away from him.

She waited for him to beg her to keep going. He knew the way she shot her eyes to the side in annoyance and wouldn't look at him until he fought for her attention again and for more of the story she was telling. He couldn't see it now. Disapproval came off her in waves, though.

"What else happened with the Annie lady?"

Tabby huffed in the dark and the sound of fabric shifting reached him. She settled lower into her sleeping bag and he half expected her to say it didn't matter and to go to sleep. She was like that sometimes.

He lay down too, rolling onto his stomach and propping his chin on his pillow, waiting.

"Devin said he seen his Mom on the stairs like a monster in the dark," Tabby finally relented. She didn't put the flashlight back under her face like before. Some of the drama of the tale was gone for the moment because he called her a liar. She clicks it off, letting a heavy dark blanket fall over the two of them.

"Yeah?" he coaxed. He felt like he did when he lost his first baby tooth. He'd dug at it with his tongue for days, sometimes tasting blood, but it wouldn't come out until finally he had to grab it and yank real hard. He didn't want to. Tabby said he should and told him he'd get money from the tooth fairy. He was digging at her, trying to pull more out of her.

"So, he calls out to her. 'Mama' he says, just like that." Her voice had gone small and scared when she said 'Mama' as if she had been there and knew how this Devin kid talked. "She doesn't say nothing back, though. She keeps down the stairs and then goes to the door. Devin follows her for a minute until he's standing in the doorway right inside, too afraid to go out onto the porch 'cause he heard wolves howling somewhere."

"There ain't wolves around here," Adam countered, puffing out his cheeks in a pout, sure she really was trying to mess with him now. Sleep-walking ladies were one thing, but wolves in the suburbs were entirely unrealistic.

"You want me to keep telling you, or what?" She shot back.

He fell silent again and let her continue.

"He hears *wolves* howling somewhere and thinks he better not go out. Mrs. Steward is walking down the street in this flowing white nightgown that's getting caught in the breeze, pulling and pulling at her like it's trying to make her go back. She keeps going, right down the road, not even blinking." Despite Adam's second interruption, Tabby got back into the flow of the story and the drama entered her voice again.

"He hurries away and goes upstairs to wake up his dad, right? The door is stuck when he starts to wriggle the handle and he pushes and shoves, but he's real small. Small as you. He finally gets it open and—" A pause, a beat where Adam was aware of the silence, and of that tree standing in stark relief against the quiet houses beyond. Waiting. "You know what he saw?"

"What?" Adam's voice came out in a barely audible wheeze.

"Blood." She said, the word a sinister whisper. "There's blood all over the floor. So much that he steps in it right when he walks in. He can't handle what he's seeing at first. He can't even move, just stares all big-eyed at what's in front of him. His Dad is in the bed. The sheets are ripped off and on the floor. His tummy is cut open, guts hanging out and strung all across the room. His mouth is wide like he'd been screaming, but Devin didn't hear anything at all through the night. Not until his Mom came creaking downstairs. His Dad's eyes are all big, almost popping out of his head, and staring straight at the ceiling.

"Devin looks up, like following his Daddy's gaze, and the ceiling is covered in paper. Someone had put up these ugly drawings all in black crayon of the Flannery house. In every picture there was someone in the windows. A man with a white face that's screaming like Devin's Dad."

Adam's tempted to say she was lying again, but worried that if he interrupted for a third time, with another utterance of disbelief, that she really would stop telling him the story.

"Devin can finally move and he screams his head off. He tries to go back out into the hall, only he turns too fast and slips, falling right into all the blood on the floor. It got on his face and all down his nightshirt. All over his hands."

Adam could vaguely make out Tabby holding up her hands as his eyes adjusted to the dark. Still, she was difficult to see; new shadows were playing across her face that made her eyes and mouth look like fuzzy black holes. He squeezed his eyes shut, an icy finger of fear running up along his spine. He hugged his pillow tight, not saying a word.

He didn't want Tabby to stop.

"He finally gets himself up, going down and out of the house the same way his Mom went. He can see her not far off so he runs as hard and as fast as he can to catch up with her. Once he's close, he can see that she's covered in blood, too. The front of her white nightgown is all stained and wet and clinging to her. Her hands are dripping drops of it onto the pavement and stuff.

"He doesn't know what to do, so he grabs her hand and starts pulling, begging her to stop and to come home. Asking her what's wrong. Trying to get her to look at him. She doesn't, just keeps walking, all the way up to the Flannery house. Devin stops when they get to it and his Mom walks up the stairs to the porch, stopping there. And then—" Tabby paused, dragging things out again. "Right there the door opens all by itself."

Adam hung on every word, and his eyes squeezed shut even tighter. In his mind's eye, he imagined he's Devin and his Mom was Annie Steward, stepping up onto the rotting brown porch of the Flannery house. The house that kids whispered about and wouldn't go near. The house where he heard Mr. Flannery died. Mr. Flannery, who one of the kids in his class said she saw standing on the porch and coaxing her to come inside.

"And in the doorway..."

Adam's heart skips a beat.

"...is the pale white man with the screaming face like in the drawings. He reaches out to Devin's mom and—" Another pause, another beat. "Grabs her!"

Something grabbed Adam's arm fast and tight, nearly making him scream as his eyes snapped open. Tabby clamped a hand over his mouth and gave a sharp laugh, soft enough not to wake their parents.

"Shut up, stupid." She sounded delighted.

Her hand is the one clamped around his arm. He'd have seen her move closer if he'd been looking.

Tears well up in his eyes and he pouted again, lowering himself back to his pillow. He was glad Tabby couldn't see him because she'd laugh at him even harder.

She called him a crybaby a lot.

"That was a dumb story."

"Scared you, though," she replied.

They both got comfortable again and she gave a pleased sigh.

Adam knew he was never going to sleep now and as the room fell quiet again, he worried about Tabby falling asleep and leaving him alone.

"What happened to Devin?" he asked.

"Uh," she thought about it for a second. "He went to a neighbors' house and told them what happened. They called the police and his whole house was closed off to be studied by detectives like in the movies. They said that Mrs. Steward had some head disorder and killed her husband. They looked for her for a long time, but then people forgot about it. Adults have short memories. They don't think about nothing for long. Even bad stuff."

"Yeah," he agreed. "What about after that?"

"Devin was all messed up after. Like anyone would be. He lived in a foster home for a little bit, right down the road."

Adam nodded. There was a house down the block that had a big family. The house was stuffed with five kids who all looked different and none of whom looked like their Mom and Dad.

"Some people came, and he got carted off in a white straight jacket. He lives in a hospital now 'cause he keeps saying he hears his Mom crying all night."

Another lie, Adam was sure. People didn't get taken away in white jackets anymore, did they?

"Why is Mr. Flannery a ghost? Why would he want Mrs. Steward to kill her husband?" Adam asked. He started going over the story in his head, looking for ways to pick apart the logic to calm his racing heart. As if logic would make the night less dark and the room less scary and the tree lurking outside less sinister.

"Mr. Flannery used to have a family. A wife and daughter. They left him. I heard he was found a long time ago, hanging from a rope inside the door."

"How?"

"I dunno." Tabby sounded annoyed again. "You don't have to believe me."

"I do."

"Good. Now, go to sleep."

Tabby's head hit her pillow with a soft *whump*.

"Did he want Mrs. Steward 'cause he doesn't have a wife anymore?" Adam asked.

"Ugh." Tabby's head lifted. "Yeah, I guess so. Maybe he's, like, trying to get another one. Or get more. I dunno. When people still talked about Devin, Mom and Dad said something about a copy-cat for something else that happened before I was born. I think before we moved here."

"Another lady?"

"Yeah."

"What was her name?"

"I dunno, Adam. Go to sleep."

Adam huffed and mumbled, "Who needs two wives? You think they go bad? Get all used up and need replacing? Or does he keep them all?"

Tabby didn't answer. Her head was back on her pillow and she was done talking for the night.

Adam shot a glance towards the hallway as a pressure built low in his stomach. The nightlight in the hall was on, washing the closed doors around it in a dim warm blush. Their parents' bedroom door was closed, too. He wondered if they had gotten up and heard Tabby telling him scary things. They'd be mad in the morning if they did.

"I have to pee." He whispered.

Tabby didn't move. He knew she wasn't asleep. She just didn't want to go with him to the bathroom.

He lay there a while longer, debating if he should stay wrapped up in his sleeping bag or make the short trek to the bathroom. He'd stopped wetting the bed for the most part with only the occasional accident. He wasn't certain he'd be able to make it through the night, though. He didn't want to find a wet sleeping bag in the morning and Mom would be upset if there was a pee stain on the carpet.

The nightlight flickered, making him swallow hard. Dad said the day before that it needed replacing. Still, his breath started to come out uneven.

Adam inhaled slowly, forcing his limbs to move. He lifted himself up, scooted out of the sleeping bag. He stood, taking stock of the room.

Everything was quiet.

Dad had stopped snoring. Outside, he couldn't even hear crickets. The old elm was still. There wasn't wind blowing through those jagged branches despite how cold it was outside.

Nothing moved. No shadows lurked. Nothing creeped around outside. Nothing out of place.

Right.

One foot after another.

He crept ahead, opened the bathroom door, and quickly shut himself inside.

Somehow, the bathroom was stuffy and suffocating. Every breath he took was heavy as if he were stuck in a steamy shower. He fumbled for the light switch and tried to flick it on, but nothing happened. The lights above the sink buzzed for a second, then died.

Fear made the bathroom air thicker. He reached out, searching for the sink's countertop and finding only air for what seemed like a decade. Relief danced its way along his arm, made him a little dizzy, when his fingertips brushed against cheap plastic. His body was tight as he felt his way past dried globs of toothpaste, superhero themed toothbrushes, and a half empty bottle of mouthwash.

He took small, unsure steps. Instinct told him he was going to bump into something slimy or furry. Something that lived in the shadows, that had crawled up from the bathtub's drain, and hunted little boys at night. It'd eat him up before he even reached the toilet.

He stopped, whimpered.

He wanted to go get his parents.

They'd be mad, he reminded himself. Tabby would get in trouble because she scared him and then she'd take it out on him for being a tattletale.

He edged further forward, letting out a sigh of relief when his knee finally bumped smooth porcelain.

Standing to relieve himself was out of the question. Blind as he was, he knew he'd make a mess. So, he dropped his pants and sat, willing himself to pee. He couldn't at first. His tiny frame had clenched up with fear and he forced himself to relax, to think of anything but Devin and Mrs. Steward and the screaming Mr. Flannery.

A whisper.

That's the sound that reached him when he finished. When he stood and tugged his pants back on. A whisper in the dark.

Near him? Right next to his ear? His heart jumped to his throat, pounded so hard he felt like he was going to throw up.

No. It came from somewhere else. Outside of the bathroom. A woman whispering something through the walls. Hinges creaked out in the hall, the whispers growing louder, seeping under the door in front of him and rising like snakes so they could tickle his ears.

"Mrs. Steward?" He squeaked out. Was she angry that he knew about her? Was Mr. Flannery? Maybe she'd been sent to silence him and Tabby for daring to make light of what happened to them.

The bathroom lights flickered and then blared on, blinding him as the room came into bright abrupt focus.

"Mama?" he called, his voice small and scared.

His hand fought to find the doorknob and he pulled it open, harsh white flooding out and breaking the dark he'd been living in since Mom and Dad went to bed. Before him were footprints on the carpet. Footprints in red that led from beneath his parents closed bedroom door. The harsh scent of copper hit his nose and he gagged.

Movement drew his attention and he looked up, looked to the living room where his Mom was. She was covered in blood. It was another thing he didn't need to see to know. He could smell it. Taste it like the time he ate a penny and swallowed it whole.

His Mom bent to scoop up a sleepy Tabitha in pale, crimson-slick arms. She stood there for a few seconds, staring at nothing, and Adam wondered if maybe some part of her was still in there, locked in a battle for control.

She lost, turning on her heels and heading to the door.

She left it wide open behind her as she stepped through it, out onto the porch. She disappeared from sight, but from where Adam stood in the bathroom doorway, staring into the hallway next to a quiet bedroom where his father lay dead, he knew she was going out to the street. Outside, far away, wolves howled low and mournful. Past that, he could almost hear her feet slapping on chilly pavement as she walked down to the Flannery House where a door would swing open and a pale screaming man would welcome in another wife and his first new daughter.

Georgie

Robert Ford

I THINK if it was only the death of our son, Maria and I would've made it, y'know? Picked each other up and worked through the grief. Healed each other. Saved our marriage.

Maria was the love of my life. Even now, after everything that's happened, there are days when I still miss her so much. I used to be angry at her for leaving, but not anymore. Not really. I know she loved me. I understand.

See, the thing is, my wife didn't leave because our son *died*.

She left because he *came back*.

* * *

You ever see those couples that are effortless?

You know the kind. They finish each other's sentences, reach for each other's hands like they have magnets in their palms. They just seem to *mesh* with each other.

Maria and I never had that.

We really had to work at our marriage but I was okay with that, y'know? It damn sure wasn't love at first sight. I thought she was just another rich girl riding Daddy's coattail and she thought I was some Irish street punk with a future of scams and back alley hustles. Hell, the thing is, that's probably the life I'd be leading if I hadn't met her. It was what I knew growing up. After I met Maria, I started to think I could rise up from the streets and actually make something of myself.

Maria was beautiful. She looked like some east coast cheerleader when I met her. Silky brunette hair pulled back in a ponytail. Innocent eyes set in a pure face. I don't know what the hell she saw in me, but when we fell for each other, we *fell hard*. Sometimes, I loved her so much it hurt.

We tied the knot about a year after we met, both of us young as hell, trying to carve our notch in the world, finding out how hard we could love each other, how hard we could fight. The temper on that woman? Oh, *goddamn*, she was full of fire back then. So full of...life.

But it was great discovering each other, y'know? Everything was new. Exciting. The two of us against the world. We had life by the short and curlies and for a while, we lived life just for ourselves.

Then one day, out of the blue, that all changed.

* * *

Her smile is what gives it away.

The alarm clock screams 05:30 in red, angry letters. Some easy listening station snaps on. It's way too damned early to be wailing about heartache, but Elton John is giving it a hell of a try. I slap the snooze button and cut him off in mid-chorus. Maria was never a morning person, so the nine extra minutes in bed is like a gift.

I go through my morning routine. Shower. Shave. Get my suit on and try to thread my five-dollar tie. I turn around and Maria's awake, watching me.

Morning sunlight streams in between the blinds, and she's washed in bands of gold. The bed sheets are wrapped around her and she's sitting up against the headboard. Her hair is all messed up, but in a good way. Sexy, y'know?

She doesn't say a word. Just gives me this funny little smile full of mischief and hope and this… it's cliché as hell, but this *glow*.

And I knew. I just… *knew*.

That was how I found out I was going to be a father.

* * *

When Georgie was born, his face was the color of wet slate. His umbilical cord was wrapped around his neck. The nurses scrambled to get the doctor some snips and he cut the cord, but Georgie lay there, still and limp as a dishrag. The doctor flipped him over on his stomach and gave him a smack on the ass. I can still remember the wet sound of latex gloves on Georgie's newborn skin.

The doctor mumbled under his breath. *Come on back, now. Death can't have you yet,* and lifted his hand for another slap.

A tiny snuffling cough, and Georgie's first cries rang out in the room. The three of us huddled there in the delivery room, tired, laughing, tears flowing down our faces. Just so relieved. Happy.

That's how we became a family.

* * *

Upstairs, the noises have stopped. Georgie was excited earlier. Angry. Throwing things. The oak bed thumped against the floor. I heard something shatter and I know I should've boarded the windows. I hope like hell he doesn't break them again.

If I go up there, I know what I'll find – the remnants of a child's tantrum. But I won't see him. He hardly ever shows himself unless he gets *really* upset. He just keeps to the shadows, but he'll never leave me.

Georgie was screaming in his *almost-voice* and even in the middle of his rage, hearing him again almost broke my heart.

He wasn't really speaking though. The noises he makes are primal, closer to the sounds a wounded animal might make. But it's quiet now, as if he's holding his breath, waiting to see what will happen.

* * *

Georgie got his looks from Maria. Would've been a real heart-breaker when he got older. Dark hair, olive skin and long lashes framing eyes the color of damp moss. He looked so full of mischief you couldn't help but smile.

Maria was a great mom y'know? You should've seen her and Georgie together, the way they laughed and carried on. Those two were best friends. They meshed. They were… *effortless*.

I used to put him to bed sometimes. Read him a story. Sing to him. We used to do this thing. He'd give me a big hug, plant a tiny, wet kiss on my lips and lay down, teddy bear pulled close, and we'd do our nightly exchange.

Night, night, Georgie.

Night, night, Daddy.

Love you.

Love you too, Daddy.

Who's your buddy?

Me. Who's your pal?

Me.

He'd yawn. His eyelids would smooth and close, flickering as he drifted off. I'd watch him as he lay there at peace. Angelic.

Nothing at all like what he is now.

* * *

Being a father changed everything. I started acting the part and got promoted at the company. Me managing employees, believe that? Maria and I bought a place out of the city and for the next few years it was yule logs and eggnog, backyard barbecues and t-ball and all the shit I used to make fun of, y'know? But it was a good life.

It was a *good* life.

Watching Georgie discover things was addictive. His excitement at learning something new. His endless questions.

Why do we call oranges, oranges, but don't call apples, reds?

Why does ice float?

Where do we go when we die?

At get-togethers, adults would have conversations with him and walk away shaking their heads, ready to mix themselves a fresh drink. They said Georgie had an old soul.

He was a smart kid, way beyond his years. We'd sidestepped questions about Santa Claus and the Easter Bunny, but Maria and I both knew, at best, we only had a few years before he figured things out.

No question he loved the presents that Christmas brought with it. Watching him run around during an Easter Egg hunt was enough to make you piss yourself laughing.

But Georgie's favorite was Halloween. Cheap plastic masks. Loose-fitting polyester costumes. Georgie loved all of it. I think it was the idea of becoming something else for the night that made it so much fun for him. But like any kid, the candy itself was what he loved most. He called it his pirate booty.

We had grilled the rules into him since his first time trick-or-treating. After we got back home, Maria or I had to check through his candy before he could eat anything. No exceptions.

He was almost five when it happened. Old enough to know better.

* * *

The night air is crisp. Downright cold really. Each time the kids yell trick-or-treat, tiny clouds of steam curl from their mouths. I can almost feel winter bullying its way past fall.

Georgie's ghost costume is stretched tight and shiny over his thin jacket. We've been out for a couple hours already and his cheeks are roses. Georgie's all smiles. His bag is heavy and he's had a pretty good haul for the night. Even so, Maria still has to bribe him with a promise of hot chocolate to steer him back home without an argument.

Just as I open the front door, the phone rings. I hurry inside, Maria and Georgie behind me. I grab the phone, praying it's not the office calling me tonight, so I'm thankful, but still groan inwardly at a telemarketer reading a script about replacement windows.

I'm tired, but I know the guy's just doing his job. I try to be polite, keep my temper in check, do my best to slip in a *thank-you-but-I'm-not-interested* so I can hang up. I'm still holding the phone as I turn around and watch it all in slow motion.

The apple is a gleaming, polished, beautiful thing. It's oversized in Georgie's tiny hands and a brilliant red against his ghost costume. His mouth opens wide. The bright rectangles of his teeth sink into the burnished skin.

A silver hairline breaks the surface of the apple but I notice it far too late.

Georgie bites in deep and so does the razor blade inside. Blood gushes from his mouth, paints the front of his costume with a red exclamation point.

The apple tumbles from his hands and falls to the carpet. It leaves a bloody trail as it rolls to a stop at my feet. Georgie looks at me, confused. He knows something's wrong, but the pain hasn't hit yet.

Georgie puts his hands to his mouth and withdraws something pink and spongy. He waves it at me and begins jumping up and down, making this high-pitched mewling. His expression turns to panic.

I run to him. I scream for Maria to call 9-1-1.

Georgie tries to talk and it comes out a garbled mess. He coughs, makes this liquid, whistling sound from the back of his throat. He claws at his neck. More blood streams from his mouth and he falls to his knees, choking. I turn him over and cradle him in my lap, try to work inside his mouth. My hands grow slick. The razor slices into the tips of my fingers, and my blood mingles with my son's. The blade's there, wedged at the back of his throat, but I can't get it free.

Georgie convulses on my lap and as little as he is, it's all I can do to hold him still. The world around me grows quiet.

I know Maria's beside me. I can see her screaming but I can't hear her. Red spirals of light twist over my living room walls. I know the paramedics are out front but I don't hear sirens.

I know they're too late.

Georgie's expression pleads with me to fix this, to put it all back together again because I'm the guy who does that. I'm the dryer of crocodile tears and the healer of boo-boos. I'm the slayer of bedtime monsters and the mechanic of broken toys.

I'm... I'm *Daddy*.

But Daddy can't fix this.

All the king's horses and all the king's men can't *fix this*.

Georgie's legs stop shaking. More blood pours from his mouth, black as oil. His body stops trembling, gets rigid. His gaze is still locked on mine.

I don't know what I expected to see in his eyes, but I didn't think it would be the anger I found. The rage.

Georgie's eyes begin to lose their shine. His small chest stops moving and his body relaxes. I feel him lift up and pass through me; a sensation like a cold breeze against sunburned skin.

Sound kicks in again. I hear the heavy footsteps of the paramedics as they run into the house. Strong hands pull Georgie away from me. They lead Maria from the room. The paramedics work on his body but it's useless. He's already gone.

And I can't stop screaming.

* * *

Two months passed before Georgie came back.

Maria and I had become little more than roommates, both of us lost in a sea of grief, unable to get to shore. She couldn't comfort me and I couldn't comfort her and to be perfectly honest, I don't think either one of us cared anymore. Something inside us died along with our son. We were both numb, drifting off into memories of when he was alive, so it took us a while to realize that Georgie was dead, but he wasn't gone.

It was little things at first. Cold pockets of air traveled around the house. Matchbox cars rolled across the hardwood floor of his bedroom. In the middle of the night, the television would flick on, blaring cartoons. I'd be standing in the kitchen and feel small, icy hands tugging at the back of my leg.

Georgie kept getting stronger.

We woke in the middle of the night to find him standing at the foot of our bed. Georgie stared at me with his angry face and milky eyes, hate streaming off him in waves. His mouth opened in a yawn and blood spilled free. Georgie pointed a single accusing finger at me. His breath carried the fetid smell of old blood and rotted apples. Then he faded into the shadows.

Maria left that night. Didn't look at me, didn't cry, just drove off. Hell, she never even came back for her goddamn clothes, just set her wedding ring on the counter, grabbed her keys and ran. Our attorneys took care of everything else. Last I heard, she moved to Seattle and started nursing school. Married an engineer I think, maybe an accountant, I can't remember. Sounds like a quiet life, though. Safe. *Predictable.*

I'm happy for Maria. Really, I am. I can't blame her. Georgie's anger lies with me, not her.

But after she left, I was alone with him.

I started sleeping with the lights on, but I could still see Georgie moving in the shadows. I tried shutting the bedroom door but could still hear him scratching, the door knob rattling, as he whispered from the hallway.

"Night, night Daddeeeeeeeeee."

Even now, sometimes I'll wake from sleep, the feeling of tiny, cold hands against my throat, choking off my air. Rows of bloody scratches cover my arms. Crescents of bite marks pattern my legs.

It's a horrible thing to be afraid of your own child. I'd be lying if I said that ending it all hasn't crossed my mind. Some days I think it would be so easy to sit in a hot bath and put a razor to my wrist. Just watch my life spool away in red ribbons.

It's ironic, really. What drove Maria away is the same thing keeping me here. Fear is its own prison and it doesn't need bars.

See, I can't help but wonder, if Georgie is this angry with me now…if he torments me this much while I'm still alive…what's he going to do to me when I'm dead?

* * *

I know why Georgie's angry. He's lonely.

Sometimes the loneliness gets to me but mostly I've learned to live with it. But Georgie…his pain I can't bear anymore.

I can hear the children outside, their excited squeals as they walk from door to door. Flashlight beams dance through the streets and I know any second I'll hear footsteps on the porch and the kids will ring my doorbell. Their painted faces will be full of smiles as they hold out their bags, waiting for the promise of candy.

This year, I've made…*special* treats for the kids.

Georgie wants a playmate and I intend to give him one.

Georgie's angry. He's lonely.

But I can fix this. I'm the guy who does that.

I'm the dryer of crocodile tears and the healer of boo-boos. I'm the slayer of bedtime monsters and the mechanic of broken toys.

I'm Daddy.

A Ghost's Revenge

Lettice Galbraith

IT WAS a dismal evening. Heavy clouds covered the sky. The air was full of a raw dampness, which hung like a veil over the flat marshy district through which the London train was winding its way, like some huge fiery serpent, now pausing in its sinuous course, now darting forward with a writhe and a shriek, to vanish under a lurid cloud of steam.

"Mallowby," shouted the hoarse voice of the porter, "Mallowby." The door of a first-class smoking carriage was reluctantly opened, and a solitary passenger alighted.

"What a beast of a night!" he muttered, hastily buttoning up his fur-lined overcoat, "and what a beast of a place!" peering discontentedly across the low white railing at the monotonous stretch of snow-powdered fallow and pasture. "What on earth has induced Forster to bury himself in such a desolate hole?"

"Any luggage, sir? Two portmanteaus and a gun-case – very good, sir. Where for – the Rectory? The cart is just outside, through the gate on the left."

With another malediction on the rawness of the atmosphere, the passenger from town picked his way across the sloppy platform and climbed into the dogcart which was in waiting for him. He was cold, hungry, and, if the truth must be told, considerably out of temper; and, as he splashed down the mile of muddy road which lay between the station and the village, Gerald Harrison was half inclined to repent his promise of spending a couple of days with his old college chum on his way to Scotland.

A hearty welcome, a sherry and bitters, a roaring fire, and a hot bath went a long way towards dispelling his ill-humour. The-Reverend Richard Forster, now acting as *locum tenens* for the absent rector of Mallowby, thoroughly understood the art of making his guests comfortable.

"You will not have too much time, old fellow," he said, when he had conducted Harrison to his room. "I am sorry to hurry you, but dinner is at half-past seven, and I cannot well put it back because I have asked another man. His name is Granville. He has lately come to the old Hall, and we are going to shoot over one of his farms tomorrow."

Twenty minutes later, when Gerald (with temperature and temper alike restored to their normal condition) descended to the library, he found his host in earnest confabulation with the visitor – a slight dark man, with an anxious, rather worried expression, and a trick of glancing nervously over his shoulder.

"I give you my word, Forster," he was saying, "that it is going on worse than ever. I can't get a servant to sleep in the front of the house, and if I were not ashamed of acknowledging myself a fool, I would cut the place tomorrow and go back to town."

The opening of the door put an end to the discussion. Forster changed the subject by introducing his guests, and as dinner was almost immediately announced, the conversation fell into general channels – such as the Irish question, pheasant-rearing, and the chances of an open season. It struck Harrison that Mr. Granville had all the appearance of a man who has received some severe mental shock. Though he talked intelligently and even well, it was evident that his attention was never wholly given to the subject in hand. He seemed to be constantly listening for some expected sound, and once, when footsteps were audible on the gravel without, he started violently and turned as white as a sheet.

"It is only Kenwell bringing back the keys of the church," remarked Forster. "He has been taking the choir practice for me this evening. There is the bell."

A servant answered the door, and the footsteps died away again, accompanied by the distant clash of the iron gate. Granville sank back in his chair with a long breath of relief. He had let his cigar out, and now looked round for a light. Harrison offered him a match, and, as the elder man took it, he could feel that his hand was cold and shaking.

The evening passed in pleasant desultory chat. At eleven o'clock Granville rose. "Will you order my cart?" he said. Then, in answer to his host's demur, he answered nervously, "Don't tempt me to stay, Forster; it only makes matters worse. Yes, I know it is quite early and all that; but they will take ten minutes to put the horse in, and," with a ghastly attempt at a smile, "I am like Cinderella, I must be indoors before midnight. You will come up early tomorrow, and of course you both lunch with me. I would ask you to dine as well, only – only I am not good company in my own house now."

Forster's hand was on the bell. He paused, and looked keenly into his friend's face.

"Don't go back, Granville," he said, earnestly. "Let me tell your man that you will stay the night here. I can easily put you up."

"No, thanks; no," with the nervous haste of one who fears that his resolution may fail him, "I cannot do that. After all I have said, I dare not show the white feather to the servants. They would think me a fool; but, my God! they don't hear it as I do. Tell them to bring the cart round, Forster. For pity's sake, man, don't waste time! It is ten minutes past eleven already."

The order was given. As the minutes wore on, Granville became increasingly uneasy. He could not restrain his restless anxiety to be off, and it was a relief to everyone when the grating of wheels outside announced that the trap was in readiness. Forster accompanied him to the door, whither Harrison presently followed.

"It is not much of a night," he commented, peering out into the chill darkness. "Your friend will have a coolish drive."

Forster was standing on the step.

"Hush!" he said, holding up his hand. "Listen! He is galloping."

From the old grey tower on their left chimed the half-hour, and, as the notes died away, they could hear the receding rattle of a cart being driven at a furious pace along the road below.

"He must be cracked to drive at that rate in the dark," cried Gerald, as the clatter of hoofs grew fainter and finally died away. "It will be more by luck than management if he doesn't upset at the first corner. What is the matter with him, Dick – does he drink, or is he off his head?"

"Neither at present. He thinks his house is haunted, and it is getting on his nerves."

"Oh, he must be cracked, then," with easy decision. "No one but a lunatic believes in ghosts in these days. Accept the possibilities of terrestrial elementaries and left-hand magic if you like; but the common or garden ghost, never."

"There is something queer about the old Hall, though," persisted Forster. "I do not believe that any consideration you could offer would induce a Mallowby man to sleep there alone. The place has a bad name. It stood empty for years before Granville bought it. He spent no end of money in repairs and furniture too, which makes it additionally hard on him to be driven out by—"

"A ghost," concluded Harrison, with a shout of laughter. "My dear Dick, it is too absurd. Let us exorcise the place. I will back my six-shooter at thirty feet against any combination of goblins and blue fire. We will arrange a match tomorrow. Fifty pounds a side, to be paid in material currency only. Come, admit now that the thing is a huge joke."

"It is a good deal more like death to Granville," returned Forster, seriously. "His nerves are regularly gone to pieces. He is not like the same fellow who came down in the autumn."

"Have the ghosts been trying to evict him ever since?"

"Sounds weak, I dare say," Dick answered, "but I am inclined to believe, Gerald, that there is more in it than meets the eye. Last October Granville was every bit as sceptical as you are. If he heard anything he treated it with contempt. When the servants complained of mysterious noises, he laughed them to scorn. You saw for yourself that he does not laugh at it now. He told me this evening that these – these – manifestations are of nightly occurrence. I am afraid it is taking serious effect upon his health. I wish I had kept him here tonight."

"Oh, he will be all right," said Harrison, lightly. "Funk is a deuced unpleasant complaint, but it don't often kill. Twelve o'clock; I think I'll be turning in. This time tomorrow, I suppose, we shall be wishing each other a happy new year."

But the glad new year was destined to be ushered in by no hearty shaking of hands, no joyous congratulations at Mallowby Rectory. In the grey dawn of the December morning Harrison was awakened by the flashing of a candle before his eyes. Forster was standing beside the bed, with a pale and horror-stricken face.

"Gerald," he said hurriedly, "will you get up at once? I want you to come with me to the Hall. Something terrible has happened. Poor Granville is dead."

"Dead!" repeated the other blankly, "Dead! Why, he only left here at eleven."

"I know that. Seven hours ago he was here, only seven hours ago, and now they are carrying his body up from the pond where it was found. Why did I not keep him?" he cried, pacing the room in deep agitation. "Why did I let him go back to that accursed house? I knew his mind was unhinged by what he had heard there. Poor fellow! Poor Granville! And now it is too late."

Harrison was already out of bed.

"I will be downstairs in five minutes," he said. "Of course, I know no particulars, but has anyone thought of sending for a doctor?"

Forster caught eagerly at the implied hope.

"Someone shall go for Mr. Tilling at once," he said, hurrying out of the room.

It was a relief to be able to do something, but long before the surgeon arrived they knew that his services would be useless. Death had sealed the master of Ravenshill for his own. The cold and rigid limbs refused to respond to the revivifying influences of hot blankets and artificial respiration.

Harrison was of opinion, as he assisted in his friend's frantic endeavours to restore some semblance of life, that poor Granville had been dead for several hours.

It was a painful task. In vain Forster tried to close the dull, lack-lustre eyes, fixed in a wide stare of indescribable horror. The tense features would not relax. Never had human being passed away from life leaving behind him so terrible an impression of fear. At seven o'clock the surgeon for whom Forster had sent appeared on the scene. One glance at the body was sufficient for him.

"He's dead," said the plain-spoken country practitioner. "Dead as a doornail. How did it happen?"

Ah! How indeed? That was a mystery. A secret known only to the dead man and to those unspeakable powers who work behind the veil.

In the early morning of the last day of the year the household at the Hall had been startled from their slumbers by a wild, agonised cry, followed by shriek upon shriek of demoniacal laughter. The horrible sounds lasted only for a minute. Before the terrified servants were fairly aroused and crowding together into the corridor, to learn the meaning of this strange alarm, the house was wrapped in its customary silence. For a few moments they had been too scared to do more than wonder at their master remaining undisturbed; then someone, bolder than the rest, suggested that it would be as well to waken him. They knocked at his door and received no answer. They called, but no voice replied. At last the butler ventured into the room. It was empty. The night lamp, which Granville had lately used, was burning brightly, the fire was nearly out. The bed had not been occupied. Thoroughly alarmed now, a search party was formed, and, armed with lights and a brace of revolvers, the men descended to the ground floor. In the library the lamp was also burning. The odour of tobacco still hung in the air; a few embers glowed in the grate; the spirit decanters and an empty soda-water bottle lay on the table beside an open book. There was no trace of any disturbance, and there was no sign of Granville.

The servants looked at each other in silence. No one dared to put into words the fear that lay chill at his heart. Suddenly the butler uttered an exclamation. His eyes had fallen on one of the windows. The long curtains were swaying gently backward and forward in the current of cold air from without.

The shutters were thrown back, and the casement stood wide open. They crowded round. "Steady, keep back a bit," protested one man, more astute than his fellows, "there is snow enough to hold footmarks. It's a pity to tread it about till we've got a lantern and struck the trail."

In a few minutes a covered light had been procured, and the threshold of the window was examined. There could be no doubt as to the way in which Granville had quitted the room. Straight from the sill the footprints were distinctly traced in the light snow. Along the path they tracked the marks, round the corner of the house, across the lawn to the edge of the pond. And there, beneath the willows, half-hidden by the drooping frost-browned ferns, they found the body of their master, still in evening dress, with clenched fingers, and features transfixed in an expression of ghastly dread.

The quiet little village was shaken to its core. All day long the people gathered in knots to discuss the awful tragedy which had been enacted in their midst. Horror was in the air. Old superstition reasserted its sway with renewed strength. Old stories were repeated with bated breath; for once again the curse of the Deverels had fallen, and the truth of the half-forgotten legend was triumphantly vindicated.

By nightfall every human being had quitted the precincts of the fateful Hall. The scared domestics absolutely refused to remain on the premises, and the big house was deserted, save for the silent form lying so still beneath the white sheet on one of the sofas in the library, in which room the body of Philip Granville had been laid to await the coroner's inquest.

To Forster this desertion of the helpless corpse seemed terrible. He would have spent the night in watching beside the poor fellow who had so lately been his guest, and was only dissuaded from his purpose by the earnest solicitations of his churchwarden, a stalwart farmer, on whose grey head seventy-odd years sat lighter than most men's fifty.

"Parson," said the old man, solemnly, "theer's noa good a fly in' in the faace o' Providence. Noa body thinks as you're a coward, but what sort o' use be theer in flingin' good loives a'ter bad uns? Yon poor lad tried it, and see how they've served him. Thirty year back Lord Broadborough's agent died in saame way. My feyther used to tell how, when he were a little lad, one of the Dawbenys caam doon hissen' and boasted as how he'd better the Deverels. It was i' the summer toime, and all went well enow. But as soon as winter caame on, 'they' were at work ag'in, and t' ould squoire, he began to grow graave and stern-like. He would na gi' in, till, on New Year's Eve, the house were fetched up by a fearful cry, and next mornin' they found his body in the pond theer, with a look on t' faace as, God forbid, should iver be sean on yours or moine. Mony an' mony a good mon has met that death, sin' the noight that Katharine Deverel stood in yon winder and cursed the mon who had robbed her of her husband's naame, an' theer lad of his lawful inheritance. 'You hev ta'an it by fraud,' she croid; 'but the Lord will avenge me. Noa good shall it bring thee. You shall neyther live in it yoursen, nor shall another receive it at your hands. Though I lose my immortal soul,' she says, 'I'll hev revenge. You may tak' my choild's birthright, you may slur ma fair naame, but noa mon – be he young or auld, good or evil, so that he does na' bear th' naame o' Deverel – shall live to see a new year dawn wi'in these walls. I'll die on Deverel land,' says she; 'and he who braves ma curse shall die even as I hev died.' Then she called on the God of the feytherless to hear her words and turned awa', and next mornin' they found her body stiff an' stark in yonder pond, with the dead baby still clasped in her arms. You'll bear in moind, sir, what the Lord did to the mon who built up the walls o' Jericho. It's His will, an' you bein' a parson, should knaw better than to goa agin' Him. What harm can taake yon poor bit o' clay now? But you hev a wark to do i' the warld, and you ain't got no reet to chuck you loife a'ter his'n."

"Mr. Dawson is right, Dick,' urged Harrison; "you can't do the poor fellow any good. Your nerves are shaken, and I am free to confess, ghost or no ghost, to spend the night in that dismal house with a dead man is more than I should care about."

Very unwillingly Forster at last agreed to yield.

Three days later the local jury brought in a verdict of 'Died by the visitation of God', and once again the spirit of Katharine Deverel had triumphed and the home of her ancestors stood empty.

* * *

Five years had come and gone, bringing with them many changes. Dick Forster, now Bishop of Honduras, was doing good work for God and man in his far-off colonial diocese. His place in Harrison's daily life had been filled by another friend of his schoolboy days, who was also shortly to become his brother-in-law. Jack Chamberlayne was a handsome, genial young fellow, blessed with a fine constitution, a sweet temper, and a very considerable fortune, and the match between his favourite sister and his special chum was a source of unmixed satisfaction to Gerald. The two men were constantly together until a matter of business obliged Harrison to visit the South of Europe. The transaction occupied him for some months, and it was not till the end of December that he found himself once more on English soil. He reached Dover at noon on the last day of the year, and went straight to the 'Lord Warden'. A packet of letters was awaiting him. They had been forwarded from San Carremo after his departure, and among them was an envelope addressed in Chamberlayne's characteristic handwriting.

Dear old boy, ran the letter, *what do you mean by spending Christmas in a dirty Italian village, instead of returning to the bosom of your family like a respectable Englishman? I don't believe a word about the vineyards. Tell your agent to go to the devil, and come to us for the new year, or neither Elaine nor I will have anything more to do with you. The Hunt Ball is on the 5th, the Cardwell's on the following evening. On the 7th Mrs. Verelst is giving some theatricals in which we are going to distinguish ourselves, and there are three or four other minor events which you ought not to miss. Also I want your valuable advice as to the wisdom of buying a place in Creamshire. I only heard of it last week, and have already made up my mind to purchase, so your counsel must tend in that direction if you wish me to profit by it. It is a jolly old house, with capital stabling, and nice gardens. There is a ripping tennis-lawn (room for two courts, if I fill up a pond at the end), and a lot of old oak indoors. I forgot to say the house is furnished. It is in the best part of the Broadborough country, and within reach of the outside meets of Lord Cremorne's and the Turton. Plenty of shooting, and the whole thing going for a mere song. I believe there is even a family ghost thrown in. I am running down on Friday for a week to see how I like it; but of course you will put up at my place as you come through town whether I am there or not—*

Harrison waited to hear no more. In a moment the letter was crushed into his pocket, and he was out in the street, and, hurrying to the nearest telegraph-office, without a second's delay he wrote the message and handed it in to the clerk:

Chamberlayne, 112 Piccadilly. – On no account go to Ravenshill Hall till you have seen me. Shall be in town this afternoon and will explain. – GERALD.

Then he hastened back to the hotel and ordered some luncheon. While he was eating he looked up the trains for town. The next was due in twenty minutes. His portmanteaus had not been unstrapped. Harrison sent for a cab, paid his bill, and in less than an hour was well on his way to London. From the moment of reading Chamberlayne's description of his projected purchase, he had decided on the course he must pursue. Though the name of the place was not mentioned he knew, by a sudden swift intuition, that it was Ravenshill Hall. Back to his mind, with the freshness of yesterday, swept the memory of that terrible night five years ago, and he shuddered as he recalled the words of the old farmer.

"No man – be he young or old, good or evil, so that he does not bear the name of Deverel – shall live to see the new year break within these walls. I will die on Deverel land, and he who braves my curse shall die even as I have died."

"Many and many a good man has met that death since." Was another victim destined to be added to the long roll-call of that terrible vengeance, and that victim his old playmate, his friend, his almost brother? No, thank God; there was yet time to avert the stroke of fate. Jack must have received his wire by now. He would be waiting for the promised explanation. The slow hours wore on; the train rattled and ground its way through the wintry landscape. The sky was leaden and dull. On the horizon lay dense masses of clouds, black and heavy with snow. By the time they ran into Charing Cross, large flakes were floating lazily down to join their crushed and mud-stained comrades on the dirty pavement. Evidently there had been a considerable fall earlier in the day, for the roofs down the Strand were gleaming white, and great heaps of snow had been scraped up from the roadway and piled behind the pillars of the station gates. Harrison got his luggage on to a hansom and drove straight to his friend's chambers. As he glanced up at the windows, it struck him as odd that no lights were to be seen.

The housekeeper answered his ring.

"Oh, is it you, Mr. Harrison? Very glad to see you back, sir. There is a letter for you upstairs and three telegrams. The first came on Wednesday, sir. The note Mr. Chamberlayne left for you; he expected you would be here on Wednesday."

"Left for me," repeated Gerald, anxiously. "He has not gone, surely? Did he not get my wire?"

"I sent it on with the other letters this morning, sir. Mr. Chamberlayne has been gone a week – him and Mr. Curtis. He is staying at Creamshire, at Ravenshill Hall, Mallowby."

Harrison's brain reeled. He saw it all now. That letter had been a week in travelling to Italy and back again to England. He had cried, "Peace, peace," when there was no peace; when all the time he was too late, and Jack had gone to that accursed house, and – this was New Year's Eve.

"Fetch the letters, Mrs. Williams; or, stay, I will get them myself."

He tore upstairs, two steps at a time, snatched the envelopes from the mantelpiece and was back to the cab before the astounded housekeeper could utter a syllable.

"King's Cross!" he shouted to the driver; "and a double fare if I catch the 7:05 for the north. It is a matter of life and death."

"I'll do my best, sir," said the man, dubiously; "but it's darned bad going."

Never had the way seemed so long; never did time go faster and horse more slowly. To Harrison's overwrought fancy they crept along, and again and again he raised the trap and implored the man to whip up. The agony and anxiety in his white drawn face moved the cabby's heart to pity, and he generously refrained from swearing at his impetuous fare.

"A cove is that onreasonable when 'e's in trouble," he growled to himself aloft. "Does 'e want me to let the mare down and make sure of losing 'is blooming train?"

At last they turned into the Euston Road. The snow was coming down in good earnest now, and Gerald could hardly see the hands of the clock for the blinding flakes. It wanted eight minutes to seven.

"Thank God!" he murmured, as the hansom turned into the yard of the Great Northern. Before the man had time to pull up, he was out on the ground.

"Mallowby," he called to the porter, "can I do it?"

"Four minutes," was the response.

Gerald flung half a sovereign to the driver, and rushed into the booking-office. The bell was ringing when he got on to the platform. The porter had put his portmanteaus into a carriage and was holding open the door. He threw himself into a seat with a sense of gratitude that he was to have the compartment to himself.

To maintain an appearance of indifferent calm at this moment would, he felt, have been impossible. He was enduring a martyrdom of suspense. If his friend's life had not already paid the forfeit for another's sin, every second that ticked its course was bringing him nearer to its end. He conjured up with horrible distinctness the dark library, the deep recesses on either side of the fireplace lined with books, the massive oak furniture. He could hear the weird murmur of voices, without, the ghostly steps on the drive; then the heavy velvet curtains trembled, parted, and a woman's figure stood framed in the long window – a woman with dripping garments and a white set face, lighted by strange, lurid eyes – eyes which were dead, and yet alive in their fierce hatred and unquenchable thirst for revenge. How they glittered! They were close to him now, looking in through the carriage window, and Harrison, who had once laughed contemptuously at the mere notion of supernatural manifestations, was perilously near raising a ghost for himself from the intensity of his nervous excitement. Fortunately, at this juncture he remembered that Jack's letter and the telegrams were still unopened in his pocket, and the break in the sequence of thought gave him time to pull himself together.

With a half-laugh at his own weakness, he drew the curtains across the windows, and, lighting a cigar, tore open the yellow envelopes.

All three messages had been handed in at Mallowby Station.

The first was dated December 29, and said:

> *Come down as soon as possible. Dull and seedy. Want cheering up.*
> *– CHAMBERLAYNE.*

"He is getting nervous," Gerald said to himself "and did not like to acknowledge it."

The second telegram was more urgent, and enclosed a reply form.

> *Must see you today. Important. Wire what train. Don't fail me. – JACK.*

The third was signed by Chamberlayne's valet.

Something seriously wrong here. Please come at once, very anxious about master.

Harrison's face grew very grave. Something must indeed have been wrong before the punctilious Curtis would take upon himself to send a wire like that. His fears returned with renewed force. It was torture to think of Jack sending message after message only to meet with blank silence. There was a piteous reproach in the last appeal, "Don't fail me."

"As if I were likely to do that so long as I am above ground," thought Gerald. "Poor old Jack, he might have known I should have answered if I'd ever got the things."

At Peterborough he went to the refreshment-room and swallowed a sandwich and a few mouthfuls of soup while his flask was replenished with brandy. Very few passengers joined the train, and no one came into Harrison's carriage. As the hours dragged out their weary length he grew more and more restless and nervous. He paced the six feet of floor like a caged animal. He let down the window. A cloud of fine snow blew in through the opening. All around hedges, fields, and trees were wrapped in a dense white mantle. It was bitterly cold. Despite his fur-lined coat, hot tin, and a couple of rugs, his teeth were chattering and his hands were like ice.

He looked at his watch. It was half-past nine. In thirty minutes the train was due at Mallowby, and they had not passed Grantham yet. Surely, too, they were slackening speed. Half doubting the evidence of his senses, he again opened the window. The train was unmistakably at a standstill, but there was not the slightest sign of a station. The wind had risen, and whistled through the telegraph-wires overhead. Between the gusts he could hear the murmur of voices. Presently a man passed along the footboard. It was the guard. Harrison inquired the cause of the delay.

"Line blocked, I'm afraid, sir," was the reply, "but I will let you know as I come back."

With an exclamation, which was almost a groan, Gerald flung himself back in his seat. Were the fates league against him, that now, when every moment might seal Jack Chamberlayne's death-warrant, he must perforce sit idle, bound hand and foot by the victory of the forces of nature over the inventions of man? Five minutes passed, ten, twenty, thirty. Then the guard put his head in at the door.

"All right, sir, line is clear; we shall go on directly."

At one minute past eleven the London train, more than an hour behind its time, set down a single passenger at Mallowby. Harrison at once addressed himself to the station master, and inquired how he could get to the old Hall. The man had been on the coroner's jury five years before, and remembered his face.

"Going to the Hall tonight, sir? Why, were not you here when poor Mr. Granville was drowned? You don't want to see it a second time, surely!"

"God forbid!" answered Gerald, quickly, "but I want to prevent it. A dear friend of mine is at that devilish house tonight. He does not know his danger, and I mean to save him."

"You can't do it," returned the man, bluntly. "Best keep clear of the black work that will be going forward up there. There is no baulking the Deverel curse. It will have its victim. God help him I say, and all those who sleep under that roof on New Year's Eve. You can do nothing for them."

"I mean to try," answered Harrison, with set teeth. "I have no time to waste. Where can I get a trap?"

"Nowhere nearer than the village. It will take you as long as walking the whole way. The roads are awful."

"Then I must walk. Can you find me a lantern? For Heaven's sake be quick. Every minute may mean his life now. What do I care about the danger? Man, I tell you he is my friend. He is to marry my sister in a fortnight, and I will either save him or die with him."

The stationmaster hesitated a moment.

"Look here, sir," he said, hurriedly, "you're a brave man, and I'll do what I can to help you. That was my last train till 1:30. I'll come with you as far as the gates. It will save you losing the way, and perhaps a bit of time getting through the drifts beside."

Gerald thanked him heartily, and side by side they turned their backs to the lights of the little station, and struck into the lonely road which lay between the railway and the haunted house. It had ceased snowing now. A few stars gleamed out between the rifts in the cloudy sky. From time to time a pale moon showed her face, now flooding the white landscape with a cold grey light, now hiding herself in a veil of fleecy vapour, as though she feared to see those things which should be done on the earth. By the help of the stationmaster's lantern the two men managed to keep to the narrow cart tract. The road was desperately bad. In places the snow was fully two feet deep. With the rising moon a keen wind had got up, which came sweeping over the level fields right in their faces, and cut like a knife. At the turning into the village where the land sloped a little, the drifts were almost impassable. At every step they sank above the knee. Harrison could hear his companion's breath coming thick and short. He was evidently getting done. For himself he was impervious to all outward discomfort. Cold, fatigue, hunger; he was vaguely conscious that he should know them all, if he were not past feeling now. His whole mind, will, nerve, aye, his very being, were centred in the one intense determination to save his friend. At length they gained the main street of the village. Here the snow was trodden down, and the going comparatively easy. Hardly a light was to be seen in any of the cottages. Involuntarily Gerald's eyes turned towards the rectory. It was wrapped in shadow and silence; but from the old grey tower, looming up behind, gleamed a small point of yellow light. Slowly it crept from window to window, steadily rising, rising. A cold shudder ran through the man who watched it. He knew what it meant; that the last sands were falling from the hour-glass of time; that the life of the old year must now be measured by minutes. The ringers were going up to the belfry.

"Oh, God!" he groaned inwardly, "give me strength, give me time."

"Have you got a drop of brandy about you, sir?" suggested the practical Miles. "It would help to keep the spirit in us a bit."

Without slackening his pace, Gerald held out his flask.

"A'ter you, sir, a'ter you."

"I don't want any, thanks." His ears were strained for the first stroke of that ominous bell.

"Oh, come now, sir, fair do's. You will need your strength more than me, and I say a'ter you."

To save discussion, Harrison put the flask to his lips. The spirit sent a warm glow through his sluggish veins. At the same moment the stillness of the night was broken by the solemn tolling of the passing bell. With a cry of horror he thrust the brandy into his companion's hands, and began to run as if for his life. Immediately before him the road curved sharply to the left, and far ahead through the skeleton branches of the leafless elms gleamed half a dozen irregular patches of light. They shone from the windows of the Hall.

Slowly, mournfully pealed the muffled notes from the belfry. The knell of the old year, dying hard in the chill winter night; the knell of a human soul, who might even now be passing from life and love to the horror of unknown darkness, through the gate of a fearful death. The thought was torture. How he lived through those moments of suspense Harrison never knew. He could not have told how he covered the ground, or when he passed the gates which led up to the house. His brain burned like molten iron, on which the slow, monotonous clang of the bell fell like the strokes of a heavy hammer.

He forgot the stationmaster, plodding along in the rear – forgot everything but that his goal was reached, if only he had not come too late.

The lower windows were closed, but from the chinks in the shutters stole the warm glow of fire and lamp, and as he reached the corner of the house he could catch the sound of approaching voices. Voices, yes! – but what sort of voices? Nearer they came, now swelling louder, now sinking to a whisper, but ever drawing nearer, till he could hear the words repeated in every shade of tone, from malignant exultation to concentrated passion of resolve.

"We shall have him tonight!" they said, with ghastly reiteration. "We shall have him tonight!"

Like a wave of ice-cold air, the horrible sounds passed by him, receded, and died away with an echo of fiendish laughter.

Despite an inexpressible thrill of fear that sent a shudder through his whole frame and nearly raised the hair on his head, Harrison was conscious of a faint hope that all was not over yet. Slowly and more slowly came the tolling of the bell. It was on the verge of midnight.

Suddenly from within the closed windows of the library issued a wild awful cry. The shutters were flung back, as if by magic the casement was thrown open, and the dark shadow of a man crossed the sill.

The moon emerging suddenly from behind a bank of clouds poured down a flood of silvery light on the stone wall, the snow-covered path, and on the figure of Jack Chamberlayne, who, with hands clenched as if in mortal pain, his eyes fixed with an expression of nameless horror on some object, invisible to all but him, was slowly following the ghostly vision along the drive, across the lawn, to—

With a supreme effort Harrison threw off the paralysing numbness which was creeping over him. Instinctively he dashed across the grass and stood between Chamberlayne and the fatal pond. Twelve paces from him his friend was advancing, slowly, unswervingly, like one who walks in his sleep.

"Jack," he shouted, "Jack, it is I, Gerald. Don't you know me?"

There was not a quiver of the tense eyeballs, not a sign that his voice had reached those ears, deaf now to all earthly sounds, but from the open window of the library a man rushed towards them, crying wildly, "Stop him, for God's sake, stop him before it is too late."

Gathering all his strength, Gerald flung himself upon the approaching figure. A frantic struggle ensued, for Chamberlayne was the taller by a head, and was at this moment, moreover, endowed with abnormal strength. It was then that his knowledge of wrestling, acquired during a 'long' spent in the Cumberland dales, stood Harrison in right good stead. He closed with his antagonist, and by a sudden dexterous manoeuvre threw him heavily to the ground, while overhead across the snowy fields the bells rang out their joyous welcome to the glad new year.

"Is he – dead?"

The valet on his knees beside his master's prostrate form had torn open Chamberlayne's vest and shirt, and was feeling for the faint pulsation which tells that the spirit has not yet quitted its earthly tenement.

"Fainted, I think; I can feel his heart beat."

"Thank God, sir, you came when you did. I should have been too late. Can you help me to carry him, Mr. Harrison? No, not to that d—d place!" as Gerald glanced involuntarily towards the lighted windows. "They are all up at the gardener's cottage. I wanted Mr. Chamberlayne to sleep there tonight; but you know what he is – told me to go myself if I was frightened. I had not been out of the room five minutes when I heard that awful cry, and – Holy Virgin! What is that?"

Harrison turned instinctively towards the library window. From the open sash a long tongue of yellow flame leaped out, curling round the edge of the curtain and licking up the thick silk cording as though it were a mere thread. Then another, and another. Fanned by the fresh breeze from without, the yellow glare broadened and deepened till the whole room was filled with a fierce lurid glow, succeeded by dense clouds of smoke and an ominous crackling sound.

"The place is on fire!" cried Gerald. "There is not a moment to lose. We must get your master into shelter and give the alarm!"

"Holy St. Patrick, defend us!" murmured Curtis, hastily crossing himself, as he stooped to raise the helpless form of poor Chamberlayne. Then, as best they could, the two men carried their burden across the lawn, along the drive, and up the side path leading to the fruit-gardens.

"Who is in the house?" gasped Harrison, as, staggering and breathless, they reached the door of the cottage. "Are any servants there?"

"Not a soul. Mrs. Bamfield here came in the day. She left directly dinner was served. There is no one in the place to burn but the devil's spawn as lighted it."

The valet's resonant knocks soon brought the gardener to the door, and while his wife was helping Curtis to restore his master to consciousness, Bamfield hurried Gerald off to the village to obtain assistance.

Just outside the gates they encountered the stationmaster, who was hanging about in great distress of mind, too anxious on Harrison's account to return to Mallowby, yet not daring to adventure himself within the fatal precincts of the Hall. His relief and joy at finding Gerald still alive knew no bounds, and he readily undertook to see a messenger despatched for the nearest doctor on his way back to the station. Meanwhile an alarm had been raised, and the sleeping village was raised by the hoarse cries of "Fire!" The ringers had been the first to see the red glare through the trees; but before long some forty men had turned out to join the little crowd already assembled before the burning house. Under Harrison's direction a body of labourers, headed by the gardener and bailiff, made an attempt to check the progress of the flames. But their efforts were scarcely perceptible. With a sharp wind blowing, and no better appliances at command than a line of buckets and a couple of garden-hose, it was evident from the first that the Hall was practically doomed. The old oak, of which the interior was chiefly built, burned like tinder. Within twenty minutes of the first outbreak the flames had spread to the upper storey. Window after window lent its aid to that weird illumination. The great carved bedsteads, the massive presses and cabinets glowed and crackled in the fierce heat. Deverel after Deverel, clothed in dainty satin or shining armour, shrivelled and cracked away from their frames, to go down calm and unflinching as became true knights and brave gentlewomen into that burning fiery furnace. Still the fire-fiend raged on, vast clouds of black smoke mingling with the glare, while from time to time could be heard the heavy crash of falling beams and flooring. As the clock of the old church chimed the first hour of the new year, with a sound like the roll of distant artillery, swelling gradually into a deafening roar, the roof fell in and there shot up to heaven one mighty sheet of flame, which turned the sky into a crimson pall, and lighted up the snow-clad country for miles around. Was it a trick of over-heated imagination, a play of superstitious fancy, or did those who stood by at that moment really hear that hideous peal of shrill triumphant laughter, which made the stoutest heart among them quail, and forced each man to edge involuntarily nearer his neighbour? It lasted but for an instant, then nothing was audible but the continuous roar of the flames. Before the pale dawn had warmed into the red flush of sunrise, Ravenshill Hall was a heap of smouldering ashes enclosed in four grim, smoke-blackened walls. From attic to cellar not a corner had been spared. The fire had done its work thoroughly, and of the original structure nothing remained save the bare tottering shell.

"It wer' th' Lord's will," said old Dawson, who had come down to inspect the scene of the late catastrophe, "that Katharine Deverel should hev her reets; and now as He's proved as mon caan't go agin' Him, He's maade awa' wi' th' dommed ould plaace, an' a good riddance too. The Lord avenges the widder and the feytherless, though He keeps 'un waitin' a bit first soomtoimes, and it seams to me," concluded the farmer, thoughtfully, "as soom o' they poor bodies in Oireland should be hevin' theer turn afore long."

"It will be a bad look-out for the Moonlighters when they do," answered Harrison, with a quiet smile.

He was a little oppressed by the situation in which he found himself; for the events of that New Year's Eve were the talk of the countryside, and Gerald the hero of the hour. A man who, single-handed, had braved the Deverel ghosts and baulked them of their prey ranked, by the Mallowby standard, above Gordon, and only a little lower than Nelson. The worthy Miles was never tired of recounting the incidents of that midnight walk, and drew upon his imagination for certain effective touches to that part of the adventure to which he had not been an eye-witness.

The rustic mind is slow to receive a new impression; but when it does get a sensation, it makes the most of it. The people would listen to the story twenty times a day. They repeated it to each other; they turned it inside and out and discussed it threadbare, beginning it over again for the benefit of every fresh comer. To Gerald, who was heartily sick of the place and the subject, this lionising was inexpressibly irritating, and he was thankful when the doctor at last gave permission for Chamberlayne to be removed.

Thanks to his splendid constitution, backed up by the devoted nursing of Curtis and his friend, Jack escaped brain fever; but he had received a terrible shock, and his nerves were sorely shaken. It was not till the snow-wreaths had melted on the Creamshire Wolds, and crocuses were showing their gold and purple heads above the dark earth in suburban gardens, that Harrison was called upon to officiate as best man at a very pretty wedding in a certain fashionable London church, after which ceremony Mr. and Mrs. Jack Chamberlayne went off to the Riviera, where it was hoped that southern sunshine and a little judicious excitement at Monte Carlo would efface from the bridegroom's memory the experiences of that terrible New Year's Eve.

Of what he had actually seen and heard in the awful interval between his servant's departure and his subsequent return to consciousness Chamberlayne never speaks.

"I used to wonder," he once said to Gerald, "why Lazarus and those other fellows who were raised from the dead never told what they did and how they felt. I think I understand now. It was too terrible. They could not put it into words, and that is how I feel about that night – as if I had been brought back from the dead."

I Exist

Lyndsay E. Gilbert

"CHARLOTTE, darling. Today we will welcome my new wife into our home." Father dabs his thin lips and ink black beard on a kerchief. In the morning light his hair is so black it sports a sheen of odd blue. He holds up his mug for a refill of coffee. "She will rejuvenate this place, she's a breeze of summer I have captured and enslaved."

"Glad tidings indeed, Papa," I say, stabbing the too-cold butter into my toast. "Again."

He sneers but does not quarrel with me. "Be ready to receive her at noon."

"As you wish," I say, and take a bite of my toast. The thick lump of butter melts on my hot tongue and helps me swallow down all words of anger.

Father pushes back his chair and leaves the room.

I smash my plate upon the floor.

* * *

My Father's house is a nightmare by day and a hell by night. Why this distinction? In the day the light of the sun stirs motes of dust to dance in the halls. And I stand at open shutters thinking I might wake. But night falls and though I stand at the shutters still, the light soon leaps around me like flame and my body burns with the desire to escape. But this is not simply a bad dream, nor even purgatory, where time is coinage paying all my debt – this is hell and hell is eternal.

I exist.

I know this because at times I wreak havoc. I pull down the paintings of debaucheries and devils that adorn every wall in the house. I shred my silken gowns. I set alight my heavy bedsheets. I shriek like a bansidhe through the darkest, hidden passageways.

I exist.

I know this because I feel the bite of the whip on my exposed back and the reluctant huffing and puffing of Hadrian, my Father's manservant as he delivers my punishments. And oh, that is a delicious pain I savour.

I no longer attempt escape – I am twenty years of age and have grown bored of concocting plans that come to nothing. I will not take my own life for in truth I tell you – *I exist* – and I will continue to exist beyond common death.

This I know by *long* experience. There are many forms of existence, and this one that pumps my salty blood through my veins is the one I choose to cling to.

* * *

She is not beautiful in the way his previous wives have been. Her features are sharp, aquiline, handsome. There is a depth to her gaze that amounts to more than the scions of innocence or vanity or terror that have been paraded into this house before.

My Father's wives are always younger than me now. I feel a little twinge in my innards, some misguided urge to protect them, but I easily tire of it.

"This is Diana," Father says, and I give a shallow curtsey.

She returns in kind. "A pleasure to meet you." But her tone says it is a curse to meet me. She cannot know, but she certainly can feel it. Diana, mistress of the hunt. I see it easily: this woman, a goddess of the wild, raven hair unkempt, bow drawn, arrow ready to fly.

But what will be her mark?

* * *

Diana is given the keys. Diana is given permission to explore. Diana is given *the warning*. And then Father takes his leave and rides away in the night, so urgent is his ungodly business.

"What a delight," she marvels over breakfast the next morning. "I get to be mistress and have no master to please for a time." She turns her face to the window as though expecting Father's coach to come thundering back. Her hooked nose and crooked lips make me think again of a bird, of a predator. She has nothing of victimhood about her.

"Will I help you to explore?" I ask.

Her gaze snaps to me, intense. She is younger and yet it seems like I am caught in the sight of an ancient crone, exposed to centuries of wisdom. "What happened to your mother?" she asks.

So blunt, rude, unexpected. It thrills me.

"I killed her on the way out," I answer. "And Father has been so dreadfully unlucky with women since."

"Perhaps you rather like that? Being the lady of the house?" She arches one heavy brow.

I sip my tea, lean back in my chair. "I welcome the woman who can finally lift the burden from my shoulders."

She smiles. "Well then, I welcome your tour around my new abode." She picks up the heavy keys by the one that is forbidden and jangles them. "This is low hanging fruit, no? Do you know what is hidden?"

It is my turn to raise an eyebrow.

* * *

I tell you there are many types of existence, and I ponder what to show Diana as we make our way through each wing of the house. She enjoys the classical scenes of orgies and of war, the paintings I have tried to destroy, the frescos of nymphs being set upon by lustful mortal men. She runs her hand along these, over the carved marble, lingering a second too long on the wood spirits' breasts. My cheeks flood with heat and she looks at me until I squirm, unable to break our locked gazes as my heartbeat skitters like a spooked gazelle.

In the music room she plays the harp as beautifully as she is playing me, and she does not seem afraid when she draws her hands away from the strings to find them coated in old flecks of blood.

"The writing on the wall is telling me the key leads to my death, no?"

I walk into the corridor and she follows. The South Wing always seems unnaturally dark. I was born here, but I hurry past my long-abandoned nursery. "Let us take a turn about the grounds," I say.

She does not protest, and I lead her through the servant quarters and out of their unassuming entrance. Autumn is queen, and her domain smells of overripe fruits and sweet rot. We walk through a sea of dead leaves in among the trees. Soon we are deep enough that I might run off and leave her lost. There is little of daylight left. But she is Diana. She could track me down and fell me with her arrow.

As if she knows my wicked thoughts of abandonment, she grasps my shoulder and pushes me hard against the sturdy trunk of a towering great oak. And then her body is flush against mine, her hands are in my hair, her lips on mine, biting down, a laughing breath ghosts into my mouth followed by her tongue.

When she draws away I lick the iron tang of blood off my swollen bottom lip. She steps aside and I am free to make a choice – run in shame, attack in anger. But I am neither angry nor ashamed. I have been so sure that I existed. But I have not *lived* until this moment.

I feel a strange sharpness at my back, and I turn. There on the tree trunk is something I have never seen before. A carving of a woman, an old, old, woman with sagging breasts and missing teeth as she leers out at me, naked, her legs spread, her fingers prying apart her nether regions, exposed like a black cave, or a second mouth that yearns to swallow me.

"That's Sheela Na Gig," Diana says. "A goddess of death and rebirth."

* * *

I lie in bed, but I cannot sleep. I live in that kiss and I know I cannot allow Diana to die.

* * *

I come to her room as dawn breaks and I pull her out of bed. Still in our nightdresses we are like two spirits as we traverse the hallways.

"This is mysterious," Diana says, though she stifles a yawn. "I would rather we breakfasted first though."

I take her to the West Wing, push aside a portrait of my dear departed grandfather and lead her down the steep stone steps, dank and miserable. There is an ancient door at the bottom.

"We didn't bring the keys," Diana says, and she sounds awake now, curious.

"You don't need keys. This is not the forbidden door, but it is its twin."

"Such riddles," she scoffs.

I take her hands in mine. "Do you believe in ghosts?"

She shakes her head. "Not in the traditional sense."

I sigh. "You must not go three paces into the room."

She frowns. "You and your Father do love your little caveats."

I hold my head high and meet her gaze solemnly.

She nods slowly, once.

I unhook the rusty latch and the door swings inward. I take two paces into the room and Diana joins me.

The room is large and holds a banquet of rotting food. It is a lady's salon, and the room teems with ladies, though none of them are alive. They exist. Luminous beings, but there is nothing angelic in their light. Instead they are like corpses, hollowed out and lit from within by a single flickering candle.

Diana holds her breath and I am glad she too can see them. Crawling on the floor is Lady Isabella, her face is waxen and she feels with her hands, ever searching for her eyes, unaware that she is dead. Lady Enna holds court at her table and her neck smiles wider than her lips. A selected group of women play at cards there, betting on pieces of flesh they have kept from my Father's regular sacrifices to them.

Diana sways. I grip her hand. "Not another step," I remind her. Three steps and you are fodder. Three steps and they will fall on your body with all their bloody fury and feast.

"These are my predecessors?" Diana asks.

"Yes." I swallow, unable to look away as Lady Eliza fits her scalp and hair back onto her skull like a French wig, only to sob mournfully as it slides away again, the sound slick and wet. Diana is Eliza's replacement. And there are women too old for me to remember, though I sometimes come here and stare at each wan face, praying I will see my own features there, for one of these surely is my Mother.

"Let's go," Diana says. Her hand is slippery in mine. When we reach the top of the stairs and go back into the hall she retches up bile. "Monstrous."

"But at least they stay in that room," I say, a strange, forced cheerfulness in my tone.

* * *

We spend the day planning an escape. I am grateful that she does not ask me if I ever showed the previous girls that hideous parlour. I showed one or two and they saw nothing, believing me mad.

"He will not kill you unless you look in the forbidden room," I say, knowing our plans are likely to be futile. "So do not look and you may live."

"And bear a man's child while I long for his daughter? It's preposterous."

I swallow. There are worse things, I think. But I say nothing.

Come nightfall I lie in bed, unable to rest my mind or my body. I am twisted in my sheets when the room begins to smell of Autumn, of that sweet decay, a heady perfume. Perhaps a servant left my window open. I sit up.

Terror freezes me as sure as an icy wind. There is a woman in my room. She is dressed in drab grey but still she has the candle glow of the other ghosts.

But at least they stay in that room.

My own words echo around me. I have not seen this ghost before. She steps forward, but it is more a stuttering stumble. She moves like a stiff marionette left too long in the attic, or one whose strings are pulled by some child in the throes of a fit.

I still cannot move but I know I am crying. My tears run salty over my lips and into my mouth. Her gown is black with blood between her legs. She stops but three feet from my bedside and then her upper body falls slack in a sudden bow. But then I see she is reaching down with her long white fingers, grasping the blood stiff hem of her gown, she begins to pull it up, exposing her skinny, stained legs, up and up, her thighs white as moonlight.

Up. God, no. I cannot look away. A baby's head, then its whole body slithers out of her. She takes it in her arms, and then cranes her neck like a curious bird. She opens her mouth, wide, so wide. Her eyes are almost white with fear.

Now I wake, her scream, my own scream. It was just a dream. Just an awful dream.

Daylight brightens the room and I take deep gulps of air, willing myself to be calm. I throw back my sheets and stand. There's something wet. Reluctant, I look down. There is blood at my feet, a pool of it, and footsteps, leading surely back to the corner of the room.

* * *

Diana continues with our plan to flee by nightfall. I sit at the table with her, but I do not hear what she says. Instead I stare at the corner of the dining room where the ghost sits in her blood, her legs wide, trying to cram the baby back inside her. I can see the baby is crying out by its open mouth and tiny screwed-up face.

I feel I will stand up and try to take it from her, but before I can it disappears. She remains, following me from room to room throughout the day. Now she holds herself apart, Sheela Na Gig. She's making a cave of herself, grinning all the while.

I know this is my Mother.

The cavern grows wider, wider and she, like some skeleton spider, grows until she's bracing herself against the walls. This is my Mother and she wants me back inside her. An image of the forbidden door blazes white in all the blackness.

"Charlotte!" Diana slaps my face and I cry out, falling from the couch and balling myself up at her feet.

"What's wrong with you?" She follows my gaze to the corner but sees nothing for she looks back at me in confusion. She reaches down and touches my forehead. "You have a fever."

I want to tell her that we are not alone here, but the words stick in my throat. "We need to get out of here, but first I must discover the truth." This I am able to say. "You must give me the keys. *I* will unlock the forbidden door and look inside. *You* will stay away. He never forbade me to go there."

I tremble as she helps me to my feet. "You seem in no fit state to be unravelling horrors."

I refuse to look at my spider Mother, though she appears in every hallway, every room, every tiny passage. Looming large. Larger. I do not believe in gods and still I cross myself.

"We will take a single horse between us," Diana says as we walk to her bedroom. "And we will ride like hell out of this place before your Father returns."

I nod, let her believe it. I wonder if my Father will slaughter me instead for opening the forbidden door and then lock Diana up for an attempt at fleeing him. She puts the keys in my hands, and they don't feel like cold, heavy iron.

They feel to me like trust and love.

* * *

I would know the way to this door even stripped of all my senses. I have spent days and nights with my back pressed against it, straining to hear a word, any sound at all. There were months when I lay outside and refused to leave, not washing, barely eating, believing that within there was the key to *not* existing. I veer dangerously between two states – wanting to exist and wanting absolute extinction, so complete that even my bone dust will dissolve into nothingness.

Such drama. I feel I have been my Father's aid since I ceased to warn the servants of the hungry ghosts. Since I ceased to warn the wives of this forsaken room. So important to my Father. So precious.

I insert the key and it turns with a delicate, harmless click. This door swings outward. I stand on the threshold and feel true emptiness. I am hollow and hungry. My eyes devour the mountain of bodies. These are not ghosts, but they *are* the corpses of the ghosts in the parlour. There is only one ghost in this room, and she sits in her pool of birthing blood eating Lady Isabella's scalp. It is cupped in her hands and she licks and sucks, bites and tears. All the while her eyes are on me.

I understand now. This is a love story. He feeds her the youth and curiosity of his brides to stop her moving on, and he feeds those sacrificed ghosts out of some strange guilt or twisted delight. It is a love story that I warped from her womb.

Still I know that I must feed the wives the remains of their own corpses now, and if that does not set them free, I know not how to help them. I will be gone by morning with my own love.

My Mother does not attack me when I enter the room. She does not stop me as I begin my gruesome excavation. The servants do not help me, but they do not stop me either, as I drag the bodies through the hallways and take them to the parlour.

One by one the ghosts go out, their inner candles snuffed out by my heaving, gasping breaths. And in the empty silence there is a sense of peace.

* * *

I do not find Mother's body but when I return to lock the door her ghost is gone. Night has fallen. A wind rises up and moves through the trees outside like laughter, or is it crying? I stink of death and sweat and guilt, but I remember Diana's plan.

I am still in my nightdress, but I throw open the front doors and see her there astride a tall, black mare. Her raven hair streams behind her. She is magnificent. She holds out one hand and helps me into the saddle. I press myself to her back. We must ride the path between the trees.

Mother staggers out from their shelter. Diana sees her now. She pulls the reins to slow our steed.

"No!" I cry. "Ride. Hard."

Diana does not question me. She tenses and goads the mare to a gallop. Mother is growing large again, and with each blink she closes in. With each breath she lifts her dress higher. But then, suddenly, she sits, and again, she pries herself apart.

I used to envy Persephone. Her mother Demeter did not give up on her, could not abandon her. But now I see Diana is my Hades. She spirits me away. My Mother's cave is now just expanding darkness. Vast and inescapable. It is the non-existence I craved all those times I lay at her door, some inner-knowing that told me she was on the other side.

But I am not a daughter now. I am myself. A creature made up of trauma, with blood on my hands and silence on my lips like poison. My Mother's ghost would never hunger again if only I turned back, but I will not. I cannot.

On we ride. I trust Diana's plans for where we are headed for I have known nothing beyond the gates of my Father's estate. Those gates lie open, a fake message from Father, willing the servants to expect him.

But then, his carriage hurtles toward us.

The darkness touches my back, I feel sorrow, thick nails sinking into my shoulders. She will get us before Father does. He has not seen us in the dark as we failed to see him at first, his carriage is sleek and black as our mare.

We pass each other, everything seems to slow to a series of still pictures.

He disappears into the abyss.

The dark is gone. I know my back is bleeding but my Mother's claws have vanished. I look behind and see only the pathway to the Manor House lit like a white ribbon by the thin crescent moon.

I press my body closer to Diana's and I feel her wild laughter reverberating through me.

Consorting with Filth

Lisa L. Hannett

THE GHOSTS are taking up too much space.

Plodding on blue-black feet, they clog roadways, airports, boardwalks. Day and night, they colonise buses, trains, trams; their haggard, translucent figures slumping on stained plastic benches, forcing the living to stand. They occupy taxis, whole families cramming into front seats. Ferries and fishing boats sit low in the water, decks weighed down by these drifters. Always arriving, more and more each day, never *leaving*.

They don't float – the burden of death has made them heavy – but they *can* swim. Herding spectres off gangplanks is futile. For a while southern seas bob with countless dead buoys that simply wash back in with the tide.

Inevitably, they migrate from this country's great unbroken shore and begin to appear inland. Skin the hue of deep bruises, arms lank by their sides, the ghosts limp from countryside to city. Avoiding farms with livestock, but sighing through quiet fields of Shiraz grapes, hops, and wheat, leaving much of the year's harvest blighted in their wake. After spoiling farmers' markets with their presence, they progress from factories to warehouses, churches to malls, waiting-rooms to welfare queues. They stop unpredictably, congregating in hotels, convenience stores, cafés. Reeking like night-shift workers – grease traps and cumin, unwashed scalp, cold lard – they suffocate banks and surgeries, the congealed air of their bodies as unbreathable as mud.

They're *everywhere*, now. Caravan parks and high-rises, petrol stations and bottle shops, the public playground down the road. They're in Ellie's suburb, even. On her street.

Ellie's mom refuses to believe some sort of heavenly war has kept the ghosts from staying where they belong. *For years these spirits have scuttled unseen*, she says. *Multiplying like cockroaches. Gathering strength. Waiting to overwhelm by sheer numbers.*

Ellie's dad says he's never seen ghouls like these. *More aimless than usual*, he comments. *More desperate.*

They're relentless, Ken, replies her mother, stabbing a knitting needle at the Channel Nine news. Her tone is fervent, almost incredulous, as if these parasites weren't the reason she deserted the overrun Northern Hemisphere and moved down here over a decade ago, soon before Ellie was born. There's no way she'd left her friends and family just because she'd fallen in love with Ellie's dad – Joy Mitchell is far from romantic. No, it was the abundance of sheep in this country that *really* drew her so far south. The hope of safety, of protection, in all that roaming fleece.

Trust me: the filthy things are trying to take over. Gaze fixed on the flat screen, Ellie's mom swaps a white skein of wool for a black and starts on another stripe. As the headlines unscroll, the scarf grows steadily longer. Between rows, she glances at Ken and gives her work a proud pat. *Thank Christ for good barriers*, she says.

Boundaries mean little to the dead, as far as Ellie can tell. If they want, ghosts can undermine walls, fences, borders. They completely ignore the 'Keep Out!' sign on her bedroom door. They slip in when she's not around, and sometimes when she is. They stand half in and half out of her wardrobe, so she can't get at her pyjamas or her clean school uniforms. They sit at the desk and muck up her homework. They lie down next to her in bed.

Their cold damp touch soothes the hot rash ever-blooming on her skin.

* * *

Last time, the ghost must've followed Ellie home after ballet.

After weeks of begging, Joy had finally relented: Ellie had been allowed to walk the two blocks between the dance studio and their unit on her own. She had taken every precaution, following her mom's instructions to the letter. She'd avoided overgrown bushes along the footpath, and bus stops, and parked cars. When the road was clear, she'd trotted right down the middle, buying herself precious seconds to escape should any strangers come flitting out of the shrubs. In one fist, she'd clutched the house keys like knuckledusters, metal prongs spiking between her small fingers; in the other, her thumb hovered over the 'Send' button on Joy's mobile phone, emergency services pre-dialled. She'd kept her head down, made no eye contact. She'd definitely spoken to no one.

Even so.

After unlatching the front door, she'd paused on the threshold to yank off the beanie and shawl Joy had made her wear – even though it was forty-odd degrees out and, as Ellie's dad would say, dry as a witch's tit. Standing on the crocheted welcome mat, fine brown hair tangled with sweat, a puff of cool air had breezed past her into the house. Maybe that's when the ghost had gotten in? Ellie still isn't sure. Might've been when she'd opened her bedroom window – it hadn't yet been nailed shut – to get some relief. Or when she'd been distracted, peeling off the mohair tights and leotard Joy had handwoven? When she'd been too busy scratching, scratching, scratching the hives erupting wherever wool had made contact with skin?

Ellie doesn't know.

That shade was taller than most of the others she'd seen. A woman, she'd thought, though with the haze all wraiths wore – oily black shrouds dripping from head to toe – it was damn near impossible to tell them apart. *Each one is vicious as the next*, or so she'd overheard the ladies in Joy's knitting circle say. But Ellie sensed curves beneath the spectral fabric, a matronly figure. It had tiptoed quite gracefully across her bedroom, inching closer and closer. Beneath its stink, there was a whiff of something comforting, something familiar. Lavender, maybe, or rosewater. Perfumed like the heart-shaped soaps in her gran's loo.

When the head had turned in Ellie's direction, she'd felt its glance brush her face. Gentle and papery, its tender palm cooled her rash-fevered brow.

The thing hadn't *seemed* all that evil.

Ellie's mother disagreed.

Within minutes of coming in with the shopping, baskets overflowing with discount yarn, Joy had hollered for Ellie to *Run, now, get the bins!* Voice shrill, her accent always more pronounced with anger. Standing there in her undies, Ellie had hesitated.

"But *Mom*," she'd begun, emphasising the 'o', trying to prove, in whatever small and spontaneous way, that she was just like Joy, really, she said 'mom' instead of 'mum', 'trunk' instead of 'boot', 'garbage' instead of 'rubbish' – and she wasn't garbage, she was her *child*, she wasn't spook-touched, she wasn't dirty garbage…

Go!

Indifferent, the ghost had watched Ellie manoeuvre two extra-large black disposal units into the room, bumping into the doorframe, snagging the wheels on her shagpile rug. Joy shouted orders as she moved from garage to kitchen, drawers clattering open and shut, directing Ellie as if this was the first time she'd hauled in the bins. Both were moulded from industrial plastic, lids secured with stainless steel padlocks. The first went into the corner, wedged between the wardrobe and desk; the other was positioned near the door for easy removal. As one, Ellie and the intruder baulked when Joy returned, dragging two tight-weaved, top-grade, angora body bags.

This one's yours, Joy snapped, swiftly unlocking the trash cans, then shoving Ellie away from the ghost. The wool sack was rough as twine, filaments bristling like nettles from every grey inch. It stung her hands as she lined the corner bin, instantly raising welts along her chest and forearms as she leaned over, smoothing the bag down. Behind her, furious grunting and slapping and scuffling, inhuman shrieks. Grave-fabric tearing. Huffing and puffing. A pong of rank spice and sweat and bogwater. A gasp of talc and lavender.

Get in! Ellie's mother snarled through gritted teeth. *Get in!*

And as Joy wrestled the phantom into its wool-bound prison, Ellie climbed into hers.

* * *

The local knitting circle is full of biddies and crackpots, Ellie's dad thinks, though he rarely says so aloud. He might roll his eyes while Joy downloads patterns – nets and carpets and bags of all sizes, jumpsuits and hoods and full-body sheaths, tents big enough to cover a yacht – and he might mutter over his beer on Saturday afternoons when his wife passes the printouts around. He might turn up the TV to drown out the ladies nattering about trash removal schedules and government sanctioned dumps. He might even threaten to take Joy's credit card if she keeps pouring his wages into the till at *Three Bags Full*.

Almost within the same breath, he'll don the cable-knit sweaters she churns out. He'll wear oversized mufflers and button-up vests over his work shirts, and that ugly yellow deerhunter cap. He'll hang every last curtain the knitters produce, bulk-blocking the whole cul-de-sac's windows and doors. He'll kiss Joy's powdered cheek, call her a loveable nutter, and pinch her flat bottom. He'll buy her a better tablet with faster internet and help her access the best knitting sites. He'll say his ute could use a set of seat and steering-wheel covers.

He'll turn a blind eye.

Whatever it takes to keep his place happily quiet.

* * *

Last time, after making a stop at the local dump, Ken had enjoyed a weekend of fishing while Ellie had spent hers locked in wool.

Jammed in the corner, the bin wouldn't roll or tip no matter how much Ellie wriggled inside it. In less than an hour – which had felt like much, much longer – her thighs had seized, calves twitched with cramps, hamstrings screamed to be straightened. Pressing her back against the container's wool-roughened sides, she flexed and relaxed her muscles. She jammed her feet *down*, shoved her shoulders *up*. She *pushed*.

The plastic creaked, thundered, but didn't give. Frustrated, she cried herself head-pounding and sweaty. The air was stifling, rancid: a mix of rubber, rotten eggs, and the piss she couldn't hold in. Her stomach was sour with hunger and worry. If only Joy would respond when she called. If only she'd listen. Then Ellie could *explain*, and her mother would understand – she hadn't done it on purpose, this time it was an accident – and Joy would see she wasn't a liar, she'd see she wasn't *befouled*, that she wasn't garbage, and she'd let her out, and everything would be fine, and Ellie wouldn't hold a grudge, she'd promise to be good, *if only she could get out.*

She wept her throat raw, pounded her knuckles bloody, but got no reply.

Exhausted, she dozed, neck painfully kinked, limbs tingling then going dead.

Two days later, Ellie emerged covered in violent sores. The wool lining had scalded her exposed skin. From face to feet, she sprouted clusters of itching red agony that kept her from school for a week.

Chicken pox, Joy had told Ellie's teachers over the phone. *She'll be right in no time.*

Blubbering quietly in a calamine bath, Ellie came up with her own diagnosis. She'd never fully feel better, she thought, since she seemed to be part ghost.

* * *

This latest drifter is about Ellie's size: same sharp elbows, same bowed thighs, same scrawny ribcage. From the way it sits, splay-legged and slouching at the foot of her bed, she reckons he's a boy. The swamp smell is faint around him – she hardly noticed it upon entering her room – and he's much less solid than the others. Light from a bare bulb on the ceiling seeps through his shroud, limning a prominent nose, weak jaw, protruding collarbone. From certain angles, Ellie can see right through him. The merino patchwork of her quilt is visible through his narrow hips and butt. The simple headboard shoots through his back like a yoke. Her flat pillow bisects his concave gut.

"You okay?" she whispers, edging towards the footboard. Moving carefully, doing her best not to generate any static. Head cocked, Ellie looks at her closed door, listens. In the living room, her dad heckles the buffoons hosting some popular footy program. The show's laugh track peters into an ad for rust-proof fences while Joy calls out from the kitchen, offering Ken a cup of tea. She hears the kettle clanking under the faucet. The cupboards opening and closing. Mugs clunking next to the sink. The squeak of her dad's pleather chair reclining.

No floorboards groaning in the hall.

No slippered steps approaching.

"Here," she says to the ghost after a moment, gaze flicking between the bed and door. "Lie down."

The boy shrinks away from the wool coverlet, navy eyes pleading. His mouth flaps, gapes. All that comes out is cold wind.

"Hang on," Ellie says."Stand up a sec."

Forearms and palms stinging, she backhands her pillow to the floor. Strips the coarse blanket and knitted sheets, exposing the mattress: floral cotton blotched with stains, but blessedly smooth. Quickly, she brushes away stray fleece fibres to prevent them both from blistering.

"Lie down," she says again, more forcefully now. "It's okay. Look."

Ellie unzips her hooded sweater, tosses her beret, kicks off the tweed culottes and tights. She slips out of her cashmere singlet, but leaves on the matching knickers. Immediately the boy's arctic breath begins to calm her body's ferocious itching. With a sigh of relief, she wraps her fingers around his clammy wrist. She pauses, listens, glances again at the door. Pulls him down onto the bed beside her.

* * *

Another time, Ellie found a tiny veiled phantom in the toy box at afterhours care. No one else noticed it – or pretended not to – so she climbed in beside it, picked it up. The abandoned little thing felt practically boneless, pliable as a blob of unbaked bread. She swaddled it in the silk handkerchief she'd traded for a week's worth of lunch vouchers at school, stuffed it under her shirt, then hurried to the cloakroom. Her homemade backpack was the perfect size for carrying a baby.

It never cried, never ate, never needed a change.

Still, Joy found it long before the fish fingers had finished frying for dinner.

"For God's sake, Ellie! Why do you *insist* on consorting with such filth? Don't you *care* about your future? Aren't you even the *tiniest* bit concerned?"

When Ellie was released the next morning, she hardly recognised her room. The desk was deprived of its drawers, the wardrobe missing its mirrored doors. On the walls, oily circles marked the spots where Blu-tack once held her favourite posters. Floating white shelves supported nothing but air. There were no colourful ponies with brushable manes. No ballerina music box. No green and gold *Good Effort* ribbons. The snowglobe Gran had given her was also gone, as was the porcelain mouse Aunty Barb had brought from overseas. Ellie's textbooks were stacked on the straight-backed chair, two plain pencils and an eraser on the desk blotter. There was no sign of the knapsack.

* * *

Behind her, the ghost is shivering.

"Get closer," Ellie whispers, schooching her bottom back, seeking the welcome crook of ethereal legs. "I'm warm enough for us both."

The bedsprings whine as the boy shifts, hesitating.

Doubt knots Ellie's throat. She tenses and for a minute imagines getting up, throwing on a nightie and socks, running out into the living room. Hair tousled, eyes wild, as though she'd just woken from a nightmare. She'd pant with feigned fear, make it seem she didn't know where she was, or when. Dragging her feet across the carpet, she'd rush to her mother, hoping to shock. Blue sparks would crackle on her fingertips as she gripped Joy's shoulder, the cardigan conducting energy, disrupting electromagnetic fields, and she'd tell her all about this new drifter, she'd shuffle while she confessed, proving with shock after shock that she was a good girl, that she'd been *fighting* this ghost's energy, armed with wool and static, that she'd been trying to dispel its electricity, that she definitely wasn't harbouring it.

But as the boy snuggles in, Ellie's vision changes. Joy isn't embracing her, she isn't cooing or patting her sweaty head. As the creature presses his chill into her scalding back – glorious relief – dream-Joy turns away, collects her discarded knitting. As he drapes a frigid sleeve across Ellie's inflamed arm, her imaginary mom casts off, then leans back to assess the piece's finish. With an unearthly face now mashed against her skull, Ellie pictures an undersized body bag dangling from sharp wooden needles. Too small for the boy. Too small for her. They'd both have to crouch to fit in it.

The way she imagines it, the sack's weave is ridged with woollen barbed wire.

Get in, says Ellie's made-up mother.

Shaking, Ellie echoes, "Get in."

The world blurs and dims as the shade embraces her, his dank clay limbs quenching her body's fierce heat. Sighing, she relaxes into his humid pressure, muscles slack as he *pushes* into her spine and neck. Into her head.

Near-smothered, Ellie sucks fresh life into her lungs. Soon the cramps in her belly stop twisting. For once, her joints are fluid, not stiff and swollen and grinding. Panic-spiders break the webs they'd spun round her heart, then swiftly tap-dance away. A serene fog settles over her, a blanket of mist and hope. She smiles and stretches to her full length, skin whole and pale and cool.

In the ghost's company, Ellie is more expansive than ever before, more free.

She's more herself.

She's blissfully, completely, alive.

"Knock knock," says Joy, switching on the light as she barges into the room. A new striped scarf pools in her arms, half-spilling onto the floor, tangling as she walks. "Try this on for size, El—"

Ellie blinks once, slowly, and a shriek tears through the soft fog hovering over her. Eyes watering, she squints as the pall fluctuates. The naked bulb is suddenly noon-bright overhead, its light shrill, screeching down onto the bed in a strong northern accent.

"Jesus Christ, Ellie!"

Rough hands force her onto her back. Fists pummel her temples and chest. Plump legs clamp her sides, and *squeeze*. Plaid trousers chafe bare skin as Joy straddles her, struggling, wrangling, failing to fully dislodge the ghost.

Strong fingers dig into Ellie's cheeks, prising the small jaw open.

"Swallow," says her mother, shoving in great mouthfuls of wool, shoving until she gags, *shoving*. "Swallow, my girl! It's for your own good!"

The Cold Earth

Sarah Hans

MY HUSBAND, Tom, killed me on the first of May, angry because I overcooked the meatloaf. It was the last straw for both of us. When he grabbed my hair and slammed my head against the kitchen counter, I thought about how I had known for years this would be my inevitable end.

Nobody survives living with a psychopath.

Tom buried me in the backyard beneath the old oak tree, where we'd shared our first kiss when I was only a blushing girl of seventeen. Even in death, I could still feel his hot breath on my face, his hands skimming my supple young body, the urgency of his erection pressed against my hip, as if it were happening at that very moment. I called out to the younger me, tried to warn her, but she just went right on kissing him.

My grave was cold beneath the oak, under the earth. My flesh melted away and my meat was eaten by worms. The tree's roots tickled my bones, wrapping around me in a woody embrace.

Mama never liked Tom. She wouldn't let us marry, so we eloped against her wishes the day I turned eighteen. Mama refused to speak to me after that. She was never a nice woman, not generous with a smile or a hug or even a kind word, but now I think maybe she did try to protect me, in the end. Maybe she did love me.

She died about a year after we eloped, killed by her two-pack-a-day habit, so we moved into the old farmhouse. It was convenient since Tom had lost his job and we were about to be evicted. He wouldn't let me work to help make ends meet. He said no wife of his would hold a job, like the concept was dirty and repulsive. I thought that was romantic, I thought he wanted to provide for me and take care of me. Wasn't that sweet? I didn't see that he was trying to control me. I didn't understand that he was cutting me off from the rest of the world and keeping me dependent on him. I didn't realize until things got bad.

Without a job, Tom turned to a life of crime. At first, he told me he was working third shift at the sandpaper factory in town. One day at the grocery store, one of the few places I was allowed to go alone, I overheard two women talking about how hard the factory closing was on their families. I confronted Tom about the lie and he hit me for the first time. Just once, on the face, just a slap, but hard enough to leave a handprint for a few days.

I packed my things and went to a friend's place. Tom came after me. He apologized. He brought me flowers. He told me he'd never hit me again. He promised things would be different, better. I was naive and silly and went back to him.

And things were better, for a while. But soon he was bringing suspicious packages home, hiding stolen cars in the barn, filing the serial numbers off firearms in the living room. My protests fell on deaf ears. He kept the only set of car keys. He canceled the phone service. My once-a-week visits to the grocery store were my only opportunity to see other people, and those were closely guarded. I became a prisoner.

I tried walking to town, once, and got picked up by a couple of Tom's 'colleagues' halfway there. They took me home. Tom locked me in the root cellar for two days in punishment and then made me burn all my shoes. I never tried to run away again.

Those days were full of so much turmoil, so many hot tears, so much fear, so much hatred. Now, below the ground, it's cool and dry and my fear is replaced by the wisdom of the earth, the songs of trees, the whispered secrets of twining roots and digging beetles. Up above, the living scurry and rush, but down here we grow and decay and wait.

I am the worms that devour my flesh, the roots that coil about my bones. I am the cool night breeze and the warm summer soil. I am forgotten and at peace.

But then I hear a voice. A woman's voice. Laughing. I am her, and she is me, flirting with Tom beneath the oak tree. He murmurs something, he smiles. He stands on my grave and seduces her with promises. *I have money, baby girl, I have a whole house.* He can protect her, he can care for her. She's as young as I was when we first met, slim as a willow, breasts like mosquito bites and hip bones jutting into his hands as he touches her, persuading her with caresses and kisses. He's kind and attentive and charming, oh so charming, with that white smile and those blue, blue eyes.

My heart hurts, even though it was devoured by worms months ago. Emotions rush into the empty space that once was me. I have no throat to scream my pain, no lips to make words, but it's too much. I can't watch him do this all over again. The earth groans, the oak tree sways, and a branch tears away from the trunk without warning, crashing to the ground below. Tom dances out of the way and the branch narrowly misses the girl, who squeaks in alarm.

They laugh in relief and he puts his arm about her possessively, protectively, pulling her toward the house. He turns and looks back at the tree as they mount the porch and I see a flicker of recognition in his eyes.

Fear races through me, stinging like that first slap to my cheek. He knows I'm down here. He knows that branch was sent for him. I shrink back into the cool embrace of my grave, trying to will myself into nonexistence. I am dirt and worms and roots now. I am nothing. If I forget myself, then maybe he'll forget me, too.

Days and weeks pass in the darkness beneath the oak tree. Tom forgets about the branch, forgets about me again. The girl moves into the farmhouse with him. I don't want to hear their voices, but I do; even through six feet of soil, I can hear them laughing, making plans, making love. If I had ears, I'd pack them full of dirt, but I don't, so there's no way to block the two of them out. I draw the tree's roots tighter around my skeleton, sinking deeper into the earth, trying to find an end for this nightmare.

Winter comes, and I get some respite. The voices are muffled now that Tom and his new bride spend most of their time indoors and the plants that serve as my eyes and ears doze in hibernation.

I hear my name, *Megan,* and the sound rouses me from slumber. Tom's friends have gathered around a bonfire in the yard, not far from my resting place. *Jessica's a real pretty girl. Don't know how you keep getting women that good looking, Tommy. That Megan was a fine piece of ass, too. Whatever happened to her?*

None of your damn business.

Rage courses through me, cold as ice and hot as a brand. The oak's roots lash beneath me in response. I seek the heat of the fire, pushing at the earth. The men shout as the bonfire bursts apart, embers flying and burning logs rolling out of the fire ring. Someone shrieks, and I can smell the gut-churning stench of searing human flesh. The others tackle him with a blanket and put out the flames. He groans. *My leg, my leg!*

Christ, his jeans are melted to his skin. Someone call 9-1-1!

No! What're you thinking? We got a barn full of hot cars. Drive him to the hospital your damn selves.

They trundle the injured man into a car. I hear the sounds of many car doors slamming, engines revving, and then a fleet of cars and motorcycles drives off the property. Left behind,

Tom curses and shouts, kicking at the smoldering logs and abandoned beer bottles. Jessica tries to calm him, telling him it'll be okay. She convinces him to go back inside and get some sleep.

The cold, blissful silence of winter snaps back into place the next morning and stays that way for another month. Then, the ground thaws. Rain falls instead of snow. Seeds begin to germinate, pushing new life into the soil. Wriggling worms breed in my eye sockets and fresh roots visit my earthy hideaway, humming the cheerful songs of green things growing.

Jessica decides to take up gardening, so Tom brings her seeds and flowers. She kneels in the yard, pulling weeds and hoeing the earth, dropping in seeds and patting the soil over them. She's very tender, very sweet, singing Guns N' Roses love ballads to the sprouting plants and walking barefoot through the grass.

She and Tom get in a fight one night when he pours a bottle of beer over her garden. He locks her out of the house. She curls up on the porch, sobbing, one hand over her throbbing jaw. I remember the sharp pain of a fresh bruise as it blossomed purple across my face. She is me and I am her. She is too tender, too kind, too young for this. It took Tom several years to be this cruel to me, and they've been married for barely one. He'll kill her soon, like he did me, without even meaning to do it. And then her body will join mine, and we'll be together, sisters in death, the roots pressing us into a cool, final caress of bone on bone.

I'm lonely, but not lonely enough to watch Tom murder again.

I can save the girl yet.

The trees sway and rattle. The flowers tremble and whisper. Jessica sits up and looks at her garden.

Jesssssssiiiiiicaaaaaaaaa.

She scrambles to her feet and runs to the door, pounding on it with her fists, shrieking and wailing. Floorboards creak as Tom moves through the house. The door opens and his fist thrusts out, catching her on the cheek, sending her tumbling back to the porch.

Please, Tommy, please don't leave me out here. It's haunted!

He pauses in the open door. *What'd you say?*

She sobs, hysterical, clutching at the porch railing as if it's a lifeline. *There's a ghost. It called my name.*

Tom strides out of the house, across the porch, to the barn. He returns with two shovels, presenting one to Jessica. He leads her to the oak tree and gestures to the place where he buried me. *Dig,* he says.

I should feel afraid. He's coming for me, again, one final time. But as they move the rain-softened soil away from my bones, I welcome them. What can he do to me in death, after all, that is worse than what he did to me in life? The earth is my flesh now, every tree and bush and blade of grass an extension of my ghostly body. I have power in death I did not possess in life.

Are...are those bones?

Keep digging. We need to get the whole skeleton.

Who is this, Tommy? Who did you bury? Is it Megan? Did you kill her?

Stop asking questions and dig, girl, if you don't want to hear no more ghost voices.

No. I won't keep going unless you tell me what happened. Who is this?

Tom raises his fist and lunges toward Jessica. My rage rushes up the oak tree and snaps another of its branches. The branch falls between them, hitting Tom's upraised arm. He bellows in pain.

Jessica scrambles for the edge of the hole while Tom is distracted. The soil is slippery and she's panicking, unable to gain purchase. I command the roots that are my fingers to make a ladder for her. She gasps for a moment, unable to comprehend what she's seeing as the roots intertwine before her very eyes.

Growling, Tom reaches for her again. She squeaks and scales the ladder, kicking away Tom's groping fingers. Tom tries to follow her up the ladder, but the roots retract as soon as Jessica is safe. He slides down the side of the hole and collapses, flailing, onto my skeleton.

The tree branches scratch and scrape together to make the sound of my terrible laughter.

I command the roots to lift me. My corpse slides from beneath Tom, rising up in the air high above him, above the hole in the earth. The moon bathes me in her silvery glow, illuminating my clean-picked bones wrapped in roots, coiled with worms, dropping beetles from above. My grin is white and menacing. The tarp in which Tom buried me trails behind me like a dark veil, fluttering and snapping in the breeze.

Until death do us part, the grasses whisper.

Jessica screams. Tom curses my name. The roots which are my arms reach up and close around him, pulling him down into the cool embrace of the grave.

* * *

Jessica plants hyacinths over my grave so I can enjoy their sweet perfume every spring. She visits the oak often to sit beneath its creaking branches. She talks to me, telling me about the life growing in her belly, the postman she's going to marry, and the family she plans to have so she can fill the farmhouse with laughter and love as it should be.

She teaches her children to swing on a tire swing from the oak's branches. The children dig holes in the earth to whisper their secrets and longings to the oak's roots. I cradle them in my branches and protect them from sudden storms beneath my canopy.

When Jessica's eldest daughter is sixteen, a boy driving a mustang arrives to take her on a date. Jessica walks out to the oak tree to lean against my trunk, pressing her forehead to my rough exterior as she has so many times before.

She wipes tears from her cheeks. *I don't like this boy, Mother Megan. He reminds me of Tommy.*

Tom writhes and gurgles at the sound of his name, but the oak's roots coil more tightly about him, like a constrictor squeezing her prey, until he silences.

I don't like the boy either.

The Story of Mimi-Nashi-Hōïchi

Lafcadio Hearn

MORE THAN seven hundred years ago, at Dan-no-ura, in the Straits of Shimonoséki, was fought the last battle of the long contest between the Heiké, or Taira clan, and the Genji, or Minamoto clan. There the Heiké perished utterly, with their women and children, and their infant emperor likewise – now remembered as Antoku Tennō. And that sea and shore have been haunted for seven hundred years... Elsewhere I told you about the strange crabs found there, called Heiké crabs, which have human faces on their backs, and are said to be the spirits of the Heiké warriors. But there are many strange things to be seen and heard along that coast. On dark nights thousands of ghostly fires hover about the beach, or flit above the waves – pale lights which the fishermen call *Oni-bi*, or demon-fires; and, whenever the winds are up, a sound of great shouting comes from that sea, like a clamor of battle.

In former years the Heiké were much more restless than they now are. They would rise about ships passing in the night, and try to sink them; and at all times they would watch for swimmers, to pull them down. It was in order to appease those dead that the Buddhist temple, Amidaji, was built at Akamagaséki. A cemetery also was made close by, near the beach; and within it were set up monuments inscribed with the names of the drowned emperor and of his great vassals; and Buddhist services were regularly performed there, on behalf of the spirits of them. After the temple had been built, and the tombs erected, the Heiké gave less trouble than before; but they continued to do queer things at intervals, proving that they had not found the perfect peace.

Some centuries ago there lived at Akamagaséki a blind man named Hōïchi, who was famed for his skill in recitation and in playing upon the *biwa*. From childhood he had been trained to recite and to play; and while yet a lad he had surpassed his teachers. As a professional *biwa-hōshi* he became famous chiefly by his recitations of the history of the Heiké and the Genji; and it is said that when he sang the song of the battle of Dan-no-ura 'even the goblins [*kijin*] could not refrain from tears'.

At the outset of his career, Hōïchi was very poor; but he found a good friend to help him. The priest of the Amidaji was fond of poetry and music; and he often invited Hōïchi to the temple, to play and recite. Afterwards, being much impressed by the wonderful skill of the lad, the priest proposed that Hōïchi should make the temple his home; and this offer was gratefully accepted. Hōïchi was given a room in the temple-building; and, in return for food and lodging, he was required only to gratify the priest with a musical performance on certain evenings, when otherwise disengaged.

One summer night the priest was called away, to perform a Buddhist service at the house of a dead parishioner; and he went there with his acolyte, leaving Hōïchi alone in the temple. It was a hot night; and the blind man sought to cool himself on the verandah before his sleeping-room. The verandah overlooked a small garden in the rear of the Amidaji. There Hōïchi waited for the priest's return, and tried to relieve his solitude by practicing upon his *biwa*. Midnight passed; and the priest did not appear. But the atmosphere was still too warm for comfort within doors; and Hōïchi remained outside. At last he heard steps approaching from the back gate. Somebody crossed the garden, advanced to the verandah, and halted directly in front of him – but it was not the priest. A deep voice called the blind man's name – abruptly and unceremoniously, in the manner of a samurai summoning an inferior:

"Hōïchi!"

"*Hai!*" answered the blind man, frightened by the menace in the voice – "I am blind! – I cannot know who calls!"

"There is nothing to fear," the stranger exclaimed, speaking more gently. "I am stopping near this temple, and have been sent to you with a message. My present lord, a person of exceedingly high rank, is now staying in Akamagaséki, with many noble attendants. He wished to view the scene of the battle of Dan-no-ura; and today he visited that place. Having heard of your skill in reciting the story of the battle, he now desires to hear your performance: so you will take your biwa and come with me at once to the house where the august assembly is waiting."

In those times, the order of a samurai was not to be lightly disobeyed. Hōïchi donned his sandals, took his *biwa*, and went away with the stranger, who guided him deftly, but obliged him to walk very fast. The hand that guided was iron; and the clank of the warrior's stride proved him fully armed – probably some palace-guard on duty. Hōïchi's first alarm was over: he began to imagine himself in good luck; for, remembering the retainer's assurance about a 'person of exceedingly high rank', he thought that the lord who wished to hear the recitation could not be less than a daimyo of the first class. Presently the samurai halted; and Hōïchi became aware that they had arrived at a large gateway – and he wondered, for he could not remember any large gate in that part of the town, except the main gate of the Amidaji. "*Kaimon*!" the samurai called, and there was a sound of unbarring; and the twain passed on. They traversed a space of garden, and halted again before some entrance; and the retainer cried in a loud voice, "Within there! I have brought Hōïchi." Then came sounds of feet hurrying, and screens sliding, and rain-doors opening, and voices of women in converse. By the language of the women Hōïchi knew them to be domestics in some noble household; but he could not imagine to what place he had been conducted. Little time was allowed him for conjecture. After he had been helped to mount several stone steps, upon the last of which he was told to leave his sandals, a woman's hand guided him along interminable reaches of polished planking, and round pillared angles too many to remember, and over widths amazing of matted floor, into the middle of some vast apartment. There he thought that many great people were assembled: the sound of the rustling of silk was like the sound of leaves in a forest. He heard also a great humming of voices, talking in undertones; and the speech was the speech of courts.

Hōïchi was told to put himself at ease, and he found a kneeling-cushion ready for him. After having taken his place upon it, and tuned his instrument, the voice of a woman – whom he divined to be the *Rōjo*, or matron in charge of the female service – addressed him, saying:

"It is now required that the history of the Heiké be recited, to the accompaniment of the *biwa*."

Now the entire recital would have required a time of many nights: therefore Hōïchi ventured a question:

"As the whole of the story is not soon told, what portion is it augustly desired that I now recite?"

The woman's voice made answer:

"Recite the story of the battle at Dan-no-ura, for the pity of it is the most deep."

Then Hōïchi lifted up his voice, and chanted the chant of the fight on the bitter sea, wonderfully making his *biwa* to sound like the straining of oars and the rushing of ships, the whirr and the hissing of arrows, the shouting and trampling of men, the crashing of steel upon helmets, the plunging of slain in the flood. And to left and right of him, in the pauses of his playing, he could hear voices murmuring praise: "How marvelous an artist!" – "Never in our own province was playing heard like this!" – "Not in all the empire is there another singer like Hōïchi!" Then fresh courage came to him, and he played and sang yet better than before; and a hush of wonder deepened about him. But when at last he came to tell the fate of the fair and helpless, the piteous perishing of the women and children, and the death-leap of Nii-no-Ama, with the imperial infant in her arms – then all the listeners uttered together one long, long shuddering cry of anguish; and thereafter they wept and wailed so loudly and so wildly that the blind man was frightened by the violence and grief that he had made. For much time the sobbing and the wailing continued. But gradually the sounds of lamentation died away; and again, in the great stillness that followed, Hōïchi heard the voice of the woman whom he supposed to be the *Rōjo*.

She said:

"Although we had been assured that you were a very skillful player upon the *biwa*, and without an equal in recitative, we did not know that anyone could be so skillful as you have proved yourself tonight. Our lord has been pleased to say that he intends to bestow upon you a fitting reward. But he desires that you shall perform before him once every night for the next six nights – after which time he will probably make his august return-journey. Tomorrow night, therefore, you are to come here at the same hour. The retainer who tonight conducted you will be sent for you... There is another matter about which I have been ordered to inform you. It is required that you shall speak to no one of your visits here, during the time of our lord's august sojourn at Akamagaséki. As he is traveling incognito, he commands that no mention of these things be made... You are now free to go back to your temple."

After Hōïchi had duly expressed his thanks, a woman's hand conducted him to the entrance of the house, where the same retainer, who had before guided him, was waiting to take him home. The retainer led him to the verandah at the rear of the temple, and there bade him farewell.

It was almost dawn when Hōïchi returned; but his absence from the temple had not been observed – as the priest, coming back at a very late hour, had supposed him asleep. During the day Hōïchi was able to take some rest; and he said nothing about his strange adventure. In the middle of the following night the samurai again came for him, and led him to the august assembly, where he gave another recitation with the same success that had attended his previous performance. But during this second visit his absence from the temple was accidentally discovered; and after his return in the morning he was summoned to the presence of the priest, who said to him, in a tone of kindly reproach:

"We have been very anxious about you, friend Hōïchi. To go out, blind and alone, at so late an hour, is dangerous. Why did you go without telling us? I could have ordered a servant to accompany you. And where have you been?"

Hōïchi answered, evasively:

"Pardon me, kind friend! I had to attend to some private business; and I could not arrange the matter at any other hour."

The priest was surprised, rather than pained, by Hōïchi's reticence: he felt it to be unnatural, and suspected something wrong. He feared that the blind lad had been bewitched or deluded by some evil spirits. He did not ask any more questions; but he privately instructed the men-servants of the temple to keep watch upon Hōïchi's movements, and to follow him in case that he should again leave the temple after dark.

On the very next night, Hōïchi was seen to leave the temple; and the servants immediately lighted their lanterns, and followed after him. But it was a rainy night, and very dark; and before the temple-folks could get to the roadway, Hōïchi had disappeared. Evidently he had walked very fast – a strange thing, considering his blindness; for the road was in a bad condition. The men hurried through the streets, making inquiries at every house which Hōïchi was accustomed to visit; but nobody could give them any news of him. At last, as they were returning to the temple by way of the shore, they were startled by the sound of a *biwa*, furiously played, in the cemetery of the Amidaji. Except for some ghostly fires – such as usually flitted there on dark nights – all was blackness in that direction. But the men at once hastened to the cemetery; and there, by the help of their lanterns, they discovered Hōïchi, sitting alone in the rain before the memorial tomb of Antoku Tennō, making his *biwa* resound, and loudly chanting the chant of the battle of Dan-no-ura. And behind him, and about him, and everywhere above the tombs, the fires of the dead were burning, like candles. Never before had so great a host of *Oni-bi* appeared in the sight of mortal man...

"Hōïchi San! – Hōïchi San!" the servants cried. "You are bewitched! Hōïchi San!"

But the blind man did not seem to hear. Strenuously he made his *biwa* to rattle and ring and clang; more and more wildly he chanted the chant of the battle of Dan-no-ura. They caught hold of him; they shouted into his ear:

"Hōïchi San! – Hōïchi San! – come home with us at once!"

Reprovingly he spoke to them:

"To interrupt me in such a manner, before this august assembly, will not be tolerated."

Whereat, in spite of the weirdness of the thing, the servants could not help laughing. Sure that he had been bewitched, they now seized him, and pulled him up on his feet, and by main force hurried him back to the temple, where he was immediately relieved of his wet clothes, by order of the priest. Then the priest insisted upon a full explanation of his friend's astonishing behavior.

Hōïchi long hesitated to speak. But at last, finding that his conduct had really alarmed and angered the good priest, he decided to abandon his reserve; and he related everything that had happened from the time of first visit of the samurai.

The priest said:

"Hōïchi, my poor friend, you are now in great danger! How unfortunate that you did not tell me all this before! Your wonderful skill in music has indeed brought you into strange trouble. By this time you must be aware that you have not been visiting any house whatever, but have been passing your nights in the cemetery, among the tombs of the Heiké – and it was before the memorial-tomb of Antoku Tennō that our people tonight found you, sitting in the rain. All that you have been imagining was illusion – except the calling of the dead. By once obeying them, you have put yourself in their power. If you obey them again, after what has already occurred, they will tear you in pieces. But they would have destroyed you, sooner or later, in any event... Now I shall not be able to remain with you tonight: I am called away to perform another service. But, before I go, it will be necessary to protect your body by writing holy texts upon it."

Before sundown the priest and his acolyte stripped Hōïchi: then, with their writing-brushes, they traced upon his breast and back, head and face and neck, limbs and hands and feet – even upon the soles of his feet, and upon all parts of his body – the text of the holy sûtra called *Hannya-Shin-Kyō*. When this had been done, the priest instructed Hōïchi, saying:

"Tonight, as soon as I go away, you must seat yourself on the verandah, and wait. You will be called. But, whatever may happen, do not answer, and do not move. Say nothing and sit still – as if meditating. If you stir, or make any noise, you will be torn asunder. Do not get frightened; and do not think of calling for help – because no help could save you. If you do exactly as I tell you, the danger will pass, and you will have nothing more to fear."

After dark the priest and the acolyte went away; and Hōïchi seated himself on the verandah, according to the instructions given him. He laid his *biwa* on the planking beside him, and, assuming the attitude of meditation, remained quite still – taking care not to cough, or to breathe audibly. For hours he stayed thus.

Then, from the roadway, he heard the steps coming. They passed the gate, crossed the garden, approached the verandah, stopped – directly in front of him.

"Hōïchi!" the deep voice called. But the blind man held his breath, and sat motionless.

"Hōïchi!" grimly called the voice a second time. Then a third time – savagely:

"Hōïchi!"

Hōïchi remained as still as a stone – and the voice grumbled:

"No answer! – that won't do! …Must see where the fellow is…"

There was a noise of heavy feet mounting upon the verandah. The feet approached deliberately, halted beside him. Then, for long minutes – during which Hōïchi felt his whole body shake to the beating of his heart – there was dead silence.

At last the gruff voice muttered close to him:

"Here is the *biwa*; but of the biwa-player I see – only two ears! So that explains why he did not answer: he had no mouth to answer with – there is nothing left of him but his ears… Now to my lord those ears I will take – in proof that the august commands have been obeyed, so far as was possible…"

At that instant Hōïchi felt his ears gripped by fingers of iron, and torn off! Great as the pain was, he gave no cry. The heavy footfalls receded along the verandah, descended into the garden, passed out to the roadway, ceased. From either side of his head, the blind man felt a thick warm trickling; but he dared not lift his hands…

Before sunrise the priest came back. He hastened at once to the verandah in the rear, stepped and slipped upon something clammy, and uttered a cry of horror; for he saw, by the light of his lantern, that the clamminess was blood. But he perceived Hōïchi sitting there, in the attitude of meditation – with the blood still oozing from his wounds.

"My poor Hōïchi!" cried the startled priest. "What is this? You have been hurt?"

At the sound of his friend's voice, the blind man felt safe. He burst out sobbing, and tearfully told his adventure of the night.

"Poor, poor Hōïchi!" the priest exclaimed. "All my fault! – my very grievous fault! Everywhere upon your body the holy texts had been written – except upon your ears! I trusted my acolyte to do that part of the work; and it was very, very wrong of me not to have made sure that he had done it! …Well, the matter cannot now be helped; we can only try to heal your hurts as soon as possible… Cheer up, friend! – the danger is now well over. You will never again be troubled by those visitors."

With the aid of a good doctor, Hōïchi soon recovered from his injuries. The story of his strange adventure spread far and wide, and soon made him famous. Many noble persons went to Akamagaséki to hear him recite; and large presents of money were given to him, so that he became a wealthy man... But from the time of his adventure, he was known only by the appellation of *Mimi-nashi-Hōïchi*: 'Hōïchi-the-Earless'.

Yuki-Onna

Lafcadio Hearn

IN A VILLAGE of Musashi Province, there lived two woodcutters: Mosaku and Minokichi. At the time of which I am speaking, Mosaku was an old man; and Minokichi, his apprentice, was a lad of eighteen years. Every day they went together to a forest situated about five miles from their village. On the way to that forest there is a wide river to cross; and there is a ferry-boat. Several times a bridge was built where the ferry is; but the bridge was each time carried away by a flood. No common bridge can resist the current there when the river rises.

Mosaku and Minokichi were on their way home, one very cold evening, when a great snowstorm overtook them. They reached the ferry; and they found that the boatman had gone away, leaving his boat on the other side of the river. It was no day for swimming; and the woodcutters took shelter in the ferryman's hut – thinking themselves lucky to find any shelter at all. There was no brazier in the hut, nor any place in which to make a fire: it was only a two-mat hut, with a single door, but no window. Mosaku and Minokichi fastened the door, and lay down to rest, with their straw rain-coats over them. At first they did not feel very cold; and they thought that the storm would soon be over.

The old man almost immediately fell asleep; but the boy, Minokichi, lay awake a long time, listening to the awful wind, and the continual slashing of the snow against the door. The river was roaring; and the hut swayed and creaked like a junk at sea. It was a terrible storm; and the air was every moment becoming colder; and Minokichi shivered under his rain-coat. But at last, in spite of the cold, he too fell asleep.

He was awakened by a showering of snow in his face. The door of the hut had been forced open; and, by the snow-light (*yuki-akari*), he saw a woman in the room – a woman all in white. She was bending above Mosaku, and blowing her breath upon him – and her breath was like a bright white smoke. Almost in the same moment she turned to Minokichi, and stooped over him. He tried to cry out, but found that he could not utter any sound. The white woman bent down over him, lower and lower, until her face almost touched him; and he saw that she was very beautiful – though her eyes made him afraid. For a little time she continued to look at him – then she smiled, and she whispered: "I intended to treat you like the other man. But I cannot help feeling some pity for you – because you are so young… You are a pretty boy, Minokichi; and I will not hurt you now. But, if you ever tell anybody – even your own mother – about what you have seen this night, I shall know it; and then I will kill you… Remember what I say!"

With these words, she turned from him, and passed through the doorway. Then he found himself able to move; and he sprang up, and looked out. But the woman was nowhere to be seen; and the snow was driving furiously into the hut. Minokichi closed the door, and secured it by fixing several billets of wood against it. He wondered if the wind had blown it open; he thought that he might have been only dreaming, and might have mistaken the gleam of the snow-light in the doorway for the figure of a white woman: but he could not be sure. He called to Mosaku, and was frightened because the old man did not answer. He put out his hand in the dark, and touched Mosaku's face, and found that it was ice! Mosaku was stark and dead…

By dawn the storm was over; and when the ferryman returned to his station, a little after sunrise, he found Minokichi lying senseless beside the frozen body of Mosaku. Minokichi was promptly cared for, and soon came to himself; but he remained a long time ill from the effects of the cold of that terrible night. He had been greatly frightened also by the old man's death; but he said nothing about the vision of the woman in white. As soon as he got well again, he returned to his calling – going alone every morning to the forest, and coming back at nightfall with his bundles of wood, which his mother helped him to sell.

One evening, in the winter of the following year, as he was on his way home, he overtook a girl who happened to be traveling by the same road. She was a tall, slim girl, very good-looking; and she answered Minokichi's greeting in a voice as pleasant to the ear as the voice of a song-bird. Then he walked beside her; and they began to talk. The girl said that her name was O-Yuki; that she had lately lost both of her parents; and that she was going to Yedo, where she happened to have some poor relations, who might help her to find a situation as a servant. Minokichi soon felt charmed by this strange girl; and the more that he looked at her, the handsomer she appeared to be. He asked her whether she was yet betrothed; and she answered, laughingly, that she was free. Then, in her turn, she asked Minokichi whether he was married, or pledged to marry; and he told her that, although he had only a widowed mother to support, the question of an 'honorable daughter-in-law' had not yet been considered, as he was very young… After these confidences, they walked on for a long while without speaking; but, as the proverb declares, *Ki ga aréba, mé mo kuchi hodo ni mono wo iu*: 'When the wish is there, the eyes can say as much as the mouth.' By the time they reached the village, they had become very much pleased with each other; and then Minokichi asked O-Yuki to rest awhile at his house. After some shy hesitation, she went there with him; and his mother made her welcome, and prepared a warm meal for her. O-Yuki behaved so nicely that Minokichi's mother took a sudden fancy to her, and persuaded her to delay her journey to Yedo. And the natural end of the matter was that Yuki never went to Yedo at all. She remained in the house, as an 'honorable daughter-in-law'.

O-Yuki proved a very good daughter-in-law. When Minokichi's mother came to die – some five years later – her last words were words of affection and praise for the wife of her son. And O-Yuki bore Minokichi ten children, boys and girls – handsome children all of them, and very fair of skin.

The country-folk thought O-Yuki a wonderful person, by nature different from themselves. Most of the peasant-women age early; but O-Yuki, even after having become the mother of ten children, looked as young and fresh as on the day when she had first come to the village.

One night, after the children had gone to sleep, O-Yuki was sewing by the light of a paper lamp; and Minokichi, watching her, said:

"To see you sewing there, with the light on your face, makes me think of a strange thing that happened when I was a lad of eighteen. I then saw somebody as beautiful and white as you are now – indeed, she was very like you."

Without lifting her eyes from her work, O-Yuki responded:

"Tell me about her… Where did you see her?"

Then Minokichi told her about the terrible night in the ferryman's hut – and about the White Woman that had stooped above him, smiling and whispering – and about the silent death of old Mosaku. And he said:

"Asleep or awake, that was the only time that I saw a being as beautiful as you. Of course, she was not a human being; and I was afraid of her – very much afraid – but she was so white! Indeed, I have never been sure whether it was a dream that I saw, or the Woman of the Snow."

O-Yuki flung down her sewing, and arose, and bowed above Minokichi where he sat, and shrieked into his face:

"It was I – I – I! Yuki it was! And I told you then that I would kill you if you ever said one word about it! But for those children asleep there, I would kill you this moment! And now you had better take very, very good care of them; for if ever they have reason to complain of you, I will treat you as you deserve!"

Even as she screamed, her voice became thin, like a crying of wind; then she melted into a bright white mist that spired to the roof-beams, and shuddered away through the smoke-hold… Never again was she seen.

My True Love Gave to Me

Sean Hogan

EACH CHRISTMAS EVE, Doctor Henry Gibbons and his old – nay, *oldest* – friend Anthony St. Clair would faithfully meet to exchange seasonal gifts. The ritual – for their arrangement had continued for so long that it was by now almost a sacred rubric, forever solemn and unchanging – would be conducted in the same fashion every year, save for the fact that, in the interests of fairness, each man took it in turns to host the other. After all, neither of them was getting any younger, and while the journey between their respective homes was not by any means long or onerous, the sapping bite of the December cold often had the unwelcome effect of making one mile feel like several, to their ageing and increasingly brittle bones at least.

Henry had welcomed Anthony into his own modest but comfortable bachelor's apartment the previous Christmas Eve, and so it was that he now found himself sequestered in his friend's book-lined study, bending stiffly down in front of the blazing fireplace to warm his numbed thighs and backside. Henry found himself quietly grateful that the room's hearth was a reasonably large one; expansive enough to warm the full span of his not-inconsiderable posterior anyway.

Anthony St. Clair himself sat in a leather armchair positioned to one side of the fire, a thick tartan blanket draped over the diminished sticks of his legs. To its left, another identical armchair awaited Henry's occupancy, and between the two chairs, a decanter of fine sherry and two crystal glasses had been placed upon a small table. Everything was precisely as it should be; indeed, as it had *always* been, for year after year, ever since the two men could remember. While one friend had physically waxed with the passage of time, just as the other had undeniably waned, their increasing age and any attendant infirmities would never be permitted to interfere with the arrangement. The unchanging nature of the exchange was the very essence of it; to alter or deviate from it in any way would suggest that their feelings about what the ritual symbolised had somehow shifted, and that could never be. The event was not simply a display of seasonal goodwill and friendship; it was an act of the utmost devotion. Accordingly, the gifts they exchanged were no mere trinkets, inevitably to be discarded and forgotten with the coming of the new year, but *sacraments*; representative of something ineffably divine.

The gifts in question lay wrapped at the foot of each of the armchairs. Neither man had learned how to properly wrap presents over the years, and so the handiwork on each was impatiently cursory, at best. Normally, such undoubtedly feminine chores would strictly be the province of each man's housekeeper, but as we shall soon see, the inexpressibly precious nature of the two gifts precluded any outside involvement in the affair.

Anthony's offering to Henry was a small box-shaped item, perhaps large enough to hold a china teacup. In contrast, Henry's own present was larger, with a dome-shaped top; to look at it, one might have surmised it was a small birdcage. Still, there could be no suggestion of disparity between the two gifts, simply for the plain fact that the pair of items concealed inside their respective wrappings never changed. Instead, much like the designated venue for the annual exchange, the two men simply alternated year on year, endlessly passing the same two presents back and forth.

Rubbing vigorously at his ample buttocks, Henry removed himself from the fireplace and settled into his seat with a relieved sigh, which Anthony took as his cue to lean over and carefully pour them both a small glass of sherry. As the two friends then held their glasses aloft in a silent toast, the reflected flames from the fireplace seemed almost to ignite the amber liquid within, and when Henry brought the glass to his mouth, he sipped at it like a wary chaffinch, as though fearing that the fiery alcohol might sear his fleshy lips. Glancing over at his companion, he noticed that Anthony had now settled back in his chair and closed his eyes, and Henry thought for an instant that he might have simply dozed off. They were both of that sort of age, after all.

But then a low rattling started to build in Anthony's chest, and without opening his eyes, he parted his lips and a reedy slur issued forth (Anthony having started sampling the sherry quite some time before his guest's arrival). "Any word of Ormsby?" he asked Henry, although as spoken, the word sounded more like *Ormshbby*.

Henry considered the question for a moment, as if pondering exactly how much he should tell his friend. "I was told he had remarried," he said finally.

Anthony opened one baleful eye. "How could he?" he growled.

Henry took another sip of sherry and sighed disapprovingly. "It just goes to show."

"Proves the point." *Proveshh.*

"Indeed." Henry's gaze drifted down to the parcel sitting at his friend's feet. "You were never tempted, I suppose?"

The question served to rouse Anthony, who finally opened both eyes and indignantly struggled upright in his chair. "There could never be anyone else," he said accusingly. "Never was, and never will be." He stared across at Henry, as if daring him to say any different.

But the other man merely gave a sorrowful shrug and sighed again. "I once thought it might get easier with the years. Time heals all wounds, as they say."

Anthony rumbled his disapproval of the homily. "Not *all* wounds. Some merely fester."

The doctor nodded wearily. "Well, one does what one can." He looked expectantly across at Anthony. "Can I see her now? I was scarcely able to sleep last night for thinking of her."

Anthony gave a long sigh, reminiscent of a dying elephant. Easing forward, he bent down and picked up his gift from the floor, which he proceeded to hand to Henry with an odd reluctance, as if to doggedly deny the old maxim about giving and receiving. As the other man took receipt of the parcel, Anthony's hands lingered on it for a moment, seemingly unwilling to part with the item.

Henry gave his friend a searching stare. "Is something the matter?"

"Nothing at all," Anthony mumbled, immediately relinquishing his grip. "Just...the thought of not seeing her for an entire year. At our age, one doesn't quite know how many years one has left, after all."

Henry brought the package protectively to his chest, cradling it there. "Well, that's the agreement. We share her, heart and soul."

Saying nothing, Anthony stared fixedly into the fire as Henry began to eagerly tear at the wrapping paper. In the hearthlight, the doctor's hungry eyes gleamed like polished obsidian. "Hello, my darling," he murmured.

What now lay revealed in his lap was a large sealed bell jar, filled with a cloudy liquid. But neither of those exterior trappings concerned Henry, any more than the length of wrapping paper now lying discarded on the rug had. The true substance of the gift, the prize he had so fervently longed to see again ever since he'd last glimpsed it, some three hundred and sixty-five days ago, was a woman's severed head.

The head bobbed gently in the jar, its features puffy and pale after long decades spent soaking in formaldehyde, and yet – if one squinted at it through aged, rheumy eyes, precisely as Henry was doing in that very moment – it was possible that the face of the dead woman might still appear just as young as it had when the two friends had originally known her, and just as beautiful.

Henry moaned softly, prompting Anthony to expel an annoyed cough. "Do come on, then," he grumbled.

Jolted from his private fantasia, the doctor immediately leaned down to fumble at his feet. "I'm sorry, please do forgive my manners," he apologised, quickly handing Anthony his own gift. "Merry Christmas, my oldest friend."

Upon receiving the parcel, Anthony's trembling hands began to fumble ineffectually at the wrapping. Cursing under his breath, he finally managed to rip aside the paper, his arthritic fingers clawing hurriedly at the small wooden box contained within, scrabbling to open its lid.

Inside lay a mummified human heart, shrunken and grey. Its new custodian gazed down at it for several long seconds, his face curdling as he ingested the cold and bitter tea of remembrance.

Eventually, Henry broke the silence, raising his glass in another toast. "To Anna. She gave her heart to another…so we were compelled to take it back," he said quietly, and with a studiedly appropriate amount of regret.

His eyes clouded with longing, Anthony gently closed the box's lid and picked up his own glass. "To Anna."

For a moment, each man silently recalled the chain of events that had led them to this macabre juncture. Their mutual obsession with the divine Anna, who (to their learned minds at least), had flightily encouraged their amorous attentions, before callously rejecting both friends in favour of the young upstart Philip Ormsby – a lowly grocer's son, at that! The poisonous humiliation of subsequently being forced to sit there in the church and watch the happy couple marry. Their determination not to let such a grievous insult go unpunished. And finally, their black revenge – snatching Anna away while Philip was out of town on business, leaving him torturously mystified as to his missing bride's fate, and ensuring that Anna – or these two deathly synedoches of her, at least – would at last belong solely to them, for as long as they both lived.

Their throats suddenly growing dry with the memory of it, the two companions quickly drained their glasses. As Anthony moved to refill them, his gaze was inescapably drawn to the jar sitting in Henry's lap. "Please," he implored his friend. "Allow me one last look at her."

Lasht. Anthony's drinking really was starting to become a problem, the doctor mused. He suddenly realised he had very strong misgivings about entrusting Anna to his friend's care for the next twelve months. But what could he do? Such was the nature of the agreement the two gentlemen had made – and who could possibly argue that the two friends were *not* gentlemen, possessing all of the attendant integrity and ethical fervour that particular title demanded?

Somewhat peevishly, Henry shifted the position of the jar just enough for Anthony to be able to glimpse Anna's face. As he gazed upon his beloved once again, the old man's sunken features visibly softened, the years seeming to fall away like autumn leaves. "Oh, her beautiful blue eyes," he breathed softly.

"What did you say?" Henry snapped.

Anthony jerked back, as if burnt. "I…I was remembering her eyes," he stammered.

"They were *brown*, not blue," Henry told him sternly.

Anthony's mouth gaped open in disbelief. "Nonsense," he said.

"I'm telling you. Brown," Henry insisted.

"Your memory grows ever more enfeebled with the years," Anthony spat. "Last Christmas you claimed that Anna's favourite colour was green, when we both know it was really red."

Bristling, Henry clutched the jar to his chest, hiding the head from his friend's sight. "I spent hours staring into those eyes," he thundered. "No, entire *days*! Through them, I gazed into the depths of her very soul. Are you honestly suggesting I don't remember what *colour* they were?"

Shaking with anger, Anthony struggled weakly to his feet. "You demented old fool! Don't you *dare* tell me I'm wrong! Her memory is all I have!"

In response, Henry also heaved himself upright and thrust his face into Anthony's, his jowls wobbling with outrage. "You don't deserve her! You never did!"

"I…? It was *me* that fought for her! *You* were resigned to her marrying Philip Ormsby! Ready to simply roll over on your back and give in, like the gutless dog that you are!"

"Then *who* was the gutless dog that cowered in their bed while I visited her on that final evening? Which one of us hid behind closed doors as I took my surgeon's scalpel and cut into Anna's flawless throat, weeping as I watched the precious life ebbing out of her…?"

"Cur!"

"Poltroon! Drunk!"

Anthony's sallow features grew uncharacteristically flushed, and his skinny hands clenched into frail, tumbleweed fists. For a moment, Henry thought his friend was about to strike him, only for the other man to dart forward and wrench the bell jar from his unsuspecting grip instead.

Holding the trophy aloft, Anthony pirouetted like a crazed stork towards the fireplace, as though performing a bizarre *danse macabre* with his lost love. "If I can't have her, then no one will!"

"No!" Henry screamed.

Too late. Anthony cast the jar into the fire with a manic screech of triumph. The glass immediately shattered with the heat, sending the formaldehyde contained inside spilling into the flames. Instantly, a loud explosion belched forth from the hearth, scorching Anthony's face and hands and sending him crashing backwards onto the carpet.

Ignoring the other man's plight, Henry watched in horror as Anna's head began to blacken and burn, the preserved flesh rapidly shrivelling away to reveal the grinning skull beneath. There was nothing he could do to prevent it – their beloved was lost to them. Grief prickling in his eyes, Henry stood and looked mutely on as the fire hungrily claimed her.

Finally, when nothing was left of Anna but bone, Henry took a hesitant step forward and picked up the poker, hoping to use it to fish what remained of his love out of the fire. But just as he turned back towards the fireplace, the skull rolled onto its side, opened its maw, and began to shriek.

Its piercing screams immediately filled the room, with sufficient force as to cause Henry's teeth to throb savagely and rattle the various framed testaments to Anthony St. Clair's eminence that adorned the study walls.

Henry gazed at the shrieking death's head in abject horror. Surely the whole town would be able to hear such a fearful noise. Now everyone would know what they had done. Everyone would know his and Anthony's secret, their shared humiliation. And it was all that old fool's fault.

He turned towards his fallen companion. Anthony lay flat on his back, the taut parchment skin of his atrophied face blackened and blistered by the explosion. His mouth opened and closed silently, like that of a halibut writhing on the deck of a fishing trawler.

"Bastard," Henry hissed. A cold fire bloomed in his chest, filling him with the strength to do what was necessary, what *had* to be done. There was simply nothing else for it: Anthony had brought it on himself. Henry had not felt this kind of icy certainty since the night of Anna's death, and quietly relished it.

He leaned forward, gazing into Anthony's eyes. "Bastard," he said again, for good measure.

Anthony goggled up at him as Henry raised the poker above his head and brought it crashing down onto his erstwhile friend's face, an action he methodically repeated until Anthony could goggle no longer.

And all the while, Anna's skull continued to scream.

Satisfied with the bloody results of his handiwork, Henry removed a handkerchief from his pocket and dabbed at the perspiration beading on his brow. His equilibrium somewhat restored, he turned his attention back to the fireplace, and what little remained of his beloved therein.

"Hush now," he murmured to the shrieking skull, bending forward to pluck it from the flames, oblivious to the scorching touch of their tongues on his flesh. As the doctor's hands closed around the skull's smoking cranium, it immediately ceased its cries.

Henry held Anna to his chest, tears flowing freely down his ruddy cheeks. Whether they were tears of joy at being reunited with his lost love, or merely caused by the pain of his burned hands, I cannot venture to say. Regardless, he stood like that for some time, swaying gently and wordlessly crooning to his prize.

Around him, a second sound slowly began to build in the room, a low whine with no apparent cause or source. Although Henry was oblivious to it at first, the noise continued to rise in pitch until it eventually drowned out the sound of his crooning; indeed, it kept on rising to a point where he soon began to wince in evident discomfort. Unwilling to relinquish Anna's skull from their jealous grip, his hands were not free to properly shield his ears from the incessant whine, and so all the doctor could think to do was retreat to the nearby corner instead. There, he began to cower and whimper, his meaty frame seeming to visibly diminish under the sonic assault, like a fallen apple withering in the hot sun.

Finally, the sound reached its terrible crescendo, shattering the two sherry glasses sitting on the small table. Relieved as he was by the sudden cessation of the noise, Henry barely even noticed their destruction, his attention now utterly transfixed by the unexpected arrival of another presence in the room.

In the shadowed far corner of the study, untouched by the throw of the firelight, stood the nebulous figure of a woman. She remained there, quite unmoving, for a short time, then slowly began to move towards the still-cowering Henry. He watched wordlessly as the woman edged into the glow cast by the fire, revealing her to be clad in a long white dress. The garment flattered her elegant figure most pleasingly, and in everyday life, his female visitor would undoubtedly have drawn many admiring glances from any menfolk in her immediate vicinity; alas, were it not for the lack of one important aspect, which at last became apparent to the doctor once she stood fully revealed in the firelight.

Her head.

Still, even without the benefit of facial recognition, Henry knew exactly who the visitor was. How could he not? He remembered every last detail of her as though it were yesterday: the small mole on her left collar bone, the exquisite, swan-like neck he had so delicately drawn his scalpel blade across all those long years ago…

"Oh Anna, my sweet, sweet darling," he whispered, his flesh aquiver with a kind of terrified ecstasy.

The headless woman loomed over him. Her only reply to his blandishment was to extend one pale hand, palm outstretched as if to seek alms.

Craving understanding, Henry gazed up at the empty space where Anna's face should have been, where it *had* been until he himself removed it. "Anything," he said desperately. "Anything for you."

The hand gestured again, more insistently this time.

Henry's gaze drifted from the absence above Anna's neck down to the swelling bosom of her dress. There, at exactly the point where the impregnable muscle that he and Anthony had so utterly failed to capture once beat, a crimson flower began to bloom on the otherwise pristine white fabric.

And he finally understood.

"All you ever had to do was ask," the doctor told her lovingly.

As he tore his shirt open to expose his hairless, sagging breasts to Anna's spectre, and she reached down to greedily claim her trophy, her long rigored fingers parting his soft flesh like putty; in the brief moments before the world went dark forever and he was once more reunited with his old – nay, *oldest* – friend Anthony St. Clair, Henry Gibbons reminded himself that his heart had always belonged to her anyway.

Jerry Bundler

W.W. Jacobs

IT WANTED a few nights to Christmas, a festival for which the small market town of Torchester was making extensive preparations. The narrow streets which had been thronged with people were now almost deserted; the cheap-jack from London, with the remnant of breath left him after his evening's exertions, was making feeble attempts to blow out his naphtha lamp, and the last shops open were rapidly closing for the night.

In the comfortable coffee-room of the old Boar's Head, half a dozen guests, principally commercial travellers, sat talking by the light of the fire. The talk had drifted from trade to politics, from politics to religion, and so by easy stages to the supernatural. Three ghost stories, never known to fail before, had fallen flat; there was too much noise outside, too much light within. The fourth story was told by an old hand with more success; the streets were quiet, and he had turned the gas out. In the flickering light of the fire, as it shone on the glasses and danced with shadows on the walls, the story proved so enthralling that George, the waiter, whose presence had been forgotten, created a very disagreeable sensation by suddenly starting up from a dark corner and gliding silently from the room. "That's what I call a good story," said one of the men, sipping his hot whisky. "Of course it's an old idea that spirits like to get into the company of human beings. A man told me once that he travelled down the Great Western with a ghost and hadn't the slightest suspicion of it until the inspector came for tickets. My friend said the way that ghost tried to keep up appearances by feeling for it in all its pockets and looking on the floor was quite touching. Ultimately it gave it up and with a faint groan vanished through the ventilator."

"That'll do, Hirst," said another man.

"It's not a subject for jesting," said a little old gentleman who had been an attentive listener. "I've never seen an apparition myself, but I know people who have, and I consider that they form a very interesting link between us and the afterlife. There's a ghost story connected with this house, you know."

"Never heard of it," said another speaker, "and I've been here some years now."

"It dates back a long time now," said the old gentleman. "You've heard about Jerry Bundler, George?"

"Well, I've just 'eard odds and ends, sir," said the old waiter, "but I never put much count to 'em. There was one chap 'ere what said 'e saw it, and the gov'ner sacked 'im prompt."

"My father was a native of this town," said the old gentleman, "and knew the story well. He was a truthful man and a steady churchgoer, but I've heard him declare that once in his life he saw the appearance of Jerry Bundler in this house."

"And who was this Bundler?" inquired a voice.

"A London thief, pickpocket, highwayman – anything he could turn his dishonest hand to," replied the old gentleman; "and he was run to earth in this house one Christmas week some eighty years ago. He took his last supper in this very room, and after he had gone up to bed a couple of Bow Street runners, who had followed him from London but lost the scent a bit, went upstairs with the landlord and tried the door. It was stout oak, and fast, so one went into the yard, and by means of a short ladder got onto the window sill, while the other stayed outside the door. Those below in the yard saw the man crouching on the sill, and then there was a sudden smash of glass, and with a cry he fell in a heap on the stones at their feet. Then in the moonlight they saw the white face of the pickpocket peeping over the sill, and while some stayed in the yard, others ran into the house and helped the other man to break the door in. It was difficult to obtain an entrance even then, for it was barred with heavy furniture, but they got in at last, and the first thing that met their eyes was the body of Jerry dangling from the top of the bed by his own handkerchief."

"Which bedroom was it?" asked two or three voices together.

The narrator shook his head. "That I can't tell you; but the story goes that Jerry still haunts this house, and my father used to declare positively that the last time he slept here the ghost of Jerry Bundler lowered itself from the top of his bed and tried to strangle him."

"That'll do," said an uneasy voice. "I wish you'd thought to ask your father which bedroom it was."

"What for?" inquired the old gentleman.

"Well, I should take care not to sleep in it, that's all," said the voice, shortly.

"There's nothing to fear," said the other. "I don't believe for a moment that ghosts could really hurt one. In fact my father used to confess that it was only the unpleasantness of the thing that upset him, and that for all practical purposes Jerry's fingers might have been made of cottonwool for all the harm they could do."

"That's all very fine," said the last speaker again; "a ghost story is a ghost story, sir; but when a gentleman tells a tale of a ghost in the house in which one is going to sleep, I call it most ungentlemanly!"

"Pooh! Nonsense!" said the old gentleman, rising; "Ghosts can't hurt you. For my own part, I should rather like to see one. Goodnight, gentlemen."

"Goodnight," said the others. "And I only hope Jerry'll pay you a visit," added the nervous man as the door closed.

"Bring some more whisky, George," said a stout commercial; "I want keeping up when the talk turns this way."

"Shall I light the gas, Mr. Malcolm?" said George.

"No; the fire's very comfortable," said the traveller. "Now, gentlemen, any of you know any more?"

"I think we've had enough," said another man; "we shall be thinking we see spirits next, and we're not all like the old gentleman who's just gone."

"Old humbug!" said Hirst. "I should like to put him to the test. Suppose I dress up as Jerry Bundler and go and give him a chance of displaying his courage?"

"Bravo!" said Malcolm, huskily, drowning one or two faint "Noes."

"Just for the joke, gentlemen."

"No, no! Drop it, Hirst," said another man.

"Only for the joke," said Hirst, somewhat eagerly. "I've got some things upstairs in which I am going to play in the Rivals – knee-breeches, buckles, and all that sort of thing. It's a rare chance. If you'll wait a bit I'll give you a full-dress rehearsal, entitled, 'Jerry Bundler; or, The Nocturnal Strangler'."

"You won't frighten us," said the commercial, with a husky laugh.

"I don't know that," said Hirst, sharply; "it's a question of acting, that's all. I'm pretty good, ain't I, Somers?"

"Oh, you're all right – for an amateur," said his friend, with a laugh.

"I'll bet you a level sov. you don't frighten me," said the stout traveller.

"Done!" said Hirst. "I'll take the bet to frighten you first and the old gentleman afterwards. These gentlemen shall be the judges."

"You won't frighten us, sir," said another man, "because we're prepared for you; but you'd better leave the old man alone. It's dangerous play."

"Well, I'll try you first," said Hirst, springing up. "No gas, mind."

He ran lightly upstairs to his room, leaving the others, most of whom had been drinking somewhat freely, to wrangle about his proceedings. It ended in two of them going to bed.

"He's crazy on acting," said Somers, lighting his pipe. "Thinks he's the equal of anybody almost. It doesn't matter with us, but I won't let him go to the old man. And he won't mind so long as he gets an opportunity of acting to us."

"Well, I hope he'll hurry up," said Malcolm, yawning; "it's after twelve now."

Nearly half an hour passed. Malcolm drew his watch from his pocket and was busy winding it, when George, the waiter, who had been sent on an errand to the bar, burst suddenly into the room and rushed towards them.

"'E's comin', gentlemen," he said breathlessly.

"Why, you're frightened, George," said the stout commercial, with a chuckle.

"It was the suddenness of it," said George, sheepishly; "and besides, I didn't look for seein' 'im in the bar. There's only a glimmer of light there, and 'e was sitting on the floor behind the bar. I nearly trod on 'im."

"Oh, you'll never make a man, George," said Malcolm.

"Well, it took me unawares," said the waiter. "Not that I'd have gone to the bar by myself if I'd known 'e was there, and I don't believe you would either, sir."

"Nonsense!" said Malcolm. "I'll go and fetch him in."

"You don't know what it's like, sir," said George, catching him by the sleeve. "It ain't fit to look at by yourself, it ain't, indeed. It's got the – What's that?"

They all started at the sound of a smothered cry from the staircase and the sound of somebody running hurriedly along the passage. Before anybody could speak, the door flew open and a figure bursting into the room flung itself gasping and shivering upon them.

"What is it? What's the matter?" demanded Malcolm. "Why, it's Mr. Hirst." He shook him roughly and then held some spirit to his lips. Hirst drank it greedily and with a sharp intake of his breath gripped him by the arm.

"Light the gas, George," said Malcolm.

The waiter obeyed hastily. Hirst, a ludicrous but pitiable figure in knee-breeches and coat, a large wig all awry and his face a mess of grease paint, clung to him, trembling.

"Now, what's the matter?" asked Malcolm.

"I've seen it," said Hirst, with a hysterical sob. "O Lord, I'll never play the fool again, never!"

"Seen what?" said the others.

"Him – it – the ghost – anything!" said Hirst, wildly.

"Rot!" said Malcolm, uneasily.

"I was coming down the stairs," said Hirst. "Just capering down – as I thought – it ought to do. I felt a tap—"

He broke off suddenly and peered nervously through the open door into the passage.

"I thought I saw it again," he whispered.

"Look – at the foot of the stairs. Can you see anything?"

"No, there's nothing there," said Malcolm, whose own voice shook a little. "Go on. You felt a tap on your shoulder—"

"I turned round and saw it – a little wicked head and a white dead face. Pah!"

"That's what I saw in the bar," said George. "'Orrid it was – devilish!"

Hirst shuddered, and, still retaining his nervous grip of Malcolm's sleeve, dropped into a chair.

"Well, it's a most unaccountable thing," said the dumbfounded Malcolm, turning round to the others. "It's the last time I come to this house."

"I leave tomorrow," said George. "I wouldn't go down to that bar again by myself, no, not for fifty pounds!"

"It's talking about the thing that's caused it, I expect," said one of the men; "we've all been talking about this and having it in our minds. Practically we've been forming a spiritualistic circle without knowing it."

"Hang the old gentleman!" said Malcolm, heartily. "Upon my soul, I'm half afraid to go to bed. It's odd they should both think they saw something."

"I saw it as plain as I see you, sir," said George, solemnly. "P'raps if you keep your eyes turned up the passage you'll see it for yourself."

They followed the direction of his finger, but saw nothing, although one of them fancied that a head peeped round the corner of the wall.

"Who'll come down to the bar?" said Malcolm, looking round.

"You can go, if you like," said one of the others, with a faint laugh; "we'll wait here for you."

The stout traveller walked towards the door and took a few steps up the passage. Then he stopped. All was quite silent, and he walked slowly to the end and looked down fearfully towards the glass partition which shut off the bar. Three times he made as though to go to it; then he turned back, and, glancing over his shoulder, came hurriedly back to the room.

"Did you see it, sir?" whispered George.

"Don't know," said Malcolm, shortly. "I fancied I saw something, but it might have been fancy. I'm in the mood to see anything just now. How are you feeling now, sir?"

"Oh, I feel a bit better now," said Hirst, somewhat brusquely, as all eyes were turned upon him. "I dare say you think I'm easily scared, but you didn't see it."

"Not at all," said Malcolm, smiling faintly despite himself.

"I'm going to bed," said Hirst, noticing the smile and resenting it. "Will you share my room with me, Somers?"

"I will with pleasure," said his friend, "provided you don't mind sleeping with the gas on full all night."

He rose from his seat, and bidding the company a friendly goodnight, left the room with his crestfallen friend. The others saw them to the foot of the stairs, and having heard their door close, returned to the coffee-room.

"Well, I suppose the bet's off?" said the stout commercial, poking the fire and then standing with his legs apart on the hearthrug; "though, as far as I can see, I won it. I never saw a man so scared in all my life. Sort of poetic justice about it, isn't there?"

"Never mind about poetry or justice," said one of his listeners; "who's going to sleep with me?"

"I will," said Malcolm, affably.

"And I suppose we share a room together, Mr. Leek?" said the third man, turning to the fourth.

"No, thank you," said the other, briskly; "I don't believe in ghosts. If anything comes into my room I shall shoot it."

"That won't hurt a spirit, Leek," said Malcolm, decisively.

"Well the noise'll be like company to me," said Leek, "and it'll wake the house too. But if you're nervous, sir," he added, with a grin, to the man who had suggested sharing his room, "George'll be only too pleased to sleep on the doormat inside your room, I know."

"That I will, sir," said George, fervently; "and if you gentlemen would only come down with me to the bar to put the gas out, I could never be sufficiently grateful."

They went out in a body, with the exception of Leek, peering carefully before them as they went. George turned the light out in the bar and they returned unmolested to the coffee-room, and, avoiding the sardonic smile of Leek, prepared to separate for the night.

"Give me the candle while you put the gas out, George," said the traveller.

The waiter handed it to him and extinguished the gas, and at the same moment all distinctly heard a step in the passage outside. It stopped at the door, and as they watched with bated breath, the door creaked and slowly opened. Malcolm fell back open-mouthed, as a white, leering face, with sunken eyeballs and close-cropped bullet head, appeared at the opening.

For a few seconds the creature stood regarding them, blinking in a strange fashion at the candle. Then, with a sidling movement, it came a little way into the room and stood there as if bewildered.

Not a man spoke or moved, but all watched with a horrible fascination as the creature removed its dirty neckcloth and its head rolled on its shoulder. For a minute it paused, and then, holding the rag before it, moved towards Malcolm.

The candle went out suddenly with a flash and a bang. There was a smell of powder, and something writhing in the darkness on the floor. A faint, choking cough, and then silence. Malcolm was the first to speak. "Matches," he said, in a strange voice. George struck one. Then he leapt at the gas and a burner flamed from the match. Malcolm touched the thing on the floor with his foot and found it soft. He looked at his companions. They mouthed inquiries at him, but he shook his head. He lit the candle, and, kneeling down, examined the silent thing on the floor. Then he rose swiftly, and dipping his handkerchief in the water-jug, bent down again and grimly wiped the white face. Then he sprang back with a cry of incredulous horror, pointing at it. Leek's pistol fell to the floor and he shut out the sight with his hands, but the others, crowding forward, gazed spell-bound at the dead face of Hirst.

Before a word was spoken the door opened and Somers hastily entered the room. His eyes fell on the floor. "Good God!" he cried. "You didn't—"

Nobody spoke.

"I told him not to," he said, in a suffocating voice. "I told him not to. I told him—"

He leaned against the wall, deathly sick, put his arms out feebly, and fell fainting into the traveller's arms.

The Turn of the Screw

Henry James

THE STORY had held us, round the fire, sufficiently breathless, but except the obvious remark that it was gruesome, as, on Christmas Eve in an old house, a strange tale should essentially be, I remember no comment uttered till somebody happened to say that it was the only case he had met in which such a visitation had fallen on a child. The case, I may mention, was that of an apparition in just such an old house as had gathered us for the occasion – an appearance, of a dreadful kind, to a little boy sleeping in the room with his mother and waking her up in the terror of it; waking her not to dissipate his dread and soothe him to sleep again, but to encounter also, herself, before she had succeeded in doing so, the same sight that had shaken him. It was this observation that drew from Douglas – not immediately, but later in the evening – a reply that had the interesting consequence to which I call attention. Someone else told a story not particularly effective, which I saw he was not following. This I took for a sign that he had himself something to produce and that we should only have to wait. We waited in fact till two nights later; but that same evening, before we scattered, he brought out what was in his mind.

"I quite agree – in regard to Griffin's ghost, or whatever it was – that its appearing first to the little boy, at so tender an age, adds a particular touch. But it's not the first occurrence of its charming kind that I know to have involved a child. If the child gives the effect another turn of the screw, what do you say to *two* children—?"

"We say, of course," somebody exclaimed, "that they give two turns! Also that we want to hear about them."

I can see Douglas there before the fire, to which he had got up to present his back, looking down at his interlocutor with his hands in his pockets. "Nobody but me, till now, has ever heard. It's quite too horrible." This, naturally, was declared by several voices to give the thing the utmost price, and our friend, with quiet art, prepared his triumph by turning his eyes over the rest of us and going on: "It's beyond everything. Nothing at all that I know touches it."

"For sheer terror?" I remember asking.

He seemed to say it was not so simple as that; to be really at a loss how to qualify it. He passed his hand over his eyes, made a little wincing grimace. "For dreadful – dreadfulness!"

"Oh, how delicious!" cried one of the women.

He took no notice of her; he looked at me, but as if, instead of me, he saw what he spoke of. "For general uncanny ugliness and horror and pain."

"Well then," I said, "just sit right down and begin."

He turned round to the fire, gave a kick to a log, watched it an instant. Then as he faced us again: "I can't begin. I shall have to send to town." There was a unanimous groan at this, and much reproach; after which, in his preoccupied way, he explained. "The story's written. It's in a locked drawer – it has not been out for years. I could write to my man and enclose the key; he could send down the packet as he finds it." It was to me in particular that he appeared to propound this – appeared almost to appeal for aid not to hesitate. He had broken a thickness of ice, the formation of many a winter; had had his reasons for a long silence. The others resented postponement, but it was just his scruples that charmed me. I adjured him to write by the first post and to agree with us for an early hearing; then I asked him if the experience in question had been his own. To this his answer was prompt. "Oh, thank God, no!"

"And is the record yours? You took the thing down?"

"Nothing but the impression. I took that *here*" – he tapped his heart. "I've never lost it."

"Then your manuscript—?"

"Is in old, faded ink, and in the most beautiful hand." He hung fire again. "A woman's. She has been dead these twenty years. She sent me the pages in question before she died." They were all listening now, and of course there was somebody to be arch, or at any rate to draw the inference. But if he put the inference by without a smile it was also without irritation. "She was a most charming person, but she was ten years older than I. She was my sister's governess," he quietly said. "She was the most agreeable woman I've ever known in her position; she would have been worthy of any whatever. It was long ago, and this episode was long before. I was at Trinity, and I found her at home on my coming down the second summer. I was much there that year – it was a beautiful one; and we had, in her off-hours, some strolls and talks in the garden – talks in which she struck me as awfully clever and nice. Oh yes; don't grin: I liked her extremely and am glad to this day to think she liked me, too. If she hadn't she wouldn't have told me. She had never told anyone. It wasn't simply that she said so, but that I knew she hadn't. I was sure; I could see. You'll easily judge why when you hear."

"Because the thing had been such a scare?"

He continued to fix me. "You'll easily judge," he repeated: "*you* will."

I fixed him, too. "I see. She was in love."

He laughed for the first time. "You *are* acute. Yes, she was in love. That is, she had been. That came out – she couldn't tell her story without its coming out. I saw it, and she saw I saw it; but neither of us spoke of it. I remember the time and the place – the corner of the lawn, the shade of the great beeches and the long, hot summer afternoon. It wasn't a scene for a shudder; but oh—!" He quitted the fire and dropped back into his chair.

"You'll receive the packet Thursday morning?" I inquired.

"Probably not till the second post."

"Well then; after dinner—"

"You'll all meet me here?" He looked us round again. "Isn't anybody going?" It was almost the tone of hope.

"Everybody will stay!"

"*I* will" – and "*I* will!" cried the ladies whose departure had been fixed. Mrs. Griffin, however, expressed the need for a little more light. "Who was it she was in love with?"

"The story will tell," I took upon myself to reply.

"Oh, I can't wait for the story!"

"The story *won't* tell," said Douglas; "not in any literal, vulgar way."

"More's the pity, then. That's the only way I ever understand."

"Won't *you* tell, Douglas?" somebody else inquired.

He sprang to his feet again. "Yes – tomorrow. Now I must go to bed. Goodnight." And quickly catching up a candlestick, he left us slightly bewildered. From our end of the great brown hall we heard his step on the stair; whereupon Mrs. Griffin spoke. "Well, if I don't know who she was in love with, I know who *he* was."

"She was ten years older," said her husband.

"*Raison de plus* – at that age! But it's rather nice, his long reticence."

"Forty years!" Griffin put in.

"With this outbreak at last."

"The outbreak," I returned, "will make a tremendous occasion of Thursday night"; and everyone so agreed with me that, in the light of it, we lost all attention for everything else. The last story, however incomplete and like the mere opening of a serial, had been told; we handshook and 'candlestuck', as somebody said, and went to bed.

I knew the next day that a letter containing the key had, by the first post, gone off to his London apartments; but in spite of – or perhaps just on account of – the eventual diffusion of this knowledge we quite let him alone till after dinner, till such an hour of the evening, in fact, as might best accord with the kind of emotion on which our hopes were fixed. Then he became as communicative as we could desire and indeed gave us his best reason for being so. We had it from him again before the fire in the hall, as we had had our mild wonders of the previous night. It appeared that the narrative he had promised to read us really required for a proper intelligence a few words of prologue. Let me say here distinctly, to have done with it, that this narrative, from an exact transcript of my own made much later, is what I shall presently give. Poor Douglas, before his death – when it was in sight – committed to me the manuscript that reached him on the third of these days and that, on the same spot, with immense effect, he began to read to our hushed little circle on the night of the fourth. The departing ladies who had said they would stay didn't, of course, thank heaven, stay: they departed, in consequence of arrangements made, in a rage of curiosity, as they professed, produced by the touches with which he had already worked us up. But that only made his little final auditory more compact and select, kept it, round the hearth, subject to a common thrill.

The first of these touches conveyed that the written statement took up the tale at a point after it had, in a manner, begun. The fact to be in possession of was therefore that his old friend, the youngest of several daughters of a poor country parson, had, at the age of twenty, on taking service for the first time in the schoolroom, come up to London, in trepidation, to answer in person an advertisement that had already placed her in brief correspondence with the advertiser. This person proved, on her presenting herself, for judgment, at a house in Harley Street, that impressed her as vast and imposing – this prospective patron proved a gentleman, a bachelor in the prime of life, such a figure as had never risen, save in a dream or an old novel, before a fluttered, anxious girl out of a Hampshire vicarage. One could easily fix his type; it never, happily, dies out. He was handsome and bold and pleasant, off-hand and gay and kind. He struck her, inevitably, as gallant and splendid, but what took her most of all and gave her the courage she afterward showed was that he put the whole thing to her as a kind of favor, an obligation he should gratefully incur. She conceived him as rich, but as fearfully extravagant – saw him all in a glow of high fashion, of good looks, of expensive habits, of charming ways with women. He had for his own town residence a big house filled with the spoils of travel and the trophies of the chase; but it was to his country home, an old family place in Essex, that he wished her immediately to proceed.

He had been left, by the death of their parents in India, guardian to a small nephew and a small niece, children of a younger, a military brother, whom he had lost two years before. These children were, by the strangest of chances for a man in his position – a lone man without the right sort of experience or a grain of patience – very heavily on his hands. It had all been a great worry and, on his own part doubtless, a series of blunders, but he immensely pitied the poor chicks and had done all he could; had in particular sent them down to his other house, the proper place for them being of course the country, and kept them there, from the first, with the best people he could find to look after them, parting even with his own servants to wait on them and going down himself, whenever he might, to see how they were doing. The awkward thing was that they had practically no other relations and that his own affairs took up all his time. He had put them in possession of

Bly, which was healthy and secure, and had placed at the head of their little establishment – but below stairs only – an excellent woman, Mrs. Grose, whom he was sure his visitor would like and who had formerly been maid to his mother. She was now housekeeper and was also acting for the time as superintendent to the little girl, of whom, without children of her own, she was, by good luck, extremely fond. There were plenty of people to help, but of course the young lady who should go down as governess would be in supreme authority. She would also have, in holidays, to look after the small boy, who had been for a term at school – young as he was to be sent, but what else could be done? – and who, as the holidays were about to begin, would be back from one day to the other. There had been for the two children at first a young lady whom they had had the misfortune to lose. She had done for them quite beautifully – she was a most respectable person – till her death, the great awkwardness of which had, precisely, left no alternative but the school for little Miles. Mrs. Grose, since then, in the way of manners and things, had done as she could for Flora; and there were, further, a cook, a housemaid, a dairywoman, an old pony, an old groom, and an old gardener, all likewise thoroughly respectable.

So far had Douglas presented his picture when someone put a question. "And what did the former governess die of? – of so much respectability?"

Our friend's answer was prompt. "That will come out. I don't anticipate."

"Excuse me – I thought that was just what you *are* doing."

"In her successor's place," I suggested, "I should have wished to learn if the office brought with it—"

"Necessary danger to life?" Douglas completed my thought. "She did wish to learn, and she did learn. You shall hear tomorrow what she learned. Meanwhile, of course, the prospect struck her as slightly grim. She was young, untried, nervous: it was a vision of serious duties and little company, of really great loneliness. She hesitated – took a couple of days to consult and consider. But the salary offered much exceeded her modest measure, and on a second interview she faced the music, she engaged." And Douglas, with this, made a pause that, for the benefit of the company, moved me to throw in—

"The moral of which was of course the seduction exercised by the splendid young man. She succumbed to it."

He got up and, as he had done the night before, went to the fire, gave a stir to a log with his foot, then stood a moment with his back to us. "She saw him only twice."

"Yes, but that's just the beauty of her passion."

A little to my surprise, on this, Douglas turned round to me. "It *was* the beauty of it. There were others," he went on, "who hadn't succumbed. He told her frankly all his difficulty – that for several applicants the conditions had been prohibitive. They were, somehow, simply afraid. It sounded dull – it sounded strange; and all the more so because of his main condition."

"Which was—?"

"That she should never trouble him – but never, never: neither appeal nor complain nor write about anything; only meet all questions herself, receive all moneys from his solicitor, take the whole thing over and let him alone. She promised to do this, and she mentioned to me that when, for a moment, disburdened, delighted, he held her hand, thanking her for the sacrifice, she already felt rewarded."

"But was that all her reward?" one of the ladies asked.

"She never saw him again."

"Oh!" said the lady; which, as our friend immediately left us again, was the only other word of importance contributed to the subject till, the next night, by the corner of the hearth, in the best chair, he opened the faded red cover of a thin old-fashioned gilt-edged album. The whole thing took indeed more nights than one, but on the first occasion the same lady put another question. "What is your title?"

"I haven't one."

"Oh, *I* have!" I said. But Douglas, without heeding me, had begun to read with a fine clearness that was like a rendering to the ear of the beauty of his author's hand.

Chapter I

I REMEMBER the whole beginning as a succession of flights and drops, a little seesaw of the right throbs and the wrong. After rising, in town, to meet his appeal, I had at all events a couple of very bad days – found myself doubtful again, felt indeed sure I had made a mistake. In this state of mind I spent the long hours of bumping, swinging coach that carried me to the stopping place at which I was to be met by a vehicle from the house. This convenience, I was told, had been ordered, and I found, toward the close of the June afternoon, a commodious fly in waiting for me. Driving at that hour, on a lovely day, through a country to which the summer sweetness seemed to offer me a friendly welcome, my fortitude mounted afresh and, as we turned into the avenue, encountered a reprieve that was probably but a proof of the point to which it had sunk. I suppose I had expected, or had dreaded, something so melancholy that what greeted me was a good surprise. I remember as a most pleasant impression the broad, clear front, its open windows and fresh curtains and the pair of maids looking out; I remember the lawn and the bright flowers and the crunch of my wheels on the gravel and the clustered treetops over which the rooks circled and cawed in the golden sky. The scene had a greatness that made it a different affair from my own scant home, and there immediately appeared at the door, with a little girl in her hand, a civil person who dropped me as decent a curtsy as if I had been the mistress or a distinguished visitor. I had received in Harley Street a narrower notion of the place, and that, as I recalled it, made me think the proprietor still more of a gentleman, suggested that what I was to enjoy might be something beyond his promise.

I had no drop again till the next day, for I was carried triumphantly through the following hours by my introduction to the younger of my pupils. The little girl who accompanied Mrs. Grose appeared to me on the spot a creature so charming as to make it a great fortune to have to do with her. She was the most beautiful child I had ever seen, and I afterward wondered that my employer had not told me more of her. I slept little that night – I was too much excited; and this astonished me, too, I recollect, remained with me, adding to my sense of the liberality with which I was treated. The large, impressive room, one of the best in the house, the great state bed, as I almost felt it, the full, figured draperies, the long glasses in which, for the first time, I could see myself from head to foot, all struck me – like the extraordinary charm of my small charge – as so many things thrown in. It was thrown in as well, from the first moment, that I should get on with Mrs. Grose in a relation over which, on my way, in the coach, I fear I had rather brooded. The only thing indeed that in this early outlook might have made me shrink again was the clear circumstance of her being so glad to see me. I perceived within half an hour that she was so glad – stout, simple, plain, clean, wholesome woman – as to be positively on her guard against showing it too much. I wondered even then a little why she should wish not to show it, and that, with reflection, with suspicion, might of course have made me uneasy.

But it was a comfort that there could be no uneasiness in a connection with anything so beatific as the radiant image of my little girl, the vision of whose angelic beauty had probably more than anything else to do with the restlessness that, before morning, made me several times rise and wander about my room to take in the whole picture and prospect; to watch, from my open window, the faint summer dawn, to look at such portions of the rest of the house as I could catch, and to listen, while, in the fading dusk, the first birds began to twitter, for the possible recurrence of a sound or two, less natural and not without, but within, that I had fancied I heard. There had been a moment when I believed I recognized, faint and far, the cry of a child; there had been another when I found myself just consciously starting as at the passage, before my door, of a light footstep. But these fancies were not marked enough not to be thrown off, and it is only in the light, or the gloom, I should rather say, of other and subsequent matters that they now come back to me. To watch, teach, 'form' little Flora would too evidently be the making of a happy and useful life. It had been agreed between us downstairs that after this first occasion I should have her as a matter of course at night, her small white bed being already arranged, to that end, in my room. What I had undertaken was the whole care of her, and she had remained, just this last time, with Mrs. Grose only as an effect of our consideration for my inevitable strangeness and her natural timidity. In spite of this timidity – which the child herself, in the oddest way in the world, had been perfectly frank and brave about, allowing it, without a sign of uncomfortable consciousness, with the deep, sweet serenity indeed of one of Raphael's holy infants, to be discussed, to be imputed to her, and to determine us – I feel quite sure she would presently like me. It was part of what I already liked Mrs. Grose herself for, the pleasure I could see her feel in my admiration and wonder as I sat at supper with four tall candles and with my pupil, in a high chair and a bib, brightly facing me, between them, over bread and milk. There were naturally things that in Flora's presence could pass between us only as prodigious and gratified looks, obscure and roundabout allusions.

"And the little boy – does he look like her? Is he too so very remarkable?"

One wouldn't flatter a child. "Oh, miss, *most* remarkable. If you think well of this one!" – and she stood there with a plate in her hand, beaming at our companion, who looked from one of us to the other with placid heavenly eyes that contained nothing to check us.

"Yes; if I do—?"

"You *will* be carried away by the little gentleman!"

"Well, that, I think, is what I came for – to be carried away. I'm afraid, however," I remember feeling the impulse to add, "I'm rather easily carried away. I was carried away in London!"

I can still see Mrs. Grose's broad face as she took this in. "In Harley Street?"

"In Harley Street."

"Well, miss, you're not the first – and you won't be the last."

"Oh, I've no pretension," I could laugh, "to being the only one. My other pupil, at any rate, as I understand, comes back tomorrow?"

"Not tomorrow – Friday, miss. He arrives, as you did, by the coach, under care of the guard, and is to be met by the same carriage."

I forthwith expressed that the proper as well as the pleasant and friendly thing would be therefore that on the arrival of the public conveyance I should be in waiting for him with his little sister; an idea in which Mrs. Grose concurred so heartily that I somehow took her manner as a kind of comforting pledge – never falsified, thank heaven! – that we should on every question be quite at one. Oh, she was glad I was there!

What I felt the next day was, I suppose, nothing that could be fairly called a reaction from the cheer of my arrival; it was probably at the most only a slight oppression produced by a fuller measure of the scale, as I walked round them, gazed up at them, took them in, of my new circumstances. They had, as it were, an extent and mass for which I had not been prepared and in the presence of which I found myself, freshly, a little scared as well as a little proud. Lessons, in this agitation, certainly suffered some delay; I reflected that my first duty was, by the gentlest arts I could contrive, to win the child into the sense of knowing me. I spent the day with her out-of-doors; I arranged with her, to her great satisfaction, that it should be she, she only, who might show me the place. She showed it step by step and room by room and secret by secret, with droll, delightful, childish talk about it and with the result, in half an hour, of our becoming immense friends. Young as she was, I was struck, throughout our little tour, with her confidence and courage with the way, in empty chambers and dull corridors, on crooked staircases that made me pause and even on the summit of an old machicolated square tower that made me dizzy, her morning music, her disposition to tell me so many more things than she asked, rang out and led me on. I have not seen Bly since the day I left it, and I daresay that to my older and more informed eyes it would now appear sufficiently contracted. But as my little conductress, with her hair of gold and her frock of blue, danced before me round corners and pattered down passages, I had the view of a castle of romance inhabited by a rosy sprite, such a place as would somehow, for diversion of the young idea, take all color out of storybooks and fairytales. Wasn't it just a storybook over which I had fallen adoze and adream? No; it was a big, ugly, antique, but convenient house, embodying a few features of a building still older, half-replaced and half-utilized, in which I had the fancy of our being almost as lost as a handful of passengers in a great drifting ship. Well, I was, strangely, at the helm!

Chapter II

THIS CAME HOME to me when, two days later, I drove over with Flora to meet, as Mrs. Grose said, the little gentleman; and all the more for an incident that, presenting itself the second evening, had deeply disconcerted me. The first day had been, on the whole, as I have expressed, reassuring; but I was to see it wind up in keen apprehension. The postbag, that evening – it came late – contained a letter for me, which, however, in the hand of my employer, I found to be composed but of a few words enclosing another, addressed to himself, with a seal still unbroken. "This, I recognize, is from the headmaster, and the headmaster's an awful bore. Read him, please; deal with him; but mind you don't report. Not a word. I'm off!" I broke the seal with a great effort – so great a one that I was a long time coming to it; took the unopened missive at last up to my room and only attacked it just before going to bed. I had better have let it wait till morning, for it gave me a second sleepless night. With no counsel to take, the next day, I was full of distress; and it finally got so the better of me that I determined to open myself at least to Mrs. Grose.

"What does it mean? The child's dismissed his school."

She gave me a look that I remarked at the moment; then, visibly, with a quick blankness, seemed to try to take it back. "But aren't they all—?"

"Sent home – yes. But only for the holidays. Miles may never go back at all."

Consciously, under my attention, she reddened. "They won't take him?"

"They absolutely decline."

At this she raised her eyes, which she had turned from me; I saw them fill with good tears. "What has he done?"

I hesitated; then I judged best simply to hand her my letter – which, however, had the effect of making her, without taking it, simply put her hands behind her. She shook her head sadly. "Such things are not for me, miss."

My counselor couldn't read! I winced at my mistake, which I attenuated as I could, and opened my letter again to repeat it to her; then, faltering in the act and folding it up once more, I put it back in my pocket. "Is he really *bad*?"

The tears were still in her eyes. "Do the gentlemen say so?"

"They go into no particulars. They simply express their regret that it should be impossible to keep him. That can have only one meaning." Mrs. Grose listened with dumb emotion; she forbore to ask me what this meaning might be; so that, presently, to put the thing with some coherence and with the mere aid of her presence to my own mind, I went on: "That he's an injury to the others."

At this, with one of the quick turns of simple folk, she suddenly flamed up. "Master Miles! *Him* an injury?"

There was such a flood of good faith in it that, though I had not yet seen the child, my very fears made me jump to the absurdity of the idea. I found myself, to meet my friend the better, offering it, on the spot, sarcastically. "To his poor little innocent mates!"

"It's too dreadful," cried Mrs. Grose, "to say such cruel things! Why, he's scarce ten years old."

"Yes, yes; it would be incredible."

She was evidently grateful for such a profession. "See him, miss, first. *Then* believe it!" I felt forthwith a new impatience to see him; it was the beginning of a curiosity that, for all the next hours, was to deepen almost to pain. Mrs. Grose was aware, I could judge, of what she had produced in me, and she followed it up with assurance. "You might as well believe it of the little lady. Bless her," she added the next moment – "*look* at her!"

I turned and saw that Flora, whom, ten minutes before, I had established in the schoolroom with a sheet of white paper, a pencil, and a copy of nice 'round O's', now presented herself to view at the open door. She expressed in her little way an extraordinary detachment from disagreeable duties, looking to me, however, with a great childish light that seemed to offer it as a mere result of the affection she had conceived for my person, which had rendered necessary that she should follow me. I needed nothing more than this to feel the full force of Mrs. Grose's comparison, and, catching my pupil in my arms, covered her with kisses in which there was a sob of atonement.

Nonetheless, the rest of the day I watched for further occasion to approach my colleague, especially as, toward evening, I began to fancy she rather sought to avoid me. I overtook her, I remember, on the staircase; we went down together, and at the bottom I detained her, holding her there with a hand on her arm. "I take what you said to me at noon as a declaration that *you've* never known him to be bad."

She threw back her head; she had clearly, by this time, and very honestly, adopted an attitude. "Oh, never known him – I don't pretend *that!*"

I was upset again. "Then you *have* known him—?"

"Yes indeed, miss, thank God!"

On reflection I accepted this. "You mean that a boy who never is—?"

"Is no boy for *me!*"

I held her tighter. "You like them with the spirit to be naughty?" Then, keeping pace with her answer, "So do I!" I eagerly brought out. "But not to the degree to contaminate—"

"To contaminate?" – my big word left her at a loss. I explained it. "To corrupt."

She stared, taking my meaning in; but it produced in her an odd laugh. "Are you afraid he'll corrupt *you?*" She put the question with such a fine bold humor that, with a laugh, a little silly doubtless, to match her own, I gave way for the time to the apprehension of ridicule.

But the next day, as the hour for my drive approached, I cropped up in another place. "What was the lady who was here before?"

"The last governess? She was also young and pretty – almost as young and almost as pretty, miss, even as you."

"Ah, then, I hope her youth and her beauty helped her!" I recollect throwing off. "He seems to like us young and pretty!"

"Oh, he *did*," Mrs. Grose assented: "it was the way he liked everyone!" She had no sooner spoken indeed than she caught herself up. "I mean that's *his* way – the master's."

I was struck. "But of whom did you speak first?"

She looked blank, but she colored. "Why, of *him*."

"Of the master?"

"Of who else?"

There was so obviously no one else that the next moment I had lost my impression of her having accidentally said more than she meant; and I merely asked what I wanted to know. "Did *she* see anything in the boy—?"

"That wasn't right? She never told me."

I had a scruple, but I overcame it. "Was she careful – particular?"

Mrs. Grose appeared to try to be conscientious. "About some things – yes."

"But not about all?"

Again she considered. "Well, miss – she's gone. I won't tell tales."

"I quite understand your feeling," I hastened to reply; but I thought it, after an instant, not opposed to this concession to pursue: "Did she die here?"

"No – she went off."

I don't know what there was in this brevity of Mrs. Grose's that struck me as ambiguous. "Went off to die?" Mrs. Grose looked straight out of the window, but I felt that, hypothetically, I had a right to know what young persons engaged for Bly were expected to do. "She was taken ill, you mean, and went home?"

"She was not taken ill, so far as appeared, in this house. She left it, at the end of the year, to go home, as she said, for a short holiday, to which the time she had put in had certainly given her a right. We had then a young woman – a nursemaid who had stayed on and who was a good girl and clever; and *she* took the children altogether for the interval. But our young lady never came back, and at the very moment I was expecting her I heard from the master that she was dead."

I turned this over. "But of what?"

"He never told me! But please, miss," said Mrs. Grose, "I must get to my work."

Chapter III

HER THUS TURNING her back on me was fortunately not, for my just preoccupations, a snub that could check the growth of our mutual esteem. We met, after I had brought home little Miles, more intimately than ever on the ground of my stupefaction, my general emotion: so monstrous was I then ready to pronounce it that such a child as had now been revealed to me should be under an interdict. I was a little late on the scene, and I felt, as he stood wistfully looking out for me before the door of the inn at which the coach had put him down, that I had seen him, on the instant, without and within, in the great glow of freshness, the same positive fragrance of purity, in which I had, from the first moment, seen his little sister. He was incredibly beautiful, and Mrs. Grose had put her finger on it: everything but a sort of passion of tenderness for him was swept away by his presence. What I then and there took him to my heart for was something divine that I have never found to the same degree in any child – his indescribable little air of knowing nothing in the world but love. It would have been impossible to carry a bad name with a greater sweetness of innocence, and by the time I had got back to Bly with him I remained merely bewildered – so far, that is, as I was not outraged – by the sense of the horrible letter locked up in my room, in a drawer. As soon as I could compass a private word with Mrs. Grose I declared to her that it was grotesque.

She promptly understood me. "You mean the cruel charge—?"

"It doesn't live an instant. My dear woman, *look* at him!"

She smiled at my pretention to have discovered his charm. "I assure you, miss, I do nothing else! What will you say, then?" she immediately added.

"In answer to the letter?" I had made up my mind. "Nothing."

"And to his uncle?"

I was incisive. "Nothing."

"And to the boy himself?"

I was wonderful. "Nothing."

She gave with her apron a great wipe to her mouth. "Then I'll stand by you. We'll see it out."

"We'll see it out!" I ardently echoed, giving her my hand to make it a vow.

She held me there a moment, then whisked up her apron again with her detached hand. "Would you mind, miss, if I used the freedom—"

"To kiss me? No!" I took the good creature in my arms and, after we had embraced like sisters, felt still more fortified and indignant.

This, at all events, was for the time: a time so full that, as I recall the way it went, it reminds me of all the art I now need to make it a little distinct. What I look back at with amazement is the situation I accepted. I had undertaken, with my companion, to see it out, and I was under a charm, apparently, that could smooth away the extent and the far and difficult connections of such an effort. I was lifted aloft on a great wave of infatuation and pity. I found it simple, in my ignorance, my confusion, and perhaps my conceit, to assume that I could deal with a boy whose education for the world was all on the point of beginning. I am unable even to remember at this day what proposal I framed for the end of his holidays and the resumption of his studies. Lessons with me, indeed, that charming summer, we all had a theory that he was to have; but I now feel that, for weeks, the lessons must have been rather my own. I learned something – at first, certainly – that had not been one of the teachings of my small, smothered life; learned to be amused, and even amusing, and not to think for the morrow. It was the first time, in a manner, that I had known space and air and freedom, all the music of summer and all the mystery of nature. And then there was consideration – and consideration was sweet. Oh, it was a trap – not designed, but deep – to my imagination, to my delicacy, perhaps to my vanity; to whatever, in me, was most excitable. The best way to picture it all is to say that I was off my guard. They gave me so little trouble – they were of a gentleness so extraordinary. I used to speculate – but even this with a dim disconnectedness – as to how the rough future (for all futures are rough!) would handle them and might bruise them. They had the bloom of health and happiness; and yet, as if I had been in charge of a pair of little grandees, of princes of the blood, for whom everything, to be right, would have to be enclosed and protected, the only form that, in my fancy, the afteryears could take for them was that of a romantic, a really royal extension of the garden and the park. It may be, of course, above all, that what suddenly broke into this gives the previous time a charm of stillness – that hush in which something gathers or crouches. The change was actually like the spring of a beast.

In the first weeks the days were long; they often, at their finest, gave me what I used to call my own hour, the hour when, for my pupils, teatime and bedtime having come and gone, I had, before my final retirement, a small interval alone. Much as I liked my companions, this hour was the thing in the day I liked most; and I liked it best of all when, as the light faded – or rather, I should say, the day lingered and the last calls of the last birds sounded, in a flushed sky, from the old trees – I could take a turn into the grounds and enjoy, almost with a sense of property that amused and flattered me, the beauty and dignity of the place. It was a pleasure at these moments to feel myself tranquil and justified; doubtless, perhaps, also to reflect that by my discretion, my quiet good sense and general high propriety, I was giving pleasure – if he ever thought of it! – to the person to whose pressure I had responded. What I was doing was what he had earnestly hoped and directly asked of me, and that I *could*, after all, do it proved even a greater joy than I had expected. I daresay I fancied myself, in short, a remarkable young woman and took comfort in the faith that this would more publicly appear. Well, I needed to be remarkable to offer a front to the remarkable things that presently gave their first sign.

It was plump, one afternoon, in the middle of my very hour: the children were tucked away, and I had come out for my stroll. One of the thoughts that, as I don't in the least shrink now from noting, used to be with me in these wanderings was that it would be as charming as a charming story suddenly to meet someone. Someone would appear there at the turn of a path and would stand before me and smile and approve. I didn't ask more than that – I only asked that he should *know;* and the only way to be sure he knew would be to see it, and the kind light of it, in his handsome face. That was exactly present to me – by which I mean the face was – when, on the first of these occasions, at the end of a long June day, I stopped short on emerging from one of the plantations and coming into view of the house. What arrested me on the spot – and with a shock much greater than any vision had allowed for – was the sense that my imagination had, in a flash, turned real. He did stand there! – but high up, beyond the lawn and at the very top of the tower to which, on that first morning, little Flora had conducted me. This tower was one of a pair – square, incongruous, crenelated structures – that were distinguished, for some reason, though I could see little difference, as the new and the old. They flanked opposite ends of the house and were probably architectural absurdities, redeemed in a measure indeed by not being wholly disengaged nor of a height too pretentious, dating, in their gingerbread antiquity, from a romantic revival that was already a respectable past. I admired them, had fancies about them, for we could all profit in a degree, especially when they loomed through the dusk, by the grandeur of their actual battlements; yet it was not at such an elevation that the figure I had so often invoked seemed most in place.

It produced in me, this figure, in the clear twilight, I remember, two distinct gasps of emotion, which were, sharply, the shock of my first and that of my second surprise. My second was a violent perception of the mistake of my first: the man who met my eyes was not the person I had precipitately supposed. There came to me thus a bewilderment of vision of which, after these years, there is no living view that I can hope to give. An unknown man in a lonely place is a permitted object of fear to a young woman privately bred; and the figure that faced me was – a few more seconds assured me – as little anyone else I knew as it was the image that had been in my mind. I had not seen it in Harley Street – I had not seen it anywhere. The place, moreover, in the strangest way in the world, had, on the instant, and by the very fact of its appearance, become a solitude. To me at least, making my statement here with a deliberation with which I have never made it, the whole feeling of the moment returns. It was as if, while I took in – what I did take in – all the rest of the scene had been stricken with death. I can hear again, as I write, the intense hush in which the sounds of evening dropped. The rooks stopped cawing in the golden sky, and the friendly hour lost, for the minute, all its voice. But there was no other change in nature, unless indeed it were a change that I saw with a stranger sharpness. The gold was still in the sky, the clearness in the air, and the man who looked at me over the battlements was as definite as a picture in a frame. That's how I thought, with extraordinary quickness, of each person that he might have been and that he was not. We were confronted across our distance quite long enough for me to ask myself with intensity who then he was and to feel, as an effect of my inability to say, a wonder that in a few instants more became intense.

The great question, or one of these, is, afterward, I know, with regard to certain matters, the question of how long they have lasted. Well, this matter of mine, think what you will of it, lasted while I caught at a dozen possibilities, none of which made a difference for the better, that I could see, in there having been in the house – and for how long, above all? – a person of whom I was in ignorance. It lasted while I just bridled a little with the sense that my office demanded that there should be no such ignorance and no such person. It lasted while this visitant, at all events – and there was a touch of the strange freedom, as I remember, in the sign of familiarity of his wearing no hat – seemed to fix me, from his position, with just the question, just the scrutiny through the fading light, that his own presence provoked. We were too far apart to call to each other, but there was a moment at which, at shorter range, some challenge between us, breaking the hush, would have been the right result of our straight mutual stare. He was in one of the angles, the one away from the house, very erect, as it struck me, and with both hands on the ledge. So I saw him as I see the letters I form on this page; then, exactly, after a minute, as if to add to the spectacle, he slowly changed his place – passed, looking at me hard all the while, to the opposite corner of the platform. Yes, I had the sharpest sense that during this transit he never took his eyes from me, and I can see at this moment the way his hand, as he went, passed from one of the crenelations to the next. He stopped at the other corner, but less long, and even as he turned away still markedly fixed me. He turned away; that was all I knew.

Chapter IV

IT WAS NOT that I didn't wait, on this occasion, for more, for I was rooted as deeply as I was shaken. Was there a 'secret' at Bly – a mystery of Udolpho or an insane, an unmentionable relative kept in unsuspected confinement? I can't say how long I turned it over, or how long, in a confusion of curiosity and dread, I remained where I had had my collision; I only recall that when I re-entered the house darkness had quite closed in. Agitation, in the interval, certainly had held me and driven me, for I must, in circling about the place, have walked three miles; but I was to be, later on, so much more overwhelmed that this mere dawn of alarm was a comparatively human chill. The most singular part of it, in fact – singular as the rest had been – was the part I became, in the hall, aware of in meeting Mrs. Grose. This picture comes back to me in the general train – the impression, as I received it on my return, of the wide white panelled space, bright in the lamplight and with its portraits and red carpet, and of the good surprised look of my friend, which immediately told me she had missed me. It came to me straightway, under her contact, that, with plain heartiness, mere relieved anxiety at my appearance, she knew nothing whatever that could bear upon the incident I had there ready for her. I had not suspected in advance that her comfortable face would pull me up, and I somehow measured the importance of what I had seen by my thus finding myself hesitate to mention it. Scarce anything in the whole history seems to me so odd as this fact that my real beginning of fear was one, as I may say, with the instinct of sparing my companion. On the spot, accordingly, in the pleasant hall and with her eyes on me, I, for a reason that I couldn't then have phrased, achieved an inward resolution – offered a vague pretext for my lateness and, with the plea of the beauty of the night and of the heavy dew and wet feet, went as soon as possible to my room.

Here it was another affair; here, for many days after, it was a queer affair enough. There were hours, from day to day – or at least there were moments, snatched even from clear duties – when I had to shut myself up to think. It was not so much yet that I was more nervous than I could bear to be as that I was remarkably afraid of becoming so; for the truth I had now to turn over was, simply and clearly, the truth that I could arrive at no account whatever of the visitor with whom I had been so inexplicably and yet, as it seemed to me, so intimately concerned. It took little time to see that I could sound without forms of inquiry and without exciting remark any domestic complications. The shock I had suffered must have sharpened all my senses; I felt sure, at the end of three days and as the result of mere closer attention, that I had not been practiced upon by the servants nor made the object of any 'game'. Of whatever it was that I knew, nothing was known around me. There was but one sane inference: someone had taken a liberty rather gross. That was what, repeatedly, I dipped into my room and locked the door to say to myself. We had been, collectively, subject to an intrusion; some unscrupulous traveler, curious in old houses, had made his way in unobserved, enjoyed the prospect from the best point of view, and then stolen out as he came. If he had given me such a bold hard stare, that was but a part of his indiscretion. The good thing, after all, was that we should surely see no more of him.

This was not so good a thing, I admit, as not to leave me to judge that what, essentially, made nothing else much signify was simply my charming work. My charming work was just my life with Miles and Flora, and through nothing could I so like it as through feeling that I could throw myself into it in trouble. The attraction of my small charges was a constant joy, leading me to wonder afresh at the vanity of my original fears, the distaste I had begun by entertaining for the probable gray prose of my office. There was to be no gray prose, it appeared, and no long grind; so how could work not be charming that presented itself as daily beauty? It was all the romance of the nursery and the poetry of the schoolroom. I don't mean by this, of course, that we studied only fiction and verse; I mean I can express no otherwise the sort of interest my companions inspired. How can I describe that except by saying that instead of growing used to them – and it's a marvel for a governess: I call the sisterhood to witness! – I made constant fresh discoveries. There was one direction, assuredly, in which these discoveries stopped: deep obscurity continued to cover the region of the boy's conduct at school. It had been promptly given me, I have noted, to face that mystery without a pang. Perhaps even it would be nearer the truth to say that – without a word – he himself had cleared it up. He had made the whole charge absurd. My conclusion bloomed there with the real rose flush of his innocence: he was only too fine and fair for the little horrid, unclean school-world, and he had paid a price for it. I reflected acutely that the sense of such differences, such superiorities of quality, always, on the part of the majority – which could include even stupid, sordid headmasters – turn infallibly to the vindictive.

Both the children had a gentleness (it was their only fault, and it never made Miles a muff) that kept them – how shall I express it? – almost impersonal and certainly quite unpunishable. They were like the cherubs of the anecdote, who had – morally, at any rate – nothing to whack! I remember feeling with Miles in especial as if he had had, as it were, no history. We expect of a small child a scant one, but there was in this beautiful little boy something extraordinarily sensitive, yet extraordinarily happy, that, more than in any creature of his age I have seen, struck me as beginning anew each day. He had never for a second suffered. I took this as a direct disproof of his having really been chastised. If he had been wicked he would have 'caught' it, and I should have caught it by the rebound – I should have found the trace. I found nothing at all, and he was therefore an angel. He never spoke of his school, never mentioned a comrade or a master; and I, for my part, was quite too much disgusted to allude to them. Of course I was under the spell, and the wonderful part is that, even at the time, I perfectly knew I was. But I gave myself up to it; it was an antidote to any pain, and I had more pains than one. I was in receipt in these days of disturbing letters from home, where things were not going well. But with my children, what things in the world mattered? That was the question I used to put to my scrappy retirements. I was dazzled by their loveliness.

There was a Sunday – to get on – when it rained with such force and for so many hours that there could be no procession to church; in consequence of which, as the day declined, I had arranged with Mrs. Grose that, should the evening show improvement, we would attend together the late service. The rain happily stopped, and I prepared for our walk, which, through the park and by the good road to the village, would be a matter of twenty minutes. Coming downstairs to meet my colleague in the hall, I remembered a pair of gloves that had required three stitches and that had received them – with a publicity perhaps not edifying – while I sat with the children at their tea, served on Sundays, by exception, in that cold, clean temple of mahogany and brass, the 'grown-up' dining room. The gloves had been dropped there, and I turned in to recover them. The day was gray enough, but the afternoon light still lingered, and it enabled me, on crossing the threshold, not only to recognize, on a chair near the wide window, then closed, the articles I wanted, but to become aware of a person on the other side of the window and looking straight in. One step into the room had sufficed; my vision was instantaneous; it was all there. The person looking straight in was the person who had already appeared to me. He appeared thus again with I won't say greater distinctness, for that was impossible, but with a nearness that represented a forward stride in our intercourse and made me, as I met him, catch my breath and turn cold. He was the same – he was the same, and seen, this time, as he had been seen before, from the waist up, the window, though the dining room was on the ground floor, not going down to the terrace on which he stood. His face was close to the glass, yet the effect of this better view was, strangely, only to show me how intense the former had been. He remained but a few seconds – long enough to convince me he also saw and recognized; but it was as if I had been looking at him for years and had known him always. Something, however, happened this time that had not happened before; his stare into my face, through the glass and across the room, was as deep and hard as then, but it quitted me for a moment during which I could still watch it, see it fix successively several other things. On the spot there came to me the added shock of a certitude that it was not for me he had come there. He had come for someone else.

The flash of this knowledge – for it was knowledge in the midst of dread – produced in me the most extraordinary effect, started as I stood there, a sudden vibration of duty and courage. I say courage because I was beyond all doubt already far gone. I bounded straight out of the door again, reached that of the house, got, in an instant, upon the drive, and, passing along the terrace as fast as I could rush, turned a corner and came full in sight. But it was in sight of nothing now – my visitor had vanished. I stopped, I almost dropped, with the real relief of this; but I took in the whole scene – I gave him time to reappear. I call it time, but how long was it? I can't speak to the purpose today of the duration of these things. That kind of measure must have left me: they couldn't have lasted as they actually appeared to me to last. The terrace and the whole place, the lawn and the garden beyond it, all I could see of the park, were empty with a great emptiness. There were shrubberies and big trees, but I remember the clear assurance I felt that none of them concealed him. He was there or was not there: not there if I didn't see him. I got hold of this; then, instinctively, instead of returning as I had come, went to the window. It was confusedly present to me that I ought to place myself where he had stood. I did so; I applied my face to the pane and looked, as he had looked, into the room. As if, at this moment, to show me exactly what his range had been, Mrs. Grose, as I had done for himself just before, came in from the hall. With this I had the full image of a repetition of what had already occurred. She saw me as I had seen my own visitant; she pulled up short as I had done; I gave her something of the shock that I had received. She turned white, and this made me ask myself if I had blanched as much. She stared, in short, and retreated on just *my* lines, and I knew she had then passed out and come round to me and that I should presently meet her. I remained where I was, and while I waited I thought of more things than one. But there's only one I take space to mention. I wondered why *she* should be scared.

Chapter V

OH, SHE let me know as soon as, round the corner of the house, she loomed again into view. "What in the name of goodness is the matter—?" She was now flushed and out of breath.

I said nothing till she came quite near. "With me?" I must have made a wonderful face. "Do I show it?"

"You're as white as a sheet. You look awful."

I considered; I could meet on this, without scruple, any innocence. My need to respect the bloom of Mrs. Grose's had dropped, without a rustle, from my shoulders, and if I wavered for the instant it was not with what I kept back. I put out my hand to her and she took it; I held her hard a little, liking to feel her close to me. There was a kind of support in the shy heave of her surprise. "You came for me for church, of course, but I can't go."

"Has anything happened?"

"Yes. You must know now. Did I look very queer?"

"Through this window? Dreadful!"

"Well," I said, "I've been frightened." Mrs. Grose's eyes expressed plainly that *she* had no wish to be, yet also that she knew too well her place not to be ready to share with me any marked inconvenience. Oh, it was quite settled that she *must* share! "Just what you saw from the dining room a minute ago was the effect of that. What *I* saw – just before – was much worse."

Her hand tightened. "What was it?"

"An extraordinary man. Looking in."

"What extraordinary man?"

"I haven't the least idea."

Mrs. Grose gazed round us in vain. "Then where is he gone?"

"I know still less."

"Have you seen him before?"

"Yes – once. On the old tower."

She could only look at me harder. "Do you mean he's a stranger?"

"Oh, very much!"

"Yet you didn't tell me?"

"No – for reasons. But now that you've guessed—"

Mrs. Grose's round eyes encountered this charge. "Ah, I haven't guessed!" she said very simply. "How can I if *you* don't imagine?"

"I don't in the very least."

"You've seen him nowhere but on the tower?"

"And on this spot just now."

Mrs. Grose looked round again. "What was he doing on the tower?"

"Only standing there and looking down at me."

She thought a minute. "Was he a gentleman?"

I found I had no need to think. "No." She gazed in deeper wonder. "No."

"Then nobody about the place? Nobody from the village?"

"Nobody – nobody. I didn't tell you, but I made sure."

She breathed a vague relief: this was, oddly, so much to the good. It only went indeed a little way. "But if he isn't a gentleman—"

"What *is* he? He's a horror."

"A horror?"

"He's – God help me if I know *what* he is!"

Mrs. Grose looked round once more; she fixed her eyes on the duskier distance, then, pulling herself together, turned to me with abrupt inconsequence. "It's time we should be at church."

"Oh, I'm not fit for church!"

"Won't it do you good?"

"It won't do *them!*" – I nodded at the house.

"The children?"

"I can't leave them now."

"You're afraid—?"

I spoke boldly. "I'm afraid of *him*."

Mrs. Grose's large face showed me, at this, for the first time, the faraway faint glimmer of a consciousness more acute: I somehow made out in it the delayed dawn of an idea I myself had not given her and that was as yet quite obscure to me. It comes back to me that I thought instantly of this as something I could get from her; and I felt it to be connected with the desire she presently showed to know more. "When was it – on the tower?"

"About the middle of the month. At this same hour."

"Almost at dark," said Mrs. Grose.

"Oh, no, not nearly. I saw him as I see you."

"Then how did he get in?"

"And how did he get out?" I laughed. "I had no opportunity to ask him! This evening, you see," I pursued, "he has not been able to get in."

"He only peeps?"

"I hope it will be confined to that!" She had now let go my hand; she turned away a little. I waited an instant; then I brought out: "Go to church. Goodbye. I must watch."

Slowly she faced me again. "Do you fear for them?"

We met in another long look. "Don't *you?*" Instead of answering she came nearer to the window and, for a minute, applied her face to the glass. "You see how he could see," I meanwhile went on.

She didn't move. "How long was he here?"

"Till I came out. I came to meet him."

Mrs. Grose at last turned round, and there was still more in her face. "*I* couldn't have come out."

"Neither could I!" I laughed again. "But I did come. I have my duty."

"So have I mine," she replied; after which she added: "What is he like?"

"I've been dying to tell you. But he's like nobody."

"Nobody?" she echoed.

"He has no hat." Then seeing in her face that she already, in this, with a deeper dismay, found a touch of picture, I quickly added stroke to stroke. "He has red hair, very red, close-curling, and a pale face, long in shape, with straight, good features and little, rather queer whiskers that are as red as his hair. His eyebrows are, somehow, darker; they look particularly arched and as if they might move a good deal. His eyes are sharp, strange – awfully; but I only know clearly that they're rather small and very fixed. His mouth's wide, and his lips are thin, and except for his little whiskers he's quite clean-shaven. He gives me a sort of sense of looking like an actor."

"An actor!" It was impossible to resemble one less, at least, than Mrs. Grose at that moment.

"I've never seen one, but so I suppose them. He's tall, active, erect," I continued, "but never – no, never! – a gentleman."

My companion's face had blanched as I went on; her round eyes started and her mild mouth gaped. "A gentleman?" she gasped, confounded, stupefied: "a gentleman *he?*"

"You know him then?"

She visibly tried to hold herself. "But he *is* handsome?"

I saw the way to help her. "Remarkably!"

"And dressed—?"

"In somebody's clothes."

"They're smart, but they're not his own."

She broke into a breathless affirmative groan: "They're the master's!"

I caught it up. "You *do* know him?"

She faltered but a second. "Quint!" she cried.

"Quint?"

"Peter Quint – his own man, his valet, when he was here!"

"When the master was?"

Gaping still, but meeting me, she pieced it all together. "He never wore his hat, but he did wear – well, there were waistcoats missed. They were both here – last year. Then the master went, and Quint was alone."

I followed, but halting a little. "Alone?"

"Alone with *us*." Then, as from a deeper depth, "In charge," she added.

"And what became of him?"

She hung fire so long that I was still more mystified. "He went, too," she brought out at last.

"Went where?"

Her expression, at this, became extraordinary. "God knows where! He died."

"Died?" I almost shrieked.

She seemed fairly to square herself, plant herself more firmly to utter the wonder of it. "Yes. Mr. Quint is dead."

Chapter VI

IT TOOK of course more than that particular passage to place us together in presence of what we had now to live with as we could – my dreadful liability to impressions of the order so vividly exemplified, and my companion's knowledge, henceforth – a knowledge half consternation and half compassion – of that liability. There had been, this evening, after the revelation left me, for an hour, so prostrate – there had been, for either of us, no attendance on any service but a little service of tears and vows, of prayers and promises, a climax to the series of mutual challenges and pledges that had straightway ensued on our retreating together to the schoolroom and shutting ourselves up there to have everything out. The result of our having everything out was simply to reduce our situation to the last rigor of its elements. She herself had seen nothing, not the shadow of a shadow, and nobody in the house but the governess was in the governess's plight; yet she accepted without directly impugning my sanity the truth as I gave it to her, and ended by showing me, on this ground, an awestricken tenderness, an expression of the sense of my more than questionable privilege, of which the very breath has remained with me as that of the sweetest of human charities.

What was settled between us, accordingly, that night, was that we thought we might bear things together; and I was not even sure that, in spite of her exemption, it was she who had the best of the burden. I knew at this hour, I think, as well as I knew later, what I was capable of meeting to shelter my pupils; but it took me some time to be wholly sure of what my honest ally was prepared for to keep terms with so compromising a contract. I was queer company enough – quite as queer as the company I received; but as I trace over what we went through I see how much common ground we must have found in the one idea that, by good fortune, *could* steady us. It was the idea, the second movement, that led me straight out, as I may say, of the inner chamber of my dread. I could take the air in the court, at least, and there Mrs. Grose could join me. Perfectly can I recall now the particular way strength came to me before we separated for the night. We had gone over and over every feature of what I had seen.

"He was looking for someone else, you say – someone who was not you?"

"He was looking for little Miles." A portentous clearness now possessed me. "*That's* whom he was looking for."

"But how do you know?"

"I know, I know, I know!" My exaltation grew. "And *you* know, my dear!"

She didn't deny this, but I required, I felt, not even so much telling as that. She resumed in a moment, at any rate: "What if *he* should see him?"

"Little Miles? That's what he wants!"

She looked immensely scared again. "The child?"

"Heaven forbid! The man. He wants to appear to *them*." That he might was an awful conception, and yet, somehow, I could keep it at bay; which, moreover, as we lingered there, was what I succeeded in practically proving. I had an absolute certainty that I should see again what I had already seen, but something within me said that by offering myself bravely as the sole subject of such experience, by accepting, by inviting, by surmounting it all, I should serve as an expiatory victim and guard the tranquility of my companions. The children, in especial, I should thus fence about and absolutely save. I recall one of the last things I said that night to Mrs. Grose.

"It does strike me that my pupils have never mentioned—"

She looked at me hard as I musingly pulled up. "His having been here and the time they were with him?"

"The time they were with him, and his name, his presence, his history, in any way."

"Oh, the little lady doesn't remember. She never heard or knew."

"The circumstances of his death?" I thought with some intensity. "Perhaps not. But Miles would remember – Miles would know."

"Ah, don't try him!" broke from Mrs. Grose.

I returned her the look she had given me. "Don't be afraid." I continued to think. "It *is* rather odd."

"That he has never spoken of him?"

"Never by the least allusion. And you tell me they were 'great friends'?"

"Oh, it wasn't *him!*" Mrs. Grose with emphasis declared. "It was Quint's own fancy. To play with him, I mean – to spoil him." She paused a moment; then she added: "Quint was much too free."

This gave me, straight from my vision of his face – *such* a face! – a sudden sickness of disgust. "Too free with *my* boy?"

"Too free with everyone!"

I forbore, for the moment, to analyze this description further than by the reflection that a part of it applied to several of the members of the household, of the half-dozen maids and men who were still of our small colony. But there was everything, for our apprehension, in the lucky fact that no discomfortable legend, no perturbation of scullions, had ever, within anyone's memory attached to the kind old place. It had neither bad name nor ill fame, and Mrs. Grose, most apparently, only desired to cling to me and to quake in silence. I even put her, the very last thing of all, to the test.

It was when, at midnight, she had her hand on the schoolroom door to take leave. "I have it from you then – for it's of great importance – that he was definitely and admittedly bad?"

"Oh, not admittedly. *I* knew it – but the master didn't."

"And you never told him?"

"Well, he didn't like tale-bearing – he hated complaints. He was terribly short with anything of that kind, and if people were all right to *him*—"

"He wouldn't be bothered with more?" This squared well enough with my impressions of him: he was not a trouble-loving gentleman, nor so very particular perhaps about some of the company *he* kept. All the same, I pressed my interlocutress. "I promise you *I* would have told!"

She felt my discrimination. "I daresay I was wrong. But, really, I was afraid."

"Afraid of what?"

"Of things that man could do. Quint was so clever – he was so deep."

I took this in still more than, probably, I showed. "You weren't afraid of anything else? Not of his effect—?"

"His effect?" she repeated with a face of anguish and waiting while I faltered.

"On innocent little precious lives. They were in your charge."

"No, they were not in mine!" she roundly and distressfully returned. "The master believed in him and placed him here because he was supposed not to be well and the country air so good for him. So he had everything to say. Yes" – she let me have it – "even about *them*."

"Them – that creature?" I had to smother a kind of howl. "And you could bear it!"

"No. I couldn't – and I can't now!" And the poor woman burst into tears.

A rigid control, from the next day, was, as I have said, to follow them; yet how often and how passionately, for a week, we came back together to the subject! Much as we had discussed it that Sunday night, I was, in the immediate later hours in especial – for it may be imagined whether I slept – still haunted with the shadow of something she had not told me. I myself had kept back nothing, but there was a word Mrs. Grose had kept back. I was sure, moreover, by morning, that this was not from a failure of frankness, but because on every side there were fears. It seems to me indeed, in retrospect, that by the time the morrow's sun was high I had restlessly read into the fact before us almost all the meaning they were to receive from subsequent and more cruel occurrences. What they gave me above all was just the sinister figure of the living man – the dead one would keep awhile! – and of the months he had continuously passed at Bly, which, added up, made a formidable stretch. The limit of this evil time had arrived only when, on the dawn of a winter's morning, Peter Quint was found, by a laborer going to early work, stone dead on the road from the village: a catastrophe explained – superficially at least – by a visible wound to his head; such a wound as might have been produced – and as, on the final evidence, *had* been – by a fatal slip, in the dark and after leaving the public house, on the steepish icy slope, a wrong path altogether, at the bottom of which he lay. The icy slope, the turn mistaken at night and in liquor, accounted for much – practically, in the end and after the inquest and boundless chatter, for everything; but there had been matters in his life – strange passages and perils, secret disorders, vices more than suspected – that would have accounted for a good deal more.

I scarce know how to put my story into words that shall be a credible picture of my state of mind; but I was in these days literally able to find a joy in the extraordinary flight of heroism the occasion demanded of me. I now saw that I had been asked for a service admirable and difficult; and there would be a greatness in letting it be seen – oh, in the right quarter! – that I could succeed where many another girl might have failed. It was an immense help to me – I confess I rather applaud myself as I look back! – that I saw my service so strongly and so simply. I was there to protect and defend the little creatures in the world the most bereaved and the most lovable, the appeal of whose helplessness had suddenly become only too explicit, a deep, constant ache of one's own committed heart. We were cut off, really, together; we were united in our danger. They had nothing but me, and I – well, I had *them*. It was in short a magnificent chance. This chance presented itself to me in an image richly material. I was a screen – I was to stand before them. The more I saw, the less they would. I began to watch them in a stifled suspense, a disguised excitement that might well, had it continued too long, have turned to something like madness. What saved me, as I now see, was that it turned to something else altogether. It didn't last as suspense – it was superseded by horrible proofs. Proofs, I say, yes – from the moment I really took hold.

This moment dated from an afternoon hour that I happened to spend in the grounds with the younger of my pupils alone. We had left Miles indoors, on the red cushion of a deep window seat; he had wished to finish a book, and I had been glad to encourage a purpose so laudable in a young man whose only defect was an occasional excess of the restless. His sister, on the contrary, had been alert to come out, and I strolled with her half an hour, seeking the shade, for the sun was still high and the day exceptionally warm. I was aware afresh, with her, as we went, of how, like her brother, she contrived – it was the charming thing in both children – to let me alone without appearing to drop me and to accompany me without appearing to surround. They were never importunate and yet never listless. My attention to them all really went to seeing them amuse themselves immensely without me: this was a spectacle they seemed actively to prepare and that engaged me as an active admirer. I walked in a world of their invention – they had no occasion whatever to draw upon mine; so that my time was taken only with being, for them, some remarkable person or thing that the game of the moment required and that was merely, thanks to my superior, my exalted stamp, a happy and highly distinguished sinecure. I forget what I was on the present occasion; I only remember that I was something very important and very quiet and that Flora was playing very hard. We were on the edge of the lake, and, as we had lately begun geography, the lake was the Sea of Azof.

Suddenly, in these circumstances, I became aware that, on the other side of the Sea of Azof, we had an interested spectator. The way this knowledge gathered in me was the strangest thing in the world – the strangest, that is, except the very much stranger in which it quickly merged itself. I had sat down with a piece of work – for I was something or other that could sit – on the old stone bench which overlooked the pond; and in this position I began to take in with certitude, and yet without direct vision, the presence, at a distance, of a third person. The old trees, the thick shrubbery, made a great and pleasant shade, but it was all suffused with the brightness of the hot, still hour. There was no ambiguity in anything; none whatever, at least, in the conviction I from one moment to another found myself forming as to what I should see straight before me and across the lake as a consequence of raising my eyes. They were attached at this juncture to the stitching in which I was engaged, and I can feel once more the spasm of my effort not to move them till I should so have steadied myself as to be able to make up my mind what to do. There was an alien object in view – a figure whose right of presence I instantly, passionately questioned. I recollect counting over perfectly the possibilities, reminding myself that nothing was more natural, for instance, than the appearance of one of the men about the place, or even of a messenger, a postman, or a tradesman's boy, from the village. That reminder had as little effect on my practical certitude as I was conscious – still even without looking – of its having upon the character and attitude of our visitor. Nothing was more natural than that these things should be the other things that they absolutely were not.

Of the positive identity of the apparition I would assure myself as soon as the small clock of my courage should have ticked out the right second; meanwhile, with an effort that was already sharp enough, I transferred my eyes straight to little Flora, who, at the moment, was about ten yards away. My heart had stood still for an instant with the wonder and terror of the question whether she too would see; and I held my breath while I waited for what a cry from her, what some sudden innocent sign either of interest or of alarm, would tell me. I waited, but nothing came; then, in the first place – and there is something more dire in this, I feel, than in anything I have to relate – I was determined by a sense that, within a minute, all sounds from her had previously dropped; and, in the second, by the circumstance that, also within the minute, she had, in her play, turned her back to the water. This was her attitude when I at last looked at her – looked with the confirmed conviction that we were still, together, under direct personal notice. She had picked up a small flat piece of wood, which happened to have in it a little hole that had evidently suggested to her the idea of sticking in another fragment that might figure as a mast and make the thing a boat. This second morsel, as I watched her, she was very markedly and intently attempting to tighten in its place. My apprehension of what she was doing sustained me so that after some seconds I felt I was ready for more. Then I again shifted my eyes – I faced what I had to face.

Chapter VII

I GOT HOLD of Mrs. Grose as soon after this as I could; and I can give no intelligible account of how I fought out the interval. Yet I still hear myself cry as I fairly threw myself into her arms: "They *know* – it's too monstrous: they know, they know!"

"And what on earth—?" I felt her incredulity as she held me.

"Why, all that *we* know – and heaven knows what else besides!" Then, as she released me, I made it out to her, made it out perhaps only now with full coherency even to myself. "Two hours ago, in the garden" – I could scarce articulate – "Flora *saw!*"

Mrs. Grose took it as she might have taken a blow in the stomach. "She has told you?" she panted.

"Not a word – that's the horror. She kept it to herself! The child of eight, *that* child!" Unutterable still, for me, was the stupefaction of it.

Mrs. Grose, of course, could only gape the wider. "Then how do you know?"

"I was there – I saw with my eyes: saw that she was perfectly aware."

"Do you mean aware of *him?*"

"No – of *her.*" I was conscious as I spoke that I looked prodigious things, for I got the slow reflection of them in my companion's face. "Another person – this time; but a figure of quite as unmistakable horror and evil: a woman in black, pale and dreadful – with such an air also, and such a face! – on the other side of the lake. I was there with the child – quiet for the hour; and in the midst of it she came."

"Came how – from where?"

"From where they come from! She just appeared and stood there – but not so near."

"And without coming nearer?"

"Oh, for the effect and the feeling, she might have been as close as you!"

My friend, with an odd impulse, fell back a step. "Was she someone you've never seen?"

"Yes. But someone the child has. Someone *you* have." Then, to show how I had thought it all out: "My predecessor – the one who died."

"Miss Jessel?"

"Miss Jessel. You don't believe me?" I pressed.

She turned right and left in her distress. "How can you be sure?"

This drew from me, in the state of my nerves, a flash of impatience. "Then ask Flora – *she's* sure!" But I had no sooner spoken than I caught myself up. "No, for God's sake, *don't!* She'll say she isn't – she'll lie!"

Mrs. Grose was not too bewildered instinctively to protest. "Ah, how *can* you?"

"Because I'm clear. Flora doesn't want me to know."

"It's only then to spare you."

"No, no – there are depths, depths! The more I go over it, the more I see in it, and the more I see in it, the more I fear. I don't know what I *don't* see – what I *don't* fear!"

Mrs. Grose tried to keep up with me. "You mean you're afraid of seeing her again?"

"Oh, no; that's nothing – now!" Then I explained. "It's of *not* seeing her."

But my companion only looked wan. "I don't understand you."

"Why, it's that the child may keep it up – and that the child assuredly *will* – without my knowing it."

At the image of this possibility Mrs. Grose for a moment collapsed, yet presently to pull herself together again, as if from the positive force of the sense of what, should we yield an inch, there would really be to give way to. "Dear, dear – we must keep our heads! And after all, if she doesn't mind it—!" She even tried a grim joke. "Perhaps she likes it!"

"Likes *such* things – a scrap of an infant!"

"Isn't it just a proof of her blessed innocence?" my friend bravely inquired.

She brought me, for the instant, almost round. "Oh, we must clutch at *that* – we must cling to it! If it isn't a proof of what you say, it's a proof of – God knows what! For the woman's a horror of horrors."

Mrs. Grose, at this, fixed her eyes a minute on the ground; then at last raising them, "Tell me how you know," she said.

"Then you admit it's what she was?" I cried.

"Tell me how you know," my friend simply repeated.

"Know? By seeing her! By the way she looked."

"At you, do you mean – so wickedly?"

"Dear me, no – I could have borne that. She gave me never a glance. She only fixed the child."

Mrs. Grose tried to see it. "Fixed her?"

"Ah, with such awful eyes!"

She stared at mine as if they might really have resembled them. "Do you mean of dislike?"

"God help us, no. Of something much worse."

"Worse than dislike?" – this left her indeed at a loss.

"With a determination – indescribable. With a kind of fury of intention."

I made her turn pale. "Intention?"

"To get hold of her." Mrs. Grose – her eyes just lingering on mine – gave a shudder and walked to the window; and while she stood there looking out I completed my statement. "*That's* what Flora knows."

After a little she turned round. "The person was in black, you say?"

"In mourning – rather poor, almost shabby. But – yes – with extraordinary beauty." I now recognized to what I had at last, stroke by stroke, brought the victim of my confidence, for she quite visibly weighed this. "Oh, handsome – very, very," I insisted; "wonderfully handsome. But infamous."

She slowly came back to me. "Miss Jessel – *was* infamous." She once more took my hand in both her own, holding it as tight as if to fortify me against the increase of alarm I might draw from this disclosure. "They were both infamous," she finally said.

So, for a little, we faced it once more together; and I found absolutely a degree of help in seeing it now so straight. "I appreciate," I said, "the great decency of your not having hitherto spoken; but the time has certainly come to give me the whole thing." She appeared to assent to this, but still only in silence; seeing which I went on: "I must have it now. Of what did she die? Come, there was something between them."

"There was everything."

"In spite of the difference—?"

"Oh, of their rank, their condition" – she brought it woefully out. "*She* was a lady."

I turned it over; I again saw. "Yes – she was a lady."

"And he so dreadfully below," said Mrs. Grose.

I felt that I doubtless needn't press too hard, in such company, on the place of a servant in the scale; but there was nothing to prevent an acceptance of my companion's own measure of my predecessor's abasement. There was a way to deal with that, and I dealt; the more readily for my full vision – on the evidence – of our employer's late clever, good-looking 'own' man; impudent, assured, spoiled, depraved. "The fellow was a hound."

Mrs. Grose considered as if it were perhaps a little a case for a sense of shades. "I've never seen one like him. He did what he wished."

"With *her?*"

"With them all."

It was as if now in my friend's own eyes Miss Jessel had again appeared. I seemed at any rate, for an instant, to see their evocation of her as distinctly as I had seen her by the pond; and I brought out with decision: "It must have been also what *she* wished!"

Mrs. Grose's face signified that it had been indeed, but she said at the same time: "Poor woman – she paid for it!"

"Then you do know what she died of?" I asked.

"No – I know nothing. I wanted not to know; I was glad enough I didn't; and I thanked heaven she was well out of this!"

"Yet you had, then, your idea—"

"Of her real reason for leaving? Oh, yes – as to that. She couldn't have stayed. Fancy it here – for a governess! And afterward I imagined – and I still imagine. And what I imagine is dreadful."

"Not so dreadful as what *I* do," I replied; on which I must have shown her – as I was indeed but too conscious – a front of miserable defeat. It brought out again all her compassion for me, and at the renewed touch of her kindness my power to resist broke down. I burst, as I had, the other time, made her burst, into tears; she took me to her motherly breast, and my lamentation overflowed. "I don't do it!" I sobbed in despair; "I don't save or shield them! It's far worse than I dreamed – they're lost!"

Chapter VIII

WHAT I HAD SAID to Mrs. Grose was true enough: there were in the matter I had put before her depths and possibilities that I lacked resolution to sound; so that when we met once more in the wonder of it we were of a common mind about the duty of resistance to extravagant fancies. We were to keep our heads if we should keep nothing else – difficult indeed as that might be in the face of what, in our prodigious experience, was least to be questioned. Late that night, while the house slept, we had another talk in my room, when she went all the way with me as to its being beyond doubt that I had seen exactly what I had seen. To hold her perfectly in the pinch of that,

I found I had only to ask her how, if I had 'made it up', I came to be able to give, of each of the persons appearing to me, a picture disclosing, to the last detail, their special marks – a portrait on the exhibition of which she had instantly recognized and named them. She wished of course – small blame to her! – to sink the whole subject; and I was quick to assure her that my own interest in it had now violently taken the form of a search for the way to escape from it. I encountered her on the ground of a probability that with recurrence – for recurrence we took for granted – I should get used to my danger, distinctly professing that my personal exposure had suddenly become the least of my discomforts. It was my new suspicion that was intolerable; and yet even to this complication the later hours of the day had brought a little ease.

On leaving her, after my first outbreak, I had of course returned to my pupils, associating the right remedy for my dismay with that sense of their charm which I had already found to be a thing I could positively cultivate and which had never failed me yet. I had simply, in other words, plunged afresh into Flora's special society and there become aware – it was almost a luxury! – that she could put her little conscious hand straight upon the spot that ached. She had looked at me in sweet speculation and then had accused me to my face of having 'cried'. I had supposed I had brushed away the ugly signs: but I could literally – for the time, at all events – rejoice, under this fathomless charity, that they had not entirely disappeared. To gaze into the depths of blue of the child's eyes and pronounce their loveliness a trick of premature cunning was to be guilty of a cynicism in preference to which I naturally preferred to abjure my judgment and, so far as might be, my agitation. I couldn't abjure for merely wanting to, but I could repeat to Mrs. Grose – as I did there, over and over, in the small hours – that with their voices in the air, their pressure on one's heart, and their fragrant faces against one's cheek, everything fell to the ground but their incapacity and their beauty. It was a pity that, somehow, to settle this once for all, I had equally to re-enumerate the signs of subtlety that, in the afternoon, by the lake had made a miracle of my show of self-possession. It was a pity to be obliged to reinvestigate the certitude of the moment itself and repeat how it had come to me as a revelation that the inconceivable communion I then surprised was a matter, for either party, of habit. It was a pity that I should have had to quaver out again the reasons for my not having, in my delusion, so much as questioned that the little girl saw our visitant even as I actually saw Mrs. Grose herself, and that she wanted, by just so much as she did thus see, to make me suppose she didn't, and at the same time, without showing anything, arrive at a guess as to whether I myself did! It was a pity that I needed once more to describe the portentous little activity by which she sought to divert my attention – the perceptible increase of movement, the greater intensity of play, the singing, the gabbling of nonsense, and the invitation to romp.

Yet if I had not indulged, to prove there was nothing in it, in this review, I should have missed the two or three dim elements of comfort that still remained to me. I should not for instance have been able to asseverate to my friend that I was certain – which was so much to the good – that *I* at least had not betrayed myself. I should not have been prompted, by stress of need, by desperation of mind – I scarce know what to call it – to invoke such further aid to intelligence as might spring from pushing my colleague fairly to the wall. She had told me, bit by bit, under pressure, a great deal; but a small shifty spot on the wrong side of it all still sometimes brushed my brow like the wing of a bat; and I remember how on this occasion – for the sleeping house and the concentration alike of our danger and our watch seemed to help – I felt the importance of giving the last jerk to the curtain. "I don't believe anything so horrible," I recollect saying; "no, let us put it definitely, my dear, that I don't. But if I did, you know, there's a thing I should require now, just without sparing you the least bit more – oh, not a scrap, come! – to get out of you. What was it you had in mind when, in our distress, before Miles came back, over the letter from his school, you said, under my insistence, that you didn't pretend for him that he had not literally *ever* been 'bad'? He has *not* literally 'ever', in these weeks that I myself have lived with him and so closely watched him; he has been an imperturbable little prodigy of delightful, lovable goodness. Therefore you might perfectly have made the claim for him if you had not, as it happened, seen an exception to take. What was your exception, and to what passage in your personal observation of him did you refer?"

It was a dreadfully austere inquiry, but levity was not our note, and, at any rate, before the gray dawn admonished us to separate I had got my answer. What my friend had had in mind proved to be immensely to the purpose. It was neither more nor less than the circumstance that for a period of several months Quint and the boy had been perpetually together. It was in fact the very appropriate truth that she had ventured to criticize the propriety, to hint at the incongruity, of so close an alliance, and even to go so far on the subject as a frank overture to Miss Jessel. Miss Jessel had, with a most strange manner, requested her to mind her business, and the good woman had, on this, directly approached little Miles. What she had said to him, since I pressed, was that *she* liked to see young gentlemen not forget their station.

I pressed again, of course, at this. "You reminded him that Quint was only a base menial?"

"As you might say! And it was his answer, for one thing, that was bad."

"And for another thing?" I waited. "He repeated your words to Quint?"

"No, not that. It's just what he *wouldn't!*" she could still impress upon me. "I was sure, at any rate," she added, "that he didn't. But he denied certain occasions."

"What occasions?"

"When they had been about together quite as if Quint were his tutor – and a very grand one – and Miss Jessel only for the little lady. When he had gone off with the fellow, I mean, and spent hours with him."

"He then prevaricated about it – he said he hadn't?" Her assent was clear enough to cause me to add in a moment: "I see. He lied."

"Oh!" Mrs. Grose mumbled. This was a suggestion that it didn't matter; which indeed she backed up by a further remark. "You see, after all, Miss Jessel didn't mind. She didn't forbid him."

I considered. "Did he put that to you as a justification?"

At this she dropped again. "No, he never spoke of it."

"Never mentioned her in connection with Quint?"

She saw, visibly flushing, where I was coming out. "Well, he didn't show anything. He denied," she repeated; "he denied."

Lord, how I pressed her now! "So that you could see he knew what was between the two wretches?"

"I don't know – I don't know!" the poor woman groaned.

"You do know, you dear thing," I replied; "only you haven't my dreadful boldness of mind, and you keep back, out of timidity and modesty and delicacy, even the impression that, in the past, when you had, without my aid, to flounder about in silence, most of all made you miserable. But I shall get it out of you yet! There was something in the boy that suggested to you," I continued, "that he covered and concealed their relation."

"Oh, he couldn't prevent—"

"Your learning the truth? I daresay! But, heavens," I fell, with vehemence, athinking, "what it shows that they must, to that extent, have succeeded in making of him!"

"Ah, nothing that's not nice *now!*" Mrs. Grose lugubriously pleaded.

"I don't wonder you looked queer," I persisted, "when I mentioned to you the letter from his school!"

"I doubt if I looked as queer as you!" she retorted with homely force. "And if he was so bad then as that comes to, how is he such an angel now?"

"Yes, indeed – and if he was a fiend at school! How, how, how? Well," I said in my torment, "you must put it to me again, but I shall not be able to tell you for some days. Only, put it to me again!" I cried in a way that made my friend stare. "There are directions in which I must not for the present let myself go." Meanwhile I returned to her first example – the one to which she had just previously referred – of the boy's happy capacity for an occasional slip. "If Quint – on your remonstrance at the time you speak of – was a base menial, one of the things Miles said to you, I find myself guessing, was that you were another." Again her admission was so adequate that I continued: "And you forgave him that?"

"Wouldn't *you?*"

"Oh, yes!" And we exchanged there, in the stillness, a sound of the oddest amusement. Then I went on: "At all events, while he was with the man—"

"Miss Flora was with the woman. It suited them all!"

It suited me, too, I felt, only too well; by which I mean that it suited exactly the particularly deadly view I was in the very act of forbidding myself to entertain. But I so far succeeded in checking the expression of this view that I will throw, just here, no further light on it than may be offered by the mention of my final observation to Mrs. Grose. "His having lied and been impudent are, I confess, less engaging specimens than I had hoped to have from you of the outbreak in him of the little natural man. Still," I mused, "They must do, for they make me feel more than ever that I must watch."

It made me blush, the next minute, to see in my friend's face how much more unreservedly she had forgiven him than her anecdote struck me as presenting to my own tenderness an occasion for doing. This came out when, at the schoolroom door, she quitted me. "Surely you don't accuse *him*—"

"Of carrying on an intercourse that he conceals from me? Ah, remember that, until further evidence, I now accuse nobody." Then, before shutting her out to go, by another passage, to her own place, "I must just wait," I wound up.

Chapter IX

I WAITED and waited, and the days, as they elapsed, took something from my consternation. A very few of them, in fact, passing, in constant sight of my pupils, without a fresh incident, sufficed to give to grievous fancies and even to odious memories a kind of brush of the sponge. I have spoken of the surrender to their extraordinary childish grace as a thing I could actively cultivate, and it may be imagined if I neglected now to address myself to this source for whatever it would yield. Stranger than I can express, certainly, was the effort to struggle against my new lights; it would doubtless have been, however, a greater tension still had it not been so frequently successful. I used to wonder how my little charges could help guessing that I thought strange things about them; and the circumstances that these things only made them more interesting was not by itself a direct aid to keeping them in the dark. I trembled lest they should see that they *were* so immensely more interesting. Putting things at the worst, at all events, as in meditation I so often did, any clouding of their innocence could only be – blameless and foredoomed as they were – a reason the more for taking risks. There were moments when, by an irresistible impulse, I found myself catching them up and pressing them to my heart. As soon as I had done so I used to say to myself: "What will they think of that? Doesn't it betray too much?" It would have been easy to get into a sad, wild tangle about how much I might betray; but the real account, I feel, of the hours of peace that I could still enjoy was that the immediate charm of my companions was a beguilement still effective even under the shadow of the possibility that it was studied. For if it occurred to me that I might occasionally excite suspicion by the little outbreaks of my sharper passion for them, so too I remember wondering if I mightn't see a queerness in the traceable increase of their own demonstrations.

They were at this period extravagantly and preternaturally fond of me; which, after all, I could reflect, was no more than a graceful response in children perpetually bowed over and hugged. The homage of which they were so lavish succeeded, in truth, for my nerves, quite as well as if I never appeared to myself, as I may say, literally to catch them at a purpose in it. They had never, I think, wanted to do so many things for their poor protectress; I mean – though they got their lessons better and better, which was naturally what would please her most – in the way of diverting, entertaining, surprising her; reading her passages, telling her stories, acting her charades, pouncing out at her, in disguises, as animals and historical characters, and above all astonishing her by the 'pieces' they had secretly got by heart and could interminably recite. I should never get to the bottom – were I to let myself go even now – of the prodigious private commentary, all under still more private correction, with which, in these days, I overscored their full hours. They had shown me from the first a facility for everything, a general faculty which, taking a fresh start, achieved remarkable flights. They got their little tasks as if they loved them, and indulged, from the mere exuberance of the gift, in the most unimposed little miracles of memory. They not only popped out at me as tigers and as Romans, but as Shakespeareans, astronomers, and navigators. This was so singularly the case that it had presumably much to do with the fact as to which, at the present day, I am at a loss for a different explanation: I allude to my unnatural composure on the subject of another school for Miles. What I remember is that I was content not, for the time, to open the question, and that contentment must have sprung from the sense of his perpetually striking show of cleverness. He was too clever for a bad governess, for a parson's daughter, to spoil; and the strangest if not the brightest thread in the pensive embroidery I just spoke of was the impression I might have got, if I had dared to work it out, that he was under some influence operating in his small intellectual life as a tremendous incitement.

If it was easy to reflect, however, that such a boy could postpone school, it was at least as marked that for such a boy to have been 'kicked out' by a schoolmaster was a mystification without end. Let me add that in their company now – and I was careful almost never to be out of it – I could follow no scent very far. We lived in a cloud of music and love and success and private theatricals. The musical sense in each of the children was of the quickest, but the elder in especial had a marvelous knack of catching and repeating. The schoolroom piano broke into all gruesome fancies; and when that failed there were confabulations in corners, with a sequel of one of them going out in the highest spirits in order to 'come in' as something new. I had had brothers myself, and it was no revelation to me that little girls could be slavish idolaters of little boys. What surpassed everything was that there was a little boy in the world who could have for the inferior age, sex, and intelligence so fine a consideration. They were extraordinarily at one, and to say that they never either quarreled or complained is to make the note of praise coarse for their quality of sweetness. Sometimes, indeed, when I dropped into coarseness, I perhaps came across traces of little understandings between them by which one of them should keep me occupied while the other slipped away. There is a *naïf* side, I suppose, in all diplomacy; but if my pupils practiced upon me, it was surely with the minimum of grossness. It was all in the other quarter that, after a lull, the grossness broke out.

I find that I really hang back; but I must take my plunge. In going on with the record of what was hideous at Bly, I not only challenge the most liberal faith – for which I little care; but – and this is another matter – I renew what I myself suffered, I again push my way through it to the end. There came suddenly an hour after which, as I look back, the affair seems to me to have been all pure suffering; but I have at least reached the heart of it, and the straightest road out is doubtless to advance. One evening – with nothing to lead up or to prepare it – I felt the cold touch of the impression that had breathed on me the night of my arrival and which, much lighter then, as I have mentioned, I should probably have made little of in memory had my subsequent sojourn been less agitated. I had not gone to bed; I sat reading by a couple of candles. There was a roomful of old books at Bly – last-century fiction, some of it, which, to the extent of a distinctly deprecated renown, but never to so much as that of a stray specimen, had reached the sequestered home and appealed to the unavowed curiosity of my youth. I remember that the book I had in my hand was Fielding's *Amelia*; also that I was wholly awake. I recall further both a general conviction that it was horribly late and a particular objection to looking at my watch. I figure, finally, that the white curtain draping, in the fashion of those days, the head of Flora's little bed, shrouded, as I had assured myself long before, the perfection of childish rest. I recollect in short that, though I was deeply interested in my author, I found myself, at the turn of a page and with his spell all scattered, looking straight up from him and hard at the door of my room. There was a moment during which I listened, reminded of the faint sense I had had, the first night, of there being something undefinably astir in the house, and noted the soft breath of the open casement just move the half-drawn blind. Then, with all the marks of a deliberation that must have seemed magnificent had there been anyone to admire it, I laid down my book, rose to my feet, and, taking a candle, went straight out of the room and, from the passage, on which my light made little impression, noiselessly closed and locked the door.

I can say now neither what determined nor what guided me, but I went straight along the lobby, holding my candle high, till I came within sight of the tall window that presided over the great turn of the staircase. At this point I precipitately found myself aware of three things. They were practically simultaneous, yet they had flashes of succession. My candle, under a bold flourish, went out, and I perceived, by the uncovered window, that the yielding dusk of earliest morning rendered it unnecessary. Without it, the next instant, I saw that there was someone on the stair. I speak of sequences, but I required no lapse of seconds to stiffen myself for a third encounter with Quint. The apparition had reached the landing halfway up and was therefore on the spot nearest the window, where at sight of me, it stopped short and fixed me exactly as it had fixed me from the tower and from the garden. He knew me as well as I knew him; and so, in the cold, faint twilight, with a glimmer in the high glass and another on the polish of the oak stair below, we faced each other in our common intensity. He was absolutely, on this occasion, a living, detestable, dangerous presence. But that was not the wonder of wonders; I reserve this distinction for quite another circumstance: the circumstance that dread had unmistakably quitted me and that there was nothing in me there that didn't meet and measure him.

I had plenty of anguish after that extraordinary moment, but I had, thank God, no terror. And he knew I had not – I found myself at the end of an instant magnificently aware of this. I felt, in a fierce rigor of confidence, that if I stood my ground a minute I should cease – for the time, at least – to have him to reckon with; and during the minute, accordingly, the thing was as human and hideous as a real interview: hideous just because it *was* human, as human as to have met alone, in the small hours, in a sleeping house, some enemy, some adventurer, some criminal. It was the dead silence of our long gaze at such close quarters that gave the whole horror, huge as it was, its only note of the unnatural. If I had met a murderer in such a place and at such an hour, we still at least would have spoken. Something would have passed, in life, between us; if nothing had passed, one of us would have moved. The moment was so prolonged that it would have taken but little more to make me doubt if even *I* were in life. I can't express what followed it save by saying that the silence itself – which was indeed in a manner an attestation of my strength – became the element into which I saw the figure disappear; in which I definitely saw it turn as I might have seen the low wretch to which it had once belonged turn on receipt of an order, and pass, with my eyes on the villainous back that no hunch could have more disfigured, straight down the staircase and into the darkness in which the next bend was lost.

Chapter X

I REMAINED awhile at the top of the stair, but with the effect presently of understanding that when my visitor had gone, he had gone: then I returned to my room. The foremost thing I saw there by the light of the candle I had left burning was that Flora's little bed was empty; and on this I caught my breath with all the terror that, five minutes before, I had been able to resist. I dashed at the place in which I had left her lying and over which (for the small silk counterpane and the sheets were disarranged) the white curtains had been deceivingly pulled forward; then my step, to my unutterable relief, produced an answering sound: I perceived an agitation of the window blind, and the child, ducking down, emerged rosily from the other side of it. She stood there in so much of her candor and so little of her nightgown, with her pink bare feet and the golden glow of her curls. She looked intensely grave, and I had never had such a sense of losing an advantage acquired (the thrill of which had just been so prodigious) as on my consciousness that she addressed me with a reproach. "You naughty: where *have* you been?" – instead of challenging her own irregularity I found myself arraigned and explaining. She herself explained, for that matter, with the loveliest, eagerest simplicity. She had known suddenly, as she lay there, that I was out of the room, and had jumped up to see what had become of me. I had dropped, with the joy of her reappearance, back into my chair – feeling then, and then only, a little faint; and she had pattered straight over to me, thrown herself upon my knee, given herself to be held with the flame of the candle full in the wonderful little face that was still flushed with sleep. I remember closing my eyes an instant, yieldingly, consciously, as before the excess of something beautiful that shone out of the blue of her own. "You were looking for me out of the window?" I said. "You thought I might be walking in the grounds?"

"Well, you know, I thought someone was" – she never blanched as she smiled out that at me.

Oh, how I looked at her now! "And did you see anyone?"

"Ah, *no!*" she returned, almost with the full privilege of childish inconsequence, resentfully, though with a long sweetness in her little drawl of the negative.

At that moment, in the state of my nerves, I absolutely believed she lied; and if I once more closed my eyes it was before the dazzle of the three or four possible ways in which I might take this up. One of these, for a moment, tempted me with such singular intensity that, to withstand it, I must have gripped my little girl with a spasm that, wonderfully, she submitted to without a cry or a sign of fright. Why not break out at her on the spot and have it all over? – give it to her straight in her lovely little lighted face? "You see, you see, you *know* that you do and that you already quite suspect I believe it; therefore, why not frankly confess it to me, so that we may at least live with it together and learn perhaps, in the strangeness of our fate, where we are and what it means?" This solicitation dropped, alas, as it came: if I could immediately have succumbed to it I might have spared myself – well, you'll see what. Instead of succumbing I sprang again to my feet, looked at her bed, and took a helpless middle way. "Why did you pull the curtain over the place to make me think you were still there?"

Flora luminously considered; after which, with her little divine smile: "Because I don't like to frighten you!"

"But if I had, by your idea, gone out—?"

She absolutely declined to be puzzled; she turned her eyes to the flame of the candle as if the question were as irrelevant, or at any rate as impersonal, as Mrs. Marcet or nine-times-nine. "Oh, but you know," she quite adequately answered, "that you might come back, you dear, and that you *have!*" And after a little, when she had got into bed, I had, for a long time, by almost sitting on her to hold her hand, to prove that I recognized the pertinence of my return.

You may imagine the general complexion, from that moment, of my nights. I repeatedly sat up till I didn't know when; I selected moments when my roommate unmistakably slept, and, stealing out, took noiseless turns in the passage and even pushed as far as to where I had last met Quint. But I never met him there again; and I may as well say at once that I on no other occasion saw him in the house. I just missed, on the staircase, on the other hand, a different adventure. Looking down it from the top I once recognized the presence of a woman seated on one of the lower steps with her back presented to me, her body half-bowed and her head, in an attitude of woe, in her hands. I had been there but an instant, however, when she vanished without looking round at me. I knew, nonetheless, exactly what dreadful face she had to show; and I wondered whether, if instead of being above I had been below, I should have had, for going up, the same nerve I had lately shown Quint. Well, there continued to be plenty of chance for nerve. On the eleventh night after my latest encounter with that gentleman – they were all numbered now – I had an alarm that perilously skirted it and that indeed, from the particular quality of its unexpectedness, proved quite my sharpest shock. It was precisely the first night during this series that, weary with watching, I had felt that I might again without laxity lay myself down at my old hour. I slept immediately and, as I afterward knew, till about one o'clock; but when I woke it was to sit straight up, as completely roused as if a hand had shook me. I had left a light burning, but it was now out, and I felt an instant certainty that Flora had extinguished it. This brought me to my feet and straight, in the darkness, to her bed, which I found she had left. A glance at the window enlightened me further, and the striking of a match completed the picture.

The child had again got up – this time blowing out the taper, and had again, for some purpose of observation or response, squeezed in behind the blind and was peering out into the night. That she now saw – as she had not, I had satisfied myself, the previous time – was proved to me by the fact that she was disturbed neither by my reillumination nor by the haste I made to get into slippers and into a wrap. Hidden, protected, absorbed, she evidently rested on the sill – the casement opened forward – and gave herself up. There was a great still moon to help her, and this fact had counted in my quick decision. She was face to face with the apparition we had met at the lake, and could now communicate with it as she had not then been able to do. What I, on my side, had to care for was, without disturbing her, to reach, from the corridor, some other window in the same quarter. I got to the door without her hearing me; I got out of it, closed it, and listened, from the other side, for some sound from her. While I stood in the passage I had my eyes on her brother's door, which was but ten steps off and which, indescribably, produced in me a renewal of the strange impulse that I lately spoke of as my temptation. What if I should go straight in and march to *his* window? – what if, by risking to his boyish bewilderment a revelation of my motive, I should throw across the rest of the mystery the long halter of my boldness?

This thought held me sufficiently to make me cross to his threshold and pause again. I preternaturally listened; I figured to myself what might portentously be; I wondered if his bed were also empty and he too were secretly at watch. It was a deep, soundless minute, at the end of which my impulse failed. He was quiet; he might be innocent; the risk was hideous; I turned away. There was a figure in the grounds – a figure prowling for a sight, the visitor with whom Flora was engaged; but it was not the visitor most concerned with my boy. I hesitated afresh, but on other grounds and only for a few seconds; then I had made my choice. There were empty rooms at Bly, and it was only a question of choosing the right one. The right one suddenly presented itself to me as the lower one – though high above the gardens – in the solid corner of the house that I have spoken of as the old tower. This was a large, square chamber, arranged with some state as a bedroom, the extravagant size of which made it so inconvenient that it had not for years, though kept by Mrs. Grose in exemplary order, been occupied. I had often admired it and I knew my way about in it; I had only, after just faltering at the first chill gloom of its disuse, to pass across it and unbolt as quietly as I could one of the shutters. Achieving this transit, I uncovered the glass without a sound and, applying my face to the pane, was able, the darkness without being much less than within, to see that I commanded the right direction. Then I saw something more. The moon made the night extraordinarily penetrable and showed me on the lawn a person, diminished by distance, who stood there motionless and as if fascinated, looking up to where I had appeared – looking, that is, not so much straight at me as at something that was apparently above me. There was clearly another person above me – there was a person on the tower; but the presence on the lawn was not in the least what I had conceived and had confidently hurried to meet. The presence on the lawn – I felt sick as I made it out – was poor little Miles himself.

Chapter XI

IT WAS NOT till late next day that I spoke to Mrs. Grose; the rigor with which I kept my pupils in sight making it often difficult to meet her privately, and the more as we each felt the importance of not provoking – on the part of the servants quite as much as on that of the children – any suspicion of a secret flurry or that of a discussion of mysteries. I drew a great security in this particular from her mere smooth aspect. There was nothing in her fresh face to pass on to others my horrible confidences. She believed me, I was sure, absolutely: if she hadn't I don't know what would have become of me, for I couldn't have borne the business alone. But she was a magnificent monument to the blessing of a want of imagination, and if she could see in our little charges nothing but their beauty and amiability, their happiness and cleverness, she had no direct communication with the sources of my trouble. If they had been at all visibly blighted or battered, she would doubtless have grown, on tracing it back, haggard enough to match them; as matters stood, however, I could feel her, when she surveyed them, with her large white arms folded and the habit of serenity in all her look, thank the Lord's mercy that if they were ruined the pieces would still serve. Flights of fancy gave place, in her mind, to a steady fireside glow, and I had already begun to perceive how, with the development of the conviction that – as time went on without a public accident – our young things could, after all, look out for themselves, she addressed her greatest solicitude to the sad case presented by their instructress. That, for myself, was a sound simplification: I could engage that, to the world, my face should tell no tales, but it would have been, in the conditions, an immense added strain to find myself anxious about hers.

At the hour I now speak of she had joined me, under pressure, on the terrace, where, with the lapse of the season, the afternoon sun was now agreeable; and we sat there together while, before us, at a distance, but within call if we wished, the children strolled to and fro in one of their most manageable moods. They moved slowly, in unison, below us, over the lawn, the boy, as they went, reading aloud from a storybook and passing his arm round his sister to keep her quite in touch. Mrs. Grose watched them with positive placidity; then I caught the suppressed intellectual creak with which she conscientiously turned to take from me a view of the back of the tapestry. I had made her a receptacle of lurid things, but there was an odd recognition of my superiority – my accomplishments and my function – in her patience under my pain. She offered her mind to my disclosures as, had I wished to mix a witch's broth and proposed it with assurance, she would have held out a large clean saucepan. This had become thoroughly her attitude by the time that, in my recital of the events of the night, I reached the point of what Miles had said to me when, after seeing him, at such a monstrous hour, almost on the very spot where he happened now to be, I had gone down to bring him in; choosing then, at the window, with a concentrated need of not alarming the house, rather that method than a signal more resonant. I had left her meanwhile in little doubt of my small hope of representing with success even to her actual sympathy my sense of the real splendor of the little inspiration with which, after I had got him into the house, the boy met my final articulate challenge. As soon as I appeared in the moonlight on the terrace, he had come to me as straight as possible; on which I had taken his hand without a word and led him, through the dark spaces, up the staircase where Quint had so hungrily hovered for him, along the lobby where I had listened and trembled, and so to his forsaken room.

Not a sound, on the way, had passed between us, and I had wondered – oh, *how* I had wondered! – if he were groping about in his little mind for something plausible and not too grotesque. It would tax his invention, certainly, and I felt, this time, over his real embarrassment, a curious thrill of triumph. It was a sharp trap for the inscrutable! He couldn't play any longer at innocence; so how the deuce would he get out of it? There beat in me indeed, with the passionate throb of this question an equal dumb appeal as to how the deuce *I* should. I was confronted at last, as never yet, with all the risk attached even now to sounding my own horrid note. I remember in fact that as we pushed into his little chamber, where the bed had not been slept in at all and the window, uncovered to the moonlight, made the place so clear that there was no need of striking a match – I remember how I suddenly dropped, sank upon the edge of the bed from the force of the idea that he must know how he really, as they say, 'had' me. He could do what he liked, with all his cleverness to help him, so long as I should continue to defer to the old tradition of the criminality of those caretakers of the young who minister to superstitions and fears. He 'had' me indeed, and in a cleft stick; for who would ever absolve me, who would consent that I should go unhung, if, by the faintest tremor of an overture, I were the first to introduce into our perfect intercourse an element so dire? No, no: it was useless to attempt to convey to Mrs. Grose, just as it is scarcely less so to attempt to suggest here, how, in our short, stiff brush in the dark, he fairly shook me with admiration. I was of course thoroughly kind and merciful; never, never yet had I placed on his little shoulders hands of such tenderness as those with which, while I rested against the bed, I held him there well under fire. I had no alternative but, in form at least, to put it to him.

"You must tell me now – and all the truth. What did you go out for? What were you doing there?"

I can still see his wonderful smile, the whites of his beautiful eyes, and the uncovering of his little teeth shine to me in the dusk. "If I tell you why, will you understand?" My heart, at this, leaped into my mouth. *Would* he tell me why? I found no sound on my lips to press it, and I was aware of replying only with a vague, repeated, grimacing nod. He was gentleness itself, and while I wagged my head at him he stood there more than ever a little fairy prince. It was his brightness indeed that gave me a respite. Would it be so great if he were really going to tell me? "Well," he said at last, "just exactly in order that you should do this."

"Do what?"

"Think me – for a change – *bad!*" I shall never forget the sweetness and gaiety with which he brought out the word, nor how, on top of it, he bent forward and kissed me. It was practically the end of everything. I met his kiss and I had to make, while I folded him for a minute in my arms, the most stupendous effort not to cry. He had given exactly the account of himself that permitted least of my going behind it, and it was only with the effect of confirming my acceptance of it that, as I presently glanced about the room, I could say—

"Then you didn't undress at all?"

He fairly glittered in the gloom. "Not at all. I sat up and read."

"And when did you go down?"

"At midnight. When I'm bad I *am* bad!"

"I see, I see – it's charming. But how could you be sure I would know it?"

"Oh, I arranged that with Flora." His answers rang out with a readiness! "She was to get up and look out."

"Which is what she did do." It was I who fell into the trap!

"So she disturbed you, and, to see what she was looking at, you also looked – you saw."

"While you," I concurred, "caught your death in the night air!"

He literally bloomed so from this exploit that he could afford radiantly to assent. "How otherwise should I have been bad enough?" he asked. Then, after another embrace, the incident and our interview closed on my recognition of all the reserves of goodness that, for his joke, he had been able to draw upon.

Chapter XII

THE PARTICULAR impression I had received proved in the morning light, I repeat, not quite successfully presentable to Mrs. Grose, though I reinforced it with the mention of still another remark that he had made before we separated. "It all lies in half a dozen words," I said to her, "words that really settle the matter. 'Think, you know, what I *might* do!' He threw that off to show me how good he is. He knows down to the ground what he 'might' do. That's what he gave them a taste of at school."

"Lord, you do change!" cried my friend.

"I don't change – I simply make it out. The four, depend upon it, perpetually meet. If on either of these last nights you had been with either child, you would clearly have understood. The more I've watched and waited the more I've felt that if there were nothing else to make it sure it would be made so by the systematic silence of each. *Never*, by a slip of the tongue, have they so much as alluded to either of their old friends, any more than Miles has alluded to his expulsion. Oh, yes, we may sit here and look at them, and they may show off to us there to their fill; but even while they pretend to be lost in their fairytale they're steeped in their vision of the dead restored. He's not reading to her," I declared; "they're talking of *them* – they're talking horrors! I go on, I know, as if I were crazy; and it's a wonder I'm not. What I've seen would have made *you* so; but it has only made me more lucid, made me get hold of still other things."

My lucidity must have seemed awful, but the charming creatures who were victims of it, passing and repassing in their interlocked sweetness, gave my colleague something to hold on by; and I felt how tight she held as, without stirring in the breath of my passion, she covered them still with her eyes. "Of what other things have you got hold?"

"Why, of the very things that have delighted, fascinated, and yet, at bottom, as I now so strangely see, mystified and troubled me. Their more than earthly beauty, their absolutely unnatural goodness. It's a game," I went on; "it's a policy and a fraud!"

"On the part of little darlings—?"

"As yet mere lovely babies? Yes, mad as that seems!" The very act of bringing it out really helped me to trace it – follow it all up and piece it all together. "They haven't been good – they've only been absent. It has been easy to live with them, because they're simply leading a life of their own. They're not mine – they're not ours. They're his and they're hers!"

"Quint's and that woman's?"

"Quint's and that woman's. They want to get to them."

Oh, how, at this, poor Mrs. Grose appeared to study them! "But for what?"

"For the love of all the evil that, in those dreadful days, the pair put into them. And to ply them with that evil still, to keep up the work of demons, is what brings the others back."

"Laws!" said my friend under her breath. The exclamation was homely, but it revealed a real acceptance of my further proof of what, in the bad time – for there had been a worse even than this! – must have occurred. There could have been no such justification for me as the plain assent of her experience to whatever depth of depravity I found credible in our brace of scoundrels. It was in obvious submission of memory that she brought out after a moment: "They *were* rascals! But what can they now do?" she pursued.

"Do?" I echoed so loud that Miles and Flora, as they passed at their distance, paused an instant in their walk and looked at us. "Don't they do enough?" I demanded in a lower tone, while the children, having smiled and nodded and kissed hands to us, resumed their exhibition. We were held by it a minute; then I answered: "They can destroy them!" At this my companion did turn, but the inquiry she launched was a silent one, the effect of which was to make me more explicit. "They don't know, as yet, quite how – but they're trying hard. They're seen only across, as it were, and beyond – in strange places and on high places, the top of towers, the roof of houses, the outside of windows, the further edge of pools; but there's a deep design, on either side, to shorten the distance and overcome the obstacle; and the success of the tempters is only a question of time. They've only to keep to their suggestions of danger."

"For the children to come?"

"And perish in the attempt!" Mrs. Grose slowly got up, and I scrupulously added: "Unless, of course, we can prevent!"

Standing there before me while I kept my seat, she visibly turned things over. "Their uncle must do the preventing. He must take them away."

"And who's to make him?"

She had been scanning the distance, but she now dropped on me a foolish face. "You, miss."

"By writing to him that his house is poisoned and his little nephew and niece mad?"

"But if they *are*, miss?"

"And if I am myself, you mean? That's charming news to be sent him by a governess whose prime undertaking was to give him no worry."

Mrs. Grose considered, following the children again. "Yes, he do hate worry. That was the great reason—"

"Why those fiends took him in so long? No doubt, though his indifference must have been awful. As I'm not a fiend, at any rate, I shouldn't take him in."

My companion, after an instant and for all answer, sat down again and grasped my arm. "Make him at any rate come to you."

I stared. "To *me?*" I had a sudden fear of what she might do. "'Him'?"

"He ought to *be* here – he ought to help."

I quickly rose, and I think I must have shown her a queerer face than ever yet. "You see me asking him for a visit?" No, with her eyes on my face she evidently couldn't. Instead of it even – as a woman reads another – she could see what I myself saw: his derision, his amusement, his contempt for the breakdown of my resignation at being left alone and for the fine machinery I had set in motion to attract his attention to my slighted charms. She didn't know – no one knew – how proud I had been to serve him and to stick to our terms; yet she nonetheless took the measure, I think, of the warning I now gave her. "If you should so lose your head as to appeal to him for me—"

She was really frightened. "Yes, miss?"

"I would leave, on the spot, both him and you."

Chapter XIII

IT WAS ALL very well to join them, but speaking to them proved quite as much as ever an effort beyond my strength – offered, in close quarters, difficulties as insurmountable as before. This situation continued a month, and with new aggravations and particular notes, the note above all, sharper and sharper, of the small ironic consciousness on the part of my pupils. It was not, I am as sure today as I was sure then, my mere infernal imagination: it was absolutely traceable that they were aware of my predicament and that this strange relation made, in a manner, for a long time, the air in which we moved. I don't mean that they had their tongues in their cheeks or did anything vulgar, for that was not one of their dangers: I do mean, on the other hand, that the element of the unnamed and untouched became, between us, greater than any other, and that so much avoidance could not have been so successfully effected without a great deal of tacit arrangement. It was as if, at moments, we were perpetually coming into sight of subjects before which we must stop short, turning suddenly out of alleys that we perceived to be blind, closing with a little bang that made us look at each other – for, like all bangs, it was something louder than we had intended – the doors we had indiscreetly opened. All roads lead to Rome, and there were times when it might have struck us that almost every branch of study or subject of conversation skirted forbidden ground. Forbidden ground was the question of the return of the dead in general and of whatever, in especial, might survive, in memory, of the friends little children had lost. There were days when I could have sworn that one of them had, with a small invisible nudge, said to the other: "She thinks she'll do it this time – but she *won't!*" To 'do it' would have been to indulge for instance – and for once in a way – in some direct reference to the lady who had prepared them for my discipline. They had a delightful endless appetite for passages in my own history, to which I had again and again treated them; they were in possession of everything that had ever happened to me, had had, with every circumstance the story of my smallest adventures and of those of my brothers and sisters and of the cat and the dog at home, as well as many particulars of the eccentric nature of my father, of the furniture and arrangement of our house, and of the conversation of the old women of our village. There were things enough, taking one with another, to chatter about, if one went very fast and knew by instinct when to go round. They pulled with an art of their own the strings of my invention and my memory; and nothing else perhaps, when I thought of such occasions afterward, gave me so the suspicion of being watched from under cover. It was in any case over *my* life, *my* past, and *my* friends alone that we could take anything like our ease – a state of affairs that led them sometimes without the least pertinence to break out into sociable reminders. I was invited – with no visible connection – to repeat afresh Goody Gosling's celebrated *mot* or to confirm the details already supplied as to the cleverness of the vicarage pony.

It was partly at such junctures as these and partly at quite different ones that, with the turn my matters had now taken, my predicament, as I have called it, grew most sensible. The fact that the days passed for me without another encounter ought, it would have appeared, to have done something toward soothing my nerves. Since the light brush, that second night on the upper landing, of the presence of a woman at the foot of the stair, I had seen nothing, whether in or out of the house, that one had better not have seen. There was many a corner round which I expected to come upon Quint, and many a situation that, in a merely sinister way, would have favored the appearance of Miss Jessel. The summer had turned, the summer had gone; the autumn had dropped upon Bly and had blown out half our lights. The place, with its gray sky and withered garlands, its bared spaces and scattered dead leaves, was like a theater after the performance – all strewn with crumpled playbills. There were exactly states of the air, conditions of sound and of stillness, unspeakable impressions of the *kind* of ministering moment, that brought back to me, long enough to catch it, the feeling of the medium in which, that June evening out of doors, I had had my first sight of Quint, and in which, too, at those other instants, I had, after seeing him through the window, looked for him in vain in the circle of shrubbery. I recognized the signs, the portents – I recognized the moment, the spot. But they remained unaccompanied and empty, and I continued unmolested; if unmolested one could call a young woman whose sensibility had, in the most extraordinary fashion, not declined but deepened. I had said in my talk with Mrs. Grose on that horrid scene of Flora's by the lake – and had perplexed her by so saying – that it would from that moment distress me much more to lose my power than to keep it. I had then expressed what was vividly in my mind: the truth that, whether the children really saw or not – since, that is, it was not yet definitely proved – I greatly preferred, as a safeguard, the fullness of my own exposure. I was ready to know the very worst that was to be known. What I had then had an ugly glimpse of was that my eyes might be sealed just while theirs were most opened. Well, my eyes *were* sealed, it appeared, at present – a consummation for which it seemed blasphemous not to thank God. There was, alas, a difficulty about that: I would have thanked him with all my soul had I not had in a proportionate measure this conviction of the secret of my pupils.

How can I retrace today the strange steps of my obsession? There were times of our being together when I would have been ready to swear that, literally, in my presence, but with my direct sense of it closed, they had visitors who were known and were welcome. Then it was that, had I not been deterred by the very chance that such an injury might prove greater than the injury to be averted, my exultation would have broken out. "They're here, they're here, you little wretches," I would have cried, "and you can't deny it now!" The little wretches denied it with all the added volume of their sociability and their tenderness, in just the crystal depths of which – like the flash of a fish in a stream – the mockery of their advantage peeped up. The shock, in truth, had sunk into me still deeper than I knew on the night when, looking out to see either Quint or Miss Jessel under the stars, I had beheld the boy over whose rest I watched and who had immediately brought in with him – had straightway, there, turned it on me – the lovely upward look with which, from the battlements above me, the hideous apparition of Quint had played. If it was a question of a scare, my discovery on this occasion had scared me more than any other, and it was in the condition of nerves produced by it that I made my actual inductions. They harassed me so that sometimes, at odd moments, I shut myself up audibly to rehearse – it was at once a fantastic relief and a renewed despair – the manner in which I might come to the point. I approached it from one side and the other while, in my room, I flung myself about, but I always broke down in the monstrous utterance of names. As they died away on my lips, I said to myself that I should indeed help them to represent something infamous, if, by pronouncing them, I should violate as rare a little case of instinctive delicacy as any schoolroom, probably, had ever known. When I said to myself: "*They* have the manners to be silent, and you, trusted as you are, the baseness to speak!" I felt myself crimson and I covered my face with my hands. After these secret scenes I chattered more than ever, going on volubly enough till one of our prodigious, palpable hushes occurred – I can call them nothing else – the strange, dizzy lift or swim (I try for terms!) into a stillness, a pause of all life, that had nothing to do with the more or less noise that at the moment we might be engaged in making and that I could hear through any deepened exhilaration or quickened recitation or louder strum of the piano. Then it was that the others, the outsiders, were there. Though they were not angels, they 'passed', as the French say, causing me, while they stayed, to tremble with the fear of their addressing to their younger victims some yet more infernal message or more vivid image than they had thought good enough for myself.

What it was most impossible to get rid of was the cruel idea that, whatever I had seen, Miles and Flora saw *more* – things terrible and unguessable and that sprang from dreadful passages of intercourse in the past. Such things naturally left on the surface, for the time, a chill which we vociferously denied that we felt; and we had, all three, with repetition, got into such splendid training that we went, each time, almost automatically, to mark the close of the incident, through the very same movements. It was striking of the children, at all events, to kiss me inveterately with a kind of wild irrelevance and never to fail – one or the other – of the precious question that had helped us through many a peril. "When do you think he *will* come? Don't you think we *ought* to write?" – there was nothing like that inquiry, we found by experience, for carrying off an awkwardness. 'He' of course was their uncle in Harley Street; and we lived in much profusion of theory that he might at any moment arrive to mingle in our circle. It was impossible to have given less encouragement than he had done to such a doctrine, but if we had not had the doctrine to fall back upon we should have deprived each other of some of our finest exhibitions. He never wrote to them – that may have been selfish, but it was a part of the flattery of his trust of me; for the way in which a man pays his highest tribute to a woman is apt to be but by the more festal celebration of one of the sacred laws of his comfort; and I held that I carried out the spirit of the pledge given not to appeal to him when I let my charges understand that their own letters were but charming literary exercises. They were too beautiful to be posted; I kept them myself; I have them all to this hour. This was a rule indeed which only added to the satiric effect of my being plied with the supposition that he might at any moment be among us. It was exactly as if my charges knew how almost more awkward than anything else that might be for me. There appears to me, moreover, as I look back, no note in all this more extraordinary than the mere fact that, in spite of my tension and of their triumph, I never lost patience with them. Adorable they must in truth have been, I now reflect, that I didn't in these days hate them! Would exasperation, however, if relief had longer been postponed, finally have betrayed me? It little matters, for relief arrived. I call it relief, though it was only the relief that a snap brings to a strain or the burst of a thunderstorm to a day of suffocation. It was at least change, and it came with a rush.

Chapter XIV

WALKING to church a certain Sunday morning, I had little Miles at my side and his sister, in advance of us and at Mrs. Grose's, well in sight. It was a crisp, clear day, the first of its order for some time; the night had brought a touch of frost, and the autumn air, bright and sharp, made the church bells almost gay. It was an odd accident of thought that I should have happened at such a moment to be particularly and very gratefully struck with the obedience of my little charges. Why did they never resent my inexorable, my perpetual society? Something or other had brought nearer home to me that I had all but pinned the boy to my shawl and that, in the way our companions were marshaled before me, I might have appeared to provide against some danger of rebellion. I was like a gaoler with an eye to possible surprises and escapes. But all this belonged – I mean their magnificent little surrender – just to the special array of the facts that were most abysmal. Turned out for Sunday by his uncle's tailor, who had had a free hand and a notion of pretty waistcoats and of his grand little air, Miles's whole title to independence, the rights of his sex and situation, were so stamped upon him that if he had suddenly struck for freedom I should have had nothing to say. I was by the strangest of chances wondering how I should meet him when the revolution unmistakably occurred. I call it a revolution because I now see how, with the word he spoke, the curtain rose on the last act of my dreadful drama, and the catastrophe was precipitated. "Look here, my dear, you know," he charmingly said, "when in the world, please, am I going back to school?"

Transcribed here the speech sounds harmless enough, particularly as uttered in the sweet, high, casual pipe with which, at all interlocutors, but above all at his eternal governess, he threw off intonations as if he were tossing roses. There was something in them that always made one 'catch', and I caught, at any rate, now so effectually that I stopped as short as if one of the trees of the park had fallen across the road. There was something new, on the spot, between us, and he was perfectly aware that I recognized it, though, to enable me to do so, he had no need to look a whit less candid and charming than usual. I could feel in him how he already, from my at first finding nothing to reply, perceived the advantage he had gained. I was so slow to find anything that he had plenty of time, after a minute, to continue with his suggestive but inconclusive smile: "You know, my dear, that for a fellow to be with a lady *always*—!" His 'my dear' was constantly on his lips for me, and nothing could have expressed more the exact shade of the sentiment with which I desired to inspire my pupils than its fond familiarity. It was so respectfully easy.

But, oh, how I felt that at present I must pick my own phrases! I remember that, to gain time, I tried to laugh, and I seemed to see in the beautiful face with which he watched me how ugly and queer I looked. "And always with the same lady?" I returned.

He neither blanched nor winked. The whole thing was virtually out between us. "Ah, of course, she's a jolly, 'perfect' lady; but, after all, I'm a fellow, don't you see? That's – well, getting on."

I lingered there with him an instant ever so kindly. "Yes, you're getting on." Oh, but I felt helpless!

I have kept to this day the heartbreaking little idea of how he seemed to know that and to play with it. "And you can't say I've not been awfully good, can you?"

I laid my hand on his shoulder, for, though I felt how much better it would have been to walk on, I was not yet quite able. "No, I can't say that, Miles."

"Except just that one night, you know—!"

"That one night?" I couldn't look as straight as he.

"Why, when I went down – went out of the house."

"Oh, yes. But I forget what you did it for."

"You forget?" – he spoke with the sweet extravagance of childish reproach. "Why, it was to show you I could!"

"Oh, yes, you could."

"And I can again."

I felt that I might, perhaps, after all, succeed in keeping my wits about me. "Certainly. But you won't."

"No, not *that* again. It was nothing."

"It was nothing," I said. "But we must go on."

He resumed our walk with me, passing his hand into my arm. "Then when *am* I going back?"

I wore, in turning it over, my most responsible air. "Were you very happy at school?"

He just considered. "Oh, I'm happy enough anywhere!"

"Well, then," I quavered, "if you're just as happy here—!"

"Ah, but that isn't everything! Of course *you* know a lot—"

"But you hint that you know almost as much?" I risked as he paused.

"Not half I want to!" Miles honestly professed. "But it isn't so much that."

"What is it, then?"

"Well – I want to see more life."

"I see; I see." We had arrived within sight of the church and of various persons, including several of the household of Bly, on their way to it and clustered about the door to see us go in. I quickened our step; I wanted to get there before the question between us opened up much further; I reflected hungrily that, for more than an hour, he would have to be silent; and I thought with envy of the comparative dusk of the pew and of the almost spiritual help of the hassock on which I might bend my knees. I seemed literally to be running a race with some confusion to which he was about to reduce me, but I felt that he had got in first when, before we had even entered the churchyard, he threw out:

"I want my own sort!"

It literally made me bound forward. "There are not many of your own sort, Miles!" I laughed. "Unless perhaps dear little Flora!"

"You really compare me to a baby girl?"

This found me singularly weak. "Don't you, then, *love* our sweet Flora?"

"If I didn't – and you, too; if I didn't—!" he repeated as if retreating for a jump, yet leaving his thought so unfinished that, after we had come into the gate, another stop, which he imposed on me by the pressure of his arm, had become inevitable. Mrs. Grose and Flora had passed into the church, the other worshippers had followed, and we were, for the minute, alone among the old, thick graves. We had paused, on the path from the gate, by a low, oblong, tablelike tomb.

"Yes, if you didn't—?"

He looked, while I waited, at the graves. "Well, you know what!" But he didn't move, and he presently produced something that made me drop straight down on the stone slab, as if suddenly to rest. "Does my uncle think what *you* think?"

I markedly rested. "How do you know what I think?"

"Ah, well, of course I don't; for it strikes me you never tell me. But I mean does *he* know?"

"Know what, Miles?"

"Why, the way I'm going on."

I perceived quickly enough that I could make, to this inquiry, no answer that would not involve something of a sacrifice of my employer. Yet it appeared to me that we were all, at Bly, sufficiently sacrificed to make that venial. "I don't think your uncle much cares."

Miles, on this, stood looking at me. "Then don't you think he can be made to?"

"In what way?"

"Why, by his coming down."

"But who'll get him to come down?"

"*I* will!" the boy said with extraordinary brightness and emphasis. He gave me another look charged with that expression and then marched off alone into church.

Chapter XV

THE BUSINESS was practically settled from the moment I never followed him. It was a pitiful surrender to agitation, but my being aware of this had somehow no power to restore me. I only sat there on my tomb and read into what my little friend had said to me the fullness of its meaning; by the time I had grasped the whole of which I had also embraced, for absence, the pretext that I was ashamed to offer my pupils and the rest of the congregation such an example of delay. What I said to myself above all was that Miles had got something out of me and that the proof of it, for him, would be just this awkward collapse. He had got out of me that there was something I was much afraid of and that he should probably be able to make use of my fear to gain, for his own purpose, more freedom. My fear was of having to deal with the intolerable question of the grounds of his dismissal from school, for that was really but the question of the horrors gathered behind. That his uncle should arrive to treat with me of these things was a solution that, strictly speaking, I ought now to have desired to bring on; but I could so little face the ugliness and the pain of it that I simply procrastinated and lived from hand to mouth. The boy, to my deep discomposure, was immensely in the right, was in a position to say to me: "Either you clear up with my guardian the mystery of this interruption of my studies, or you cease to expect me to lead with you a life that's so unnatural for a boy." What was so unnatural for the particular boy I was concerned with was this sudden revelation of a consciousness and a plan.

That was what really overcame me, what prevented my going in. I walked round the church, hesitating, hovering; I reflected that I had already, with him, hurt myself beyond repair. Therefore I could patch up nothing, and it was too extreme an effort to squeeze beside him into the pew: he would be so much more sure than ever to pass his arm into mine and make me sit there for an hour in close, silent contact with his commentary on our talk. For the first minute since his arrival I wanted to get away from him. As I paused beneath the high east window and listened to the sounds of worship, I was taken with an impulse that might master me, I felt, completely should I give it the least encouragement. I might easily put an end to my predicament by getting away altogether. Here was my chance; there was no one to stop me; I could give the whole thing up – turn my back and retreat. It was only a question of hurrying again, for a few preparations, to the house which the attendance at church of so many of the servants would practically have left unoccupied. No one, in short, could blame me if I should just drive desperately off. What was it to get away if I got away only till dinner? That would be in a couple of hours, at the end of which – I had the acute prevision – my little pupils would play at innocent wonder about my nonappearance in their train.

"What *did* you do, you naughty, bad thing? Why in the world, to worry us so – and take our thoughts off, too, don't you know? – did you desert us at the very door?" I couldn't meet such questions nor, as they asked them, their false little lovely eyes; yet it was all so exactly what I should have to meet that, as the prospect grew sharp to me, I at last let myself go.

I got, so far as the immediate moment was concerned, away; I came straight out of the churchyard and, thinking hard, retraced my steps through the park. It seemed to me that by the time I reached the house I had made up my mind I would fly. The Sunday stillness both of the approaches and of the interior, in which I met no one, fairly excited me with a sense of opportunity. Were I to get off quickly, this way, I should get off without a scene, without a word. My quickness would have to be remarkable, however, and the question of a conveyance was the great one to settle. Tormented, in the hall, with difficulties and obstacles, I remember sinking down at the foot of the staircase – suddenly collapsing there on the lowest step and then, with a revulsion, recalling that it was exactly where more than a month before, in the darkness of night and just so bowed with evil things, I had seen the specter of the most horrible of women. At this I was able to straighten myself; I went the rest of the way up; I made, in my bewilderment, for the schoolroom, where there were objects belonging to me that I should have to take. But I opened the door to find again, in a flash, my eyes unsealed. In the presence of what I saw I reeled straight back upon my resistance.

Seated at my own table in clear noonday light I saw a person whom, without my previous experience, I should have taken at the first blush for some housemaid who might have stayed at home to look after the place and who, availing herself of rare relief from observation and of the schoolroom table and my pens, ink, and paper, had applied herself to the considerable effort of a letter to her sweetheart. There was an effort in the way that, while her arms rested on the table, her hands with evident weariness supported her head; but at the moment I took this in I had already become aware that, in spite of my entrance, her attitude strangely persisted. Then it was – with the very act of its announcing itself – that her identity flared up in a change of posture. She rose, not as if she had heard me, but with an indescribable grand melancholy of indifference and detachment, and, within a dozen feet of me, stood there as my vile predecessor. Dishonored and tragic, she was all before me; but even as I fixed and, for memory, secured it, the awful image passed away. Dark as midnight in her black dress, her haggard beauty and her unutterable woe, she had looked at me long enough to appear to say that her right to sit at my table was as good as mine to sit at hers. While these instants lasted, indeed, I had the extraordinary chill of feeling that it was I who was the intruder. It was as a wild protest against it that, actually addressing her – "You terrible, miserable woman!" – I heard myself break into a sound that, by the open door, rang through the long passage and the empty house. She looked at me as if she heard me, but I had recovered myself and cleared the air. There was nothing in the room the next minute but the sunshine and a sense that I must stay.

Chapter XVI

I HAD SO perfectly expected that the return of my pupils would be marked by a demonstration that I was freshly upset at having to take into account that they were dumb about my absence. Instead of gaily denouncing and caressing me, they made no allusion to my having failed them, and I was left, for the time, on perceiving that she too said nothing, to study Mrs. Grose's odd face. I did this to such purpose that I made sure they had in some way bribed her to silence; a silence that, however, I would engage to break down on the first private opportunity. This opportunity came before tea: I secured five minutes with her in the housekeeper's room, where, in the twilight, amid a smell of lately baked bread, but with the place all swept and garnished, I found her sitting in pained placidity before the fire. So I see her still, so I see her best: facing the flame from her straight chair in the dusky, shining room, a large clean image of the 'put away' – of drawers closed and locked and rest without a remedy.

"Oh, yes, they asked me to say nothing; and to please them – so long as they were there – of course I promised. But what had happened to you?"

"I only went with you for the walk," I said. "I had then to come back to meet a friend."

She showed her surprise. "A friend – *you?*"

"Oh, yes, I have a couple!" I laughed. "But did the children give you a reason?"

"For not alluding to your leaving us? Yes; they said you would like it better. Do you like it better?"

My face had made her rueful. "No, I like it worse!" But after an instant I added: "Did they say why I should like it better?"

"No; Master Miles only said, 'We must do nothing but what she likes!'"

"I wish indeed he would. And what did Flora say?"

"Miss Flora was too sweet. She said, 'Oh, of course, of course!' – and I said the same."

I thought a moment. "You were too sweet, too – I can hear you all. But nonetheless, between Miles and me, it's now all out."

"All out?" My companion stared. "But what, miss?"

"Everything. It doesn't matter. I've made up my mind. I came home, my dear," I went on, "for a talk with Miss Jessel."

I had by this time formed the habit of having Mrs. Grose literally well in hand in advance of my sounding that note; so that even now, as she bravely blinked under the signal of my word, I could keep her comparatively firm. "A talk! Do you mean she spoke?"

"It came to that. I found her, on my return, in the schoolroom."

"And what did she say?" I can hear the good woman still, and the candor of her stupefaction.

"That she suffers the torments—!"

It was this, of a truth, that made her, as she filled out my picture, gape. "Do you mean," she faltered, "—of the lost?"

"Of the lost. Of the damned. And that's why, to share them—" I faltered myself with the horror of it.

But my companion, with less imagination, kept me up. "To share them—?"

"She wants Flora." Mrs. Grose might, as I gave it to her, fairly have fallen away from me had I not been prepared. I still held her there, to show I was. "As I've told you, however, it doesn't matter."

"Because you've made up your mind? But to what?"

"To everything."

"And what do you call 'everything'?"

"Why, sending for their uncle."

"Oh, miss, in pity do," my friend broke out.

"Ah, but I will, I *will!* I see it's the only way. What's 'out', as I told you, with Miles is that if he thinks I'm afraid to – and has ideas of what he gains by that – he shall see he's mistaken. Yes, yes; his uncle shall have it here from me on the spot (and before the boy himself, if necessary) that if I'm to be reproached with having done nothing again about more school—"

"Yes, miss—" my companion pressed me.

"Well, there's that awful reason."

There were now clearly so many of these for my poor colleague that she was excusable for being vague. "But – a – which?"

"Why, the letter from his old place."

"You'll show it to the master?"

"I ought to have done so on the instant."

"Oh, no!" said Mrs. Grose with decision.

"I'll put it before him," I went on inexorably, "that I can't undertake to work the question on behalf of a child who has been expelled—"

"For we've never in the least known what!" Mrs. Grose declared.

"For wickedness. For what else – when he's so clever and beautiful and perfect? Is he stupid? Is he untidy? Is he infirm? Is he ill-natured? He's exquisite – so it can be only *that*; and that would open up the whole thing. After all," I said, "it's their uncle's fault. If he left here such people—!"

"He didn't really in the least know them. The fault's mine." She had turned quite pale.

"Well, you shan't suffer," I answered.

"The children shan't!" she emphatically returned.

I was silent awhile; we looked at each other. "Then what am I to tell him?"

"You needn't tell him anything. *I'll* tell him."

I measured this. "Do you mean you'll write—?" Remembering she couldn't, I caught myself up. "How do you communicate?"

"I tell the bailiff. *He* writes."

"And should you like him to write our story?"

My question had a sarcastic force that I had not fully intended, and it made her, after a moment, inconsequently break down. The tears were again in her eyes. "Ah, miss, *you* write!"

"Well – tonight," I at last answered; and on this we separated.

Chapter XVII

I WENT so far, in the evening, as to make a beginning. The weather had changed back, a great wind was abroad, and beneath the lamp, in my room, with Flora at peace beside me, I sat for a long time before a blank sheet of paper and listened to the lash of the rain and the batter of the gusts. Finally I went out, taking a candle; I crossed the passage and listened a minute at Miles's door. What, under my endless obsession, I had been impelled to listen for was some betrayal of his not being at rest, and I presently caught one, but not in the form I had expected. His voice tinkled out. "I say, you there – come in." It was a gaiety in the gloom!

I went in with my light and found him, in bed, very wide awake, but very much at his ease. "Well, what are *you* up to?" he asked with a grace of sociability in which it occurred to me that Mrs. Grose, had she been present, might have looked in vain for proof that anything was 'out'.

I stood over him with my candle. "How did you know I was there?"

"Why, of course I heard you. Did you fancy you made no noise? You're like a troop of cavalry!" he beautifully laughed.

"Then you weren't asleep?"

"Not much! I lie awake and think."

I had put my candle, designedly, a short way off, and then, as he held out his friendly old hand to me, had sat down on the edge of his bed. "What is it," I asked, "that you think of?"

"What in the world, my dear, but *you?*"

"Ah, the pride I take in your appreciation doesn't insist on that! I had so far rather you slept."

"Well, I think also, you know, of this queer business of ours."

I marked the coolness of his firm little hand. "Of what queer business, Miles?"

"Why, the way you bring me up. And all the rest!"

I fairly held my breath a minute, and even from my glimmering taper there was light enough to show how he smiled up at me from his pillow. "What do you mean by all the rest?"

"Oh, you know, you know!"

I could say nothing for a minute, though I felt, as I held his hand and our eyes continued to meet, that my silence had all the air of admitting his charge and that nothing in the whole world of reality was perhaps at that moment so fabulous as our actual relation. "Certainly you shall go back to school," I said, "if it be that that troubles you. But not to the old place – we must find another, a better. How could I know it did trouble you, this question, when you never told me so, never spoke of it at all?" His clear, listening face, framed in its smooth whiteness, made him for the minute as appealing as some wistful patient in a children's hospital; and I would have given, as the resemblance came to me, all I possessed on earth really to be the nurse or the sister of charity who might have helped to cure him. Well, even as it was, I perhaps might help! "Do you know you've never said a word to me about your school – I mean the old one; never mentioned it in any way?"

He seemed to wonder; he smiled with the same loveliness. But he clearly gained time; he waited, he called for guidance. "Haven't I?" It wasn't for *me* to help him – it was for the thing I had met!

Something in his tone and the expression of his face, as I got this from him, set my heart aching with such a pang as it had never yet known; so unutterably touching was it to see his little brain puzzled and his little resources taxed to play, under the spell laid on him, a part of innocence and consistency. "No, never – from the hour you came back. You've never mentioned to me one of your masters, one of your comrades, nor the least little thing that ever happened to you at school. Never, little Miles – no, never – have you given me an inkling of anything that *may* have happened there. Therefore you can fancy how much I'm in the dark. Until you came out, that way, this morning, you had, since the first hour I saw you, scarce even made a reference to anything in your previous life. You seemed so perfectly to accept the present." It was extraordinary how my absolute conviction of his secret precocity (or whatever I might call the poison of an influence that I dared but half to phrase) made him, in spite of the faint breath of his inward trouble, appear as accessible as an older person – imposed him almost as an intellectual equal. "I thought you wanted to go on as you are."

It struck me that at this he just faintly colored. He gave, at any rate, like a convalescent slightly fatigued, a languid shake of his head. "I don't – I don't. I want to get away."

"You're tired of Bly?"

"Oh, no, I like Bly."

"Well, then—?"

"Oh, *you* know what a boy wants!"

I felt that I didn't know so well as Miles, and I took temporary refuge. "You want to go to your uncle?"

Again, at this, with his sweet ironic face, he made a movement on the pillow. "Ah, you can't get off with that!"

I was silent a little, and it was I, now, I think, who changed color. "My dear, I don't want to get off!"

"You can't, even if you do. You can't, you can't!" – he lay beautifully staring. "My uncle must come down, and you must completely settle things."

"If we do," I returned with some spirit, "you may be sure it will be to take you quite away."

"Well, don't you understand that that's exactly what I'm working for? You'll have to tell him – about the way you've let it all drop: you'll have to tell him a tremendous lot!"

The exultation with which he uttered this helped me somehow, for the instant, to meet him rather more. "And how much will *you*, Miles, have to tell him? There are things he'll ask you!"

He turned it over. "Very likely. But what things?"

"The things you've never told me. To make up his mind what to do with you. He can't send you back—"

"Oh, I don't want to go back!" he broke in. "I want a new field."

He said it with admirable serenity, with positive unimpeachable gaiety; and doubtless it was that very note that most evoked for me the poignancy, the unnatural childish tragedy, of his probable reappearance at the end of three months with all this bravado and still more dishonor. It overwhelmed me now that I should never be able to bear that, and it made me let myself go. I threw myself upon him and in the tenderness of my pity I embraced him. "Dear little Miles, dear little Miles—!"

My face was close to his, and he let me kiss him, simply taking it with indulgent good humor. "Well, old lady?"

"Is there nothing – nothing at all that you want to tell me?"

He turned off a little, facing round toward the wall and holding up his hand to look at as one had seen sick children look. "I've told you – I told you this morning."

Oh, I was sorry for him! "That you just want me not to worry you?"

He looked round at me now, as if in recognition of my understanding him; then ever so gently, "To let me alone," he replied.

There was even a singular little dignity in it, something that made me release him, yet, when I had slowly risen, linger beside him. God knows I never wished to harass him, but I felt that merely, at this, to turn my back on him was to abandon or, to put it more truly, to lose him. "I've just begun a letter to your uncle," I said.

"Well, then, finish it!"

I waited a minute. "What happened before?"

He gazed up at me again. "Before what?"

"Before you came back. And before you went away."

For some time he was silent, but he continued to meet my eyes. "What happened?"

It made me, the sound of the words, in which it seemed to me that I caught for the very first time a small faint quaver of consenting consciousness – it made me drop on my knees beside the bed and seize once more the chance of possessing him. "Dear little Miles, dear little Miles, if you *knew* how I want to help you! It's only that, it's nothing but that, and I'd rather die than give you a pain or do you a wrong – I'd rather die than hurt a hair of you. Dear little Miles" – oh, I brought it out now even if I *should* go too far – "I just want you to help me to save you!" But I knew in a moment after this that I had gone too far. The answer to my appeal was instantaneous, but it came in the form of an extraordinary blast and chill, a gust of frozen air, and a shake of the room as great as if, in the wild wind, the casement had crashed in. The boy gave a loud, high shriek, which, lost in the rest of the shock of sound, might have seemed, indistinctly, though I was so close to him, a note either of jubilation or of terror. I jumped to my feet again and was conscious of darkness. So for a moment we remained, while I stared about me and saw that the drawn curtains were unstirred and the window tight. "Why, the candle's out!" I then cried.

"It was I who blew it, dear!" said Miles.

Chapter XVIII

THE NEXT DAY, after lessons, Mrs. Grose found a moment to say to me quietly: "Have you written, miss?"

"Yes – I've written." But I didn't add – for the hour – that my letter, sealed and directed, was still in my pocket. There would be time enough to send it before the messenger should go to the village. Meanwhile there had been, on the part of my pupils, no more brilliant, more exemplary morning. It was exactly as if they had both had at heart to gloss over any recent little friction. They performed the dizziest feats of arithmetic, soaring quite out of *my* feeble range, and perpetrated, in higher spirits than ever, geographical and historical jokes. It was conspicuous of course in Miles in particular that he appeared to wish to show how easily he could let me down. This child, to my memory, really lives in a setting of beauty and misery that no words can translate; there was a distinction all his own in every impulse he revealed; never was a small natural creature, to the uninitiated eye all frankness and freedom, a more ingenious, a more extraordinary little gentleman. I had perpetually to guard against the wonder of contemplation into which my initiated view betrayed me; to check the irrelevant gaze and discouraged sigh in which I constantly both attacked and renounced the enigma of what such a little gentleman could have done that deserved a penalty. Say that, by the dark prodigy I knew, the imagination of all evil *had* been opened up to him: all the justice within me ached for the proof that it could ever have flowered into an act.

He had never, at any rate, been such a little gentleman as when, after our early dinner on this dreadful day, he came round to me and asked if I shouldn't like him, for half an hour, to play to me. David playing to Saul could never have shown a finer sense of the occasion. It was literally a charming exhibition of tact, of magnanimity, and quite tantamount to his saying outright: "The true knights we love to read about never push an advantage too far. I know what you mean now: you mean that – to be let alone yourself and not followed up – you'll cease to worry and spy upon me, won't keep me so close to you, will let me go and come. Well, I 'come', you see – but I don't go! There'll be plenty of time for that. I do really delight in your society, and I only want to show you that I contended for a principle." It may be imagined whether I resisted this appeal or failed to accompany him again, hand in hand, to the schoolroom. He sat down at the old piano and played as he had never played; and if there are those who think he had better have been kicking a football I can only say that I wholly agree with them. For at the end of a time that under his influence I had quite ceased to measure, I started up with a strange sense of having literally slept at my post. It was after luncheon, and by the schoolroom fire, and yet I hadn't really, in the least, slept: I had only done something much worse – I had forgotten. Where, all this time, was Flora? When I put the question to Miles, he played on a minute before answering and then could only say: "Why, my dear, how do *I* know?" – breaking moreover into a happy laugh which, immediately after, as if it were a vocal accompaniment, he prolonged into incoherent, extravagant song.

I went straight to my room, but his sister was not there; then, before going downstairs, I looked into several others. As she was nowhere about she would surely be with Mrs. Grose, whom, in the comfort of that theory, I accordingly proceeded in quest of. I found her where I had found her the evening before, but she met my quick challenge with blank, scared ignorance. She had only supposed that, after the repast, I had carried off both the children; as to which she was quite in her right, for it was the very first time I had allowed the little girl out of my sight without some special provision. Of course now indeed she might be with the maids, so that the immediate thing was to look for her without an air of alarm. This we promptly arranged between us; but when, ten minutes later and in pursuance of our arrangement, we met in the hall, it was only to report on either side that after guarded inquiries we had altogether failed to trace her. For a minute there, apart from observation, we exchanged mute alarms, and I could feel with what high interest my friend returned me all those I had from the first given her.

"She'll be above," she presently said – "in one of the rooms you haven't searched."

"No; she's at a distance." I had made up my mind. "She has gone out."

Mrs. Grose stared. "Without a hat?"

I naturally also looked volumes. "Isn't that woman always without one?"

"She's with *her?*"

"She's with *her!*" I declared. "We must find them."

My hand was on my friend's arm, but she failed for the moment, confronted with such an account of the matter, to respond to my pressure. She communed, on the contrary, on the spot, with her uneasiness. "And where's Master Miles?"

"Oh, *he's* with Quint. They're in the schoolroom."

"Lord, miss!" My view, I was myself aware – and therefore I suppose my tone – had never yet reached so calm an assurance.

"The trick's played," I went on; "they've successfully worked their plan. He found the most divine little way to keep me quiet while she went off."

"'Divine'?" Mrs. Grose bewilderedly echoed.

"Infernal, then!" I almost cheerfully rejoined. "He has provided for himself as well. But come!"

She had helplessly gloomed at the upper regions. "You leave him—?"

"So long with Quint? Yes – I don't mind that now."

She always ended, at these moments, by getting possession of my hand, and in this manner she could at present still stay me. But after gasping an instant at my sudden resignation, "Because of your letter?" she eagerly brought out.

I quickly, by way of answer, felt for my letter, drew it forth, held it up, and then, freeing myself, went and laid it on the great hall table. "Luke will take it," I said as I came back. I reached the house door and opened it; I was already on the steps.

My companion still demurred: the storm of the night and the early morning had dropped, but the afternoon was damp and gray. I came down to the drive while she stood in the doorway. "You go with nothing on?"

"What do I care when the child has nothing? I can't wait to dress," I cried, "and if you must do so, I leave you. Try meanwhile, yourself, upstairs."

"With *them?*" Oh, on this, the poor woman promptly joined me!

Chapter XIX

WE WENT straight to the lake, as it was called at Bly, and I daresay rightly called, though I reflect that it may in fact have been a sheet of water less remarkable than it appeared to my untraveled eyes. My acquaintance with sheets of water was small, and the pool of Bly, at all events on the few occasions of my consenting, under the protection of my pupils, to affront its surface in the old flat-bottomed boat moored there for our use, had impressed me both with its extent and its agitation. The usual place of embarkation was half a mile from the house, but I had an intimate conviction that, wherever Flora might be, she was not near home. She had not given me the slip for any small adventure, and, since the day of the very great one that I had shared with her by the pond, I had been aware, in our walks, of the quarter to which she most inclined. This was why I had now given to Mrs. Grose's steps so marked a direction – a direction that made her, when she perceived it, oppose a resistance that showed me she was freshly mystified. "You're going to the water, Miss? – you think she's *in*—?"

"She may be, though the depth is, I believe, nowhere very great. But what I judge most likely is that she's on the spot from which, the other day, we saw together what I told you."

"When she pretended not to see—?"

"With that astounding self-possession? I've always been sure she wanted to go back alone. And now her brother has managed it for her."

Mrs. Grose still stood where she had stopped. "You suppose they really *talk* of them?"

"I could meet this with a confidence! They say things that, if we heard them, would simply appall us."

"And if she *is* there—"

"Yes?"

"Then Miss Jessel is?"

"Beyond a doubt. You shall see."

"Oh, thank you!" my friend cried, planted so firm that, taking it in, I went straight on without her. By the time I reached the pool, however, she was close behind me, and I knew that, whatever, to her apprehension, might befall me, the exposure of my society struck her as her least danger. She exhaled a moan of relief as we at last came in sight of the greater part of the water without a sight of the child. There was no trace of Flora on that nearer side of the bank where my observation of her had been most startling, and none on the opposite edge, where, save for a margin of some twenty yards, a thick copse came down to the water. The pond, oblong in shape, had a width so scant compared to its length that, with its ends out of view, it might have been taken for a scant river. We looked at the empty expanse, and then I felt the suggestion of my friend's eyes. I knew what she meant and I replied with a negative headshake.

"No, no; wait! She has taken the boat."

My companion stared at the vacant mooring place and then again across the lake. "Then where is it?"

"Our not seeing it is the strongest of proofs. She has used it to go over, and then has managed to hide it."

"All alone – that child?"

"She's not alone, and at such times she's not a child: she's an old, old woman." I scanned all the visible shore while Mrs. Grose took again, into the queer element I offered her, one of her plunges of submission; then I pointed out that the boat might perfectly be in a small refuge formed by one of the recesses of the pool, an indentation masked, for the hither side, by a projection of the bank and by a clump of trees growing close to the water.

"But if the boat's there, where on earth's *she?*" my colleague anxiously asked.

"That's exactly what we must learn." And I started to walk further.

"By going all the way round?"

"Certainly, far as it is. It will take us but ten minutes, but it's far enough to have made the child prefer not to walk. She went straight over."

"Laws!" cried my friend again; the chain of my logic was ever too much for her. It dragged her at my heels even now, and when we had got halfway round – a devious, tiresome process, on ground much broken and by a path choked with overgrowth – I paused to give her breath. I sustained her with a grateful arm, assuring her that she might hugely help me; and this started us afresh, so that in the course of but few minutes more we reached a point from which we found the boat to be where I had supposed it. It had been intentionally left as much as possible out of sight and was tied to one of the stakes of a fence that came, just there, down to the brink and that had been an assistance to disembarking. I recognized, as I looked at the pair of short, thick oars, quite safely drawn up, the prodigious character of the feat for a little girl; but I had lived, by this time, too long among wonders and had panted to too many livelier measures. There was a gate in the fence, through which we passed, and that brought us, after a trifling interval, more into the open. Then, "There she is!" we both exclaimed at once.

Flora, a short way off, stood before us on the grass and smiled as if her performance was now complete. The next thing she did, however, was to stoop straight down and pluck – quite as if it were all she was there for – a big, ugly spray of withered fern. I instantly became sure she had just come out of the copse. She waited for us, not herself taking a step, and I was conscious of the rare solemnity with which we presently approached her. She smiled and smiled, and we met; but it was all done in a silence by this time flagrantly ominous. Mrs. Grose was the first to break the spell: she threw herself on her knees and, drawing the child to her breast, clasped in a long embrace the little tender, yielding body. While this dumb convulsion lasted I could only watch it – which I did the more intently when I saw Flora's face peep at me over our companion's shoulder. It was serious now – the flicker had left it; but it strengthened the pang with which I at that moment envied Mrs. Grose the simplicity of *her* relation. Still, all this while, nothing more passed between us save that Flora had let her foolish fern again drop to the ground. What she and I had virtually said to each other was that pretexts were useless now. When Mrs. Grose finally got up she kept the child's hand, so that the two were still before me; and the singular reticence of our communion was even more marked in the frank look she launched me. "I'll be hanged," it said, "if *I'll* speak!"

It was Flora who, gazing all over me in candid wonder, was the first. She was struck with our bareheaded aspect. "Why, where are your things?"

"Where yours are, my dear!" I promptly returned.

She had already got back her gaiety, and appeared to take this as an answer quite sufficient. "And where's Miles?" she went on.

There was something in the small valor of it that quite finished me: these three words from her were, in a flash like the glitter of a drawn blade, the jostle of the cup that my hand, for weeks and weeks, had held high and full to the brim that now, even before speaking, I felt overflow in a deluge. "I'll tell you if you'll tell *me*—" I heard myself say, then heard the tremor in which it broke.

"Well, what?"

Mrs. Grose's suspense blazed at me, but it was too late now, and I brought the thing out handsomely. "Where, my pet, is Miss Jessel?"

Chapter XX

JUST AS in the churchyard with Miles, the whole thing was upon us. Much as I had made of the fact that this name had never once, between us, been sounded, the quick, smitten glare with which the child's face now received it fairly likened my breach of the silence to the smash of a pane of glass. It added to the interposing cry, as if to stay the blow, that Mrs. Grose, at the same instant, uttered over my violence – the shriek of a creature scared, or rather wounded, which, in turn, within a few seconds, was completed by a gasp of my own. I seized my colleague's arm. "She's there, she's there!"

Miss Jessel stood before us on the opposite bank exactly as she had stood the other time, and I remember, strangely, as the first feeling now produced in me, my thrill of joy at having brought on a proof. She was there, and I was justified; she was there, and I was neither cruel nor mad. She was there for poor scared Mrs. Grose, but she was there most for Flora; and no moment of my monstrous time was perhaps so extraordinary as that in which I consciously threw out to her – with the sense that, pale and ravenous demon as she was, she would catch and understand it – an inarticulate message of gratitude. She rose erect on the spot my friend and I had lately quitted, and there was not, in all the long reach of her desire, an inch of her evil that fell short. This first vividness of vision and emotion were things of a few seconds, during which Mrs. Grose's dazed blink across to where I pointed struck me as a sovereign sign that she too at last saw, just as it carried my own eyes precipitately to the child. The revelation then of the manner in which Flora was affected startled me, in truth, far more than it would have done to find her also merely agitated, for direct dismay was of course not what I had expected. Prepared and on her guard as our pursuit had actually made her, she would repress every betrayal; and I was therefore shaken, on the spot, by my first glimpse of the particular one for which I had not allowed. To see her, without a convulsion of her small pink face, not even feign to glance in the direction of the prodigy I announced, but only, instead of that, turn at *me* an expression of hard, still gravity, an expression absolutely new and unprecedented and that appeared to read and accuse and judge me – this was a stroke that somehow converted the little girl herself into the very presence that could make me quail. I quailed even though my certitude that she thoroughly saw was never greater than at that instant, and in the immediate need to defend myself I called it passionately to witness. "She's there, you little unhappy thing – there, there, *there*, and you see her as well as you see me!" I had said shortly before to Mrs. Grose that she was not at these times a child, but an old, old woman, and that description of her could not have been more strikingly confirmed than in the way in which, for all answer to this, she simply showed me, without a concession, an admission, of her eyes, a countenance of deeper and deeper, of indeed suddenly quite fixed, reprobation. I was by this time – if I can put the whole thing at all together – more appalled at what I may properly call her manner than at anything else, though it was simultaneously with this that I became aware of having Mrs. Grose also, and very formidably, to reckon with. My elder companion, the next moment, at any rate, blotted out everything but her own flushed face and her loud, shocked protest, a burst of high disapproval. "What a dreadful turn, to be sure, miss! Where on earth do you see anything?"

I could only grasp her more quickly yet, for even while she spoke the hideous plain presence stood undimmed and undaunted. It had already lasted a minute, and it lasted while I continued, seizing my colleague, quite thrusting her at it and presenting her to it, to insist with my pointing hand. "You don't see her exactly as *we* see? – you mean to say you don't now – *now?* She's as big as a blazing fire! Only look, dearest woman, *look*—!" She looked, even as I did, and gave me, with her deep groan of negation, repulsion, compassion – the mixture with her pity of her relief at her exemption – a sense, touching to me even then, that she would have backed me up if she could. I might well have needed that, for with this hard blow of the proof that her eyes were hopelessly sealed I felt my own situation horribly crumble, I felt – I saw – my livid predecessor press, from her position, on my defeat, and I was conscious, more than all, of what I should have from this instant to deal with in the astounding little attitude of Flora. Into this attitude Mrs. Grose immediately and violently entered, breaking, even while there pierced through my sense of ruin a prodigious private triumph, into breathless reassurance.

"She isn't there, little lady, and nobody's there – and you never see nothing, my sweet! How can poor Miss Jessel – when poor Miss Jessel's dead and buried? *We* know, don't we, love?" – and she appealed, blundering in, to the child. "It's all a mere mistake and a worry and a joke – and we'll go home as fast as we can!"

Our companion, on this, had responded with a strange, quick primness of propriety, and they were again, with Mrs. Grose on her feet, united, as it were, in pained opposition to me. Flora continued to fix me with her small mask of reprobation, and even at that minute I prayed God to forgive me for seeming to see that, as she stood there holding tight to our friend's dress, her incomparable childish beauty had suddenly failed, had quite vanished. I've said it already – she was literally, she was hideously, hard; she had turned common and almost ugly. "I don't know what you mean. I see nobody. I see nothing. I never *have*. I think you're cruel. I don't like you!" Then, after this deliverance, which might have been that of a vulgarly pert little girl in the street, she hugged Mrs. Grose more closely and buried in her skirts the dreadful little face. In this position she produced an almost furious wail. "Take me away, take me away – oh, take me away from *her!*"

"From *me?*" I panted.

"From you – from you!" she cried.

Even Mrs. Grose looked across at me dismayed, while I had nothing to do but communicate again with the figure that, on the opposite bank, without a movement, as rigidly still as if catching, beyond the interval, our voices, was as vividly there for my disaster as it was not there for my service. The wretched child had spoken exactly as if she had got from some outside source each of her stabbing little words, and I could therefore, in the full despair of all I had to accept, but sadly shake my head at her. "If I had ever doubted, all my doubt would at present have gone. I've been living with the miserable truth, and now it has only too much closed round me. Of course

I've lost you: I've interfered, and you've seen – under *her* dictation" – with which I faced, over the pool again, our infernal witness – "the easy and perfect way to meet it. I've done my best, but I've lost you. Goodbye." For Mrs. Grose I had an imperative, an almost frantic "Go, go!" before which, in infinite distress, but mutely possessed of the little girl and clearly convinced, in spite of her blindness, that something awful had occurred and some collapse engulfed us, she retreated, by the way we had come, as fast as she could move.

Of what first happened when I was left alone I had no subsequent memory. I only knew that at the end of, I suppose, a quarter of an hour, an odorous dampness and roughness, chilling and piercing my trouble, had made me understand that I must have thrown myself, on my face, on the ground and given way to a wildness of grief. I must have lain there long and cried and sobbed, for when I raised my head the day was almost done. I got up and looked a moment, through the twilight, at the gray pool and its blank, haunted edge, and then I took, back to the house, my dreary and difficult course. When I reached the gate in the fence the boat, to my surprise, was gone, so that I had a fresh reflection to make on Flora's extraordinary command of the situation. She passed that night, by the most tacit, and I should add, were not the word so grotesque a false note, the happiest of arrangements, with Mrs. Grose. I saw neither of them on my return, but, on the other hand, as by an ambiguous compensation, I saw a great deal of Miles. I saw – I can use no other phrase – so much of him that it was as if it were more than it had ever been. No evening I had passed at Bly had the portentous quality of this one; in spite of which – and in spite also of the deeper depths of consternation that had opened beneath my feet – there was literally, in the ebbing actual, an extraordinarily sweet sadness. On reaching the house I had never so much as looked for the boy; I had simply gone straight to my room to change what I was wearing and to take in, at a glance, much material testimony to Flora's rupture. Her little belongings had all been removed. When later, by the schoolroom fire, I was served with tea by the usual maid, I indulged, on the article of my other pupil, in no inquiry whatever. He had his freedom now – he might have it to the end! Well, he did have it; and it consisted – in part at least – of his coming in at about eight o'clock and sitting down with me in silence. On the removal of the tea things I had blown out the candles and drawn my chair closer: I was conscious of a mortal coldness and felt as if I should never again be warm. So, when he appeared, I was sitting in the glow with my thoughts. He paused a moment by the door as if to look at me; then – as if to share them – came to the other side of the hearth and sank into a chair. We sat there in absolute stillness; yet he wanted, I felt, to be with me.

Chapter XXI

BEFORE a new day, in my room, had fully broken, my eyes opened to Mrs. Grose, who had come to my bedside with worse news. Flora was so markedly feverish that an illness was perhaps at hand; she had passed a night of extreme unrest, a night agitated above all by fears that had for their subject not in the least her former, but wholly her present, governess. It was not against the possible re-entrance of Miss Jessel on the scene that she protested – it was conspicuously and passionately against mine. I was promptly on my feet of course, and with an immense deal to ask; the more that my friend had discernibly now girded her loins to meet me once more. This I felt as soon as I had put to her the question of her sense of the child's sincerity as against my own. "She persists in denying to you that she saw, or has ever seen, anything?"

My visitor's trouble, truly, was great. "Ah, miss, it isn't a matter on which I can push her! Yet it isn't either, I must say, as if I much needed to. It has made her, every inch of her, quite old."

"Oh, I see her perfectly from here. She resents, for all the world like some high little personage, the imputation on her truthfulness and, as it were, her respectability. 'Miss Jessel indeed – *she!*' Ah, she's 'respectable', the chit! The impression she gave me there yesterday was, I assure you, the very strangest of all; it was quite beyond any of the others. I *did* put my foot in it! She'll never speak to me again."

Hideous and obscure as it all was, it held Mrs. Grose briefly silent; then she granted my point with a frankness which, I made sure, had more behind it. "I think indeed, miss, she never will. She do have a grand manner about it!"

"And that manner" – I summed it up – "is practically what's the matter with her now!"

Oh, that manner, I could see in my visitor's face, and not a little else besides! "She asks me every three minutes if I think you're coming in."

"I see – I see." I, too, on my side, had so much more than worked it out. "Has she said to you since yesterday – except to repudiate her familiarity with anything so dreadful – a single other word about Miss Jessel?"

"Not one, miss. And of course you know," my friend added, "I took it from her, by the lake, that, just then and there at least, there *was* nobody."

"Rather! And, naturally, you take it from her still."

"I don't contradict her. What else can I do?"

"Nothing in the world! You've the cleverest little person to deal with. They've made them – their two friends, I mean – still cleverer even than nature did; for it was wondrous material to play on! Flora has now her grievance, and she'll work it to the end."

"Yes, miss; but to *what* end?"

"Why, that of dealing with me to her uncle. She'll make me out to him the lowest creature—!"

I winced at the fair show of the scene in Mrs. Grose's face; she looked for a minute as if she sharply saw them together. "And him who thinks so well of you!"

"He has an odd way – it comes over me now," I laughed, "– of proving it! But that doesn't matter. What Flora wants, of course, is to get rid of me."

My companion bravely concurred. "Never again to so much as look at you."

"So that what you've come to me now for," I asked, "is to speed me on my way?" Before she had time to reply, however, I had her in check. "I've a better idea – the result of my reflections. My going *would* seem the right thing, and on Sunday I was terribly near it. Yet that won't do. It's *you* who must go. You must take Flora."

My visitor, at this, did speculate. "But where in the world—?"

"Away from here. Away from *them*. Away, even most of all, now, from me. Straight to her uncle."

"Only to tell on you—?"

"No, not 'only'! To leave me, in addition, with my remedy."

She was still vague. "And what *is* your remedy?"

"Your loyalty, to begin with. And then Miles's."

She looked at me hard. "Do you think he—?"

"Won't, if he has the chance, turn on me? Yes, I venture still to think it. At all events, I want to try. Get off with his sister as soon as possible and leave me with him alone." I was amazed, myself, at the spirit I had still in reserve, and therefore perhaps a trifle the more disconcerted at the way in which, in spite of this fine example of it, she hesitated. "There's one thing, of course," I went on: "they mustn't, before she goes, see each other for three seconds." Then it came over me that, in spite of Flora's presumable sequestration from the instant of her return from the pool, it might already be too late. "Do you mean," I anxiously asked, "that they *have* met?"

At this she quite flushed. "Ah, miss, I'm not such a fool as that! If I've been obliged to leave her three or four times, it has been each time with one of the maids, and at present, though she's alone, she's locked in safe. And yet – and yet!" There were too many things.

"And yet what?"

"Well, are you so sure of the little gentleman?"

"I'm not sure of anything but *you*. But I have, since last evening, a new hope. I think he wants to give me an opening. I do believe that – poor little exquisite wretch! – he wants to speak. Last evening, in the firelight and the silence, he sat with me for two hours as if it were just coming."

Mrs. Grose looked hard, through the window, at the gray, gathering day. "And did it come?"

"No, though I waited and waited, I confess it didn't, and it was without a breach of the silence or so much as a faint allusion to his sister's condition and absence that we at last kissed for good night. All the same," I continued, "I can't, if her uncle sees her, consent to his seeing her brother without my having given the boy – and most of all because things have got so bad – a little more time."

My friend appeared on this ground more reluctant than I could quite understand. "What do you mean by more time?"

"Well, a day or two – really to bring it out. He'll then be on *my* side – of which you see the importance. If nothing comes, I shall only fail, and you will, at the worst, have helped me by doing, on your arrival in town, whatever you may have found possible." So I put it before her, but she continued for a little so inscrutably embarrassed that I came again to her aid. "Unless, indeed," I wound up, "you really want *not* to go."

I could see it, in her face, at last clear itself; she put out her hand to me as a pledge. "I'll go – I'll go. I'll go this morning."

I wanted to be very just. "If you *should* wish still to wait, I would engage she shouldn't see me."

"No, no: it's the place itself. She must leave it." She held me a moment with heavy eyes, then brought out the rest. "Your idea's the right one. I myself, miss—"

"Well?"

"I can't stay."

The look she gave me with it made me jump at possibilities. "You mean that, since yesterday, you *have* seen—?"

She shook her head with dignity. "I've *heard*—!"

"Heard?"

"From that child – horrors! There!" she sighed with tragic relief. "On my honor, miss, she says things—!" But at this evocation she broke down; she dropped, with a sudden sob, upon my sofa and, as I had seen her do before, gave way to all the grief of it.

It was quite in another manner that I, for my part, let myself go. "Oh, thank God!"

She sprang up again at this, drying her eyes with a groan. "'Thank God'?"

"It so justifies me!"

"It does that, miss!"

I couldn't have desired more emphasis, but I just hesitated. "She's so horrible?"

I saw my colleague scarce knew how to put it. "Really shocking."

"And about me?"

"About you, miss – since you must have it. It's beyond everything, for a young lady; and I can't think wherever she must have picked up—"

"The appalling language she applied to me? I can, then!" I broke in with a laugh that was doubtless significant enough.

It only, in truth, left my friend still more grave. "Well, perhaps I ought to also – since I've heard some of it before! Yet I can't bear it," the poor woman went on while, with the same movement, she glanced, on my dressing table, at the face of my watch. "But I must go back."

I kept her, however. "Ah, if you can't bear it—!"

"How can I stop with her, you mean? Why, just *for* that: to get her away. Far from this," she pursued, "far from *them*—"

"She may be different? She may be free?" I seized her almost with joy. "Then, in spite of yesterday, you *believe*—"

"In such doings?" Her simple description of them required, in the light of her expression, to be carried no further, and she gave me the whole thing as she had never done. "I believe."

Yes, it was a joy, and we were still shoulder to shoulder: if I might continue sure of that I should care but little what else happened. My support in the presence of disaster would be the same as it had been in my early need of confidence, and if my friend would answer for my honesty, I would answer for all the rest. On the point of taking leave of her, nonetheless, I was to some extent embarrassed. "There's one thing, of course – it occurs to me – to remember. My letter, giving the alarm, will have reached town before you."

I now perceived still more how she had been beating about the bush and how weary at last it had made her. "Your letter won't have got there. Your letter never went."

"What then became of it?"

"Goodness knows! Master Miles—"

"Do you mean *he* took it?" I gasped.

She hung fire, but she overcame her reluctance. "I mean that I saw yesterday, when I came back with Miss Flora, that it wasn't where you had put it. Later in the evening I had the chance to question Luke, and he declared that he had neither noticed nor touched it." We could only exchange, on this, one of our deeper mutual soundings, and it was Mrs. Grose who first brought up the plumb with an almost elated "You see!"

"Yes, I see that if Miles took it instead he probably will have read it and destroyed it."

"And don't you see anything else?"

I faced her a moment with a sad smile. "It strikes me that by this time your eyes are open even wider than mine."

They proved to be so indeed, but she could still blush, almost, to show it. "I make out now what he must have done at school." And she gave, in her simple sharpness, an almost droll disillusioned nod. "He stole!"

I turned it over – I tried to be more judicial. "Well – perhaps."

She looked as if she found me unexpectedly calm. "He stole *letters!*"

She couldn't know my reasons for a calmness after all pretty shallow; so I showed them off as I might. "I hope then it was to more purpose than in this case! The note, at any rate, that I put on the table yesterday," I pursued, "will have given him so scant an advantage – for it contained only the bare demand for an interview – that he is already much ashamed of having gone so far for so little, and that what he had on his mind last evening was precisely the need of confession." I seemed to myself, for the instant, to have mastered it, to see it all. "Leave us, leave us" – I was already, at the door, hurrying her off. "I'll get it out of him. He'll meet me – he'll confess. If he confesses, he's saved. And if he's saved—"

"Then *you* are?" The dear woman kissed me on this, and I took her farewell. "I'll save you without him!" she cried as she went.

Chapter XXII

YET IT WAS when she had got off – and I missed her on the spot – that the great pinch really came. If I had counted on what it would give me to find myself alone with Miles, I speedily perceived, at least, that it would give me a measure. No hour of my stay in fact was so assailed with apprehensions as that of my coming down to learn that the carriage containing Mrs. Grose and my younger pupil had already rolled out of the gates. Now I *was*, I said to myself, face to face with the elements, and for much of the rest of the day, while I fought my weakness, I could consider that I had been supremely rash. It was a tighter place still than I had yet turned round in; all the more that, for the first time, I could see in the aspect of others a confused reflection of the crisis. What had happened naturally caused them all to stare; there was too little of the explained, throw out whatever we might, in the suddenness of my colleague's act. The maids and the men looked blank; the effect of which on my nerves was an aggravation until I saw the necessity of making it a positive aid. It was precisely, in short, by just clutching the helm that I avoided total wreck; and I dare say that, to bear up at all, I became, that morning, very grand and very dry. I welcomed the consciousness that I was charged with much to do, and I caused it to be known as well that, left thus to myself, I was quite remarkably firm. I wandered with that manner, for the next hour or two, all over the place and looked, I have no doubt, as if I were ready for any onset. So, for the benefit of whom it might concern, I paraded with a sick heart.

The person it appeared least to concern proved to be, till dinner, little Miles himself. My perambulations had given me, meanwhile, no glimpse of him, but they had tended to make more public the change taking place in our relation as a consequence of his having at the piano, the day before, kept me, in Flora's interest, so beguiled and befooled. The stamp of publicity had of course been fully given by her confinement and departure, and the change itself was now ushered in by our nonobservance of the regular custom of the schoolroom. He had already disappeared when, on my way down, I pushed open his door, and I learned below that he had breakfasted – in the presence of a couple of the maids – with Mrs. Grose and his sister. He had then gone out, as he said, for a stroll; than which nothing, I reflected, could better have expressed his frank view of the abrupt transformation of my office. What he would not permit this office to consist of was yet to be settled: there was a queer relief, at all events – I mean for myself in especial – in the renouncement of one pretension. If so much had sprung to the surface, I scarce put it too strongly in saying that what had perhaps sprung highest was the absurdity of our prolonging the fiction that I had anything more to teach him. It sufficiently stuck out that, by tacit little tricks in which even more than myself he carried out the care for my dignity, I had had to appeal to him to let me off straining to meet him on the ground of his true capacity. He had at any rate his freedom now; I was never to touch it again; as I had amply shown, moreover, when, on his joining me in the schoolroom the previous night, I had uttered, on the subject of the interval just concluded, neither challenge nor hint. I had too much, from this moment, my other ideas. Yet when he at last arrived, the difficulty of applying them, the accumulations of my problem, were brought straight home to me by the beautiful little presence on which what had occurred had as yet, for the eye, dropped neither stain nor shadow.

To mark, for the house, the high state I cultivated I decreed that my meals with the boy should be served, as we called it, downstairs; so that I had been awaiting him in the ponderous pomp of the room outside of the window of which I had had from Mrs. Grose, that first scared Sunday, my flash of something it would scarce have done to call light. Here at present I felt afresh – for I had felt it again and again – how my equilibrium depended on the success of my rigid will, the will to shut my eyes as tight as possible to the truth that what I had to deal with was, revoltingly, against nature. I could only get on at all by taking 'nature' into my confidence and my account, by treating my monstrous ordeal as a push in a direction unusual, of course, and unpleasant, but demanding, after all, for a fair front, only another turn of the screw of ordinary human virtue. No attempt, nonetheless, could well require more tact than just this attempt to supply, one's self, *all* the nature. How could I put even a little of that article into a suppression of reference to what had occurred? How, on the other hand, could I make reference without a new plunge into the hideous obscure? Well, a sort of answer, after a time, had come to me, and it was so far confirmed as that I was met, incontestably, by the quickened vision of what was rare in my little companion. It was indeed as if he had found even now – as he had so often found at lessons – still some other delicate way to ease me off. Wasn't there light in the fact which, as we shared our solitude, broke out with a specious glitter it had never yet quite worn? – the fact that (opportunity aiding, precious opportunity which had now come) it would be preposterous, with a child so endowed, to forego the help one might wrest from absolute intelligence? What had his intelligence been given him for but to save him? Mightn't one, to reach his mind, risk the stretch of an angular arm over his character? It was as if, when we were face to face in the dining room, he had literally shown me the way. The roast mutton was on the table, and I had dispensed with attendance. Miles, before he sat down, stood a moment with his hands in his pockets and looked at the joint, on which he seemed on the point of passing some humorous judgment. But what he presently produced was: "I say, my dear, is she really very awfully ill?"

"Little Flora? Not so bad but that she'll presently be better. London will set her up. Bly had ceased to agree with her. Come here and take your mutton."

He alertly obeyed me, carried the plate carefully to his seat, and, when he was established, went on. "Did Bly disagree with her so terribly suddenly?"

"Not so suddenly as you might think. One had seen it coming on."

"Then why didn't you get her off before?"

"Before what?"

"Before she became too ill to travel."

I found myself prompt. "She's *not* too ill to travel: she only might have become so if she had stayed. This was just the moment to seize. The journey will dissipate the influence" – oh, I was grand! – "and carry it off."

"I see, I see" – Miles, for that matter, was grand, too. He settled to his repast with the charming little 'table manner' that, from the day of his arrival, had relieved me of all grossness of admonition. Whatever he had been driven from school for, it was not for ugly feeding. He was irreproachable, as always, today; but he was unmistakably more conscious. He was discernibly trying to take for granted more things than he found, without assistance, quite easy; and he dropped into peaceful silence while he felt his situation. Our meal was of the briefest – mine a vain pretense, and I had the things immediately removed. While this was done Miles stood again with his hands in his little pockets and his back to me – stood and looked out of the wide window through which, that other day, I had seen what pulled me up. We continued silent while the maid was with us – as silent, it whimsically occurred to me, as some young couple who, on their wedding journey, at the inn, feel shy in the presence of the waiter. He turned round only when the waiter had left us. "Well – so we're alone!"

Chapter XXIII

"OH, MORE or less." I fancy my smile was pale. "Not absolutely. We shouldn't like that!" I went on.

"No – I suppose we shouldn't. Of course we have the others."

"We have the others – we have indeed the others," I concurred.

"Yet even though we have them," he returned, still with his hands in his pockets and planted there in front of me, "they don't much count, do they?"

I made the best of it, but I felt wan. "It depends on what you call 'much'!"

"Yes" – with all accommodation – "everything depends!" On this, however, he faced to the window again and presently reached it with his vague, restless, cogitating step. He remained there awhile, with his forehead against the glass, in contemplation of the stupid shrubs I knew and the dull things of November. I had always my hypocrisy of 'work', behind which, now, I gained the sofa. Steadying myself with it there as I had repeatedly done at those moments of torment that I have described as the moments of my knowing the children to be given to something from which I was barred, I sufficiently obeyed my habit of being prepared for the worst. But an extraordinary impression dropped on me as I extracted a meaning from the boy's embarrassed back – none other than the impression that I was not barred now. This inference grew in a few minutes to sharp intensity and seemed bound up with the direct perception that it was positively *he* who was. The frames and squares of the great window were a kind of image, for him, of a kind of failure. I felt that I saw him, at any rate, shut in or shut out. He was admirable, but not comfortable: I took it in with a throb of hope. Wasn't he looking, through the haunted pane, for something he couldn't see? – and wasn't it the first time in the whole business that he had known such a lapse? The first, the very first: I found it a splendid portent. It made him anxious, though he watched himself; he had been anxious all day and, even while in his usual sweet little manner he sat at table, had needed all his small strange genius to give it a gloss. When he at last turned round to meet me, it was almost as if this genius had succumbed. "Well, I think I'm glad Bly agrees with *me!*"

"You would certainly seem to have seen, these twenty-four hours, a good deal more of it than for some time before. I hope," I went on bravely, "that you've been enjoying yourself."

"Oh, yes, I've been ever so far; all round about – miles and miles away. I've never been so free."

He had really a manner of his own, and I could only try to keep up with him. "Well, do you like it?"

He stood there smiling; then at last he put into two words – "Do *you?*" – more discrimination than I had ever heard two words contain. Before I had time to deal with that, however, he continued as if with the sense that this was an impertinence to be softened. "Nothing could be more charming than the way you take it, for of course if we're alone together now it's you that are alone most. But I hope," he threw in, "you don't particularly mind!"

"Having to do with you?" I asked. "My dear child, how can I help minding? Though I've renounced all claim to your company – you're so beyond me – I at least greatly enjoy it. What else should I stay on for?"

He looked at me more directly, and the expression of his face, graver now, struck me as the most beautiful I had ever found in it. "You stay on just for *that?*"

"Certainly. I stay on as your friend and from the tremendous interest I take in you till something can be done for you that may be more worth your while. That needn't surprise you." My voice trembled so that I felt it impossible to suppress the shake. "Don't you remember how I told you, when I came and sat on your bed the night of the storm, that there was nothing in the world I wouldn't do for you?"

"Yes, yes!" He, on his side, more and more visibly nervous, had a tone to master; but he was so much more successful than I that, laughing out through his gravity, he could pretend we were pleasantly jesting. "Only that, I think, was to get me to do something for *you!*"

"It was partly to get you to do something," I conceded. "But, you know, you didn't do it."

"Oh, yes," he said with the brightest superficial eagerness, "you wanted me to tell you something."

"That's it. Out, straight out. What you have on your mind, you know."

"Ah, then, is *that* what you've stayed over for?"

He spoke with a gaiety through which I could still catch the finest little quiver of resentful passion; but I can't begin to express the effect upon me of an implication of surrender even so faint. It was as if what I had yearned for had come at last only to astonish me. "Well, yes – I may as well make a clean breast of it, it was precisely for that."

He waited so long that I supposed it for the purpose of repudiating the assumption on which my action had been founded; but what he finally said was: "Do you mean now – here?"

"There couldn't be a better place or time." He looked round him uneasily, and I had the rare – oh, the queer! – impression of the very first symptom I had seen in him of the approach of immediate fear. It was as if he were suddenly afraid of me – which struck me indeed as perhaps the best thing to make him. Yet in the very pang of the effort I felt it vain to try sternness, and I heard myself the next instant so gentle as to be almost grotesque. "You want so to go out again?"

"Awfully!" He smiled at me heroically, and the touching little bravery of it was enhanced by his actually flushing with pain. He had picked up his hat, which he had brought in, and stood twirling it in a way that gave me, even as I was just nearly reaching port, a perverse horror of what I was doing. To do it in *any* way was an act of violence, for what did it consist of but the obtrusion of the idea of grossness and guilt on a small helpless creature who had been for me a revelation of the possibilities of beautiful intercourse? Wasn't it base to create for a being so exquisite a mere alien awkwardness? I suppose I now read into our situation a clearness it couldn't have had at the time, for I seem to see our poor eyes already lighted with some spark of a prevision of the anguish that was to come. So we circled about, with terrors and scruples, like fighters not daring to close. But it was for each other we feared! That kept us a little longer suspended and unbruised. "I'll tell you everything," Miles said – "I mean I'll tell you anything you like. You'll stay on with me, and we shall both be all right, and I *will* tell you – I *will*. But not now."

"Why not now?"

My insistence turned him from me and kept him once more at his window in a silence during which, between us, you might have heard a pin drop. Then he was before me again with the air of a person for whom, outside, someone who had frankly to be reckoned with was waiting. "I have to see Luke."

I had not yet reduced him to quite so vulgar a lie, and I felt proportionately ashamed. But, horrible as it was, his lies made up my truth. I achieved thoughtfully a few loops of my knitting. "Well, then, go to Luke, and I'll wait for what you promise. Only, in return for that, satisfy, before you leave me, one very much smaller request."

He looked as if he felt he had succeeded enough to be able still a little to bargain. "Very much smaller—?"

"Yes, a mere fraction of the whole. Tell me" – oh, my work preoccupied me, and I was offhand! – "if, yesterday afternoon, from the table in the hall, you took, you know, my letter."

Chapter XXIV

MY SENSE of how he received this suffered for a minute from something that I can describe only as a fierce split of my attention – a stroke that at first, as I sprang straight up, reduced me to the mere blind movement of getting hold of him, drawing him close, and, while I just fell for support against the nearest piece of furniture, instinctively keeping him with his back to the window. The appearance was full upon us that I had already had to deal with here: Peter Quint had come into view like a sentinel before a prison. The next thing I saw was that, from outside, he had reached the window, and then I knew that, close to the glass and glaring in through it, he offered once more to the room his white face of damnation. It represents but grossly what took place within me at the sight to say that on the second my decision was made; yet I believe that no woman so overwhelmed ever in so short a time recovered her grasp of the *act*. It came to me in the very horror of the immediate presence that the act would be, seeing and facing what I saw and faced, to keep the boy himself unaware. The inspiration – I can call it by no other name – was that I felt how voluntarily, how transcendently, I *might*. It was like fighting with a demon for a human soul, and when I had fairly so appraised it I saw how the human soul – held out, in the tremor of my hands, at arm's length – had a perfect dew of sweat on a lovely childish forehead. The face that was close to mine was as white as the face against the glass, and out of it presently came a sound, not low nor weak, but as if from much further away, that I drank like a waft of fragrance.

"Yes – I took it."

At this, with a moan of joy, I enfolded, I drew him close; and while I held him to my breast, where I could feel in the sudden fever of his little body the tremendous pulse of his little heart, I kept my eyes on the thing at the window and saw it move and shift its posture. I have likened it to a sentinel, but its slow wheel, for a moment, was rather the prowl of a baffled beast. My present quickened courage, however, was such that, not too much to let it through, I had to shade, as it were, my flame. Meanwhile the glare of the face was again at the window, the scoundrel fixed as if to watch and wait. It was the very confidence that I might now defy him, as well as the positive certitude, by this time, of the child's unconsciousness, that made me go on. "What did you take it for?"

"To see what you said about me."

"You opened the letter?"

"I opened it."

My eyes were now, as I held him off a little again, on Miles's own face, in which the collapse of mockery showed me how complete was the ravage of uneasiness. What was prodigious was that at last, by my success, his sense was sealed and his communication stopped: he knew that he was in presence, but knew not of what, and knew still less that I also was and that I did know. And what did this strain of trouble matter when my eyes went back to the window only to see that the air was clear again and – by my personal triumph – the influence quenched? There was nothing there. I felt that the cause was mine and that I should surely get *all*. "And you found nothing!" – I let my elation out.

He gave the most mournful, thoughtful little headshake. "Nothing."

"Nothing, nothing!" I almost shouted in my joy.

"Nothing, nothing," he sadly repeated.

I kissed his forehead; it was drenched. "So what have you done with it?"

"I've burned it."

"Burned it?" It was now or never. "Is that what you did at school?"

Oh, what this brought up! "At school?"

"Did you take letters? – or other things?"

"Other things?" He appeared now to be thinking of something far off and that reached him only through the pressure of his anxiety. Yet it did reach him. "Did I *steal?*"

I felt myself redden to the roots of my hair as well as wonder if it were more strange to put to a gentleman such a question or to see him take it with allowances that gave the very distance of his fall in the world. "Was it for that you mightn't go back?"

The only thing he felt was rather a dreary little surprise. "Did you know I mightn't go back?"

"I know everything."

He gave me at this the longest and strangest look. "Everything?"

"Everything. Therefore *did* you—?" But I couldn't say it again.

Miles could, very simply. "No. I didn't steal."

My face must have shown him I believed him utterly; yet my hands – but it was for pure tenderness – shook him as if to ask him why, if it was all for nothing, he had condemned me to months of torment. "What then did you do?"

He looked in vague pain all round the top of the room and drew his breath, two or three times over, as if with difficulty. He might have been standing at the bottom of the sea and raising his eyes to some faint green twilight. "Well – I said things."

"Only that?"

"They thought it was enough!"

"To turn you out for?"

Never, truly, had a person 'turned out' shown so little to explain it as this little person! He appeared to weigh my question, but in a manner quite detached and almost helpless. "Well, I suppose I oughtn't."

"But to whom did you say them?"

He evidently tried to remember, but it dropped – he had lost it. "I don't know!"

He almost smiled at me in the desolation of his surrender, which was indeed practically, by this time, so complete that I ought to have left it there. But I was infatuated – I was blind with victory, though even then the very effect that was to have brought him so much nearer was already that of added separation. "Was it to everyone?" I asked.

"No; it was only to—" But he gave a sick little headshake. "I don't remember their names."

"Were they then so many?"

"No – only a few. Those I liked."

Those he liked? I seemed to float not into clearness, but into a darker obscure, and within a minute there had come to me out of my very pity the appalling alarm of his being perhaps innocent. It was for the instant confounding and bottomless, for if he *were* innocent, what then on earth was *I?* Paralyzed, while it lasted, by the mere brush of the question, I let him go a little, so that, with a deep-drawn sigh, he turned away from me again; which, as he faced toward the clear window, I suffered, feeling that I had nothing now there to keep him from. "And did they repeat what you said?" I went on after a moment.

He was soon at some distance from me, still breathing hard and again with the air, though now without anger for it, of being confined against his will. Once more, as he had done before, he looked up at the dim day as if, of what had hitherto sustained him, nothing was left but an unspeakable anxiety. "Oh, yes," he nevertheless replied – "they must have repeated them. To those *they* liked," he added.

There was, somehow, less of it than I had expected; but I turned it over. "And these things came round—?"

"To the masters? Oh, yes!" he answered very simply. "But I didn't know they'd tell."

"The masters? They didn't – they've never told. That's why I ask you."

He turned to me again his little beautiful fevered face. "Yes, it was too bad."

"Too bad?"

"What I suppose I sometimes said. To write home."

I can't name the exquisite pathos of the contradiction given to such a speech by such a speaker; I only know that the next instant I heard myself throw off with homely force: "Stuff and nonsense!" But the next after that I must have sounded stern enough. "What *were* these things?"

My sternness was all for his judge, his executioner; yet it made him avert himself again, and that movement made *me*, with a single bound and an irrepressible cry, spring straight upon him. For there again, against the glass, as if to blight his confession and stay his answer, was the hideous author of our woe – the white face of damnation. I felt a sick swim at the drop of my victory and all the return of my battle, so that the wildness of my veritable leap only served as a great betrayal. I saw him, from the midst of my act, meet it with a divination, and on the perception that even now he only guessed, and that the window was still to his own eyes free, I let the impulse flame up to convert the climax of his dismay into the very proof of his liberation. "No more, no more, no more!" I shrieked, as I tried to press him against me, to my visitant.

"Is she *here?*" Miles panted as he caught with his sealed eyes the direction of my words. Then as his strange 'she' staggered me and, with a gasp, I echoed it, "Miss Jessel, Miss Jessel!" he with a sudden fury gave me back.

I seized, stupefied, his supposition – some sequel to what we had done to Flora, but this made me only want to show him that it was better still than that. "It's not Miss Jessel! But it's at the window – straight before us. It's *there* – the coward horror, there for the last time!"

At this, after a second in which his head made the movement of a baffled dog's on a scent and then gave a frantic little shake for air and light, he was at me in a white rage, bewildered, glaring vainly over the place and missing wholly, though it now, to my sense, filled the room like the taste of poison, the wide, overwhelming presence. "It's *he?*"

I was so determined to have all my proof that I flashed into ice to challenge him. "Whom do you mean by 'he'?"

"Peter Quint – you devil!" His face gave again, round the room, its convulsed supplication. "*Where?*"

They are in my ears still, his supreme surrender of the name and his tribute to my devotion. "What does he matter now, my own? – what will he *ever* matter? *I* have you," I launched at the beast, "but he has lost you forever!" Then, for the demonstration of my work, "There, *there!*" I said to Miles.

But he had already jerked straight round, stared, glared again, and seen but the quiet day. With the stroke of the loss I was so proud of he uttered the cry of a creature hurled over an abyss, and the grasp with which I recovered him might have been that of catching him in his fall. I caught him, yes, I held him – it may be imagined with what a passion; but at the end of a minute I began to feel what it truly was that I held. We were alone with the quiet day, and his little heart, dispossessed, had stopped.

"Oh Whistle, and I'll Come to You, My Lad"

M.R. James

"I SUPPOSE you will be getting away pretty soon, now Full Term is over, Professor," said a person not in the story to the Professor of Ontography, soon after they had sat down next to each other at a feast in the hospitable hall of St James's College.

The Professor was young, neat, and precise in speech.

"Yes," he said; "my friends have been making me take up golf this term, and I mean to go to the East Coast – in point of fact to Burnstow – (I dare say you know it) for a week or ten days, to improve my game. I hope to get off tomorrow."

"Oh, Parkins," said his neighbour on the other side, "if you are going to Burnstow, I wish you would look at the site of the Templars' preceptory, and let me know if you think it would be any good to have a dig there in the summer."

It was, as you might suppose, a person of antiquarian pursuits who said this, but, since he merely appears in this prologue, there is no need to give his entitlements.

"Certainly," said Parkins, the Professor: "if you will describe to me whereabouts the site is, I will do my best to give you an idea of the lie of the land when I get back; or I could write to you about it, if you would tell me where you are likely to be."

"Don't trouble to do that, thanks. It's only that I'm thinking of taking my family in that direction in the Long, and it occurred to me that, as very few of the English preceptories have ever been properly planned, I might have an opportunity of doing something useful on off-days."

The Professor rather sniffed at the idea that planning out a preceptory could be described as useful. His neighbour continued:

"The site – I doubt if there is anything showing above ground – must be down quite close to the beach now. The sea has encroached tremendously, as you know, all along that bit of coast. I should think, from the map, that it must be about three-quarters of a mile from the Globe Inn, at the north end of the town. Where are you going to stay?"

"Well, *at* the Globe Inn, as a matter of fact," said Parkins; "I have engaged a room there. I couldn't get in anywhere else; most of the lodging-houses are shut up in winter, it seems; and, as it is, they tell me that the only room of any size I can have is really a double-bedded one, and that they haven't a corner in which to store the other bed, and so on. But I must have a fairly large room, for I am taking some books down, and mean to do a bit of work; and though I don't quite fancy having an empty bed – not to speak of two – in what I may call for the time being my study, I suppose I can manage to rough it for the short time I shall be there."

"Do you call having an extra bed in your room roughing it, Parkins?" said a bluff person opposite. "Look here, I shall come down and occupy it for a bit; it'll be company for you."

The Professor quivered, but managed to laugh in a courteous manner.

"By all means, Rogers; there's nothing I should like better. But I'm afraid you would find it rather dull; you don't play golf, do you?"

"No, thank Heaven!" said rude Mr. Rogers.

"Well, you see, when I'm not writing I shall most likely be out on the links, and that, as I say, would be rather dull for you, I'm afraid."

"Oh, I don't know! There's certain to be somebody I know in the place; but, of course, if you don't want me, speak the word, Parkins; I shan't be offended. Truth, as you always tell us, is never offensive."

Parkins was, indeed, scrupulously polite and strictly truthful. It is to be feared that Mr. Rogers sometimes practised upon his knowledge of these characteristics. In Parkins's breast there was a conflict now raging, which for a moment or two did not allow him to answer. That interval being over, he said:

"Well, if you want the exact truth, Rogers, I was considering whether the room I speak of would really be large enough to accommodate us both comfortably; and also whether (mind, I shouldn't have said this if you hadn't pressed me) you would not constitute something in the nature of a hindrance to my work."

Rogers laughed loudly.

"Well done, Parkins!" he said. "It's all right. I promise not to interrupt your work; don't you disturb yourself about that. No, I won't come if you don't want me; but I thought I should do so nicely to keep the ghosts off." Here he might have been seen to wink and to nudge his next neighbour. Parkins might also have been seen to become pink. "I beg pardon, Parkins," Rogers continued; "I oughtn't to have said that. I forgot you didn't like levity on these topics."

"Well," Parkins said, "as you have mentioned the matter, I freely own that I do *not* like careless talk about what you call ghosts. A man in my position," he went on, raising his voice a little, "cannot, I find, be too careful about appearing to sanction the current beliefs on such subjects. As you know, Rogers, or as you ought to know; for I think I have never concealed my views—"

"No, you certainly have not, old man," put in Rogers *sotto voce.*

"—I hold that any semblance, any appearance of concession to the view that such things might exist is equivalent to a renunciation of all that I hold most sacred. But I'm afraid I have not succeeded in securing your attention."

"Your *undivided* attention, was what Dr. Blimber actually *said*,"[1] Rogers interrupted, with every appearance of an earnest desire for accuracy. "But I beg your pardon, Parkins: I'm stopping you."

"No, not at all," said Parkins. "I don't remember Blimber; perhaps he was before my time. But I needn't go on. I'm sure you know what I mean."

"Yes, yes," said Rogers, rather hastily – "just so. We'll go into it fully at Burnstow, or somewhere."

In repeating the above dialogue I have tried to give the impression which it made on me, that Parkins was something of an old woman – rather henlike, perhaps, in his little ways; totally destitute, alas! of the sense of humour, but at the same time dauntless and sincere in his convictions, and a man deserving of the greatest respect. Whether or not the reader has gathered so much, that was the character which Parkins had.

* * *

On the following day Parkins did, as he had hoped, succeed in getting away from his college, and in arriving at Burnstow. He was made welcome at the Globe Inn, was safely installed in the large double-bedded room of which we have heard, and was able before retiring to rest to arrange his materials for work in apple-pie order upon a commodious table which occupied the outer end of the room, and was surrounded on three sides by windows looking out seaward; that is to say, the central window looked straight out to sea, and those on the left and right commanded prospects along the shore to the north and south respectively. On the south you saw the village of Burnstow. On the north no houses were to be seen, but only the beach and the low cliff backing it. Immediately in front was a strip – not considerable – of rough grass, dotted with old anchors, capstans, and so forth; then a broad path; then the beach. Whatever may have been the original distance between the Globe Inn and the sea, not more than sixty yards now separated them.

The rest of the population of the inn was, of course, a golfing one, and included few elements that call for a special description. The most conspicuous figure was, perhaps, that of an *ancien militaire*, secretary of a London club, and possessed of a voice of incredible strength, and of views of a pronouncedly Protestant type. These were apt to find utterance after his attendance upon the ministrations of the Vicar, an estimable man with inclinations towards a picturesque ritual, which he gallantly kept down as far as he could out of deference to East Anglian tradition.

Professor Parkins, one of whose principal characteristics was pluck, spent the greater part of the day following his arrival at Burnstow in what he had called improving his game, in company with this Colonel Wilson: and during the afternoon – whether the process of improvement were to blame or not, I am not sure – the Colonel's demeanour assumed a colouring so lurid that even Parkins jibbed at the thought of walking home with him from the links. He determined, after a short and furtive look at that bristling moustache and those incarnadined features, that it would be wiser to allow the influences of tea and tobacco to do what they could with the Colonel before the dinner-hour should render a meeting inevitable.

"I might walk home tonight along the beach," he reflected – "yes, and take a look – there will be light enough for that – at the ruins of which Disney was talking. I don't exactly know where they are, by the way; but I expect I can hardly help stumbling on them."

This he accomplished, I may say, in the most literal sense, for in picking his way from the links to the shingle beach his foot caught, partly in a gorse-root and partly in a biggish stone, and over he went. When he got up and surveyed his surroundings, he found himself in a patch of somewhat broken ground covered with small depressions and mounds. These latter, when he came to examine them, proved to be simply masses of flints embedded in mortar and grown over with turf. He must, he quite rightly concluded, be on the site of the preceptory he had promised to look at. It seemed not unlikely to reward the spade of the explorer; enough of the foundations was probably left at no great depth to throw a good deal of light on the general plan. He remembered vaguely that the Templars, to whom this site had belonged, were in the habit of building round churches, and he thought a particular series of the humps or mounds near him did appear to be arranged in something of a circular form. Few people can resist the temptation to try a little amateur research in a department quite outside their own, if only for the satisfaction of showing how successful they would have been had they only taken it up seriously. Our Professor, however, if he felt something of this mean desire, was also truly anxious to oblige Mr. Disney. So he paced with care the circular area he had noticed, and wrote down its rough dimensions in his pocket-book. Then he proceeded to examine an oblong eminence which lay east of the centre of the circle, and seemed to his thinking likely to be the base of a platform or altar. At one end of it, the northern, a patch of the turf was gone – removed by some boy or other creature *ferae naturae*. It might, he thought, be as well to probe the soil here for evidences of masonry, and he took out his knife and began scraping away the earth. And now followed another little discovery: a portion of soil fell inward as he scraped, and disclosed a small cavity. He lighted one match after another to help him to see of what nature the hole was, but the wind was too strong for them all. By tapping and scratching the sides with his knife, however, he was able to make out that it must be an artificial hole in masonry. It was rectangular, and the sides, top, and bottom, if not actually plastered, were smooth and regular. Of course it was empty. No! As he withdrew the knife he heard a metallic clink, and when he introduced his hand it met with a cylindrical object lying on the floor of the hole. Naturally enough, he picked it up, and when he brought it into the light, now fast fading, he could see that it, too, was of man's making – a metal tube about four inches long, and evidently of some considerable age.

By the time Parkins had made sure that there was nothing else in this odd receptacle, it was too late and too dark for him to think of undertaking any further search. What he had done had proved so unexpectedly interesting that he determined to sacrifice a little more of the daylight on the morrow to archaeology. The object which he now had safe in his pocket was bound to be of some slight value at least, he felt sure.

Bleak and solemn was the view on which he took a last look before starting homeward. A faint yellow light in the west showed the links, on which a few figures moving towards the club-house were still visible, the squat martello tower, the lights of Aldsey village, the pale ribbon of sands intersected at intervals by black wooden groynes, the dim and murmuring sea. The wind was bitter from the north, but was at his back when he set out for the Globe. He quickly rattled and clashed through the shingle and gained the sand, upon which, but for the groynes which had to be got over every few yards, the going was both good and quiet. One last look behind, to measure the distance he had made since leaving the ruined Templars' church, showed him a prospect of company on his walk, in the shape of a rather indistinct personage, who seemed to be making great efforts to catch up with him, but made little, if any, progress. I mean that there was an appearance of running about his movements, but that the distance between him and Parkins did not seem materially to lessen. So, at least, Parkins thought, and decided that he almost certainly did not know him, and that it would be absurd to wait until he came up. For all that, company, he began to think, would really be very welcome on that lonely shore, if only you could choose your companion. In his unenlightened days he had read of meetings in such places which even now would hardly bear thinking of. He went on thinking of them, however, until he reached home, and particularly of one which catches most people's fancy at some time of their childhood. 'Now I saw in my dream that Christian had gone but a very little way when he saw a foul fiend coming over the field to meet him.'

"What should I do now," he thought, "if I looked back and caught sight of a black figure sharply defined against the yellow sky, and saw that it had horns and wings? I wonder whether I should stand or run for it. Luckily, the gentleman behind is not of that kind, and he seems to be about as far off now as when I saw him first. Well, at this rate, he won't get his dinner as soon as I shall; and, dear me! it's within a quarter of an hour of the time now. I must run!"

Parkins had, in fact, very little time for dressing. When he met the Colonel at dinner, Peace – or as much of her as that gentleman could manage – reigned once more in the military bosom; nor was she put to flight in the hours of bridge that followed dinner, for Parkins was a more than respectable player. When, therefore, he retired towards twelve o'clock, he felt that he had spent his evening in quite a satisfactory way, and that, even for so long as a fortnight or three weeks, life at the Globe would be supportable under similar conditions – "especially," thought he, "if I go on improving my game."

As he went along the passages he met the boots of the Globe, who stopped and said:

"Beg your pardon, sir, but as I was abrushing your coat just now there was something fell out of the pocket. I put it on your chest of drawers, sir, in your room, sir – a piece of a pipe or somethink of that, sir. Thank you, sir. You'll find it on your chest of drawers, sir – yes, sir. Goodnight, sir."

The speech served to remind Parkins of his little discovery of that afternoon. It was with some considerable curiosity that he turned it over by the light of his candles. It was of bronze, he now saw, and was shaped very much after the manner of the modern dog-whistle; in fact it was – yes, certainly it was – actually no more nor less than a whistle. He put it to his lips, but it was quite full of a fine, caked-up sand or earth, which would not yield to knocking, but must be loosened with a knife. Tidy as ever in his habits, Parkins cleared out the earth on to a piece of paper, and took the latter to the window to empty it out. The night was clear and bright, as he saw when he had opened the casement, and he stopped for an instant to look at the sea and note a belated wanderer stationed on the shore in front of the inn. Then he shut the window, a little surprised at the late hours people kept at Burnstow, and took his whistle to the light again. Why, surely there were marks on it, and not merely marks, but letters! A very little rubbing rendered the deeply-cut inscription quite legible, but the Professor had to confess, after some earnest thought, that the meaning of it was as obscure to him as the writing on the wall to Belshazzar. There were legends both on the front and on the back of the whistle. The one read thus:

FLA FUR BIS FLE

The other:

QUIS EST ISTE QUI VENIT

"I ought to be able to make it out," he thought; "but I suppose I am a little rusty in my Latin. When I come to think of it, I don't believe I even know the word for a whistle. The long one does seem simple enough. It ought to mean: "Who is this who is coming?" Well, the best way to find out is evidently to whistle for him."

He blew tentatively and stopped suddenly, startled and yet pleased at the note he had elicited. It had a quality of infinite distance in it, and, soft as it was, he somehow felt it must be audible for miles round. It was a sound, too, that seemed to have the power (which many scents possess) of forming pictures in the brain. He saw quite clearly for a moment a vision of a wide, dark expanse at night, with a fresh wind blowing, and in the midst a lonely figure – how employed, he could not tell. Perhaps he would have seen more had not the picture been broken by the sudden surge of a gust of wind against his casement, so sudden that it made him look up, just in time to see the white glint of a seabird's wing somewhere outside the dark panes.

The sound of the whistle had so fascinated him that he could not help trying it once more, this time more boldly. The note was little, if at all, louder than before, and repetition broke the illusion – no picture followed, as he had half hoped it might. "But what is this? Goodness! What force the wind can get up in a few minutes! What a tremendous gust! There! I knew that window-fastening was no use! Ah! I thought so – both candles out. It is enough to tear the room to pieces."

The first thing was to get the window shut. While you might count twenty Parkins was struggling with the small casement, and felt almost as if he were pushing back a sturdy burglar, so strong was the pressure. It slackened all at once, and the window banged to and latched itself. Now to relight the candles and see what damage, if any, had been done. No, nothing seemed amiss; no glass even was broken in the casement. But the noise had evidently roused at least one member of the household: the Colonel was to be heard stumping in his stockinged feet on the floor above, and growling. Quickly as it had risen, the wind did not fall at once. On it went, moaning and rushing past the house, at times rising to a cry so desolate that, as Parkins disinterestedly said, it might have made fanciful people feel quite uncomfortable; even the unimaginative, he thought after a quarter of an hour, might be happier without it.

Whether it was the wind, or the excitement of golf, or of the researches in the preceptory that kept Parkins awake, he was not sure. Awake he remained, in any case, long enough to fancy (as I am afraid I often do myself under such conditions) that he was the victim of all manner of fatal disorders: he would lie counting the beats of his heart, convinced that it was going to stop work every moment, and would entertain grave suspicions of his lungs, brain, liver, etc. – suspicions which he was sure would be dispelled by the return of daylight, but which until then refused to be put aside. He found a little vicarious comfort in the idea that someone else was in the same boat. A near neighbour (in the darkness it was not easy to tell his direction) was tossing and rustling in his bed, too.

The next stage was that Parkins shut his eyes and determined to give sleep every chance. Here again over-excitement asserted itself in another form – that of making pictures. *Experto crede*, pictures do come to the closed eyes of one trying to sleep, and are often so little to his taste that he must open his eyes and disperse them.

Parkins's experience on this occasion was a very distressing one. He found that the picture which presented itself to him was continuous. When he opened his eyes, of course, it went; but when he shut them once more it framed itself afresh, and acted itself out again, neither quicker nor slower than before. What he saw was this:

A long stretch of shore – shingle edged by sand, and intersected at short intervals with black groynes running down to the water – a scene, in fact, so like that of his afternoon's walk that, in the absence of any landmark, it could not be distinguished therefrom. The light was obscure, conveying an impression of gathering storm, late winter evening, and slight cold rain. On this bleak stage at first no actor was visible. Then, in the distance, a bobbing black object appeared; a moment more, and it was a man running, jumping, clambering over the groynes, and every few seconds looking eagerly back. The nearer he came the more obvious it was that he was not only anxious, but even terribly frightened, though his face was not to be distinguished. He was, moreover, almost at the end of his strength. On he came; each successive obstacle seemed to cause him more difficulty than the last. "Will he get over this next one?" thought Parkins; "it seems a little higher than the others." Yes; half climbing, half throwing himself, he did get over, and fell all in a heap on the other side (the side nearest to the spectator). There, as if really unable to get up again, he remained crouching under the groyne, looking up in an attitude of painful anxiety.

So far no cause whatever for the fear of the runner had been shown; but now there began to be seen, far up the shore, a little flicker of something light-coloured moving to and fro with great swiftness and irregularity. Rapidly growing larger, it, too, declared itself as a figure in pale, fluttering draperies, ill-defined. There was something about its motion which made Parkins very unwilling to see it at close quarters. It would stop, raise arms, bow itself towards the sand, then run stooping across the beach to the water-edge and back again; and then, rising upright, once more continue its course forward at a speed that was startling and terrifying. The moment came when the pursuer was hovering about from left to right only a few yards beyond the groyne where the runner lay in hiding. After two or three ineffectual castings hither and thither it came to a stop, stood upright, with arms raised high, and then darted straight forward towards the groyne.

It was at this point that Parkins always failed in his resolution to keep his eyes shut. With many misgivings as to incipient failure of eyesight, overworked brain, excessive smoking, and so on, he finally resigned himself to light his candle, get out a book, and pass the night waking, rather than be tormented by this persistent panorama, which he saw clearly enough could only be a morbid reflection of his walk and his thoughts on that very day.

The scraping of match on box and the glare of light must have startled some creatures of the night – rats or whatnot – which he heard scurry across the floor from the side of his bed with much rustling. Dear, dear! The match is out! Fool that it is! But the second one burnt better, and a candle and book were duly procured, over which Parkins pored till sleep of a wholesome kind came upon him, and that in no long space. For about the first time in his orderly and prudent life he forgot to blow out the candle, and when he was called next morning at eight there was still a flicker in the socket and a sad mess of guttered grease on the top of the little table.

After breakfast he was in his room, putting the finishing touches to his golfing costume – fortune had again allotted the Colonel to him for a partner – when one of the maids came in.

"Oh, if you please," she said, "would you like any extra blankets on your bed, sir?"

"Ah! thank you," said Parkins. "Yes, I think I should like one. It seems likely to turn rather colder."

In a very short time the maid was back with the blanket.

"Which bed should I put it on, sir?" she asked.

"What? Why, that one – the one I slept in last night," he said, pointing to it.

"Oh yes! I beg your pardon, sir, but you seemed to have tried both of 'em; leastways, we had to make 'em both up this morning."

"Really? How very absurd!" said Parkins. "I certainly never touched the other, except to lay some things on it. Did it actually seem to have been slept in?"

"Oh yes, sir!" said the maid. "Why, all the things was crumpled and throwed about all ways, if you'll excuse me, sir – quite as if anyone 'adn't passed but a very poor night, sir."

"Dear me," said Parkins. "Well, I may have disordered it more than I thought when I unpacked my things. I'm very sorry to have given you the extra trouble, I'm sure. I expect a friend of mine soon, by the way – a gentleman from Cambridge – to come and occupy it for a night or two. That will be all right, I suppose, won't it?"

"Oh yes, to be sure, sir. Thank you, sir. It's no trouble, I'm sure," said the maid, and departed to giggle with her colleagues.

Parkins set forth, with a stern determination to improve his game.

I am glad to be able to report that he succeeded so far in this enterprise that the Colonel, who had been rather repining at the prospect of a second day's play in his company, became quite chatty as the morning advanced; and his voice boomed out over the flats, as certain also of our own minor poets have said, 'like some great bourdon in a minster tower'.

"Extraordinary wind, that, we had last night," he said. "In my old home we should have said someone had been whistling for it."

"Should you, indeed!" said Perkins. "Is there a superstition of that kind still current in your part of the country?"

"I don't know about superstition," said the Colonel. "They believe in it all over Denmark and Norway, as well as on the Yorkshire coast; and my experience is, mind you, that there's generally something at the bottom of what these country-folk hold to, and have held to for generations. But it's your drive" (or whatever it might have been: the golfing reader will have to imagine appropriate digressions at the proper intervals).

When conversation was resumed, Parkins said, with a slight hesitancy:

"A propos of what you were saying just now, Colonel, I think I ought to tell you that my own views on such subjects are very strong. I am, in fact, a convinced disbeliever in what is called the 'supernatural'."

"What!" said the Colonel. "Do you mean to tell me you don't believe in second-sight, or ghosts, or anything of that kind?"

"In nothing whatever of that kind," returned Parkins firmly.

"Well," said the Colonel, "but it appears to me at that rate, sir, that you must be little better than a Sadducee."

Parkins was on the point of answering that, in his opinion, the Sadducees were the most sensible persons he had ever read of in the Old Testament; but feeling some doubt as to whether much mention of them was to be found in that work, he preferred to laugh the accusation off.

"Perhaps I am," he said; "but – Here, give me my cleek, boy! – Excuse me one moment, Colonel." A short interval. "Now, as to whistling for the wind, let me give you my theory about it. The laws which govern winds are really not at all perfectly known – to fisherfolk and such, of course, not known at all. A man or woman of eccentric habits, perhaps, or a stranger, is seen repeatedly on the beach at some unusual hour, and is heard whistling. Soon afterwards a violent wind rises; a man who could read the sky perfectly or who possessed a barometer could have foretold that it would. The simple people of a fishing-village have no barometers, and only a few rough rules for prophesying weather. What more natural than that the eccentric personage I postulated should be regarded as having raised the wind, or that he or she should clutch eagerly at the reputation of being able to do so? Now, take last night's wind: as it happens, I myself was whistling. I blew a whistle twice, and the wind seemed to come absolutely in answer to my call. If anyone had seen me—"

The audience had been a little restive under this harangue, and Parkins had, I fear, fallen somewhat into the tone of a lecturer; but at the last sentence the Colonel stopped.

"Whistling, were you?" he said. "And what sort of whistle did you use? Play this stroke first." Interval.

"About that whistle you were asking, Colonel. It's rather a curious one. I have it in my – No; I see I've left it in my room. As a matter of fact, I found it yesterday."

And then Parkins narrated the manner of his discovery of the whistle, upon hearing which the Colonel grunted, and opined that, in Parkins's place, he should himself be careful about using a thing that had belonged to a set of Papists, of whom, speaking generally, it might be affirmed that you never knew what they might not have been up to. From this topic he diverged to the enormities of the Vicar, who had given notice on the previous Sunday that Friday would be the Feast of St. Thomas the Apostle, and that there would be service at eleven o'clock in the church. This and other similar proceedings constituted in the Colonel's view a strong presumption that the Vicar was a concealed Papist, if not a Jesuit; and Parkins, who could not very readily follow the Colonel in this region, did not disagree with him. In fact, they got on so well together in the morning that there was not talk on either side of their separating after lunch.

Both continued to play well during the afternoon, or at least, well enough to make them forget everything else until the light began to fail them. Not until then did Parkins remember that he had meant to do some more investigating at the preceptory; but it was of no great importance, he reflected. One day was as good as another; he might as well go home with the Colonel.

As they turned the corner of the house, the Colonel was almost knocked down by a boy who rushed into him at the very top of his speed, and then, instead of running away, remained hanging on to him and panting. The first words of the warrior were naturally those of reproof and objurgation, but he very quickly discerned that the boy was almost speechless with fright. Inquiries were useless at first. When the boy got his breath he began to howl, and still clung to the Colonel's legs. He was at last detached, but continued to howl.

"What in the world is the matter with you? What have you been up to? What have you seen?" said the two men.

"Ow, I seen it wive at me out of the winder," wailed the boy, "and I don't like it."

"What window?" said the irritated Colonel. "Come pull yourself together, my boy."

"The front winder it was, at the 'otel," said the boy.

At this point Parkins was in favour of sending the boy home, but the Colonel refused; he wanted to get to the bottom of it, he said; it was most dangerous to give a boy such a fright as this one had had, and if it turned out that people had been playing jokes, they should suffer for it in some way. And by a series of questions he made out this story: The boy had been playing about on the grass in front of the Globe with some others; then they had gone home to their teas, and he was just going, when he happened to look up at the front winder and see it a-wiving at him. *It* seemed to be a figure of some sort, in white as far as he knew – couldn't see its face; but it wived at him, and it warn't a right thing – not to say not a right person. Was there a light in the room? No, he didn't think to look if there was a light. Which was the window? Was it the top one or the second one? The seckind one it was – the big winder what got two little uns at the sides.

"Very well, my boy," said the Colonel, after a few more questions. "You run away home now. I expect it was some person trying to give you a start. Another time, like a brave English boy, you just throw a stone – well, no, not that exactly, but you go and speak to the waiter, or to Mr. Simpson, the landlord, and – yes – and say that I advised you to do so."

The boy's face expressed some of the doubt he felt as to the likelihood of Mr. Simpson's lending a favourable ear to his complaint, but the Colonel did not appear to perceive this, and went on:

"And here's a sixpence – no, I see it's a shilling – and you be off home, and don't think any more about it."

The youth hurried off with agitated thanks, and the Colonel and Parkins went round to the front of the Globe and reconnoitred. There was only one window answering to the description they had been hearing.

"Well, that's curious," said Parkins; "it's evidently my window the lad was talking about. Will you come up for a moment, Colonel Wilson? We ought to be able to see if anyone has been taking liberties in my room."

They were soon in the passage, and Parkins made as if to open the door. Then he stopped and felt in his pockets.

"This is more serious than I thought," was his next remark. "I remember now that before I started this morning I locked the door. It is locked now, and, what is more, here is the key." And he held it up. "Now," he went on, "if the servants are in the habit of going into one's room during the day when one is away, I can only say that – well, that I don't approve of it at all." Conscious of a somewhat weak climax, he busied himself in opening the door (which was indeed locked) and in lighting candles. "No," he said, "nothing seems disturbed."

"Except your bed," put in the Colonel.

"Excuse me, that isn't my bed," said Parkins. "I don't use that one. But it does look as if someone had been playing tricks with it."

It certainly did: the clothes were bundled up and twisted together in a most tortuous confusion. Parkins pondered.

"That must be it," he said at last. "I disordered the clothes last night in unpacking, and they haven't made it since. Perhaps they came in to make it, and that boy saw them through the window; and then they were called away and locked the door after them. Yes, I think that must be it."

"Well, ring and ask," said the Colonel, and this appealed to Parkins as practical.

The maid appeared, and, to make a long story short, deposed that she had made the bed in the morning when the gentleman was in the room, and hadn't been there since. No, she hadn't no other key. Mr. Simpson, he kep' the keys; he'd be able to tell the gentleman if anyone had been up.

This was a puzzle. Investigation showed that nothing of value had been taken, and Parkins remembered the disposition of the small objects on tables and so forth well enough to be pretty sure that no pranks had been played with them. Mr. and Mrs. Simpson furthermore agreed that neither of them had given the duplicate key of the room to any person whatever during the day. Nor could Parkins, fair-minded man as he was, detect anything in the demeanour of master, mistress, or maid that indicated guilt. He was much more inclined to think that the boy had been imposing on the Colonel.

The latter was unwontedly silent and pensive at dinner and throughout the evening. When he bade goodnight to Parkins, he murmured in a gruff undertone:

"You know where I am if you want me during the night."

"Why, yes, thank you, Colonel Wilson, I think I do; but there isn't much prospect of my disturbing you, I hope. By the way," he added, "did I show you that old whistle I spoke of? I think not. Well, here it is."

The Colonel turned it over gingerly in the light of the candle.

"Can you make anything of the inscription?" asked Parkins, as he took it back.

"No, not in this light. What do you mean to do with it?"

"Oh, well, when I get back to Cambridge I shall submit it to some of the archaeologists there, and see what they think of it; and very likely, if they consider it worth having, I may present it to one of the museums."

"'M!" said the Colonel. "Well, you may be right. All I know is that, if it were mine, I should chuck it straight into the sea. It's no use talking, I'm well aware, but I expect that with you it's a case of live and learn. I hope so, I'm sure, and I wish you a good night."

He turned away, leaving Parkins in act to speak at the bottom of the stair, and soon each was in his own bedroom.

By some unfortunate accident, there were neither blinds nor curtains to the windows of the Professor's room. The previous night he had thought little of this, but tonight there seemed every prospect of a bright moon rising to shine directly on his bed, and probably wake him later on. When he noticed this he was a good deal annoyed, but, with an ingenuity which I can only envy, he succeeded in rigging up, with the help of a railway-rug, some safety-pins, and a stick and umbrella, a screen which, if it only held together, would completely keep the moonlight off his bed. And shortly afterwards he was comfortably in that bed. When he had read a somewhat solid work long enough to produce a decided wish to sleep, he cast a drowsy glance round the room, blew out the candle, and fell back upon the pillow.

He must have slept soundly for an hour or more, when a sudden clatter shook him up in a most unwelcome manner. In a moment he realised what had happened: his carefully-constructed screen had given way, and a very bright frosty moon was shining directly on his face. This was highly annoying. Could he possibly get up and reconstruct the screen? or could he manage to sleep if he did not?

For some minutes he lay and pondered over all the possibilities; then he turned over sharply, and with his eyes open lay breathlessly listening. There had been a movement, he was sure, in the empty bed on the opposite side of the room. Tomorrow he would have it moved, for there must be rats or something playing about in it. It was quiet now. No! the commotion began again. There was a rustling and shaking: surely more than any rat could cause.

I can figure to myself something of the Professor's bewilderment and horror, for I have in a dream thirty years back seen the same thing happen; but the reader will hardly, perhaps, imagine how dreadful it was to him to see a figure suddenly sit up in what he had known was an empty bed. He was out of his own bed in one bound, and made a dash towards the window, where lay his only weapon, the stick with which he had propped his screen. This was, as it turned out, the worst thing he could have done, because the personage in the empty bed, with a sudden smooth motion, slipped from the bed and took up a position, with outspread arms, between the two beds, and in front of the door. Parkins watched it in a horrid perplexity. Somehow, the idea of getting past it and escaping through the door was intolerable to him; he could not have borne – he didn't know why – to touch it; and as for its touching him, he would sooner dash himself through the window than have that happen. It stood for the moment in a band of dark shadow, and he had not seen what its face was like. Now it began to move, in a stooping posture, and all at once the spectator realised, with some horror and some relief, that it must be blind, for it seemed to feel about it with its muffled arms in a groping and random fashion. Turning half away from him, it became suddenly conscious of the bed he had just left, and darted towards it, and bent and felt over the pillows in a way which made Parkins shudder as he had never in his life thought it possible. In a very few moments it seemed to know that the bed was empty, and then, moving forward into the area of light and facing the window, it showed for the first time what manner of thing it was.

Parkins, who very much dislikes being questioned about it, did once describe something of it in my hearing, and I gathered that what he chiefly remembers about it is a horrible, an intensely horrible, face *of crumpled linen.* What expression he read upon it he could not or would not tell, but that the fear of it went nigh to maddening him is certain.

But he was not at leisure to watch it for long. With formidable quickness it moved into the middle of the room, and, as it groped and waved, one corner of its draperies swept across Parkins's face. He could not, though he knew how perilous a sound was – he could not keep back a cry of disgust, and this gave the searcher an instant clue. It leapt towards him upon the instant, and the next moment he was halfway through the window backwards, uttering cry upon cry at the utmost pitch of his voice, and the linen face was thrust close into his own. At this, almost the last possible second, deliverance came, as you will have guessed: the Colonel burst the door open, and was just in time to see the dreadful group at the window. When he reached the figures only one was left. Parkins sank forward into the room in a faint, and before him on the floor lay a tumbled heap of bedclothes.

Colonel Wilson asked no questions, but busied himself in keeping everyone else out of the room and in getting Parkins back to his bed; and himself, wrapped in a rug, occupied the other bed, for the rest of the night. Early on the next day Rogers arrived, more welcome than he would have been a day before, and the three of them held a very long consultation in the Professor's room. At the end of it the Colonel left the hotel door carrying a small object between his finger and thumb, which he cast as far into the sea as a very brawny arm could send it. Later on the smoke of a burning ascended from the back premises of the Globe.

Exactly what explanation was patched up for the staff and visitors at the hotel I must confess I do not recollect. The Professor was somehow cleared of the ready suspicion of delirium tremens, and the hotel of the reputation of a troubled house.

There is not much question as to what would have happened to Parkins if the Colonel had not intervened when he did. He would either have fallen out of the window or else lost his wits. But it is not so evident what more the creature that came in answer to the whistle could have done than frighten. There seemed to be absolutely nothing material about it save the bedclothes of which it had made itself a body. The Colonel, who remembered a not very dissimilar occurrence in India, was of the opinion that if Parkins had closed with it it could really have done very little, and that its one power was that of frightening. The whole thing, he said, served to confirm his opinion of the Church of Rome.

There is really nothing more to tell, but, as you may imagine, the Professor's views on certain points are less clear-cut than they used to be. His nerves, too, have suffered: he cannot even now see a surplice hanging on a door quite unmoved, and the spectacle of a scarecrow in a field late on a winter afternoon has cost him more than one sleepless night.

Footnotes for *Oh Whistle, and I'll Come to You, My Lad*

1. Mr. Rogers was wrong, *vide Dombey and Son*, chapter xii.

The Ash Tree

M.R. James

EVERYONE WHO has travelled over Eastern England knows the smaller country-houses with which it is studded – the rather dank little buildings, usually in the Italian style, surrounded with parks of some eighty to a hundred acres. For me they have always had a very strong attraction: with the grey paling of split oak, the noble trees, the meres with their reed-beds, and the line of distant woods. Then, I like the pillared portico – perhaps stuck on to a red-brick Queen Anne house which has been faced with stucco to bring it into line with the 'Grecian' taste of the end of the eighteenth century; the hall inside, going up to the roof, which hall ought always to be provided with a gallery and a small organ. I like the library, too, where you may find anything from a Psalter of the thirteenth century to a Shakespeare quarto. I like the pictures, of course; and perhaps most of all I like fancying what life in such a house was when it was first built, and in the piping times of landlords' prosperity, and not least now, when, if money is not so plentiful, taste is more varied and life quite as interesting. I wish to have one of these houses, and enough money to keep it together and entertain my friends in it modestly.

But this is a digression. I have to tell you of a curious series of events which happened in such a house as I have tried to describe. It is Castringham Hall in Suffolk. I think a good deal has been done to the building since the period of my story, but the essential features I have sketched are still there – Italian portico, square block of white house, older inside than out, park with fringe of woods, and mere. The one feature that marked out the house from a score of others is gone. As you looked at it from the park, you saw on the right a great old ash tree growing within half a dozen yards of the wall, and almost or quite touching the building with its branches. I suppose it had stood there ever since Castringham ceased to be a fortified place, and since the moat was filled in and the Elizabethan dwelling-house built. At any rate, it had well nigh attained its full dimensions in the year 1690.

In that year the district in which the Hall is situated was the scene of a number of witch-trials. It will be long, I think, before we arrive at a just estimate of the amount of solid reason – if there was any – which lay at the root of the universal fear of witches in old times. Whether the persons accused of this offence really did imagine that they were possessed of unusual powers of any kind; or whether they had the will at least, if not the power, of doing mischief to their neighbours; or whether all the confessions, of which there are so many, were extorted by the mere cruelty of the witch-finders – these are questions which are not, I fancy, yet solved. And the present narrative gives me pause. I cannot altogether sweep it away as mere invention. The reader must judge for himself.

Castringham contributed a victim to the *auto-da-fé*. Mrs. Mothersole was her name, and she differed from the ordinary run of village witches only in being rather better off and in a more influential position. Efforts were made to save her by several reputable farmers of the parish. They did their best to testify to her character, and showed considerable anxiety as to the verdict of the jury.

But what seems to have been fatal to the woman was the evidence of the then proprietor of Castringham Hall – Sir Matthew Fell. He deposed to having watched her on three different occasions from his window, at the full of the moon, gathering sprigs "from the ash tree near my house." She had climbed into the branches, clad only in her shift, and was cutting off small twigs with a peculiarly curved knife, and as she did so she seemed to be talking to herself. On each occasion Sir Matthew had done his best to capture the woman, but she had always taken alarm at some accidental noise he had made, and all he could see when he got down to the garden was a hare running across the park in the direction of the village.

On the third night he had been at the pains to follow at his best speed, and had gone straight to Mrs. Mothersole's house; but he had had to wait a quarter of an hour battering at her door, and then she had come out very cross, and apparently very sleepy, as if just out of bed; and he had no good explanation to offer of his visit.

Mainly on this evidence, though there was much more of a less striking and unusual kind from other parishioners, Mrs. Mothersole was found guilty and condemned to die. She was hanged a week after the trial, with five or six more unhappy creatures, at Bury St. Edmunds.

Sir Matthew Fell, then Deputy-Sheriff, was present at the execution. It was a damp, drizzly March morning when the cart made its way up the rough grass hill outside Northgate, where the gallows stood. The other victims were apathetic or broken down with misery; but Mrs. Mothersole was, as in life so in death, of a very different temper. Her 'poysonous Rage', as a reporter of the time puts it, 'did so work upon the Bystanders – yea, even upon the Hangman – that it was constantly affirmed of all that saw her that she presented the living Aspect of a mad Divell. Yet she offer'd no Resistance to the Officers of the Law; onely she looked upon those that laid Hands upon her with so direfull and venomous an Aspect that – as one of them afterwards assured me – the meer Thought of it preyed inwardly upon his Mind for six Months after.'

However, all that she is reported to have said was the seemingly meaningless words: "There will be guests at the Hall." Which she repeated more than once in an undertone.

Sir Matthew Fell was not unimpressed by the bearing of the woman. He had some talk upon the matter with the Vicar of his parish, with whom he travelled home after the assize business was over. His evidence at the trial had not been very willingly given; he was not specially infected with the witch-finding mania, but he declared, then and afterwards, that he could not give any other account of the matter than that he had given, and that he could not possibly have been mistaken as to what he saw. The whole transaction had been repugnant to him, for he was a man who liked to be on pleasant terms with those about him; but he saw a duty to be done in this business, and he had done it. That seems to have been the gist of his sentiments, and the Vicar applauded it, as any reasonable man must have done.

A few weeks after, when the moon of May was at the full, Vicar and Squire met again in the park, and walked to the Hall together. Lady Fell was with her mother, who was dangerously ill, and Sir Matthew was alone at home; so the Vicar, Mr. Crome, was easily persuaded to take a late supper at the Hall.

Sir Matthew was not very good company this evening. The talk ran chiefly on family and parish matters, and, as luck would have it, Sir Matthew made a memorandum in writing of certain wishes or intentions of his regarding his estates, which afterwards proved exceedingly useful.

When Mr. Crome thought of starting for home, about half-past nine o'clock, Sir Matthew and he took a preliminary turn on the gravelled walk at the back of the house. The only incident that struck Mr. Crome was this: they were in sight of the ash tree which I described as growing near the windows of the building, when Sir Matthew stopped and said:

"What is that that runs up and down the stem of the ash? It is never a squirrel? They will all be in their nests by now."

The Vicar looked and saw the moving creature, but he could make nothing of its colour in the moonlight. The sharp outline, however, seen for an instant, was imprinted on his brain, and he could have sworn, he said, though it sounded foolish, that, squirrel or not, it had more than four legs.

Still, not much was to be made of the momentary vision, and the two men parted. They may have met since then, but it was not for a score of years.

Next day Sir Matthew Fell was not downstairs at six in the morning, as was his custom, nor at seven, nor yet at eight. Hereupon the servants went and knocked at his chamber door. I need not prolong the description of their anxious listenings and renewed batterings on the panels. The door was opened at last from the outside, and they found their master dead and black. So much you have guessed. That there were any marks of violence did not at the moment appear; but the window was open.

One of the men went to fetch the parson, and then by his directions rode on to give notice to the coroner. Mr. Crome himself went as quick as he might to the Hall, and was shown to the room where the dead man lay. He has left some notes among his papers which show how genuine a respect and sorrow was felt for Sir Matthew, and there is also this passage, which I transcribe for the sake of the light it throws upon the course of events, and also upon the common beliefs of the time:

> *There was not any the least Trace of an Entrance having been forc'd to the Chamber: but the Casement stood open, as my poor Friend would always have it in this Season. He had his Evening Drink of small Ale in a silver vessel of about a pint measure, and tonight had not drunk it out. This Drink was examined by the Physician from Bury, a Mr. Hodgkins, who could not, however, as he afterwards declar'd upon his Oath, before the Coroner's quest, discover that any matter of a venomous kind was present in it. For, as was natural, in the great Swelling and Blackness of the Corpse, there was talk made among the Neighbours of Poyson. The Body was very much Disorder'd as it laid in the Bed, being twisted after so extream a sort as gave too probable Conjecture that my worthy Friend and Patron had expir'd in great Pain and Agony. And what is as yet unexplain'd, and to myself the Argument of some Horrid and Artfull Designe in the Perpetrators of this Barbarous Murther, was this, that the Women which were entrusted with the laying-out of the Corpse and washing it, being both sad Persons and very well Respected in their Mournfull Profession, came to me in a great Pain and Distress both of Mind and Body, saying, what was indeed confirmed upon the first View, that they had no sooner touch'd the Breast of the Corpse with their naked Hands than they were sensible of a more than ordinary violent Smart and Acheing in their Palms, which, with their whole Forearms, in no long time swell'd so immoderately, the Pain still continuing, that, as afterwards proved, during many weeks they were forc'd to lay by the exercise of their Calling; and yet no mark seen on the Skin.*
>
> *Upon hearing this, I sent for the Physician, who was still in the House, and we made as carefull a Proof as we were able by the Help of a small Magnifying Lens of Crystal of the condition of the Skinn on this Part of the Body: but could not detect with the Instrument we had any Matter of Importance beyond a couple of small Punctures or Pricks, which we then concluded were the Spotts by which the Poyson might be introduced, remembering that Ring of Pope Borgia, with other known Specimens of the Horrid Art of the Italian Poysoners of the last age.*
>
> *So much is to be said of the Symptoms seen on the Corpse. As to what I am to add, it is meerly my own Experiment, and to be left to Posterity to judge whether there be*

anything of Value therein. There was on the Table by the Beddside a Bible of the small size, in which my Friend – punctuall as in Matters of less Moment, so in this more weighty one – used nightly, and upon his First Rising, to read a sett Portion. And I taking it up – not without a Tear duly paid to him which from the Study of this poorer Adumbration was now pass'd to the contemplation of its great Originall – it came into my Thoughts, as at such moments of Helplessness we are prone to catch at any the least Glimmer that makes promise of Light, to make trial of that old and by many accounted Superstitious Practice of drawing the Sortes: of which a Principall Instance, in the case of his late Sacred Majesty the Blessed Martyr King Charles and my Lord Falkland, was now much talked of. I must needs admit that by my Trial not much Assistance was afforded me: yet, as the Cause and Origin of these Dreadful Events may hereafter be search'd out, I set down the Results, in the case it may be found that they pointed the true Quarter of the Mischief to a quicker Intelligence than my own.

I made, then, three trials, opening the Book and placing my Finger upon certain Words: which gave in the first these words, from Luke xiii. 7, Cut it down*; in the second, Isaiah xiii. 20,* It shall never be inhabited*; and upon the third Experiment, Job xxxix. 30,* Her young ones also suck up blood.

This is all that need be quoted from Mr. Crome's papers. Sir Matthew Fell was duly coffined and laid into the earth, and his funeral sermon, preached by Mr. Crome on the following Sunday, has been printed under the title of 'The Unsearchable Way; or, England's Danger and the Malicious Dealings of Anti-christ', it being the Vicar's view, as well as that most commonly held in the neighbourhood, that the Squire was the victim of a recrudescence of the Popish Plot.

His son, Sir Matthew the second, succeeded to the title and estates. And so ends the first act of the Castringham tragedy. It is to be mentioned, though the fact is not surprising, that the new Baronet did not occupy the room in which his father had died. Nor, indeed, was it slept in by anyone but an occasional visitor during the whole of his occupation. He died in 1735, and I do not find that anything particular marked his reign, save a curiously constant mortality among his cattle and live-stock in general, which showed a tendency to increase slightly as time went on.

Those who are interested in the details will find a statistical account in a letter to the *Gentleman's Magazine* of 1772, which draws the facts from the Baronet's own papers. He put an end to it at last by a very simple expedient, that of shutting up all his beasts in sheds at night, and keeping no sheep in his park. For he had noticed that nothing was ever attacked that spent the night indoors. After that the disorder confined itself to wild birds, and beasts of chase. But as we have no good account of the symptoms, and as all-night watching was quite unproductive of any clue, I do not dwell on what the Suffolk farmers called the 'Castringham sickness'.

The second Sir Matthew died in 1735, as I said, and was duly succeeded by his son, Sir Richard. It was in his time that the great family pew was built out on the north side of the parish church. So large were the Squire's ideas that several of the graves on that unhallowed side of the building had to be disturbed to satisfy his requirements. Among them was that of Mrs. Mothersole, the position of which was accurately known, thanks to a note on a plan of the church and yard, both made by Mr. Crome.

A certain amount of interest was excited in the village when it was known that the famous witch, who was still remembered by a few, was to be exhumed. And the feeling of surprise, and indeed disquiet, was very strong when it was found that, though her coffin was fairly sound and unbroken, there was no trace whatever inside it of body, bones, or dust. Indeed, it is a curious phenomenon, for at the time of her burying no such things were dreamt of as resurrection-men, and it is difficult to conceive any rational motive for stealing a body otherwise than for the uses of the dissecting-room.

The incident revived for a time all the stories of witch-trials and of the exploits of the witches, dormant for forty years, and Sir Richard's orders that the coffin should be burnt were thought by a good many to be rather foolhardy, though they were duly carried out.

Sir Richard was a pestilent innovator, it is certain. Before his time the Hall had been a fine block of the mellowest red brick; but Sir Richard had travelled in Italy and become infected with the Italian taste, and, having more money than his predecessors, he determined to leave an Italian palace where he had found an English house. So stucco and ashlar masked the brick; some indifferent Roman marbles were planted about in the entrance-hall and gardens; a reproduction of the Sibyl's temple at Tivoli was erected on the opposite bank of the mere; and Castringham took on an entirely new, and, I must say, a less engaging, aspect. But it was much admired, and served as a model to a good many of the neighbouring gentry in after-years.

* * *

One morning (it was in 1754) Sir Richard woke after a night of discomfort. It had been windy, and his chimney had smoked persistently, and yet it was so cold that he must keep up a fire. Also something had so rattled about the window that no man could get a moment's peace. Further, there was the prospect of several guests of position arriving in the course of the day, who would expect sport of some kind, and the inroads of the distemper (which continued among his game) had been lately so serious that he was afraid for his reputation as a game-preserver. But what really touched him most nearly was the other matter of his sleepless night. He could certainly not sleep in that room again.

That was the chief subject of his meditations at breakfast, and after it he began a systematic examination of the rooms to see which would suit his notions best. It was long before he found one. This had a window with an eastern aspect and that with a northern; this door the servants would be always passing, and he did not like the bedstead in that. No, he must have a room with a western look-out, so that the sun could not wake him early, and it must be out of the way of the business of the house. The housekeeper was at the end of her resources.

"Well, Sir Richard," she said, "you know that there is but one room like that in the house."

"Which may that be?" said Sir Richard.

"And that is Sir Matthew's – the West Chamber."

"Well, put me in there, for there I'll lie tonight," said her master. "Which way is it? Here, to be sure"; and he hurried off.

"Oh, Sir Richard, but no one has slept there these forty years. The air has hardly been changed since Sir Matthew died there."

Thus she spoke, and rustled after him.

"Come, open the door, Mrs. Chiddock. I'll see the chamber, at least."

So it was opened, and, indeed, the smell was very close and earthy. Sir Richard crossed to the window, and, impatiently, as was his wont, threw the shutters back, and flung open the casement. For this end of the house was one which the alterations had barely touched, grown up as it was with the great ash tree, and being otherwise concealed from view.

"Air it, Mrs. Chiddock, all today, and move my bed-furniture in in the afternoon. Put the Bishop of Kilmore in my old room."

"Pray, Sir Richard," said a new voice, breaking in on this speech, "might I have the favour of a moment's interview?"

Sir Richard turned round and saw a man in black in the doorway, who bowed.

"I must ask your indulgence for this intrusion, Sir Richard. You will, perhaps, hardly remember me. My name is William Crome, and my grandfather was Vicar here in your grandfather's time."

"Well, sir," said Sir Richard, "the name of Crome is always a passport to Castringham. I am glad to renew a friendship of two generations' standing. In what can I serve you? For your hour of calling – and, if I do not mistake you, your bearing – shows you to be in some haste."

"That is no more than the truth, sir. I am riding from Norwich to Bury St. Edmunds with what haste I can make, and I have called in on my way to leave with you some papers which we have but just come upon in looking over what my grandfather left at his death. It is thought you may find some matters of family interest in them."

"You are mighty obliging, Mr. Crome, and, if you will be so good as to follow me to the parlour, and drink a glass of wine, we will take a first look at these same papers together. And you, Mrs. Chiddock, as I said, be about airing this chamber… Yes, it is here my grandfather died… Yes, the tree, perhaps, does make the place a little dampish… No; I do not wish to listen to any more. Make no difficulties, I beg. You have your orders – go. Will you follow me, sir?"

They went to the study. The packet which young Mr. Crome had brought – he was then just become a Fellow of Clare Hall in Cambridge, I may say, and subsequently brought out a respectable edition of Polyaenus – contained among other things the notes which the old Vicar had made upon the occasion of Sir Matthew Fell's death. And for the first time Sir Richard was confronted with the enigmatical *Sortes Biblicae* which you have heard. They amused him a good deal.

"Well," he said, "my grandfather's Bible gave one prudent piece of advice – *Cut it down*. If that stands for the ash tree, he may rest assured I shall not neglect it. Such a nest of catarrhs and agues was never seen."

The parlour contained the family books, which, pending the arrival of a collection which Sir Richard had made in Italy, and the building of a proper room to receive them, were not many in number.

Sir Richard looked up from the paper to the bookcase.

"I wonder," says he, "whether the old prophet is there yet? I fancy I see him."

Crossing the room, he took out a dumpy Bible, which, sure enough, bore on the flyleaf the inscription: 'To Matthew Fell, from his Loving Godmother, Anne Aldous, 2 September, 1659.'

"It would be no bad plan to test him again, Mr. Crome. I will wager we get a couple of names in the Chronicles. H'm! What have we here? 'Thou shalt seek me in the morning, and I shall not be.' Well, well! Your grandfather would have made a fine omen of that, hey? No more prophets for me! They are all in a tale. And now, Mr. Crome, I am infinitely obliged to you for your packet. You will, I fear, be impatient to get on. Pray allow me – another glass."

So with offers of hospitality, which were genuinely meant (for Sir Richard thought well of the young man's address and manner), they parted.

In the afternoon came the guests – the Bishop of Kilmore, Lady Mary Hervey, Sir William Kentfield, etc. Dinner at five, wine, cards, supper, and dispersal to bed.

Next morning Sir Richard is disinclined to take his gun with the rest. He talks with the Bishop of Kilmore. This prelate, unlike a good many of the Irish Bishops of his day, had visited his see, and, indeed, resided there for some considerable time. This morning, as the two were walking along the terrace and talking over the alterations and improvements in the house, the Bishop said, pointing to the window of the West Room:

"You could never get one of my Irish flock to occupy that room, Sir Richard."

"Why is that, my lord? It is, in fact, my own."

"Well, our Irish peasantry will always have it that it brings the worst of luck to sleep near an ash tree, and you have a fine growth of ash not two yards from your chamber window. Perhaps," the Bishop went on, with a smile, "it has given you a touch of its quality already, for you do not seem, if I may say it, so much the fresher for your night's rest as your friends would like to see you."

"That, or something else, it is true, cost me my sleep from twelve to four, my lord. But the tree is to come down tomorrow, so I shall not hear much more from it."

"I applaud your determination. It can hardly be wholesome to have the air you breathe strained, as it were, through all that leafage."

"Your lordship is right there, I think. But I had not my window open last night. It was rather the noise that went on – no doubt from the twigs sweeping the glass – that kept me open-eyed."

"I think that can hardly be, Sir Richard. Here – you see it from this point. None of these nearest branches even can touch your casement unless there were a gale, and there was none of that last night. They miss the panes by a foot."

"No, sir, true. What, then, will it be, I wonder, that scratched and rustled so – ay, and covered the dust on my sill with lines and marks?"

At last they agreed that the rats must have come up through the ivy. That was the Bishop's idea, and Sir Richard jumped at it.

So the day passed quietly, and night came, and the party dispersed to their rooms, and wished Sir Richard a better night.

And now we are in his bedroom, with the light out and the Squire in bed. The room is over the kitchen, and the night outside still and warm, so the window stands open.

There is very little light about the bedstead, but there is a strange movement there; it seems as if Sir Richard were moving his head rapidly to and fro with only the slightest possible sound. And now you would guess, so deceptive is the half-darkness, that he had several heads, round and brownish, which move back and forward, even as low as his chest. It is a horrible illusion. Is it nothing more? There! Something drops off the bed with a soft plump, like a kitten, and is out of the window in a flash; another – four – and after that there is quiet again.

'Thou shalt seek me in the morning, and I shall not be.'

As with Sir Matthew, so with Sir Richard – dead and black in his bed!

A pale and silent party of guests and servants gathered under the window when the news was known. Italian poisoners, Popish emissaries, infected air – all these and more guesses were hazarded, and the Bishop of Kilmore looked at the tree, in the fork of whose lower boughs a white tom-cat was crouching, looking down the hollow which years had gnawed in the trunk. It was watching something inside the tree with great interest.

Suddenly it got up and craned over the hole. Then a bit of the edge on which it stood gave way, and it went slithering in. Everyone looked up at the noise of the fall.

It is known to most of us that a cat can cry; but few of us have heard, I hope, such a yell as came out of the trunk of the great ash. Two or three screams there were – the witnesses are not sure which – and then a slight and muffled noise of some commotion or struggling was all that came. But Lady Mary Hervey fainted outright, and the housekeeper stopped her ears and fled till she fell on the terrace.

The Bishop of Kilmore and Sir William Kentfield stayed. Yet even they were daunted, though it was only at the cry of a cat; and Sir William swallowed once or twice before he could say:

"There is something more than we know of in that tree, my lord. I am for an instant search."

And this was agreed upon. A ladder was brought, and one of the gardeners went up, and, looking down the hollow, could detect nothing but a few dim indications of something moving. They got a lantern, and let it down by a rope.

"We must get at the bottom of this. My life upon it, my lord, but the secret of these terrible deaths is there."

Up went the gardener again with the lantern, and let it down the hole cautiously. They saw the yellow light upon his face as he bent over, and saw his face struck with an incredulous terror and loathing before he cried out in a dreadful voice and fell back from the ladder – where, happily, he was caught by two of the men – letting the lantern fall inside the tree.

He was in a dead faint, and it was some time before any word could be got from him.

By then they had something else to look at. The lantern must have broken at the bottom, and the light in it caught upon dry leaves and rubbish that lay there, for in a few minutes a dense smoke began to come up, and then flame; and, to be short, the tree was in a blaze.

The bystanders made a ring at some yards' distance, and Sir William and the Bishop sent men to get what weapons and tools they could; for, clearly, whatever might be using the tree as its lair would be forced out by the fire.

So it was. First, at the fork, they saw a round body covered with fire – the size of a man's head – appear very suddenly, then seem to collapse and fall back. This, five or six times; then a similar ball leapt into the air and fell on the grass, where after a moment it lay still. The Bishop went as near as he dared to it, and saw – what but the remains of an enormous spider, veinous and seared! And, as the fire burned lower down, more terrible bodies like this began to break out from the trunk, and it was seen that these were covered with greyish hair.

All that day the ash burned, and until it fell to pieces the men stood about it, and from time to time killed the brutes as they darted out. At last there was a long interval when none appeared, and they cautiously closed in and examined the roots of the tree.

"They found," says the Bishop of Kilmore, "below it a rounded hollow place in the earth, wherein were two or three bodies of these creatures that had plainly been smothered by the smoke; and, what is to me more curious, at the side of this den, against the wall, was crouching the anatomy or skeleton of a human being, with the skin dried upon the bones, having some remains of black hair, which was pronounced by those that examined it to be undoubtedly the body of a woman, and clearly dead for a period of fifty years."

A Soap Opera for One

O.R. Kennett

ETHEL CLARKE is lonely. She lives in the same small cottage that she grew up in though now the rear garden is wild and unkempt.

Within, it is full of ghosts, though they are ghosts that make her smile.

Her father sitting in his nebula of pipe smoke reading the funnies to her, both laughing.

Here, her brother, as handsome as a movie star and as charming as the devil himself, has an unending parade of pretty girls that he brings to dinner to 'Meet the folks' though few reappear.

The tickling excitement of hide and seek as she hears, from beyond this door, or that curtain, footsteps draw near, nearer… And then pass, never finding her, she is too good.

And now, her mother walking in with the gravy boat, tripping over their dog and dumping the whole lot on the floor and, here, dear old Wolf, a beagle with flopping ears and huffing halitosis, thinking he'd died and gone to doggy heaven. How they all laugh.

The laughter, the scent of pipe smoke, the excited barks echo down the years to Ethel as she sits in her rocking chair, blue TV screen light making her as insubstantial as her absent family.

Beyond the peeling paint of her front door with its rusted knocker, beyond the windows that have become cataracts of grime, the world is in turmoil.

Every night she watches the news, woollen blanket clutched to her sunken mouth as numbers of dead soar, knitting a tight glove of worry about her heart.

She understands the anxiety, the fear, but, for her, the worst has already come.

"High risk," the man on TV warns. "Self-isolate" and "save lives" he says, as Ethel sees her own life, such that it is, slip away.

* * *

Ethel's age-softened mouth twitches as she recalls how she would rush, as fast as her arthritic hips would allow, to the door when the lion knocker went, shouting "Coming," trying not to sound excited and failing. Was that only two months ago? It feels like forever.

She swirls the chicken soup in its bowl. Despite her meagre appetite and her rationing, she is down to her last few tins. She has hoarded her supplies, unsure of when she will get more. Bread, so simple yet such a comfort, has become something to eke out. She has two slices left in her freezer and a special treat for when she reaches her lowest point and needs, as her dad would have said, "A pick-me-up", a choc-ice, the last one. She'd unearthed it as the mounds of frozen peas, boil in the bag fish and other staples of her life, were mined away. Each evening after her scant supper she thinks of it, hiding in the frozen dark.

"One more day," she promises herself because, once it is gone, there is nothing left to look forward to.

* * *

It begins when she is sat, sipping her morning tea, no milk, and looking out of the window at the same scene she has looked at for the last eighty odd years. The faces may change, grow older, vanish, but the stage, for the most part, has remained the same. She thinks of the window as her own TV channel, just for her, the sound turned down, a soap opera for one.

Since the virus came the cast has dwindled. The few characters that appear are furtive, scurrying, heads down. The mothers that walked children to the little primary school around the corner are gone. Car-washing neighbours are absent, their vehicles as stationary as the houses they squat before. There is no one chatting on drives or slipping inside to be followed an hour or so later by the smells of cooking, the soft murmur of voices and music. It is as if the rising numbers that the man quotes are only a fraction of the people who have vanished.

Ethel is a person who believes in tidiness, in order; she also believes in keeping herself to herself, so, when she sees the green wheelie bin toppled on the other side of her silent street, its lid flopped open and its contents disgorged over the pavement, she is indecisive. It is not her bin, it's none of her business. She resolves that someone else, the owners of the white-fronted house with the shiny red car, the owners of the bin, will sort it.

But, as the day draws on, her small eyes, behind her bifocals, are drawn to the mess which remains, occasionally investigated by flapping birds and once by a grey cat.

"If it's not tidied up," she says to the silent house, "I will call the council tomorrow."

* * *

Next morning, in her dressing gown and limping into the front room, Ethel is dismayed to see that the bin remains. She peers at the house, at its lightless windows, curtains closed, and attempts to recall the last time she saw any sign of life there.

She blinks behind her bifocals, time has become stretched, like hot toffee. Was it a week ago that she saw the elegant woman leave the house, or a month? Did the elegant woman, Ethel doesn't know her name, ever return?

She shakes her head, makes her morning tea, no sugar, and settles in her rocking chair, the yellow pages open in her lap, the phone in reach, and waits for nine o'clock.

When the man answers and Ethel starts speaking, something happens, it is as if a creeping darkness that had been filling her all these months begins to lift, a darkness so slow to assert itself that she hadn't noticed and is now only aware of it with its leaving.

With a rare smile she lays the black Bakelite receiver back in its cradle. It's not the man's vague assurances that the bin will be seen to, it is simply talking to someone. She is surprised when she feels the hitch in her chest, a combination of a laugh and a sob, and has to wipe under her spectacles.

She pushes herself out of the deep chair and heads toward the kitchen.

A cup of tea is in order, she thinks happily.

For the rest of the day Ethel is happy. Not once does her emergency choc-ice cross her mind.

* * *

The feeling, like her food supplies, dwindles. She attempts to ration it, thinking of the conversation only briefly. She limits herself to tiny speculations of who the voice on the other end of the phone belongs to, if he is married, what he might be doing now.

Finally, two days later she has to admit that the joy of speaking with another human being has joined the ghosts in her little house, never gone but as tangible as a rising shadow on the wall.

Worse still, the tumbled green bin remains tumbled.

* * *

Ethel, though she would never admit it, starts scrutinising her personal TV channel, peering out night and day, looking for anything that is amiss, anything that needs reporting. She tells herself that it is her neighbourly duty but, when she awakes in her chair in the small hours having sat and watched all day and most of the night, she has to admit that she is becoming obsessive. What she is looking for, she doesn't know: the bin to be cleared up? For something else to legitimately report? For something to break the monotony of this haunted isolation?

She has decided that the man on the phone is called Dennis, like her brother, and has a dog, a wife called Sue and two, no three, lovely blonde-haired daughters that squabble but ultimately love one another dearly.

She thinks about his nasal voice, the way he listened to her, the way he used her name, and she craves talking to him more than the two lonely slices of bread in her freezer.

Ethel has never been in love, as a quiet girl and a timid woman she has never been outgoing. She has passed through her long life with her head down, trying not to exist, trying not to upset or disturb. She has never been in love but concedes that this heartache she feels might be something like it and it's not for Dennis, he's married after all, it's an infatuation with contact. She knows it's pathetic and self-pitying but she wants to speak with someone, anyone.

She is left with no choice but to wrap herself in the gossamer blanket of memory. It is patched, it is frayed, there are holes that spread bigger year after year.

Shivering in this thin blanket, Ethel is lonely.

* * *

Hurrying back from the spiderweb-infested tomb of the garden shed, Ethel heard a sound, laughter. Looking up, she stopped, the thing she went to fetch dangling from one hand.

"Girls are seen and not heard." Her mother had told her many times, but Ethel, as she gazed in the kitchen window, wondered if she was seen at all.

Her family and her brother's new girl were clustered about the kitchen table, her mother's prized cake stand between them, dirty empty plates before each. They had forgotten about her, again.

She was a ghost of frost trembling on the winter air, peering in on a warm living world, as welcome in that cozy scene as the icy breath of wind that slapped at her coat and bit at her ears.

Shadows flitted over her, cast by dashing clouds, a forgotten girl, secateurs dangling from one dirty, broken nailed hand.

Her brother's 'girls', Ethel noticed, never had broken nails or chapped fingers and lips. They were always fine, oh yes, very fine indeed.

* * *

Waking next morning, her midnight vigil having caused her to sleep in until ten o'clock, Ethel resolves to call the council again about the tumbled bin. It has been long enough, hasn't it? She doesn't want to be a pest but, well, maybe they've forgotten, that's it.

She shuffles from her room, past her brother's bedroom door and then her parents', both closed all these years, holding their secrets, and creaks down the stairs, hands tight on the pair of rails that have been gripped by these hands countless times, her heart light and her conscience clean. She's doing the right thing, keeping the neighbourhood tidy. If she gets something out of it too, well, that's alright, isn't it?

* * *

Ethel makes a cup of tea, having to reuse her last teabag, and is settling herself next to the black Bakelite phone, the yellow pages in her lap when she glances across the road. In the stark light of late morning she sees something that makes her heart plummet all the way down to her tartan slippers. The tumbled green bin has been righted, its contents gone or returned to its green gullet. Whilst she slept it had been tidied up, by the council or maybe by some nosy neighbour.

As she glares at the green bin, she feels a stab of frustration that could easily become the snip and chop of anger, but Ethel doesn't get angry, not since she lost her family. She releases the feeling, reluctantly letting it trickle away. It is replaced by the hollowness of disappointment. Slowly, she closes the yellow pages and puts them back under the little table beside her chair.

Without anything to report, the telephone goes unused. Her mind turns to the choc-ice.

* * *

Daydreaming. Ethel catches herself doing it more and more these days. This one is about something buried out there in the tangled wilderness of her garden. Maybe it is the feel of the teapot in her hands but she is thinking about the biscuit-brown gravy boat or, at least, its jigsawed remains. She can't recall how it came to be shattered, nor how it came to be buried in the garden, but it is out there, under a cool blanket of earth, isn't it?

* * *

A gravy boat, a Sunday lunch staple, its contents glossy and rich. She always got the biscuit-brown gravy boat last.

"Don't be greedy," her mother chided as Ethel, ten now, attempted to spoon out the scant remains of unctuous liquid onto her plate.

* * *

Ethel blinks as a blackbird flutters into view and lights on a branch thick with blossoms. The kettle grows cold.

She can almost feel the weight of the biscuit-brown gravy boat, its heavy slosh. She'd carried it from the kitchen, trying to help, and into the cramped dining room. She held it in both hands, careful not to spill and thinking:

"This time I'll go first. No sad dregs for Ethel. So what if mother calls me greedy."

And then there was the floating, sickening shock that she was tipping forwards, her feet tangled under the sprawled body of Wolf.

The gravy boat seemed to hang for a moment, forever in a shaft of dusty sunlight, turning, tipping its thick dark cargo out. Ethel hit the ground, arms thrust out to catch the precious vessel, her teeth snapping on her tongue as her chin smacked into the thin carpet. She hardly tasted the penny tang of blood in her mouth for she was holding up the gravy boat, unbroken, perfect, and safe.

Her heart thudded against the floor, triumph rushed through her veins. She gazed at the unbroken, biscuit brown gravy boat in wonderment. She was smiling.

* * *

Ethel rests the teapot on the draining board, hands trembling. She'd caught hell for that, not only the mess of gravy on the floor but she had to endure the frantic panic of her mother, hand to her throat, gasping:

"My heart oh God, but my poor heart." As if she were trying to push it back down into its rightful place.

The worst part of it all though, was her father, his glance at her, the first all that day, maybe all that week, and then the slight shake of his head. She had finally been seen, and she had been deemed a disappointment.

She had hated her mother for her hysteria, her brother for his laughing eyes above the hand he'd put to his mouth as if trying to hold in his mirth, and her father for his dismissive disdain, and yet… she had felt a prickle of excitement, a blush of joy.

After she had been left to "think about what you've done", and stood in the centre of her small bedroom, gazing down into the neat patch of garden, she smiled. For the first time in as long as she could remember, little Ethel Clarke felt seen.

* * *

Ethel knows it's wrong, shuffling back inside her warm house and softly shutting out the chill night air, but it's only a little wrong. Surely she, Ethel, who has lived her life so gently, so quietly, is allowed just a little naughtiness, for that's all it is, naughtiness.

"Hello," she says several hours later having been too excited to go back to bed. "I need to report a mess in my street. Yes, a bin has been knocked over, it looks awful."

* * *

Ethel is elated, she doesn't have just one conversation but two, the council ring her back, her concerns of vandalism having caused alarm in the halls of power, but the emotion starts to ebb before twilight. In an attempt to prolong the good feeling Ethel shuffles to the freezer and takes out one of her last slices of bread, goes to the pantry and gets a small tin of beans.

It helps, but not for long. It is with a hot water bottle and an addict's scratching need that Ethel slips into bed that night.

* * *

Ethel has been told that it is now a police matter and is given the name of one Constable Philips her 'Overseeing officer'.

Her night-time activities have left her prickle-eyed and aching but happy. She has moved on from bins, attacking hedges with her father's ancient secateurs, rust-coloured flakes from a night a lifetime ago scattering from the blades.

Rude words are now painstakingly chalked in a shaky hand on the road:

'Ninny', 'Toe rag' and, her hand had trembled even more writing this, 'Bastard'.

The officer, young and, in her mind, handsome as her brother had been, is suitably appalled that someone would do this in such a quiet and nice neighbourhood.

"I am very sorry it's fallen to you to report this," Philips says on one of their bi-weekly telephone conversations. "We've received similar reports from your neighbours but you are always the first one," he chuckles, a kind sound Ethel thinks, "first to the scene".

"Just want to help out." Ethel tells him, only feeling a tiny twinge of guilt. It is soon overpowered with the simple and honest joy of talking.

"I would hate for you to feel unsafe in your home, Miss Clarke."

"Please, call me Ethy," she says, but it's not the first time she's asked, and he's still not stretched to that familiarity.

"I am taking a personal interest in this." He lowers his voice, understanding, gentle and heartachingly kind, "I know this is a very difficult time for those who are living by themselves. There are opportunists out there too, and I want you to know, you are not alone."

"Thank you," Ethel whispers. She blinks away tears.

* * *

"Is your brother home?" the young women would shyly ask, standing on the doorstep in their lovely dresses and gentle clouds of perfume.

Ethel, with all the grace of one still wandering the marshes between childhood and adulthood, always felt awkward and ugly, and when he was out she'd let that ugliness bubble up, just a tiny bit.

"He is otherwise engaged," she would say, a term she liked the taste of. It had an adult taste and the sour suggestion of truth.

Ethel would feel equal pleasure and guilt at the look of disappointment in their long-lashed eyes, the bent bow of their full-painted lips. Ethel's lips were thin, pale things and she wasn't allowed to wear makeup.

"Do you want to look like a tart?" her mother had asked, but Ethel had seen the admiring glances of her father and heard the gushing compliments from her mother when her brother brought those girls to their dinner table, eclipsing little dull Ethel with her forgettable face and bland quiet clothes, when Ethel became a ghost in her own home.

"You don't need makeup," one of these visiting beauties had cried, pinching her cheek painfully, "You're pretty enough." But then the girl's bright blue eyes in their sockets of blue dusk slid off her like rain off a rockery, and, as Ethel watched those plump red kissable lips move, talking, smiling, hooping in to an O of surprise at one of her brother's stories, she thought: She can't see me anymore. None of them can.

And little Ethel, grey as a February day, slipped from the table, unnoticed.

* * *

It's less than a week later that Ethel is caught, in this case, white handed, the chalk dust coating her fingers and palms.

Constable Philips doesn't raise his voice but Ethel can tell he is annoyed and, worst of all, disappointed. She feels terrible, she has let him down.

He tells her, in a cool tone, that in this case, he is willing to look the other way if she stops. He understands that she is lonely but the police are not the ones she should be reaching out to. He tells her that there are phone lines out there for the elderly, for the depressed.

Ethel, who doesn't think of herself as something so self-pitiable as 'depressed' and doesn't like to think of herself as 'Elderly', agrees that she will not do it again. She will seek help elsewhere, but the sheet of paper from the constable's notebook with the numbers he wrote down from the websites he visited is balled up and thrown away. Ethel doesn't want to talk to someone who patronises her, tells her everything is fine, she wants to talk to Constable Philips, he is her friend. She has spoken more with him in the last month than she has with anyone else in the last fifty years, ever since her parents and brother went into the ground, leaving her alone without company, without the social skills to cultivate any.

She sits in her chair, her house, her prison. It breathes with memory, things tucked in shadow staring out with dead eyes. For the first time in a long time, Ethel feels the brush of fear.

* * *

Afterwards, after her family and the girl had gone away, people called. Later, they stopped calling. Ethel, a little older now, understood better why they stopped coming even if the people didn't. They couldn't see her. Like her family before, they couldn't see dull Ethel, quiet Ethel, invisible Ethel. There may have been people who worried for her, a young woman all alone, her family gone, but they couldn't see her either.

She still did her weekly shop, now cheaper, now just for one, and the man behind the counter at the grocers saw her a bit then, but only enough to take the crumpled money from her, and then Ethel would vanish once again.

But is this true? Is any of this true? Ethel can't remember. She can feel her family about her, her father no longer laughing at the funnies in the Sunday paper but at something else, at her?

The endless games of hide and seek. Did they even look for her? Had she just been a small child tucked away, trembling with anticipation whilst a careless world went on without her?

They went away, but they are here. Ethel's eyes are clouded with time, with tears.

* * *

She is crying, the Bakelite handset pressed to her ear, and she keeps calling Constable Philips by her brother's name. He is as polite as his office dictates but he is not friendly, not anymore.

"There are people in the garden," she says. Things have started to blur in her head, some nights she wakes and thinks she can hear the playful bark of Wolf, but that can't be true, he's buried in the garden too, long ago turned to pale white bones alongside her vanished family.

"Someone's here," she says, her voice hardly more than a breath. "They can see me."

"That is enough." His voice in her ear is as close to angry as Ethel has ever heard. "I have enough to deal with. You need to stop calling me. Is that understood?"

She can hear voices in the background, whooping voices, laughter, people living.

All Ethel wants is to not be alone anymore, to be released from this solitary confinement. She is sick of the ghosts that whisper her name in the dark, in the quiet, and she thought that this man, her knight in blue, could save her from the guilt, from the fear, from her haunted solitude.

"Yes," Ethel whispers.

After he hangs up, she settles the handset back into its cradle. Tears blur her vision. In the smear of light she thinks she sees someone move. Someone here, someone inside.

She blinks and rises, feeling her eighty-odd years in every joint and, turning her back on the blur of figures – her absent family – that stand in the doorway out to the front hall, she shuffles into her neat, cramped kitchen.

There is nowhere for her out there, no one for her. She is locked down, locked in, a prisoner in this house, her memories are her warders.

All her life Ethel Clarke wanted to be seen and now, God forgive her, she is.

With trembling fingers she unwraps the choc-ice.

An Inverted Haunting

John Kiste

CAROLYN FOLLOWED ME to my cubicle this morning. I saw her drowned pale face floating sideways in the water cooler, her long white hair billowing into every bubble at the waterline. I spilled my coffee at once, but while I cleaned the floor on my knees, watching her eyeballs float in and out of their black sockets, my co-workers commiserated regarding my accident and kept filling little dunce cap paper cups from the tap as though nothing were amiss. They flanked the gurgling head in the blue plastic tank, drank the liquid that her bloody neck had stained pink in my sight, and chatted obliviously about the game and some reality show finale, and no one even asked why my own eyes were starting from their sockets or why I was gibbering as I sponged up Starbucks latte.

I retreated madly to my cubicle and tried to catch my breath. Such a scene I had not envisioned when I occupied my house on the little hill near the cemetery just beyond the outskirts of town. No one had denied it was haunted; the legends were common knowledge. I had known the tale of Carolyn Waiteman since I was a child. She should have been my great, great grandmother, but my forbearer Simon Harding had thrown her over during a dinner party at his home – now my home – and she had offed herself in the boudoir bathtub during dessert. I had heard the cake was exquisitely decorated, but never cut, unlike her lovely throat.

Afterwards, though all trace of her was carefully removed, Carolyn's ghost would appear to my ancestor in sudden frightful manners, sometimes floating upside down before him with blood dripping rapidly from her throat at his feet and transforming from ectoplasm to actual plasma. Once she had materialized commingling with his body, and the chill he caught had confined him to bed for a week, while she peered out from every corner of his quilts and blankets.

Finally Simon had sealed the house and stables, and he eventually married my actual great, great grandmother, and the property, though remaining in the family, had been rented to strangers for decades. Strangers who never encountered Carolyn. Ever. No Harding, though, could cross the threshold without witnessing a horrible incarnation of her specter, but now, without friends or close kin and in my relative poverty, I had determined to reclaim the ancestral home and try to bear the consequences.

I had first seen her reflected in the mirror of the Victorian hall tree as soon as I stepped across the dusty threshold. Her form was lithe and willowy, enfolded as she was in snowy gauze that covered her from throat to toe. Her long hair swirled as though a gale blew behind the glass, and her bright blue eyes stared unblinking, following each move I made. The gash beneath her chin was evident, and blood spotted her breast, but no part of her body or visage inspired fear. Quite the opposite. She seemed curious, as was I. I stood before her for a long time, and she touched her side of the glass longingly wherever I touched my side. A soft scent of rosewater enwrapped me. She studied me intimately, and I suddenly understood why. My grandmother had once told me I was the spitting image of Simon. Still, Carolyn's apparition seemed to indicate approval. I thought she liked me; I saw the tiniest smile touch the corners of her red lips, and it looked in no manner nefarious. I sensed no threat. Then she disappeared, and in the gloom of the hall I found myself gazing back at myself.

In the weeks and months it had taken to restore the huge house, mostly on my own during an extended vacation from the office, Carolyn had never manifested again. I began to think she had simply approved of me, based on that tinge of smile I had seen, and had moved on to a further realm. She had never been seen by any of my family – or anyone else – outside of Harding Manor. Until today.

My first day back at the office, and she was metaphysically polluting the drinking water. My confusion and my shock left me dizzy and shaking. One of the pool secretaries asked if I felt okay, and I could only nod unconvincingly. I shuffled some papers and sorted several file folders. I opened one and found a tress of gory white hair dampening the pages. I slammed it shut. Diluted blood sprayed across the desk. I clutched for tissues and dabbed at the mess like a lunatic.

Suddenly I realized my boss was standing over me, staring suspiciously. "Is everything all right?" he asked, while one of his thick eyebrows moved toward his receding forehead.

"Just getting reacclimated," I lied, convincingly enough. I took a very deep breath and grinned, though a pale hand rested casually on his shoulder. He grunted and left, unaware of the arm that trailed down his back and ended in nothing. A mist flooded about my head, but not because of my dizziness. This dank gray fog was filling my cubicle, smelling of rosewater but cloying and stale, and body parts of poor dead Carolyn kept popping up in its tendrils. I took an early lunch.

I got glimpses of her, or at least glimpses of pieces of her, the rest of the day, and by five o'clock had largely learned to ignore the intrusions, but my work suffered badly, to say the least. She must be waiting to really bedevil me at the house. We would be having a long chat. If she would not listen to reason, I would threaten her with priests and exorcists or even the demolition of the house that had never been hers, though she had dwelt there more than a century.

But I was fortunate to make it home. Just as I crossed the city limits, a caricature of her face, more livid and rotted than the one in the water cooler, leapt up in front of the windshield. I screamed and yanked the steering wheel of the car, and came inches from driving head-on into a tractor trailer truck in the other lane. The driver blared his horn as the bulk of the vehicle whizzed by my door. I veered into a pull-off and slammed the shifter into park, swearing and crying. I was both angry and horrified. What had prompted such a long-distance haunting? I drove the rest of the way home very slowly. Several times cars passed me beeping and cussing. At length I turned onto the lane that skirted the cemetery and saw the large brick edifice outlined on the steep hill against the darkening fall sky. One light was on in the study to the left; the remainder of the house was a hulking silhouette that looked hunched on the ridge crest, ready to pounce toward me. I climbed the long set of front stairs to the porch and stood poised with my key shaking slightly above the lock, afraid to guess what I might encounter within. I opened the door and sidled cautiously around it. It slowly shut behind me.

I felt Carolyn's presence at once, but this was not the seething, sinister aura of malice I had encountered throughout the day. This was the calm, introspective, half-smiling visitant I had come upon the first day; the one from whom I had felt approval and, almost, kindness. In fact, though I knew her shade was here, the house did not feel haunted at all. I wandered the halls and staircases, pausing at every reflective surface, and breathing deeply each dusty scent. I smelled no rosewater, and though I asked repeatedly why she had done what she had done, I discovered no trace of her. My home felt safe and welcoming, but I was sorely bewildered.

My sleep refreshed me without dreams, but the moment I stepped from my front door, multiple morning mists spat rotted clones of Carolyn rapidly toward my face, each one dissolving as it splashed the sickly sweet taste of rosewater past my lips. I shrieked and coughed and turned inside to sit on the hall tiles and cry. "Why!" I shouted, and my voice echoed through the long empty spaces. I called the office and told my boss I was sick, and he said he was not surprised – I had looked peaked the day before – and that I should get some rest. I retreated to my study and sat in my favorite recliner there, awaiting further atmospherics, but she did not come. I finally dozed awhile, and decided upon awakening that I would buy a bottle of wine at a shop about three-quarters of a mile toward town and therefore within walking distance.

I trudged down the lane for about one hundred yards without incident when my guts began to roil. I twisted about, and watched a gauze-shrouded, disembodied arm withdraw from my body near my right kidney. The white fingertips were the same blood color as the nails, and I felt my insides knot and threw up on the asphalt. I staggered to a tree just outside the gates of the graveyard, but suddenly Carolyn was hanging there, a thick noose cutting into the deep, gaping self-inflicted gash in her neck. My breath coming fitfully, I sat beside her manifestation and stared at her ghastly face. Her purple tongue hung thick on one side. The blue eyes had rolled over steel gray. I reached out and grasped at her bare feet, which brushed the grass. My fingers went through her, but I shivered with sudden chill.

"Were you murdered, Carolyn?" I asked slowly. "Is that why you remain? Did Simon kill you? Is that why the Hardings are cursed?"

I expected no answer, but I looked up from the swaying body to see the head and hair move from side to side. A chime inside my own head began to form soft, tinkling sorts of words. "I understood the possibility of my fate when I crawled into that tub those eons ago. Still, I like Harding Manor. But I have been lonely there for so very long. Then you came…"

I sensed a melancholy happiness wrapped somewhere in those last words. "I don't understand," I whispered. "I never see you inside the house."

Now it became a certainty that her essence had somehow mixed inside me, blended with my psyche to explain what I needed to comprehend. I felt her words more than heard them, and the bitter sadness they imparted drained my spirit. "You were there – and your face was so like his – and I was content. You made the place a home once more, and I did not let you see me, for I wanted not to frighten you, and I wished for you to stay. But you left me yesterday, and I could not bear it. So I will employ the means I can to keep you to the house, and will ensure you are comfortable nowhere else."

All fell into place as I sat calmly, watching gouts of blood and tissue plop into the grass from her torn and strangled throat. I was the owner of a haunted house that was haunted everywhere on earth except inside. "Carolyn," I said with sudden assurance in my voice. "I have no one. There is nothing in my life but my job, my work to keep me in Harding Manor, and to keep me alive. I know my ancestor betrayed you, but I have no reason to. Make a pact with me. Allow me to pursue the financial means to keep us in peace, and I promise, I swear I will never abandon the house – or you. I will remain there always, if possible even after death." I paused. "But if you cause me to be killed outside our home, I cannot guarantee my vow – or my continued presence."

I heard no further chimes within me, and Carolyn's form floated away on the autumn air. I sat in the grass watching the mare's tail clouds for a long time before turning back home. I still see hints of her only rarely, a slight smile from a brass doorknob or a gentle tap of guidance from my shaving mirror. Her eyes gleam back from my dinner plate on chilly nights. But I know two things that warm my heart each winter evening. She is waiting for me when I cross into our home. And she no longer inhabits the water cooler.

On Bricks and Bronze

Spencer Koelle

"EXCUSE ME—" Marina Sanchez broke off in mid-sentence.

The man on the park bench she had started to address was gone. What was more, there was no indication that anyone had been there. She didn't catch a flicker of movement or see somebody fleeing. There was just an empty bench, between two gingko trees, unoccupied, with no strange shadows or circumstances to account for the illusion.

Marina shrugged and sat down on the bench. It was wide enough she wouldn't feel like she took up too much space if somebody else came to sit there. It was pleasantly cool, despite being in the full sun. The air smelled of lilies instead of the rotting ginko fruit. Dogs barked joyfully. A breeze ruffled her hair like gentle fingers.

Life was good, Marina reflected, as a lovely black pigeon picked at a pretzel. She'd finally passed the probation period for her job. The hormone treatments were working, and she could actually afford them thanks to the sliding scale at Mazzoni Center of LGBTQ healthcare. Her girlfriend had gotten a raise. Nobody had misgendered her or catcalled her for days.

The bird's violet feathers shone like amethysts in the sunshine. It was joined by little brown birds, competing for the prize. She thought about crushing the pretzel with her foot, so they could share easily, but that might scare them off.

A white child hurried up the path, trailing after an enormous Pitbull. The shadow of a cloud passed over Marina. Daisy had died over three months ago, but the grief was still sharp in her chest. She clutched her rosary and the sterling silver icon of La Santa Muerte.

"Please take care of my puppy, sweet saint," she murmured.

The cold wet smack made Marina jump out of her seat. She turned around, expecting to see a burst water balloon or a wet leaf, but there was nothing. The park bench was completely dry.

In her survey of the seat, she noticed the dedication on the bench.

In memory of Reverend Matthew Everett Stith:
The angels shall cast out all abominations and heaven will sing,
till Gabriel's hounds return.

Marina decided not to sit back down. Nothing else strange happened to her on that day.

* * *

Nothing happened to distress Marina, aside from the harassment in a Burger King restroom, for three days. Even then, she enjoyed most of the night serving drinks for the Emerald City Drag Show.

Wicked Witch of the Southeast was tearing up the stage to a *When Doves Cry* remix in a slinky black dress and green body paint. The crowd was lively, but she wasn't overwhelmed by the forest of people clambering for her attention. There was a good balance of interest between the show on stage, the bar, and light conversation. Marina distributed the drops of grenadine, eased the tequila over the barspoon, and topped the pony glasses off with eggnog. It wasn't until she served the nice older couple in black leather that she realized her mistake.

She'd made three drinks for two people. She could have sworn, though, that there had been a third person leaning on the bar. The one on the left had ordered a Tornado, the person on the right said "me too", and the one in the middle had raised a hand, as if to say "me three". But there was no seat between the two, just a carelessly abandoned crate. Had somebody been squatting on it? "Where did your friend go?" Marina said.

The couple stared at her. She twisted her spiked cuffs and brushed back her purple hair. "Was someone sitting between you?"

The couple shook their heads.

"Nevermind," She set the third drink between them. "This one's on the house." She put her tip into the register.

No incidents marked the appearance of the drag king Toto, or the queen Ozma (named after the true ruler of Oz that the wizard deposed). It was late at night when she ran out of white rum. Alex and Jamal were both serving, so she had to head down the stairs to get another case.

The naked bulb swung gently, shedding its stingy light on the classic Philadelphia murder-basement. Marina focused on the walls of boxes and crates ahead and wrestled with her memory. She didn't want to come back up and have to ask the manager where the white rum was. He always managed to point it out in a way that made her feel incredibly stupid for wasting his time.

The bulb hung still. Something squelched under her heel. Her leg shot forward and the basement swung around her. She mashed the side of her face against the cold stone wall. Marina just caught the edge of the railing with two fingers, stopping herself from a slide down the stairs.

Gasping and shivering, Marina carefully drew herself upright. She kept hold of the railing with both hands. She crept down the remaining stairs, thankful that she hadn't been carrying a case of heavy bottles when she'd slipped.

Marina turned to see what she'd slipped on. There was nothing on the stairs. No plastic wrappers or lemon peels lay on any step. She couldn't even see the shine of a wet spot against the dull grey stairs. She leaned down and felt along the stairs with her hands. She caught a faint whiff of lilies, but found nothing to explain her fall.

Confused and nervous, Marina carried up all the bottles one at a time. The boss might chew her out about it later, but she hadn't reached her thirties by prioritizing other people's demands over her own safety.

* * *

Marina sighed as the second number ten Trolley in a row pulled up. She'd just finished this month's street paper. Transmissions in the Philly Gay News had been replaced with some letters to the editor, and she really didn't feel like reading Metro today. She pulled out her phone instead, thinking she'd wade through some newsletters or cry over short videos of dogs being wonderful.

Instead, she thought of that warm afternoon last week, the momentary trick of the eye, and that cold little park bench. The quote had been rather odd; most park benches just had 'In Memory of Name', with maybe a date. She typed Matthew Everett Stith into Goodsearch. A mother shouted at her child nearby. Marina clarified that, no, she was not trying to search Matthew Everest Smith.

A mouse ran out on the tracks and vanished again. The smells of old urine, lily perfume, and cigarettes struggled for dominance. A gray-bearded white man asked her for a light. Mechanically, Marina took out her lighter and obliged him. A cold wind rose up inside her.

The articles mentioned Reverend Stith's generous legacy of philanthropy, the churches he restored, the food pantries he opened, and the buildings named after him. Some articles mentioned controversy over Reverend Stith's conversion therapy. A lot of the results were obituaries or news coverage of the reverend's improbable death.

A weak hand tugged on Marina's coat. She pulled loose and shuffled aside without looking.

"You stop bothering that man," a tired mother snapped. "Get your ass right back here."

Marina groaned. She wasn't going to bother correcting the woman. That might start an argument or draw unwanted attention. She really tried her best, but maybe she should have worn something more slimming today, or a skirt instead of pants. She tried to focus on the tiny screen in front of her. It wasn't much better.

Reverend Matthew Stith had lead a bipartisan alliance against the city ordinance that required bathrooms in new buildings be gender neutral. He had also given sermons at a lot of funerals where parents buried their children in the wrong clothes and put the birth name instead of the chosen name on the headstone.

Somebody across the tracks shouted "Woo woo! Look here! Woo woo! Look here!" Marina jerked back from the yellow line. He didn't seem to be shouting at her, but it took a moment to catch her breath. She fantasized about answering him with a hurled soda can to the face, but reflected that she didn't want to be beaten into a thin slime by police. Anyway, her aim wasn't that good.

She peeked down the tunnel, looking for distant lights, and coughed as a very thick fog of floral perfume assailed her. She returned to her phone.

Despite her low opinion of Reverend Stith's doctrine, it was still a shock to see the photographs of his final moments. Marina made a little choking noise as she staggered back.

Reverend Stith had been engaged in a public interfaith debate on issues of gender and sexuality at the time. There were representatives from Whosoever Metropolitan Church, Mt Olive Church, Temple Beth Zion, The Love of God the Lord Almighty Community Church, Masjid Al-Jamia, Beth Am Israel, and a few more. The important thing was the sheet-metal sign with Leviticus 20:13 painted on it in gold letters, and the way Stith had been leaning forward. There was something about an inquiry into the subcontractors who had put up the sign. It should have been secured better. It shouldn't have been so heavy. The jagged bottom edge of the sign should have been finished properly. The reverend had leaned forward and banged his fist at exactly the wrong moment.

The police had drawn a chalk outline during the inquiry. Two chalk outlines, actually. One of the outlines, up behind the podium, had two legs. The other had a long, trailing zigzag. Attempts at rendering first aid had been almost comically futile.

Reverend Stith must have been a very determined man to get as far as he did after the sign fell. A great hill of lilies had been assembled in his honor at the public funeral.

"I told you to leave that nice man alone! You just wait till we get home."

Marina looked up. A small child was tugging on an elderly figure's overcoat. "I'm so sorry," said the mother who had spoken earlier, as she yanked the child away. The mother hadn't misgendered Marina after all.

The sense of relief curdled quickly. There was another tugging.

Marina turned around slowly. She saw nobody behind her. Maybe somebody had tried to pickpocket her and then darted away. Her wallet was still there, along with her travel pass and keys.

The thirteen trolley had pulled up while she was distracted. Other people rushed to board it. Marina got in just as the doors were closing, and a cold, wet grip yanked her ankle.

No, that couldn't have happened. She'd just stepped in a wet patch. Right?

A wet handprint smeared across the trolley door just as they took off. Marina clutched her wooden cross and began to pray, starting with La Santa Muerte. She spent the rest of the ride working through the list of saints.

* * *

At four in the morning, Marina Sanchez gave up on trying to sleep. When the sun rose, she called her girlfriend, asking her to come over. Shakima wasn't perfect, but thank God and the Virgin Mary, she was the kind of person who had your back in a tight corner. Woken up at ass-o-clock, she'd just accepted that Marina would try to give an explanation when she came over, but that she really couldn't stand to be alone right now.

Marina sat on her orange loveseat and drummed her fingers on the collapsible table. She'd cleaned the whole apartment, from the dust on the windows to the scum behind the toilet. When everything was spotless, she'd gone through the motions of cleaning again. She'd worked away to the soundtrack of pop rock, barking dogs, and screaming birds.

On one end of her bookshelf was a simple urn containing Daisy's ashes and collar. The other end had a framed picture of her tia, who had warned her when her parents were about to throw her out with only the clothes on her back. Thanks to that, she'd been able to grab a bug-out bag and pack her silver, along with a fifty her tia had slipped into her pocket. Those times after had been hard, but they'd have been a lot harder without her tia's kindness and prayers.

Marina had filled the space between these relics with votive candles. She had used tall white ones, set in glass; she had the kind you get from the corner store, and the blue ones for protection, and the illustrated special ones, like the Sacred Heart of Jesus candle and Saint John the Baptist and the Lady of Guadalupe. When she'd run out of those, Marina had lit some apple-cinnamon tea light candles.

Technically, they must represent a fire hazard. She needed the light and heat they gave. It was almost enough to soften the goosebumps on her skin. It wasn't enough to make her forget the cold touch on her ankle, or the cold shadow on the bench, or the wet slip on the stairs.

She'd tried to read her collection of short stories by trans authors. She'd tried to read her trashy lesbian werewolf romance novel. She'd tried to read her bible. She hadn't been able to get more than a few pages into any of them. Her mind was like a bare foot on a hot tarmac.

Last year, when they were up late, exhausted and happy, Shakima had told Marina about her own grandmother painting places haint blue. It fooled dead things into thinking there was running water that they couldn't cross. Marina wished she had a bucket of haint blue paint. She felt like rolling in the stuff. A lonely dog howled in the distance and set the rest of the neighborhood off barking.

Marina pulled her finger out of her mouth when she realized she'd been chewing on it like a twig. She tapped her feet. She got up, strode to the aging refrigerator, and stared at the contents. There were no leftovers, only things she'd have to prepare and cook. She didn't even feel up to making rice and veggies, never mind a full meal, but just now she realized how hungry she was. She'd forgotten dinner and breakfast.

Marina turned to her cabinet. She stared at the meager collection of cans she'd picked up at Aldi. She grabbed the spaghetti rings and a bottle of hot sauce.

Marina opened the can, slurped out some of the contents, then poured some sauce and mixed it in with a spoon. She was always careful about her appearance and table manners, always careful to avoid seeming gross. She had a lot of double-standards to fight against as a fat trans Latina. Right now she didn't give a damn that she was eating cold spaghetti-rings straight from the can, standing up, dripping sauce on her favorite lavender top that already stank of fear sweat. Right now, survival meant something other than passing well.

Halfway through the can, she grabbed a fifth of Bacardi. She didn't bother with ice or even a glass. She forced the stuff down, taking another spoonful of uncooked rings with tomato sauce and meatballs every time the burning in her throat became too sharp. She brought the can and the bottle to her loveseat. The bottle had started out half-full, but now it was less than a third.

Marina finished the can in seconds, then set it down. She didn't feel like lugging it to the recycling bin now. She wiped her mouth on her sleeve. She'd probably ruined this shirt with the red sauce smears. Anything strong enough to remove the stains would also fade the color.

Marina opened the window a crack. The song of birds and the smell of lilies greeted her. She felt a little better now that the sun was properly up and the clinging gray of twilight had left.

A knock on the door made her jump. Marina wanted to clean herself up a bit, but she was shaking too hard. She could barely fumble the door chain open.

"Come in!"

A hand pounded on the door. Marina hesitated. The dogs outside were silent. She pulled out her phone. A new text appeared.

Stuck in traffic. Will b therf in 15 mins.

She tried to fit the chain back into place. The door shook under the hammerings.

"No, don't come in! I take it back! Keep out!"

The stench of lilies overwhelmed her. The birdsong outside seemed to mock her. The door unlocked by itself.

Marina was strong, even for a trans woman her size. Sometimes she resented her physique. Now she was thankful for every inch of muscular bulk as she slammed her back against the door. The knob turned but the thing on the other side was weaker than her. It couldn't force the door open.

She shouted "Go to the devil or whatever crazy saint let you out of your pit!"

The hammering increased. Somebody wheezed and panted outside in the hall. She didn't want to see the half-sized figure. She didn't even want to know if there was anything to be seen.

She fit the chain lock back in place with one sweaty hand. She slid it home.

Marina pulled away from the door. She clicked the main lock. The door unlocked. She locked it again.

"I can keep this up all day," she shouted. Laughter leaked from the painful corners of her mouth.

The weak, wet hands continued to pound away. "*Chingate*!" she shouted, locking it again. The hammering stopped. She backed up, slowly. She grabbed her wooden cross in one hand, tight enough to hurt, and said the Lord's prayer.

Would that work, though? Would the words and symbols of God have any power to ward off a thing that claimed to speak in God's name and wielded His authority like a bullwhip?

Some sixth sense made her turn and look at the bookshelf. She had a little shrine to La Santa Muerte there, a grim reaper figure she'd brought at an overpriced jewelry shop with birthday money and outfitted in a Barbie's dress. The candle in front of it was guttering as if in a wet breeze.

The blue candle right next to Daisy's urn flickered. All the other blue candles extinguished at once.

The pet-flap on her door slapped down into place.

* * *

All Marina could see was that the pet flap hadn't closed completely. All she could smell were fresh lilies. She could hear a lot more, though. She could hear something slippery-wet, tugging through the pet flap a few inches at a time. She could hear hands thud down on the shag carpeting. They should make little handprints there, just like they'd formed a smear on the trolley window. The only impression they left was their sound. There was no heavy depression where the bulk of the bodiless body dragged itself, just the sound of that slow, heavy, determined movement.

Marina raised up her cross and prayed with all the breath she could muster. The sound dragged closer and closer. She called on Santa Muerte, on the Virgin Mary, on Jesus Christ and John the Baptist and the angel Michael. She drew up every holy name her shaking mind could grip.

The thing dragged nearer and nearer to her. It would have cold, wet hands, and they would grip her, weakly at first like a sick old man. They would dig in harder, growing stronger as she weakened, and they would never ever let her go.

Marina could hear her own ragged breathing. She heard a man outside selling loosies and a motorcycle revving. She heard the wet thing pull itself nearer to her. Her fingers grew numb around the cross.

She tried to stomp on it. Her foot passed through chill air and her sock became soaking wet, but the dragging sounds continued. She felt cold arms reach back and quickly withdrew her foot. She backed away from it until her head smacked against the wall. The candles rattled dangerously.

She picked up a candle at random and thrust it at the shape. It went out before reaching it. She flung it. Wax smeared on the floor and received no impression from the shape dragging over it.

Every candle except the one by the urn died. That last one sputtered and gave off smoke. She remembered the silence of distant dogs, the quote on the park bench, and the warmth of Daisy's breath against her skin. Her heart ached as she lifted the urn from the shelf. She drew in a breath.

It shattered against something that couldn't have been there. Pale ash outlined the form of a man, his collar turned up with bands, his head raised, crawling on two outstretched arms. Behind it, the remains revealed something long and deflated. The figure raised a hand towards her, and then it began to recede. Steam rose. Ash and bone shards fell to the floor with nothing to support them.

Marina prodded the ashes with her foot. The dogs outside started barking again. She gave an involuntary gasp of relief. After minutes of shuddering numbness, tears followed. She clutched the collar to her heart.

Marina wasn't safe yet. One of her friends made jewelry out of ethically collected animal bones. She would set a shard in a necklace she could wear everywhere, as long as she lived in this city. She needed her beloved Daisy close to hand, because the name of Reverend Stith was engraved all over this city, on bricks and bronze.

Floating Ghosts

Jessica Landry

I WAS ASLEEP when my mother died. Warm, comfy, dreaming of a rose garden, one with no leaves, no greenery, only black petals attached to thorny stems. As I walked through the garden, the dirt grew rougher, rigid. Thorns pushed themselves through the dirt until the path I was on disappeared completely. I thought I'd feel it then – the thorns winding up my legs, piercing my skin – but when I looked down, my feet were drifting over the tangles. I dreamt she was there, my mother, underneath the knots, her hands outreached, not to me, but something beyond me. Something small.

My mother loved to garden, said it was the one thing that kept her sane.

That, and the floating ghost.

* * *

When I was nine, we found ourselves in Dover, along England's east coast. My mother had packed us up and moved us across Europe, all in search of answers to questions she never shared. She moved us on whims, when the air didn't feel right in the places we were resting; she moved us on whispers, on words slurred from the mouths of drunken bar patrons. She moved us because standing still for too long frightened her. The moments when I did pry about our constant travels, her response was always, "I'll tell you when you're older."

My mother was a small-built woman, one who floated more than walked, and wherever she went, the weight of the world followed. I saw it in her shoulders, how they slouched inward ever so slightly. I saw it in her face, how it would light up at the beginning of our journeys and fade out by the end. It was around those times, when the light had gone, that I knew to say my goodbyes to any friends I'd made and start culling any toys I'd collected – we could never take them with us.

Though I didn't remember much of my younger years, I could recall certain places, certain attractions. Whenever the scent of lilacs found my nose, I was reminded of a shoppe my mother had taken me somewhere, one filled with dried flowers and tiny vials full of strange salts. My mother had sat around a table across from a woman dressed in gold who glared into a glass ball. They spoke in hushed tones, and whatever the woman had whispered to my mother was enough for us to move on to another town that very night.

We had visited many women like that in our travels, and I expected no less when we arrived in Dover. I tried to take it all in, just as with any town. I loved that here, as we strolled along the boardwalk, I could hear the waves crashing against the rocks, that the air left a taste of salt in my mouth, that the grey clouds above made me feel as though I were in a snowglobe, preserved and protected, and permanently ensconced in a glass ball.

But nothing was ever permanent. It was only a matter of time.

Until my mother saw the poster hanging off a boarded-up shop.

Come see the floating ghost! it said in bold, bright letters next to a photo of a blurry face. *Look through the veil into the spirit world, and if you dare, see what looks back at you.*

* * *

Twenty minutes later we were on the water, just her and I and the small boat's captain. I clutched onto my mother's arm as the boat lurched forward into the grey afternoon, watching the shoreline grow smaller and smaller until any sign of land disappeared.

It was a strange sensation being out in the open water. I felt uneasy, unsettled, as though millions of unseen eyes had turned toward me. The feeling only grew stronger the closer we got to our destination.

I found my mother's hand as we puttered to a stop but she pulled away before I could grasp it. My eyes found her face as she stood, the light burning bright inside her.

She stepped toward the boat's handrail at a speed that caused me to steady myself, and only when I turned my head did I see what had caught her attention.

A wall of mist sat before us, thick yet glinting like strands of opalescent pearls strung together. They shimmered in a light that did not exist and swayed in a wind different than the one that blew around us. From that wind, a sickly sweet scent tickled my nose, one that I couldn't quite place though I knew I had encountered it before.

The captain turned the motor off, the only sound now coming from the tiny waves batting against the hull. I stayed in my seat, tiny fingers wrapped around the solidity of wood.

My mother gripped onto the rails, leaning forward more than I was comfortable with.

Then, her shoulders straightened and a quiet gasp escaped her lips.

With a shaky foot and a queasy stomach, I made my way next to her.

As I grabbed onto the rail, I looked to the pearls.

And in them, a face looked back.

* * *

We purchased a quaint Victorian manor on the edge of town that overlooked the water the next day. I spent hours curled up on my windowsill, listening to the waves caught against the white cliffs, eyes searching for strange things while scanning the rolling green hills, looking down into the blooming rose garden half expecting to see my mother tending to the smallest flower. At night, when my mother did most of her gardening, the red of the flowers dulled, casting an even darker black around them so it looked as though she held pure darkness in the palm of her hands.

We spent that first day covering all the mirrors that had come with the house with black veils. "To keep the house clear," my mother said.

And not long after the purchase of the house, my mother bought a boat, even though she had never so much as driven a car. She hired the captain to give her lessons, leaving me on the shore to watch as she steered up and down the coast.

I didn't attend school, as my mother often said, "Eliza, you've seen more in your life than any classroom could teach you." So days were spent at her side, strolling through town, where she would recite any knowledge she held to me. It was on those rolling hills and sandy shores that I learned about politics, about war, about how my mother had escaped Treblinka, though she never lingered too long on her personal history. After lessons, we often found ourselves on the boardwalk, even on rainy days. I'd point out music boxes that I wanted or five-cent games to play, and though she always nodded at what I said, her eyes were never on me.

They always found their way to the water.

My mother had sent for our things – her things, mostly. Things in storage god knows where for god knows how long, things I had no idea existed – and within days, the house started to feel fuller. Still, nearly half the rooms remained empty and the things in storage were from another era, a time prior to myself, a time when my mother's travel companion had been someone else, a name she never shared with me.

I took it upon myself during my free time to place at least one trinket from this new treasure trove of old, dusty items in the empty rooms so that way it wouldn't feel so lonely. I'd go from room to room and play with each toy as though it were my own. But when I went to place a music box in the attic, I found the door locked.

Being a curious child, I peered through the keyhole and saw a moonlit room stripped down to the studs. Tucked away under the window sat a chest.

"You're not to go in there," my mother said when I later inquired.

I nodded, already planning my entry.

* * *

My mother left the house every night after tucking me into bed, though as soon as I heard the back door open and shut, I'd leap from under my sheets and watch her go. She'd slink through the rose garden first, checking her flowers, picking at dead leaves. Then she'd saunter down the dirt path to the boathouse, her black coat turning her into another moving piece of the darkness. I'd watch until she became a fleck of dust, a star in the sky.

I sat at the window every night until she floated home just before the sun.

Her steps seemed heavier as she climbed the stairs, like wet, bare feet slapping against the waters' surface. She'd hover at my door, her silhouette blocking the hallway light, but she would never come in. She'd never knock. She'd simply shuffle away and I'd hear the click and latch of her bedroom door.

I knew where she went those nights, that was no secret. But what I didn't know was why she kept going back to the mist, to the floating ghost.

* * *

One grey morning when my mother went out to tend to the garden, I decided to try my luck. She left the keyring with the skeleton key in her nightstand, assuming I would never seek it out. Assuming her never-questioning child would continue staying silent.

The stairs moaned under my weight as I made my way up. I was sure she could hear the creaks from the garden, that I would be caught and punished, but when I peered out the window in the staircase, I saw her blissfully going about her work, not a care in the world.

I held my breath as I slid the key into the hole with ease, and promptly released when I turned and the click echoed through the house.

I stepped inside, immediately sneezing at the stirring dust, my eyes trying to focus in the dark room. The floorboards shuddered under my weight with every step I took.

Tucked away at the corner of the open space sat a floor-length mirror.

I approached it with caution – my mother insisted all mirrors be covered in her presence, though she never told me why. It was just another secret that died with her.

I examined the mirror – it seemed frail, the pegs holding it up at the back had all but whittled away. Through the surface, the moonlight caught the trunk's golden metal, causing it to twinkle. I left the mirror, quietly sitting in front of the chest. I examined my mother's keychain. One key in particular matched the style of the chest, so I placed the key in and turned.

The lock clicked open.

"Eliza?" My mother's voice sounded out from down below.

The stairs began to creak.

I unlatched the lock.

"Are you up here?"

I flipped the lid open.

"Eliza?"

I glanced over the contents and found myself disappointed. Inside were more toys, more photos, more clothes – more things I didn't recognize. It was as though my mother had been a collector of meaningless trinkets.

But a sickly sweet scent rose off the chest, sparking something inside me that I couldn't quite grasp.

No, these items weren't familiar, but I knew them. Somehow, I knew them.

Her footsteps inched closer. With no other options, I closed the chest and ran to the darkest corner, the one behind the mirror, tucking myself away.

"Elizabeth Bauer, you better not be in here," her voice asserted as she stepped into the room.

I held my breath, the sweet scent following me.

My mother stood in the centre of the attic, her eyes tracing over the closed chest. It seemed to pass her test as she started to the mirror.

"You must keep the door closed," she whispered.

At first I thought she had found me, my hiding spot not nearly as good as I had imagined. I waited for my punishment. I waited to be reprimanded.

But then her hands grasped the side of the mirror, and she spoke directly into it. "Be patient," she said. "There's no more lost time between us."

She let a hand rest against the surface before stepping out of the room, closing the door behind her.

As I listened to her go down the stairs, I wormed out of my hiding spot and slowly turned to face the mirror.

In its reflection, nothing seemed different. The attic was dark, the door was closed, and the chest's lid sat open.

* * *

That night, I feigned being sick, opting to go to bed long before my mother's usual departure. I told her to leave me be, that I needed to sleep, so she tucked me in, feeling my forehead in concern, but let me on my own.

Shortly before she left, I got out of bed and got dressed, then propped my pillow under my sheets to mimic my shape.

In the stillness of the house, I carefully unlatched my door, sure to pause in case I was heard.

From across the hall, I saw my mother's shadow pacing from under her door, a constant string of movement. It almost looked as though she were floating.

I crept down the stairs, imagining myself as light as a feather, slinking to the front door. Under the shadow of the night, I rounded the house, passing by the black rose garden, following the dirt path to the boathouse.

* * *

My mother came to the boat some time later, blissfully unaware that I had tucked myself away behind the back bench. I could only watch as she started the boat and began backing out of the boathouse.

Soon enough, we were out on the open water, the salt taste blossoming on my tongue. My mother steered as a seasoned professional, a smooth ride on an otherwise calm sea.

Some time later, I felt the boat reduce in speed, then the engine stopped. We drifted as the water lapped against the hull.

I watched as she left the boat's wheel and went to the side, clutching onto the rail.

It was only when my mother reached an arm out that I saw the mist. Still as opulent as the first time I had seen it, still swaying to its own breeze.

And the smell, sickly sweet like rotten fruit on a hot summer's day.

A smile crossed my mother's face, a laugh escaping her lips – a sound I hadn't heard often. Then I watched as she kicked off her shoes and propped herself up onto the thin ledge of the boat, crouching at first to steady herself, then, in sync with the waves, coming to a stand, her arms outstretched in front of her for balance.

"Mama!" I shouted, springing from my hiding spot.

But as I stood, she pitched herself forward.

Her body disappeared into the mist.

"Mama no!" I ran to the spot she had stood, my eyes on the water below.

But she wasn't there.

And when I looked up into the fog, I saw her floating, holding onto the hand of a little girl.

* * *

Sleep had overtaken me at some point during the night, so when I awoke some time later, the boat was docked at the boathouse and the birds were chirping somewhere distant.

I groggily made my way up the path to the house. The closer I came, the clearer I could see my mother pacing back and forth in the kitchen, hands to her mouth, eyes red from tears.

"Eliza!" she screamed as she saw me, running out to the path. She held me in her arms, her bony fingers clutching me nearly as tight as she clutched the boat's railing. "Where were you? You had me worried sick."

"Sorry, mama," was all I could say.

* * *

I spent the day in my room, silently building up the courage to confront my mother once and for all. I needed to know why we had stayed here. No more secrets. No more ghosts.

* * *

We sat around the kitchen table, the sun long set, picking away at our dinners. My mother seemed lost in thought, her fork lightly tapping against the china, her eyes focused ahead of her.

I took a nibble of bread, swallowing fast, wiping my sweaty palms against my dress.

It was now or never. I had to say something.

"I'd like to come with you tonight," I managed. "Out on the water."

"Hm?" she turned her eyes on me, snapping out of her reverie.

I started again, "I'd like to come—"

"That's not a good idea, Eliza," she interrupted, going back to picking at her plate.

"Why not?" I felt my face growing flush, the blood pulsing through my veins.

"Are you finished?" she smiled, looking down at my plate.

"Mother—"

"I'll fetch your dessert."

"Enough!" I shouted louder than I anticipated, slamming my fists against the table.

My mother jumped in her seat. "Eliza—"

"You've moved us around for years with no explanations," I continued, the words pouring from my mouth. "You've packed us up more times than I can remember. Why are we staying here? What is it that you're trying to find?"

She looked at me with a stunned silence, calmly setting her fork and knife down.

"It's not so easy to explain…"

"Tell me."

She sighed, the slouch in her shoulders ever-present. "I'll tell you when you're—"

I screamed at her then, a scream that sounded nothing like my voice, as though a foreign presence had taken over my vocal chords. I jumped from my chair, knocking it over behind me.

"Elizabeth Bauer, stop immediately," my mother said, reaching out for me. But I pulled away and ran into the parlour. She followed after me.

"I know where you go," I spat. "I know you go out there to the water. To see the floating ghost."

Her eyes fell to the floor then. I could see the breath caught in her chest. She exhaled, slowly, deliberately, but said nothing.

"Who do you see out there, in the mist?"

Still nothing.

"Who? Tell me!"

"Eliza—"

"No more, mother!" I screamed as the tears spilled onto my cheeks. "I can't do this anymore."

We locked eyes.

And then I began yanking the black veils from all the mirrors.

"Stop, Eliza! You'll let her out!" My mother panted, desperately trying to place them back on.

"Tell me who you see," I said, but she didn't respond.

So I ran up the stairs, to the second floor, to the attic door. She gave chase, her small build too slow to catch up.

I stood at the door, the door I hadn't locked since the last time I had been up. She watched me from the bottom step like a curious child.

I opened the door. Her eyes widened.

I ran into the room and grabbed hold of the chest.

I threw it down the stairs.

She screamed.

In a tizzy, she dropped to her knees as the chest burst open, toys and photos and baby clothes raining down around her. Things from storage. Things that were not mine. Things that smelled of rotten fruit on a hot summer's day.

"Vera," she said quietly, clutching onto a knitted onesie. She brought it to her mouth and kissed it. She wailed, a noise I had never heard emanate from her lips. She looked up at me as tears spilled onto her cheeks, a look of betrayal. Of heartache. "I just wanted to see her again."

I stood speechless at the top of the stairs, my stomach a bottomless pit.

I watched my mother stand, still clutching the onesie, and walk out of sight, downstairs. I heard the front door open and shut.

That night I stayed in bed, I didn't watch her from the window. I could see her clearly in my mind's eye stopping to check her roses; her ankle boots kicking up dirt along the path to the boathouse. I imagined her getting into the boat, her eyes black and wet. I hope she looked back to the house one last time, up to my window, maybe to see if I was sitting there watching her as I had every other night.

But as the faint sound of the boat's engine started, and eventually grew farther away, I dozed off to sleep, where I dreamed of roses.

* * *

I returned to Dover years later, having spent my formative years in Canada with an aunt who treated me as her own. I strolled down the boardwalk, most of the old storefronts sealed up, not a soul in sight. Though I didn't want to see it, I kept looking for the poster of the floating ghost. But there were none to be found.

From the boardwalk, I found myself on the rolling hills until I was outside what was left of the house, windows broken, half the front door missing. I only peered inside from as far back as I could, the light catching the glint of the mirror near the door, the wind catching the black veil that had remained over it all these years. The house seemed to sway in its own invisible wind, a creak and a moan sounding out from somewhere inside.

I went around to the back and stepped around what remained of the rose garden: dead earth that could never grow any new life. Then I followed the path down to the shore, to the boathouse.

Taking a deep breath, I opened the door and found the boat still intact. She had taken it out that night. A local fisherman had found the boat floating carelessly on its own near the mist, and after her body had been pulled from under it, it was returned home.

I carefully stepped on the boat, found the keys still in the ignition, and tried it – the boat coughed several times but came to life. Even after all these years.

It was a grey day, the waters a little rougher than what I had remembered. I followed the sea outward until the house and the hills and any sign of life disappeared from view.

Until I saw the mist.

It wavered before me, thick yet glinting, shimmering in a light that did not exist, swaying in a wind different than the one around me. I turned the motor off and let the boat drift alongside the fog. I knew it would never cross that threshold.

I went along the rails, leaning forward more than I should have.

As I clutched onto the cold, wet metal, I looked to the pearls.

And in them, a face looked back.

Schalken the Painter

Joseph Sheridan Le Fanu

'For he is not a man as I am that we should come together; neither is there any that might lay his hand upon us both. Let him, therefore, take his rod away from me, and let not his fear terrify me.'

THERE EXISTS, at this moment, in good preservation a remarkable work of Schalken's. The curious management of its lights constitutes, as usual in his pieces, the chief apparent merit of the picture. I say *apparent*, for in its subject, and not in its handling, however exquisite, consists its real value. The picture represents the interior of what might be a chamber in some antique religious building; and its foreground is occupied by a female figure, in a species of white robe, part of which is arranged so as to form a veil. The dress, however, is not that of any religious order. In her hand the figure bears a lamp, by which alone her figure and face are illuminated; and her features wear such an arch smile, as well becomes a pretty woman when practising some prankish roguery; in the background, and, excepting where the dim red light of an expiring fire serves to define the form, in total shadow, stands the figure of a man dressed in the old Flemish fashion, in an attitude of alarm, his hand being placed upon the hilt of his sword, which he appears to be in the act of drawing.

There are some pictures, which impress one, I know not how, with a conviction that they represent not the mere ideal shapes and combinations which have floated through the imagination of the artist, but scenes, faces, and situations which have actually existed. There is in that strange picture, something that stamps it as the representation of a reality.

And such in truth it is, for it faithfully records a remarkable and mysterious occurrence, and perpetuates, in the face of the female figure, which occupies the most prominent place in the design, an accurate portrait of Rose Velderkaust, the niece of Gerard Douw, the first, and, I believe, the only love of Godfrey Schalken. My great grandfather knew the painter well; and from Schalken himself he learned the fearful story of the painting, and from him too he ultimately received the picture itself as a bequest. The story and the picture have become heir-looms in my family, and having described the latter, I shall, if you please, attempt to relate the tradition which has descended with the canvas.

There are few forms on which the mantle of romance hangs more ungracefully than upon that of the uncouth Schalken – the boorish but most cunning worker in oils, whose pieces delight the critics of our day almost as much as his manners disgusted the refined of his own; and yet this man, so rude, so dogged, so slovenly, in the midst of his celebrity, had in his obscure, but happier days, played the hero in a wild romance of mystery and passion.

When Schalken studied under the immortal Gerard Douw, he was a very young man; and in spite of his phlegmatic temperament, he at once fell over head and ears in love with the beautiful niece of his wealthy master. Rose Velderkaust was still younger than he, having not yet attained her seventeenth year, and, if tradition speaks truth, possessed all the soft and dimpling charms of the fair, light-haired Flemish maidens. The young painter loved honestly and fervently. His frank adoration was rewarded. He declared his love, and extracted a faltering confession in return. He was the happiest and proudest painter in all Christendom. But there was somewhat to dash his elation; he was poor and undistinguished. He dared not ask old Gerard for the hand of his sweet ward. He must first win a reputation and a competence.

There were, therefore, many dread uncertainties and cold days before him; he had to fight his way against sore odds. But he had won the heart of dear Rose Velderkaust, and that was half the battle. It is needless to say his exertions were redoubled, and his lasting celebrity proves that his industry was not unrewarded by success.

These ardent labours, and worse still, the hopes that elevated and beguiled them, were however, destined to experience a sudden interruption – of a character so strange and mysterious as to baffle all inquiry and to throw over the events themselves a shadow of preternatural horror.

Schalken had one evening outstayed all his fellow-pupils, and still pursued his work in the deserted room. As the daylight was fast falling, he laid aside his colours, and applied himself to the completion of a sketch on which he had expressed extraordinary pains. It was a religious composition, and represented the temptations of a pot-bellied Saint Anthony. The young artist, however destitute of elevation, had, nevertheless, discernment enough to be dissatisfied with his own work, and many were the patient erasures and improvements which saint and devil underwent, yet all in vain. The large, old-fashioned room was silent, and, with the exception of himself, quite emptied of its usual inmates. An hour had thus passed away, nearly two, without any improved result. Daylight had already declined, and twilight was deepening into the darkness of night. The patience of the young painter was exhausted, and he stood before his unfinished production, angry and mortified, one hand buried in the folds of his long hair, and the other holding the piece of charcoal which had so ill-performed its office, and which he now rubbed, without much regard to the sable streaks it produced, with irritable pressure upon his ample Flemish inexpressibles. "Curse the subject!" said the young man aloud. "Curse the picture, the devils, the saint—"

At this moment a short, sudden sniff uttered close beside him made the artist turn sharply round, and he now, for the first time, became aware that his labours had been overlooked by a stranger. Within about a yard and half, and rather behind him, there stood the figure of an elderly man in a cloak and broad-brimmed, conical hat; in his hand, which was protected with a heavy gauntlet-shaped glove, he carried a long ebony walking stick, surmounted with what appeared, as it glittered dimly in the twilight, to be a massive head of gold, and upon his breast, through the folds of the cloak, there shone the links of a rich chain of the same metal. The room was so obscure that nothing further of the appearance of the figure could be ascertained, and his hat threw his features into profound shadow. It would not have been easy to conjecture the age of the intruder; but a quantity of dark hair escaping from beneath this sombre hat, as well as his firm and upright carriage served to indicate that his years could not yet exceed threescore, or thereabouts. There was an air of gravity and importance about the garb of the person, and something indescribably odd, I might say awful, in the perfect, stone-like stillness of the figure, that effectually checked the testy comment which had at once risen to the lips of the irritated artist. He, therefore, as soon as he had sufficiently recovered his surprise, asked the stranger, civilly, to be seated, and desired to know if he had any message to leave for his master.

"Tell Gerard Douw," said the unknown, without altering his attitude in the smallest degree, "that Minheer Vanderhausen, of Rotterdam, desires to speak with him on tomorrow evening at this hour, and if he please, in this room, upon matters of weight; that is all."

The stranger, having finished this message, turned abruptly, and, with a quick but silent step quitted the room, before Schalken had time to say a word in reply. The young man felt a curiosity to see in what direction the burgher of Rotterdam would turn, on quitting the studio, and for that purpose he went directly to the window which commanded the door. A lobby of considerable extent intervened between the inner door of the painter's room and the street entrance, so that Schalken occupied the post of observation before the old man could possibly have reached the street. He watched in vain, however. There was no other mode of exit. Had the queer old man vanished, or was he lurking about the recesses of the lobby for some sinister purpose? This last suggestion filled the mind of Schalken with a vague uneasiness, which was so unaccountably intense as to make him alike afraid to remain in the room alone, and reluctant to pass through the lobby. However, with an effort which appeared very disproportioned to the occasion, he summoned resolution to leave the room, and, having locked the door and thrust the key in his pocket, without looking to the right or left, he traversed the passage which had so recently, perhaps still, contained the person of his mysterious visitant, scarcely venturing to breathe till he had arrived in the open street.

"Minheer Vanderhausen!" said Gerard Douw within himself, as the appointed hour approached, "Minheer Vanderhausen, of Rotterdam! I never heard of the man till yesterday. What can he want of me? A portrait, perhaps, to be painted; or a poor relation to be apprenticed; or a collection to be valued; or – pshaw! there's no one in Rotterdam to leave me a legacy. Well, whatever the business may be, we shall soon know it all."

It was now the close of day, and again every easel, except that of Schalken, was deserted. Gerard Douw was pacing the apartment with the restless step of impatient expectation, sometimes pausing to glance over the work of one of his absent pupils, but more frequently placing himself at the window, from whence he might observe the passengers who threaded the obscure by-street in which his studio was placed.

"Said you not, Godfrey," exclaimed Douw, after a long and fruitful gaze from his post of observation, and turning to Schalken, "that the hour he appointed was about seven by the clock of the Stadhouse?"

"It had just told seven when I first saw him, sir," answered the student.

"The hour is close at hand, then," said the master, consulting a horologe as large and as round as an orange. "Minheer Vanderhausen from Rotterdam – is it not so?"

"Such was the name."

"And an elderly man, richly clad?" pursued Douw, musingly.

"As well as I might see," replied his pupil; "he could not be young, nor yet very old, neither; and his dress was rich and grave, as might become a citizen of wealth and consideration."

At this moment the sonorous boom of the Stadhouse clock told, stroke after stroke, the hour of seven; the eyes of both master and student were directed to the door; and it was not until the last peal of the bell had ceased to vibrate, that Douw exclaimed:

"So, so; we shall have his worship presently, that is, if he means to keep his hour; if not, you may wait for him, Godfrey, if you court his acquaintance. But what, after all, if it should prove but a mummery got up by Vankarp, or some such wag? I wish you had run all risks, and cudgelled the old burgomaster soundly. I'd wager a dozen of Rhenish, his worship would have unmasked, and pleaded old acquaintance in a trice."

"Here he comes, sir," said Schalken, in a low monitory tone; and instantly, upon turning towards the door, Gerard Douw observed the same figure which had, on the day before, so unexpectedly greeted his pupil Schalken.

There was something in the air of the figure which at once satisfied the painter that there was no masquerading in the case, and that he really stood in the presence of a man of worship; and so, without hesitation, he doffed his cap, and courteously saluting the stranger, requested him to be seated. The visitor waved his hand slightly, as if in acknowledgment of the courtesy, but remained standing.

"I have the honour to see Minheer Vanderhausen of Rotterdam?" said Gerard Douw.

"The same," was the laconic reply of his visitor.

"I understand your worship desires to speak with me," continued Douw, "and I am here by appointment to wait your commands."

"Is that a man of trust?" said Vanderhausen, turning towards Schalken, who stood at a little distance behind his master.

"Certainly," replied Gerard.

"Then let him take this box, and get the nearest jeweller or goldsmith to value its contents, and let him return hither with a certificate of the valuation."

At the same time, he placed a small case about nine inches square in the hands of Gerard Douw, who was as much amazed at its weight as at the strange abruptness with which it was handed to him. In accordance with the wishes of the stranger, he delivered it into the hands of Schalken, and repeating his direction, despatched him upon the mission.

Schalken disposed his precious charge securely beneath the folds of his cloak, and rapidly traversing two or three narrow streets, he stopped at a corner house, the lower part of which was then occupied by the shop of a Jewish goldsmith. He entered the shop, and calling the little Hebrew into the obscurity of its back recesses, he proceeded to lay before him Vanderhausen's casket. On being examined by the light of a lamp, it appeared entirely cased with lead, the outer surface of which was much scraped and soiled, and nearly white with age. This having been partially removed, there appeared beneath a box of some hard wood; which also they forced open and after the removal of two or three folds of linen, they discovered its contents to be a mass of golden ingots, closely packed, and, as the Jew declared, of the most perfect quality. Every ingot underwent the scrutiny of the little Jew, who seemed to feel an epicurean delight in touching and testing these morsels of the glorious metal; and each one of them was replaced in its berth with the exclamation: "*Mein Gott*, how very perfect! Not one grain of alloy – beautiful, beautiful!" The task was at length finished, and the Jew certified under his hand the value of the ingots submitted to his examination, to amount to many thousand rix-dollars. With the desired document in his pocket, and the rich box of gold carefully pressed under his arm, and concealed by his cloak, he retraced his way, and entering the studio, found his master and the stranger in close conference. Schalken had no sooner left the room, in order to execute the commission he had taken in charge, than Vanderhausen addressed Gerard Douw in the following terms:

"I cannot tarry with you tonight more than a few minutes, and so I shall shortly tell you the matter upon which I come. You visited the town of Rotterdam some four months ago, and then I saw in the church of St. Lawrence your niece, Rose Velderkaust. I desire to marry her; and if I satisfy you that I am wealthier than any husband you can dream of for her, I expect that you will forward my suit with your authority. If you approve my proposal, you must close with it here and now, for I cannot wait for calculations and delays."

Gerard Douw was hugely astonished by the nature of Minheer Vanderhausen's communication, but he did not venture to express surprise; for besides the motives supplied by prudence and politeness, the painter experienced a kind of chill and oppression like that which is said to intervene when one is placed in unconscious proximity with the object of a natural antipathy – an undefined but overpowering sensation, while standing in the presence of the eccentric stranger, which made him very unwilling to say anything which might reasonably offend him.

"I have no doubt," said Gerard, after two or three prefatory hems, "that the alliance which you propose would prove alike advantageous and honourable to my niece; but you must be aware that she has a will of her own, and may not acquiesce in what *we* may design for her advantage."

"Do not seek to deceive me, sir painter," said Vanderhausen; "you are her guardian – she is your ward – she is mine if *you* like to make her so."

The man of Rotterdam moved forward a little as he spoke, and Gerard Douw, he scarce knew why, inwardly prayed for the speedy return of Schalken.

"I desire," said the mysterious gentleman, "to place in your hands at once an evidence of my wealth, and a security for my liberal dealing with your niece. The lad will return in a minute or two with a sum in value five times the fortune which she has a right to expect from her husband. This shall lie in your hands, together with her dowry, and you may apply the united sum as suits her interest best; it shall be all exclusively hers while she lives: is that liberal?"

Douw assented, and inwardly acknowledged that fortune had been extraordinarily kind to his niece; the stranger, he thought, must be both wealthy and generous, and such an offer was not to be despised, though made by a humourist, and one of no very prepossessing presence. Rose had no very high pretensions for she had but a modest dowry, which she owed entirely to the generosity of her uncle; neither had she any right to raise exceptions on the score of birth, for her own origin was far from splendid, and as the other objections, Gerald resolved, and indeed, by the usages of the time, was warranted in resolving, not to listen to them for a moment.

"Sir," said he, addressing the stranger, "your offer is liberal, and whatever hesitation I may feel in closing with it immediately, arises solely from my not having the honour of knowing anything of your family or station. Upon these points you can, of course, satisfy me without difficulty?"

"As to my respectability," said the stranger, drily, "you must take that for granted at present; pester me with no inquiries; you can discover nothing more about me than I choose to make known. You shall have sufficient security for my respectability – my word, if you are honourable: if you are sordid, my gold."

"A testy old gentleman," thought Douw, "he must have his own way; but, all things considered, I am not justified to declining his offer. I will not pledge myself unnecessarily, however."

"You will not pledge yourself unnecessarily," said Vanderhausen, strangely uttering the very words which had just floated through the mind of his companion; "but you will do so if it is necessary, I presume; and I will show you that I consider it indispensable. If the gold I mean to leave in your hands satisfy you, and if you don't wish my proposal to be at once withdrawn, you must, before I leave this room, write your name to this engagement."

Having thus spoken, he placed a paper in the hands of the master, the contents of which expressed an engagement entered into by Gerard Douw, to give to Wilken Vanderhausen of Rotterdam, in marriage, Rose Velderkaust, and so forth, within one week of the date thereof. While the painter was employed in reading this covenant, by the light of a twinkling oil lamp in the far wall of the room, Schalken, as we have stated, entered the studio, and having delivered the box and the valuation of the Jew, into the hands of the stranger, he was about to retire, when Vanderhausen called to him to wait; and, presenting the case and the certificate to Gerard Douw, he paused in silence until he had satisfied himself, by an inspection of both, respecting the value of the pledge left in his hands. At length he said:

"Are you content?"

The painter said he would fain have another day to consider.

"Not an hour," said the suitor, apathetically.

"Well then," said Douw, with a sore effort, "I am content, it is a bargain."

"Then sign at once," said Vanderhausen, "for I am weary."

At the same time he produced a small case of writing materials, and Gerard signed the important document.

"Let this youth witness the covenant," said the old man; and Godfrey Schalken unconsciously attested the instrument which forever bereft him of his dear Rose Velderkaust.

The compact being thus completed, the strange visitor folded up the paper, and stowed it safely in an inner pocket.

"I will visit you tomorrow night at nine o'clock, at your own house, Gerard Douw, and will see the object of our contract." And so saying Wilken Vanderhausen moved stiffly, but rapidly, out of the room.

Schalken, eager to resolve his doubts, had placed himself by the window, in order to watch the street entrance; but the experiment served only to support his suspicions, for the old man did not issue from the door. This was *very* strange, odd, nay fearful. He and his master returned together, and talked but little on the way, for each had his own subjects of reflection, of anxiety, and of hope. Schalken, however, did not know the ruin which menaced his dearest projects.

Gerard Douw knew nothing of the attachment which had sprung up between his pupil and his niece; and even if he had, it is doubtful whether he would have regarded its existence as any serious obstruction to the wishes of Minheer Vanderhausen. Marriages were then and there matters of traffic and calculation; and it would have appeared as absurd in the eyes of the guardian to make a mutual attachment an essential element in a contract of the sort, as it would have been to draw up his bonds and receipts in the language of romance.

The painter, however, did not communicate to his niece the important step which he had taken in her behalf, a forebearance caused not by any anticipated opposition on her part, but solely by a ludicrous consciousness that if she were to ask him for a description of her destined bridegroom, he would be forced to confess that he had not once seen his face, and if called upon, would find it absolutely impossible to identify him. Upon the next day, Gerard Douw, after dinner, called his niece to him and having scanned her person with an air of satisfaction, he took her hand, and looking upon her pretty innocent face with a smile of kindness, he said:

"Rose, my girl, that face of yours will make your fortune." Rose blushed and smiled. "Such faces and such tempers seldom go together, and when they do, the compound is a love charm, few heads or hearts can resist; trust me, you will soon be a bride, girl. But this is trifling, and I am pressed for time, so make ready the large room by eight o'clock tonight, and give directions for supper at nine. I expect a friend; and observe me, child, do you trick yourself out handsomely. I will not have him think us poor or sluttish."

With these words he left her, and took his way to the room in which his pupils worked.

When the evening closed in, Gerard called Schalken, who was about to take his departure to his own obscure and comfortless lodgings, and asked him to come home and sup with Rose and Vanderhausen. The invitation was, of course, accepted and Gerard Douw and his pupil soon found themselves in the handsome and, even then, antique chamber, which had been prepared for the reception of the stranger. A cheerful wood fire blazed in the hearth, a little at one side of which an old-fashioned table, which shone in the firelight like burnished gold, was awaiting the supper, for which preparations were going forward; and ranged with exact regularity, stood the tall-backed chairs, whose ungracefulness was more than compensated by their comfort. The little party, consisting of Rose, her uncle, and the artist, awaited the arrival of the expected visitor with considerable impatience. Nine o'clock at length came, and with it a summons at the street door, which being speedily answered, was followed by a slow and emphatic tread upon the staircase; the steps moved heavily across the lobby, the door of the room in which the party we have described were assembled slowly opened, and there entered a figure which startled, almost appalled, the phlegmatic Dutchmen, and nearly made Rose scream with terror. It was the form, and arrayed in the garb of Minheer Vanderhausen; the air, the gait, the height were the same, but the features had never been seen by any of the party before. The stranger stopped at the door of the room, and displayed his form and face completely. He wore a dark-coloured cloth cloak, which was short and full, not falling quite to his knees; his legs were cased in dark purple silk stockings, and his shoes were adorned with roses of the same colour. The opening of the cloak in front showed the under-suit to consist of some very dark, perhaps sable material, and his hands were enclosed in a pair of heavy leather gloves, which ran up considerably above the wrist, in the manner of a gauntlet. In one hand he carried his walking stick and his hat, which he had removed, and the other hung heavily by his side. A quantity of grizzled hair descended in long tresses from his head, and rested upon the plaits of a stiff ruff, which effectually concealed his neck. So far all was well; but the face! – all the flesh of the face was coloured with the bluish leaden hue, which is sometimes produced by metallic medicines, administered in excessive quantities; the eyes showed an undue proportion of muddy white, and had a certain indefinable character of insanity; the hue of the lips bearing the usual relation to that of the face, was, consequently, nearly black; and the entire character of the face was sensual, malignant, and even satanic. It was remarkable that the worshipful stranger suffered as little as possible of his flesh to appear, and that during his visit he did not once remove his gloves. Having stood for some moments at the door, Gerard Douw at length found breath and collectedness to bid him welcome, and with a mute inclination of the head, the stranger stepped forward into the room. There was something indescribably odd, even horrible, about all his motions, something undefinable, that was unnatural, unhuman; it was as if the limbs were guided and directed by a spirit unused to the management of bodily machinery. The stranger spoke hardly at all during his visit, which did not exceed half an hour; and the host himself could scarcely muster courage enough to utter the few necessary salutations and courtesies; and, indeed, such was the nervous terror which the presence of Vanderhausen inspired, that very little would have made all his entertainers fly in downright panic from the room. They had not so far lost all self-possession, however, as to fail to observe two strange peculiarities of their visitor. During his stay his eyelids did not once close, or, indeed, move in the slightest degree; and farther, there was a deathlike stillness in his whole person, owing to the absence of the heaving motion of the chest, caused by the process of respiration. These two peculiarities, though when told they may appear trifling, produced a very striking and unpleasant effect when seen and observed. Vanderhausen at length relieved the painter of Leyden of his inauspicious presence; and with no trifling sense of relief the little party heard the street door close after him.

"Dear uncle," said Rose, "what a frightful man! I would not see him again for the wealth of the States."

"Tush, foolish girl," said Douw, whose sensations were anything but comfortable. "A man may be as ugly as the devil, and yet, if his heart and actions are good, he is worth all the pretty-faced perfumed puppies that walk the Mall. Rose, my girl, it is very true he has not thy pretty face, but I know him to be wealthy and liberal; and were he ten times more ugly, these two virtues would be enough to counter balance all his deformity, and if not sufficient actually to alter the shape and hue of his features, at least enough to prevent one thinking them so much amiss."

"Do you know, uncle," said Rose, "when I saw him standing at the door, I could not get it out of my head that I saw the old painted wooden figure that used to frighten me so much in the Church of St. Laurence at Rotterdam."

Gerard laughed, though he could not help inwardly acknowledging the justness of the comparison. He was resolved, however, as far as he could, to check his niece's disposition to dilate upon the ugliness of her intended bridegroom, although he was not a little pleased, as well as puzzled, to observe that she appeared totally exempt from that mysterious dread of the stranger which, he could not disguise it from himself, considerably affected him, as also his pupil Godfrey Schalken.

Early on the next day there arrived, from various quarters of the town, rich presents of silks, velvets, jewellery, and so forth, for Rose; and also a packet directed to Gerard Douw, which on being opened, was found to contain a contract of marriage, formally drawn up, between Wilken Vanderhausen of the *Boom-quay*, in Rotterdam, and Rose Velderkaust of Leyden, niece to Gerard Douw, master in the art of painting, also of the same city; and containing engagements on the part of Vanderhausen to make settlements upon his bride, far more splendid than he had before led her guardian to believe likely, and which were to be secured to her use in the most unexceptionable manner possible – the money being placed in the hand of Gerard Douw himself.

I have no sentimental scenes to describe, no cruelty of guardians, no magnanimity of wards, no agonies, or transport of lovers. The record I have to make is one of sordidness, levity, and heartlessness. In less than a week after the first interview which we have just described, the contract of marriage was fulfilled, and Schalken saw the prize which he would have risked existence to secure, carried off in solemn pomp by his repulsive rival. For two or three days he absented himself from the school; he then returned and worked, if with less cheerfulness, with far more dogged resolution than before; the stimulus of love had given place to that of ambition. Months passed away, and, contrary to his expectation, and, indeed, to the direct promise of the parties, Gerard Douw heard nothing of his niece or her worshipful spouse. The interest of the money, which was to have been demanded in quarterly sums, lay unclaimed in his hands.

He began to grow extremely uneasy. Minheer Vanderhausen's direction in Rotterdam he was fully possessed of; after some irresolution he finally determined to journey thither – a trifling undertaking, and easily accomplished – and thus to satisfy himself of the safety and comfort of his ward, for whom he entertained an honest and strong affection. His search was in vain, however; no one in Rotterdam had ever heard of Minheer Vanderhausen. Gerard Douw left not a house in the *Boom-quay* untried, but all in vain. No one could give him any information whatever touching the object of his inquiry, and he was obliged to return to Leyden nothing wiser and far more anxious than when he had left it.

On his arrival he hastened to the establishment from which Vanderhausen had hired the lumbering, though, considering the times, most luxurious vehicle, which the bridal party had employed to convey them to Rotterdam. From the driver of this machine he learned, that having proceeded by slow stages, they had late in the evening approached Rotterdam; but that before they entered the city, and while yet nearly a mile from it, a small party of men, soberly clad, and after the old fashion, with peaked beards and moustaches, standing in the centre of the road, obstructed the further progress of the carriage. The driver reined in his horses, much fearing, from the obscurity of the hour, and the loneliness, of the road, that some mischief was intended. His fears were, however, somewhat allayed by his observing that these strange men carried a large litter, of an antique shape, and which they immediately set down upon the pavement, whereupon the bridegroom, having opened the coach-door from within, descended, and having assisted his bride to do likewise, led her, weeping bitterly, and wringing her hands, to the litter, which they both entered. It was then raised by the men who surrounded it, and speedily carried towards the city, and before it had proceeded very far, the darkness concealed it from the view of the Dutch coachman. In the inside of the vehicle he found a purse, whose contents more than thrice paid the hire of the carriage and man. He saw and could tell nothing more of Minheer Vanderhausen and his beautiful lady.

This mystery was a source of profound anxiety and even grief to Gerard Douw. There was evidently fraud in the dealing of Vanderhausen with him, though for what purpose committed he could not imagine. He greatly doubted how far it was possible for a man possessing such a countenance to be anything but a villain, and every day that passed without his hearing from or of his niece, instead of inducing him to forget his fears, on the contrary tended more and more to aggravate them. The loss of her cheerful society tended also to depress his spirits; and in order to dispel the gloom, which often crept upon his mind after his daily occupations were over, he was wont frequently to ask Schalken to accompany him home, and share his otherwise solitary supper.

One evening, the painter and his pupil were sitting by the fire, having accomplished a comfortable meal, and had yielded to the silent and delicious melancholy of digestion, when their ruminations were disturbed by a loud sound at the street door, as if occasioned by some person rushing and scrambling vehemently against it. A domestic had run without delay to ascertain the cause of the disturbance, and they heard him twice or thrice interrogate the applicant for admission, but without eliciting any other answer but a sustained reiteration of the sounds. They heard him then open the hall-door, and immediately there followed a light and rapid tread on the staircase. Schalken advanced towards the door. It opened before he reached it, and Rose rushed into the room. She looked wild, fierce and haggard with terror and exhaustion, but her dress surprised them as much as even her unexpected appearance. It consisted of a kind of white woollen wrapper, made close about the neck, and descending to the very ground. It was much deranged and travel-soiled. The poor creature had hardly entered the chamber when she fell senseless on the floor. With some difficulty they succeeded in reviving her, and on recovering her senses, she instantly exclaimed, in a tone of terror rather than mere impatience:

"Wine! Wine! Quickly, or I'm lost!"

Astonished and almost scared at the strange agitation in which the call was made, they at once administered to her wishes, and she drank some wine with a haste and eagerness which surprised them. She had hardly swallowed it, when she exclaimed, with the same urgency:

"Food, for God's sake, food, at once, or I perish."

A considerable fragment of a roast joint was upon the table, and Schalken immediately began to cut some, but he was anticipated, for no sooner did she see it than she caught it, a more than mortal image of famine, and with her hands, and even with her teeth, she tore off the flesh, and swallowed it. When the paroxysm of hunger had been a little appeased, she appeared on a sudden overcome with shame, or it may have been that other more agitating thoughts overpowered and scared her, for she began to weep bitterly and to wring her hands.

"Oh, send for a minister of God," said she; "I am not safe till he comes; send for him speedily."

Gerard Douw despatched a messenger instantly, and prevailed on his niece to allow him to surrender his bedchamber to her use. He also persuaded her to retire to it at once to rest; her consent was extorted upon the condition that they would not leave her for a moment.

"Oh that the holy man were here," she said; "he can deliver me: the dead and the living can never be one: God has forbidden it."

With these mysterious words she surrendered herself to their guidance, and they proceeded to the chamber which Gerard Douw had assigned to her use.

"Do not, do not leave me for a moment," said she; "I am lost for ever if you do."

Gerard Douw's chamber was approached through a spacious apartment, which they were now about to enter. He and Schalken each carried a candle, so that a sufficiency of light was cast upon all surrounding objects. They were now entering the large chamber, which as I have said, communicated with Douw's apartment, when Rose suddenly stopped, and, in a whisper which thrilled them both with horror, she said:

"Oh, God! He is here! He is here! See, see! There he goes!"

She pointed towards the door of the inner room, and Schalken thought he saw a shadowy and ill-defined form gliding into that apartment. He drew his sword, and, raising the candle so as to throw its light with increased distinctness upon the objects in the room, he entered the chamber into which the shadow had glided. No figure was there – nothing but the furniture which belonged to the room, and yet he could not be deceived as to the fact that something had moved before them into the chamber. A sickening dread came upon him, and the cold perspiration broke out in heavy drops upon his forehead; nor was he more composed, when he heard the increased urgency and agony of entreaty, with which Rose implored them not to leave her for a moment.

"I saw him," said she; "he's here. I cannot be deceived; I know him; he's by me; he is with me; he's in the room. Then, for God's sake, as you would save me, do not stir from beside me."

They at length prevailed upon her to lie down upon the bed, where she continued to urge them to stay by her. She frequently uttered incoherent sentences, repeating, again and again, "The dead and the living cannot be one: God has forbidden it." And then again, "Rest to the wakeful – sleep to the sleep-walkers." These and such mysterious and broken sentences, she continued to utter until the clergyman arrived. Gerard Douw began to fear, naturally enough, that terror or ill-treatment had unsettled the poor girl's intellect, and he half suspected, by the suddenness of her appearance, the unseasonableness of the hour, and above all, from the wildness and terror of her manner, that she had made her escape from some place of confinement for lunatics, and was in imminent fear of pursuit. He resolved to summon medical advice as soon as the mind of his niece had been in some measure set at rest by the offices of the clergyman whose attendance she had so earnestly desired; and until this object had been attained, he did not venture to put any questions to her, which might possibly, by reviving painful or horrible recollections, increase her agitation. The clergyman soon arrived – a man of ascetic countenance and venerable age – one whom Gerard Douw respected very much, forasmuch as he was a veteran polemic, though one perhaps more dreaded as a combatant than beloved as a Christian – of pure morality, subtle brain, and frozen heart. He entered the chamber which communicated with that in which Rose reclined and immediately on his arrival, she requested him to pray for her, as for one who lay in the hands of Satan, and who could hope for deliverance only from heaven.

That you may distinctly understand all the circumstances of the event which I am going to describe, it is necessary to state the relative position of the parties who were engaged in it. The old clergyman and Schalken were in the anteroom of which I have already spoken; Rose lay in the inner chamber, the door of which was open; and by the side of the bed, at her urgent desire, stood her guardian; a candle burned in the bedchamber, and three were lighted in the outer apartment. The old man now cleared his voice as if about to commence, but before he had time to begin, a sudden gust of air blew out the candle which served to illuminate the room in which the poor girl lay, and she, with hurried alarm, exclaimed:

"Godfrey, bring in another candle; the darkness is unsafe."

Gerard Douw forgetting for the moment her repeated injunctions, in the immediate impulse, stepped from the bedchamber into the other, in order to supply what she desired.

"Oh God! Do not go, dear uncle," shrieked the unhappy girl – and at the same time she sprung from the bed, and darted after him, in order, by her grasp, to detain him. But the warning came too late, for scarcely had he passed the threshold, and hardly had his niece had time to utter the startling exclamation, when the door which divided the two rooms closed violently after him, as if swung by a strong blast of wind. Schalken and he both rushed to the door, but their united and desperate efforts could not avail so much as to shake it. Shriek after shriek burst from the inner chamber, with all the piercing loudness of despairing terror. Schalken and Douw applied every nerve to force open the door; but all in vain. There was no sound of struggling from within, but the screams seemed to increase in loudness, and at the same time they heard the bolts of the latticed window withdrawn, and the window itself grated upon the sill as if thrown open. One *last* shriek, so long and piercing and agonised as to be scarcely human, swelled from the room, and suddenly there followed a death-like silence. A light step was heard crossing the floor, as if from the bed to the window; and almost at the same instant the door gave way, and, yielding to the pressure of the external applicants, nearly precipitated them into the room. It was empty. The window was open, and Schalken sprung to a chair and gazed out upon the street and canal below. He saw no form, but he saw, or thought he saw, the waters of the broad canal beneath settling ring after ring in heavy circles, as if a moment before disturbed by the submission of some ponderous body.

No trace of Rose was ever after found, nor was anything certain respecting her mysterious wooer discovered or even suspected – no clue whereby to trace the intricacies of the labyrinth and to arrive at its solution, presented itself. But an incident occurred, which, though it will not be received by our rational readers in lieu of evidence, produced nevertheless a strong and a lasting impression upon the mind of Schalken. Many years after the events which we have detailed, Schalken, then residing far away, received an intimation of his father's death, and of his intended burial upon a fixed day in the church of Rotterdam. It was necessary that a very considerable journey should be performed by the funeral procession, which as it will be readily believed, was not very numerously attended. Schalken with difficulty arrived in Rotterdam late in the day upon which the funeral was appointed to take place. It had not then arrived. Evening closed in, and still it did not appear.

Schalken strolled down to the church; he found it open; notice of the arrival of the funeral had been given, and the vault in which the body was to be laid had been opened. The sexton, on seeing a well-dressed gentleman, whose object was to attend the expected obsequies, pacing the aisle of the church, hospitably invited him to share with him the comforts of a blazing fire, which, as was his custom in winter time upon such occasions, he had kindled in the hearth of a chamber in which he was accustomed to await the arrival of such grisly guests and which communicated, by a flight of steps, with the vault below. In this chamber, Schalken and his entertainer seated themselves; and the sexton, after some fruitless attempts to engage his guest in conversation, was obliged to apply himself to his tobacco-pipe and can, to solace his solitude. In spite of his grief and cares, the fatigues of a rapid journey of nearly forty hours gradually overcame the mind and body of Godfrey Schalken, and he sank into a deep sleep, from which he awakened by someone's shaking him gently by the shoulder. He first thought that the old sexton had called him, but *he* was no longer in the room. He roused himself, and as soon as he could clearly see what was around him, he perceived a female form, clothed in a kind of light robe of white, part of which was so disposed as to form a veil, and in her hand she carried a lamp. She was moving rather away from him, in the direction of the flight of steps which conducted towards the vaults. Schalken felt a vague alarm at the sight of this figure and at the same time an irresistible impulse to follow its guidance. He followed it towards the vaults, but when it reached the head of the stairs, he paused; the figure paused also, and, turning gently round, displayed, by the light of the lamp it carried, the face and features of his first love, Rose Velderkaust. There was nothing horrible, or even sad, in the countenance. On the contrary, it wore the same arch smile which used to enchant the artist long before in his happy days. A feeling of awe and interest, too intense to be resisted, prompted him to follow the spectre, if spectre it were. She descended the stairs – he followed – and turning to the left, through a narrow passage, she led him, to his infinite surprise, into what appeared to be an old-fashioned Dutch apartment, such as the pictures of Gerard Douw have served to immortalise. Abundance of costly antique furniture was disposed about the room, and in one corner stood a four-post bed, with heavy black cloth curtains around it; the figure frequently turned towards him with the same arch smile; and when she came to the side of the bed, she drew the curtains, and, by the light of the lamp, which she held towards its contents, she disclosed to the horror-stricken painter, sitting bolt upright in the bed, the livid and demoniac form of Vanderhausen. Schalken had hardly seen him, when he fell senseless upon the floor, where he lay until discovered, on the next morning, by persons employed in closing the passages into the vaults. He was lying in a cell of considerable size, which had not been disturbed for a long time, and he had fallen beside a large coffin, which was supported upon small pillars, a security against the attacks of vermin.

To his dying day Schalken was satisfied of the reality of the vision which he had witnessed, and he has left behind him a curious evidence of the impression which it wrought upon his fancy, in a painting executed shortly after the event I have narrated, and which is valuable as exhibiting not only the peculiarities which have made Schalken's pictures sought after, but even more so as presenting a portrait of his early love, Rose Velderkaust, whose mysterious fate must always remain matter of speculation.

Green Branches

Fiona Macleod

IN THE YEAR that followed the death of Manus MacCodrum, James Achanna saw nothing of his brother Gloom. He might have thought himself alone in the world, of all his people, but for a letter that came to him out of the west. True, he had never accepted the common opinion that his brothers had both been drowned on that night when Anne Gillespie left Eilanmore with Manus.

In the first place he had nothing of that inner conviction concerning the fate of Gloom which he had concerning that of Marcus; in the next, had he not heard the sound of the *feadan*, which no one that he knew played except Gloom; and, for further token, was not the tune that which he hated above all others – the 'Dance of the Dead' – for who but Gloom would be playing that, he hating it so, and the hour being late, and no one else on Eilanmore? It was no sure thing that the dead had not come back; but the more he thought of it the more Achanna believed that his sixth brother was still alive. Of this, however, he said nothing to anyone.

It was as a man set free that, at last, after long waiting and patient trouble, with the disposal of all that was left of the Achanna heritage, he left the island. It was a grey memory for him. The bleak moorland of it, the blight that had lain so long and so often upon the crops, the rains that had swept the isle for grey days and grey weeks and grey months, the sobbing of the sea by day and its dark moan by night, its dim relinquishing sigh in the calm of dreary ebbs, its hollow, baffling roar when the storm-shadow swept up out of the sea – one and all oppressed him, even in memory. He had never loved the island, even when it lay green and fragrant in the green and white seas under white and blue skies, fresh and sweet as an Eden of the sea.

He had ever been lonely and weary, tired of the mysterious shadow that lay upon his folk, caring little for any of his brothers except the eldest – long since mysteriously gone out of the ken of man – and almost hating Gloom, who had ever borne him a grudge because of his beauty, and because of his likeness to and reverent heed for Alison. Moreover, ever since he had come to love Katreen Macarthur, the daughter of Donald Macarthur who lived in the Sleat of Skye, he had been eager to live near her; the more eager as he knew that Gloom loved the girl also, and wished for success not only for his own sake, but so as to put a slight upon his younger brother.

So, when at last he left the island, he sailed southward gladly. He was leaving Eilanmore; he was bound to a new home in Skye, and perhaps he was going to his long-delayed, long dreamed-of happiness. True, Katreen was not pledged to him; he did not even know for sure if she loved him. He thought, hoped, dreamed, almost believed that she did; but then there was her cousin Ian, who had long wooed her, and to whom old Donald Macarthur had given his blessing. Nevertheless, his heart would have been lighter than it had been for long, but for two things. First, there was the letter. Some weeks earlier he had received it, not recognising the writing, because of the few letters he had ever seen, and, moreover, as it was in a feigned hand. With difficulty he had deciphered the manuscript, plain printed though it was. It ran thus:

Well, Sheumais, my brother, it is wondering if I am dead, you will be. Maybe ay, and maybe no. But I send you this writing to let you know that I know all you do and think of.

So you are going to leave Eilanmore without an Achanna upon it? And you will be going to Sleat in Skye? Well, let me be telling you this thing. Do not go. I see blood there. And there is this, too: neither you nor any man shall take Katreen away from me. You know that; and Ian Macarthur knows it; and Katreen knows it; and that holds whether I am alive or dead. I say to you: do not go. It will be better for you, and for all. Ian Macarthur is away in the north sea with the whaler-captain who came to us at Eilanmore, and will not be back for three months yet. It will be better for him not to come back. But if he comes back he will have to reckon with the man who says that Katreen Macarthur is his. I would rather not have two men to speak to, and one my brother. It does not matter to you where I am. I want no money just now. But put aside my portion for me. Have it ready for me against the day I call for it. I will not be patient that day; so have it ready for me. In the place that I am I am content. You will be saying: why is my brother away in a remote place (I will say this to you: that it is not further north than St. Kilda nor further south than the Mull of Cantyre!), and for what reason? That is between me and silence. But perhaps you think of Anne sometimes. Do you know that she lies under the green grass? And of Manus MacCodrum? They say that he swam out into the sea and was drowned; and they whisper of the seal-blood, though the minister is wrath with them for that. He calls it a madness. Well, I was there at that madness, and I played to it on my feadan. And now, Sheumais, can you be thinking of what the tune was that I played?

Your brother, who waits his own day,
GLOOM

Do not be forgetting this thing: I would rather not be playing the 'Damhsa-na-Mairbh'. It was an ill hour for Manus when he heard the 'Dan-nan-Ron'; it was the song of his soul, that; and yours is the 'Davsa-na-Mairv'.

This letter was ever in his mind; this, and what happened in the gloaming when he sailed away for Skye in the herring-smack of two men who lived at Armandale in Sleat. For, as the boat moved slowly out of the haven, one of the men asked him if he was sure that no one was left upon the island; for he thought he had seen a figure on the rocks, waving a black scarf. Achanna shook his head; but just then his companion cried that at that moment he had seen the same thing. So the smack was put about, and when she was moving slowly through the haven again, Achanna sculled ashore in the little coggly punt. In vain he searched here and there, calling loudly again and again. Both men could hardly have been mistaken, he thought. If there were no human creature on the island, and if their eyes had not played them false, who could it be? The wraith of Marcus, mayhap; or might it be the old man himself (his father), risen to bid farewell to his youngest son, or to warn him?

It was no use to wait longer, so, looking often behind him, he made his way to the boat again, and rowed slowly out toward the smack.

Jerk – jerk – jerk across the water came, low but only too loud for him, the opening motif of the 'Damhsa-na-Mairbh'. A horror came upon him, and he drove the boat through the water so that the sea splashed over the bows. When he came on deck he cried in a hoarse voice to the man next him to put up the helm, and let the smack swing to the wind.

"There is no one there, Callum Campbell," he whispered.

"And who is it that will be making that strange music?"

"What music?"

"Sure it has stopped now, but I heard it clear, and so did Anndra MacEwan. It was like the sound of a reed pipe, and the tune was an eery one at that."

"It was the Dance of the Dead."

"And who will be playing that?" asked the man, with fear in his eyes.

"No living man."

"No living man?"

"No. I'm thinking it will be one of my brothers who was drowned here, and by the same token that it is Gloom, for he played upon the *feadan*. But if not, then – then—"

The two men waited in breathless silence, each trembling with superstitious fear; but at last the elder made a sign to Achanna to finish.

"Then – it will be the Kelpie."

"Is there – is there one of the – cave-women here?"

"It is said; and you know of old that the Kelpie sings or plays a strange tune to wile seamen to their death."

At that moment the fantastic, jerking music came loud and clear across the bay. There was a horrible suggestion in it, as if dead bodies were moving along the ground with long jerks, and crying and laughing wild. It was enough; the men, Campbell and MacEwan, would not now have waited longer if Achanna had offered them all he had in the world. Nor were they, or he, out of their panic haste till the smack stood well out at sea, and not a sound could be heard from Eilanmore.

They stood watching, silent. Out of the dusky mass that lay in the seaward way to the north came a red gleam. It was like an eye staring after them with blood-red glances.

"What is that, Achanna?"

"It looks as though a fire had been lighted in the house up in the island. The door and the window must be open. The fire must be fed with wood, for no peats would give that flame; and there were none lighted when I left. To my knowing, there was no wood for burning except the wood of the shelves and the bed."

"And who would be doing that?"

"I know of that no more than you do, Callum Campbell."

No more was said, and it was a relief to all when the last glimmer of the light was absorbed in the darkness.

At the end of the voyage Campbell and MacEwan were well pleased to be quit of their companion; not so much because he was moody and distraught as because they feared that a spell was upon him – a fate in the working of which they might become involved. It needed no vow of the one to the other for them to come to the conclusion that they would never land on Eilanmore, or, if need be, only in broad daylight, and never alone.

* * *

The days went well for James Achanna, where he made his home at Ranza-beag, on Ranza Water in the Sleat of Skye. The farm was small but good, and he hoped that with help and care he would soon have the place as good a farm as there was in all Skye.

Donald Macarthur did not let him see much of Katreen, but the old man was no longer opposed to him. Sheumais must wait till Ian Macarthur came back again, which might be any day now. For sure, James Achanna of Ranza-beag was a very different person from the youngest of the Achanna-folk, who held by on lonely Eilanmore; moreover, the old man could not but think with pleasure that it would be well to see Katreen able to walk over the whole land of Ranza, from the cairn at the north of his own Ranza-Mòr to the burn at the south of Ranza-beag, and know it for her own.

But Achanna was ready to wait. Even before he had the secret word of Katreen he knew from her beautiful dark eyes that she loved him. As the weeks went by they managed to meet often, and at last Katreen told him that she loved him too, and would have none but him; but that they must wait till Ian came back, because of the pledge given to him by her father. They were days of joy for him. Through many a hot noon-tide hour, through many a gloaming he went as one in a dream. Whenever he saw a birch swaying in the wind, or a wave leaping upon Loch Laith, that was near his home, or passed a bush covered with wild roses, or saw the moonbeams lying white on the boles of the pines, he thought of Katreen – his fawn for grace, and so lithe and tall, with sunbrown face and wavy, dark mass of hair, and shadowy eyes and rowan-red lips. It is said that there is a god clothed in shadow who goes to and fro among the human kind, putting silence between lovers with his waving hands, and breathing a chill out of his cold breath, and leaving a gulf of deep water flowing between them because of the passing of his feet. That shadow never came their way. Their love grew as a flower fed by rains and warmed by sunlight.

When midsummer came, and there was no sign of Ian Macarthur, it was already too late. Katreen had been won.

During the summer months it was the custom for Katreen and two of the farm-girls to go up Maol-Ranza, to reside at the shealing of Cnoc-an-Fhraoch: and this because of the hill-pasture for the sheep. Cnoc-an-Fhraoch is a round, boulder-studded hill covered with heather, which has a precipitous corrie on each side, and in front slopes down to Lochan Fraoch, a lochlet surrounded by dark woods. Behind the hill, or great hillock rather, lay the shealing. At each weekend Katreen went down to Ramza-Mòr, and on every Monday morning at sunrise returned to her heather-girt eerie. It was on one of these visits that she endured a cruel shock. Her father told her that she must marry someone else than Sheumais Achanna. He had heard words about him which made a union impossible, and indeed, he hoped that the man would leave Ranza-beag. In the end he admitted that what he had heard was to the effect that Achanna was under a doom of some kind, that he was involved in a blood-feud; and, moreover, that he was fey. The old man would not be explicit as to the person from whom his information came, but hinted that he was a stranger of rank, probably a laird of the isles. Besides this, there was word of Ian Macarthur. He was at Thurso, in the far north, and would be in Skye before long, and he – her father – had written to him that he might wed Katreen as soon as was practicable.

"Do you see that lintie yonder, father?" was her response to this.

"Ay, lass, and what about the birdeen?"

"Well, when she mates with a hawk, so will I be mating with Ian Macarthur, but not till then."

With that she turned and left the house, and went back to Cnoc-an-Fhraoch. On the way she met Achanna.

It was that night that for the first time he swam across Lochan Fraoch to meet Katreen.

The quickest way to reach the shealing was to row across the lochlet, and then ascend by a sheep-path that wound through the hazel copses at the base of the hill. Fully half an hour was thus saved, because of the steepness of the precipitous corries to right and left. A boat was kept for this purpose, but it was fastened to a shore boulder by a padlocked iron chain, the key of which was kept by Donald Macarthur. Latterly he had refused to let this key out of his possession. For one thing, no doubt, he believed he could thus restrain Achanna from visiting his daughter. The young man could not approach the shealing from either side without being seen.

But that night, soon after the moon was whitening slow in the dark, Katreen stole down to the hazel copse and awaited the coming of her lover. The lochan was visible from almost any point on Cnoc-an-Fhraoch, as well as from the south side. To cross it in a boat unseen, if any watcher were near, would be impossible, nor could even a swimmer hope to escape notice unless in the gloom of night or, mayhap, in the dusk. When, however, she saw, halfway across the water, a spray of green branches slowly moving athwart the surface, she knew that Sheumais was keeping his tryst.

If, perchance, anyone else saw, he or she would never guess that those derelict rowan branches shrouded Sheumais Achanna.

It was not till the estray had drifted close to the hedge, where, hid among the bracken and the hazel undergrowth, she awaited him, that Katreen descried the face of her lover, as with one hand he parted the green sprays, and stared longingly and lovingly at the figure he could just discern in the dim, fragrant obscurity.

And as it was this night so was it many of the nights that followed. Katreen spent the days as in a dream. Not even the news of her cousin Ian's return disturbed her much.

One day the inevitable meeting came. She was at Ranza-Mòr, and when a shadow came into the dairy where she was standing she looked up, and saw Ian before her. She thought he appeared taller and stronger than ever, though still not so tall as Sheumais, who would appear slim beside the Herculean Skyeman. But as she looked at his close curling black hair and thick bull-neck and the sullen eyes in his dark wind-red face, she wondered that she had ever tolerated him at all.

He broke the ice at once.

"Tell me, Katreen, are you glad to see me back again?"

"I am glad that you are home once more safe and sound."

"And will you make it my home for me by coming to live with me, as I've asked you again and again?"

"No: as I've told you again and again."

He gloomed at her angrily for a few moments before he resumed.

"I will be asking you this one thing, Katreen, daughter of my father's brother: do you love that man Achanna who lives at Ranza-beag?"

"You may ask the wind why it is from the east or the west, but it won't tell you. You're not the wind's master."

"If you think I will let this man take you away from me, you are thinking a foolish thing."

"And you saying a foolisher."

"Ay?"

"Ah, sure. What could you do, Ian Mhic Ian? At the worst, you could do no more than kill James Achanna. What then? I too would die. You cannot separate us. I would not marry you, now, though you were the last man in the world and I the last woman."

"You are a fool, Katreen Macarthur. Your father has promised you to me, and I tell you this: if you love Achanna you'll save his life only by letting him go away from here. I promise you he will not be here long."

"Ah, you promise *me*; but you will not say that thing to James Achanna's face. You are a coward."

With a muttered oath the man turned on his heel.

"Let him beware o' me, and you, too, Katreen-mo-nighean-donn. I swear it by my mother's grave and by St. Martin's Cross that you will be mine by hook or by crook."

The girl smiled scornfully. Slowly she lifted a milk-pail.

"It would be a pity to waste the good milk, Ian-gòrach, but if you don't go it is I that will be emptying the pail on you, and then you will be as white without as your heart is within."

"So you call me witless, do you? *Ian-gòrach!* Well, we shall be seeing as to that. And as for the milk, there will be more than milk spilt because of *you*, Katreen-donn."

From that day, though neither Sheumais nor Katreen knew of it, a watch was set upon Achanna.

It could not be long before their secret was discovered, and it was with a savage joy overmastering his sullen rage that Ian Macarthur knew himself the discoverer, and conceived his double vengeance. He dreamed, gloatingly, on both the black thoughts that roamed like ravenous beasts through the solitudes of his heart. But he did not dream that another man was filled with hate because of Katreen's lover, another man who had sworn to make her his own, the man who, disguised, was known in Armandale as Donald McLean, and in the north isles would have been hailed as Gloom Achanna.

There had been steady rain for three days, with a cold, raw wind. On the fourth the sun shone, and set in peace. An evening of quiet beauty followed, warm, fragrant, dusky from the absence of moon or star, though the thin veils of mist promised to disperse as the night grew.

There were two men that eve in the undergrowth on the south side of the lochlet. Sheumais had come earlier than his wont. Impatient for the dusk, he could scarce await the waning of the afterglow; surely, he thought, he might venture. Suddenly his ears caught the sound of cautious footsteps. Could it be old Donald, perhaps with some inkling of the way in which his daughter saw her lover in despite of all; or, mayhap, might it be Ian Macarthur, tracking him as a hunter stalking a stag by the water-pools? He crouched, and waited. In a few minutes he saw Ian carefully picking his way. The man stopped as he descried the green branches; smiled as, with a low rustling, he raised them from the ground.

Meanwhile yet another man watched and waited, though on the farther side of the lochan, where the hazel copses were. Gloom Achanna half hoped, half feared the approach of Katreen. It would be sweet to see her again, sweet to slay her lover before her eyes, brother to him though he was. But, there was chance that she might descry him, and, whether recognisingly or not, warn the swimmer.

So it was that he had come there before sundown, and now lay crouched among the bracken underneath a projecting mossy ledge close upon the water, where it could scarce be that she or any should see him.

As the gloaming deepened a great stillness reigned. There was no breath of wind. A scarce audible sigh prevailed among the spires of the heather. The churring of a night-jar throbbed through the darkness. Somewhere a corncrake called its monotonous *crek-craik*; the dull, harsh sound emphasising the utter stillness. The pinging of the gnats hovering over and among the sedges made an incessant murmur through the warm, sultry air.

There was a splash once as of a fish. Then, silence. Then a lower but more continuous splash, or rather wash of water. A slow *susurrus* rustled through the dark.

Where he lay among the fern Gloom Achanna slowly raised his head, stared through the shadows and listened intently. If Katreen were waiting there she was not near.

Noiselessly he slid into the water. When he rose it was under a clump of green branches. These he had cut and secured three hours before. With his left hand he swam slowly, or kept his equipoise in the water; with his right he guided the heavy rowan bough. In his mouth were two objects, one long and thin and dark, the other with an occasional glitter as of a dead fish.

His motion was scarcely perceptible. Nonetheless he was near the middle of the loch almost as soon as another clump of green branches. Doubtless the swimmer beneath it was confident that he was now safe from observation.

The two clumps of green branches drew nearer. The smaller seemed a mere estray, a spray blown down by the recent gale. But all at once the larger clump jerked awkwardly and stopped. Simultaneously a strange, low strain of music came from the other.

The strain ceased. The two clumps of green branches remained motionless. Slowly, at last, the larger moved forward. It was too dark for the swimmer to see if anyone lay hid behind the smaller. When he reached it he thrust aside the leaves.

It was as though a great salmon leaped. There was a splash, and a narrow, dark body shot through the gloom. At the end of it something gleamed. Then suddenly there was a savage struggle. The inanimate green branches tore this way and that, and surged and swirled. Gasping cries came from the leaves. Again and again the gleaming thing leaped. At the third leap an awful scream shrilled through the silence. The echo of it wailed thrice, with horrible distinctness, in the corrie beyond Cnoc-an-Fhraoch. Then, after a faint splashing, there was silence once more. One clump of green branches drifted slowly up the lochlet. The other moved steadily toward the place whence, a brief while before, it had stirred.

Only one thing lived in the heart of Gloom Achanna – the joy of his exultation. He had killed his brother Sheumais. He had always hated him because of his beauty; of late he had hated him because he had stood between him, Gloom, and Katreen Macarthur – because he had become her lover. They were all dead now except himself, all the Achannas. He was 'Achanna'. When the day came that he would go back to Galloway, there would be a magpie on the first birk, and a screaming jay on the first rowan, and a croaking raven on the first fir; ay, he would be their suffering, though they knew nothing of him meanwhile! He would be Achanna of Achanna again. Let those who would stand in his way beware. As for Katreen: perhaps he would take her there, perhaps not. He smiled.

These thoughts were the wandering fires in his brain while he slowly swam shoreward under the floating green branches, and as he disengaged himself from them and crawled upward through the bracken. It was at this moment that a third man entered the water from the further shore.

Prepared as he was to come suddenly upon Katreen, Gloom was startled when, in a place of dense shadow, a hand touched his shoulder, and her voice whispered:

"Sheumais, Sheumais!"

The next moment she was in his arms. He could feel her heart beating against his.

"What is it, Sheumais? What was that awful cry?" she whispered.

For answer he put his lips to hers, and kissed her again and again.

The girl drew back. Some vague instinct warned her.

"What is it, Sheumais? Why don't you speak?"

He drew her close again.

"Pulse of my heart, it is I who love you, I who love you best of all; it is I, Gloom Achanna!"

With a cry she struck him full in the face. He staggered and in that moment she freed herself.

"You *coward*!"

"Katreen, I—"

"Come no nearer. If you do, it will be the death of you!"

"The death o' me! Ah, bonnie fool that you are, and is it you that will be the death o' me?"

"Ay, Gloom Achanna, for I have but to scream and Sheumais will be here, an' he would kill you like a dog if he knew you did me harm."

"Ah, but if there were no Sheumais, or any man to come between me an' my will!"

"Then there would be a woman! Ay, if you overbore me I would strangle you with my hair, or fix my teeth in your false throat!"

"I was not for knowing you were such a wild-cat; but I'll tame you yet, my lass! Aha, wild-cat!" And as he spoke he laughed low.

"It is a true word, Gloom of the black heart. I am a wild-cat, and, like a wild-cat, I am not to be seized by a fox; and that you will be finding to your cost, by the holy St. Bridget! But now, off with you, brother of my man!"

"Your man – ha! ha!"

"Why do you laugh?"

"Sure, I am laughing at a warm, white lass like yourself having a dead man as your lover!"

"A – dead – man?"

No answer came. The girl shook with a new fear. Slowly she drew closer, till her breath fell warm against the face of the other.

He spoke at last: "Ay, a dead man."

"It is a lie."

"Where would you be that you were not hearing his goodbye? I'm thinking it was loud enough!"

"It is a lie – it is a lie!"

"No, it is no lie. Sheumais is cold enough now. He's low among the weeds by now. Ay, by now: down there in the lochan."

"*What* – you, *you devil*! Is it for killing your own brother you would be?"

"I killed no one. He died his own way. Maybe the cramp took him. Maybe – maybe a Kelpie gripped him. I watched. I saw him beneath the green branches. He was dead before he died. I saw it in the white face o' him. Then he sank. He's dead. Sheumais is dead. Look here, girl, I've always loved you. I swore the oath upon you. You're mine. Sure, you're mine now, Katreen! It is loving you I am! It will be a south wind for you from this day, muirnean mochree! See here, I'll show you how I—"

"Back – back – *murderer*!"

"Be stopping that foolishness now, Katreen Macarthur! By the Book, I am tired of it. I am loving you, and it's having you for mine I am! And if you won't come to me like the dove to its mate, I'll come to you like the hawk to the dove!"

With a spring he was upon her. In vain she strove to beat him back. His arms held her as a stoat grips a rabbit.

He pulled her head back, and kissed her throat till the strangulating breath sobbed against his ear. With a last despairing effort she screamed the name of the dead man: "Sheumais! Sheumais! Sheumais!" The man who struggled with her laughed.

"Ay, call away! The herrin' will be coming through the bracken as soon as Sheumais comes to your call! Ah, it is mine you are now, Katreen! He's dead and cold – an' you'd best have a living man – an'—"

She fell back, her balance lost in the sudden releasing. What did it mean? Gloom still stood there, but as one frozen. Through the darkness she saw, at last, that a hand gripped his shoulder; behind him a black mass vaguely obtruded.

For some moments there was absolute silence. Then a hoarse voice came out of the dark:

"You will be knowing now who it is, Gloom Achanna!"

The voice was that of Sheumais, who lay dead in the lochan. The murderer shook as in a palsy. With a great effort, slowly he turned his head. He saw a white splatch, the face of the corpse; in this white splatch flamed two burning eyes, the eyes of the soul of the brother whom he had slain.

He reeled, staggered as a blind man, and, free now of that awful clasp, swayed to and fro as one drunken.

Slowly Sheumais raised an arm and pointed downward through the wood toward the lochan. Still pointing, he moved swiftly forward.

With a cry like a beast, Gloom Achanna swung to one side, stumbled, rose, and leaped into the darkness.

For some minutes Sheumais and Katreen stood, silent, apart, listening to the crashing sound of his flight – the race of the murderer against the pursuing shadow of the Grave.

We Were Supposed to Be Happy

J.A.W. McCarthy

I DIDN'T BELIEVE my sister until I watched her cough up our mother into the bathroom sink. There, surrounded by pale pink tile, she hovered over the basin as a pearlescent form, bruise-grey and burst-veined like a diseased organ, slithered from her mouth. No bigger than my fist, it shuddered in the sink before bursting open and releasing what looked like a puff of smoke that swirled around our heads then raced out the open window. After wiping the oily bile from her mouth, my sister said she felt much better.

Before our mother died, June had been the optimistic one. When Mother called me a whore for wanting to attend a school dance, June told me she hoped I got kissed that night so I could tell her what it was like. When Mother locked her in the broom closet for laughing during church television, June said she was relieved because she would rather be reading the back of the Clorox bottle. When our mother pinned her across her lap and spanked her at age sixteen for stealing her cigarettes, June never cried as I whispered that I was sorry. June was the first to call our wounds battle scars. Throughout our childhood she came up with the most outrageous, elaborate plans to murder our mother, describing iced-over porch steps and unstable shelves laden with dog shit and raccoon carcasses ("The shelf would knock her out and then she would smother in the dog shit, Edie. The raccoons are just there because she hates them.") until I was blind and doubled-over from laughter. Even under our mother's judgmental eye, June found joy in what we could one day have.

June had just finished high school when our mother took a tumble down the stairs. In her will she left us the house and the burden of planning a funeral that no one would attend. We didn't care, though; we lounged around the house in our new party dresses, singing along with Stevie Nicks on the radio and gorging ourselves on cinnamon coffee cake and vanilla fudge during the body-less wake we had so carefully arranged. We stayed up all night watching movies where people kissed and took off their clothes and sometimes got murdered by madmen in the woods. We dug up our records from the backyard and played them so loud that the windows rattled. For the first time June talked about college and maybe becoming an architect or a graphic designer or a veterinarian. It wasn't until we saw our mother lowered into the ground that June started to change.

"It's a waste of money," she said one day after I found the college brochures in the garbage. "No point in squandering what little we have on something so prideful."

She started complaining about how her clothes touched her body and said we could have nicer things if I got a better job than bakery cashier. She stopped listening to our records and took up humming instead, these strange, strangled dirges that I had at first mistaken for grumbling under her breath. Often I would awaken to find her sitting at the kitchen table smoking our mother's Virginia Slims, the ashtray already overflowing as if she'd been up since before dawn. When I stayed out late on the weekends, she waited at the window for me, telling me I should be charging if I was going to spread my legs all over town.

At first I thought June was having a delayed reaction to Mother's death, perhaps some lingering guilt from our celebration. Her eyes weighed on me every moment I was in that house and her voice followed me out. I yelled, I shook her hard, I begged her to be my little sister again. I took extra shifts at the bakery even though it hurt to be there. I started dating a man who encouraged me to move to the city with him.

One night, in a rare moment of clarity, June came to my bed in tears, sweat rolling from her hairline and beading along her collarbones. The heat coming off her was so intense that I thought our palms would sear together when she grasped my hand. This was when she first said it.

"Mother's in me, Edie. I see her sometimes when I look in the mirror. She's suffocating me. I can feel her in my chest. I can't breathe."

This is why, after I finally believed her, after I saw her cough up our mother into the bathroom sink, that I try to stay out of her lungs, even though it really is the best place to be.

* * *

I died six months after moving to the city, though I wasn't left for dead in an alley with my panties around my ankles as Mother had predicted. It was after the funeral that I slipped in through June's left nostril, when the casket was being lowered into the ground and I realized I didn't want to go down with it. Outside of my body I was a rush of air, a ghost without a form blindly searching for soft walls to contain me. My sister June was a magnet, all velvet and steam and the irresistible comfort of familiarity. I remember wondering if our mother had felt the same when she chose June, when she gladly let June pull her in.

It wasn't the lure of getting to live again inside a human body that gets to taste and touch and dance and sing. The truth is, I had been abruptly expelled into the stinging cold and I needed warmth again, like when you first step out of a bath. I knew what our mother had done to June, and I didn't want to be that thing that wormed its way through my sister's heart and lungs, smothering and overtaking until June herself was nothing more than a tiny knot in the back of her own mind. Racing around in my sister's throat, I whispered apologies and promised that we could coexist.

Now I mostly alternate between her ear, her eyes, her right hand, and her belly. Curled in the cool tunnel of her ear I can talk to her and know that she understands me. I slide down into her right hand whenever she touches bathwater or kitten fur. When she visits the bakery where I used to work, I linger in her eyes so I can watch Louisa's round hips sway and dip as she bends to take the perfect cupcake from the front of the case. For just a moment I'm back in June's ear as Louisa says she's sorry about Edie – about me – and I hope she means more than my death. Later, at home, I pool in June's belly so I can remember what it felt like to lay my head there and be comforted by the gurgling of her stomach like we used to do as children.

We've been listening to T. Rex and The Pretenders and Leonard Cohen, indulging in sporadic jumping and slow glides around the living room like right after Mother died. I wrap myself around June's tongue whenever she licks the salt off the French fries from our favorite diner in town. She's started wearing my old clothes, taking in the waist a touch and shortening hems, slipping into the lacy things I kept well-hidden when our mother was alive. She preens and poses in front of the mirror in our room, making me gasp when she rips a skirt's seam all the way up her thigh. I can see myself in her reflection, a softly diffused form roughly in the shape I used to hold, crackling and smoking like live flames along the lines of my sister's body. I know she sees me too: she smiles and says, "Your favorite, Edie" as she steps into my green silk dress.

There's lipstick and the tiny gold hoops I used to keep in an envelope under my mattress, then the heels from my apartment in the city. She dabs perfume in the places I thought only I knew: the back of her neck, between her breasts, along her thighs where her stockings clutch her skin.

I don't have to ask; I know where she is going because I was in her right hand when she dialed my husband.

* * *

I can tell that he misses me: boxes of half-eaten pizzas litter every surface of the living room; every ashtray is overflowing, my lipstick-coated butts still lining the bottom of each dish; my purse is still where I left it on the kitchen counter; my plants are all dead; and he looks like shit. He's still buttoning his shirt when he opens the front door, and I can feel my sister's disappointment as she peers over his shoulder to see that he hasn't bothered to clean up for her.

"You look good, Adam," she says, stepping inside.

He's too dampened from the whisky and last night's pills to be taken aback. I know June isn't being sarcastic, though. My husband was always sexiest to me when he was wearing three days of stubble and begging for a haircut, and the smell of stale cigarettes and congealed cheese isn't enough to cool the heat I feel spreading through June's lower belly and down her thighs. She makes him coffee and tells him to eat the cake she brought, all the while making flustered little noises about how thin he's gotten and how he's got to start taking care of himself and how *Edie wouldn't want to see you like this, Adam*. She sits too close to him on the couch, and I race to her nose so I can smell him, so I can burrow through the musk of dried sweat and three-day-old soap and the salt still on his skin from the nights when the whisky ran out.

"I haven't finished boxing up her stuff yet, but I can do it now," he offers, tensing as he starts to rise.

I rush into June's hand and guide it over his, relishing the familiar roughness of his knuckles, his once constant restless energy tame under what's left of me, so grateful to my sister for letting me linger here. "There's no rush. I really just wanted to see how you're doing," June says.

"Shitty, obviously," Adam chuckles, taking back his hand and pushing it through his dark, grease-clumped hair.

It was always easy for me. From the first time I saw him sitting alone in the far corner of the pub, hunched over a tattered paperback and losing his place every time he took a drink, I knew I wanted him, and I made sure he wanted me too. I acted like I didn't enjoy being pushed up against the backs of couches and bathroom stalls, like I was embarrassed by his hand up my skirt under restaurant tables and when our dinner party hosts left the room, but he knew the thrill it gave me and we both loved the game. We kept our hands and our minds busy, and he didn't ever have to swear that he wasn't thinking of anyone else when he was with me. Now I see the spark of recognition in my husband's eyes as June flips her skirt above her knee and guides his hand there. I feel the moisture transfer from his skin to hers, her pulse quickening with his, both their chests seizing in a held breath. I know that look. It's easy for my sister too.

I can't stay out of her lungs. They're exactly where I want to be, riding every quick and heavy breath as she unzips his jeans and slips her hand inside. I'm in her fingers again as she pulls her black lace panties off and presses them into his fist. On my sister's tongue I taste the flesh I never thought I'd know again. I roll inside her chest and slide down her throat and am propelled throughout her body by her racing heart, touching on fingers, filling her lips, alighting for just a moment in her ear. As she straddles him, I spread myself along her thighs, pouring back into her chest at the end so that I can feel his heart speed against hers.

After, while Adam is zipping up and June is smoothing my green silk dress over her knees, a darkness unfurls inside her head, a thick choking haze like city smog that makes it difficult to see through her eyes. She picks up her panties from where they have fallen between the couch cushions and regards them as if they are the stray cats our mother used to shoo away with rocks from the yard. When she next speaks, Adam can barely look at her.

"I know all about it," June says, rising to her feet, towering over my husband as he sits splayed on the brown leather. I am still flushed and pleasantly electric along her limbs, but her words pinch and constrict me. "I know what you did with her and you know it's why she's dead," she continues, the haze between us thickening. "You took my Edie away."

Adam picks up one of the many beer cans from the coffee table, shakes it, then polishes off its stale contents in one sloppy gulp. "You can show yourself out," he says.

* * *

I sit inside my sister's ear and beg her to explain herself as she stands in the shower scrubbing every inch until her skin is glowing red and raw. *Why were you so cruel to him?* I ask. *You always liked him.* She shakes her head so hard that I tumble down into her pelvis.

Once she's satisfied and clean, a growing hunger tosses me around in June's belly, and the heat spreading through her chest makes her lungs too stifling for me to rest. I'm in her mouth, dodging behind teeth and under her tongue as she rampages through a box of saltines then so many eggs fried in butter that I feel a nausea that makes me believe that I have a body again. She sleeps fitfully, sweating even though I make a point to settle in her always-cold feet. She's anxious for morning, and I'm afraid of what's going to happen when she's up at dawn and already rubbing my perfume along the length of her neck.

The bakery doesn't open until seven, but June is there just after six, tapping daintily on the door before the employees arrive. Of course I've been in her eyes, watching through the glass as Louisa heaves enormous trays of mantecados and almond schnicken and cinnamon apple empanadas into the cases. She's already wiped her hands on her apron so many times that the pink-frosting streaked fabric is wadded like a corsage at her waist, and every time she bends to adjust a row of pastel tea cakes I can see the outline of her breasts swing inside her white T-shirt. I didn't fall in love with Louisa because her sweat smelled like yeast dough or her lips tasted of powdered sugar. I loved her because she was generous and stubborn, and she put her back into everything she did, and for a brief time she gave me something better than what I had at home. June was the one who held me and promised me my heart would heal as she pushed her fingers along the back of my head, unaware that Louisa used to do the same for me.

"Hey, sweetie," Louisa greets June as she unlocks the door for her. "The register's not up yet, but I can give you some schnicken for breakfast if you like."

"Yes, that would be nice," June agrees.

My sister sits at a table by the window, absently picking at her pastry while watching my boss putter behind the counter. We take in the smell of warm milk and sugar-frosted steam from the ovens in the back. Louisa starts a pot of coffee and pours June a cup, jovially teasing my sister for being up so early and how it must be because she couldn't wait for one of her famous treats. June doesn't respond, doesn't even smile. She turns her gaze out the window, observing the sky as it lightens in warm bursts of orange into blue into white.

"Did you love my sister?"

Back behind the counter, Louisa drops one of the little cards meant to label a tray of ham and cheddar tarts. She keeps her eyes on it as she retrieves the paper and brushes it against her skirt. "Of course I did. She was a lovely girl, a great employee, she—"

"You know what I mean."

"She was a good friend."

Now I'm on June's tongue, and I'm rolling and bouncing and screaming as if her mouth were my own. I'm screaming *liar* and *coward* and *you told me you loved me every night*, but my sister's teeth don't so much as rattle. Louisa keeps the counter between herself and June as June rises and crosses towards her. I move to my sister's ear so I can hear Louisa's breath quicken as she glances nervously at the clock, expecting JoAnn or Terry to walk in any minute now. *"What would he think?"* she had asked when I grew tired of after-hours gropings and dropped kisses every time her son arrived to take her home. *"He'd never forgive me,"* she had sighed more than once into my hair. Even though I knew he was just an excuse, I joined my mother in hurling vulgarities at the sweet boy who would sometimes deliver his mother's apology cakes to our house.

Why were you so ashamed? I whisper before sliding from June's ear.

Louisa jumps when June slams her palms down on the counter.

"Why were you so ashamed?"

"I don't know what—"

"Don't lie. I know everything."

Louisa's shoulders slump first, this folding in on herself as if her lungs have completely deflated, taking a couple of inches off her already small stature. A tendril of her long black hair slips from the loose bun at the back of her head, a thick loop of shiny silk snaking around her neck, threatening to tighten around her throat.

"You're a coward," June chastises her. "Your son, he's a grown man now – he knows about these things. Don't you think he'd want his mother to be happy? You broke my sister's heart."

"She…she got married. She moved on," Louisa stammers.

"Edie moved to the city. Edie ended up dead."

That's what does it. *Dead*, in the voice of my sister, a voice that sounds just like mine used to. Louisa's lips press into a wavering line against each other and her eyes blur with the sudden weight of tears. I wonder if she's ever really thought about it before this moment, about what she's lost. I wonder if she cried alone like I did that night after she told me it was over. I wonder if she regretted spending her day kneading dough while my funeral took place across town with only my sister and the priest our mother complained was 'too liberal' in attendance.

Louisa wipes her arm roughly over her eyes. Flour mixes with tears across her reddening cheeks. "I'm sorry."

"*Sorry*? That's it? That's hardly even an apology."

"I don't know what else to say, June."

"Tell Edie you love her. Then tell your son. Tell him everything."

"I can't…."

"She died thinking she was nothing to you, thinking you just threw her away."

Louisa doesn't look scared or even surprised when June reaches across the counter and grabs the loose rope of hair curled around her neck. Her dark, wet eyes struggle to stay on June's face as my sister drags the edge of her fingernail slowly across Louisa's fat lower lip, and I race to June's hand so I can relive the tremor of those lips against my skin all warm and soft and pliant. It occurs to me that I have all of eternity to think about those lips the same way I think about my husband's hands.

Louisa closes her eyes for just a moment. With her face now pulled close to June's, I see the recognition surface as she breathes in my perfume. She looks confused by the intimacy, by something I used to do.

"You'll never be happy," my sister says.

I'm in June's chest when she grips the back of Louisa's head and slams it into the side of the pastry case. Nestled against her heart, every staccato beat jolts me like the glass against Louisa's temple. There's a little blood and a crack racing towards the cupcakes, and Louisa is flailing and screaming and grabbing more of her own hair than June's hands. It's easy for my sister, easier than it ever was for me.

Once Louisa is quiet and slumped behind the counter, June grabs a handful of napkins and wipes the blood and stray strands of hair from the pastry case. I allow myself to settle in her lungs, surprised at how her breathing has slowed and how the heat in her chest has cooled to a perfect warm bath that cradles me. I still remember what it feels like to have a heart with its jackrabbit highs and smothering lows and the engine-beat of contentment in between. It's this contentment that fills me, that gives me a shape again, when June smiles at the first employee in as she passes him through the bakery's double doors.

* * *

This is not my sister. This is not my June. This is all me.

I was the one who pocketed cigarettes and lipsticks, and dreamt of humiliating revenge, and plotted arsons. June was the one who told me people are weak and not to dwell and to be patient. She took the hammer from my hands when I stood over Mother's bed at night. She reminded me of who was worth my tears and who wasn't. When I screamed and broke dishes and poured cold water all over the porch steps, June talked me down with promises of what we deserved.

I try to make her expel me, make her cough me up into the bathroom sink like she did with our mother. After she eats, I push my way through her stomach, bouncing up into her throat and back into her gut over and over until she's doubled over and retching, but she always manages to keep me locked in behind her teeth. While she sleeps, I lodge myself in her throat so that she's forced to cough unconsciously, but her tongue always rolls me back inside. It doesn't matter what happens to me, if I will become smoke out the window or if I will cease to exist once I'm outside of her body – I just have to get out so I don't keep hurting my sister the way our mother did.

"We were supposed to be happy," June says one night as she stands in front of the mirror in her nightgown, her fingers busy working through her long blonde hair. I can see myself in her reflection, diffused and crackling at the same time, outlining her body like angry marker strokes over and over again as I race along her edges. I know she can feel me too by the way she rolls her arm, tumbling me back into her chest. "I tried, but I was too late, wasn't I?" she sighs, her words a dull reverberation inside her ribcage.

You have to let me go, June, I say inside her ear.

"Again? Like I let you go when you said you knew what you were doing? Like when you said it wasn't too much and you could handle it?"

I made a mistake.

June finishes braiding her hair, considers herself in the mirror, then shakes her hair loose again, knocking me into the base of her skull. I've been here before, of course, gliding over the surface of my sister's brain, desperately trying to get inside, but never even able to work my way between the folds.

"I had a plan, Edie. It was slow, but it was working. First Mother, then Louisa – I would've left Adam alone, but then all that shit you did together.... If you had any kind of patience, Edie, we could've been happy."

Please, June. This isn't you.

"This isn't me? You think Mother was controlling me? You think *you*'ve been controlling me?" She lets out a huge, gaping laugh, jarring and so much crueler than the ones I remember when she talked about smothering our mother in dog shit or the irony of Louisa's son falling in love with a man. "I'm the one who pushed Mother down the stairs, Edie," she tells me, going back to fussing with her hair. "I'm the one who made sure Louisa got what's coming and I'll be the one who does the same for Adam. All those things you wanted but couldn't do – it's me, Edie. Maybe this is who I really am."

I think about the day our mother died, seeing June frozen at the top of the stairs, one hand on the railing and the other braced against the wall as she stared down at the woman I'd wished dead a thousand times over. I remember envisioning myself there, close behind Mother as she rattled off that day's chores and how I could do them better, my foot jutting out just enough to catch her heel and knock her off her feet. I remember holding June's hand as her tears started right as the paramedics arrived, amazed at her capacity for tenderness towards the woman who had been so cruel to us. As a thick, choking haze falls between my sister and me again, I imagine Adam standing on the roof with her, drunk and leaning farther and farther over the ledge while she asks him if he can still see my blood on the sidewalk below.

You have to let me go, June. You won't be happy as long as I'm here.

My sister smooths down her hair one last time then drops her hands, bracing her palms against the mirror as she leans in close to the glassy surface, squinting a little as if she can see me inside of her reflection. "What about you, Edie? You didn't get to be happy when you were alive, but I'm fixing that now. Then we can both be happy."

We shared more than just blood – I see that now. All night and into the next day I roil and jump, struggling to break myself apart, to dissolve myself fully into the person who has always been half of me like I was half of her. Despite my efforts, she sleeps soundly, and she eats without nausea or vomiting, and I stay lodged in her body for days that could be weeks that could be months.

When June walks by the bakery, I am afraid to look, so I tense in her ear hoping to hear Louisa's laugh as she greets her favorite customers or wishes my old coworkers a good night.

When June stops in the corner store, I'm in her fingers as she turns the heavy bottle of Adam's favorite whisky over in her hands.

When June climbs the stairs to the apartment where I last lived, I linger in her feet so I can feel each weathered groove and remember what it was like to stumble and yell and laugh, tipsy from gin, cheeks and chest hot with anticipation as my husband tugs at my skirt.

And when Adam opens the door and takes the whisky and accepts my sister's suggestion to enjoy a drink on the roof, I wonder if after this, if after we are done, June and I will finally be happy.

Fudakaeshi

Marshall J. Moore

SHIKOKU, JAPAN. 1577.

* * *

"You must be very polite to Minoru-sama," Goro said. "She receives few visitors, and is eager for your company."

Yukiko smiled slightly as she followed the elderly servant up the winding trail. The wind blew strongly from the sea, and she pulled her ragged kimono more tightly about her shoulders.

"Courtesy is one of the seven tenets of the warrior," she told him. "I will strive to exhibit it to my host."

"That is good," Goro said, glancing over his shoulder at her. "My lord and lady have need of a capable *bushi*."

"Even a ronin?"

The old man paused at the top of the slope and gave her an appraising look.

"It is not for me to say," he said at last. "But if you are the same Okabe Yukiko that we have heard of, I think my masters will be glad of your service."

* * *

Kagawa Minoru knelt at the top of the hill, bent over a long *kakemono* scroll, its four corners weighted down with round stones. She ran her brush carefully across the scroll in long, elegant strokes, humming quietly to herself. The sea breeze tugged at the few strands of dark hair that had fallen loose from her bun.

Her back was to Yukiko and Goro as they approached. The old servant slowly lowered himself to his knees, beckoning Yukiko to do the same. He placed his hands flat on the ground and bent so low that his brow nearly touched the grass. Yukiko knelt as well, though she did not bow nearly as low.

"Minoru-sama," Goro said, loudly enough to draw her attention. "I have the honor of introducing you to Okabe Yukiko."

Minoru stood and turned around, hiding her ink-stained hands in the sleeves of her kimono. She bowed from the waist, though her eyes never left Yukiko.

The ronin was a striking woman: tall and long-limbed, with the lean features of one acquainted with hardship and hunger. Her kimono with its cherry blossom *mon* was well-worn, and the two swords tucked into the *obi* sash about her waist looked as though they had been drawn often.

"*Konnichiwa,* Okabe-san," Minoru greeted her. "Have you had rice today?"

"Thank you, Minoru-sama," Yukiko replied, straightening to look her in the eye. Minoru's breath caught. Yukiko's eyes were as grey as the sea. "I have eaten."

"Good," Minoru nodded. "Come and sit with me. You may go, Goro-chan."

The old servant bowed once more, then turned and set off slowly back down the hill. Yukiko rose and walked over to Minoru. She pulled both her swords from her *obi,* still sheathed in their *saya*, and set them down on her right side as she knelt. This was a gesture of trust and respect; if she meant Minoru violence, it would be difficult to draw her blades from this angle.

"Thank you, Yukiko-san," Minoru said, returning to her brushwork. "I appreciate you meeting with me."

"The pleasure is mine, Minoru-sama." Yukiko's gaze fell to the scroll in front of her host. Minoru was painting the seascape before them: the broad sweep of the rolling hills to either side giving way to the wide grey plain of the Seto Sea dividing the island of Shikoku from its larger neighbor, Honshu. The day was overcast, and Yukiko could just make out the distant shoreline on the horizon.

"You paint well," she said.

"Thank you," Minoru flushed. "Are you a painter?"

"No," Yukiko shook her head. She glanced down at the swords beside her. "But one artist recognizes another's skill."

"I suppose that is so." Minoru drew a long, winding brushstroke near the top of the scroll, representing the far horizon. "Did Goro tell you why I wished to meet with you?"

"No." Yukiko shifted slightly. "But in my experience, there is only one reason a noble lady seeks out a ronin."

Minoru dipped her brush once again. "You speak bluntly, Okabe Yukiko."

"Some have told me so," Yukiko shrugged. "I prefer to think of it as candor. Is it a tongue you require, or a blade?"

That earned her a faint smile. "Neither, I hope. It is your keen grey eyes I need."

"Ah." Yukiko gazed out at the roiling sea. "You need me to banish a ghost."

The salt wind blew cold. Yukiko's long black hair fluttered in the breeze, and Minoru felt the chill bite at her exposed hands.

"Yes," Minoru said, not looking at Yukiko. "Let us speak directly, Yukiko-san. My family is being haunted. I believe this *yūrei* seeks to kill my husband."

Her dark brown eyes met Yukiko's sea-grey ones. "And that someone is helping it."

* * *

"It appeared on the last full moon," Minoru explained, steam rising from the teapot as she poured into Yukiko's cup. "It wailed and moaned for three nights, trying to break into our home."

Nodding her thanks, Yukiko raised the porcelain cup to her mouth with both hands. She breathed deeply, savoring the grassy aroma. It had been many seasons since she had tasted good matcha.

"I trust the *o-fuda* kept it out?" she asked.

A look passed between her hosts – Minoru and her husband, Kagawa Ryo, daimyo of this stretch of Shikoku's northern coast. They knelt on woven tatami mats facing Yukiko, in the tearoom of the family home. It was a small manor, nicer than any building Yukiko had been allowed inside in the past year.

"Yes," Ryo said. He had a deep voice, one that was slightly at odds with his refined, birdlike features. Yukiko judged him to be at least a decade older than her own thirty years, and twice the age of his young wife. "We keep three *o-fuda* in our house. One hanging from the ceiling outside our bedroom. One mounted above the door to our home. And one outside the children's window."

Yukiko nodded. *O-fuda* were protective amulets, charms inscribed with the name of a *kami* spirit on paper, wood, or metal. When placed throughout a home, they were meant to protect against invasion from hostile spirits or angry ghosts.

Like the one Yukiko had been hired to dispatch, for instance.

"And this happened last month," she said, taking a sip of tea.

"Yes," Minoru nodded. "The *o-fuda* kept the *yūrei* out, though it wailed and howled something terrible. The children hardly slept those three nights."

"How many children do you have?"

"Two," Ryo said. "Sato and Kaede. Both are under the age of three."

"And they saw this *yūrei*?"

"Yes." Minoru shuddered, her face pale at the memory. "It appeared outside their window, but could not get in because of the *o-fuda* we had placed there."

"And now the ghost has appeared again?"

"It has." Ryo looked at Yukiko with a direct, unblinking gaze. "It appeared again last night, the first night of the full moon, just as it did a month ago."

"Did the *o-fuda* still keep it out?"

"No," Minoru broke in before her husband could answer. "I awoke in the night to hear it screaming in the garden. I ran to see that the *o-fuda* were holding it at bay – only to find that the one outside our door had been torn down and trampled on. I raced to the children's room and hurried them from their beds just as the ghost tore in through the window. The *o-fuda* there was gone, too."

Yukiko listened in silence, fingers tight around her porcelain teacup. Ryo watched his wife tell her story, his own face pained. Yukiko sympathized. She knew what it was to fear for the life of one's child.

Tea sloshed onto her shaking hands, painfully hot. But Minoru was so rapt in her retelling that she failed to notice.

"I took the children to the bedroom and locked them inside. Then I stood on the threshold, the last *o-fuda* hanging over me. The ghost howled and raged, but she could not touch me while it was there." She shivered. "I stayed there until dawn, when the ghost left. Then I sent Goro to the village, to see if any ronin there had dealt with ghosts before."

A wry smile touched Kagawa Ryo's lips. "Imagine our surprise when he returned with Okabe Yukiko, the Ghost Hunter herself."

"The Seven Lucky Gods have smiled upon us both," Yukiko said. "For I am in need of work, and you have ghost in need of hunting."

"You will help us, then?" Minoru asked, leaning forward eagerly. Ryo's expression was more guarded.

"I will. All I ask in return is food and shelter through the winter." Yukiko met Kagawa Ryo's gaze directly. "You will have my aid and service until the spring thaws."

"Impertinent," came a voice from the corner of the tearoom. "Lord Ryo already has one *bushi* retainer. He does not need a second."

He leaned against the door, a gaunt, hard-featured man wearing the *chonmage* topknot of the samurai caste, both swords tucked into his *obi*. Yukiko's own swords were on the far side of the manor, resting in a *daishō* stand provided for visitors.

"Peace, Hayate," Ryo said. "Okabe-san is our guest, and deserves our courtesy."

He had not introduced his *yojimbo* by family name. That and his hardened looks told Yukiko that Hayate was a masterless ronin, like herself. Until now, he had not spoken; merely gazed at Yukiko with undisguised mistrust.

"It is no offense," Yukiko said, gazing levelly at the daimyo's bodyguard. "I am sure that Hayate-san and I will become fast friends, given time."

One corner of the *yojimbo's* mouth twitched, though his expression remained unfriendly. Yukiko turned back to the daimyo and his wife.

"What did the *yūrei* look like?"

Ryo's shoulder twitched in a shrug. "Like all ghosts look. A woman in a kimono with long hair. You could see through her, and she faded away at the legs."

Yukiko sipped her tea. Many ghosts looked like that, though not all. But for it to have sabotaged the protective charms around the house…no ghost could have torn them down without help.

Which meant she was dealing with a *fudakaeshi.*

"Your *o-fuda*," she said at last, careful not to let her thoughts show on her face. "Have they been replaced yet?"

"Yes," Minoru spoke up. "The one outside our bedroom remains. The other two have been replaced with paper charms by Shichiro, the village priest."

"Excellent." Yukiko stood, and Minoru's fan once again fluttered in front of her face. Rising before one's host was highly rude.

Good. Yukiko wanted their full attention.

"I mean no disrespect, Kagawa-sama," she said, inclining her head, "but if you want this *yūrei* dealt with, you must do as I say. Do you agree?"

"Yes," Minoru said, as her husband opened his mouth. "Of course."

Ryo frowned at his wife but nodded his assent.

"Good. Then here is what must be done. The children must sleep with you in your room, in case the *o-fuda* above their window is tampered with again. How many servants do you have?"

"Goro and his wife, Nanako," Ryo answered. "They live in a servant's cottage on the grounds."

"Bar their door, then, when nightfall comes." Yukiko's gaze turned to Hayate. "You are Kagawa-sama's *yojimbo,* yes?"

"*Hai*," Hayate said, somehow making the affirmative a challenge.

"Then you must wait in the family's room with them. If the *yūrei* devours me, you will be all that stands between your lord and an angry ghost."

"And you?" Kagawa Ryo asked. "What will you do, while we cower in our beds?"

Yukiko's eyes were as grey as the evening sky. "I will sit outside your room and wait for the ghost to reveal herself."

The ghost, she thought, *and the one who serves it.*

* * *

The night wind gusted quietly through the sliding *shoji* screens. Yukiko knelt in the center of the manor with her back to the Kagawas' bedroom door, resting her buttocks on her heels. It was an uncomfortable position, but she had maintained it for hours, ever since night had fallen and the Kagawa family had retired to their bedroom. The discomfort helped sharpen her senses, keeping her awake and aware through the long hours of her vigil.

Her swords lay sheathed on the floor beside her on her left. In one swift, practiced motion she could stand, draw, and strike with either blade, should the need arise.

The ghost that haunted Kagawa Ryo and his family was a *fudakaeshi,* a charm-ripper. Yukiko was certain of that. No *yūrei* could touch an *o-fuda*, but the *fudakaeshi* was a master deceiver, adept at tricking the living into tearing down their protective charms and letting them inside their homes.

Yukiko gazed at the *shoji* screen before her, a watercolor painting of a *kitsune* fox spirit darting between the trees of a lush forest. A *fudakaeshi* knew the inmost desires of the heart. It would promise, plead, threaten – whatever it thought would subvert the living into serving it.

Lies, always.

It must be the Hour of the Tiger by now; the last stretch of night before grey dawn. Yukiko fought the urge to rub at her eyes. It was not the first time she had remained awake all through the night, but each time she did so she felt more tired the following day.

A wail split the silence, a piercing feminine cry. Yukiko's breath caught, the hairs on her neck standing on end. Still she waited patiently, her eyes fixed on the *shoji* leading to the front of the house.

A shadow appeared on the screen, a dark shape with long hair. A woman stood on the other side – or at least, the shadow of a woman.

"Let me in," the shadow whispered. Yukiko heard its voice as plainly and clearly as though it had been sitting beside her. "Let me in, little *onna-bugeisha*."

Yukiko said nothing. The shadow raised one hand and scratched a fingernail along the *shoji* screen, leaving a trail like an ink stain.

"Let me in, Okabe Yukiko," the shadow whispered again. Its voice was plaintive, pleading. "Let me into the room behind you. You need not even open the door. Merely take down that terrible charm above you."

Yukiko looked up at the *o-fuda* dangling over her head; a single strip of thin metal hanging from the ceiling rafters.

"Take it down," the shadow pleaded.

"I will not," she said, her voice dry. Speaking to the *fudakaeshi* was a mistake, but she could not help herself.

"There is much I can give you," the shadow whispered. It pressed its hand flat against the screen, fingers spread. "I can bring you to the home of the general with the *oni* mask."

Yukiko's breath caught. The darkest corners of her memory summoned that mask to her mind: a war *menpō* of demonic aspect, flames gleaming off its curling tusks.

"Tear down the charm, and I will lead you to where the *oni* dwells," the shadow promised. "I will dance in the flames as you burn his home to the ground. Surely he deserves to have his own sins visited upon him, Yukiko-san."

Yukiko looked down at her hands. She remembered how they had looked, covered in her husband's blood. She remembered the heat of the fire blistering her face.

"No," she said, her voice barely a whisper.

"The other charms are gone," the shadow said. "Only this last remains. Tear it down, and I will take you to where your daughter is."

Yukiko did not remember standing, but she was suddenly on her feet, her wakizashi in hand.

"My daughter is *dead*."

"Is she?" the shadow whispered.

Yukiko stood there, her shaking hands tight around the sword.

"Tear the *o-fuda* down, and I will tell you where little Izumi is."

"You lie," Yukiko hissed into the darkness.

"No," the shadow said softly. "Not about this. Remove the charm, Yukiko-san."

Yukiko shut her eyes as tightly as she could, her hand trembling on the wakizashi's grip.

"I will not," she whispered.

Distantly, a rooster crowed, heralding the approach of dawn.

When Yukiko opened her eyes, the shadow had vanished. Only its handprint remained; a dark smudge on the painted screen.

* * *

"I have a question for you, Shichiro-san."

"Oh?" The rotund little priest turned, fixing Yukiko with an appraising gaze. "I may have an answer."

Yukiko gave him a tired smile. The night's vigil had left her weary.

"Is Minoru-sama the daimyo's first wife?"

Shichiro chuckled. "Noticed the difference in age, did you?"

"It is hard to miss."

The village priest, Shichiro had arrived that afternoon, bearing paper *o-fuda* to replace those destroyed the night before.

The ghost had not lied about that, at least. Once the sun had cleared the horizon and she was certain the *fudakaeshi* was gone, she had patrolled the grounds. Surely enough, the protective charms over the front door and the children's window had been torn down and ripped into little pieces.

No *yūrei* could touch the *o-fuda* or cross a threshold protected by one.

Which meant that someone had been up and about, moving through the house on silent feet even as Yukiko had maintained her vigil.

"Well?" she prompted, returning her thoughts to the present. "Is she?"

"No," Shichiro admitted, as they reached the front door of the manor house. Yukiko was most of a foot taller than him, so he handed her the paper *o-fuda*. "He had another wife, Aiko. They were wed nearly ten years but had no children."

Sometimes it is easier not to be a mother, Yukiko thought, standing on tiptoe to tie the charm to the rafters. "How did she die?"

"Tragically," Shichiro said. The good-humored smile faded from his round face. "She and Ryo-sama took a walk along the cliffs one night. The moon was full, like tonight, and so bright that they could see every step. But even so she slipped, and fell into the waves."

"That is tragic," Yukiko agreed, tying the knot that kept the *o-fuda* in place. She stepped back and admired her handiwork. "I've another question, Shichiro-san."

"And I may have another answer."

"When I—" she cleared her throat and started again, reminding herself to leave the past in the past. "Some daimyos have secret passageways in their castles, for when they must escape an enemy invasion. Kagawa-sama has a fine house, but it is not a castle."

"You are asking if there is such an escape here?" Shichiro asked as they walked to the children's room.

"I am."

The priest chuckled. "You are a shrewd one, Yukiko-san. As it happens, there are two loose boards in the daimyo's bedroom. If things were dire enough, the family could be smuggled out that way."

"That is well," Yukiko nodded. "I hope it will not come to that, but it is good to know that they might flee while I hold off the *yūrei*."

They reached the children's room. This must have been where the ghost had entered the house last night. Clawmarks scored the wooden exterior walls, and the *shoji* screens had been torn to little more than shreds.

"Do you really think you can defeat such a ghost?" Shichiro asked, all color drained from his face.

Yukiko surveyed the wreckage grimly. "I can try."

But first, she reminded herself, *I must deal with the one who let it in.*

* * *

The second night of her vigil wore on much the same as the first. Again Yukiko knelt patiently outside the daimyo's bedroom, the single metal *o-fuda* dangling from the ceiling directly above her. Her swords lay at her left side.

Yukiko waited as the hours passed, her eyes and ears alert to every breath of wind and rustle of the leaves. Once, towards midnight, she heard the soft, mournful hooting of an owl. A good omen, or so she hoped.

The rhythms of the night shifted, and she judged it must be near the Hour of the Tiger. The *fudakaeshi* would soon make its appearance. Its living collaborator would tear down the *o-fuda* she and Shichiro had placed earlier that day, leaving the one directly above Yukiko as the only remaining ward protecting the daimyo's family from the ghost. It and its mortal servant would have to go through her to reach them.

And Yukiko would be ready for them.

* * *

The Hour of the Tiger drew on. Still, the ghost did not appear. Slowly, Yukiko's eyes closed. Her head fell to her chest, shoulders slumping. Her breathing changed, coming slower and deeper, a slight snore whistling through her half-open mouth.

There was a subtle, nearly undetectable shift in the air around her. A slight change in pressure, gentle as the wings of a moth fluttering through the room.

It was enough.

Yukiko's eyes snapped open, two points of grey light in the blackness. In one fluid motion she rose to her feet and turned around, raising her sheathed wakizashi in her left hand.

Her attacker's blade hummed as it cut through the air, only to bounce off the wakizashi's lacquered *saya*. Yukiko drew the sword, keeping its *saya* in her off hand. She lay the scabbard along the flat of her blade, using both to parry the attacker's backswing. Steel clashed against steel, breaking the tranquil nighttime silence.

Yukiko swept her wakizashi in a horizontal cut, feeling resistance as the blade bit deeply across her enemy's stomach. She knew it to be a mortal wound, but that was not the end of the fight. An enemy wounded to death was still an enemy that could kill.

Her attacker grunted in surprise and pain and thrust his sword at her. Yukiko sidestepped, though not quickly enough. She let out a pained hiss as the tip of the blade pierced her side, drawing a long, shallow cut just above her left hip.

It had been a reckless attack, one that left him open to her counterstrike. She stepped forward, inside the reach of his blade, and drove her wakizashi into his middle. Hot blood washed over her hand, and her foe let out a startled gurgle. His sword clattered to the floor.

Only then, in the light of the full moon, did she see her attacker's face.

"Hayate-san," Yukiko breathed, her heartbeat pounding in her chest. The fight had been brief, but nothing set the heart to racing like battle.

The *yojimbo's* eyes were wide, his face draining swiftly of color. Blood seeped from one corner of his mouth.

"You fought well," he managed to gasp. He stumbled forward, clutching at her. Yukiko lowered him to the floor, kneeling over him. She heard the sound of commotion in the room behind her; Kagawa Ryo and his family must have been awakened by the struggle.

"Tell me why," she whispered to Hayate. "Why betray your lord?"

"Never," Hayate breathed. His eyes fixed on the metal *o-fuda* dangling above Yukiko's head. "I tore down the charms at his command."

A shiver crawled down Yukiko's spine.

The ghost's low, mournful wail echoed through the house.

The *shoji* screen behind Yukiko slid open.

She threw herself to the side, acting on sheer instinct. The long blade of a katana whipped through the air where her head had been only seconds before.

Yukiko rolled, grabbing her own katana from the floor and drawing it as she stood, assuming the classic fighter's pose: one foot forward, sword gripped in both hands, the blade pointing at her foe.

Kagawa Ryo stood opposite her, his own stance mirroring hers. Awoken from sleep, he wore only his underclothes, his bare feet padding silently over the wooden floor as he and Yukiko circled one another.

"You," Yukiko said as the ghost's wailing drew closer. "You ordered Hayate to tear down the wards. You *wanted* the *fudakaeshi* to come inside."

"I did," Ryo said. A bead of sweat stood out on his forehead as he gripped his katana tighter. "And he obeyed, as a good samurai should."

The ghost let out another long, ghastly moan, even closer. It was inside the house by now.

Understanding dawned.

"Your wife," Yukiko breathed. "Your *first* wife, Aiko. She is the *fudakaeshi.*"

"Yes," Ryo said. There was a strange gleam in his eyes. "I loved her, you know."

"Yet you killed her."

He did not deny it, only gave her a tired, sad smile. "Ten years we were together, Yukiko-san. Ten years, and not one child from the union. A daimyo must have heirs."

Kagawa Ryo's gaze shifted to the bedroom. Yukiko could see movement through the *shoji* screens; Minoru rousing her children from sleep.

"So you pushed her into the sea," Yukiko said. She advanced a step, the tip of her katana unwavering. Ryo took a corresponding step back, his own blade unsteady. "You found a new, young wife. A fertile wife."

A shadow appeared beside the shadow Ryo cast on the *shoji* behind him. It had the outline of a woman with long hair and fingers like claws.

At the same time Minoru appeared in the bedroom doorway, her eyes wide with fear. She held her two children against her sides, sheltering them in the folds of her kimono. Her face glanced from Yukiko and her husband standing with drawn swords to the fallen body of Hayate, then drifted up to the shadow on the *shoji* behind Ryo. Her mouth fell open in a scream, but no sound came out.

"Stay back," Yukiko ordered her. "Do not cross the threshold."

Minoru swayed in place, paralyzed by fear.

"Minoru gave you what you sought," Yukiko said, advancing so that the *o-fuda* hung directly over her head. Now she stood directly between Ryo and his living wife. "Children. And then the ghost appeared."

"The ghost of my wife!" Ryo shouted, his eyes wild. "Aiko, who I loved! She came back from death to be with me once again! She *promised* me we would be together, once I disposed of her usurper!"

The blade of his katana suddenly pointed at Minoru. A stifled gasp escaped her lips, mirrored by the rising wail of the *fudakaeshi* behind the *shoji* screen.

"Be with her, then," Yukiko said, and cut down the last *o-fuda*.

The katana was a longer blade than the wakizashi, meant for use outdoors on the battlefield, not within the confines of a home. But with its greater reach, Yukiko severed the cords of the protective charm in a single stroke.

The *o-fuda* dropped to the floor with a dull thud.

The ghostly wail grew to a piercing shriek. Long-fingered claws ripped through the *shoji* screen and seized Ryo around his neck and shoulders. The daimyo turned with a start, as the translucent visage of his first wife burst through the tattered screen, her face twisted into a mask of hunger and hate.

Behind Yukiko, Minoru screamed.

The *fudakaeshi* that had once been Aiko wrapped its ghostly arms tight around Ryo, He flailed helplessly, katana forgotten, as the ghost's implacable strength hauled him off his feet, dragging him through the *shoji*.

Minoru stood horrorstruck, rooted to the spot, her children clinging to her legs. Only once Ryo's screams had faded into the night did she sway like a tree in the wind. Her eyes rolled back into her head, and Yukiko barely caught her before she fell into a swoon.

"Shh," Yukiko murmured, cradling the other woman's head against her shoulder. "It's alright, Minoru-san. It's over. You're safe now."

Minoru did not open her eyes. "Truly?"

"Truly," Yukiko assured her. "The *fudakaeshi* wanted your husband, as you first told me. Now that it has him, you are safe."

"Are you certain?" Minoru's narrow shoulders shook. "Ryo…he said that the ghost loved him. That it promised to replace me."

"No. They are gone now, both of them."

Of that, Yukiko was certain. The *fudakaeshi* had dragged Ryo off in the direction of the sea, no doubt towards the cliffs where Ryo had thrown his first wife into the hungry sea.

Minoru sobbed, and buried her face against Yukiko's neck. Yukiko held Minoru tightly in her arms, comforting her as she would a small child. Minoru's own children, too small and frightened to understand what they had just witnessed, joined them, throwing their arms against their mother.

"I will tell you where your daughter is," the ghost whispered in Yukiko's memory.

Yukiko squeezed her eyes shut and shook her head.

"Ghosts always lie," she whispered.

Theater Crowd

Joe Nazare

BERRIMAN cringed at the sound of the girl's chuckle, automatically hearing derision directed at him. He ventured a glance to his right and spotted a curvy brunette in a cleavage-showcasing pink V-neck top. The figure slouched in the seat alongside her wore a denim jacket and a smirk, the latter pinching the corner of his mouth much like that thin silver hoop did to the flesh around the tail of his left eyebrow. Both the guy and girl appeared to be teenagers, their faces young enough to make Berriman wonder why they weren't staring at a high school blackboard right now. Then the door to Theater 8 swung shut behind him, its clatter knocking the hitch out of his step and propelling him down the sloping aisle.

Just a coincidence, Berriman assured himself about the teens' mirth as he pressed his steps into the maroon carpeting. He moved empty-handed, having bypassed the concession stand in the lobby when he laid eyes on the attendant: a petite Filipina-looking girl, as cute as the brunette back there in the last row was overripe. Seeing her, he'd instantly resolved to go without his customary pretzel and Sprite.

The theater, Berriman noted as he navigated the walkway, was a study in asymmetry: long rows running right of the aisle comprised the bulk of the seating area, while those on the left jutted only five seats wide of the velvet-curtained wall. Berriman didn't care that the latter section forced you to angle your view onto the movie screen; he broke off his descent about ten rows from bottom and sidestepped into the patron-barren area. The peculiarity of the situation enveloped him even as he squatted into the fourth seat in from the aisle. Though he'd been to this particular multiplex on countless occasions, this was the first time in his thirty-three years that he'd ever gone to the movies alone.

He and Elise had a deal: she came with him to the slasher flicks, and he in turn agreed to sit through the alleged comedy of Will Ferrell or Jim Carrey, actors whose antics rivaled a pepper-spraying for irritating. Not that Elise was any more a fan of his favorite genre. *I don't know how you can watch those movies, Brad*, she'd told him on countless occasions over the last three and a half years. And every time, Berriman heard the two extra, unspoken words hidden within her comment: how *someone like him* could watch those movies.

He wasn't a timid man – 'reserved' would be the better adjective. He simply disliked raising his voice (Elise might understand why if she'd grown up listening to the blaring soundtrack of his parents' arguments). So what if horror films – as the Wes Craven franchise was so self-aware – aimed to make you scream. Berriman could experience such fare just fine without indulging in exclamation.

The lingering raunchiness of bygone popcorn infiltrated his nostrils, a virtual smelling salt that snapped him from his momentary daze. Berriman twisted his neck to survey his surroundings in the giant cube of a theater. Scattered pairs, couples or at least friends, occupied less than a dozen total seats, the attendees mumbling to each other as the pre-preview slideshow of local advertisements played silently onscreen. Just as Berriman had expected, not many people were at the movies on a Tuesday afternoon.

Tu-uesdaaay…afternoon, the words echoed, before Berriman squelched the old song trying to play in his head. Turning himself back around, he caught glimpse of a balding, unshaven man sitting front-row, center-screen. The man's T-shirt, dull white save for the urine-colored crescent below the armpit, looked thin to the point of translucence. Something about the solitary figure – perhaps his stooped posture as much as his appearance – marked him a drunk. Sure enough, as Berriman watched from a good thirty feet off, the man tucked his chin to his chest and raised a palmed flask to his lips. You had to admire his ingenuity at least: for the mere price of a matinee ticket, the rummy could enter the multiplex and drink away the early-September day in air-conditioned peace.

A fleshy slap resounded from the back of the theater. "Antonio," Berriman misheard at first, then parsed the cry as "Tony, no." He suspected that the eyebrow-ringed teen just tried to take advantage of his companion's plunging neckline and had his access denied. Still, the brunette's verbal rebuff had sounded half-hearted, full of false modesty. "No" meant "not yet."

The mating ritual in the last row only made a frowning Berriman think of Elise. He wished the two of them could just sit down and discuss whatever problems she thought they had – such as her gripes about his never being the one to initiate foreplay, and his hushed nature during sex – but she had nixed all types of intercourse. She just needed to be on her own right now, she'd said. And she'd made it clear that trying to contact her would only hurt his cause, so Berriman had no choice but to suffer through the past sixteen days – and counting – of separation and silence.

Self-consciousness dogged him throughout these days. Being single again after all this time had left him feeling Elephant-Man freakish. His DUMPED status (was there really any difference between being broken up and 'on a break'?) must've been obvious as a forehead stamp.

Work provided anything but relief from this perceived conspicuousness; manning his post turned into an eight-hour ordeal. Finally his boss Joan – who always called him by his surname, casually as Scully to Mulder – had encouraged Berriman to make use of some of the time off he'd accrued. He realized his mistake, though, in taking up that suggestion after only a day and a half of moping around his apartment. Utter solitude wasn't the answer; he needed to get out of the house and out of his own head. That desperation, coupled with his summer-long anticipation of the release of the *Halloween* sequel, drove him into the movie theater this afternoon.

Suddenly the house lights dimmed, having the same effect on Berriman as a muscle relaxant. He could sit back and breathe easier now. He wasn't a lonesome loser, just another shadow-draped shape in the audience.

The obligatory 'Silence is Golden' p.s.a. segued into coming attractions. For the latest *Saw*. And the adaptation of Cormac McCarthy's most recent novel – no country for anyone, by the looks of that post-apocalyptic landscape. A new sci-fi extravaganza starring Bruce Willis in a toupee, a reliable index that the film wouldn't be any good. Finally the screen blanked, and darkness eclipsed the theater in the few seconds before the start of the feature presentation.

"Showtime," Tony announced unabashedly, his identity betrayed by his date's responding chuckle.

The action picked up right where the first remake left off, or so it seemed until the opening proved to be an extended dream sequence. Berriman knew the twist was coming, from having read the cover story on *H2* in last month's *Fangoria*, but the foreknowledge did nothing to diminish his entertainment. And while the Carpenter loyalists no doubt were all over the message boards right now excoriating Rob Zombie and the white-horse-symbolism he rode in on, Berriman actually appreciated the risks the latter director took in re-envisioning the *Halloween* movies. Just like in the first remake, Zombie tried to provide a glimpse of Michael Myers' psyche, to make him more than another masked killing machine. More important than the film's determination to get inside Myers' head, though, was its success in drawing Berriman out of his own. He lost himself in the screened fantasy, forgetting his own woes and shucking all sense of his present surroundings.

Right up until the point when someone in the audience tried to pre-empt a startle moment via a hokey scream.

No, not just someone, an anonymous anybody. Berriman was certain of the exact source of the disturbance.

Maybe it was because he'd had to put up with his unfair share of disruptive teens in his past nine years behind the Reference desk of the Clifton Public Library; maybe, deep down, he still smarted from Elise's remark about his characteristic muteness; or maybe he just couldn't stand to have his moviegoing experience spoiled, given everything that'd gone sour in his life of late, but before Berriman was even aware of his own intention, he barked the reprimand: *"Hey, cut it out, asshole!"*

Astonishment at his own outburst slackened his jaw. Yet he also felt relieved, as if he'd finally managed to belch out indigestion. Meanwhile the air seemed to have been vacuumed from the theater. You couldn't call the condition silence – not with the onscreen havoc being wreaked on Haddonfield by the slaughtering Myers – but the seating area was conspicuously devoid of noise.

A satisfied smile remolded Berriman's features. See, he told himself, that's all it takes. Sometimes you just had to speak up, and put a person in his place.

Sensing the tacit approval of the other audience members, Berriman settled back into his seat and refocused on the screen. The incident faded from his thoughts within moments as the movie engrossed him again. All the more surprising, then, when the echo came, minutes later:

"Cut it out, asshole."

The words were mocking, falsetto-pitched and lisping. More disconcerting still, they did not seem to emanate from the rear right corner of the theater.

Berriman pointed his chin over his right shoulder. The seats behind him all stretched back emptily, save for three occupied about five rows down from the top. A mother and her pre-adolescent kids, their faces wan and shimmering, frontlit by the reflected glow of the movie screen. Berriman hadn't noted the family during his previous scan of the audience; studying the trio now, he had a hard time imagining any of them responsible for the mimicry.

He flicked his gaze toward the far corner, wondering about the ventriloquist skills of Tony and Chesty. Distance blurred the two figures, but he could still make out that they sat quiescent, for all appearances behaved.

His brow furrowed, Berriman stared for a few seconds more and then turned back to the woman and children. And spotted what he'd missed a moment ago – the tiny old couple perched directly behind the family. He could remember glimpsing them when he'd entered Theater 8. Noticeable for the white manes sitting thick as colonial wigs atop their heads, the seniors had then occupied two seats just right of the aisle, mid-theater.

Berriman, who prided himself on being able to complete the Word Jumble in the newspaper in less than a minute, struggled to unscramble this present arrangement into any semblance of sense. For what possible reason would the two old-timers relocate to a tougher vantage point?

A shriek erupted, wrenching Berriman's attention toward the front of the theater. But the culprit was only Laurie Strode (played by an actress infinitely less mature than Jamie Lee Curtis had been in her turn in the role). Berriman sighed, chagrined not just by his own jumpiness but at the fact that he was missing the movie. Pledging to hell with the audience, he concentrated on the screen. But no sooner than he sat back, he heard the stage-whispered heckle:

"Hey...asshole."

Berriman whipped around. *There a problem here?* he wanted to voice, but then stifled himself, recognizing the absurdity of the question. Damned straight there was a problem here.

A quintet of viewers now filled the row in front of the mother and her two children. Side by side sat a long-necked blonde, an elderly black woman, a candy-chomping young boy, a middle-aged Asian man in a white dress shirt, and an obese teen sporting a Titans cap. An odd assortment, to be sure, but that wasn't what bothered Berriman. He was dead certain he hadn't heard the theater's door swing open in the past minute (and even if the group had somehow just entered, why would they crowd over there, with so many other empty seats to choose from?).

Where'd they come from, then? Berriman had no answer to that riddle. They might as well have materialized through the pores of their seat cushions, coalesced from dandruff and dried sweat and spilt emotion.

The people in the two rows behind the latecomers ignored their curious presence. In fact, all ten of the viewers now congregated in that area just sat placidly, their eyes locked onto the movie screen.

Eager to seize on some rational explanation, Berriman twisted further around and searched for another entrance, one occluded by the curtained left wall of the theater. Naturally, there was no such aperture. And when he returned his gaze to those gathered a dozen rows behind him, he saw that the crowd had again multiplied, amassing as surreptitiously as cancer cells in a victim's body.

Berriman uncoiled, squaring his shoulders to the movie screen. He closed his eyes and shook his head. *Can't be happening*, he told himself. He must be hallucinating. Maybe someone had slipped something into his Sprite.

Then he remembered that he'd balked at purchasing a soda.

Warily, Berriman glanced back over his shoulder. More viewers had joined the impossible mob in the brief interval since his last check. Packed into the stunted rows on this side of the aisle, the people suggested passengers on the deck of a careening ship. The image sent Berriman mentally listing, riddling him with a sense of skewed equilibrium that was not entirely unfamiliar, more like some awful exacerbation of the state he'd been staggering around in for the past few Elise-less weeks.

Concern for his own stability emboldened his study. He peered at the crowd, scrutinizing the ostensible visual evidence. Some of the members were transplants, had been sitting elsewhere in the theater at the start of the movie; others were just-as-inexplicable newcomers. Like that pruneface in the bifocals, and the ginger-bearded man alongside him. Something about the latter figure snagged Berriman's gaze; it took him a moment to process the significance of that white square centered in the collar of the black shirt.

What the hell was a priest doing at a horror movie?

Berriman's legs started twitching like the limbs of an electrocuted frog carcass as a terrible conviction surged through him: the priest hadn't come for a horror movie. Nor was anyone else in that bizarre cluster of patrons here to be entertained by Rob Zombie.

The thought widened his eyes, and seemed to sharpen his awareness of the scene. He realized that the crowd hadn't just expanded. It'd *descended*. When he wasn't looking, the entire group had shifted a few rows down. The figures all kept up with the charade of watching the screen, acted as if they were not targeting him.

Berriman swept his own sights across the theater. Spotted a handful of human viewers – he shuddered at the need for such classification – still scattered about. But they were encapsulated in their own little world, fixated on the drama projected onto the outsized rectangle, totally unaware of the silent predation transpiring in their midst.

When Berriman tried to call out to them, he discovered that fear had stuffed his mouth like a giant ball-gag. He sat there with his lips peeled back from his teeth in grimace, his windpipe constricted. His imploring stares alone failed to rouse the other moviegoers; no timely rescue would be coming from that quarter.

Drowning in panic, he darted a look at the rows trailing his. The crowd had advanced again, simultaneously, pushed ahead like the chess pieces of the world's worst cheater.

As Berriman jerked around in his seat, his sightline slanted toward the front left corner of the theater. There below the screen, an escape route beckoned him. Berriman deliberated, all the while sensing the crowd's encroachment. But he couldn't make the requisite break – just couldn't chance that darkened doorway beneath the gleaming sign. For all he knew, EXIT was TRAP encrypted.

He forced himself to look behind him once more, and immediately felt as if he had a pair of frigid hands inside him, wringing his stomach and threatening to undam his bowels. The crowd lurked only two rows back now, but what terrorized Berriman most was the sight of the pair now forming the vanguard of the movement: Tony and his chuckling sidekick.

Entranced by the movie, the brunette scratched absently at her cleavage with a long, lacquered nail. Her chomping jaws tormented a red wad of gum. On her immediate left, in the fourth seat in from the aisle, Tony sat with his mouth slit into a grin. His eyes were all pupil, two dark marbles beaming blackness not up at the screen but directly at Berriman.

Unable to bear the sight of such malicious focus, Berriman spun face-forward. A small part of his consciousness marveled that the force of his grip hadn't shattered the armrests. While he knew he should bolt without another second's delay, he couldn't get his tremor-wracked legs to oblige. He fretted that the attempt would fail, that the cement floor's grime would grip the soles of his Nikes like flypaper. Then he'd be caught out in naked fear, and Tony and his entourage would be free to pounce.

Dread clapped him in an invisible neck brace, rendered him incapable of twisting around again to check the antagonists' advance. But his worst fears were confirmed anyhow when he heard the unmistakable snick of a switchblade coming from the seat directly behind him.

That flick of noise ravaged Berriman's entire worldview. His mind boggled at the thought of the cosmos encompassing such a horde as the one stalking him. And he had a whole new conception (though not appreciation) of the act of moviegoing: he'd come here to experience fear vicariously, in a controlled environment, but was now forced to recognize his own vulnerability, as he sat alone in the dark.

The bristling of the hairs on his nape told him that Tony was leaning forward. Out of the corner of his popping eye, Berriman spotted flecks dancing in the air above his shoulder, and wondered if Tony had produced the dust motes rather than just stirred existing ones. The figure's breath had a surprising absence of stench, a non-smell that Berriman equated with Death.

"*Cut it out*," Tony whispered, and Berriman felt his own heart jackhammer the bones of his chest as he contemplated all the possible organs the neuter pronoun referenced.

Yet ultimately it wasn't a simple evisceration by Tony that he had to fear. Without having to turn around, Berriman could envision the whole throng in motion now, crowding in on him, invading his most personal space, their insubstantial but smothering bulk breaking over him like some oily wave. Berriman squeezed his eyes shut and braced for impact.

Explosion rather than concussion: the feeling of innumerable hands tugging him in every direction at once, yanking not on his clothes but on the underlying fabric of his being. Agony locked Berriman's jaws, prevented him from voicing the merest protest. Within moments (which seemed like epochs), he resigned himself to his own decimation.

Because of the squall of noise battering his eardrums, Berriman failed to hear the music at first. Catching the brash notes, he was still too overwhelmed to identify the tune he'd selected as alert sound months earlier. A beat after the brief electronic clamor finished, though, Berriman clearly heard the slurred grouse emanating from front-row, center-screen:

"*S'posed to shut that off, jackass.*"

Berriman bounced against his seat, the jolt from the unhanding snapping his eyes open. As his head lolled on his shoulder, he looked over towards the source of the censure. Thirty diagonal feet away, the rummy lounged with his flask tilted once more to his pursed lips.

The seats behind the drinker were all empty – and yet not. A black static seemed to charge the shadows there, mobilizing them into a nebulous mass that strained toward the lone occupant of the front row. Meantime the man just sat staring at the masked slasher onscreen, perhaps mercifully oblivious to the horror he'd just sicced on himself.

Berriman didn't wait for the fade out. His self-preservation instinct kicked in at last, booting him from his seat. He bounded up the aisle and banged through the theater door, and didn't look back once as he raced straight out of the multiplex.

The smack of sunshine against his chill-bumped skin felt like ecstasy, and Berriman couldn't help but whoop. Nor could he stifle his laughter – which kept coming in strings of loud barks, uncontrollable as a bronchitic cough – when he unpocketed his cell phone and read the salvational text:

Hey, Elise reached out intangibly. *This a good time to talk?*

The Portent of the Shadow

Edith Nesbit

THIS IS NOT an artistically rounded off ghost story and nothing is explained in it; and there seems to be no reason why any of it should have happened. But that is no reason why it should not be told. You must have noticed that all the real ghost stories you ever come close to are like this in these respects: no explanation, no logical coherence. Here is the story.

* * *

There were three of us – and another. But she had fainted suddenly at the second extra of the Christmas Dance, and had been put to bed in the dressing room next to the room which we three shared. It had been one of those jolly old-fashioned dances, where nearly everybody stays the night, and the big country house is stretched to its utmost containing power; guests harbouring on sofas, couches, cots, and even mattresses on the floor. Some of the young men, even, I believe, slept on the great dining table. We had talked of our partners, as girls will, and then the stillness of the Manor House, broken only by the whisper of the wind in the cedar branches, and the scraping of their lean fingers against our window panes, had pricked us to such a luxurious confidence in our surroundings of bright chintz and candle-flame and firelight, that we had dared to talk of ghosts – in which, said we all, we did not believe one bit. We had told the story of the phantom coach, and the horribly strange bed, and the lady in the sacque, and the house in Berkeley Square. Not one of us believed in ghosts, but my heart, at least, seemed to leap to my throat and choke me, when a tap came to our door – a tap faint, but not to be mistaken.

"Who's there?" said the youngest of us, craning a lean neck towards the door. It opened slowly – and I give you my word the instant of suspense that followed is still reckoned among my life's least confident moments. Almost at once the door opened fully, and Miss Eastwich, my aunt's housekeeper, companion and general standby, looked in on us.

We all said "Come in," but she stood there. She was, at all normal hours, the most silent woman I have ever known. She stood and looked at us, and shivered a little. So did we – for in those days corridors were not warmed by hot-water pipes, and the air from the door was keen.

"I saw your light," she said at last, "and I thought it was late for you to be up – after all this gaiety. I thought perhaps—" her glance turned towards the door of the dressing room.

"No," I said, "she's fast asleep." I should have added a "goodnight", but the youngest of us forestalled my speech. She did not know Miss Eastwich as we others did. Did not know how her persistent silence had built a wall round her, a wall that no one dared to break down with the commonplaces of talk or the littlenesses of mere human relationship. Miss Eastwich's silence had taught us to treat her as a machine, and as other than a machine we never dreamed of treating her. But the youngest of us had seen Miss Eastwich for the first time that day. She was young and crude and ill-balanced, and the victim of blind calf-like impulse. She was also the heiress of a rich tallow-chandler, but that has nothing to do with this part of the story. She jumped up from the hearthrug, her unsuitably rich silk, lace-trimmed dressing gown falling back from her lean neck, and ran to the door and put an arm round Miss Eastwich's prim lisse-encircled neck. I gasped. I should as soon have dared embrace Cleopatra's Needle.

"Come in," said the youngest of us, "come in and get warm. There's lots of cocoa left." She drew Miss Eastwich in and shut the door.

The vivid light of pleasure in the housekeeper's pale eyes went through my heart like a knife. It would have been so easy to put an arm round her neck if one had only thought she wanted it. But it was not I who had thought that, and, indeed, my arm might not have brought the light invoked by the lean arm of the youngest of us.

"Now," the youngest went on eagerly, "you shall have the very biggest, nicest chair, and the cocoa pot's here on the hob as hot as hot, and we've all been telling ghost stories, only we don't believe in them a bit, and when you get warm you ought to tell one too."

Miss Eastwich, that model of decorum and decently done duties, tell a ghost story! The child was mad!

"You're sure I'm not in your way?" Miss Eastwich said, stretching her hands to the blaze. I wondered whether housekeepers have fires in their rooms even at Christmas time.

"Not a bit." I said it and I hope I said it as warmly as I felt it. "I – Miss Eastwich – I'd have asked you to come in other times – only I didn't think you'd care for girls' chatter."

The third girl, who was really of no account, and that's why I have not said anything about her before, poured cocoa for our guest; I put my fleecy Madeira shawl round her shoulders. I could not think of anything else to do for her, and I suddenly found myself wishing desperately to do something. The smile she gave us was quite pretty. People can smile prettily at forty or fifty, or even later, though girls don't realise this. It occurred to me, and this was another knife-thrust, that I had never seen Miss Eastwich smile – a real smile – before. The pale smiles of dutiful acquiescence were not of the same blood as this dimpling, happy transfiguring look.

"This is very pleasant," she said, and it seemed to me that I had never before heard her real voice. It did not please me to think that at the cost of cocoa and fire and my arms round her neck I might have heard this new voice any time these six years.

"We've been telling ghost stories," I said, "the worst of it is we don't believe in ghosts. No one anyone knows has ever seen one."

"It's always what somebody told somebody who told somebody, you know," said the youngest of us. "And you can't believe that, can you?"

"What the soldier said is not evidence," said Miss Eastwich. Will it be believed that the little Dickens quotation pierced me more keenly than the new smile or the new voice?

"And all ghost stories are so beautifully rounded off – a murder committed on the spot – or a hidden treasure or a warning – I think that makes them harder to believe. The most horrid ghost story I ever heard was one that was quite silly."

"Tell it."

"I can't – it doesn't sound anything to tell. Miss Eastwich ought to tell one."

"Oh, do!" said the youngest of us. and her salt-cellars loomed dark as she stretched her neck eagerly and laid an entreating arm on our guest's knee.

"The only thing that I ever knew of was – was hearsay," she said slowly, "at least half of it was."

I knew she would tell her story, and I knew she had never before told it, and I knew she was only telling it now because she was proud, and this seemed the only way to pay for the fire and the cocoa and the laying of that thin arm round her neck.

"Don't tell it," I said suddenly, "I know you'd rather not."

"I daresay it would bore you," she said meekly, and the youngest of us, who after all, did not understand everything, glared resentfully at me.

"We should just love it," she said, "do tell us. Never mind if it isn't a real proper fixed-up story. I'm certain anything you think ghostly would be quite too beautifully horrid for anything."

Miss Eastwich finished her cocoa and reached up to set the cup on the mantelpiece.

"It can't do any harm," she said to herself, "they don't believe in ghosts, and it wasn't exactly a ghost either. And they're all over twenty – they're not babies." There was a breathing time of hush and expectancy. The fire crackled and the gas flared higher because the billiard lights had been put out. We heard the steps and voices of the men going along the corridors.

"It is really hardly worth telling," Miss Eastwich said doubtfully, shading her faded face from the fire with her thin hand.

We all said, "Go on; oh, go on, do!"

"Well," she said, "twenty years ago, and more than that, I had two friends, and I loved them more than anything in the world. And they married each other."

She paused, and I knew just in what way she had loved each of them. The youngest of us said, "How awfully nice for you! Do go on."

She patted the youngest's shoulder, and I was glad that I had understood what the youngest of all hadn't. She went on.

"Well, after they were married I didn't see much of them for a year or two, and then he wrote and asked me to come and stay, because his wife was ill, and I should cheer her up, and cheer him up as well, for it was a gloomy house, and he himself was growing gloomy too."

I knew as she spoke that she had every line of that letter by heart.

"Well, I went. The address was in Lee, near London, and in those days there were streets and streets of new villa-houses growing up round old brick mansions standing in their own grounds, with red walls round, you know, and a sort of flavour of coaching days and post-chaises and Blackheath highwaymen about them. He had said the house was gloomy, and it was called 'The Firs', and I imagined my cab going through a dark winding shrubbery and drawing up in front of one of those sedate old square houses. Instead, we drew up in front of a large, smart villa, with iron railings, gay, encaustic tiles leading from the iron gate to the stained-glass panelled door, and for shrubbery, only a few stunted cypresses and acubas in the tiny front garden. But inside it was all warm and welcoming. He met me at the door.

She was gazing into the fire, and I knew she had forgotten us. But the youngest girl of all still thought that it was to us she was telling her story.

"He met me at the door," she said again, "and thanked me for coming, and asked me to forgive the past."

"What past?" asked that high priestess of the inapropos, the youngest of all.

"Oh, I suppose he meant because they hadn't invited me before, or something," said Miss Eastwich, worriedly. "But it's a very dull story, I find, after all, and—"

"Do go on," I said. Then I kicked the youngest of us and got up to re-arrange Miss Eastwich's shawl, and said in blatant dumb show, over the shawled shoulders:

"Shut up, you little idiot!"

After another silence the housekeeper's new voice went on:

"They were very glad to see me, and I was very glad to be there. You girls now have such troops of friends, but these two were all I had, all I had ever had. Mabel wasn't exactly ill, only weak and excitable. I thought he seemed more ill than she did. She went to bed early, and before she went, she asked me to keep him company through his last pipe, so we went into the dining room and sat in the two armchairs on each side of the fireplace. They were covered with green leather, I remember. There were bronze groups of horses and a black marble clock on the mantelpiece – all wedding presents. He poured out some whisky for himself, but he hardly touched it. He sat looking into the fire. At last I said:

"'What's wrong? Mabel looks as well as you could expect.'

"He said 'Yes, but I don't know from one day to another that she won't begin to notice something wrong. That's why I wanted you to come. You were always so sensible and strong-minded, and Mabel's like a little bird, or a flower.'

"I said 'Yes, of course,' and waited for him to go on. I thought he must be in debt or in trouble of some sort. So I just waited. Presently he said:

"'Margaret, this is a very peculiar house.' He always called me Margaret; you see, we'd been such old friends. I told him I thought the house was very pretty, and fresh, and homelike, only a little too new, but that fault would mend with time. He said:

"'It is new; that's just it. We're the first people who've ever lived in it. If it were an old house, Margaret, I should think it was haunted.'

"I asked if he had seen anything. 'No,' he said, 'not yet.'

"'Heard, then?' said I.

"'No, nor heard either,' he said, 'but there's a sort of feeling, I can't describe it. I've seen nothing and I've heard nothing, but I've been so near to seeing and hearing! Just not, that's all. And something follows me about – only when I turn round there's never anything but my shadow. And I always feel that I shall see the thing, or hear it, next minute; but I never do, not quite, it's always just not visible.'

"I thought he'd been working rather hard, and I tried to cheer him up by making light of all this. 'It was just nerves,' I said. Then he said he had thought I could help him. and did I think anyone he had wronged could have laid a curse on him, and did I believe in curses? I said I didn't, and the only person anyone could have said he had wronged forgave him freely, I knew, if there was anything to forgive. So I told him this too."

It was I, not the youngest of us, who knew the name of that person wronged and forgiving.

"So then I said 'He ought to take Mabel away from the house and have a complete change.' But he said, 'No, Mabel had got everything in order, and he could never manage to get her away just now without explaining everything, and above all,' he said, 'she mustn't guess there's anything wrong. I daresay I shall not feel quite such a lunatic now you're here.'

"So we said 'Goodnight'."

"Is that all the story?" said the third girl, striving to convey that even as it stood it was a good story.

"That is only the beginning." said Miss Eastwich. "Whenever I was alone with him, he used to tell me the same thing over and over again, and at first when I began to notice things I tried to think that it was his talk that had upset my nerves. The odd thing was that it wasn't only at night – but in broad daylight, and particularly on the stairs and passages. On the staircase the feeling used to be so awful that I have had to bite my lips till they bled, to keep myself from running up the stairs at full speed. Only I knew if I did I should go mad at the top. There was always something behind me – exactly as he had said – something that one could just not see. And, a sound that one could just not hear. There was a long corridor at the top of the house. I have sometimes almost seen something – you know how one sees things without looking – but if I turned round it seemed as if the thing dropped and melted into my shadow. There was a little window at the end of the corridor.

"Downstairs there was another corridor, something like it, with a cupboard at one end and the kitchen at the other. One night I went down into the kitchen to warm some milk for Mabel. The servants had gone to bed. As I stood by the fire waiting for the milk to boil I glanced through the open door and along the passage. I never could keep my eyes on what I was doing, in that house. The cupboard door was partly open; they used to keep empty bottles and things in it. And as I looked I knew that now it was not going to be 'almost' anymore. Yet I said 'Mabel?' not because I thought it could be Mabel who was crouching down there, half in and half out of the cupboard. The thing was grey at first and then it was black. And when I whispered 'Mabel', it seemed to sink down till it lay like a pool of ink on the floor, and then its edges drew in, and it seemed to flow, like ink, when you tilt up the paper you have spilt it on, and it flowed into the cupboard till it was all gathered into the shadow there. I saw it go quite plainly. The gas was full on in the kitchen. I screamed aloud, but even then I'm thankful to say I had enough sense to upset the boiling milk, so that when he came downstairs three steps at a time, I had the excuse for my scream of a scalded hand. The explanation was satisfactory to Mabel, but next night he said:

"'Why didn't you tell me? It was that cupboard. All the horror of the house comes out of that. Tell me, have you seen anything yet? Or is it only the nearly seeing and nearly hearing still?'

"I said. 'You must tell me first what you've seen.' He told me, and his eyes wandered as he spoke to the shadows by the curtains, and I turned up all three gaslights and lit the candles on the mantelpiece. Then we looked at each other and said we were both mad, and thanked God that Mabel was at least sane. For what he had seen was what I had seen.

"After that I hated to be alone with a shadow, because at any moment I might see something that would crouch and sink and lie like a black pool and then slowly draw itself into the shadow that was nearest. Often that shadow was my own. The thing came first at night, but afterwards there was no hour safe from it. I saw it at dawn, and at noon, in the dusk and in the firelight, and always it crouched and sank, and was a pool that flowed into some shadow and became part of it. And always I saw it with a straining of the eyes, a pricking and aching. It seemed as though I could only just see it, as if my sight, to see it, had to be strained to the uttermost. And still the sound was in the house, the sound that I could just not hear. At last one morning early I did hear it. It was close behind me, and it was only a sigh. It was worse than the thing that crept among the shadows.

"I don't know how I bore it. I couldn't have borne it if I hadn't been so fond of them both. But I knew in my heart that if he had no one to whom he could speak openly he would go mad, or tell Mabel. His was not a very strong character. Very sweet and kind and gentle, but not strong. He was always easily led. So I stayed on and bore up, and we were very cheerful and made little jokes and tried to be amusing when Mabel was with us. But when we were alone we did not try to he amusing.

"And sometimes a day or two would go by without our seeing or hearing anything, and we should perhaps have fancied that we had fancied what we had seen and heard, only there was always the feeling of there being something about the house that one could just not hear and not see. Sometimes we used to try not to talk about it, but generally we talked of nothing else at all. And the weeks went by, and Mabel's baby was born. The nurse and the doctor said that both mother and child were doing well. He and I sat late in the dining room that night. We had neither of us seen or heard anything for three days – our anxiety about Mabel was lessened. We talked of the future: it seemed then so much brighter than the past. We arranged that the moment she was fit to be moved he should take her away to the sea, and I should superintend the moving of their furniture into the new house he had already chosen. He was gayer than I had seen him since his marriage, almost like his old self. When I said 'goodnight' to him he said a lot of things about my having been a comfort to them both. I hadn't done anything much of course, but still I am glad he said that.

"Then I went upstairs – almost for the first time without that feeling of something following me. I listened at Mabel's door. Everything was quiet. I went on towards my own room, and in an instant I felt that there was something behind me. I turned. It was crouching there; it sank, and the black fluidness of it seemed to be sucked under the door of Mabel's room.

"I went back. I opened the door a listening inch. All was still. And then I heard a sigh – close behind me. I opened the door and went in. The nurse and the baby were asleep. Mabel was asleep too; she looked so pretty, like a tired child – the baby was cuddled up into one of her arms with its tiny head against her side. I prayed then that Mabel might never know the terrors that he and I had known – that those little ears might never hear any but pretty sounds, those dear eyes never see any but pretty sights. I did not dare to pray for a long time after that. Because my prayer was answered. She never saw, never heard anything more in this world. And now I could do nothing more for him or for her.

"When they had put her in her coffin I lighted wax candles round her, and laid the horrible white flowers that people will send, near to her, and then I saw he had followed me. I took his hand to lead him away.

"At the door we both turned. It seemed to us that we heard a sigh. He would have sprung to her side in I don't know what mad glad hope. But at that instant we both saw it. Between us and the coffin, first grey, then black, it crouched an instant, then sank and liquified, and was gathered together and drawn till it ran into the nearest shadow. And the nearest shadow was the shadow of Mabel's coffin. I left the next day. His mother came. She had never liked me."

Miss Eastwich paused. I think she had quite forgotten us.

"Didn't you see him again?" asked the youngest of all.

"Only once," Miss Eastwich answered, "and something black crouched then between him and me. But it was only his second wife crying beside his coffin. It's not a cheerful story, is it? And it doesn't lead anywhere. I've never told anyone else. I think it was seeing his daughter that brought it all back."

She looked toward the dressing-room door. "Mabel's baby," said the youngest of all.

"Yes, and exactly like Mabel, only with his eyes."

The youngest of all had Miss Eastwich's hands and was petting them.

Suddenly the woman wrenched her hands away and stood at her gaunt height, hands clenched, eyes straining. She was looking at something that we could not see, and I know now what the man in the Bible meant when he said "the hair of my flesh stood up—"

What she saw seemed not quite to reach the height of the dressing-room door handle. Her eyes following it down, down, widened and widened. Mine followed them, and all the nerves of my eyes seemed strained to the uttermost – and I almost saw – or did I quite see? I can't be certain. But we all heard the long-drawn, quivering sigh. And to each of us it seemed to be breathed just behind each.

It was I who caught up the candle – it dropped wax all over my trembling hands – it was I who was dragged by Miss Eastwich to the side of the girl who had fainted during the second extra. But it was the youngest of all whose lean arms were round the housekeeper when we turned away, and that have been round her many a time since in the new home where she keeps house for the youngest of us all.

The doctor, who came in the morning, said that Mabel's daughter had died of heart disease, which she inherited from her mother. That was what made her faint during the second extra. But I have sometimes wondered whether she may not have inherited something from her father. I have never been able to forget the look on her dead face.

They Walk and Weep

Michael Nethercott

A WINTER'S NIGHT on the outskirts of Boston, and I a young man. The dim little bar was half-filled, yet I happened to be the one he latched onto when I went up to order. Swiveling on his barstool, he pointed a somewhat palsied finger at me and snapped out his question: "Who is the greatest writer that ever there was?"

His brogue marked him as an Irishman. He was a skinny, fairly dapper-looking elder in a plaid Sinatra hat. He had obviously downed a few drinks, and there hung about him a decided air of gloom.

I paid for my beer and accepted the challenge. "Oh, Shakespeare, I'd say."

The aged man clicked his tongue. "Incorrect. Not too heinous a guess, though. We can't dismiss the fellow who did so well by mad old Lear and treacherous Macbeth."

I happened to know a little *Macbeth.* "Slain by a man who'd been 'from his mother's womb untimely ripped.'"

He lit up. "Admirable! A pup who knows his Bard. Here, have a seat. You'll not pay for another drink tonight, I swear. Meet Eachan Clooney, your benefactor. Sure, Shakespeare he's a worthy, no denying; but for sheer power of verse, there's none can touch My Lord Swinburne."

"Who?"

"*Who,* you dare ask? *Who?*" Eachan grimaced. "You're back on your own coin for your drinks, lad. It's a vulgar crime that so few today remember the grandness of him. Algernon Charles Swinburne. I call him My Lord Swinburne, the poet beyond poets. Even if he *was* an Englishman, through no fault of his own. Are you Irish then? With your round face and black curls, you look the part."

"My mother's folks were from County Kerry," I conceded.

"A Kerryman!" he chuckled. "They're a queer lot, you know. But they *do* crave their poetry down there on the rough shores. You should really know your Swinburne, young man. He'll speak for you if you listen. He surely speaks for me on this wretched night." Eachan took in a deep breath and intoned:

"The burden of long living. Thou shalt fear
Waking, and sleeping mourn upon thy bed;
And say at night 'Would God the day were here,'
And say at dawn 'Would God the day were dead.'"

He finished off his whiskey and called for another.

"It's fine verse," I said.

"Of course it is," Eachan concurred. "And like all fine verse, it sings of truth. It sings, surely, of *my* dismal truth."

"How so?"

He appraised me with red, weary eyes. "You're thinking I'm just another old drunk out on his rounds, aren't you? Well, you'd be wrong. I'm not a drinking man at all. Just these last several days.

The burden of long living... But even we who've lived long want to keep on living. Death, death clinging to my throat – *that's* the fierce burden I now bear."

"You're afraid of dying?" I surprised myself with my bluntness.

"It's not common death I fear!" He grew agitated. "It's death that comes from an evil place! Death from—" He caught himself and lowered his voice. "From the schemings of a *corpse man.* An entity who spits on the very laws of God. Look now, I fancy myself an honest Christian and a humble being, but a man's faith can be shaken. Savagely shaken..."

Hailing the bartender, I ordered a whiskey for myself. I sensed that I needed to brace up for this. Eachan went silent for a minute until my drink arrived. Then he glanced about to make sure we were unobserved, reached into his coat pocket, and withdrew a small cloth pouch. From this, he shook something dark and crumpled into his hand and held it out to me.

"This is what it's about," he whispered.

It looked to me like a strip of old leather. "What is it?"

"A caul."

"A what?"

"A *caul.*" His eyes widened. "A birth membrane. It happens ever so rarely that a babe is born with its face covered over by a caul. Like a veil of flesh, it is. No harm to the child; it can be just lifted off. But those born with the veil are said to possess the second sight. And some individuals, if they apply themselves, can beckon up even greater powers."

I gazed at the object with some disdain. "Jesus. How old is this one?"

"Over eighty years," said Eachan. "The sailor who first owned it must have treated it with some chemical. Shriveled it a bit, but preserved it to this day."

"Why did a sailor have it?"

He offered me a cold smile. "So you're to be my holy confessor, are you, lad? Well, Lord knows, I need one. My cousin here in town thinks I've gone mad and won't hear a word from me. And there's not a priest in the state I'd trust with my suffering. You're a wee little Kerryman who can quote *Macbeth*, so you'll do for me. Come on then, walk me to my door and I'll tell it as we go."

He put away the caul, swallowed his whiskey and headed out. I drained my own glass and followed him. When you are young and untethered, master of your own evenings, the call to adventure is hard to ignore. I had nothing to lose, I reasoned, by lending an ear to this character's odd, bleak fantasies. We stepped out into the winter night. A light, lively snowfall whirled about us. Eachan pulled up the collar of his overcoat and shivered visibly.

"Yeah, it's chilly," I observed.

"It's not just the temperature," said my companion. "It's the fear in me, if you must know. He could be out here in the darkness. Waiting."

"You're talking about someone who's dead? You said—"

"Let's walk," he insisted, leading the way down the narrow sidewalk. "You need first to understand about the caul. It's considered great good luck to keep one on your person. Seamen say it can protect against shipwrecks. That's why that sailor bought this one off a midwife. Came from a baby boy. This was back in Ireland, 'round turn of the century. The sailor kept the caul for about two decades. Then, when he was a man of middle years, he met this lovely young lass in Galway. He was struck mightily by her and gave over the caul as a gift."

"Quite the Romeo." The whiskey had made me cocky. "He sure knew how to charm the ladies, eh?"

"Quiet!" Eachan barked. "This is no amusement, believe me. He was killed in a boarding house fire not a week later. His luck had forsaken him, don't you see?"

"He was lucky up till then?"

The old man nodded. "Very, according to the tales he told her. In the years he owned the caul, that sailor survived several brushes with death. Once, he was attacked with a knife, and the blade broke on a harmonica in his breast pocket, sparing his life. Another time he missed a passage on a fishing trawler and the boat went down that night with all hands. Several near misses like that. But then he gave away the veil, and he burned..."

"What about the girl?"

"She later became a nun. It's true. I'm sure it was her way of balancing out the fact that the sailor perished in giving her his gift. Yes, she became a bride of Jesus, but she always kept the caul hidden in her robes. The holy bishops in Rome wouldn't much care for *that* bit of paganry, I'm guessing."

We turned a corner. "So you yourself got the caul from the nun?"

"That's right. I got it from the nun."

"And did the same thing happen as with the sailor?" I asked. "Did the nun die right after she gave it away?"

"Yes," said Eachan softly. "She died. More than forty years ago."

"How many years have you lived in America?"

"Nearly five. I never had wife or child back in Ireland; but I had a cousin over here, and I'd always wanted to see the States. Foolish for a man to make such a drastic change so late in his game. But then, many are the foolish things I've done in this life."

The snowfall was growing bolder, agitated by a strong wind. We were now alone on the street. I noticed just ahead of us a little spiral of flakes, about five feet above the sidewalk, spinning energetically beneath a street lamp. It seemed almost as if the snow at that certain spot was struggling to achieve some form.

Eachan saw it too, for he clutched my arm and pointed frantically. "Dear God, do you not see it? The eyes! And the terrible mouth! It's himself again, keeping after me..."

I strained my eyes. There appeared to be *something* there, but I could not tell what. In a moment, the phenomenon had played itself out.

At this point, Eachan was fairly hanging onto me to stay on his feet. He closed his eyes and choked down a sob. "It's just as My Lord Swinburne has written:

"The burden of dead faces. Out of sight
And out of love, beyond the reach of hands
Changed in the changing of the dark and light,
They walk and weep about the barren lands."

Putting an arm around him, I forced my companion to continue forward. We passed under the street lamp without incident.

Eachan was trembling, but trying hard to regain his composure. "Our poor, troubled world is filled with them, lad. All those who won't take their slumber beyond the black curtain. *They walk and weep...* I heard of a farmer once who would leave his grave to stride the fields every harvest time. And my mother told of a noblewoman who hanged herself in her stables and was often seen there swinging and moaning to herself. And now I, too, know one. I have my own tormenting specter. This is the fourth time I've seen him, and he draws nearer each visit."

I was not yet ready to abandon reason. "I don't know if we saw anything, really. Maybe just some weird, little meteorological thing. What dead man do you think is following you, anyway? The sailor?"

"No, not him," Eachan answered. "*The man born with the caul*. He who had it lifted from his face as a newborn babe. It's said that those who've had their veils sold must get them back in death or they'll never rest. He's hounding me for his veil, don't you see? But if I give it up, I'll perish like the others."

I wanted to laugh away this fable, to declare it a pathetic blend of whiskey and senility. But somehow I couldn't. "How would you even know what he looked like? Did you ever meet him?"

Eachan shook his head. "No, never. Yet I know it in every inch of me. He's a very old little man, older than I. He must have died just recently, because the visits began only a week ago. I believe he's of the type I mentioned to you who've taken their caul-power and raised it to something unworldly."

"You're saying this man is – was – some kind of sorcerer?"

"Call him what you will," snapped Eachan. "All I know is that he has the means to quit his grave and track me down here in the States. I've seen him and, God protect me, I've *heard* him. That hideous bloody wailing…"

It was getting hard to ignore the storm. The snow-filled wind bit into our faces and pushed forcefully against our bodies. Then, as we were passing a row of closed shop fronts, something unsettling occurred. A whirlwind of sorts sprang up around us, a tight cyclone of frenzied snow that threw us against each other and sucked away our air. It was like being squeezed inside an icy, rotating cylinder.

"Leave me be!" Eachan screamed out. "Keep to your damned coffin!"

With extraordinary effort, he hurled himself through that circling white wall. By this action, the whirlwind seemed to instantly dissipate. Eachan continued down the street in a stumbling run. I overcame my shock and went after him. He had taken to pounding on the darkened shop windows, shouting for someone to open up for him. Only one tiny grocery remained lit within. Through the glass front, we could see a large black woman intent on her sweeping.

"I know her!" Eachan was almost giddy. "Marie! Marie, let me in!"

The woman looked up and called out in a West Indies accent, "Sorry, I'm closed for the night."

Eachan rapped insistently on the glass. "It's me, Marie – Mr. Clooney, don't you know. I buy my sardines here twice a week. Twice a week! Let me in, Marie…"

She came forward and unlocked the door. Standing in the threshold, leaning on her broom, she smiled tiredly at us. "I'm all out of sardines, Mr. Clooney. You come back Monday, please."

As Marie was pulling the door closed, Eachan suddenly shoved past her and planted himself firmly inside her little shop. "I just need to get myself out of the dark for a bit, that's all."

"Hey!" Marie stepped close to him. "I said to you I'm closed!"

Eachan's eyes twitched spasmodically and his lower lip quivered. "Now look, Marie, we're both island people, you and I. We know of the fierce things that can move through the night. We know the dead aren't always dead. Please let me—"

The shopkeeper looked greatly disturbed. Her voice got very low, "Go, both of you. Go, or I'll call up the policemen."

"Come on, Eachan," I insisted. "Let's go. *Now.*" I gripped his arm and began leading him towards the door.

With a cry, Eachan broke loose and yanked the broom away from Marie. He wielded it high like a club and shook his head frantically. "No, no, no. I'll not go back out there."

This was getting very out of hand. Marie shifted her footing and Eachan took a swing at her, missing by inches. The motion put him off balance, and I used the opportunity to snatch away his weapon and bustle him outside.

"I'm sorry, ma'am" I called over my shoulder. The last glimpse I had of Marie, she had retrieved her broom and was holding it across her chest in a protective stance.

This evening had turned into more than I had bargained for. Why couldn't I have met some lovely, wanton young adventuress at that bar? Why, instead, had I saddled myself with this old lunatic? And, more troublingly, why couldn't I seem to disengage myself from him? As we pressed on through the storm, Eachan appeared drained and defeated.

"It's a bad thing I did back there," he mumbled. "But I'll make it up to Marie. I'll buy her some flowers tomorrow. I will – red roses. Nice red roses."

A taxi sped down our empty street, splattering us with thick slush. In Eachan's frayed condition, this mundane misfortune was enough to unravel him. He slid down to the sidewalk and began to loudly whimper.

"I deserve whatever comes to me. For I stole it, didn't I? Didn't I?" He was talking rapidly, gasping out his words. "But I was going to war, you see. Needed the luck. I was young, young as you. I didn't want to die. She'd left the pouch on a table. She didn't know I took it."

I crouched down beside him. "The caul? You mean you stole it from the nun?"

"Yes, yes. I was going to war. She was just a nun, I told myself. Her life was safe, sheltered. It was *me* that was going to face the bullets. Wasn't *I* the one that deserved the luck? And, indeed, I came through the war unscratched. But at what a wretched cost! The day after I shipped out, she was strolling across a field to hear Mass. There was a hunter in the woods. He didn't see her…" Eachan dissolved into tears.

I tried to help him up, but he resisted. "Come on, Eachan," I said gently. "It was a long time ago. More than forty years, you told me."

He fixed his damp, burning eyes on mine. "But, dear God, what I did to her. To her! *And I her own brother.*"

A terrible understanding came to me. "The nun was your sister?"

He smiled grimly. "My eldest one. Only thirty-six the day she died. I stole the caul from her and sentenced her to death. Her own darling brother."

It was all more than I could take in. I suddenly wanted very much to be done with Mr. Eachan Clooney and all his occult blatherings. "Are we almost to where you live?"

He stared into the darkness. "Not too far."

I stood. "Then get up and I'll walk you there."

Eachan remained on the sidewalk. He dropped his head.

"I said get up."

"Four hundred and ninety." With his head lowered, I could barely make out the words.

"What's that?"

"Four hundred and ninety." Eachan looked back up at me, his eyes still moist.

"It's in the gospels. The Christ is asked by his man Peter how often should a sinner be forgiven. Would seven times be a reasonable amount? And Jesus replies, no, seven times isn't adequate – a man should be forgiven seventy times seven. See? Seventy times seven. If you cipher that out it comes to four hundred and ninety."

"Eachan…"

"But I'll not be getting that allotment will I?" The tears were running freely now. "Tell me, lad, where's *my* Christian forgiveness?"

I'd had enough. "Get up right now or you're on your own. I mean it." I reached down my hand to him. "Well?"

He looked up at me with a weak grin. "Ah, my good little Kerryman."

The next moment, an impossible blast of snow slammed me from behind and sent me sprawling over Eachan. When I raised my head, I saw something coming towards us from down the street. Or rather, the thing approaching us was motion itself; for there was nothing of substance to it, only a moving point within which the enraged snows seemed to be gathering. Then, all at once, the heavy spiraling flakes convened themselves into a rough form. It was, I swear, that of a diminutive man.

"Himself," Eachan groaned.

I scrambled to my feet, grabbed my companion violently by his shirtfront and hauled him upright. "Move!" I began to run, dragging Eachan along with me. The storm's accumulation underfoot slowed our pace. Stealing a glance backwards, I saw the figure dissipate into snow again. I didn't pause. Coming to an intersection, I shouted into Eachan's face, "Which way? Which way?" He pointed left and I turned us onto a dim-lit side street.

We had not gone a block, when the swirling mass of snow swooped down again, just a few yards ahead of us. As before, the form of a man abruptly appeared, but now more fully articulated. I could make out a beard, narrow eyes, wrinkled jowls. His whole figure had a grayish-white hue, like a blending of snow and shadow. He stretched out an arm towards us.

We were next to an alleyway. Instinctively, I pushed Eachan into it and forced him forward. I could see the low glow of a street lamp at the other end. We overturned several trashcans in our flight. Eachan was panting dangerously and I was not doing much better. We had almost reached the end, when something suddenly blocked our exit. There, in jaundiced lamplight, stood our pursuer. He parted his lips and a disturbing, incomprehensible sound came forth. It was the high-pitched, tremulous cry of a newborn child.

The storm's brutal chill was nothing compared to what now seized my blood. To hear an infant's distressed wail from the mouth of an ancient man was hideous to the nth degree. The scream seemed to be amplified, as if it echoed from the depths of some endless cavern, and it throbbed deafeningly within the confines of the alleyway. Like a pair of maze rats, we pivoted and fled back towards where we had entered. Eachan was apparently energized by the horror of it all, for he hurtled past me and became the first to escape. A tumble over one of the trashcans delayed me, and when I finally reached the street I could not find Eachan. Peering through the snowfall, I at last spied him leaning against the wall of a building, his back turned towards me. I ran to his side and spun him about.

An exclamation died in my throat. What greeted me was not Eachan's face, but a white, featureless mask. A gruesome caul of snow. Fighting for breath, he began to claw convulsively at the thing. I stood transfixed, unable to make myself help him. After a struggle, he somehow managed to free himself. The snow that had enwrapped his face now cast itself back into the wind.

I saw that Eachan had torn his cheeks with several long, deep scratches. His eyes were wild with fear. He opened his mouth to beg some mercy of me, but what came out horrified us both. Here again rose the unearthly baby's cry, though now it issued from Eachan's own lungs.

It was at this moment that something from the common world intruded on our nightmare. A delivery van lurched out of the darkness and came racing up the road. Swifter than thought, Eachan flung himself from the sidewalk to accept the full impact of the speeding vehicle.

I took it all in: the vicious thud, the ragdoll flight through air, the merciless descent. Then the driver, a teenaged boy, was hopping crazily about the street, chanting: "Didn't see him, didn't see him…"

"I know," I said to him. "We need an ambulance. Run down the street and find a phone."

He nodded desperately and sprinted away. I went over and sat down in the snow beside Eachan. Somehow, I thought he'd be already gone, but he opened his eyes to me.

"Stay still now," I said. "We're getting help."

He offered up a little smile. His voice was barely audible. "No need. No need. Young man, it's not so hard to die after all."

I took his hand. "Rest now, Eachan."

"I will. Let him have his damned thing, anyway. All my piss and poetry's done." He went silent for a few long moments, then said, "I'm content. And I believe I'm forgiven. I didn't need seven times seven after all..."

A great howl of wind made me look up. The snowstorm seemed to be drawing itself rapidly away across the black skies.

"Ah, pup," Eachan groaned softly. "An Irishman should leave with verse upon his lips.

"We thank with brief thanksgiving whatever gods may be
That no life lives for ever; that dead men rise up never;
That even the weariest river winds somewhere safe to sea."

Eachan swallowed hard and whispered, "Oh, My Lord Swinburne..." Then he closed his eyes and his hand slipped from mine.

I sat there by him for several minutes, drained and numb. I would never be able to make sense of this evening. In fact, would I ever be able to make sense of *anything* ever again? When I heard the van driver's footfalls coming up the street, I snapped to and quickly reached into Eachan's coat pocket. Pulling out the cloth pouch, I turned it upside down over my palm. Nothing. It was gone. I tossed the pouch aside.

The boy ran up. "They're coming. They should be – Hey, he's not dead, is he? Please don't tell me he died."

"It's all right," I said. "It's really all right. His luck just ran out after all these years. That's all."

Then I thought to myself: *Roses. I should buy Marie her roses.*

Enlivened

Adam L.G. Nevill

BEFORE US, a rock. About us, darkness.

Aged limestone dimly lit from below. A dolmen, pale in patches on its raised features but mostly weathered green, blotched like verdigris on copperplate. A pillar stained the tinge of dried mucus or dead seaweed; a palette of nausea when observed for more than moments. A monolith of stone pored and burrowed by creatures no longer infesting the rock; the uneven surface pockmarked with sinuses, tiny tunnels that end in black. Honeycombed from the myriad of tiny mouths that chewed stone during a vast swathe of time in the sea, or perhaps a cave where it patiently awaited excavation.

A rough design is inscribed on the front of the menhir. Unsavoury form emerges upon this crude column that stands within an iron caliper, rooted to the floorboards. Is that a bulbous abdomen fashioned by Neolithic hands, from a time of frost and tundra, wild times without words? Are they wings, foetal and insubstantial, that cling to the sides of the rock? Was this a likeness, or an impression, wrought by an artist, or priest? And what does the faint, ghastly image depict? Can we assume that the pointed or beaked shape crowning this lumpen bas-relief was once a fearsome head tilted to shriek? Is this an ancient royal crest hewn into rock? Or an image of something once worshipped? A symbol? A territorial marker? Was it brought here from a lonely vigil in a misted, wet landscape, or from the ruins of a temple? The rock's carving conjures all such purposes and settings.

From its cold breast an aroma wafts and lingers in heavy air. An ecclesiastical flavour, mingling with the mineral scent of damp stone. Something has been sprinkled, consecrating the crude rock. Frankincense, a sweet piney resin. Vetiver, a twist of citron. And something more pungent, like almonds, adorns, honours and respects this stone.

About the foundations of the pillar, a myriad tealight candles glimmer in the last of the liquefied wax upon which they float like small yellow hands waving from tiny grey seas. Close to extinction, the dimming candlelight ripples the engulfing dark and the silent, hallowed air that surrounds the rock.

Two bowls sit at the foot of the column. Simple, unadorned wooden containers.

The contents of the first bowl glimmer the black of treacle or fresh oil. A tidemark, the red of beets, is visible above the slippery onyx surface of the liquid.

In the second bowl, two egg-shapes slump together. Soft and dull, partially squashed or collapsed: eyes. And now that sight has left the pair of discarded orbs inside the bowl, the sclera has tarnished an unhealthy grey and the irises have misted and been sheathed with a pellucid veil. These sticky misshapen lumps were once blue eyes. There is still a trace of a dark sea where they bulge at the front and a vague sheen persists about the dead flesh, mere memory of the lustre these eyes once possessed when alive and blinking and seeing and rotating within a human face.

About the rock, the bowl of blood, the bowl of eyes, and the many candles whose flames shrink to feeble points the size of match-heads, the dark oppresses. This space, this sanctum, is tuned to a frequency of the deepest silence. The profound stillness creates an uncomfortable pressure as if the space has been lowered into an unseen water that slops beyond the encroaching walls of darkness. The narrowing space about the rock is the last portion of dimming illumination within a mute void that laps at the room and flows from the ceiling. A place smothered by an uncanny quiescence.

Two steps back and withdraw across spiky patterns: lines and angles mark the wooden floor, carefully fashioned from strips of black electrician's tape. Within the shapes marked out by the black lines, messy symbols, curved or jagged, have been fashioned from blood that crusts. An arrangement that indicates an established practice, a rite, a procedure that has been repeated many times in this space.

Against the murky floor, a new shape takes form within the darkness. A body curled into itself. A wretched, uneven, glistening silhouette, its face black with blood. Sunken to inky pulps, the eye sockets gape. From scalp to heel the figure has been peeled and thinned, is wetly gelid.

Wrists bound with green twine, dark fingers knot beneath a glossy chin in supplication. The figure prays. Perhaps for mercy, even now the possibility of reprieve is gone. Thin ankles are tethered like a hen in the window of a restaurant; long feet swell blue below the pinch of their bindings.

The gender is impossible to discern but the figure on the floor was dispatched by the leather thong entwined about their neck. A throttling string knotted about a piece of wood toggles the victim's nape. Strangled. As the wood was turned the leather tightened. Before the votive candles, before the bowls, before the rock, before the dark, they choked.

Further back from the dolmen and the lifeless and stripped body before it, a perimeter marked out by another four candles: one positioned to the front of the dolmen, one behind, one at either side of it, equidistant apart. Thick vanilla candles are mounted on iron stands, still lit but with recalcitrant flames that do little to beat back a darkness near solid.

Four candles that stand before four arches. Apertures appearing as pale eclipses, their dim curvatures positioned at the four points of a compass, the monolith occupying the centre where invisible lines would cross between the arches. A room offering a quartet of opposing entrances, or exits.

Beyond each arched portal little to nothing is visible save more of the dark.

Closer to the first arch, it is possible to see that the empty frame is made of wood, painted black. This door faces south. The floor beneath this oval void feels unstable. An unpleasant vibration runs below the wooden floorboards, one strong enough to interfere with the heart's rhythm, the mind's ability to form thoughts, the respiratory system's essential inhalations and exhalations.

Step away.

To the east.

Where it is not possible to pass from the sanctum and its smothering darkness, or the clinging pall of almonds, frankincense and vetiver. From the blank depth beyond this door, a muscular force of moving air funnels inwards like a bloated river's mightiest current. A hot wind belches from a region as sun-blanched as the hottest desert on earth.

To the west.

Where something worse than wind or the thrumming of an unstable energy exists. Beyond the depthless oblivion of the third portal comes the distant noise of a great beast, sniffing. Too easy to imagine a large muzzle lapping across a floor beyond the aperture; a form wary of entry, but reluctant to retreat.

North.

The northern arch reeks of sulphur. From the centre of the arch, water drips and splashes in minute, invisible explosions, barely discernible slaps against sodden wood.

Beyond the arch, an object glimmers in what light struggles to reach here from beyond this room. A wooden floor can be seen to extend along a narrow passage to the foot of a staircase, the walls on either side impossible to see in any detail. At the summit of the wooden stairs, a dirty yellow light settles.

The object upon the floor of the narrow passage is a scabbard for a sword. The unsheathed sword is not visible, but hard brown leather once gripped the absent blade, the hide now brittle and flaking with age. Brass fittings glimmer where they rib the scabbard, cold to the touch.

Along the passage and up the stairs to an obstacle. A second body.

An old man, his thin face stiffened into a scream that left his mouth in the lightless past of this place; his lips are peeled back from bony gums, fossilised to a rictus. A grimace missing any augmentation from the eyes, which are missing. Empty black wells leer up at the dark from beneath a pale scalp freckled like eggshell. What hair exists at the back and sides of the skull is in wispy disarray. Nostrils ungroomed, eyebrows tangled like wires at the end of a severed cable. A head that has turned too far backwards. The figure might have been looking over its shoulder before the whole head became unmoored at the furthest extent of the intended rotation.

His clothing is ordinary: a woollen cardigan, bottle-green corduroy trousers, belted tight, maroon socks on shrivelled ankles, innocuous black shoes, still laced. But the man's slight and pointed frame appears flatter than it should, as if his body has been pressed into the stairs. The figure may have been stepped upon. A closer scrutiny of the clothing also suggests a lumpiness caused by the breaking of the body inside the surrounding, confining fabric, so that the garments now function as bags to hold the limbs and trunk together.

The steel of a ceremonial sword lies two steps above one outstretched and frail hand, the polished blade a dull smear in thin light.

At the summit of the staircase, an open door.

Electric light glows within a hallway beyond the door, tainted the hue of a faded photograph.

A pall of stale air reeking of almonds is trapped behind the curtained windows of the ground floor. A closeness further compressed by drab wallpaper and yellowing ceilings.

On the far left of the reception, a cluttered kitchen, its fittings and fixtures not modernised in decades. Once white doors of cabinets and drawers sallowed by sunlight and cooking stains. Orange lino worn to ivory by decades of feet shuffling between aged, enamelled appliances, whose surfaces are a murder scene of baked grease and spills transformed from liquid to solid.

Fragile wooden blinds, their ties impenetrable knots bunching like fibrous grapes, shut out most of the light, leaving a little glaring from the corners of the window frames.

Across the counter tops a spiky battlefield of unwashed crockery and murky containers. The tins and jars with their congealed contents are like beakers in an abandoned laboratory. A toaster is pressed into the wall, blackened as a car-wreck. Breadbin: its door kicked in. A coloured tongue of unwashed clothes pours onto the floor from the washing machine's porthole.

A third body. Jammed into the corner of the kitchen.

Beside the metal sink that grows a tower of stained bowls and rimed pans, and amidst a scaffolding of begrimed utensils, part of a woman is visible. From the waist upwards, she has disappeared inside the confines of a cupboard between the cooker and sink. The door of the wooden unit has been smashed inwards from the force of her entry. Fresh splinters of timber spike from the frame around buckled hinges. A pair of fat legs inside taut taupe slacks jut into the room. White socks cover thick ankles. Cream shoes fastened with a velcro strap conceal oddly small feet that look silly despite the shock of their owner being thrust through the door of a kitchen unit.

Beside the legs and portion of abdomen not crammed inside the fitted cupboard lies a small, round shield. The kind of artefact seen in museums of antiquity. It is fashioned from leather stretched across wood, with a wheel-shaped rim and spherical boss of highly polished brass. A shield ceremonial and untested in battle, perhaps until now, but its incongruity amidst the domestic rubble of a messy and unhygienic household is as striking as the discarded sword and scabbard in the cellar: old weapons that offered scant protection against the kind of force that smote these bodies.

A noise from further down the hallway. A sign of life.

From that sound of exertion, it would be easy to imagine that a new-born foal or calf was struggling to get onto spindly legs; hooves skittering in amniotic fluid splashed about a sordid barn; the swollen walnuts of knee-joints banging about a hollow floor. A scrabbling. Then a knocking of hard feet on the hall floor before it moves up thinly carpeted stairs.

We are not alone in here. Whatever was just outside has gone upstairs.

From the open doorway of the kitchen, the locked rear of a front door is visible, the fanlight blacked out with messily cut cardboard, sealed in place by black electrician's tape. One panel of cardboard displays the brand of a dog food, stamped in black ink.

The dull, brownish corridor that reeks of frankincense tunnels away, like a pipe-smoker's throat, to a pair of dim rooms on the ground floor.

A glance into the next room on the ground floor. A few patches of red carpet remain visible beneath what looks like earthquake damage. On the floor, what isn't obscured is salted with lint and wormed with ribbons of grey dust. The two lumps might be chairs, but so blanketed are they by rubbish that not even their style nor the patterns of their upholstery are discoverable. Old papers, clothes, cardboard boxes, plastic crates, sloping tiers of books, their covers concealed by poor light, cover the sitting room's furniture, save the top shelf of a cream-coloured bookcase that stands against the far wall, swamped and intimidated.

On the opposite side of this room, the landfill of twisted and neglected belongings reaches to head-height where old Christmas cards, bleached by time, hang on a red string affixed to the dreary floral wallpaper by brass drawing pins.

The door of the neighbouring room lies flat against the floor inside the living room. It has been torn down. The rents in the doorframe, where a hinge was tugged right out of the wood, are fresh.

This room is beset by a shut-in's gloom. Blackout curtains conceal the windows and patio doors. A small lamp on a pile of newspapers casts an undersea glow over a table. Meals were eaten upon it, but the crockery was never cleared. At least a dozen mugs, the insides stained by tannin to the colour of unclean mouths, litter the surface. Dark tidemarks of grime tapestry the odd-coloured ceramic bowls; stale toast turned to wood rests in a galaxy of black crumbs. An open packet of shortbread biscuits slouches atop magazines and puzzle books.

Beside an easy chair, its cream and rose fabric darkened by the grease of use and spills, a cloth bag is open like a sloppy drunk's mouth from which wool and knitting paraphernalia spill.

Between the gas fire and the messy table, the fourth body.

A woman, face-down on a dirty red rug before the fire's grate. A shock of white hair, cotton-wool-wild on one side but matted wet and dark on the other. Her legs shoot out at angles impossible to effect within the ball-and-socket joints of a human pelvis. One slip-on shoe has left a foot. Her arms reach out, in line with her narrow back, like a skydiver's. One hand still clutches a wooden cup shaped like a goblet, its style suggesting it was made centuries ago. Nothing spills from the cup.

The rest of the room's furnishings and artefacts are mundane, ordinary, in disarray, lazily cast down and never picked up again. Except for the picture above the mantel. A large oil, the palette so sombre it is difficult to determine the subject of the portrait, save that something the colour of shadow wears a crown and spreads murky wings.

Incongruously, despite the meagreness, dirt and orderless nature of this home, the frame of the painting is coated in a lavish gold-leaf and moulded like an extravagant cornice. Within the frame, scores of small, naked human figures are depicted. They entwine as if climbing over each other.

Back down the tobacco-stained chute of the hallway to the staircase. Almonds. Vetiver. Frankincense.

Silence upstairs, the stairwell as close and murky as a grimy maw opened to yawn behind the bars of a zoo.

First floor: four closed doors. Upon the landing, a dull thump, muted through the ceiling. Followed by the scraping of a substantial weight along a carpeted floor. When the dragging noise ceases, as if the process has been abandoned, hard feet scatter across the floorboards. A door is slammed shut further along the landing, towards the front of the property.

We are not alone here.

Up the stairs to the next storey of a grim building that remains in permanent night, as if the rising of each new dawn was an insult to whatever morbid preoccupations gripped the sleepers, residents or guests, who woke here each day until their last.

Four doors, all thickly painted a red so dark that it appears brown in what dismal light wafts up the stairwell. Three of the doors are shut. One doorway gapes, the door hanging from a single hinge, the upper hinge smashed free of the timber. The master bedroom.

Looking inside the master bedroom from the landing, what sunlight strains through thin yellowy curtains casts a malarial sheen over a murky space crowded with furniture. A vast unkempt bed the centrepiece. Shabby bedclothes, tangled and hopelessly creased, hang from the divan's side and rear. The floor at its side a veritable swamp of discarded garments, newspapers, books, crockery.

From the doorway of this immediately accessible room, two large wardrobes become visible, as dark and cumbersome as upright coffins, filling the two gloomy far corners like sentries unwilling to be seen and unlikely to issue challenges. At the foot of the bed, forming an antique bridge between the two wardrobes, a chest of drawers or dresser. It's hard to imagine being able to pass between the end of the bed and this article of furniture if its drawers were left open. Atop the dresser, running its entire length, a silvery rectangle of mirror reflects the opposite side of the room: tangled bedclothes upon the unhealthy bed become visible, grey pillows indented with the shape of a head, two bedside cabinets, their surfaces step-pyramids of medication packets and empty cups atop books and discarded tissues. A pair of reading glasses peers at a dim ceiling.

A few steps inside the room and the feet of the fifth body become visible, trapped between the end of the bed and the dresser. Ordinary black shoes, schoolish in appearance, are neatly laced up beneath the turnups of a pair of grey trousers.

A glance into the shadowy trench between bed and dresser reveals a thin, elderly male body lying on its back. Each arm is still partly raised, as if flung outwards at the last moment. The fingers of one hand still grip the brass handle of a dresser drawer; the other hand and wrist remain coiled within the bedclothes, presumably fisted as the victim faced the violence of the attack that left him lifeless. Perhaps he clutched the sides of the ravine to prevent himself being dragged out.

Sticking upwards, like an antenna or aerial, a thin wooden stick protrudes from the hand lost within the bed sheets. The wooden stick, or wand, was gripped until the last moment. A close and knowledgeable scrutiny would identify the wood as oak.

Above the extended arms, the head resembles smashed pottery partly held together by a pale-coloured sack. As the body was pulled along the floor from where it was dispatched, and perhaps from beneath the bed where the man had been hiding, the top of the head has smeared away into the darkness. The stain spreads into discarded clothing and the pages of a broadsheet, the paper called upon to demonstrate the absorbent properties of newsprint. The lower jaw of the face is intact, though a pair of detached false teeth seem to form a second mouth within the one stretched so unnaturally wide.

A door clicks open.

Outside the room, somewhere on the dim landing, cumbersome feet bump, scrabble and kick like a panicked animal compelled from its pen. The pervasive smell that has lingered inside the building intensifies. Heavy and sickly, a tinge of almonds amidst a new perfume of tropical flowers and sweet rot, spills across the landing and into the dim master bedroom.

Moments after the hard, stamping feet become audible on the landing outside, the mirror of the dresser at the end of the unkempt bed where the broken man is wedged is busy with motion. Framed within the rectangle of the doorway but partly obscured by the tilting door, a brief moment of revelation is granted. The aperture darkens, is filled.

A flash of torso beneath embryonic wings, raised as if for a fledgling's first flight. Long ribs as if glimpsed through a tadpole's abdomen. What functions for a head is intricately boned, the beak stained, not unlike that of a great plucked bird. A crown of wood upon the ghastly skull.

What lopes across the open doorway of the master bedroom is soon gone, crossing the landing to reach the staircase in a single stride. Then it vanishes from sight, the rickety legs and long toes carrying it away and down.

A skittering of sharp, heavy feet from below in the hall.

A thumping of an ungainly body through the aperture of the cellar door.

A far-off scratching of claws on bare wooden steps, diminishing, descending. Gone.

Silence.

Almonds. Vetiver. Frankincense.

What Was It? A Mystery

Fitz-James O'Brien

IT IS, I confess, with considerable diffidence that I approach the strange narrative which I am about to relate. The events which I purpose detailing are of so extraordinary and unheard-of a character that I am quite prepared to meet with an unusual amount of incredulity and scorn. I accept all such beforehand. I have, I trust, the literary courage to face unbelief. I have, after mature consideration, resolved to narrate, in as simple and straightforward a manner as I can compass, some facts that passed under my observation in the month of July last, and which, in the annals of the mysteries of physical science, are wholly unparalleled.

I live at No.— Twenty-sixth Street, in this city. The house is in some respects a curious one. It has enjoyed for the last two years the reputation of being haunted. It is a large and stately residence, surrounded by what was once a garden, but which is now only a green inclosure used for bleaching clothes. The dry basin of what has been a fountain, and a few fruit-trees, ragged and unpruned, indicate that this spot, in past days, was a pleasant, shady retreat, filled with fruits and flowers and the sweet murmur of waters.

The house is very spacious. A hall of noble size leads to a vast spiral staircase winding through its center, while the various apartments are of imposing dimensions. It was built some fifteen or twenty years since by Mr. A—, the well-known New York merchant, who five years ago threw the commercial world into convulsions by a stupendous bank fraud. Mr. A—, as everyone knows, escaped to Europe, and died not long after of a broken heart. Almost immediately after the news of his decease reached this country, and was verified, the report spread in Twenty-sixth Street that No.— was haunted. Legal measures had dispossessed the widow of its former owner, and it was inhabited merely by a caretaker and his wife, placed there by the house agent into whose hands it had passed for purposes of renting or sale. These people declared that they were troubled with unnatural noises. Doors were opened without any visible agency. The remnants of furniture scattered through the various rooms were, during the night, piled one upon the other by unknown hands. Invisible feet passed up and down the stairs in broad daylight, accompanied by the rustle of unseen silk dresses, and the gliding of viewless hands along the massive balusters. The caretaker and his wife declared that they would live there no longer. The house agent laughed, dismissed them, and put others in their place. The noises and supernatural manifestations continued. The neighborhood caught up the story, and the house remained untenanted for three years. Several persons negotiated for it; but somehow, always before the bargain was closed, they heard the unpleasant rumors, and declined to treat any further.

It was in this state of things that my landlady – who at that time kept a boarding-house in Bleecker Street, and who wished to move farther up town – conceived the bold idea of renting No.— Twenty-sixth Street. Happening to have in her house rather a plucky and philosophical set of boarders, she laid down her scheme before us, stating candidly everything she had heard respecting the ghostly qualities of the establishment to which she wished to remove us. With the exception of two timid persons – a sea captain and a returned Californian, who immediately gave notice that they would leave – all of Mrs. Moffat's guests declared that they would accompany her in her chivalric incursion into the abode of spirits.

Our removal was effected in the month of May, and we were all charmed with our new residence. The portion of Twenty-sixth Street where our house is situated – between Seventh and Eighth Avenues – is one of the pleasantest localities in New York. The gardens back of the houses, running down nearly to the Hudson, form, in the summer time, a perfect avenue of verdure. The air is pure and invigorating, sweeping, as it does, straight across the river from the Weehawken heights, and even the ragged garden which surrounded the house on two sides, although displaying on washing days rather too much clothesline, still gave us a piece of greensward to look at, and a cool retreat in the summer evenings, where we smoked our cigars in the dusk, and watched the fireflies flashing their dark-lanterns in the long grass.

Of course we had no sooner established ourselves at No.— than we began to expect the ghosts. We absolutely awaited their advent with eagerness. Our dinner conversation was supernatural. One of the boarders, who had purchased Mrs. Crowe's 'Night Side of Nature' for his own private delectation, was regarded as a public enemy by the entire household for not having bought twenty copies. The man led a life of supreme wretchedness while he was reading this volume. A system of espionage was established, of which he was the victim. If he incautiously laid the book down for an instant and left the room, it was immediately seized and read aloud in secret places to a select few. I found myself a person of immense importance, it having leaked out that I was tolerably well versed in the history of supernaturalism, and had once written a story, entitled 'The Pot of Tulips', for *Harper's Monthly,* the foundation of which was a ghost. If a table or a wainscot panel happened to warp when we were assembled in the large drawing room, there was an instant silence, and everyone was prepared for an immediate clanking of chains and a spectral form.

After a month of psychological excitement, it was with the utmost dissatisfaction that we were forced to acknowledge that nothing in the remotest degree approaching the supernatural had manifested itself. Once the black butler asseverated that his candle had been blown out by some invisible agency while he was undressing himself for the night; but as I had more than once discovered this colored gentleman in a condition when one candle must have appeared to him like two, I thought it possible that, by going a step farther in his potations, he might have reversed his phenomenon, and seen no candle at all where he ought to have beheld one.

Things were in this state when an incident took place so awful and inexplicable in its character that my reason fairly reels at the bare memory of the occurrence. It was the tenth of July. After dinner was over I repaired with my friend, Dr. Hammond, to the garden to smoke my evening pipe. The Doctor and myself found ourselves in an unusually metaphysical mood. We lit our large meerschaums, filled with fine Turkish tobacco; we paced to and fro, conversing. A strange perversity dominated the currents of our thought. They would *not* flow through the sunlit channels into which we strove to divert them. For some unaccountable reason they constantly diverged into dark and lonesome beds, where a continual gloom brooded. It was in vain that, after our old fashion, we flung ourselves on the shores of the East, and talked of its gay bazaars, of the splendors of the time of Haroun, of harems and golden palaces. Black afreets continually arose from the depths of our talk, and expanded, like the one the fisherman released from the copper vessel, until they blotted everything bright from our vision. Insensibly, we yielded to the occult force that swayed us, and indulged in gloomy speculation. We had talked some time upon the proneness of the human mind to mysticism, and the almost universal love of the Terrible, when Hammond suddenly said to me, "What do you consider to be the greatest element of Terror?"

The question, I own, puzzled me. That many things were terrible, I knew. Stumbling over a corpse in the dark; beholding, as I once did, a woman floating down a deep and rapid river, with wildly lifted arms, and awful, upturned face, uttering, as she sank, shrieks that rent one's heart, while we, the spectators, stood frozen at a window which overhung the river at a height of sixty feet, unable to make the slightest effort to save her, but dumbly watching her last supreme agony and her disappearance. A shattered wreck, with no life visible, encountered floating listlessly on the ocean, is a terrible object, for it suggests a huge terror, the proportions of which are veiled. But it now struck me for the first time that there must be one great and ruling embodiment of fear, a King of Terrors to which all others must succumb. What might it be? To what train of circumstances would it owe its existence?

"I confess, Hammond," I replied to my friend, "I never considered the subject before. That there must be one Something more terrible than any other thing, I feel. I cannot attempt, however, even the most vague definition."

"I am somewhat like you, Harry," he answered. "I feel my capacity to experience a terror greater than anything yet conceived by the human mind – something combining in fearful and unnatural amalgamation hitherto supposed incompatible elements. The calling of the voices in Brockden Brown's novel of 'Wieland' is awful; so is the picture of the Dweller of the Threshold, in Bulwer's 'Zanoni'; but," he added, shaking his head gloomily, "there is something more horrible still than these."

"Look here, Hammond," I rejoined, "let us drop this kind of talk, for Heaven's sake!"

"I don't know what's the matter with me tonight," he replied, "but my brain is running upon all sorts of weird and awful thoughts. I feel as if I could write a story like Hoffman tonight, if I were only master of a literary style."

"Well, if we are going to be Hoffmanesque in our talk, I'm off to bed. How sultry it is! Goodnight, Hammond."

"Goodnight, Harry. Pleasant dreams to you."

"To you, gloomy wretch, afreets, ghouls, and enchanters."

We parted, and each sought his respective chamber. I undressed quickly and got into bed, taking with me, according to my usual custom, a book, over which I generally read myself to sleep. I opened the volume as soon as I had laid my head upon the pillow, and instantly flung it to the other side of the room. It was Goudon's 'History of Monsters' – a curious French work, which I had lately imported from Paris, but which, in the state of mind I had then reached, was anything but an agreeable companion. I resolved to go to sleep at once; so, turning down my gas until nothing but a little blue point of light glimmered on the top of the tube, I composed myself to rest.

The room was in total darkness. The atom of gas that still remained lighted did not illuminate a distance of three inches round the burner. I desperately drew my arm across my eyes, as if to shut out even the darkness, and tried to think of nothing. It was in vain. The confounded themes touched on by Hammond in the garden kept obtruding themselves on my brain. I battled against them. I erected ramparts of would-be blankness of intellect to keep them out. They still crowded upon me. While I was lying still as a corpse, hoping that by a perfect physical inaction I should hasten mental repose, an awful incident occurred. A Something dropped, as it seemed, from the ceiling, plumb upon my chest, and the next instant I felt two bony hands encircling my throat, endeavoring to choke me.

I am no coward, and am possessed of considerable physical strength. The suddenness of the attack, instead of stunning me, strung every nerve to its highest tension. My body acted from instinct, before my brain had time to realize the terrors of my position. In an instant I wound two muscular arms around the creature, and squeezed it, with all the strength of despair, against my chest. In a few seconds the bony hands that had fastened on my throat loosened their hold, and I was free to breathe once more. Then commenced a struggle of awful intensity. Immersed in the most profound darkness, totally ignorant of the nature of the Thing by which I was so suddenly attacked, finding my grasp slipping every moment, by reason, it seemed to me, of the entire nakedness of my assailant, bitten with sharp teeth in the shoulder, neck, and chest, having every moment to protect my throat against a pair of sinewy, agile hands, which my utmost efforts could not confine – these were a combination of circumstances to combat which required all the strength and skill and courage that I possessed.

At last, after a silent, deadly, exhausting struggle, I got my assailant under by a series of incredible efforts of strength. Once pinned, with my knee on what I made out to be its chest, I knew that I was victor. I rested for a moment to breathe. I heard the creature beneath me panting in the darkness, and felt the violent throbbing of a heart. It was apparently as exhausted as I was; that was one comfort. At this moment I remembered that I usually placed under my pillow, before going to bed, a large yellow silk pocket handkerchief, for use during the night. I felt for it instantly; it was there. In a few seconds more I had, after a fashion, pinioned the creature's arms.

I now felt tolerably secure. There was nothing more to be done but to turn on the gas, and, having first seen what my midnight assailant was like, arouse the household. I will confess to being actuated by a certain pride in not giving the alarm before; I wished to make the capture alone and unaided.

Never losing my hold for an instant, I slipped from the bed to the floor, dragging my captive with me. I had but a few steps to make to reach the gas-burner; these I made with the greatest caution, holding the creature in a grip like a vice. At last I got within arm's-length of the tiny speck of blue light which told me where the gas-burner lay. Quick as lightning I released my grasp with one hand and let on the full flood of light. Then I turned to look at my captive.

I cannot even attempt to give any definition of my sensations the instant after I turned on the gas. I suppose I must have shrieked with terror, for in less than a minute afterward my room was crowded with the inmates of the house. I shudder now as I think of that awful moment. *I saw nothing!* Yes; I had one arm firmly clasped round a breathing, panting, corporeal shape, my other hand gripped with all its strength a throat as warm, and apparently fleshly, as my own; and yet, with this living substance in my grasp, with its body pressed against my own, and all in the bright glare of a large jet of gas, I absolutely beheld nothing! Not even an outline – a vapor!

I do not, even at this hour, realize the situation in which I found myself. I cannot recall the astounding incident thoroughly. Imagination in vain tries to compass the awful paradox.

It breathed. I felt its warm breath upon my cheek. It struggled fiercely. It had hands. They clutched me. Its skin was smooth, like my own. There it lay, pressed close up against me, solid as stone – and yet utterly invisible!

I wonder that I did not faint or go mad on the instant. Some wonderful instinct must have sustained me; for, absolutely, in place of loosening my hold on the terrible Enigma, I seemed to gain an additional strength in my moment of horror, and tightened my grasp with such wonderful force that I felt the creature shivering with agony.

Just then Hammond entered my room at the head of the household. As soon as he beheld my face – which, I suppose, must have been an awful sight to look at – he hastened forward, crying, "Great heaven, Harry! What has happened?"

"Hammond! Hammond!" I cried. "Come here. Oh! This is awful! I have been attacked in bed by something or other, which I have hold of; but I can't see it – I can't see it!"

Hammond, doubtless struck by the unfeigned horror expressed in my countenance, made one or two steps forward with an anxious yet puzzled expression. A very audible titter burst from the remainder of my visitors. This suppressed laughter made me furious. To laugh at a human being in my position! It was the worst species of cruelty. *Now,* I can understand why the appearance of a man struggling violently, as it would seem, with an airy nothing, and calling for assistance against a vision, should have appeared ludicrous. *Then,* so great was my rage against the mocking crowd that had I the power I would have stricken them dead where they stood.

"Hammond! Hammond!" I cried again, despairingly. "For God's sake come to me. I can hold the – the Thing but a short while longer. It is overpowering me. Help me! Help me!"

"Harry," whispered Hammond, approaching me, "you have been smoking too much."

"I swear to you, Hammond, that this is no vision," I answered, in the same low tone. "Don't you see how it shakes my whole frame with its struggles? If you don't believe me, convince yourself. Feel it – touch it."

Hammond advanced and laid his hand on the spot I indicated. A wild cry of horror burst from him. He had felt it!

In a moment he had discovered somewhere in my room a long piece of cord, and was the next instant winding it and knotting it about the body of the unseen being that I clasped in my arms.

"Harry," he said, in a hoarse, agitated voice, for, though he preserved his presence of mind, he was deeply moved, "Harry, it's all safe now. You may let go, old fellow, if you're tired. The Thing can't move."

I was utterly exhausted, and I gladly loosed my hold.

Hammond stood holding the ends of the cord that bound the Invisible, twisted round his hand, while before him, self-supporting as it were, he beheld a rope laced and interlaced, and stretching tightly round a vacant space. I never saw a man look so thoroughly stricken with awe. Nevertheless his face expressed all the courage and determination which I knew him to possess. His lips, although white, were set firmly, and one could perceive at a glance that, although stricken with fear, he was not daunted.

The confusion that ensued among the guests of the house who were witnesses of this extraordinary scene between Hammond and myself – who beheld the pantomime of binding this struggling Something – who beheld me almost sinking from physical exhaustion when my task of jailer was over – the confusion and terror that took possession of the bystanders, when they saw all this, was beyond description. The weaker ones fled from the apartment. The few who remained clustered near the door, and could not be induced to approach Hammond and his Charge. Still incredulity broke out through their terror. They had not the courage to satisfy themselves, and yet they doubted. It was in vain that I begged of some of the men to come near and convince themselves by touch of the existence in that room of a living being which was invisible. They were incredulous, but did not dare to undeceive themselves. How could a solid, living, breathing body be invisible, they asked. My reply was this. I gave a sign to Hammond, and both of us – conquering our fearful repugnance to touch the invisible creature – lifted it from the ground, manacled as it was, and took it to my bed. Its weight was about that of a boy of fourteen.

"Now, my friends," I said, as Hammond and myself held the creature suspended over the bed, "I can give you self-evident proof that here is a solid, ponderable body which, nevertheless, you cannot see. Be good enough to watch the surface of the bed attentively."

I was astonished at my own courage in treating this strange event so calmly; but I had recovered from my first terror, and felt a sort of scientific pride in the affair which dominated every other feeling.

The eyes of the bystanders were immediately fixed on my bed. At a given signal Hammond and I let the creature fall. There was the dull sound of a heavy body alighting on a soft mass. The timbers of the bed creaked. A deep impression marked itself distinctly on the pillow, and on the bed itself. The crowd who witnessed this gave a sort of low, universal cry, and rushed from the room. Hammond and I were left alone with our Mystery.

We remained silent for some time, listening to the low, irregular breathing of the creature on the bed, and watching the rustle of the bedclothes as it impotently struggled to free itself from confinement. Then Hammond spoke.

"Harry, this is awful."

"Aye, awful."

"But not unaccountable."

"Not unaccountable! What do you mean? Such a thing has never occurred since the birth of the world. I know not what to think, Hammond. God grant that I am not mad, and that this is not an insane fantasy!"

"Let us reason a little, Harry. Here is a solid body which we touch, but which we cannot see. The fact is so unusual that it strikes us with terror. Is there no parallel, though, for such a phenomenon? Take a piece of pure glass. It is tangible and transparent. A certain chemical coarseness is all that prevents its being so entirely transparent as to be totally invisible. It is not *theoretically impossible,* mind you, to make a glass which shall not reflect a single ray of light – a glass so pure and homogeneous in its atoms that the rays from the sun shall pass through it as they do through the air, refracted but not reflected. We do not see the air, and yet we feel it."

"That's all very well, Hammond, but these are inanimate substances. Glass does not breathe, air does not breathe. *This* thing has a heart that palpitates – a will that moves it – lungs that play, and inspire and respire."

"You forget the strange phenomena of which we have so often heard of late," answered the Doctor, gravely. "At the meetings called 'spirit circles', invisible hands have been thrust into the hands of those persons round the table – warm, fleshly hands that seemed to pulsate with mortal life."

"What? Do you think, then, that this thing is—"

"I don't know what it is," was the solemn reply; "but please the gods I will, with your assistance, thoroughly investigate it."

We watched together, smoking many pipes, all night long, by the bedside of the unearthly being that tossed and panted until it was apparently wearied out. Then we learned by the low, regular breathing that it slept.

The next morning the house was all astir. The boarders congregated on the landing outside my room, and Hammond and myself were lions. We had to answer a thousand questions as to the state of our extraordinary prisoner, for as yet not one person in the house except ourselves could be induced to set foot in the apartment.

The creature was awake. This was evidenced by the convulsive manner in which the bedclothes were moved in its efforts to escape. There was something truly terrible in beholding, as it were, those second-hand indications of the terrible writhings and agonized struggles for liberty which themselves were invisible.

Hammond and myself had racked our brains during the long night to discover some means by which we might realize the shape and general appearance of the Enigma. As well as we could make out by passing our hands over the creature's form, its outlines and lineaments were human. There was a mouth; a round, smooth head without hair; a nose, which, however, was little elevated above the cheeks; and its hands and feet felt like those of a boy. At first we thought of placing the being on a smooth surface and tracing its outline with chalk, as shoemakers trace the outline of the foot. This plan was given up as being of no value. Such an outline would give not the slightest idea of its conformation.

A happy thought struck me. We would take a cast of it in plaster of Paris. This would give us the solid figure, and satisfy all our wishes. But how to do it? The movements of the creature would disturb the setting of the plastic covering, and distort the mold. Another thought. Why not give it chloroform? It had respiratory organs – that was evident by its breathing. Once reduced to a state of insensibility, we could do with it what we would. Doctor X— was sent for; and after the worthy physician had recovered from the first shock of amazement, he proceeded to administer the chloroform. In three minutes afterward we were enabled to remove the fetters from the creature's body, and a well-known modeler of this city was busily engaged in covering the invisible form with the moist clay. In five minutes more we had a mold, and before evening a rough *facsimile* of the mystery. It was shaped like a man,– distorted, uncouth, and horrible, but still a man. It was small, not over four feet and some inches in height, and its limbs revealed a muscular development that was unparalleled. Its face surpassed in hideousness anything I had ever seen. Gustave Doré, or Callot, or Tony Johannot, never conceived anything so horrible. There is a face in one of the latter's illustrations to 'Un Voyage où il vous plaira', which somewhat approaches the countenance of this creature, but does not equal it. It was the physiognomy of what I should have fancied a ghoul to be. It looked as if it was capable of feeding on human flesh.

Having satisfied our curiosity, and bound everyone in the house to secrecy, it became a question what was to be done with our Enigma. It was impossible that we should keep such a horror in our house; it was equally impossible that such an awful being should be let loose upon the world. I confess that I would have gladly voted for the creature's destruction. But who would shoulder the responsibility? Who would undertake the execution of this horrible semblance of a human being? Day after day this question was deliberated gravely. The boarders all left the house. Mrs. Moffat was in despair, and threatened Hammond and myself with all sorts of legal penalties if we did not remove the Horror. Our answer was, "We will go if you like, but we decline taking this creature with us. Remove it yourself if you please. It appeared in your house. On you the responsibility rests." To this there was, of course, no answer. Mrs. Moffat could not obtain for love or money a person who would even approach the Mystery.

The most singular part of the transaction was that we were entirely ignorant of what the creature habitually fed on. Everything in the way of nutriment that we could think of was placed before it, but was never touched. It was awful to stand by, day after day, and see the clothes toss, and hear the hard breathing, and know that it was starving.

Ten, twelve days, a fortnight passed, and it still lived. The pulsations of the heart, however, were daily growing fainter, and had now nearly ceased altogether. It was evident that the creature was dying for want of sustenance. While this terrible life struggle was going on, I felt miserable. I could not sleep of nights. Horrible as the creature was, it was pitiful to think of the pangs it was suffering.

At last it died. Hammond and I found it cold and stiff one morning in the bed. The heart had ceased to beat, the lungs to inspire. We hastened to bury it in the garden. It was a strange funeral, the dropping of that viewless corpse into the damp hole. The cast of its form I gave to Dr. X—, who keeps it in his museum in Tenth Street.

As I am on the eve of a long journey from which I may not return, I have drawn up this narrative of an event the most singular that has ever come to my knowledge.

NOTE – It was rumored that the proprietors of a well-known museum in this city had made arrangements with Dr. X— to exhibit to the public the singular cast which Mr. Escott deposited with him. So extraordinary a history cannot fail to attract universal attention.

Metzengerstein

A Tale in Imitation of the German

Edgar Allan Poe

'Pestis eram vivus – moriens tua mors ero.'[1]
Martin Luther

HORROR AND FATALITY have been stalking abroad in all ages. Why then give a date to this story I have to tell? Let it suffice to say, that at the period of which I speak, there existed, in the interior of Hungary, a settled although hidden belief in the doctrines of the Metempsychosis. Of the doctrines themselves – that is, of their falsity, or of their probability – I say nothing. I assert, however, that much of our incredulity – as La Bruyère says of all our unhappiness – *'vient de ne pouvoir être seuls.'*[2]

But there are some points in the Hungarian superstition which were fast verging to absurdity. They – the Hungarians – differed very essentially from their Eastern authorities. For example, *'The soul,'* said the former – I give the words of an acute and intelligent Parisian – *'ne demeure qu'un seul fois dans un corps sensible: au reste – un cheval, un chien, un homme meme, n'est que la ressemblance peu tangible de ces animaux.'*[3]

The families of Berlifitzing and Metzengerstein had been at variance for centuries. Never before were two houses so illustrious, mutually embittered by hostility so deadly. The origin of this enmity seems to be found in the words of an ancient prophecy – 'A lofty name shall have a fearful fall when, as the rider over his horse, the mortality of Metzengerstein shall triumph over the immortality of Berlifitzing.'

To be sure the words themselves had little or no meaning. But more trivial causes have given rise – and that no long while ago – to consequences equally eventful. Besides, the estates, which were contiguous, had long exercised a rival influence in the affairs of a busy government. Moreover, near neighbors are seldom friends; and the inhabitants of the Castle Berlifitzing might look, from their lofty buttresses, into the very windows of the palace Metzengerstein. Least of all had the more than feudal magnificence, thus discovered, a tendency to allay the irritable feelings of the less ancient and less wealthy Berlifitzings. What wonder then, that the words, however silly, of that prediction, should have succeeded in setting and keeping at variance two families already predisposed to quarrel by every instigation of hereditary jealousy? The prophecy seemed to imply – if it implied anything – a final triumph on the part of the already more powerful house; and was of course remembered with the more bitter animosity by the weaker and less influential.

Wilhelm, Count Berlifitzing, although loftily descended, was, at the epoch of this narrative, an infirm and doting old man, remarkable for nothing but an inordinate and inveterate personal antipathy to the family of his rival, and so passionate a love of horses, and of hunting, that neither bodily infirmity, great age, nor mental incapacity, prevented his daily participation in the dangers of the chase.

Frederick, Baron Metzengerstein, was, on the other hand, not yet of age. His father, the Minister G—, died young. His mother, the Lady Mary, followed him quickly after. Frederick was, at that time, in his fifteenth year. In a city, fifteen years are no long period – a child may be still a child in his third lustrum: but in a wilderness – in so magnificent a wilderness as that old principality, fifteen years have a far deeper meaning.

From some peculiar circumstances attending the administration of his father, the young Baron, at the decease of the former, entered immediately upon his vast possessions. Such estates were seldom held before by a nobleman of Hungary. His castles were without number. The chief in point of splendor and extent was the 'Chateau Metzengerstein'. The boundary line of his dominions was never clearly defined; but his principal park embraced a circuit of fifty miles.

Upon the succession of a proprietor so young, with a character so well known, to a fortune so unparalleled, little speculation was afloat in regard to his probable course of conduct. And, indeed, for the space of three days, the behavior of the heir out-heroded Herod, and fairly surpassed the expectations of his most enthusiastic admirers. Shameful debaucheries – flagrant treacheries – unheard-of atrocities – gave his trembling vassals quickly to understand that no servile submission on their part – no punctilios of conscience on his own – were thenceforward to prove any security against the remorseless fangs of a petty Caligula. On the night of the fourth day, the stables of the castle Berlifitzing were discovered to be on fire; and the unanimous opinion of the neighborhood added the crime of the incendiary to the already hideous list of the Baron's misdemeanors and enormities.

But during the tumult occasioned by this occurrence, the young nobleman himself sat apparently buried in meditation, in a vast and desolate upper apartment of the family palace of Metzengerstein. The rich although faded tapestry hangings which swung gloomily upon the walls represented the shadowy and majestic forms of a thousand illustrious ancestors. *Here*, rich-ermined priests, and pontifical dignitaries, familiarly seated with the autocrat and the sovereign, put a veto on the wishes of a temporal king, or restrained with the fiat of papal supremacy the rebellious sceptre of the Arch-enemy. *There*, the dark, tall statures of the Princes Metzengerstein – their muscular war-coursers plunging over the carcasses of fallen foes – startled the steadiest nerves with their vigorous expression; and *here*, again, the voluptuous and swan-like figures of the dames of days gone by, floated away in the mazes of an unreal dance to the strains of imaginary melody.

But as the Baron listened, or affected to listen, to the gradually increasing uproar in the stables of Berlifitzing – or perhaps pondered upon some more novel, some more decided act of audacity – his eyes became unwittingly riveted to the figure of an enormous, and unnaturally colored horse, represented in the tapestry as belonging to a Saracen ancestor of the family of his rival. The horse itself, in the foreground of the design, stood motionless and statue-like – while farther back, its discomfited rider perished by the dagger of a Metzengerstein.

On Frederick's lip arose a fiendish expression, as he became aware of the direction which his glance had, without his consciousness, assumed. Yet he did not remove it. On the contrary, he could by no means account for the overwhelming anxiety which appeared falling like a pall upon his senses. It was with difficulty that he reconciled his dreamy and incoherent feelings with the certainty of being awake. The longer he gazed the more absorbing became the spell – the more impossible did it appear that he could ever withdraw his glance from the fascination of that tapestry. But the tumult without becoming suddenly more violent, with a compulsory exertion he diverted his attention to the glare of ruddy light thrown full by the flaming stables upon the windows of the apartment.

The action, however, was but momentary, his gaze returned mechanically to the wall. To his extreme horror and astonishment, the head of the gigantic steed had, in the meantime, altered its position. The neck of the animal, before arched, as if in compassion, over the prostrate body of its lord, was now extended, at full length, in the direction of the Baron. The eyes, before invisible, now wore an energetic and human expression, while they gleamed with a fiery and unusual red; and the distended lips of the apparently enraged horse left in full view his gigantic and disgusting teeth.

Stupified with terror, the young nobleman tottered to the door. As he threw it open, a flash of red light, streaming far into the chamber, flung his shadow with a clear outline against the quivering tapestry, and he shuddered to perceive that shadow – as he staggered awhile upon the threshold – assuming the exact position, and precisely filling up the contour, of the relentless and triumphant murderer of the Saracen Berlifitzing.

To lighten the depression of his spirits, the Baron hurried into the open air. At the principal gate of the palace he encountered three equerries. With much difficulty, and at the imminent peril of their lives, they were restraining the convulsive plunges of a gigantic and fiery-colored horse.

"Whose horse? Where did you get him?" demanded the youth, in a querulous and husky tone of voice, as he became instantly aware that the mysterious steed in the tapestried chamber was the very counterpart of the furious animal before his eyes.

"He is your own property, sire," replied one of the equerries, "at least he is claimed by no other owner. We caught him flying, all smoking and foaming with rage, from the burning stables of the Castle Berlifitzing. Supposing him to have belonged to the old Count's stud of foreign horses, we led him back as an estray. But the grooms there disclaim any title to the creature; which is strange, since he bears evident marks of having made a narrow escape from the flames."

"The letters W.V.B. are also branded very distinctly on his forehead," interrupted a second equerry, "I supposed them, of course, to be the initials of Wilhelm Von Berlifitzing – but all at the castle are positive in denying any knowledge of the horse."

"Extremely singular!" said the young Baron, with a musing air, and apparently unconscious of the meaning of his words. "He is, as you say, a remarkable horse – a prodigious horse! Although, as you very justly observe, of a suspicious and untractable character, let him be mine, however," he added, after a pause, "perhaps a rider like Frederick of Metzengerstein, may tame even the devil from the stables of Berlifitzing."

"You are mistaken, my lord; the horse, as I think we mentioned, is *not* from the stables of the Count. If such had been the case, we know our duty better than to bring him into the presence of a noble of your family."

"True!" observed the Baron, dryly, and at that instant a page of the bedchamber came from the palace with a heightened color, and a precipitate step. He whispered into his master's ear an account of the sudden disappearance of a small portion of the tapestry, in an apartment which he designated; entering, at the same time, into particulars of a minute and circumstantial character; but from the low tone of voice in which these latter were communicated, nothing escaped to gratify the excited curiosity of the equerries.

The young Frederick, during the conference, seemed agitated by a variety of emotions. He soon, however, recovered his composure, and an expression of determined malignancy settled upon his countenance, as he gave peremptory orders that a certain chamber should be immediately locked up, and the key placed in his own possession.

"Have you heard of the unhappy death of the old hunter Berlifitzing?" said one of his vassals to the Baron, as, after the departure of the page, the huge steed which that nobleman had adopted as his own, plunged and curvetted, with redoubled fury, down the long avenue which extended from the chateau to the stables of Metzengerstein.

"No!" said the Baron, turning abruptly toward the speaker, "Dead! say you?"

"It is indeed true, my lord; and, to a noble of your name, will be, I imagine, no unwelcome intelligence."

A rapid smile shot over the countenance of the listener. "How died he?"

"In his rash exertions to rescue a favorite portion of his hunting stud, he has himself perished miserably in the flames."

"I-n-d-e-e-d-!" ejaculated the Baron, as if slowly and deliberately impressed with the truth of some exciting idea.

"Indeed"; repeated the vassal.

"Shocking!" said the youth, calmly, and turned quietly into the chateau.

From this date a marked alteration took place in the outward demeanor of the dissolute young Baron Frederick Von Metzengerstein. Indeed, his behavior disappointed every expectation, and proved little in accordance with the views of many a manoeuvering mamma; while his habits and manner, still less than formerly, offered anything congenial with those of the neighboring aristocracy. He was never to be seen beyond the limits of his own domain, and, in this wide and social world, was utterly companionless – unless, indeed, that unnatural, impetuous, and fiery-colored horse, which he henceforward continually bestrode, had any mysterious right to the title of his friend.

Numerous invitations on the part of the neighborhood for a long time, however, periodically came in. "Will the Baron honor our festivals with his presence?"

"Will the Baron join us in a hunting of the boar?" – "Metzengerstein does not hunt"; "Metzengerstein will not attend," were the haughty and laconic answers.

These repeated insults were not to be endured by an imperious nobility. Such invitations became less cordial – less frequent – in time they ceased altogether. The widow of the unfortunate Count Berlifitzing was even heard to express a hope "that the Baron might be at home when he did not wish to be at home, since he disdained the company of his equals; and ride when he did not wish to ride, since he preferred the society of a horse." This to be sure was a very silly explosion of hereditary pique; and merely proved how singularly unmeaning our sayings are apt to become, when we desire to be unusually energetic.

The charitable, nevertheless, attributed the alteration in the conduct of the young nobleman to the natural sorrow of a son for the untimely loss of his parents – forgetting, however, his atrocious and reckless behavior during the short period immediately succeeding that bereavement. Some there were, indeed, who suggested a too haughty idea of self-consequence and dignity. Others again (among them may be mentioned the family physician) did not hesitate in speaking of morbid melancholy, and hereditary ill-health; while dark hints, of a more equivocal nature, were current among the multitude.

Indeed, the Baron's perverse attachment to his lately-acquired charger – an attachment which seemed to attain new strength from every fresh example of the animal's ferocious and demon-like propensities – at length became, in the eyes of all reasonable men, a hideous and unnatural fervor. In the glare of noon – at the dead hour of night – in sickness or in health – in calm or in tempest – the young Metzengerstein seemed riveted to the saddle of that colossal horse, whose intractable audacities so well accorded with his own spirit.

There were circumstances, moreover, which coupled with late events, gave an unearthly and portentous character to the mania of the rider, and to the capabilities of the steed. The space passed over in a single leap had been accurately measured, and was found to exceed, by an astounding difference, the wildest expectations of the most imaginative. The Baron, besides, had no particular *name* for the animal, although all the rest in his collection were distinguished by characteristic appellations. His stable, too, was appointed at a distance from the rest; and with regard to grooming and other necessary offices, none but the owner in person had ventured to officiate, or even to enter the enclosure of that particular stall. It was also to be observed, that although the three grooms, who had caught the steed as he fled from the conflagration at Berlifitzing, had succeeded in arresting his course, by means of a chain-bridle and noose – yet no one of the three could with any certainty affirm that he had, during that dangerous struggle, or at any period thereafter, actually placed his hand upon the body of the beast. Instances of peculiar intelligence in the demeanor of a noble and high-spirited horse are not to be supposed capable of exciting unreasonable attention – especially among men who, daily trained to the labors of the chase, might appear well acquainted with the sagacity of a horse – but there were certain circumstances which intruded themselves per force upon the most skeptical and phlegmatic; and it is said there were times when the animal caused the gaping crowd who stood around to recoil in horror from the deep and impressive meaning of his terrible stamp – times when the young Metzengerstein turned pale and shrunk away from the rapid and searching expression of his earnest and human-looking eye.

Among all the retinue of the Baron, however, none were found to doubt the ardor of that extraordinary affection which existed on the part of the young nobleman for the fiery qualities of his horse; at least, none but an insignificant and misshapen little page, whose deformities were in everybody's way, and whose opinions were of the least possible importance. He – if his ideas are worth mentioning at all – had the effrontery to assert that his master never vaulted into the saddle without an unaccountable and almost imperceptible shudder, and that, upon his return from every long-continued and habitual ride, an expression of triumphant malignity distorted every muscle in his countenance.

One tempestuous night, Metzengerstein, awaking from a heavy slumber, descended like a maniac from his chamber, and, mounting in hot haste, bounded away into the mazes of the forest. An occurrence so common attracted no particular attention, but his return was looked for with intense anxiety on the part of his domestics, when, after some hours' absence, the stupendous and magnificent battlements of the Chateau Metzengerstein, were discovered crackling and rocking to their very foundation, under the influence of a dense and livid mass of ungovernable fire.

As the flames, when first seen, had already made so terrible a progress that all efforts to save any portion of the building were evidently futile, the astonished neighborhood stood idly around in silent and pathetic wonder. But a new and fearful object soon riveted the attention of the multitude, and proved how much more intense is the excitement wrought in the feelings of a crowd by the contemplation of human agony, than that brought about by the most appalling spectacles of inanimate matter.

Up the long avenue of aged oaks which led from the forest to the main entrance of the Chateau Metzengerstein, a steed, bearing an unbonneted and disordered rider, was seen leaping with an impetuosity which outstripped the very Demon of the Tempest.

The career of the horseman was indisputably, on his own part, uncontrollable. The agony of his countenance, the convulsive struggle of his frame, gave evidence of superhuman exertion: but no sound, save a solitary shriek, escaped from his lacerated lips, which were bitten through and through in the intensity of terror. One instant, and the clattering of hoofs resounded sharply and shrilly above the roaring of the flames and the shrieking of the winds – another, and, clearing at a single plunge the gateway and the moat, the steed bounded far up the tottering staircases of the palace, and, with its rider, disappeared amid the whirlwind of chaotic fire.

The fury of the tempest immediately died away, and a dead calm sullenly succeeded. A white flame still enveloped the building like a shroud, and, streaming far away into the quiet atmosphere, shot forth a glare of preternatural light; while a cloud of smoke settled heavily over the battlements in the distinct colossal figure of – *a horse.*

Footnotes for *Metzengerstein*

1. 'Living, I was your plague – dying, I shall be your death.'
2. 'Just cannot be alone.'
3. '...remains only once in a sensitive body: the rest – a horse, a dog, even a man, is that little tangible likeness of these animals.'

The Victim

May Sinclair

Chapter I

STEVEN ACROYD, Mr. Greathead's chauffeur, was sulking in the garage.

Everybody was afraid of him. Everybody hated him except Mr. Greathead, his master, and Dorsy, his sweetheart.

And even Dorsy now, after yesterday!

Night had come. On one side the yard gates stood open to the black tunnel of the drive. On the other the high moor rose above the wall, immense, darker than the darkness. Steven's lantern in the open doorway of the garage and Dorsy's lamp in the kitchen window threw a blond twilight into the yard between. From where he sat, slantways on the step of the car, he could see, through the lighted window, the table with the lamp and Dorsy's sewing huddled up in a white heap as she left it just now, when she had jumped up and gone away. Because she was afraid of him.

She had gone straight to Mr. Greathead in his study, and Steven, sulking, had flung himself out into the yard.

He stared into the window, thinking, thinking. Everybody hated him. He could tell by the damned spiteful way they looked at him in the bar of the 'King's Arms'; kind of sideways and slink-eyed, turning their dirty tails and shuffling out of his way.

He had said to Dorsy he'd like to know what he'd done. He'd just dropped in for his glass as usual; he'd looked round and said "Good evening", civil, and the dirty tykes took no more notice of him than if he'd been a toad. Mrs. Oldishaw, Dorsy's aunt, *she* hated him, boiled-ham-face, swelling with spite, shoving his glass at the end of her arm, without speaking, as if he'd been a bloody cockroach.

All because of the thrashing he'd given young Ned Oldishaw. If she didn't want the cub's neck broken she'd better keep him out of mischief. Young Ned knew what he'd get if he came meddling with *his* sweetheart.

It had happened yesterday afternoon, Sunday, when he had gone down with Dorsy to the 'King's Arms' to see her aunt. They were sitting out on the wooden bench against the inn wall when young Ned began it. He could see him now with his arm round Dorsy's neck and his mouth gaping.

And Dorsy laughing like a silly fool and the old woman snorting and shaking.

He could hear him. "She's my cousin if she *is* your sweetheart. You can't stop me kissing her." *Couldn't* he!

Why, what did they think? When he'd given up his good job at the Darlington Motor Works to come to Eastthwaite and black Mr. Greathead's boots, chop wood, carry coal and water for him, and drive his shabby secondhand car. Not that he cared what he did so long as he could live in the same house with Dorsy Oldishaw. It wasn't likely he'd sit like a bloody Moses, looking on, while Ned—

To be sure, he had half killed him. He could feel Ned's neck swelling and rising up under the pressure of his hands, his fingers. He had struck him first, flinging him back against the inn wall, then he had pinned him – till the men ran up and dragged him off.

And now they were all against him. Dorsy was against him. She had said she was afraid of him.

"Steven," she had said, "tha med 'a killed him."

"Well – p'r'aps next time he'll knaw better than to coom meddlin' with *my* lass."

"I'm not thy lass, ef tha canna keep thy hands off folks. I should be feared for my life of thee. Ned wum't doing naw 'arm."

"Ef he doos it again, ef he cooms between thee and me, Dorsy, I shall do 'im in."

"Naw, tha maunna talk that road."

"It's Gawd's truth. Anybody that cooms between thee and me, loove, I shall do 'im in. Ef 'twas thy aunt, I should wring 'er neck, same as I wroong Ned's."

"And ef it was me, Steven?"

"Ef it wur thee, ef tha left me – Aw, doan't tha assk me, Dorsy."

"There – that's 'ow tha scares me."

"But tha' 'astna left me – 'tes thy wedding daithes tha'rt making."

"Aye, 'tes my wedding claithes."

She had started fingering the white stuff, looking at it with her head on one side, smiling prettily. Then all of a sudden she had flung it down in a heap and burst out crying. When he tried to comfort her she pushed him off and ran out of the room, to Mr. Greathead.

It must have been half an hour ago and she had not come back yet.

He got up and went through the yard gates into the dark drive. Turning there, he came to the house front and the lighted window of the study. Hidden behind a clump of yew he looked in.

Mr. Greathead had risen from his chair. He was a little old man, shrunk and pinched, with a bowed narrow back and slender neck under his grey hanks of hair.

Dorsy stood before him, facing Steven. The lamplight fell full on her. Her sweet flower-face was flushed. She had been crying.

Mr. Greathead spoke.

"Well, that's my advice," he said. "Think it over, Dorsy, before you do anything."

That night Dorsy packed her boxes, and the next day at noon, when Steven came in for his dinner, she had left the Lodge. She had gone back to her father's house in Garthdale.

She wrote to Steven saying that she had thought it over and found she daren't marry him. She was afraid of him. She would be too unhappy.

Chapter II

THAT WAS the old man, the old man. He had made her give him up. But for that, Dorsy would never have left him. She would never have thought of it herself. And she would never have got away if he had been there to stop her. It wasn't Ned. Ned was going to marry Nancy Peacock down at Morfe. Ned hadn't done any harm.

It was Mr. Greathead who had come between them. He hated Mr. Greathead.

His hate became a nausea of physical loathing that never ceased. Indoors he served Mr. Greathead as footman and valet, waiting on him at meals, bringing the hot water for his bath, helping him to dress and undress. So that he could never get away from him. When he came to call him in the morning, Steven's stomach heaved at the sight of the shrunken body under the bedclothes, the flushed, pinched face with its peaked, finicking nose upturned, the thin silver tuft of hair pricked up above the pillow's edge. Steven shivered with hate at the sound of the rattling, old-man's cough, and the *shoob-shoob* of the feet shuffling along the flagged passages.

He had once had a feeling of tenderness for Mr. Greathead as the tie that bound him to Dorsy. He even brushed his coat and hat tenderly, as if he loved them. Once Mr. Greathead's small, close smile – the greyish bud of the lower lip pushed out, the upper lip lifted at the corners – and his kind, thin "Thank you, my lad," had made Steven smile back, glad to serve Dorsy's master. And Mr. Greathead would smile again and say, "It does me good to see your bright face, Steven." Now Steven's face writhed in a tight contortion to meet Mr. Greathead's kindliness, while his throat ran dry and his heart shook with hate.

At meal-times from his place by the sideboard he would look on at Mr. Greathead eating, in a long contemplative disgust. He could have snatched the plate away from under the slow, fumbling hands that hovered and hesitated. He would catch words coming into his mind: "He ought to be dead. He ought to be dead." To think that this thing that ought to be dead, this old, shrivelled skin-bag of creaking bones should come between him and Dorsy, should have power to drive Dorsy from him.

One day when he was brushing Mr. Greathead's soft felt hat a paroxysm of hatred gripped him. He hated Mr. Greathead's hat. He took a stick and struck at it again and again; he threw it on the flags and stamped on it, clenching his teeth and drawing in his breath with a sharp hiss. He picked up the hat, looking round furtively, for fear lest Mr. Greathead or Dorsy's successor, Mrs. Blenkiron, should have seen him. He pinched and pulled it back into shape and brushed it carefully and hung it on the stand. He was ashamed, not of his violence, but of its futility.

Nobody but a damned fool, he said to himself, would have done that. He must have been mad.

It wasn't as if he didn't know what he was going to do. He had known ever since the day when Dorsy left him.

"I shan't be myself again till I've done him in," he thought.

He was only waiting till he had planned it out; till he was sure of every detail; till he was fit and cool. There must be no hesitation, no uncertainty at the last minute, above all, no blind, headlong violence. Nobody but a fool would kill in mad rage, and forget things, and be caught and swing for it. Yet that was what they all did. There was always something they hadn't thought of that gave them away.

Steven had thought of everything, even the date, even the weather.

Mr. Greathead was in the habit of going up to London to attend the debates of a learned Society he belonged to that held its meetings in May and November. He always travelled up by the five o'clock train, so that he might go to bed and rest as soon as he arrived. He always stayed for a week and gave his housekeeper a week's holiday. Steven chose a dark, threatening day in November, when Mr. Greathead was going up to his meeting and Mrs. Blenkiron had left Eastthwaite for Morfe by the early morning bus. So that there was nobody in the house but Mr. Greathead and Steven.

Eastthwaite Lodge stands alone, grey, hidden between the shoulder of the moor and the ash trees of its drive. It is approached by a bridle-path across the moor, a turning off the road that runs from Eastthwaite in Rathdale to Shawe in Westleydale, about a mile from the village and a mile from Hardraw Pass. No tradesmen visited it. Mr. Greathead's letters and his newspaper were shot into a post-box that hung on the ash tree at the turn.

The hot water laid on in the house was not hot enough for Mr. Greathead's bath, so that every morning, while Mr. Greathead shaved, Steven came to him with a can of boiling water.

Mr. Greathead, dressed in a mauve and grey striped sleeping-suit, stood shaving himself before the looking-glass that hung on the wall beside the great white bath. Steven waited with his hand on the cold tap, watching the bright curved rod of water falling with a thud and a splash.

In the white, stagnant light from the muffed window-pane the knife-blade flame of a small oil-stove flickered queerly. The oil sputtered and stank.

Suddenly the wind hissed in the water-pipes and cut off the glittering rod. To Steven it seemed the suspension of all movement. He would have to wait there till the water flowed again before he could begin. He tried not to look at Mr. Greathead and the lean wattles of his lifted throat. He fixed his eyes on the long crack in the soiled green distemper of the wall. His nerves were on edge with waiting for the water to flow again. The fumes of the oil-stove worked on them like a rank intoxicant. The soiled green wall gave him a sensation of physical sickness.

He picked up a towel and hung it over the back of a chair. Thus he caught sight of his own face in the glass above Mr. Greathead's; it was livid against the soiled green wall. Steven stepped aside to avoid it.

"Don't you feel well, Steven?"

"No, sir." Steven picked up a small sponge and looked at it.

Mr. Greathead had laid down his razor and was wiping the lather from his chin. At that instant, with a gurgling, spluttering haste, the water leaped from the tap.

It was then that Steven made his sudden, quiet rush. He first gagged Mr. Greathead with the sponge, then pushed him back and back against the wall and pinned him there with both hands round his neck, as he had pinned Ned Oldishaw. He pressed in on Mr. Greathead's throat, strangling him.

Mr. Greathead's hands flapped in the air, trying feebly to beat Steven off; then his arms, pushed back by the heave and thrust of Steven's shoulders, dropped. Then Mr. Greathead's body sank, sliding along the wall, and fell to the floor, Steven still keeping his hold, mounting it, gripping it with his knees. His fingers tightened, pressing back the blood. Mr. Greathead's face swelled up; it changed horribly. There was a groaning and rattling sound in his throat. Steven pressed in till it had ceased.

Then he stripped himself to the waist. He stripped Mr. Greathead of his sleeping-suit and hung his naked body face downwards in the bath. He took the razor and cut the great arteries and veins in the neck. He pulled up the plug of the waste-pipe, and left the body to drain in the running water.

He left it all day and all night.

He had noticed that murderers swung just for want of attention to little things like that; messing up themselves and the whole place with blood; always forgetting something essential. He had no time to think of horrors. From the moment he had murdered Mr. Greathead his own neck was in danger; he was simply using all his brain and nerve to save his neck. He worked with the stern, cool hardness of a man going through with an unpleasant, necessary job. He had thought of everything.

He had even thought of the dairy.

It was built on to the back of the house under the shelter of the high moor. You entered it through the scullery, which cut it off from the yard. The window-panes had been removed and replaced by sheets of perforated zinc. A large corrugated glass sky-light lit it from the roof. Impossible either to see in or to approach it from the outside. It was fitted up with a long, black slate shelf, placed, for the convenience of butter-makers, at the height of an ordinary work-bench. Steven had his tools, a razor, a carving-knife, a chopper and a meat-saw, laid there ready, beside a great pile of cotton waste.

Early the next day he took Mr. Greathead's body out of the bath, wrapped a thick towel round the neck and head, carried it down to the dairy and stretched it out on the slab. And there he cut it up into seventeen pieces.

These he wrapped in several layers of newspaper, covering the face and the hands first, because, at the last moment, they frightened him. He sewed them up in two sacks and hid them in the cellar.

He burnt the towel and the cotton waste in the kitchen fire; he cleaned his tools thoroughly and put them back in their places; and he washed down the marble slab. There wasn't a spot on the floor except for one flagstone where the pink rinsing of the slab had splashed over. He scrubbed it for half an hour, still seeing the rusty edges of the splash long after he had scoured it out.

He then washed and dressed himself with care.

As it was war-time Steven could only work by day, for a light in the dairy roof would have attracted the attention of the police. He had murdered Mr. Greathead on a Tuesday; it was now three o'clock on Thursday afternoon. Exactly at ten minutes past four he had brought out the car, shut in close with its black hood and side curtains. He had packed Mr. Greathead's suitcase and placed it in the car with his umbrella, railway rug, and travelling cap. Also, in a bundle, the clothes that his victim would have gone to London in.

He stowed the body in the two sacks beside him on the front.

By Hardraw Pass, halfway between Eastthwaite and Shawe, there are three round pits, known as the Churns, hollowed out of the grey rock and said to be bottomless. Steven had thrown stones, big as a man's chest, down the largest pit, to see whether they would be caught on any ledge or boulder. They had dropped clean, without a sound.

It poured with rain, the rain that Steven had reckoned on. The Pass was dark under the clouds and deserted. Steven turned his car so that the headlights glared on the pit's mouth. Then he ripped open the sacks and threw down, one by one, the seventeen pieces of Mr. Greathead's body, and the sacks after them, and the clothes.

It was not enough to dispose of Mr. Greathead's dead body; he had to behave as though Mr. Greathead were alive. Mr. Greathead had disappeared and he had to account for his disappearance. He drove on to Shawe station to the five o'clock train, taking care to arrive close on its starting. A troop-train was due to depart a minute earlier. Steven, who had reckoned on the darkness and the rain, reckoned also on the hurry and confusion on the platform.

As he had foreseen, there were no porters in the station entry; nobody to notice whether Mr. Greathead was or was not in the car. He carried his things through on to the platform and gave the suitcase to an old man to label. He dashed into the booking-office and took Mr. Greathead's ticket, and then rushed along the platform as if he were following his master. He heard himself shouting to the guard, "Have you seen Mr. Greathead?" And the guard's answer, "Naw!" And his own inspired statement, "He must have taken his seat in the front, then." He ran to the front of the train, shouldering his way among the troops. The drawn blinds of the carriages favoured him.

Steven thrust the umbrella, the rug, and the travelling cap into an empty compartment, and slammed the door to. He tried to shout something through the open window; but his tongue was harsh and dry against the roof of his mouth, and no sound came. He stood, blocking the window, till the guard whistled. When the train moved he ran alongside with his hand on the window ledge, as though he were taking the last instructions of his master. A porter pulled him back.

"Quick work, that," said Steven.

Before he left the station he wired to Mr. Greathead's London hotel, announcing the time of his arrival.

He felt nothing, nothing but the intense relief of a man who has saved himself by his own wits from a most horrible death. There were even moments, in the week that followed, when, so powerful was the illusion of his innocence, he could have believed that he had really seen Mr. Greathead off by the five o'clock train. Moments when he literally stood still in amazement before his own incredible impunity. Other moments when a sort of vanity uplifted him. He had committed a murder that for sheer audacity and cool brain work surpassed all murders celebrated in the history of crime. Unfortunately the very perfection of his achievement doomed it to oblivion. He had left not a trace.

Not a trace.

Only when he woke in the night a doubt sickened him. There was the rusted ring of that splash on the dairy floor. He wondered, had he really washed it out clean. And he would get up and light a candle and go down to the dairy to make sure. He knew the exact place; bending over it with the candle, he could imagine that he still saw a faint outline.

Daylight reassured him. *He* knew the exact place, but nobody else knew. There was nothing to distinguish it from the natural stains in the flagstone. Nobody would guess. But he was glad when Mrs. Blenkiron came back again.

On the day that Mr. Greathead was to have come home by the four o'clock train. Steven drove into Shawe and bought a chicken for the master's dinner. He met the four o'clock train and expressed surprise that Mr. Greathead had not come by it. He said he would be sure to come by the seven. He ordered dinner for eight; Mrs. Blenkiron roasted the chicken, and Steven met the seven o'clock train. This time he showed uneasiness.

The next day he met all the trains and wired to Mr. Greathead's hotel for information. When the manager wired back that Mr. Greathead had not arrived, he wrote to his relatives and gave notice to the police.

Three weeks passed. The police and Mr. Greathead's relatives accepted Steven's statements, backed as they were by the evidence of the booking office clerk, the telegraph clerk, the guard, the porter who had labelled Mr. Greathead's luggage and the hotel manager who had received his telegram. Mr. Greathead's portrait was published in the illustrated papers with requests for any information which might lead to his discovery. Nothing happened, and presently he and his disappearance were forgotten. The nephew who came down to Eastthwaite to look into his affairs was satisfied. His balance at his bank was low owing to the non-payment of various dividends, but the accounts and the contents of Mr. Greathead's cash-box and bureau were in order and Steven had put down every penny he had spent. The nephew paid Mrs. Blenkiron's wages and dismissed her and arranged with the chauffeur to stay on and take care of the house. And as Steven saw that this was the best way to escape suspicion, he stayed on.

Only in Westleydale and Rathdale excitement lingered. People wondered and speculated. Mr. Greathead had been robbed and murdered in the train (Steven said he had had money on him). He had lost his memory and wandered goodness knew where. He had thrown himself out of the railway carriage. Steven said Mr. Greathead wouldn't do *that*, but he shouldn't be surprised if he had lost his memory. He knew a man who forgot who he was and where he lived. Didn't know his own wife and children. Shell-shock. And lately Mr. Greathead's memory hadn't been what it was. Soon as he got it back he'd turn up again. Steven wouldn't be surprised to see him walking in any day.

But on the whole people noticed that he didn't care to talk much about Mr. Greathead. They thought this showed very proper feeling. They were sorry for Steven. He had lost his master and he had lost Dorsy Oldishaw. And if he *did* half kill Ned Oldishaw, well, young Ned had no business to go meddling with his sweetheart. Even Mrs. Oldishaw was sorry for him. And when Steven came into the bar of the King's Arms everybody said "Good evening, Steve," and made room for him by the fire.

Chapter III

STEVEN came and went now as if nothing had happened. He made a point of keeping the house as it would be kept if Mr. Greathead were alive. Mrs. Blenkiron, coming in once a fortnight to wash and clean, found the fire lit in Mr. Greathead's study and his slippers standing on end in the fender. Upstairs his bed was made, the clothes folded back, ready. This ritual guarded Steven not only from the suspicions of outsiders, but from his own knowledge. By behaving as though he believed that Mr. Greathead was still living he almost made himself believe it. By refusing to let his mind dwell on the murder he came to forget it. His imagination saved him, playing the play that kept him sane, till the murder became vague to him and fantastic like a thing done in a dream. He had waked up and this was the reality; this round of caretaking, this look the house had of waiting for Mr. Greathead to come back to it. He had left off getting up in the night to examine the place on the dairy floor. He was no longer amazed at his impunity.

Then suddenly, when he really had forgotten, it ended. It was on a Saturday in January, about five o'clock. Steven had heard that Dorsy Oldishaw was back again, living at the 'King's Arms' with her aunt. He had a mad, uncontrollable longing to see her again.

But it was not Dorsy that he saw.

His way from the Lodge kitchen into the drive was through the yard gates and along the flagged path under the study window. When he turned on to the flags he saw it shuffling along before him. The lamplight from the window lit it up. He could see distinctly the little old man in the long, shabby black overcoat, with the grey woollen muffler round his neck hunched up above his collar, lifting the thin grey hair that stuck out under the slouch of the black hat.

In the first moment that he saw it Steven had no fear. He simply felt that the murder had not happened, that he really *had* dreamed it, and that this was Mr. Greathead come back, alive among the living. The phantasm was now standing at the door of the house, its hand on the doorknob as if about to enter.

But when Steven came up to the door it was not there.

He stood, fixed, staring at the space which had emptied itself so horribly. His heart heaved and staggered, snatching at his breath. And suddenly the memory of the murder rushed at him. He saw himself in the bathroom, shut in with his victim by the soiled green walls. He smelt the reek of the oil-stove; he heard the water running from the tap. He felt his feet springing forward, and his fingers pressing, tighter and tighter, on Mr. Greathead's throat. He saw Mr. Greathead's hands flapping helplessly, his terrified eyes, his face swelling and discoloured, changing horribly, and his body sinking to the floor.

He saw himself in the dairy, afterwards; he could hear the thudding, grinding, scraping noises of his tools. He saw himself on Hardraw Pass and the headlights glaring on the pit's mouth. And the fear and the horror he had not felt then came on him now.

He turned back; he bolted the yard gates and all the doors of the house, and shut himself up in the lighted kitchen. He took up his magazine. *The Autocar*, and forced himself to read it. Presently his terror left him. He said to himself it was nothing. Nothing but his fancy. He didn't suppose he'd ever see anything again.

Three days passed. On the third evening, Steven had lit the study lamp and was bolting the window when he saw it again.

It stood on the path outside, close against the window, looking in. He saw its face distinctly, the greyish, stuck-out bud of the under-lip, and the droop of the pinched nose. The small eyes peered at him, glittering. The whole figure had a glassy look between the darkness behind it and the pane. One moment it stood outside, looking in; and the next it was mixed up with the shimmering picture of the lighted room that hung there on the blackness of the trees. Mr. Greathead then showed as if reflected, standing with Steven in the room.

And now he was outside again, looking at him, looking at him through the pane.

Steven's stomach sank and dragged, making him feel sick. He pulled down the blind between him and Mr. Greathead, clamped the shutters to and drew the curtains over them. He locked and double-bolted the front door, all the doors, to keep Mr. Greathead out. But, once that night, as he lay in bed, he heard the *shoob-shoob* of feet shuffling along the flagged passages, up the stairs, and across the landing outside his door. The door handle rattled; but nothing came. He lay awake till morning, the sweat running off his skin, his heart plunging and quivering with terror.

When he got up he saw a white, scared face in the looking-glass. A face with a half-open mouth, ready to blab, to blurt out his secret; the face of an idiot. He was afraid to take that face into Eastthwaite or into Shawe. So he shut himself up in the house, half starved on his small stock of bread, bacon and groceries.

Two weeks passed; and then it came again in broad daylight.

It was Mrs. Blenkiron's morning. He had lit the fire in the study at noon and set up Mr. Greathead's slippers in the fender. When he rose from his stooping and turned round he saw Mr. Greathead's phantasm standing on the hearthrug close in front of him. It was looking at him and smiling in a sort of mockery, as if amused at what Steven had been doing. It was solid and completely lifelike at first. Then, as Steven in his terror backed and backed away from it (he was afraid to turn and feel it there behind him), its feet became insubstantial. As if undermined, the whole structure sank and fell together on the floor, where it made a pool of some whitish glistening substance that mixed with the pattern of the carpet and sank through.

That was the most horrible thing it had done yet, and Steven's nerve broke under it. He went to Mrs. Blenkiron, whom he found scrubbing out the dairy.

She sighed as she wrung out the floor-cloth.

"Eh, these owd yeller stawnes, scroob as you will they'll nawer look clean."

"Naw," he said. "Scroob and scroob, you'll nawer get them clean."

She looked up at him.

"Eh, lad, what ails 'ee? Ye've got a faace like a wroong dishdout hanging ower t' sink."

"I've got the colic."

"Aye, an' naw woonder wi' the damp, and they misties, an' your awn bad cooking. Let me roon down t' 'King's Arms' and get you a drop of whisky."

"Naw, I'll gaw down mysen."

He knew now he was afraid to be left alone in the house. Down at the 'King's Arms' Dorsy and Mrs. Oldishaw were sorry for him. By this time he was really ill with fright. Dorsy and Mrs. Oldishaw said it was a chill. They made him lie down on the settle by the kitchen fire and put a rug over him, and gave him stiff hot grog to drink. He slept. And when he woke he found Dorsy sitting beside him with her sewing.

He sat up and her hand was on his shoulder.

"Lay still, lad."

"I maun get oop and gaw."

"Nay, there's naw call for 'ee to gaw. Lay still and I'll make thee a coop o' tea."

He lay still.

Mrs. Oldishaw had made up a bed for him in her son's room, and they kept him there that night and till four o'clock the next day.

When he got up to go Dorsy put on her coat and hat.

"Is tha gawing out, Dorsy?"

"Aye. I canna let thee gaw and set there by thysen. I'm cooming oop to set with 'ee till nighttime."

She came up and they sat side by side in the Lodge kitchen by the fire as they used to sit when they were together there, holding each other's hands and not talking.

"Dorsy," he said at last, "what astha coom for? Astha coom to tall me tha'll nawer speak to me again?"

"Nay. Tha knaws what I've coom for."

"To saay tha'll marry me?"

"Aye."

"I maunna marry thee, Dorsy. 'Twouldn' be right."

"Right? What dostha mean? 'Twouldn't be right for me to coom and set wi' thee this road ef I doan't marry thee."

"Nay. I darena'. Tha said tha was afraid of me, Dorsy. I doan't want 'ee to be afraid. Tha said tha'd be unhappy. I doan't want 'ee to be unhappy."

"That was lasst year. I'm not afraid of 'ee, now, Steve."

"Tha doan't knaw me, lass."

"Aye, I knaw thee. I knaw tha's sick and starved for want of me. Tha canna live wi'out thy awn lass to take care of 'ee."

She rose.

"I maun gaw now. But I'll be oop tomorrow and the next day."

And tomorrow and the next day and the next, at dusk, the hour that Steven most dreaded, Dorsy came. She sat with him till long after the night had fallen.

Steven would have felt safe so long as she was with him, but for his fear that Mr. Greathead would appear to him while she was there and that she would see him. If Dorsy knew he was being haunted she might guess why. Or Mr. Greathead might take some horrible blood-dripping and dismembered shape that would show her how he had been murdered. It would be like him, dead, to come between them as he had come when he was living.

They were sitting at the round table by the fireside. The lamp was lit and Dorsy was bending over her sewing. Suddenly she looked up, her head on one side, listening. Far away inside the house, on the flagged passage from the front door, he could hear the *shoob-shoob* of the footsteps. He could almost believe that Dorsy shivered. And somehow, for some reason, this time he was not afraid.

"Steven," she said, "didsta 'ear anything?"

"Naw. Nobbut t' wind oonder t' roogs."

She looked at him; a long wondering look. Apparently it satisfied her, for she answered: "Aye. Mebbe 'tes nobbut wind," and went on with her sewing.

He drew his chair nearer to her to protect her if it came. He could almost touch her where she sat.

The latch lifted. The door opened, and, his entrance and his passage unseen, Mr. Greathead stood before them.

The table hid the lower half of his form; but above it he was steady and solid in his terrible semblance of flesh and blood.

Steven looked at Dorsy. She was staring at the phantasm with an innocent, wondering stare that had no fear in it at all. Then she looked at Steven. An uneasy, frightened, searching look, as though to make sure whether he had seen it.

That was her fear – that *he* should see it, that *he* should be frightened, that *he* should be haunted.

He moved closer and put his hand on her shoulder. He thought, perhaps, she might shrink from him because she knew that it *was* he who was haunted. But no, she put up her hand and held his, gazing up into his face and smiling.

Then, to his amazement, the phantasm smiled back at them; not with mockery, but with a strange and terrible sweetness. Its face lit up for one instant with a sudden, beautiful, shining light; then it was gone.

"Did tha see 'im, Steve?"

"Aye."

"Astha seen annything afore?"

"Aye, three times I've seen 'im."

"Is it that 'as scared thee?"

"'Oo tawled 'ee I was scared?"

"I knawed. Because nowt can 'appen to thee but I maun knaw it."

"What dostha think, Dorsy?"

"I think tha needna be scared, Steve. 'E's a kind ghawst. Whatever 'e is 'e doan't mean thee no 'arm. T' owd gentleman nawer did when he was alive."

"Didn' 'e? Didn' 'e? 'E served me the woorst turn 'e could when 'e coomed between thee and me."

"Whatever makes 'ee think that, lad?"

"I doan' think it. I *know*."

"Nay, loove, tha dostna."

"'E did. 'E did, I tell thee."

"Doan' tha say that," she cried. "Doan' tha say it, Stevey."

"Why shouldn't I?"

"Tha'll set folk talking that road."

"What do they knaw to talk about?"

"Ef they was to remember what tha said."

"And what did I say?"

"Why, that ef annybody was to coom between thee and me, tha'd do them in."

"I wasna thinking of *'im*. Gawd knaws I wasna."

"*They* doan't," she said.

"*Tha* knaws? Tha knaws I didna mean 'im?"

"Aye, *I* knaw, Steve."

"An', Dorsy, tha 'm't afraid of me? Tha 'm't afraid of me anny more?"

"Nay, lad. I loove thee too mooch. I shall nawer be afraid of 'ee again. Would I coom to thee this road ef I was afraid?"

"Tha'll be afraid now."

"And what should I be afraid of?"

"Why – 'm."

"*'Im?* I should be a deal more afraid to think of 'ee setting with 'im oop 'ere, by thysen. Wuntha coom down and sleep at aunt's?"

"That I wunna. But I shall set 'ee on t' road passt t' moor."

He went with her down the bridle-path and across the moor and along the main road that led through Eastthwaite. They parted at the turn where the lights of the village came in sight.

The moon had risen as Steven went back across the moor. The ash tree at the bridle-path stood out clear, its hooked, bending branches black against the grey moor-grass. The shadows in the ruts laid stripes along the bridle-path, black on grey. The house was black-grey in the darkness of the drive. Only the lighted study window made a golden square in its long wall.

Before he could go up to bed he would have to put out the study lamp. He was nervous; but he no longer felt the sickening and sweating terror of the first hauntings. Either he was getting used to it, or – something had happened to him.

He had closed the shutters and put out the lamp. His candle made a ring of light round the table in the middle of the room. He was about to take it up and go when he heard a thin voice calling his same: "Steven." He raised his head to listen. The thin thread of sound seemed to come from outside, a long way off, at the end of the bridle-path.

"Steven, Steven—"

This time he could have sworn the sound came from inside his head, like the hiss of air in his ears.

"Steven—"

He knew the voice now. It was behind him in the room. He turned, and saw the phantasm of Mr. Greathead sitting, as he used to sit, in the armchair by the fire. The form was dim in the dusk of the room outside the ring of candlelight. Steven's first movement was to snatch up the candlestick and hold it between him and the phantasm, hoping that the light would cause it to disappear. Instead of disappearing the figure became clear and solid, indistinguishable from a figure of flesh and blood dressed in black broadcloth and white linen. Its eyes had the shining transparency of blue crystal; they were fixed on Steven with a look of quiet, benevolent attention. Its small, narrow mouth was lifted at the corners, smiling.

It spoke.

"You needn't be afraid," it said.

The voice was natural now, quiet, measured, slightly quavering. Instead of frightening Steven it soothed and steadied him.

He put the candle on the table behind him and stood up before the phantasm, fascinated.

"*Why* are you afraid?" it asked.

Steven couldn't answer. He could only stare, held there by the shining, hypnotizing eyes.

"You are afraid," it said, "because you think I'm what you call a ghost, a supernatural thing. You think I'm dead and that you killed me. You think you took a horrible revenge for a wrong you thought I did you. You think I've come back to frighten you, to revenge myself in my turn.

"And everyone of those thoughts of yours, Steven, is wrong. I'm real, and my appearance is as natural and real as anything in this room – *more* natural and more real if you did but know. You didn't kill me, as you see; for here I am, as alive, more alive than you are. Your revenge consisted in removing me from a state which had become unbearable to a state more delightful than you can imagine. I don't mind telling you, Steven, that I was in serious financial difficulties (which, by the way, is a good thing for you, as it provides a plausible motive for my disappearance). So that, as far as revenge goes, the thing was a complete frost. You were my benefactor. Your methods were somewhat violent, and I admit you gave me some disagreeable moments before my actual deliverance; but as I was already developing rheumatoid arthritis there can be no doubt that in your hands my death was more merciful than if it had been left to Nature. As for the subsequent arrangements, I congratulate you, Steven, on your coolness and resource. I always said you were equal to any emergency, and that your brains would pull you safe through any scrape. You committed an appalling and dangerous crime, a crime of all things the most difficult to conceal, and you contrived so that it was not discovered and never will be discovered. And no doubt the details of this crime seemed to you horrible and revolting to the last degree; and the more horrible and the more revolting they were, the more you piqued yourself on your nerve in carrying the thing through without a hitch.

"I don't want to put you entirely out of conceit with your performance. It was very creditable for a beginner, very creditable indeed. But let me tell you, this idea of things being horrible and revolting is all illusion. The terms are purely relative to your limited perceptions.

"I'm speaking now to your intelligence – I don't mean that practical ingenuity which enabled you to dispose of me so neatly. When I say intelligence I mean intelligence. All you did, then, was to redistribute matter. To our incorruptible sense matter never takes any of those offensive forms in which it so often appears to you. Nature has evolved all this horror and repulsion just to prevent people from making too many little experiments like yours. You mustn't imagine that these things have any eternal importance. Don't flatter yourself you've electrified the universe. For minds no longer attached to flesh and blood, that horrible butchery you were so proud of, Steven, is simply silly. No more terrifying than the spiffing of red ink or the rearrangement of a jigsaw puzzle. I saw the whole business, and I can assure you I felt nothing but intense amusement. Your face, Steven, was so absurdly serious. You've no idea what you looked like with that chopper. I'd have appeared to you then and told you so, only I knew I should frighten you into fits.

"And there's another grand mistake, my lad – your thinking that I'm haunting you out of revenge, that I'm trying to frighten you… My dear Steven, if I'd wanted to frighten you I'd have appeared in a very different shape. I needn't remind you what shape I *might* have appeared in… What do you suppose I've come for?"

"I don't know," said Steven in a husky whisper. "Tell me."

"I've come to forgive you. And to save you from the horror you *would* have felt sooner or later. And to stop your going on with your crime."

"You needn't," Steven said. "I'm not going on with it. I shall do no more murders."

"There you are again. Can't you understand that I'm not talking about your silly butcher's work? I'm talking about your *real* crime. Your real crime was hating me.

"And your very hate was a blunder, Steven. You hated me for something I hadn't done."

"Aye, what did you do? Tell me that."

"You thought I came between you and your sweetheart. That night when Dorsy spoke to me, you thought I told her to throw you over, didn't you?"

"Aye. And what did you tell her?"

"I told her to stick to you. It was you, Steven, who drove her away. You frightened the child. She said she was afraid for her life of you. Not because you half killed that poor boy, but because of the look on your face before you did it. The look of hate, Steven.

"I told her not to be afraid of you. I told her that if she threw you over you might go altogether to the devil; that she might even be responsible for some crime. I told her that if she married you and was faithful – *if she loved you* – I'd answer for it you'd never go wrong.

"She was too frightened to listen to me. Then I told her to think over what I'd said before she did anything. You heard me say that."

"Aye. That's what I heard you say. I didn' knaw. I didn' knaw. I thought you'd set her agen me."

"If you don't believe me, you can ask her, Steven."

"That's what she said t' other night. That you nawer coom between her and me. Nawer."

"Never," the phantasm said. "And you don't hate me now."

"Naw. Naw. I should nawer 'a hated 'ee. I should nawer 'a laid a finger on thee, ef I'd knawn."

"It's not your laying fingers on me, it's your hatred that matters. If that's done with, the whole thing's done with."

"Is it? Is it? Ef it was knawn, I should have to hang for it. Maunna I gie mysen oop? Tell me, maun I gie mysen oop?"

"You want me to decide that for you?"

"Aye. Doan't gaw," he said. "Doan't gaw."

It seemed to him that Mr. Greathead's phantasm was getting a little thin, as if it couldn't last more than an instant. He had never so longed for it to go, as he longed now for it to stay and help him.

"Well, Steven, any flesh-and-blood man would tell you to go and get hanged tomorrow; that it was no more than your plain duty. And I daresay there are some mean, vindictive spirits even in my world who would say the same, not because *they* think death important but because they know *you* do, and want to get even with you that way.

"It isn't *my* way. I consider this little affair is strictly between ourselves. There isn't a jury of flesh-and-blood men who would understand it. They all think death so important."

"What do you want me to do, then? Tell me and I'll do it! Tell me!"

He cried it out loud; for Mr. Greathead's phantasm was getting thinner and thinner; it dwindled and fluttered, like a light going down. Its voice came from somewhere away outside, from the other end of the bridle-path.

"Go on living," it said. "Marry Dorsy."

"I darena'. She doan' knaw I killed 'ee."

"Oh, yes" – the eyes flickered up, gentle and ironic – "she does. She knew all the time."

And with that the phantasm went out.

The Sounds of a Bamboo Forest

Michelle Tang

THE BAMBOO TREES loomed over the rental car, their branches bending with the wind. The forest had moved in closer since the last time he was here, encroaching on the gravel that made up the already narrow road. Finger-thin leaves brushed against the windows and pattered against the sides of the car.

Lisa stared through the sunroof to see where tree met sky. "This is amazing."

"You should have seen it when Mitch first started planting," Brad said, "A few rows of these skinny little plants around some cherry blossom trees. The bamboo's really taken over." His eyes darted to the rearview mirror at the box strapped into the backseat.

"When did he start all this?" Lisa gestured at her window. The trees seemed to blur together as they passed.

"When his ex-wife first moved in with him, about ten years ago. He wanted to give her a little piece of home."

"That's really sweet. Every time she looked outside she'd see how much he loved her."

"Mitch is – *was* that kind of guy." Brad's older brother had always taken care of everyone around him. And how had Brad returned a lifetime of support?

He gazed into the rearview mirror at the small box again, squeezed the steering wheel tight. "I shouldn't have…it was his last request, for Pete's sake."

His wife rubbed his thigh. "He'd understand, Brad. If he knew how hard this would be on you, I feel like he'd be okay with it. We'll do what we have to do here, and then we'll leave, and the urn will come with us. Don't worry about it, okay?"

The gravel road curved around a large rock outcropping, and Brad recognized the landmark. "Too late to turn back now."

The small wooden house came into view a moment later. Brad was relieved to see something familiar: the land had turned strange and unfamiliar since he'd last come. The trees were stretched so high they blotted out everything but a narrow strip of dusky sky, and the shadows beneath the bamboo's slender leaves transformed into opaque, creeping things that seemed to dodge his headlights and coalesce behind the car. Since they'd turned onto the forest road, they hadn't seen another car.

Lisa pulled forward against her seatbelt and stared at the cabin as they approached. The gravel road gave way to the even, packed dirt that encircled the wooden house. Brad parked close to the front door. He handed his wife the key and moved to the backseat, unbuckling the small cardboard box and holding it carefully. With his other hand, he grabbed his overnight bag and their groceries.

Once inside, Lisa flipped the light on. The worn spot on the couch and Mitch's chipped, unwashed coffee mug made Brad flinch. It was like no time had passed since he'd last been here: clean wood floors and furniture, plain blue curtains at the windows, not even a TV. Mitch's thin laptop lay closed on his desk.

"Where's the bathroom?" Lisa asked, and followed his pointed finger to one of the two doors at the back of the main room.

"Why wouldn't you want to come back? You loved this place." Brad muttered to the urn as he took it from the box. He slid it on the counter right where Mitch used to lean his hip, sipping coffee and staring out at the trees. "I'm sorry, Mitch." Brad's voice broke. "I just couldn't be here without you."

He was boiling pasta when his jaw began to ache. The sound outside – the wind groaning between the bamboo trees – set his nerves on edge, and his teeth had been clenched, probably since they'd arrived.

"I don't know how he ever lived with this noise." Brad said. "Last time I visited, God, it had to have been five years ago, the trees were smaller and further back. Barely heard a sound."

Lisa went to set the table. "He probably got used to it. Like people who live by the ocean."

"Maybe that's why Mari split, Mitch. She needed some peace and quiet." Brad's joke felt wrong. Ever since Mari had left, saying her name felt taboo, like a curse.

"He never said why?" Lisa asked.

Brad shook his head. "That was Mitch. He'd listen to everyone else's problems for days, but didn't want to burden anyone with his own. I've probably only heard him cry once in my life."

Brad remembered the helpless frustration that filled him as Mitch sobbed over the phone to him. "She's gone, Brad. She's gone."

"What was she like?"

Brad shrugged. "She didn't talk much, but she seemed nice. I figured she wanted me to have quality time with my brother. In the day she'd go for long walks in the forest. At night, she'd just sit and laugh at our bickering. I spent four days here and didn't get to know her well at all."

They streamed a radio station from Lisa's phone while they ate. There were moments of static, but he wanted to hear other people's voices. Toronto always sounded so alive with light and noise, even in the dead of night. Here, the darkness and silence pressed in on Brad, hushing his voice. He went around the two-room space, making sure the curtains were all closed, convinced that the lit windows shone like a beacon in the black emptiness outside.

In the space between one song ending and before another began, an unfamiliar sound came from outside. Brad set down the soapy plate and wiped his hands.

"Lisa, can you mute your phone for a second?"

She did. The groaning of the bamboo trees filled the cabin once more. "What?"

"Listen." Brad crossed the room to pull aside the curtain and peer out the window. There was no point – the glass reflected his own tired face and the single light that hung over the kitchen sink. The squat, dark blue urn on the counter drew his eye.

The sound came again. It was high-pitched and short-lived, loud before it trailed off into silence.

"There's got to be a bunch of animals in the forest, right?" Lisa asked. "Or maybe neighbours?"

Brad shrugged, let the curtain fall from his fingers before he returned to the sink. "Mitch owns a lot of land here. I've never seen signs of anyone else living nearby. But who knows? A lot could have changed in five years."

Brad brushed his teeth. The water had an earthy smell to it and had a metallic aftertaste. He was checking the windows and door to make sure everything was locked, when the thought struck him: Mitch had had his heart attack mid-morning, so the curtains should have been pulled back. They were all drawn closed.

He laid his head on the pillow, and the smell of Mitch's shampoo and aftershave tickled his nose. Mitch had used the same product for years, and out of all the memories the scent stirred up, Brad remembered the time they'd gone hiking in Killarney Park. He'd landed wrong, jumping off a boulder onto the trail, and pain exploded up his left leg.

"I can't walk, Mitch. I think I broke something." Pain made his voice thin.

They'd been hours away from help, their cell phone signals as empty of bars as the path was of other hikers. Mitch hoisted Brad onto his back and had carried him all the way back. Brad had clutched onto his brother's shoulders and tried to distract them with stupid stories, while his brother's familiar scent surrounded and soothed him. Brad's eyes prickled. *This will be the last time I smell you.*

Lisa lay down, her own soapy smell overwhelming his brother's, and grief clanged inside him.

Outside, the strange call sounded again.

"There's got to be new neighbours. Campers, maybe. That's a human sound." Lisa cuddled closer.

Brad grabbed his phone off the nightstand to search for answers."Maybe a fox or a bobcat," he said. "Their cries can sound like a human screaming."

"Are there bobcats up here?"

"This far north? Who knows what the bamboo forest hides?" Brad tried to sound playful, but the sense of wrongness struck again, even though he hadn't mentioned Mari. The groaning of the trees and the wild animal calls weren't enough to keep him awake and he drifted to sleep.

When he woke, Brad opened all the curtains to let the light in, but the morning had dawned dim and cloudy. The smooth grey-green bamboo greeted him, closer than he liked. They were planted so densely that the space between the trees always held shadows.

After breakfast, Brad sorted through Mitch's desk. His brother never kept much: the drawers held printer paper and cartridges, a few pens, and one thick file folder with important documents. Brad avoided the closed silver laptop for now: he wasn't ready to see the shows Mitch would never be able to finish, the music he'd been listening to, the recent photos.

"Guess the animal was nocturnal." Brad gestured outside. "We should find where it's sleeping and scream, see how it likes that."

Lisa paused the show she was streaming on her phone.

"There has to be people nearby. I heard a woman talking last night when I got up to pee."

Brad stared at his wife. "How loud was she talking? My brother's property goes out pretty far."

"She wasn't yelling or anything. She sounded pretty close." Lisa restarted her show. "Maybe they heard your brother passed away and thought they'd have the place to themselves. I'm sure seeing lights on here surprised them."

Organizing his brother's things was harder than Brad thought, and when Lisa offered to pack up Mitch's clothes, he accepted.

"Babe, look at this." Lisa came out of the bedroom, holding a small square of paper. "It was tucked between two sweaters in his drawer."

"It looks like a baby ultrasound." Brad's shaking fingers made the sonogram hard to read. He steadied it with his other hand. Mari's name was printed in white against the black background. It was dated six years ago. "I didn't even know they were expecting." His grief became tinged with regret. Why hadn't Mitch told him?

"Do you think something went wrong?" Lisa traced the tiny profile on the black printout.

"My brother was pretty private, but he'd have mentioned if he'd had a kid."

"That's so sad." Lisa placed the sonograph on the kitchen counter beside the urn. "Let's go outside and get some fresh air. We can go for a walk in the forest. Didn't you say that he planted a bunch of cherry blossom trees?"

Brad shook his head. "I don't want to go in there. I don't like how the place feels anymore."

Lisa frowned and gestured out the window. "You grew up hiking in forests, didn't you?"

He nodded. "My mom and dad used to take us camping every summer."

"Why is this one different then?"

"It was fine the last time I came to visit, but now…it's weird. There's no sounds of birds, or insects. There's not even any undergrowth, just dirt and bamboo. It creeps me out." That wrong feeling came back, and he rubbed at his arms.

Lisa raised her eyebrows. "I didn't realize there weren't birds. It's so noisy from the trees itself that I didn't… but you're right. What's that popping sound I keep hearing?"

"Bamboo have these air chambers inside them, and when there's a pressure change outside the tree, the air on the inside pops. That's the official explanation that I've heard, but…" Despite his discomfort, Brad enjoyed the way Lisa's eyes widened and how she leaned closer.

"But what?" She sounded like she was holding her breath.

"A guy I knew in my university biology class told me that his family believed bamboo would pop when there were ghosts present. He said that in the bamboo forests in Japan, the ones where there were a lot of suicides would make a lot more noise, like the spirits were restless and trying to talk."

"Brad!" Lisa punched his arm, hard. Her eyes flashed with real anger. "How dare you tell me this when we're in the middle of a damn bamboo forest? How can I keep from freaking out now?"

Brad grinned. "It's a jerk move, I'll admit, but it feels so good to be able to share that creepy story with someone. At least I didn't tell you last night."

Lisa tapped an app on her phone. "Let's watch a happy movie. I'm freaked out."

After the movie, they went back to packing and sorting until full night settled around the cabin. Brad was making instant macaroni and cheese for dinner when Lisa spoke up from the couch.

"Brad, that sound again."

The sonograph was still in his mind when the high-pitched cry came from the darkness. "It's a baby, isn't it?" Brad's skin prickled into gooseflesh.

Brad went into both rooms with Lisa, closing the curtains and re-checking the window latches. They bolted the door shut and ate without tasting the food. Lisa had loaded up a comedy to watch, but hadn't pressed play. They barely spoke, but dinner was far from silent. The meal was accompanied by the creaking wood, the wailing of a baby, and the popping cracks.

"How much longer till we can leave?" Lisa stared at the food in front of her.

"One more night, okay? Let me make sure I haven't missed anything important."

Afterwards, the dishes were abandoned in favor of retreating to Mitch's bed, huddling beneath his heavy covers. Lisa woke him. He blinked open bleary eyes: the bedside lamp was still on.

"Brad, that woman from last night is back," Lisa hissed.

He listened. It was faint and muffled, but the stranger's voice came from just outside. Brad signalled to Lisa to turn off the lamp and crept to the bedroom window. When it was dark inside, he nudged open the curtains to peek. The trees stood like ghostly figures just two meters from the house, filled with shadows. There was nothing that resembled a human silhouette.

A loud bang from the front of the cabin made them both jump. Lisa whimpered. Brad walked towards the front door, Lisa pulling futilely at him to return to the bed. For once, Brad was grateful for the bamboo creaking, which drowned out his footsteps as he tiptoed towards the door.

Brad listened again. "She's saying, 'Mitchell, Mitchell'." He rubbed at his eyes with the heel of his hands. "Her voice sounds familiar." He reached for the door.

"Don't, Brad! Oh my God." Lisa pushed him away and stood in front of the bolt, eyes wide, palms out.

"It's Mari, Lisa. She probably heard about his heart attack and came right away."

"Brad, why the hell would she come visit him in the middle of the night?"

"I don't know. But we can't leave her out there, Lisa. She's probably freezing."

The baby cried again, just outside. Brad reached for the door, pushing Lisa away from the locks. Lisa moved towards the counter, and even as he thought to reach for her, to apologize, something turned him back towards the door.

His hand was on the deadbolt when Lisa slid in front of him once more. She held Mitch's urn, the lid rattling with the force of her shaking. Her jaw was set.

"Babe, I love you, but if you open this door I swear to God I'll smash your brother's ashes all over the floor."

Brad glared at her. He took a step back, forced open clenched fists, nostrils flaring with the force of his breaths. "That's really cruel."

"You're not thinking clearly, Brad. That isn't Mari, or if it is, she was out there last night too. Something isn't right."

A loud crack of thunder startled him into awareness, and he retreated from the voice outside, grabbing for Lisa's hand. Her hand, or his, was shaking. "You're right. You're right, Lisa. I'm so sorry."

She slid the urn back onto the counter. Brad held his arms out to her, and tears stung the back of his eyes when she returned the embrace.

"I'm so sorry. I can't believe I pushed you."

The splatter of rain against the windows almost drowned out the voice calling for Brad's brother, and the baby's faint cry.

They sat together on the bed, feeling exposed despite the bolted door and locked windows.

Lisa spoke slowly, as though trying to sound calm. "This is the second night I've heard her. Last night she was outside the bathroom window, and tonight she's knocking on the door. What if she tries to get in, or knows where Mitch kept a key?"

Imagining the front door unlocking and footsteps entering the house while they lay defenceless in the bedroom sent a chill through Brad, but he shook his head. "The deadbolt is in place. And she was here last night and didn't try anything, right?"

"I'm not going to get any sleep tonight." Lisa sat up, leaning against the headboard, and swiped at her phone. "We're leaving first thing tomorrow."

"Agreed," Brad said. He would take the important documents and Mitch's valuables, do a final once-over of the drawers. The rest could be sold in the estate sale. Mitch had kept nothing of sentimental value here. Except, of course, for one old sonograph.

When Brad awoke, it was morning. The rain had stopped, and he heard nothing outside except for the tortuous creaks of the bamboo, punctuated by the occasional cracking *pop*. Lisa was already dressed, zipping up her duffel bag.

"I can't believe you slept," she said. "When she got quiet, it was even scarier because I didn't know where she was."

"I must have been more tired than I thought. Are you okay to drive the rental?" Brad wanted to keep Mitch's SUV. Lisa had come so they could each drive a car home.

"I'll be fine. Just… can you come with me to load the car?"

Brad dressed and they walked towards the front of the small cabin together. The bolts and locks were intact, and when he opened the front door, it was unmarred. The rain had softened the packed dirt of the driveway, and mud sucked at their shoes.

There were marks on the ground – mostly around the front door, but they seemed to circle around the house.

"Oh my God… are those footprints?" Lisa gasped and crouched, her long hair almost skimming the tracks.

"Yeah." They had been small feet, and bare. Brad could see each individual toe print, and something else, thin and long, that seemed to trail between both feet. He stood up and grabbed Mitch's urn from inside. "Lisa, will you take him with you?"

"Of course." Lisa's eyes were curious, but her face was tense. Brad knew that she didn't want to ask, didn't want to know what he was afraid of. He wasn't sure, himself. Lisa drove off without eating breakfast, and Brad watched the back of her car getting smaller on the narrow road until the forest seemed to devour it.

He loaded Mitch's SUV and sat down to have a coffee before leaving. For the first time, he flipped open his brother's laptop. The background image was a photo they'd taken together, years ago when they'd vacationed in Cuba, and Brad touched Mitch's smiling face with a finger. *Have to cancel his internet, too.*

He began to type 'bamboo tree' into the search bar. The auto-population field dropped down and he saw his brother's previous searches. *Bamboo trees ward off evil; bamboo trees and spirits; Bamboo trees superstition…* it went on and on.

Brad finished washing up and locked the front door. His car was packed, and if he had any sense, he'd drive out of here without a backward glance. The muddy ground drew his eye again: he stared at the tracks of bare feet that had circled the cabin while he slept and Lisa kept watch. At the strange line that trailed in between each footprint. He had to know.

Brad took some rope from the cabin and tied one end to the front door. He unrolled rope as he walked, following the small prints into the bamboo forest that remained dark and damp even beneath the afternoon sun.

There was no clear path. The footprints soon disappeared in the soft loam. Brad walked in as straight a line as he could, not sure what he was searching for, checking his diminishing coil of rope. The bamboo shoots were so tall overhead that he only saw small, bright patches of sky. The density of the plants obliterated any obvious landmarks, and soon everywhere he turned had the same green-grey creaking trees. The smell of wet earth and chlorophyll surrounded him, cloying and close.

He jumped at the occasional loud *pop*. The time between each staccato explosion varied, and the anticipation left him feeling on edge. Brad walked until he saw the blackened cherry tree, barren of leaf or blossom, and the small headstone beneath it. It was a tiny grave, and he pictured the perfect profile he'd seen on a sonogram lying amidst twisted roots and cold earth.

The gravestone was inscribed with words in Mitch's careful hand. "You are loved." Brad's finger traced the cold letters. The creaking around him became louder, and he straightened up, keeping his gaze on the grave. It was no longer the creak of the wind in the bamboo, or a stranger walking over a wooden floor. The sound became the noise of a straining rope, of a tree bough groaning under sudden, heavy weight. Above the small mound of dirt, the rotting threads of a rope hung from the cherry tree and entwined with its dead branches.

Amidst the groans of tortured wood, soft footsteps approached. Brad gripped his own rope in a sweating hand and didn't dare turn his head, not even when the footsteps stopped beside him. His legs locked and he shivered like the bamboo leaves around him. His mind kept seeing the thin length that trailed behind small footprints in the mud. He could fill in the blanks now. Beside his own booted feet stepped smaller ones, bare and blue-grey with decay, and a frayed rope that dragged on the ground like a braided umbilical cord.

He sensed the question, and forced the answer out of lungs gone tight with terror. "He had a heart attack. Mitch is dead." The sense of wrongness that had plagued him every time he'd mentioned Mari returned, but with it came Brad's relief that his brother was free – that Mitch wouldn't remain staring at his forest like it was a penance, hearing his dead child and his dead wife calling for him. Around Brad, the air was full of cracking pops. They filled the air like gunshots.

Eventually the feet turned and left, but Brad didn't dare move until all sounds of her footsteps had faded. With a last look at the gravestone, he followed his rope back through the forest.

The rope went slack in his hand as he walked. Panic building, Brad stopped pulling at it and tried to follow the rope where it lay. He walked until he found the end of it, coiled neatly on the ground.

Brad walked for hours in the same direction, cursing the phone that sat forgotten in Mitch's SUV, swearing at the darkening sky above him that gave no sign of the sun's direction. The shadows that hid between the dense bamboo grew and merged to surround him in blackness, until he was disoriented and thirsty and praying for help. Soon it was too dark to see. Brad wandered, goodbyes to his wife running like an incantation in his head. Lisa would suspect, but would never know, what had happened to him. Would she come back, perhaps, to search for him? Would she enter the forest?

The thought made him speak out. "His remains aren't here. He wanted to leave, Mari. You have to let him go." He said it again, quieter, to himself. "You have to let him go."

The trees moaned again, mournful and haunting. As he stumbled onwards, they grew thinner, until he saw the brown wood of the cabin in the distance. He sprinted to his car, afraid the forest would change its mind.

Brad sped under leering bamboo trees, glanced at the mirrors too often, afraid of seeing Mari's small frame behind his car, or in the encroaching line of trees. Had Mitch found her body, swaying above their child's grave? Brad didn't bother to wipe the tears that rolled down his cheeks when he remembered the brokenness of his brother's voice saying, "She's gone, Brad. She's gone," and the gravestone carved by hand.

He drove past the border of Mitch's property. The forest was replaced with small shrubs and rocky ground. Only then did Brad breathe a sigh of relief. He lowered his windows to feel the fresh air. As he left the trees, a baby cried.

Praying That You Feel Better Soon

Jeffrey Thomas

WHEN I half-fainted in the close, carpeted aisle of *Taylor's Cards and Gifts*, I fell heavily backwards against a display of ceramic knick-knacks and brought a row of them shattering down in little glittering fragments like the bones of faeries.

The proprietor, more concerned about my health or a lawsuit than the knick-knacks, called an ambulance, no doubt thinking this old lady had suffered a heart attack on the premises. I assured her and the few customers who gathered around that I was fine, if shaken. But I offered no explanation except to mumble that I hadn't eaten enough that morning. I did not tell them about the card I had just picked up. It still lay on the floor where I had dropped it, and I saw the proprietor half-consciously stoop for it and return it to its place in the wall of GET WELL cards. For a moment I again saw the front of the card, before I looked sharply away.

There was no type on the front, which was simply a gray, soft-focus black and white photograph of a statue in front of a vague background of trees. The statue was of a little girl, with the prepubescent wings of a child angel. Her hands were pressed together under her chin in an attitude of prayer, her lids lowered and the subtlest smile on her tiny lips. The flowing lines of her light soft gown were remarkably rendered in the unwavering stone, as if you might expect to see the material begin to float and ripple. The lines of her hair and feathers of her small spread wings were also realistic if a bit more stylized.

These days, a lot can be done to alter photographs. Another person picking up that card might think that the dark stains on the angel child's cheeks had been added in by a computer program. It looked as though heavy black mascara had run down from both eyes as a result of tears the child had shed. It put one in mind of pictures of the Madonna in which tears of blood are said to have flowed.

But I knew those stains were not an embellishment. I had had this angel statue meticulously described to me, some twenty odd years before.

The ambulance arrived. I balked at going with them, but a policeman who came wouldn't let me drive until I had been checked out. At last I gave in...but before I left *Taylor's Cards and Gifts* – as loathe as I was to touch it again – I bought that card of the angel child, though I had no intention of sending the thing to my ailing cousin in Minnesota.

While seated in the back of the ambulance (no, I told the officer, I had no children to drive me to the hospital – and my husband had died years ago) I took the card from my bag with trembling hands and heart, and opened it at last to read its inside sentiment. There was a closer shot of just the statue's prim folded hands, screened to look lighter, and the cursive words:

Praying That You Feel Better Soon.

* * *

It was my husband William who described the angel child to me.

Will had been an employee of the town Department of Public Works, and it often fell to him not only to plow snow from the roads of Eastborough during the winter, but from the roads and pathways of the several town cemeteries as well. After the blizzard of '78, Eastborough was like Pompeii after all the ash fell, and for a week it seemed that I didn't see Will at all, as if those two feet of bright heavy snow had buried him as well.

The town's four cemeteries took little precedence when some people couldn't even get to work for a week, but when at last the DPW could take the time, it fell to Will to plow out the Pine Grove Cemetery, which borders on Eastborough Swamp.

Will told me later that evening that although the sky was a blazing blue that afternoon, a biting wind had been whipping up mists of sparkling snow dust like wraiths that billowed between the ranks of stones. Well, Will didn't say it like that – Will wasn't one for embellishments, or for much talk at all. But I could visualize the scene as he related it to me that evening. And Will's emotion made the visualization all the more vivid, because he was shaken that evening – and Will wasn't one to be shaken, either.

The snow lay in as yet unbroken dunes and drifts, and he could only tell where the paths lay because there were spaces winding between the rows of gravestones. He lowered his plow and began what would prove to be a long afternoon's work, Pine Grove being the largest of Eastborough's graveyards.

Up front when one enters into Pine Grove, the plots tend to be newer, the rows neater, the headstones more polished and modern in their outlines. The cemetery began at the periphery of the swamp, and grew out from there. There are no old willow-and-urn eighteenth century slates, as there are in the Midtown Cemetery just down the street from my house; the oldest stones in Pine Grove date back to the mid-nineteenth century. At the back of Pine Grove, Will must have seen those pitted, slanting white tombstones with their raised or indented words nearly erased by rains and many previous blizzards and biting winds. There is a section along one side path that is entirely devoted to children…many of them stillborn, or dead in their infancy. It's a sad little spot, a tragic reminder of a time when such deaths were more common than now.

But that isn't where Will struck the stone angel.

He was turning down a fresh pathway when his blade caught against something buried in an especially deep drift. He said he heard a screeching as the metal ground against stone. Hissing a curse under his breath – he never swore outright, and certainly not at me – Will stopped his truck and got out with a shovel in hand. A less conscientious worker wouldn't have thought twice about the accident, and kept going on despite whatever damage he might have caused. I sometimes wish Will hadn't stopped, and dug out the thing he had struck so as to inspect it. But then, he wouldn't have been my Will if he hadn't.

The first thing he laid bare was the top of a head. As he dug further, he uncovered a child's head with dreamily lowered lids, streaked stains down both cheeks, and a smile so subtle the Mona Lisa might seem like a grinning fool. He dug further like a less than enthusiastic archeologist, and he didn't stop until he had found the spot where he had struck the little statue. There was only a scrape across one of her stylized miniature wings, a white scratch against the age-stained gray of the rest of her. Will was relieved. The statue leaned a bit to one side, but he didn't know if he had caused that or if it had been a natural occurrence. There was nothing he could do about that either way, and so he got back into his truck, poured a fresh coffee from his large plaid thermos, had a few sips, and resumed his work.

He circled about the cemetery, and the winds picked up in speed, like waves breaking across his windshield. He told me that as he turned into yet another pathway – though nearly finished now, as the sun began to lower and the snow began to turn a dark violet color – he saw an odd thing through a cloud of this whipped-up dust.

Distantly, through the glittering veil and the naked branches of intervening trees, Will saw a child that seemed to be having a violent seizure. The figure was vague, but it seemed to be tightly bound, so that it couldn't move its arms or legs...could only whip its body madly from side to side. It was as if a child were being terribly electrocuted, as Will described it (his deep, low voice in a raspy whisper, tinged with shame at the tinge of fear I heard in it). Violent, jerking spasms. The child's clothing seemed to be snapping and blowing behind it in a blur. He heard no cries, but he said he could see the steamy exhalations of the child billowing around its head, obscuring its face.

Needless to say, Will turned his truck around as quickly as he could manage and headed back that way. But as he rounded a bend and neared the spot, he realized what he had really seen...

It was the angel statue he had struck. It was not moving, its face as placid as when he had uncovered it. What he had taken to be clothing blowing behind it were only its granite wings, incapable of any blurred, frenetic movement. Will shuddered, and told himself he had gone without enough sleep and with too much coffee over the past week.

Still, he couldn't account for the steamy clouds that were still dispersing in the air around the head of the angel child.

* * *

Will was not the fanciful type. He wasn't superstitious, wasn't even religious (much to the disapproval of my parents early on, though they came to accept him for the kind man he was). So I didn't feel he was lying about or imagining what came later. If he told me he hadn't been dreaming that night, then I had to accept that. It didn't mean I believed what he saw was fact. It only meant that I didn't disbelieve him.

It was nearly a week after Will had plowed out the cemetery that I awoke to an awful cry in the middle of the night. I had never heard my husband utter such a sound before – for it was him I had heard. As I sat up in bed, my heart galloping, I saw his large body silhouetted at one of the room's windows.

When I asked him what was wrong he spun around startled and frightened me as much as I had frightened him. I clawed a lamp on, and saw a face so transfigured that for a wild moment I wondered if I hadn't surprised a burglar in the bedroom, a stranger with crazed eyes. But it was Will, and he cast one more look – a timid look of dread – out the window before he came to the bed to tell me what he'd seen.

He told me that a scraping sound had awakened him, a sound against the clapboards outside as if a tree branch were blowing against them. But there was no tree outside that window close enough to rake across the boards. So Will stole out of bed, and went to peek around the shade to see what it might be.

It had been dark, but the street lamps had given off enough illumination to glow white on the figure he saw climbing up the side of the house toward our second floor bedroom window.

It was a child, all white from her skin to her hair to her gown...poised on the side of our house like a fly...a fly with stone wings...and he said when he parted the shade, the child lifted her head to look up at him. Her eyes were open and had black pupils and rolled like the eyes of a panicking horse. But she was grinning, grinning in such a way that her lips were pulled far back from white gums like the lips of a snarling dog, revealing little clenched granite teeth.

But when he cried out, he said, he saw the child drop from the house to her feet and scamper off madly across the yard, disappearing into a line of trees that separated our yard from the next. She had thrown one look back at him over her shoulder, he told me in a shaky voice. She had still been grinning.

We slept with the bedside light on that night. I admit, the light made me feel better, too.

In the morning, I saw Will out that same window. He was examining the yard for footprints in the snow...but if any had been there, a light snow that had fallen in the early morning hours and a gusty wind had obliterated them. What was left could have been made by a dog. But I thought there was something suggestive to them, at least. Because when Will had left for work, I snuck out to look at them myself.

He had been afraid to leave me alone in the house, but promised me he would be home before dark. And again, I'll admit that I was grateful for his promise.

The snows of the early morning returned the next night with more vigor. By the next day, Will was out plowing again. I filled his big plaid thermos for him, kissed his cheek before he left. It was unshaven. That wasn't like Will.

Those who examined him later decided it was a massive heart attack that killed my husband sometime that afternoon.

When he didn't answer his radio calls, his friends Donny McNeil and John Thompson drove out to Pine Grove Cemetery, where they knew Will was supposed to be plowing.

They found his yellow truck there. The plow was down, and he had begun his job. But inside the cold tomb of its cab, Will sat dead behind the wheel. I'm told his eyes were tightly squinted shut, as if to block out intense pain...or as if to block out something terrible he had seen.

Through my tears, I asked Donny and John later if they had seen any odd footprints in the snow. If they had seen any children about in the graveyard. Both of them wagged their heads, but when Donny began to ask me why, I waved for him not to.

Well, John said as if in an afterthought, he *had* heard something funny when he opened the door of Will's cab – something he had dismissed or hadn't really taken in at the time, considering the shock of the discovery of his friend. He remembered now that he had heard a child giggling behind a tree, not too far away. He hadn't seen anyone when he glanced that way, but he believed he saw a little white mist of breath curling out from around the trunk...and maybe...just maybe... tiny white fingers peeking out from behind, clutching the bark.

* * *

I discovered one thing about the statue of the angel child just several weeks after Will's funeral. And more than twenty years later – after my trip to *Taylor's Cards and Gifts* – I have now uncovered another fact.

The first discovery came with the aid of the DPW, the Eastborough Antiquarian Society, and through my own investigation of Pine Grove Cemetery, once the snows had receded enough for me to explore it.

Try as I might, and filled with dread though I was, I could not locate within all of Pine Grove any statue of an angel, let alone that of a child angel. And when I asked Will's boss at the DPW, he told me that despite Will's having struck the statue, it had not been removed – at least, not by any of his crew. He began to suggest that Will himself had removed it, if he had been feeling guilty about the thing, so as to set it straight in the earth come spring...but he dropped his theory when he noticed my glare.

It was Jo Torrey at the Antiquarian Society who was the most helpful, the most informed, and whose information stunned me the most. Jo was into gravestone rubbing. She would have known these things.

She told me there had never been any angel statues in Pine Grove Cemetery.

And that was where it ended, for twenty years. And though Will and I had plots already purchased in Pine Grove, I had Will cremated and scattered his ashes along a path in Acadia

National Park where he had kissed me on our honeymoon. I did not want him left helpless in that cold ground, under future snows.

The get well card with the angel was printed by a large corporation that was not immediately receptive to my letters, but I persisted with more letters and several phone calls and my niece contacted them over the internet, until finally I was given the address of the photographer who had taken the photograph of the angel with her dark-stained cheeks, and her little hands pressed together demurely under her chin.

The photographer, a Richard Bedard, has since told me that he chanced upon the statue in a small, back road cemetery in Oakton, Virginia.

Which is a long way away from Eastborough, Massachusetts.

I do not want to visualize a small white figure scampering along dark roads in the dead of night, in its mysterious migration. Or perhaps, even, flying...

I try to tell myself, some nights as I lie awake in the same bedroom where my Will stood in terror at that window, that it couldn't be the same statue. Couldn't be...

But it's clear in the photo, you see. White against the gray of the stone.

There is a long shallow scratch across one of the angel's wings.

Mrs. Lunt

Hugh Walpole

Chapter I

"DO YOU believe in ghosts?" I asked Runciman. I had to ask him this very platitudinous question more because he was so difficult a man to spend an hour with than for any other reason. You know his books, perhaps, or more probably you don't know them – *The Running Man, The Elm Tree,* and *Crystal and Candlelight.* He is one of those little men who are constant enough in this age of immense over-production of books, men who publish every autumn their novel, who arouse by that publication in certain critics eager appreciation and praise, who have a small and faithful public, whose circulation is very small indeed, who when you meet them have little to say, are often shy and nervous, pessimistic and remote from daily life. Such men do fine work, are made but little of in their own day, and perhaps fifty years after their death are rediscovered by some digging critic and become a sort of cult with a new generation.

I asked Runciman that question because, for some unknown reason, I had invited him to dinner at my flat, and was now faced with a long evening filled with that most tiresome of all conversations, talk that dies every two minutes and has to be revived with terrific exertions. Being myself a critic, and having on many occasions praised Runciman's work, he was the more nervous and shy with me; had I abused it, he would perhaps have had plenty to say – he was that kind of man. But my question was a lucky one: it roused him instantly, his long, bony body became full of a new energy, his eyes stared into a rich and exciting reminiscence, he spoke without pause, and I took care not to interrupt him. He certainly told me one of the most astounding stories I have ever heard. Whether it was true or not I cannot, of course, say: these ghost stories are nearly always at second or third hand. I had, at any rate, the good fortune to secure mine from the source. Moreover, Runciman was not a liar: he was too serious for that. He himself admitted that he was not sure, at this distance of time, as to whether the thing had gained as the years passed. However, here it is as he told it.

"It was some fifteen years ago," he said. "I went down to Cornwall to stay with Robert Lunt. Do you remember his name? No, I suppose you do not. He wrote several novels; some of those half-and-half things that are not quite novels, not quite poems, rather mystical and picturesque, and are the very devil to do well. De la Mare's *Return* is a good example of the kind of thing. I had reviewed somewhere his last book, and reviewed it favourably, and received from him a really touching letter showing that the man was thirsting for praise, and also, I fancied, for company. He lived in Cornwall somewhere on the sea-coast, and his wife had died a year ago; he said he was quite alone there, and would I come and spend Christmas with him; he hoped I would not think this impertinent; he expected that I would be engaged already, but he could not resist the chance. Well, I wasn't engaged; far from it. If Lunt was lonely, so was I; if Lunt was a failure, so was I; I was touched, as I have said, by his letter, and I accepted his invitation. As I went down in the train to Penzance I wondered what kind of a man he would be. I had never seen any photographs of him; he was not the sort of author whose picture the newspapers publish. He must be, I fancied, about my own age – perhaps rather older. I know when we're lonely how some of us are forever imagining that a friend will somewhere turn up, that ideal friend who will understand all one's feelings, who will give one affection without being sentimental, who will take an interest in one's affairs without being impertinent – yes, the sort of friend one never finds.

"I fancy that I became quite romantic about Lunt before I reached Penzance. We would talk, he and I, about all those literary questions that seemed to me at that time so absorbing; we would perhaps often stay together and even travel abroad on those little journeys that are so swiftly melancholy when one is alone, so delightful when one has a perfect companion. I imagined him as sparse and delicate and refined, with a sort of wistfulness and rather childish play of fancy. We had both, so far, failed in our careers, but perhaps together we would do great things.

"When I arrived at Penzance it was almost dark, and the snow, threatened all day by an overhanging sky, had begun gently and timorously to fall. He had told me in his letter that a fly would be at the station to take me to his house; and there I found it – a funny old weather-beaten carriage with a funny old weather-beaten driver. At this distance of time my imagination may have created many things, but I fancy that from the moment I was shut into that carriage some dim suggestion of fear and apprehension attacked me. I fancy that I had some absurd impulse to get out of the thing and take the night train back to London again – an action that would have been very unlike me, as I had always a sort of obstinate determination to carry through anything that I had begun. In any case, I was uncomfortable in that carriage; it had, I remember, a nasty, musty smell of damp straw and stale eggs, and it seemed to confine me so closely as though it were determined that, once I was in, I should never get out again. Then, it was bitterly cold; I was colder during that drive than I have ever been before or since. It was that penetrating cold that seems to pierce your very brain, so that I could not think with any clearness, but only wish again and again that I hadn't come. Of course, I could see nothing – only feel the jolt over the uneven road – and once and again we seemed to fight our way through dark paths, because I could feel the overhanging branches of the trees knock against the cab with mysterious taps, as though they were trying to give me some urgent message.

"Well, I mustn't make more of it than the facts allow, and I mustn't see into it all the significance of the events that followed. I only know that as the drive proceeded I became more and more miserable: miserable with the cold of my body, the misgivings of my imagination, the general loneliness of my case.

"At last we stopped. The old scarecrow got slowly off his box, with many heavings and sighings, came to the cab door, and, with great difficulty and irritating slowness, opened it. I got out of it, and found that the snow was now falling very heavily indeed, and that the path was lighted with its soft, mysterious glow. Before me was a humped and ungainly shadow: the house that was to receive me. I could make nothing of it in that darkness, but only stood there shivering while the old man pulled at the doorbell with a sort of frantic energy as though he were anxious to be rid of the whole job as quickly as possible and return to his own place. At last, after what seemed an endless time, the door opened, and an old man, who might have been own brother to the driver, poked out his head. The two old men talked together, and at last my bag was shouldered and I was permitted to come in out of the piercing cold.

"Now this, I know, is not imagination. I have never at any period of my life hated at first sight so vigorously any dwelling-place into which I have ever entered as I did that house. There was nothing especially disagreeable about my first vision of the hall. It was a large, dark place, lit by two dim lamps, cold and cheerless; but I got no particular impression of it because at once I was conducted out of it, led along a passage, and then introduced into a room which was, I saw, as warm and comfortable as the hall had been dark and dismal. I was, in fact, so eagerly pleased at the large and leaping fire that I moved towards it at once, not noting, at the first moment, the presence of my host; and when I did see him I could not believe that it was he. I have told you the kind of man that I had expected; but, instead of the sparse, sensitive artist, I found facing me a large burly man, over six foot, I should fancy, as broad-shouldered as he was tall, giving evidence of great muscular strength, the lower part of his face hidden by a black, pointed beard.

"But if I was astonished at the sight of him, I was doubly amazed when he spoke. His voice was thin and piping, like that of some old woman, and the little nervous gestures that he made with his hands were even more feminine than his voice. But I had to allow, perhaps, for excitement, for excited he was; he came up to me, took my hand in both of his, and held it as though he would never let it go. In the evening he apologised for this. "I was so glad to see you," he said; "I couldn't believe that really you would come; you are the first visitor of my own kind that I have had here for ever so long. I was ashamed, indeed, of asking you, but I had to snatch at the chance – it means so much to me."

"His eagerness, in fact, had something disturbing about it; something pathetic, too. He simply couldn't do too much for me: he led me through funny crumbling old passages, the boards creaking under us at every step, up some dark stairs, the walls hung, so far as I could see in the dim light, with faded yellow photographs of places, and showed me into my room with a deprecating agitated gesture as though he expected me at the first sight of it to turn and run. I didn't like it any more than I liked the rest of the house; but that was not my host's fault. He had done everything he possibly could for me: there was a large fire flaming in the open fireplace, there was a hot bottle, as he explained to me, in the big four-poster bed, and the old man who had opened the door to me was already taking my clothes out of my bag and putting them away. Lunt's nervousness was almost sentimental. He put both his hands on my shoulders and said, looking at me pleadingly: "If you only knew what it is for me to have you here, the talks we'll have. Well, well, I must leave you. You'll come down and join me, won't you, as soon as you can?"

"It was then, when I was left alone in my room, that I had my second impulse to flee. Four candles in tall old silver candlesticks were burning brightly, and these, with the blazing fire, gave plenty of light; and yet the room was in some way dim, as though a faint smoke pervaded it, and I remember that I went to one of the old lattice windows and threw it open for a moment as though I felt stifled. Two things quickly made me close it. One was the intense cold which, with a fluttering scamper of snow, blew into the room; the other was the quite deafening roar of the sea, which seemed to fling itself at my very face as though it wanted to knock me down. I quickly shut the window, turned round, and saw an old woman standing just inside the door. Now every story of this kind depends for its interest on its verisimilitude. Of course, to make my tale convincing I should be able to prove to you that I saw that old woman; but I can't. I can only urge upon you my rather dreary reputation of probity. You know that I'm a teetotaller, and always have been, and, most important evidence of all, I was not expecting to see an old woman; and yet I hadn't the least doubt in the world but that it was an old woman I saw. You may talk about shadows, clothes hanging on the back of the door, and the rest of it. I don't know. I've no theories about this story, I'm not a spiritualist, I don't know that I believe in anything especially, except the beauty of beautiful things. We'll put it, if you like, that I fancied that I saw an old woman, and my fancy was so strong that I can give you to this day a pretty detailed account of her appearance. She wore a black silk dress and on her breast was a large, ugly, gold brooch; she had black hair, brushed back from her forehead and parted down the middle; she wore a collar of some white stuff round her throat; her face was one of the wickedest, most malignant and furtive that I have ever seen – very white in colour. She was shrivelled enough now, but might once have been rather beautiful. She stood there quietly, her hands at her side. I thought that she was some kind of housekeeper. 'I have everything I want, thank you,' I said. 'What a splendid fire!' I turned for a moment towards it, and when I looked back she was gone. I thought nothing of this, of course, but drew up an old chair covered with green faded tapestry, and thought that I would read a little from some book that I had brought down with me before I went to join my host. The fact was that I was not very intent upon joining him before I must. I didn't like him. I had already made up my mind that I would find some excuse to return to London as soon as possible. I can't tell you why I didn't like him, except that I was myself very reserved and had, like many Englishmen, a great distrust of demonstrations, especially from another man. I hadn't cared for the way in which he had put his hands on my shoulders, and I felt perhaps that I wouldn't be able to live up to all his eager excitement about me.

"I sat in my chair and took up my book, but I had not been reading for more than two minutes before I was conscious of a most unpleasant smell. Now, there are all sorts of smells – healthy and otherwise – but I think the nastiest is that chilly kind of odour that comes from bad sanitation and stuffy rooms combined; you meet it sometimes at little country inns and decrepit town lodgings. This smell was so definite that I could almost locate it; it came from near the door. I got up, approached the door, and at once it was as though I were drawing near to somebody who, if you'll forgive the impoliteness, was not accustomed to taking too many baths. I drew back just as I might had an actual person been there. Then quite suddenly the smell was gone, the room was fresh, and I saw, to my surprise, that one of the windows had opened and that snow was again blowing in. I closed it and went downstairs.

"The evening that followed was odd enough. My host was not in himself an unlikeable man; he did his very utmost to please me. He had a fine culture and a wide knowledge of books and things. He became quite cheerful as the evening went on; gave me a good dinner in a funny little dining room hung with some admirable mezzotints. The serving-man looked after us – a funny old man, with a long white beard like a goat – and, oddly enough, it was from him that I first recaught my earlier apprehension. He had just put the dessert on the table, had arranged my plate in front of me, when I saw him give a start and look towards the door. My attention was attracted to this because his hand, as it touched the plate, suddenly trembled. My eyes followed, but I could see nothing. That he was frightened of something was perfectly clear, and then (it may, of course, very easily have been fancy) I thought that I detected once more that strange unwholesome smell.

"I forgot this again when we were both seated in front of a splendid fire in the library. Lunt had a very fine collection of books, and it was delightful to him, as it is to every book collector, to have somebody with him who could really appreciate them. We stood looking at one book after another and talking eagerly about some of the minor early English novelists who were my especial hobby – Bage, Godwin, Henry Mackenzie, Mrs. Shelley, Mat Lewis and others – when once again he affected me most unpleasantly by putting his arm round my shoulders. I have all my life disliked intensely to be touched by certain people. I suppose we all feel like this. It is one of those inexplicable things; and I disliked this so much that I abruptly drew away.

"Instantly he was changed into a man of furious and ungovernable rage; I thought that he was going to strike me. He stood there quivering all over, the words pouring out of his mouth incoherently, as though he were mad and did not know what he was saying. He accused me of insulting him, of abusing his hospitality, of throwing his kindness back into his face, and of a thousand other ridiculous things; and I can't tell you how strange it was to hear all this coming out in that shrill piping voice as though it were from an agitated woman, and yet to see with one's eyes that big, muscular frame, those immense shoulders and that dark-bearded face.

"I said nothing. I am, physically, a coward. I dislike, above anything else in the world, any sort of quarrel. At last I brought out, 'I am very sorry. I didn't mean anything. Please forgive me,' and then hurriedly turned to leave the room. At once he changed again; now he was almost in tears. He implored me not to go; said it was his wretched temper, but that he was so miserable and unhappy, and had for so long now been alone and desolate that he hardly knew what he was doing. He begged me to give him another chance, and if I would only listen to his story I would perhaps be more patient with him.

"At once, so oddly is man constituted, I changed in my feelings towards him. I was very sorry for him. I saw that he was a man on the edge of his nerves, and that he really did need some help and sympathy, and would be quite distracted if he could not get it. I put my hand on his shoulder to quieten him and to show him that I bore no malice, and I felt that his great body was quivering from head to foot. We sat down again, and in an odd, rambling manner he told me his story. It amounted to very little, and the gist of it was that, rather to have some sort of companionship than from any impulse of passion, he had married some fifteen years before the daughter of a neighbouring clergyman. They had had no very happy life together, and at the last, he told me quite frankly, he had hated her. She had been mean, overbearing, and narrow-minded; it had been, he confessed, nothing but a relief to him when, just a year ago, she had suddenly died from heart failure. He had thought then that things would go better with him, but they had not; nothing had gone right with him since. He hadn't been able to work, many of his friends had ceased to come to see him, he had found it even difficult to get servants to stay with him, he was desperately lonely, he slept badly – that was why his temper was so terribly on edge. He had no one in the house with him save the old man, who was, fortunately, an excellent cook, and a boy – the old man's grandson. 'Oh, I thought,' I said, 'that that excellent meal tonight was cooked by your housekeeper.' 'My housekeeper?' he answered. 'There's no woman in the house.' 'Oh, but one came to my room,' I replied, 'this evening – an old lady-like-looking person in a black silk dress.' 'You were mistaken,' he answered in the oddest voice, as though he were exerting all the strength that he possessed to keep himself quiet and controlled. 'I am sure that I saw her,' I answered. 'There couldn't be any mistake.' And I described her to him. 'You were mistaken,' he repeated again. 'Don't you see that you must have been when I tell you there is no woman in the house?' I reassured him quickly lest there should be another outbreak of rage. Then there followed the strangest kind of appeal. Urgently, as though his very life depended upon it, he begged me to stay with him for a few days. He implied, although he said nothing definitely, that he was in great trouble, that if only I would stay for a few days all would be well, that if ever in all my life I had had a chance of doing a kind action I had one now, that he couldn't expect me to stop in so dreary a place, but that he would never forget it if I did. He spoke in a voice of such urgent distress that I comforted him as I might a child, promising that I would stay and shaking hands with him on it as though it were a kind of solemn oath between us."

Chapter II

"I AM SURE that you would wish me to give you this incident as it occurred, and if the final catastrophe seems to come, as it were, accidentally, I can only say to you that that was how it happened. It is since the event that I have tried to put two and two together, and that they don't altogether make four is the fault that mine shares, I suppose, with every true ghost story.

"But the truth is that after that very strange episode between us I had a very good night. I slept the sleep of all justice, cosy and warm, in my four-poster, with the murmur of the sea beyond the windows to rock my slumbers. Next morning too was bright and cheerful, the sun sparkling down on the snow, and the snow sparkling back to the sun as though they were glad to see one another. I had a very pleasant morning looking at Lunt's books, talking to him, and writing one or two letters. I must say that, after all, I liked the man. His appeal to me on the night before had touched me. So few people, you see, had ever appealed to me about anything. His nervousness was there and the constant sense of apprehension, yet he seemed to be putting the best face on it, doing his utmost to set me at my ease in order to induce me to stay, I suppose, and to give him a little of that company that he so terribly needed. I dare say if I had not been so busy about the books I would not have been so happy. There was a strange eerie silence about that house if one ever stopped to listen; and once, I remember, sitting at the old bureau writing a letter, I raised my head and looked up, and caught Lunt watching as though he wondered whether I had heard or noticed anything. And so I listened too, and it seemed to me as though someone were on the other side of the library door with their hand raised to knock; a quaint notion, with nothing to support it, but I could have sworn that if I had gone to the door and opened it suddenly someone would have been there.

"However, I was cheerful enough, and after lunch quite happy. Lunt asked me if I would like a walk, and I said I would; and we started out in the sunshine over the crunching snow towards the sea. I don't remember what we talked of; we seemed to be now quite at our ease with one another. We crossed the fields to a certain point, looked down at the sea – smooth now, like silk – and turned back. I remember that I was so cheerful that I seemed suddenly to take a happy view of all my prospects. I began to confide in Lunt, telling him of my little plans, of my hopes for the book that I was then writing, and even began rather timidly to suggest to him that perhaps we should do something together; that what we both needed was a friend of common taste with ourselves. I know that I was talking on, that we had crossed a little village street, and were turning up the path towards the dark avenue of trees that led to his house, when suddenly the change came.

"What I first noticed was that he was not listening to me; his gaze was fixed beyond me, into the very heart of the black clump of trees that fringed the silver landscape. I looked too, and my heart bounded. There was, standing just in front of the trees, as though she were waiting for us, the old woman whom I had seen in my room the night before. I stopped. 'Why, there she is!' I said. 'That's the old woman of whom I was speaking – the old woman who came to my room.' He caught my shoulder with his hand. 'There's nothing there,' he said. 'Don't you see that that's shadow? What's the matter with you? Can't you see that there's nothing?' I stepped forward, and there was nothing, and I wouldn't, to this day, be able to tell you whether it was hallucination or not. I can only say that, from that moment, the afternoon appeared to become dark. As we entered into the avenue of trees, silently and hurrying as though someone were behind us, the dusk seemed to have fallen so that I could scarcely see my way. We reached the house breathless. He hastened into his study as though I were not with him, but I followed and, closing the door behind me, said, with all the force that I had at command: 'Now, what is this? What is it that's troubling you? You must tell me! How can I help you if you don't?' And he replied, in so strange a voice that it was as though he had gone out of his mind: 'I tell you there's nothing! Can't you believe me when I tell you there's nothing at all? I'm quite all right…Oh, my God! – my God!…don't leave me!…This is the very day – the very night she said… But I did nothing, I tell you – I did nothing – it's only her beastly malice…' He broke off. He still held my arm with his hand. He made strange movements, wiping his forehead as though it were damp with sweat, almost pleading with me; then suddenly angry again, then beseeching once more, as though I had refused him the one thing he wanted.

"I saw that he was truly not far from madness, and I began myself to have a sudden terror of this damp, dark house, this great, trembling man, and something more that was worse than they. But I pitied him. How could you or any man have helped it? I made him sit down in the armchair beside the fire, which had now dwindled to a few glimmering red coals. I let him hold me close to him with his arm and clutch my hand with his, and I repeated, as quietly as I might: 'But tell me; don't be afraid, whatever it is you have done. Tell me what danger it is you fear, and then we can face it together.' 'Fear! Fear!' he repeated; and then, with a mighty effort which I could not but admire, he summoned all his control. 'I'm off my head,' he said, 'with loneliness and depression. My wife died a year ago on this very night. We hated one another. I couldn't be sorry when she died, and she knew it. When that last heart attack came on, between her gasps she told me that she would return, and I've always dreaded this night. That's partly why I asked you to come, to have someone here, anybody, and you've been very kind – more kind than I had any right to expect. You must think me insane going on like this, but see me through tonight and we'll have splendid times together. Don't desert me now – now, of all times!' I promised that I would not. I soothed him as best I could. We sat there, for I know not how long, through the gathering dark; we neither of us moved, the fire died out, and the room was lit with a strange dim glow that came from the snowy landscape beyond the uncurtained windows. Ridiculous, perhaps, as I look back at it. We sat there, I in a chair close to his, hand in hand, like a couple of lovers; but, in real truth, two men terrified, fearful of what was coming, and unable to do anything to meet it.

"I think that that was perhaps the queerest part of it; a sort of paralysis that crept over me. What would you or anyone else have done – summoned the old man, gone down to the village inn, fetched the local doctor? I could do nothing, but see the snow-shine move like trembling water about the furniture and hear, through the urgent silence, the faint hoot of an owl from the trees in the wood."

Chapter III

"ODDLY ENOUGH, I can remember nothing, try as I may, between that strange vigil and the moment when I myself, wakened out of a brief sleep, sat up in bed to see Lunt standing inside my room holding a candle. He was wearing a nightshirt, and looked huge in the candlelight, his black beard falling intensely dark on the white stuff of his shirt. He came very quietly towards my bed, the candle throwing flickering shadows about the room. When he spoke it was in a voice low and subdued, almost a whisper. 'Would you come,' he asked, 'only for half an hour – just for half an hour?' he repeated, staring at me as though he didn't know me. 'I'm unhappy without somebody – very unhappy.' Then he looked over his shoulder, held the candle high above his head, and stared piercingly at every part of the room. I could see that something had happened to him, that he had taken another step into the country of Fear – a step that had withdrawn him from me and from every other human being. He whispered: 'When you come, tread softly; I don't want anyone to hear us.' I did what I could. I got out of bed, put on my dressing-gown and slippers, and tried to persuade him to stay with me. The fire was almost dead, but I told him that we would build it up again, and that we would sit there and wait for the morning; but no, he repeated again and again: 'It's better in my own room; we're safer there.' 'Safe from what?' I asked him, making him look at me. 'Lunt, wake up! You're as though you were asleep. There's nothing to fear. We've nobody but ourselves. Stay here and let us talk, and have done with this nonsense.' But he wouldn't answer; only drew me forward down the dark passage, and then turned into his room, beckoning me to follow. He got into bed and sat hunched up there, his hands holding his knees, staring at the door, and every once and again shivering with a little tremor. The only light in the room was that from the candle, now burning low, and the only sound was the purring whisper of the sea.

"It seemed to make little difference to him that I was there. He did not look at me, but only at the door, and when I spoke to him he did not answer me nor seem to hear what I had said. I sat down beside the bed and, in order to break the silence, talked on about anything, about nothing, and was dropping off, I think, into a confused doze, when I heard his voice breaking across mine.

Very clearly and distinctly he said: 'If I killed her, she deserved it; she was never a good wife to me, not from the first; she shouldn't have irritated me as she did – she knew what my temper was. She had a worse one than mine, though. She can't touch me; I'm as strong as she is.' And it was then, as clearly as I can now remember, that his voice suddenly sank into a sort of gentle whisper, as though he were almost glad that his fears had been confirmed. He whispered: 'She's there!' I cannot possibly describe to you how that whisper seemed to let Fear loose like water through my body. I could see nothing – the candle was flaming high in the last moments of its life – I could see nothing; but Lunt suddenly screamed, with a shrill cry like a tortured animal in agony: 'Keep her off me, keep her away from me, keep her off – keep her off!' He caught me, his hands digging into my shoulders; then, with an awful effect of constricted muscles, as though rigor had caught and held him, his arms slowly fell away, he slipped back on to the bed as though someone were pushing him, his hands fell against the sheet, his whole body jerked with a convulsive effort, and then he rolled over. I saw nothing; only, quite distinctly, in my nostrils was that same fetid odour that I had known on the preceding evening. I rushed to the door, opened it, shouted down the long passage again and again, and soon the old man came running. I sent him for the doctor, and then could not return to the room, but stood there listening, hearing nothing save the whisper of the sea, the loud ticking of the hall clock. I flung open the window at the end of the passage; the sea rushed in with its precipitant roar; some bells chimed the hour. Then at last, beating into myself more courage, I turned back towards the room…"

"Well?" I asked as Runciman paused. "He was dead, of course?"

"Dead, the doctor afterwards said, of heart failure."

"Well?" I asked again.

"That's all." Runciman paused. "I don't know whether you can even call it a ghost story. My idea of the old woman may have been all hallucination. I don't even know whether his wife was like that when she was alive. She may have been large and fat. Lunt died of an evil conscience."

"Yes," I said.

"The only thing," Runciman added at last, after a long pause, "is that on Lunt's body there were marks – on his neck especially, some on his chest – as of fingers pressing in, scratches and dull blue marks. He may, in his terror, have caught at his own throat…"

"Yes," I said again.

"Anyway" – Runciman shivered – "I don't like Cornwall – beastly county. Queer things happen there – something in the air…"

"So I've heard," I answered.

The Moth

H.G. Wells

PROBABLY you have heard of Hapley – not W.T. Hapley, the son, but the celebrated Hapley, the Hapley of *Periplaneta Hapliia*, Hapley the entomologist.

If so you know at least of the great feud between Hapley and Professor Pawkins, though certain of its consequences may be new to you. For those who have not, a word or two of explanation is necessary, which the idle reader may go over with a glancing eye, if his indolence so incline him.

It is amazing how very widely diffused is the ignorance of such really important matters as this Hapley–Pawkins feud. Those epoch-making controversies, again, that have convulsed the Geological Society are, I verily believe, almost entirely unknown outside the fellowship of that body. I have heard men of fair general education even refer to the great scenes at these meetings as vestry-meeting squabbles. Yet the great hate of the English and Scotch geologists has lasted now half a century, and has 'left deep and abundant marks upon the body of the science.' And this Hapley-Pawkins business, though perhaps a more personal affair, stirred passions as profound, if not profounder. Your common man has no conception of the zeal that animates a scientific investigator, the fury of contradiction you can arouse in him. It is the *odium theologicum* in a new form. There are men, for instance, who would gladly burn Professor Ray Lankester at Smithfield for his treatment of the Mollusca in the Encyclopaedia. That fantastic extension of the Cephalopods to cover the Pteropods… But I wander from Hapley and Pawkins.

It began years and years ago, with a revision of the Microlepidoptera (whatever these may be) by Pawkins, in which he extinguished a new species created by Hapley. Hapley, who was always quarrelsome, replied by a stinging impeachment of the entire classification of Pawkins. Pawkins in his 'Rejoinder' suggested that Hapley's microscope was as defective as his power of observation, and called him an 'irresponsible meddler' – Hapley was not a professor at that time. Hapley in his retort, spoke of 'blundering collectors', and described, as if inadvertently, Pawkins' revision as a 'miracle of ineptitude'. It was war to the knife. However, it would scarcely interest the reader to detail how these two great men quarrelled, and how the split between them widened until from the Microlepidoptera they were at war upon every open question in entomology. There were memorable occasions. At times the Royal Entomological Society meetings resembled nothing so much as the Chamber of Deputies. On the whole, I fancy Pawkins was nearer the truth than Hapley. But Hapley was skilful with his rhetoric, had a turn for ridicule rare in a scientific man, was endowed with vast energy, and had a fine sense of injury in the matter of the extinguished species; while Pawkins was a man of dull presence, prosy of speech, in shape not unlike a water-barrel, over-conscientious with testimonials, and suspected of jobbing museum appointments. So the young men gathered round Hapley and applauded him. It was a long struggle, vicious from the beginning and growing at last to pitiless antagonism. The successive turns of fortune, now an advantage to one side and now to another – now Hapley tormented by some success of Pawkins, and now Pawkins outshone by Hapley, belong rather to the history of entomology than to this story.

But in 1891 Pawkins, whose health had been bad for some time, published some work upon the 'mesoblast' of the Death's Head Moth. What the mesoblast of the Death's Head Moth may be does not matter a rap in this story. But the work was far below his usual standard, and gave Hapley an opening he had coveted for years. He must have worked night and day to make the most of his advantage.

In an elaborate critique he rent Pawkins to tatters – one can fancy the man's disordered black hair, and his queer dark eyes flashing as he went for his antagonist – and Pawkins made a reply, halting, ineffectual, with painful gaps of silence, and yet malignant. There was no mistaking his will to wound Hapley, nor his incapacity to do it. But few of those who heard him – I was absent from that meeting – realised how ill the man was.

Hapley got his opponent down, and meant to finish him. He followed with a simply brutal attack upon Pawkins, in the form of a paper upon the development of moths in general, a paper showing evidence of a most extraordinary amount of mental labour, and yet couched in a violently controversial tone. Violent as it was, an editorial note witnesses that it was modified. It must have covered Pawkins with shame and confusion of face. It left no loophole; it was murderous in argument, and utterly contemptuous in tone; an awful thing for the declining years of a man's career.

The world of entomologists waited breathlessly for the rejoinder from Pawkins. He would try one, for Pawkins had always been game. But when it came it surprised them. For the rejoinder of Pawkins was to catch influenza, proceed to pneumonia, and die.

It was perhaps as effectual a reply as he could make under the circumstances, and largely turned the current of feeling against Hapley. The very people who had most gleefully cheered on those gladiators became serious at the consequence. There could be no reasonable doubt the fret of the defeat had contributed to the death of Pawkins. There was a limit even to scientific controversy, said serious people. Another crushing attack was already in the press and appeared on the day before the funeral. I don't think Hapley exerted himself to stop it. People remembered how Hapley had hounded down his rival, and forgot that rival's defects. Scathing satire reads ill over fresh mould. The thing provoked comment in the daily papers. This it was that made me think that you had probably heard of Hapley and this controversy. But, as I have already remarked, scientific workers live very much in a world of their own; half the people, I dare say, who go along Piccadilly to the Academy every year, could not tell you where the learned societies abide. Many even think that research is a kind of happy-family cage in which all kinds of men lie down together in peace.

In his private thoughts Hapley could not forgive Pawkins for dying. In the first place, it was a mean dodge to escape the absolute pulverisation Hapley had in hand for him, and in the second, it left Hapley's mind with a queer gap in it. For twenty years he had worked hard, sometimes far into the night, and seven days a week, with microscope, scalpel, collecting-net, and pen, and almost entirely with reference to Pawkins. The European reputation he had won had come as an incident in that great antipathy. He had gradually worked up to a climax in this last controversy. It had killed Pawkins, but it had also thrown Hapley out of gear, so to speak, and his doctor advised him to give up work for a time, and rest. So Hapley went down into a quiet village in Kent, and thought day and night of Pawkins, and good things it was now impossible to say about him.

At last Hapley began to realise in what direction the preoccupation tended. He determined to make a fight for it, and started by trying to read novels. But he could not get his mind off Pawkins, white in the face and making his last speech – every sentence a beautiful opening for Hapley. He turned to fiction – and found it had no grip on him. He read the *Island Nights' Entertainments* until his 'sense of causation' was shocked beyond endurance by 'The Bottle Imp'. Then he went to Kipling, and found he 'proved nothing', besides being irreverent and vulgar. These scientific people have their limitations. Then unhappily, he tried Besant's *Inner House*, and the opening chapter set his mind upon learned societies and Pawkins at once.

So Hapley turned to chess, and found it a little more soothing. He soon mastered the moves and the chief gambits and commoner closing positions, and began to beat the Vicar. But then the cylindrical contours of the opposite king began to resemble Pawkins standing up and gasping ineffectually against checkmate, and Hapley decided to give up chess.

Perhaps the study of some new branch of science would after all be better diversion. The best rest is change of occupation. Hapley determined to plunge at diatoms, and had one of his smaller microscopes and Halibut's monograph sent down from London. He thought that perhaps if he could get up a vigorous quarrel with Halibut, he might be able to begin life afresh and forget Pawkins. And very soon he was hard at work in his habitual strenuous fashion, at these microscopic denizens of the way-side pool.

It was on the third day of the diatoms that Hapley became aware of a novel addition to the local fauna. He was working late at the microscope, and the only light in the room was the brilliant little lamp with the special form of green shade. Like all experienced microscopists, he kept both eyes open. It is the only way to avoid excessive fatigue. One eye was over the instrument, and bright and distinct before that was the circular field of the microscope, across which a brown diatom was slowly moving. With the other eye Hapley saw, as it were, without seeing. He was only dimly conscious of the brass side of the instrument, the illuminated part of the tablecloth, a sheet of notepaper, the foot of the lamp, and the darkened room beyond.

Suddenly his attention drifted from one eye to the other. The tablecloth was of the material called tapestry by shopmen, and rather brightly coloured. The pattern was in gold, with a small amount of crimson and pale blue upon a greyish ground. At one point the pattern seemed displaced, and there was a vibrating movement of the colours at this point.

Hapley suddenly moved his head back and looked with both eyes. His mouth fell open with astonishment.

It was a large moth or butterfly; its wings spread in butterfly fashion!

It was strange it should be in the room at all, for the windows were closed. Strange that it should not have attracted his attention when fluttering to its present position. Strange that it should match the tablecloth. Stranger far that to him, Hapley, the great entomologist, it was altogether unknown. There was no delusion. It was crawling slowly towards the foot of the lamp.

"New Genus, by heavens! And in England!" said Hapley, staring.

Then he suddenly thought of Pawkins. Nothing would have maddened Pawkins more… And Pawkins was dead!

Something about the head and body of the insect became singularly suggestive of Pawkins, just as the chess king had been.

"Confound Pawkins!" said Hapley. "But I must catch this." And looking round him for some means of capturing the moth, he rose slowly out of his chair. Suddenly the insect rose, struck the edge of the lampshade – Hapley heard the 'ping' – and vanished into the shadow.

In a moment Hapley had whipped off the shade, so that the whole room was illuminated. The thing had disappeared, but soon his practised eye detected it upon the wallpaper near the door. He went towards it poising the lampshade for capture. Before he was within striking distance, however, it had risen and was fluttering round the room. After the fashion of its kind, it flew with sudden starts and turns, seeming to vanish here and reappear there. Once Hapley struck, and missed; then again.

The third time he hit his microscope. The instrument swayed, struck and overturned the lamp, and fell noisily upon the floor. The lamp turned over on the table and, very luckily, went out. Hapley was left in the dark. With a start he felt the strange moth blunder into his face.

It was maddening. He had no lights. If he opened the door of the room the thing would get away. In the darkness he saw Pawkins quite distinctly laughing at him. Pawkins had ever an oily laugh. He swore furiously and stamped his foot on the floor.

There was a timid rapping at the door.

Then it opened, perhaps a foot, and very slowly. The alarmed face of the landlady appeared behind a pink candle flame; she wore a night-cap over her grey hair and had some purple garment over her shoulders. "What *was* that fearful smash?" she said. "Has anything—" The strange moth appeared fluttering about the chink of the door. "Shut that door!" said Hapley, and suddenly rushed at her.

The door slammed hastily. Hapley was left alone in the dark. Then in the pause he heard his landlady scuttle upstairs, lock her door, and drag something heavy across the room and put against it.

It became evident to Hapley that his conduct and appearance had been strange and alarming. Confound the moth! And Pawkins! However, it was a pity to lose the moth now. He felt his way into the hall and found the matches, after sending his hat down upon the floor with a noise like a drum. With the lighted candle he returned to the sitting-room. No moth was to be seen. Yet once for a moment it seemed that the thing was fluttering round his head. Hapley very suddenly decided to give up the moth and go to bed. But he was excited. All night long his sleep was broken by dreams of the moth, Pawkins, and his landlady. Twice in the night he turned out and soused his head in cold water.

One thing was very clear to him. His landlady could not possibly understand about the strange moth, especially as he had failed to catch it. No one but an entomologist would understand quite how he felt. She was probably frightened at his behaviour, and yet he failed to see how he could explain it. He decided to say nothing further about the events of last night. After breakfast he saw her in her garden, and decided to go out and talk to reassure her. He talked to her about beans and potatoes, bees, caterpillars, and the price of fruit. She replied in her usual manner, but she looked at him a little suspiciously, and kept walking as he walked, so that there was always a bed of flowers, or a row of beans, or something of the sort, between them. After a while he began to feel singularly irritated at this, and to conceal his vexation went indoors and presently went out for a walk.

The moth, or butterfly, trailing an odd flavour of Pawkins with it, kept coming into that walk, though he did his best to keep his mind off it. Once he saw it quite distinctly, with its wings flattened out, upon the old stone wall that runs along the west edge of the park, but going up to it he found it was only two lumps of grey and yellow lichen. "This," said Hapley, "is the reverse of mimicry. Instead of a butterfly looking like a stone, here is a stone looking like a butterfly!" Once something hovered and fluttered round his head, but by an effort of will he drove that impression out of his mind again.

In the afternoon Hapley called upon the Vicar, and argued with him upon theological questions. They sat in the little arbour covered with briar, and smoked as they wrangled. "Look at that moth!" said Hapley, suddenly, pointing to the edge of the wooden table.

"Where?" said the Vicar.

"You don't see a moth on the edge of the table there?" said Hapley.

"Certainly not," said the Vicar.

Hapley was thunderstruck. He gasped. The Vicar was staring at him. Clearly the man saw nothing. "The eye of faith is no better than the eye of science," said Hapley awkwardly.

"I don't see your point," said the Vicar, thinking it was part of the argument.

That night Hapley found the moth crawling over his counterpane. He sat on the edge of the bed in his shirt sleeves and reasoned with himself. Was it pure hallucination? He knew he was slipping, and he battled for his sanity with the same silent energy he had formerly displayed against Pawkins. So persistent is mental habit, that he felt as if it were still a struggle with Pawkins. He was well versed in psychology. He knew that such visual illusions do come as a result of mental strain. But the point was, he did not only *see* the moth, he had heard it when it touched the edge of the lampshade, and afterwards when it hit against the wall, and he had felt it strike his face in the dark.

He looked at it. It was not at all dreamlike, but perfectly clear and solid-looking in the candlelight. He saw the hairy body, and the short feathery antennae, the jointed legs, even a place where the down was rubbed from the wing. He suddenly felt angry with himself for being afraid of a little insect.

His landlady had got the servant to sleep with her that night, because she was afraid to be alone. In addition she had locked the door, and put the chest of drawers against it. They listened and talked in whispers after they had gone to bed, but nothing occurred to alarm them. About eleven they had ventured to put the candle out, and had both dozed off to sleep. They woke up with a start, and sat up in bed, listening in the darkness.

Then they heard slippered feet going to and fro in Hapley's room. A chair was overturned, and there was a violent dab at the wall. Then a china mantel ornament smashed upon the fender. Suddenly the door of the room opened, and they heard him upon the landing. They clung to one another, listening. He seemed to be dancing upon the staircase. Now he would go down three or four steps quickly, then up again, then hurry down into the hall. They heard the umbrella stand go over, and the fanlight break. Then the bolt shot and the chain rattled. He was opening the door.

They hurried to the window. It was a dim grey night; an almost unbroken sheet of watery cloud was sweeping across the moon, and the hedge and trees in front of the house were black against the pale roadway. They saw Hapley, looking like a ghost in his shirt and white trousers, running to and fro in the road, and beating the air. Now he would stop, now he would dart very rapidly at something invisible, now he would move upon it with stealthy strides. At last he went out of sight up the road towards the down. Then, while they argued who should go down and lock the door, he returned. He was walking very fast, and he came straight into the house, closed the door carefully, and went quietly up to his bedroom. Then everything was silent.

"Mrs. Colville," said Hapley, calling down the staircase next morning, "I hope I did not alarm you last night."

"You may well ask that!" said Mrs. Colville.

"The fact is, I am a sleep-walker, and the last two nights I have been without my sleeping mixture. There is nothing to be alarmed about, really. I am sorry I made such an ass of myself. I will go over the down to Shoreham, and get some stuff to make me sleep soundly. I ought to have done that yesterday."

But halfway over the down, by the chalk pits, the moth came upon Hapley again. He went on, trying to keep his mind upon chess problems, but it was no good. The thing fluttered into his face, and he struck at it with his hat in self-defence. Then rage, the old rage – the rage he had so often felt against Pawkins – came upon him again. He went on, leaping and striking at the eddying insect. Suddenly he trod on nothing, and fell headlong.

There was a gap in his sensations, and Hapley found himself sitting on the heap of flints in front of the opening of the chalk-pits, with a leg twisted back under him. The strange moth was still fluttering round his head. He struck at it with his hand, and turning his head saw two men approaching him. One was the village doctor. It occurred to Hapley that this was lucky. Then it came into his mind with extraordinary vividness, that no one would ever be able to see the strange moth except himself, and that it behoved him to keep silent about it.

Late that night, however, after his broken leg was set, he was feverish and forgot his self-restraint. He was lying flat on his bed, and he began to run his eyes round the room to see if the moth was still about. He tried not to do this, but it was no good. He soon caught sight of the thing resting close to his hand, by the night-light, on the green tablecloth. The wings quivered. With a sudden wave of anger he smote at it with his fist, and the nurse woke up with a shriek. He had missed it.

"That moth!" he said; and then, "It was fancy. Nothing!"

All the time he could see quite clearly the insect going round the cornice and darting across the room, and he could also see that the nurse saw nothing of it and looked at him strangely. He must keep himself in hand. He knew he was a lost man if he did not keep himself in hand. But as the night waned the fever grew upon him, and the very dread he had of seeing the moth made him see it. About five, just as the dawn was grey, he tried to get out of bed and catch it, though his leg was afire with pain. The nurse had to struggle with him.

On account of this, they tied him down to the bed. At this the moth grew bolder, and once he felt it settle in his hair. Then, because he struck out violently with his arms, they tied these also. At this the moth came and crawled over his face, and Hapley wept, swore, screamed, prayed for them to take it off him, unavailingly.

The doctor was a blockhead, a just-qualified general practitioner, and quite ignorant of mental science. He simply said there was no moth. Had he possessed the wit, he might still, perhaps, have saved Hapley from his fate by entering into his delusion, and covering his face with gauze, as he prayed might be done. But, as I say, the doctor was a blockhead, and until the leg was healed Hapley was kept tied to his bed, and with the imaginary moth crawling over him. It never left him while he was awake and it grew to a monster in his dreams. While he was awake he longed for sleep, and from sleep he awoke screaming.

So now Hapley is spending the remainder of his days in a padded room, worried by a moth that no one else can see. The asylum doctor calls it hallucination; but Hapley, when he is in his easier mood, and can talk, says it is the ghost of Pawkins, and consequently a unique specimen and well worth the trouble of catching.

Pomegranate Seed

Edith Wharton

Chapter I

CHARLOTTE ASHBY paused on her doorstep. Dark had descended on the brilliancy of the March afternoon, and the grinding, rasping street life of the city was at its highest. She turned her back on it, standing for a moment in the old-fashioned, marble-flagged vestibule before she inserted her key in the lock. The sash curtains drawn across the panes of the inner door softened the light within to a warm blur through which no details showed. It was the hour when, in the first months of her marriage to Kenneth Ashby, she had most liked to return to that quiet house in a street long since deserted by business and fashion. The contrast between the soulless roar of New York, its devouring blaze of lights, the oppression of its congested traffic, congested houses, lives, minds and this veiled sanctuary she called home, always stirred her profoundly. In the very heart of the hurricane she had found her tiny islet – or thought she had. And now, in the last months, everything was changed, and she always wavered on the doorstep and had to force herself to enter.

While she stood there she called up the scene within: the hall hung with old prints, the ladder-like stairs, and on the left her husband's long shabby library, full of books and pipes and worn armchairs inviting to meditation. How she had loved that room! Then, upstairs, her own drawing room, in which, since the death of Kenneth's first wife, neither furniture nor hangings had been changed, because there had never been money enough, but which Charlotte had made her own by moving furniture about and adding more books, another lamp, a table for the new reviews. Even on the occasion of her only visit to the first Mrs. Ashby – a distant, self-centered woman, whom she had known very slightly – she had looked about her with an innocent envy, feeling it to be exactly the drawing room she would have liked for herself; and now for more than a year it had been hers to deal with as she chose – the room to which she hastened back at dusk on winter days, where she sat reading by the fire, or answering notes at the pleasant roomy desk, or going over her stepchildren's copybooks, till she heard her husband's step.

Sometimes friends dropped in; sometimes – oftener – she was alone; and she liked that best, since it was another way of being with Kenneth, thinking over what he had said when they parted in the morning, imagining what he would say when he sprang up the stairs, found her by herself and caught her to him.

Now, instead of this, she thought of one thing only – the letter she might or might not find on the hall table. Until she had made sure whether or not it was there, her mind had no room for anything else. The letter was always the same – a square grayish envelope with 'Kenneth Ashby, Esquire', written on it in bold but faint characters. From the first it had struck Charlotte as peculiar that anyone who wrote such a firm hand should trace the letters so lightly; the address was always written as though there were not enough ink in the pen, or the writer's wrist were too weak to bear upon it. Another curious thing was that, in spite of its masculine curves, the writing was so visibly feminine. Some hands are sexless, some masculine, at first glance; the writing on the gray envelope, for all its strength and assurance, was without doubt a woman's. The envelope never bore anything but the recipient's name; no stamp, no address. The letter was presumably delivered by hand – but by whose? No doubt it was slipped into the letterbox, whence the parlormaid, when she closed the shutters and lit the lights, probably extracted it. At any rate, it was always in the evening, after dark, that Charlotte saw it lying there. She thought of the letter in the singular, as 'it', because, though there had been several since her marriage – seven, to be exact – they were so alike in appearance that they had become merged in one another in her mind, become one letter, become 'it'.

The first had come the day after their return from their honeymoon – a journey prolonged to the West Indies, from which they had returned to New York after an absence of more than two months. Re-entering the house with her husband, late on that first evening – they had dined at his mother's – she had seen, alone on the hall table, the gray envelope. Her eye fell on it before Kenneth's, and her first thought was: "Why, I've seen that writing before"; but where she could not recall. The memory was just definite enough for her to identify the script whenever it looked up at her faintly from the same pale envelope; but on that first day she would have thought no more of the letter if, when her husband's glance lit on it, she had not chanced to be looking at him. It all happened in a flash – his seeing the letter, putting out his hand for it, raising it to his shortsighted eyes to decipher the faint writing, and then abruptly withdrawing the arm he had slipped through Charlotte's, and moving away to the hanging light, his back turned to her. She had waited – waited for a sound, an exclamation; waited for him to open the letter; but he had slipped it into his pocket without a word and followed her into the library. And there they had sat down by the fire and lit their cigarettes, and he had remained silent, his head thrown back broodingly against the armchair, his eyes fixed on the hearth, and presently had passed his hand over his forehead and said: "Wasn't it unusually hot at my mother's tonight? I've got a splitting head. Mind if I take myself off to bed?"

That was the first time. Since then Charlotte had never been present when he had received the letter. It usually came before he got home from his office, and she had to go upstairs and leave it lying there. But even if she had not seen it, she would have known it had come by the change in his face when he joined her – which, on those evenings, he seldom did before they met for dinner. Evidently, whatever the letter contained, he wanted to be by himself to deal with it; and when he reappeared he looked years older, looked emptied of life and courage, and hardly conscious of her presence. Sometimes he was silent for the rest of the evening; and if he spoke, it was usually to hint some criticism of her household arrangements, suggest some change in the domestic administration, to ask, a little nervously, if she didn't think Joyce's nursery governess was rather young and flighty, or if she herself always saw to it that Peter – whose throat was delicate – was properly wrapped up when he went to school. At such times Charlotte would remember the friendly warnings she had received when she became engaged to Kenneth Ashby: "Marrying a heartbroken widower! Isn't that rather risky? You know Elsie Ashby absolutely dominated him"; and how she had jokingly replied: "He may be glad of a little liberty for a change." And in this respect she had been right. She had needed no one to tell her, during the first months, that her husband was perfectly happy with her. When they came back from their protracted honeymoon the same friends said: "What have you done to Kenneth? He looks twenty years younger"; and this time she answered with careless joy: "I suppose I've got him out of his groove."

But what she noticed after the gray letters began to come was not so much his nervous tentative faultfinding – which always seemed to be uttered against his will – as the look in his eyes when he joined her after receiving one of the letters. The look was not unloving, not even indifferent; it was the look of a man who had been so far away from ordinary events that when he returns to familiar things they seem strange. She minded that more than the faultfinding.

Though she had been sure from the first that the handwriting on the gray envelope was a woman's, it was long before she associated the mysterious letters with any sentimental secret. She was too sure of her husband's love, too confident of filling his life, for such an idea to occur to her. It seemed far more likely that the letters – which certainly did not appear to cause him any sentimental pleasure – were addressed to the busy lawyer than to the private person. Probably they were from some tiresome client – women, he had often told her, were nearly always tiresome as clients – who did not want her letters opened by his secretary and therefore had them carried to his house. Yes; but in that case the unknown female must be unusually troublesome, judging from the effect her letters produced. Then again, though his professional discretion was exemplary, it was odd that he had never uttered an impatient comment, never remarked to Charlotte, in a moment of expansion, that there was a nuisance of a woman who kept badgering him about a case that had gone against her. He had made more than one semi-confidence of the kind – of course without giving names or details; but concerning this mysterious correspondent his lips were sealed.

There was another possibility: what is euphemistically called an 'old entanglement'. Charlotte Ashby was a sophisticated woman. She had few illusions about the intricacies of the human heart; she knew that there were often old entanglements. But when she had married Kenneth Ashby, her friends, instead of hinting at such a possibility, had said: "You've got your work cut out for you. Marrying a Don Juan is a sinecure to it. Kenneth's never looked at another woman since he first saw Elsie Corder. During all the years of their marriage he was more like an unhappy lover than a comfortably contented husband. He'll never let you move an armchair or change the place of a lamp; and whatever you venture to do, he'll mentally compare with what Elsie would have done in your place."

Except for an occasional nervous mistrust as to her ability to manage the children – a mistrust gradually dispelled by her good humor and the children's obvious fondness for her – none of these forebodings had come true. The desolate widower, of whom his nearest friends said that only his absorbing professional interests had kept him from suicide after his first wife's death, had fallen in love, two years later, with Charlotte Gorse, and after an impetuous wooing had married her and carried her off on a tropical honeymoon. And ever since he had been as tender and lover-like as during those first radiant weeks. Before asking her to marry him he had spoken to her frankly of his great love for his first wife and his despair after her sudden death; but even then he had assumed no stricken attitude, or implied that life offered no possibility of renewal. He had been perfectly simple and natural, and had confessed to Charlotte that from the beginning he had hoped the future held new gifts for him. And when, after their marriage, they returned to the house where his twelve years with his first wife had been spent, he had told Charlotte at once that he was sorry he couldn't afford to do the place over for her, but that he knew every woman had her own views about furniture and all sorts of household arrangements a man would never notice, and had begged her to make any changes she saw fit without bothering to consult him. As a result, she made as few as possible; but his way of beginning their new life in the old setting was so frank and unembarrassed that it put her immediately at her ease, and she was almost sorry to find that the portrait of Elsie Ashby, which used to hang over the desk in his library, had been transferred in their absence to the children's nursery. Knowing herself to be the indirect cause of this banishment, she spoke of it to her husband; but he answered: "Oh, I thought they ought to grow up with her looking down on them." The answer moved Charlotte, and satisfied her; and as time went by she had to confess that she felt more at home in her house, more at ease and in confidence with her husband, since that long coldly beautiful face on the library wall no longer followed her with guarded eyes. It was as if Kenneth's love had penetrated to the secret she hardly acknowledged to her own heart – her passionate need to feel herself the sovereign even of his past.

With all this stored-up happiness to sustain her, it was curious that she had lately found herself yielding to a nervous apprehension. But there the apprehension was; and on this particular afternoon – perhaps because she was more tired than usual, or because of the trouble of finding a new cook or, for some other ridiculously trivial reason, moral or physical – she found herself unable to react against the feeling. Latchkey in hand, she looked back down the silent street to the whirl and illumination of the great thoroughfare beyond, and up at the sky already aflare with the city's nocturnal life. "Outside there," she thought, "skyscrapers, advertisements, telephones, wireless, airplanes, movies, motors, and all the rest of the twentieth century; and on the other side of the door something I can't explain, can't relate to them. Something as old as the world, as mysterious as life…Nonsense! What am I worrying about? There hasn't been a letter for three months now – not since the day we came back from the country after Christmas…Queer that they always seem to come after our holidays! …Why should I imagine there's going to be one tonight!"

No reason why, but that was the worst of it – one of the worst! – that there were days when she would stand there cold and shivering with the premonition of something inexplicable, intolerable, to be faced on the other side of the curtained panes; and when she opened the door and went in, there would be nothing; and on other days when she felt the same premonitory chill, it was justified by the sight of the gray envelope. So that ever since the last had come she had taken to feeling cold and premonitory every evening, because she never opened the door without thinking the letter might be there.

Well, she'd had enough of it: that was certain. She couldn't go on like that. If her husband turned white and had a headache on the days when the letter came, he seemed to recover afterward; but she couldn't. With her the strain had become chronic, and the reason was not far to seek. Her husband knew from whom the letter came and what was in it; he was prepared beforehand for whatever he had to deal with, and master of the situation, however bad; whereas she was shut out in the dark with her conjectures.

"I can't stand it! I can't stand it another day!" she exclaimed aloud, as she put her key in the lock. She turned the key and went in; and there, on the table, lay the letter.

Chapter II

SHE WAS ALMOST glad of the sight. It seemed to justify everything, to put a seal of definiteness on the whole blurred business. A letter for her husband; a letter from a woman – no doubt another vulgar case of 'old entanglement'. What a fool she had been ever to doubt it, to rack her brains for less obvious explanations! She took up the envelope with a steady contemptuous hand, looked closely at the faint letters, held it against the light and just discerned the outline of the folded sheet within. She knew that now she would have no peace till she found out what was written on that sheet.

Her husband had not come in; he seldom got back from his office before half-past six or seven, and it was not yet six. She would have time to take the letter up to the drawing room, hold it over the tea kettle which at that hour always simmered by the fire in expectation of her return, solve the mystery and replace the letter where she had found it. No one would be the wiser, and her gnawing uncertainty would be over. The alternative, of course, was to question her husband; but to do that seemed even more difficult. She weighed the letter between thumb and finger, looked at it again under the light, started up the stairs with the envelope – and came down again and laid it on the table.

"No, I evidently can't," she said, disappointed.

What should she do, then? She couldn't go up alone to that warm welcoming room, pour out her tea, look over her correspondence, glance at a book or review – not with that letter lying below and the knowledge that in a little while her husband would come in, open it and turn into the library alone, as he always did on the days when the gray envelope came.

Suddenly she decided. She would wait in the library and see for herself; see what happened between him and the letter when they thought themselves unobserved. She wondered the idea had never occurred to her before. By leaving the door ajar, and sitting in the corner behind it, she could watch him unseen... Well, then, she would watch him! She drew a chair into the corner, sat down, her eyes on the crack, and waited.

As far as she could remember, it was the first time she had ever tried to surprise another person's secret, but she was conscious of no compunction. She simply felt as if she were fighting her way through a stifling fog that she must at all costs get out of.

At length she heard Kenneth's latchkey and jumped up. The impulse to rush out and meet him had nearly made her forget why she was there; but she remembered in time and sat down again. From her post she covered the whole range of his movements – saw him enter the hall, draw the key from the door and take off his hat and overcoat. Then he turned to throw his gloves on the hall table, and at that moment he saw the envelope. The light was full on his face, and what Charlotte first noted there was a look of surprise. Evidently he had not expected the letter – had not thought of the possibility of its being there that day. But though he had not expected it, now that he saw it he knew well enough what it contained. He did not open it immediately, but stood motionless, the color slowly ebbing from his face. Apparently he could not make up his mind to touch it; but at length he put out his hand, opened the envelope, and moved with it to the light. In doing so he turned his back on Charlotte, and she saw only his bent head and slightly stooping shoulders. Apparently all the writing was on one page, for he did not turn the sheet but continued to stare at it for so long that he must have reread it a dozen times – or so it seemed to the woman breathlessly watching him. At length she saw him move; he raised the letter still closer to his eyes, as though he had not fully deciphered it. Then he lowered his head, and she saw his lips touch the sheet.

"Kenneth!" she exclaimed, and went on out into the hall.

The letter clutched in his hand, her husband turned and looked at her. "Where were you?" he said, in a low bewildered voice, like a man waked out of his sleep.

"In the library, waiting for you." She tried to steady her voice: "What's the matter! What's in that letter? You look ghastly."

Her agitation seemed to calm him, and he instantly put the envelope into his pocket with a slight laugh. "Ghastly? I'm sorry. I've had a hard day in the office – one or two complicated cases. I look dog-tired, I suppose."

"You didn't look tired when you came in. It was only when you opened that letter—"

He had followed her into the library, and they stood gazing at each other. Charlotte noticed how quickly he had regained his self-control; his profession had trained him to rapid mastery of face and voice. She saw at once that she would be at a disadvantage in any attempt to surprise his secret, but at the same moment she lost all desire to maneuver, to trick him into betraying anything he wanted to conceal. Her wish was still to penetrate the mystery, but only that she might help him to bear the burden it implied. "Even if it *is* another woman," she thought.

"Kenneth," she said, her heart beating excitedly, "I waited here on purpose to see you come in. I wanted to watch you while you opened that letter."

His face, which had paled, turned to dark red; then it paled again. "That letter? Why especially that letter?"

"Because I've noticed that whenever one of those letters comes it seems to have such a strange effect on you."

A line of anger she had never seen before came out between his eyes, and she said to herself: "The upper part of his face is too narrow; this is the first time I ever noticed it."

She heard him continue, in the cool and faintly ironic tone of the prosecuting lawyer making a point: "Ah, so you're in the habit of watching people open their letters when they don't know you're there?"

"Not in the habit. I never did such a thing before. But I had to find out what she writes to you, at regular intervals, in those gray envelopes."

He weighed this for a moment; then: "The intervals have not been regular," he said.

"Oh, I dare say you've kept a better account of the dates than I have," she retorted, her magnanimity vanishing at his tone. "All I know is that every time that woman writes to you—"

"Why do you assume it's a woman?"

"It's a woman's writing. Do you deny it?"

He smiled. "No, I don't deny it. I asked only because the writing is generally supposed to look more like a man's."

Charlotte passed this over impatiently. "And this woman – what does she write to you about?"

Again he seemed to consider a moment. "About business."

"Legal business?"

"In a way, yes. Business in general."

"You look after her affairs for her?"

"Yes."

"You've looked after them for a long time?"

"Yes. A very long time."

"Kenneth, dearest, won't you tell me who she is?"

"No. I can't." He paused, and brought out, as if with a certain hesitation:

"Professional secrecy."

The blood rushed from Charlotte's heart to her temples. "Don't say that – don't!"

"Why not?"

"Because I saw you kiss the letter."

The effect of the words was so disconcerting that she instantly repented having spoken them. Her husband, who had submitted to her cross-questioning with a sort of contemptuous composure, as though he were humoring an unreasonable child, turned on her a face of terror and distress. For a minute he seemed unable to speak; then, collecting himself, with an effort, he stammered out: "The writing is very faint; you must have seen me holding the letter close to my eyes to try to decipher it."

"No; I saw you kissing it." He was silent. "Didn't I see you kissing it?"

He sank back into indifference. "Perhaps."

"Kenneth! You stand there and say that – to me?"

"What possible difference can it make to you? The letter is on business, as I told you. Do you suppose I'd lie about it? The writer is a very old friend whom I haven't seen for a long time."

"Men don't kiss business letters, even from women who are very old friends, unless they have been their lovers, and still regret them."

He shrugged his shoulders slightly and turned away, as if he considered the discussion at an end and were faintly disgusted at the turn it had taken.

"Kenneth!" Charlotte moved toward him and caught hold of his arm.

He paused with a look of weariness and laid his hand over hers. "Won't you believe me?" he asked gently.

"How can I? I've watched these letters come to you – for months now they've been coming. Ever since we came back from the West Indies – one of them greeted me the very day we arrived. And after each one of them I see their mysterious effect on you, I see you disturbed, unhappy, as if someone were trying to estrange you from me."

"No, dear; not that. Never!"

She drew back and looked at him with passionate entreaty. "Well, then, prove it to me, darling. It's so easy!"

He forced a smile. "It's not easy to prove anything to a woman who's once taken an idea into her head."

"You've only got to show me the letter."

His hand slipped from hers and he drew back and shook his head.

"You won't?"

"I can't."

"Then the woman who wrote it is your mistress."

"No, dear. No."

"Not now, perhaps. I suppose she's trying to get you back, and you're struggling, out of pity for me. My poor Kenneth!"

"I swear to you she never was my mistress."

Charlotte felt the tears rushing to her eyes. "Ah, that's worse, then – that's hopeless! The prudent ones are the kind that keep their hold on a man. We all know that." She lifted her hands and hid her face in them.

Her husband remained silent; he offered neither consolation nor denial, and at length, wiping away her tears, she raised her eyes almost timidly to his.

"Kenneth, think! We've been married such a short time. Imagine what you're making me suffer. You say you can't show me this letter. You refuse even to explain it."

"I've told you the letter is on business. I will swear to that too."

"A man will swear to anything to screen a woman. If you want me to believe you, at least tell me her name. If you'll do that, I promise you I won't ask to see the letter."

There was a long interval of suspense, during which she felt her heart beating against her ribs in quick admonitory knocks, as if warning her of the danger she was incurring.

"I can't," he said at length.

"Not even her name?"

"No."

"You can't tell me anything more?"

"No."

Again a pause; this time they seemed both to have reached the end of their arguments and to be helplessly facing each other across a baffling waste of incomprehension.

Charlotte stood breathing rapidly, her hands against her breast. She felt as if she had run a hard race and missed the goal. She had meant to move her husband and had succeeded only in irritating him; and this error of reckoning seemed to change him into a stranger, a mysterious incomprehensible being whom no argument or entreaty of hers could reach. The curious thing was that she was aware in him of no hostility or even impatience, but only of a remoteness, an inaccessibility, far more difficult to overcome. She felt herself excluded, ignored, blotted out of his life. But after a moment or two, looking at him more calmly, she saw that he was suffering as much as she was. His distant guarded face was drawn with pain; the coming of the gray envelope, though it always cast a shadow, had never marked him as deeply as this discussion with his wife.

Charlotte took heart; perhaps, after all, she had not spent her last shaft. She drew nearer and once more laid her hand on his arm. "Poor Kenneth! If you knew how sorry I am for you—"

She thought he winced slightly at this expression of sympathy, but he took her hand and pressed it.

"I can think of nothing worse than to be incapable of loving long," she continued, "to feel the beauty of a great love and to be too unstable to bear its burden."

He turned on her a look of wistful reproach. "Oh, don't say that of me. Unstable!"

She felt herself at last on the right tack, and her voice trembled with excitement as she went on: "Then what about me and this other woman? Haven't you already forgotten Elsie twice within a year?"

She seldom pronounced his first wife's name; it did not come naturally to her tongue. She flung it out now as if she were flinging some dangerous explosive into the open space between them, and drew back a step, waiting to hear the mine go off.

Her husband did not move; his expression grew sadder, but showed no resentment. "I have never forgotten Elsie," he said.

Charlotte could not repress a faint laugh. "Then, you poor dear, between the three of us—"

"There are not—" he began; and then broke off and put his hand to his forehead.

"Not what?"

"I'm sorry; I don't believe I know what I'm saying. I've got a blinding headache." He looked wan and furrowed enough for the statement to be true, but she was exasperated by his evasion.

"Ah, yes; the gray envelope headache!"

She saw the surprise in his eyes. "I'd forgotten how closely I've been watched," he said coldly. "If you'll excuse me, I think I'll go up and try an hour in the dark, to see if I can get rid of this neuralgia."

She wavered; then she said, with desperate resolution: "I'm sorry your head aches. But before you go I want to say that sooner or later this question must be settled between us. Someone is trying to separate us, and I don't care what it costs me to find out who it is." She looked him steadily in the eyes. "If it costs me your love, I don't care! If I can't have your confidence I don't want anything from you."

He still looked at her wistfully. "Give me time."

"Time for what? It's only a word to say."

"Time to show you that you haven't lost my love or my confidence."

"Well, I'm waiting."

He turned toward the door, and then glanced back hesitatingly. "Oh, do wait, my love," he said, and went out of the room.

She heard his tired step on the stairs and the closing of his bedroom door above. Then she dropped into a chair and buried her face in her folded arms. Her first movement was one of compunction; she seemed to herself to have been hard, unhuman, unimaginative. "Think of telling him that I didn't care if my insistence cost me his love! The lying rubbish!" She started up to follow him and unsay the meaningless words. But she was checked by a reflection. He had had his way, after all; he had eluded all attacks on his secret, and now he was shut up alone in his room, reading that other woman's letter.

Chapter III

SHE WAS STILL reflecting on this when the surprised parlormaid came in and found her. No, Charlotte said, she wasn't going to dress for dinner; Mr. Ashby didn't want to dine. He was very tired and had gone up to his room to rest; later she would have something brought on a tray to the drawing room. She mounted the stairs to her bedroom. Her dinner dress was lying on the bed, and at the sight the quiet routine of her daily life took hold of her and she began to feel as if the strange talk she had just had with her husband must have taken place in another world, between two beings who were not Charlotte Gorse and Kenneth Ashby, but phantoms projected by her fevered imagination. She recalled the year since her marriage – her husband's constant devotion; his persistent, almost too insistent tenderness; the feeling he had given her at times of being too eagerly dependent on her, too searchingly close to her, as if there were not air enough between her soul and his. It seemed preposterous, as she recalled all this, that a few moments ago she should have been accusing him of an intrigue with another woman! But, then, what—

Again she was moved by the impulse to go up to him, beg his pardon and try to laugh away the misunderstanding. But she was restrained by the fear of forcing herself upon his privacy. He was troubled and unhappy, oppressed by some grief or fear; and he had shown her that he wanted to fight out his battle alone. It would be wiser, as well as more generous, to respect his wish. Only, how strange, how unbearable, to be there, in the next room to his, and feel herself at the other end of the world! In her nervous agitation she almost regretted not having had the courage to open the letter and put it back on the hall table before he came in. At least she would have known what his secret was, and the bogy might have been laid. For she was beginning now to think of the mystery as something conscious, malevolent: a secret persecution before which he quailed, yet from which he could not free himself. Once or twice in his evasive eyes she thought she had detected a desire for help, an impulse of confession, instantly restrained and suppressed. It was as if he felt she could have helped him if she had known, and yet had been unable to tell her!

There flashed through her mind the idea of going to his mother. She was very fond of old Mrs. Ashby, a firm-fleshed clear-eyed old lady, with an astringent bluntness of speech which responded to the forthright and simple in Charlotte's own nature. There had been a tacit bond between them ever since the day when Mrs. Ashby Senior, coming to lunch for the first time with her new daughter-in-law, had been received by Charlotte downstairs in the library, and glancing up at the empty wall above her son's desk, had remarked laconically: "Elsie gone, eh?" adding, at Charlotte's murmured explanation: "Nonsense. Don't have her back. Two's company." Charlotte, at this reading of her thoughts, could hardly refrain from exchanging a smile of complicity with her mother-in-law; and it seemed to her now that Mrs. Ashby's almost uncanny directness might pierce to the core of this new mystery. But here again she hesitated, for the idea almost suggested a betrayal. What right had she to call in anyone, even so close a relation, to surprise a secret which her husband was trying to keep from her? "Perhaps, by and by, he'll talk to his mother of his own accord," she thought, and then ended: "But what does it matter? He and I must settle it between us."

She was still brooding over the problem when there was a knock on the door and her husband came in. He was dressed for dinner and seemed surprised to see her sitting there, with her evening dress lying unheeded on the bed.

"Aren't you coming down?"

"I thought you were not well and had gone to bed," she faltered.

He forced a smile. "I'm not particularly well, but we'd better go down." His face, though still drawn, looked calmer than when he had fled upstairs an hour earlier.

"There it is; he knows what's in the letter and has fought his battle out again, whatever it is," she reflected, "while I'm still in darkness." She rang and gave a hurried order that dinner should be served as soon as possible – just a short meal, whatever could be got ready quickly, as both she and Mr. Ashby were rather tired and not very hungry.

Dinner was announced, and they sat down to it. At first neither seemed able to find a word to say; then Ashby began to make conversation with an assumption of ease that was more oppressive than his silence. "How tired he is! How terribly overtired!" Charlotte said to herself, pursuing her own thoughts while he rambled on about municipal politics, aviation, an exhibition of modern French painting, the health of an old aunt and the installing of the automatic telephone. "Good heavens, how tired he is!"

When they dined alone they usually went into the library after dinner, and Charlotte curled herself up on the divan with her knitting while he settled down in his armchair under the lamp and lit a pipe. But this evening, by tacit agreement, they avoided the room in which their strange talk had taken place, and went up to Charlotte's drawing room.

They sat down near the fire, and Charlotte said: "Your pipe?" after he had put down his hardly tasted coffee.

He shook his head. "No, not tonight."

"You must go to bed early; you look terribly tired. I'm sure they overwork you at the office."

"I suppose we all overwork at times."

She rose and stood before him with sudden resolution. "Well, I'm not going to have you use up your strength slaving in that way. It's absurd. I can see you're ill." She bent over him and laid her hand on his forehead. "My poor old Kenneth. Prepare to be taken away soon on a long holiday."

He looked up at her, startled. "A holiday?"

"Certainly. Didn't you know I was going to carry you off at Easter? We're going to start in a fortnight on a month's voyage to somewhere or other. On any one of the big cruising steamers." She paused and bent closer, touching his forehead with her lips. "I'm tired, too, Kenneth."

He seemed to pay no heed to her last words, but sat, his hands on his knees, his head drawn back a little from her caress, and looked up at her with a stare of apprehension. "Again? My dear, we can't; I can't possibly go away."

"I don't know why you say 'again', Kenneth; we haven't taken a real holiday this year."

"At Christmas we spent a week with the children in the country."

"Yes, but this time I mean away from the children, from servants, from the house. From everything that's familiar and fatiguing. Your mother will love to have Joyce and Peter with her."

He frowned and slowly shook his head. "No, dear; I can't leave them with my mother."

"Why, Kenneth, how absurd! She adores them. You didn't hesitate to leave them with her for over two months when we went to the West Indies."

He drew a deep breath and stood up uneasily. "That was different."

"Different? Why?"

"I mean, at that time I didn't realize—" He broke off as if to choose his words and then went on: "My mother adores the children, as you say. But she isn't always very judicious. Grandmothers always spoil children. And sometimes she talks before them without thinking." He turned to his wife with an almost pitiful gesture of entreaty. "Don't ask me to, dear."

Charlotte mused. It was true that the elder Mrs. Ashby had a fearless tongue, but she was the last woman in the world to say or hint anything before her grandchildren at which the most scrupulous parent could take offense. Charlotte looked at her husband in perplexity.

"I don't understand."

He continued to turn on her the same troubled and entreating gaze. "Don't try to," he muttered.

"Not try to?"

"Not now – not yet." He put up his hands and pressed them against his temples. "Can't you see that there's no use in insisting? I can't go away, no matter how much I might want to."

Charlotte still scrutinized him gravely. "The question is, *do* you want to?"

He returned her gaze for a moment; then his lips began to tremble, and he said, hardly above his breath: "I want – anything you want."

"And yet—"

"Don't ask me. I can't leave – I can't!"

"You mean that you can't go away out of reach of those letters!"

Her husband had been standing before her in an uneasy half-hesitating attitude; now he turned abruptly away and walked once or twice up and down the length of the room, his head bent, his eyes fixed on the carpet.

Charlotte felt her resentfulness rising with her fears. "It's that," she persisted. "Why not admit it? You can't live without them."

He continued his troubled pacing of the room; then he stopped short, dropped into a chair and covered his face with his hands. From the shaking of his shoulders, Charlotte saw that he was weeping. She had never seen a man cry, except her father after her mother's death, when she was a little girl; and she remembered still how the sight had frightened her. She was frightened now; she felt that her husband was being dragged away from her into some mysterious bondage, and that she must use up her last atom of strength in the struggle for his freedom, and for hers.

"Kenneth – Kenneth!" she pleaded, kneeling down beside him. "Won't you listen to me? Won't you try to see what I'm suffering? I'm not unreasonable, darling, really not. I don't suppose I should ever have noticed the letters if it hadn't been for their effect on you. It's not my way to pry into other people's affairs; and even if the effect had been different – yes, yes, listen to me – if I'd seen that the letters made you happy, that you were watching eagerly for them, counting the days between their coming, that you wanted them, that they gave you something I haven't known how to give – why, Kenneth, I don't say I shouldn't have suffered from that, too; but it would have been in a different way, and I should have had the courage to hide what I felt, and the hope that someday you'd come to feel about me as you did about the writer of the letters. But what I can't bear is to see how you dread them, how they make you suffer, and yet how you can't live without them and won't go away lest you should miss one during your absence. Or perhaps," she added, her voice breaking into a cry of accusation – "perhaps it's because she's actually forbidden you to leave. Kenneth, you must answer me! Is that the reason? Is it because she's forbidden you that you won't go away with me?"

She continued to kneel at his side, and raising her hands, she drew his gently down. She was ashamed of her persistence, ashamed of uncovering that baffled disordered face, yet resolved that no such scruples should arrest her. His eyes were lowered, the muscles of his face quivered; she was making him suffer even more than she suffered herself. Yet this no longer restrained her.

"Kenneth, is it that? She won't let us go away together?"

Still he did not speak or turn his eyes to her; and a sense of defeat swept over her. After all, she thought, the struggle was a losing one. "You needn't answer. I see I'm right," she said.

Suddenly, as she rose, he turned and drew her down again. His hands caught hers and pressed them so tightly that she felt her rings cutting into her flesh. There was something frightened, convulsive in his hold; it was the clutch of a man who felt himself slipping over a precipice. He was staring up at her now as if salvation lay in the face she bent above him. "Of course we'll go away together. We'll go wherever you want," he said in a low confused voice; and putting his arm about her, he drew her close and pressed his lips on hers.

Chapter IV

CHARLOTTE had said to herself: "I shall sleep tonight," but instead she sat before her fire into the small hours, listening for any sound that came from her husband's room. But he, at any rate, seemed to be resting after the tumult of the evening. Once or twice she stole to the door and in the faint light that came in from the street through his open window she saw him stretched out in heavy sleep – the sleep of weakness and exhaustion. "He's ill," she thought "he's undoubtedly ill. And it's not overwork; it's this mysterious persecution."

She drew a breath of relief. She had fought through the weary fight and the victory was hers – at least for the moment. If only they could have started at once – started for anywhere! She knew it would be useless to ask him to leave before the holidays; and meanwhile the secret influence – as to which she was still so completely in the dark – would continue to work against her, and she would have to renew the struggle day after day till they started on their journey. But after that everything would be different. If once she could get her husband away under other skies, and all to herself, she never doubted her power to release him from the evil spell he was under. Lulled to quiet by the thought, she too slept at last.

When she woke, it was long past her usual hour, and she sat up in bed surprised and vexed at having overslept herself. She always liked to be down to share her husband's breakfast by the library fire; but a glance at the clock made it clear that he must have started long since for his office. To make sure, she jumped out of bed and went into his room, but it was empty. No doubt he had looked in on her before leaving, seen that she still slept, and gone downstairs without disturbing her; and their relations were sufficiently lover-like for her to regret having missed their morning hour.

She rang and asked if Mr. Ashby had already gone. Yes, nearly an hour ago, the maid said. He had given orders that Mrs. Ashby should not be waked and that the children should not come to her till she sent for them… Yes, he had gone up to the nursery himself to give the order. All this sounded usual enough, and Charlotte hardly knew why she asked: "And did Mr. Ashby leave no other message?"

Yes, the maid said, he did; she was so sorry she'd forgotten. He'd told her, just as he was leaving, to say to Mrs. Ashby that he was going to see about their passages, and would she please be ready to sail tomorrow?

Charlotte echoed the woman's "Tomorrow", and sat staring at her incredulously. "Tomorrow – you're sure he said to sail tomorrow?"

"Oh, ever so sure, ma'am. I don't know how I could have forgotten to mention it."

"Well, it doesn't matter. Draw my bath, please." Charlotte sprang up, dashed through her dressing, and caught herself singing at her image in the glass as she sat brushing her hair. It made her feel young again to have scored such a victory. The other woman vanished to a speck on the horizon, as this one, who ruled the foreground, smiled back at the reflection of her lips and eyes. He loved her, then – he loved her as passionately as ever. He had divined what she had suffered, had understood that their happiness depended on their getting away at once, and finding each other again after yesterday's desperate groping in the fog. The nature of the influence that had come between them did not much matter to Charlotte now; she had faced the phantom and dispelled it. "Courage – that's the secret! If only people who are in love weren't always so afraid of risking their happiness by looking it in the eyes." As she brushed back her light abundant hair it waved electrically above her head, like the palms of victory. Ah, well, some women knew how to manage men, and some didn't – and only the fair – she gaily paraphrased – deserve the brave! Certainly she was looking very pretty.

The morning danced along like a cockleshell on a bright sea – such a sea as they would soon be speeding over. She ordered a particularly good dinner, saw the children off to their classes, had her trunks brought down, consulted with the maid about getting out summer clothes – for of course they would be heading for heat and sunshine – and wondered if she oughtn't to take Kenneth's flannel suits out of camphor. "But how absurd," she reflected, "that I don't yet know where we're going!" She looked at the clock, saw that it was close on noon, and decided to call him up at his office. There was a slight delay; then she heard his secretary's voice saying that Mr. Ashby had looked in for a moment early, and left again almost immediately… Oh, very well; Charlotte would ring up later. How soon was he likely to be back? The secretary answered that she couldn't tell; all they knew in the office was that when he left he had said he was in a hurry because he had to go out of town.

Out of town! Charlotte hung up the receiver and sat blankly gazing into new darkness. Why had he gone out of town? And where had he gone? And of all days, why should he have chosen the eve of their suddenly planned departure? She felt a faint shiver of apprehension. Of course he had gone to see that woman – no doubt to get her permission to leave. He was as completely in bondage as that; and Charlotte had been fatuous enough to see the palms of victory on her forehead. She burst into a laugh and, walking across the room, sat down again before her mirror. What a different face she saw! The smile on her pale lips seemed to mock the rosy vision of the other Charlotte. But gradually her color crept back. After all, she had a right to claim the victory, since her husband was doing what she wanted, not what the other woman exacted of him. It was natural enough, in view of his abrupt decision to leave the next day, that he should have arrangements to make, business matters to wind up; it was not even necessary to suppose that his mysterious trip was a visit to the writer of the letters. He might simply have gone to see a client who lived out of town. Of course they would not tell Charlotte at the office; the secretary had hesitated before imparting even such meager information as the fact of Mr. Ashby's absence. Meanwhile she would go on with her joyful preparations, content to learn later in the day to what particular island of the blest she was to be carried.

The hours wore on, or rather were swept forward on a rush of eager preparations. At last the entrance of the maid who came to draw the curtains roused Charlotte from her labors, and she saw to her surprise that the clock marked five. And she did not yet know where they were going the next day! She rang up her husband's office and was told that Mr. Ashby had not been there since the early morning. She asked for his partner, but the partner could add nothing to her information, for he himself, his suburban train having been behind time, had reached the office after Ashby had come and gone. Charlotte stood perplexed; then she decided to telephone to her mother-in-law. Of course Kenneth, on the eve of a month's absence, must have gone to see his mother. The mere fact that the children – in spite of his vague objections – would certainly have to be left with old Mrs. Ashby, made it obvious that he would have all sorts of matters to decide with her. At another time Charlotte might have felt a little hurt at being excluded from their conference, but nothing mattered now but that she had won the day, that her husband was still hers and not another woman's. Gaily she called up Mrs. Ashby, heard her friendly voice, and began: "Well, did Kenneth's news surprise you? What do you think of our elopement?"

Almost instantly, before Mrs. Ashby could answer, Charlotte knew what her reply would be. Mrs. Ashby had not seen her son, she had had no word from him and did not know what her daughter-in-law meant. Charlotte stood silent in the intensity of her surprise. "But then, where *has* he been?" she thought. Then, recovering herself, she explained their sudden decision to Mrs. Ashby, and in doing so, gradually regained her own self-confidence, her conviction that nothing could ever again come between Kenneth and herself. Mrs. Ashby took the news calmly and approvingly. She, too, had thought that Kenneth looked worried and overtired, and she agreed with her daughter-in-law that in such cases change was the surest remedy. "I'm always so glad when he gets away. Elsie hated traveling; she was always finding pretexts to prevent his going anywhere. With you, thank goodness, it's different." Nor was Mrs. Ashby surprised at his not having had time to let her know of his departure. He must have been in a rush from the moment the decision was taken; but no doubt he'd drop in before dinner. Five minutes' talk was really all they needed. "I hope you'll gradually cure Kenneth of his mania for going over and over a question that could be settled in a dozen words. He never used to be like that, and if he carried the habit into his professional work he'd soon lose all his clients... Yes, do come in for a minute, dear, if you have time; no doubt he'll turn up while you're here." The tonic ring of Mrs. Ashby's voice echoed on reassuringly in the silent room while Charlotte continued her preparations.

Toward seven the telephone rang, and she darted to it. Now she would know! But it was only from the conscientious secretary, to say that Mr. Ashby hadn't been back, or sent any word, and before the office closed she thought she ought to let Mrs. Ashby know. "Oh, that's all right. Thanks a lot!" Charlotte called out cheerfully, and hung up the receiver with a trembling hand. But perhaps by this time, she reflected, he was at his mother's. She shut her drawers and cupboards, put on her hat and coat and called up to the nursery that she was going out for a minute to see the children's grandmother.

Mrs. Ashby lived nearby, and during her brief walk through the cold spring dusk Charlotte imagined that every advancing figure was her husband's. But she did not meet him on the way, and when she entered the house she found her mother-in-law alone. Kenneth had neither telephoned nor come. Old Mrs. Ashby sat by her bright fire, her knitting needles flashing steadily through her active old hands, and her mere bodily presence gave reassurance to Charlotte. Yes, it was certainly odd that Kenneth had gone off for the whole day without letting any of them know; but, after all, it was to be expected. A busy lawyer held so many threads in his hands that any sudden change of plan would oblige him to make all sorts of unforeseen arrangements and adjustments. He might have gone to see some client in the suburbs and been detained there; his mother remembered his telling her that he had charge of the legal business of a queer old recluse somewhere in New Jersey, who was immensely rich but too mean to have a telephone. Very likely Kenneth had been stranded there.

But Charlotte felt her nervousness gaining on her. When Mrs. Ashby asked her at what hour they were sailing the next day and she had to say she didn't know – that Kenneth had simply sent her word he was going to take their passages – the uttering of the words again brought home to her the strangeness of the situation. Even Mrs. Ashby conceded that it was odd; but she immediately added that it only showed what a rush he was in.

"But, mother, it's nearly eight o'clock! He must realize that I've got to know when we're starting tomorrow."

"Oh, the boat probably doesn't sail till evening. Sometimes they have to wait till midnight for the tide. Kenneth's probably counting on that. After all, he has a level head."

Charlotte stood up. "It's not that. Something has happened to him."

Mrs. Ashby took off her spectacles and rolled up her knitting. "If you begin to let yourself imagine things—"

"Aren't you in the least anxious?"

"I never am till I have to be. I wish you'd ring for dinner, my dear. You'll stay and dine? He's sure to drop in here on his way home."

Charlotte called up her own house. No, the maid said, Mr. Ashby hadn't come in and hadn't telephoned. She would tell him as soon as he came that Mrs. Ashby was dining at his mother's. Charlotte followed her mother-in-law into the dining room and sat with parched throat before her empty plate, while Mrs. Ashby dealt calmly and efficiently with a short but carefully prepared repast. "You'd better eat something, child, or you'll be as bad as Kenneth... Yes, a little more asparagus, please, Jane."

She insisted on Charlotte's drinking a glass of sherry and nibbling a bit of toast; then they returned to the drawing room, where the fire had been made up, and the cushions in Mrs. Ashby's armchair shaken out and smoothed. How safe and familiar it all looked; and out there, somewhere in the uncertainty and mystery of the night, lurked the answer to the two women's conjectures, like an indistinguishable figure prowling on the threshold.

At last Charlotte got up and said: "I'd better go back. At this hour Kenneth will certainly go straight home."

Mrs. Ashby smiled indulgently. "It's not very late, my dear. It doesn't take two sparrows long to dine."

"It's after nine." Charlotte bent down to kiss her. "The fact is, I can't keep still."

Mrs. Ashby pushed aside her work and rested her two hands on the arms of her chair. "I'm going with you," she said, helping herself up.

Charlotte protested that it was too late, that it was not necessary, that she would call up as soon as Kenneth came in, but Mrs. Ashby had already rung for her maid. She was slightly lame, and stood resting on her stick while her wraps were brought. "If Mr. Kenneth turns up, tell him he'll find me at his own house," she instructed the maid as the two women got into the taxi which had been summoned. During the short drive Charlotte gave thanks that she was not returning home alone. There was something warm and substantial in the mere fact of Mrs. Ashby's nearness, something that corresponded with the clearness of her eyes and the texture of her fresh firm complexion. As the taxi drew up she laid her hand encouragingly on Charlotte's. "You'll see; there'll be a message."

The door opened at Charlotte's ring and the two entered. Charlotte's heart beat excitedly; the stimulus of her mother-in-law's confidence was beginning to flow through her veins.

"You'll see – you'll see," Mrs. Ashby repeated.

The maid who opened the door said no, Mr. Ashby had not come in, and there had been no message from him.

"You're sure the telephone's not out of order?" his mother suggested; and the maid said, well, it certainly wasn't half an hour ago; but she'd just go and ring up to make sure. She disappeared, and Charlotte turned to take off her hat and cloak. As she did so her eyes lit on the hall table, and there lay a gray envelope, her husband's name faintly traced on it. "Oh!" she cried out, suddenly aware that for the first time in months she had entered her house without wondering if one of the gray letters would be there.

"What is it, my dear?" Mrs. Ashby asked with a glance of surprise.

Charlotte did not answer. She took up the envelope and stood staring at it as if she could force her gaze to penetrate to what was within. Then an idea occurred to her. She turned and held out the envelope to her mother-in-law.

"Do you know that writing?" she asked.

Mrs. Ashby took the letter. She had to feel with her other hand for her eyeglasses, and when she had adjusted them she lifted the envelope to the light. "Why!" she exclaimed; and then stopped. Charlotte noticed that the letter shook in her usually firm hand. "But this is addressed to Kenneth,"

Mrs. Ashby said at length, in a low voice. Her tone seemed to imply that she felt her daughter-in-law's question to be slightly indiscreet.

"Yes, but no matter," Charlotte spoke with sudden decision. "I want to know – do you know the writing?"

Mrs. Ashby handed back the letter. "No," she said distinctly.

The two women had turned into the library. Charlotte switched on the electric light and shut the door. She still held the envelope in her hand.

"I'm going to open it," she announced.

She caught her mother-in-law's startled glance. "But, dearest – a letter not addressed to you? My dear, you can't!"

"As if I cared about that – now!" She continued to look intently at Mrs. Ashby. "This letter may tell me where Kenneth is."

Mrs. Ashby's glossy bloom was effaced by a quick pallor; her firm cheeks seemed to shrink and wither. "Why should it? What makes you believe – It can't possibly—"

Charlotte held her eyes steadily on that altered face. "Ah, then you *do* know the writing?" she flashed back.

"Know the writing? How should I? With all my son's correspondents… What I do know is—" Mrs. Ashby broke off and looked at her daughter-in-law entreatingly, almost timidly.

Charlotte caught her by the wrist. "Mother! What do you know? Tell me! You must!"

"That I don't believe any good ever came of a woman's opening her husband's letters behind his back."

The words sounded to Charlotte's irritated ears as flat as a phrase culled from a book of moral axioms. She laughed impatiently and dropped her mother-in-law's wrist. "Is that all? No good can come of this letter, opened or unopened. I know that well enough. But whatever ill comes, I mean to find out what's in it." Her hands had been trembling as they held the envelope, but now they grew firm, and her voice also. She still gazed intently at Mrs. Ashby. "This is the ninth letter addressed in the same hand that has come for Kenneth since we've been married. Always these same gray envelopes. I've kept count of them because after each one he has been like a man who has had some dreadful shock. It takes him hours to shake off their effect. I've told him so. I've told him I must know from whom they come, because I can see they're killing him. He won't answer my questions; he says he can't tell me anything about the letters; but last night he promised to go away with me – to get away from them."

Mrs. Ashby, with shaking steps, had gone to one of the armchairs and sat down in it, her head drooping forward on her breast. "Ah," she murmured.

"So now you understand—"

"Did he tell you it was to get away from them?"

"He said, to get away – to get away. He was sobbing so that he could hardly speak. But I told him I knew that was why."

"And what did he say?"

"He took me in his arms and said he'd go wherever I wanted."

"Ah, thank God!" said Mrs. Ashby. There was a silence, during which she continued to sit with bowed head, and eyes averted from her daughter-in-law. At last she looked up and spoke. "Are you sure there have been as many as nine?"

"Perfectly. This is the ninth. I've kept count."

"And he has absolutely refused to explain?"

"Absolutely."

Mrs. Ashby spoke through pale contracted lips. "When did they begin to come? Do you remember?"

Charlotte laughed again. "Remember? The first one came the night we got back from our honeymoon."

"All that time?" Mrs. Ashby lifted her head and spoke with sudden energy. "Then – yes, open it."

The words were so unexpected that Charlotte felt the blood in her temples, and her hands began to tremble again. She tried to slip her finger under the flap of the envelope, but it was so tightly stuck that she had to hunt on her husband's writing table for his ivory letter opener. As she pushed about the familiar objects his own hands had so lately touched, they sent through her the icy chill emanating from the little personal effects of someone newly dead. In the deep silence of the room the tearing of the paper as she slit the envelope sounded like a human cry. She drew out the sheet and carried it to the lamp.

"Well?" Mrs. Ashby asked below her breath.

Charlotte did not move or answer. She was bending over the page with wrinkled brows, holding it nearer and nearer to the light. Her sight must be blurred, or else dazzled by the reflection of the lamplight on the smooth surface of the paper, for, strain her eyes as she would, she could discern only a few faint strokes, so faint and faltering as to be nearly undecipherable.

"I can't make it out," she said.

"What do you mean, dear?"

"The writing's too indistinct… Wait."

She went back to the table and, sitting down close to Kenneth's reading lamp, slipped the letter under a magnifying glass. All this time she was aware that her mother-in-law was watching her intently.

"Well?" Mrs. Ashby breathed.

"Well, it's no clearer. I can't read it."

"You mean the paper is an absolute blank?"

"No, not quite. There is writing on it. I can make out something like 'mine' – oh, and 'come'. It might be 'come'."

Mrs. Ashby stood up abruptly. Her face was even paler than before. She advanced to the table and, resting her two hands on it, drew a deep breath. "Let me see," she said, as if forcing herself to a hateful effort.

Charlotte felt the contagion of her whiteness. "She knows," she thought. She pushed the letter across the table. Her mother-in-law lowered her head over it in silence, but without touching it with her pale wrinkled hands.

Charlotte stood watching her as she herself, when she had tried to read the letter, had been watched by Mrs. Ashby. The latter fumbled for her glasses, held them to her eyes, and bent still closer to the outspread page, in order, as it seemed, to avoid touching it. The light of the lamp fell directly on her old face, and Charlotte reflected what depths of the unknown may lurk under the clearest and most candid lineaments. She had never seen her mother-in-law's features express any but simple and sound emotions – cordiality, amusement, a kindly sympathy; now and again a flash of wholesome anger. Now they seemed to wear a look of fear and hatred, of incredulous dismay and almost cringing defiance. It was as if the spirits warring within her had distorted her face to their own likeness. At length she raised her head. "I can't – I can't," she said in a voice of childish distress.

"You can't make it out either?"

She shook her head, and Charlotte saw two tears roll down her cheeks.

"Familiar as the writing is to you?" Charlotte insisted with twitching lips.

Mrs. Ashby did not take up the challenge. "I can make out nothing – nothing."

"But you do know the writing?"

Mrs. Ashby lifted her head timidly; her anxious eyes stole with a glance of apprehension around the quiet familiar room. "How can I tell? I was startled at first…"

"Startled by the resemblance?"

"Well, I thought—"

"You'd better say it out, mother! You knew at once it was *her* writing?"

"Oh, wait, my dear – wait."

"Wait for what?"

Mrs. Ashby looked up; her eyes, traveling slowly past Charlotte, were lifted to the blank wall behind her son's writing table.

Charlotte, following the glance, burst into a shrill laugh of accusation. "I needn't wait any longer! You've answered me now! You're looking straight at the wall where her picture used to hang!"

Mrs. Ashby lifted her hand with a murmur of warning. "Sh-h."

"Oh, you needn't imagine that anything can ever frighten me again!" Charlotte cried.

Her mother-in-law still leaned against the table. Her lips moved plaintively. "But we're going mad – we're both going mad. We both know such things are impossible."

Her daughter-in-law looked at her with a pitying stare. "I've known for a long time now that everything was possible."

"Even this?"

"Yes, exactly this."

"But this letter – after all, there's nothing in this letter—"

"Perhaps there would be to him. How can I tell? I remember his saying to me once that if you were used to a handwriting the faintest stroke of it became legible. Now I see what he meant. He *was* used to it."

"But the few strokes that I can make out are so pale. No one could possibly read that letter."

Charlotte laughed again. "I suppose everything's pale about a ghost," she said stridently.

"Oh, my child – my child – don't say it!"

"Why shouldn't I say it, when even the bare walls cry it out? What difference does it make if her letters are illegible to you and me? If even you can see her face on that blank wall, why shouldn't he read her writing on this blank paper? Don't you see that she's everywhere in this house, and the closer to him because to everyone else she's become invisible?" Charlotte dropped into a chair and covered her face with her hands. A turmoil of sobbing shook her from head to foot. At length a touch on her shoulder made her look up, and she saw her mother-in-law bending over her. Mrs. Ashby's face seemed to have grown still smaller and more wasted, but it had resumed its usual quiet look. Through all her tossing anguish, Charlotte felt the impact of that resolute spirit.

"Tomorrow – tomorrow. You'll see. There'll be some explanation tomorrow."

Charlotte cut her short. "An explanation? Who's going to give it, I wonder?"

Mrs. Ashby drew back and straightened herself heroically. "Kenneth himself will," she cried out in a strong voice. Charlotte said nothing, and the old woman went on: "But meanwhile we must act; we must notify the police. Now, without a moment's delay. We must do everything – everything."

Charlotte stood up slowly and stiffly; her joints felt as cramped as an old woman's. "Exactly as if we thought it could do any good to do anything?"

Resolutely Mrs. Ashby cried: "Yes!" and Charlotte went up to the telephone and unhooked the receiver.

Biographies & Sources

S. Baring-Gould
A Dead Finger
(Originally Published in *A Book of Ghosts*, 1904)
The Devon-born clergyman S. Baring Gould (1834–1924) is most famous as author of the hymn 'Onward Christian Soldiers' (1865). (Arthur 'Gilbert &' Sullivan wrote the famous tune.) But, along with more ambitious religious works, including a sixteen-volume study of *The Lives of the Saints* (1872–77), Baring-Gould was a keen collector of folk songs. His folkloric interests inspired a major work on *Curious Myths of the Middle Ages* (1866–68) and a *Book of Werewolves* (1865). It's no surprise, then, that his short stories should so often have taken a supernatural or macabre theme: *A Book of Ghosts* appeared in 1904.

A.C. Benson
Out of the Sea
(Originally Published in *The Isles of Sunset*, 1904)
Very much a child of the Establishment, Arthur Christopher Benson (1862–1925) was literally born at Berkshire's Wellington College, where his father – a future Archbishop of Canterbury – was headmaster. Benson himself was later to teach at Eton and ultimately to be Master of Magdalene College, Cambridge. Notoriously, he wrote the words to Elgar's patriotic anthem 'Land of Hope and Glory', though (like the composer) he came to question this contribution after seeing so many former students slaughtered in the First World War. Such misgivings only underlined the melancholy (possibly bipolar) streak which tormented him – exacerbated by his struggles with his sexuality.

E.F. Benson
The Face
(Originally Published in *Hutchinson's Magazine*, 1924)
The Step
(Originally Published in *Windsor Magazine*, 1926)
Edward Frederic ('E.F.') Benson (1867–1940) was born at Wellington College in Berkshire, England, where his father, the future Archbishop of Canterbury Edward White Benson, was headmaster. Benson is widely known for being a writer of reminiscences, fiction, satirical novels, biographies and autobiographical studies. His first published novel, *Dodo*, initiated his success, followed by a series of comic novels such as *Queen Lucia* and *Trouble for Lucia*. Later in life, Benson moved to Rye where he was elected mayor. It was here that he was inspired to write several macabre ghost story and supernatural collections and novels, including *Paying Guests* and *Mrs. Ames*.

Ambrose Bierce
The Secret of Macarger's Gulch
(Originally Published in *The Wave*, 1891)
Ambrose Bierce (1842–*c*. 1914) was born in Meigs County, Ohio. He was a famous journalist and author known for writing *The Devil's Dictionary*. After fighting in the American Civil War, Bierce

used his combat experience to write stories based on the war, such as in 'An Occurrence at Owl Creek Bridge'. Following the separate deaths of his ex-wife and two of his three children he gained a sardonic view of human nature and earned the name 'Bitter Bierce'. His disappearance at the age of seventy-one on a trip to Mexico remains a great mystery and continues to spark speculation.

Die Booth

Of Water

(Originally Published in *Unfading Daydream: Issue 7*, 2019)

Die Booth likes wild beaches and exploring dark places. When not writing, he DJs at Chester's best (and only) goth club. You can read his stories in places like *LampLight Magazine*, *The Fiction Desk* and *The Cheshire Prize for Literature* anthologies. His books *My Glass is Runn*, *365 Lies* (profits go to the MNDA) and *Spirit Houses* are available online and *Making Friends (and Other Fictions)* is due out soon. He's currently working on a collection of spooky stories featuring transgender protagonists. You can find out more about his writing at diebooth.wordpress.com or say hi on Twitter @diebooth.

Mary Elizabeth Braddon

Eveline's Visitant

(Originally Published in *Belgravia*, 1867)

Mary Elizabeth Braddon (1835–1915) was born in London, England. During her lifetime, Braddon was a productive writer, producing over eighty novels. Her most notable novel, *Lady Audley's Secret* (1862), brought Braddon much recognition and fortune. In addition to her tales of intrigue, Braddon wrote a number of works on the supernatural, including, *Gerard, or, the World, the Flesh and the Devil*, 'The Cold Embrace' and 'At Chrighton Abbey'. Beyond her literary endeavours, Braddon founded the magazine *Belgravia* (1866), showcasing the latest serialized sensation novels, poems and travel narratives alongside essays on fashion, history and science.

Nancy Brewka-Clark

The Rebus

(First Publication)

Nancy Brewka-Clark's poems, short stories, drama, and nonfiction have appeared in periodicals and anthologies published by Red Hen Press, University of Iowa Press, Southeast Missouri State University Press, Smith and Kraus, YouthPLAYS of Los Angeles, and Routledge U.K. among others. Her poetry collection *Beautiful Corpus* is available at Kelsay Books and Amazon. She lives on the northern coast of Boston, Massachusetts with her husband Tom, who is a direct descendant of Susanna Martin, hanged as a witch in Salem in 1692.

Ramsey Campbell

Passing Through Peacehaven

(Originally Published in *Portents*, 2011)

The Oxford Companion to English Literature describes Ramsey Campbell as 'Britain's most respected living horror writer'. He has been given more awards than any other writer in the field, including the Grand Master Award of the World Horror Convention, the Lifetime Achievement Award of the Horror Writers Association, the Living Legend Award of the International Horror Guild and the World Fantasy Lifetime Achievement Award. In 2015 he was made an Honorary

Fellow of Liverpool John Moores University for outstanding services to literature. Among his novels available from Flame Tree Press are *Thirteen Days by Sunset Beach*, *Think Yourself Lucky*, *The Wise Friend*, and *The Searching Dead*, the first volume of his trilogy *The Three Births of Daoloth.*

Bernard Capes
William Tyrwhitt's 'Copy'
(Originally Published in *At a Winter's Fire*, 1899)
Bernard Capes (1854–1918) was born in London, England, and was one of eleven children. He was a very prolific writer and published over forty books, including romances, ghost stories, poetry, and history. He won a prize offered by the Chicago Record in 1898 for his story *The Lake of Wine*. He died in 1918 during the Spanish flu epidemic and a memorial plaque was placed in Winchester Cathedral (where he lived for his last years).

Dan Coxon
Ones and Zeros
(Originally Published in *The Ghastling: Issue 10*, 2019)
Dan Coxon is an editor and writer based in London, UK. His fiction has appeared in *Black Static*, *Nightscript*, *Unsung Stories*, *Not One of Us*, *Humanagerie* and Bram Stoker Award nominated anthology *Nox Pareidolia*, among others. His anthology *This Dreaming Isle* was shortlisted for both a Shirley Jackson Award and a British Fantasy Award. His non-fiction has appeared everywhere from *Salon* to *The Guardian*, and a collection of his short fiction, *Only the Broken Remain*, was published by Black Shuck Books in November 2020.

Ralph Adams Cram
In Kropfsberg Keep
(Originally Published in *Black Spirits and White: A Book of Ghost Stories*, 1895)
Ralph Adams Cram (1863–1942) was born in Hampton Falls, New Hampshire, United States. He wrote a number of fiction stories and was praised by H.P. Lovecraft for his horror. In addition to his work as a writer, Cram was also one of the foremost architects of the Gothic revival in the United States. His influence helped to establish Gothic as the standard style of the period for American college and university buildings.

Dick Donovan
The Corpse Light
(Originally Collected in *Tales of Terror*, 1899)
Dick Donovan (1843–1934) was the pseudonym of J.E. Preston Muddock. Born near Southampton, England, Muddock became a journalist and travelled the globe. 'Dick Donovan' was the name of his fictional Glasgow detective – a character who so rivalled the popularity of Sherlock Holmes that Muddock later chose Donovan as his own pen name. This technique of using a fictional detective as a pseudonym was used later by Ellery Queen and Nick Carter. He was incredibly prolific in crime and horror genres in particular, and some suggest that the origin of the term 'Dick' to mean an American private detective may be linked back to him.

Arthur Conan Doyle
The Captain of the Polestar
(Originally Published in *Temple Bar*, 1883)

Arthur Conan Doyle (1859–1930) was born in Edinburgh, Scotland. As a medical student Doyle was so impressed by his professor's powers of deduction that he was inspired to create the illustrious and much-loved figure Sherlock Holmes. However, he became increasingly interested in spiritualism and the supernatural, leaving him keen to explore fantastical elements in his stories. Doyle's vibrant and remarkable characters have breathed life into all of his stories, engaging readers throughout the decades.

Amelia B. Edwards
The Phantom Coach
(Originally Published in *All the Year Round*, 1864)
Amelia B. Edwards (1831–92) was born in London, England. Enjoying a rich and varied career as a writer, journalist and Egyptologist, Edwards was a precocious talent, as her first poem was published when she was only seven years old. Her most successful works included the short story 'The Phantom Coach' – one of her many ghost stories, and the novels *Barbara's History* and *Lord Brackenbury*, alongside her Egyptian travelogue *A Thousand Miles up the Nile*, which detailed her extensive 1873–74 voyage through the country.

Clare Frances Elliott
Foreword: Terrifying Ghosts Short Stories
Clare Frances Elliott is Senior Lecturer in English Literature at Northumbria University, Newcastle upon Tyne, and she has published widely on transatlantic connections in literature of the long nineteenth century. Clare has taught gothic literature at several institutions, including ghost stories that range from nineteenth-century gothic writing by Sheridan Le Fanu, through to Toni Morrison's magic-realist novel *Beloved* (1987) in which a ghost is the titular character. Clare's favourite ghost story to date is Sarah Waters's spooky novel, *The Little Stranger* (2009).

Felix Flynn
Flannery House
(First Publication)
Felix is a lifelong writer and lover of horror. Raised in the hellious heat of south Georgia, he has moved to central Illinois with his fiancée to enjoy proper winters and try avoiding frostbite. His works can be found on podcasts like *The No-Sleep Podcast* and *Monsters Out of the Closet*. In print, he has been published in a number of anthologies, most notably *The Third Corona Book of Horror Stories*, *Wickedly Abled*, and *Black Rainbow Vol. 1*. He spends his free time playing video games, petting his cats, or scrolling endlessly through social media.

Robert Ford
Georgie
(Originally Published in *Shroud: Issue 10*, 2010)
Robert Ford has written the novels *Burner*, and *The Compound*. He also has a collection of his short fiction *The God Beneath My Garden*, and a novella collection, *Inner Demons*. He collaborated, with John Boden, on the novellas *Rattlesnake Kisses*, *Cattywampus*, and *Black Salve*, in the *Knucklebucket Thang* series. Robert lives in Central Pennsylvania, and is usually hard at work on at least two projects at a time. You can find out more about his upcoming releases at robertfordauthor.com.

Lettice Galbraith
A Ghost's Revenge
(Originally Published in *New Ghost Stories*, 1893)
Lettice Galbraith (fl. 1893–97) might have been a ghost herself, so unobtrusively did she flit on to the fin-de-siècle supernatural scene; so untraceably did she slip away once she was done. Nothing is known of her life before or after. In between, however, she contributed some of the period's most memorable stories of the supernatural – not just 'The Ghost's Revenge' but 'The Empty Picture Frame', 'The Case of Sir Nigel Otterburne', 'The Trainer's Ghost' and 'The Séance Room'.

Lyndsay E. Gilbert
I Exist
(First Publication)
Lyndsay E. Gilbert is a hopeful YA author from Northern Ireland. She lives by an ancient castle looking out to sea. Her interests are reading, writing, science fiction and fantasy, horror, music, playing the fiddle, movies, fairy tales, cats, dogs and the ancient art of belly dance. Lyndsay has a few stories published in anthologies such as *Steampunk Universe*, *Fae Visions of the Mediterranean* and the up-and-coming *Trouble the Waters*. She is currently working on a horror novel about post-apocalyptic witches and can be found writing terrible poetry and procrastinating on Instagram @lyndsayegilbert.

Lisa L. Hannett
Consorting with Filth
(Originally Published in *Blurring the Line*, 2015)
Lisa L. Hannett has had over seventy-five short stories appear in venues including *Clarkesworld*, *Fantasy*, *Weird Tales*, *Apex*, *The Dark* and *Year's Best* anthologies in Australia, Canada and the US. She has won four Aurealis Awards, including Best Collection for her first book, *Bluegrass Symphony*, which was also nominated for a World Fantasy Award. Her new collection, *Songs for Dark Seasons*, is out now. You can find her online at lisahannett.com and on Instagram @LisaLHannett.

Sarah Hans
The Cold Earth
(Originally Published in *Familiar Spirits*, 2015)
Sarah Hans is an award-winning writer, editor, and teacher whose stories have appeared in more than thirty publications, including *The Arcanist* and *Pseudopod*. Her first dark fantasy novel, *Entomophobia*, will be published in Winter 2021 by Omnium Gatherum. You can read more of Sarah's short stories in the collection *Dead Girls Don't Love*, published by Dragon's Roost Press, or by backing her Patreon for just $1. You can also find her on Twitter under the handle @steampunkpanda.

Lafcadio Hearn
The Story of Mimi-Nashi-Hōïchi
(Originally Published in *The Atlantic Monthly*, 1903)
Yuki-Onna
(Originally Published in *Kwaidan: Stories and Studies of Strange Things*, 1904)
Lafcadio Hearn (1850–1904) was a writer and translator best known in the English-speaking world for the works he wrote (as Koizumi Yakumo) on Japan, the adoptive homeland in which

he spent the last years of his life. He'd previously lived in Ireland, the United States and the French West Indies, and was born in Lefkada, in the Ionian Islands, to an Irish father and Greek mother. The distinguished translator of modern French classics by Gautier, Flaubert, Zola and Maupassant, he was a literary force in his own right, with a longstanding interest in the supernatural.

Sean Hogan
My True Love Gave to Me
(First Publication)
Sean Hogan is a writer and filmmaker based in Margate. He has published two acclaimed books of metafictional film criticism: *England's Screaming* (named one of the five best SFF books of 2020 by *The Financial Times*) and *Three Mothers, One Father*, as well as a monograph on the cult film *Death Line*. His feature film credits include *The Devil's Business*, *Future Shock! The Story of 2000AD*, and *The Borderlands*. In collaboration with Kim Newman, he co-created the anthology plays *The Hallowe'en Sessions* and *The Ghost Train Doesn't Stop Here Anymore*, and directed both their West End runs.

W.W. Jacobs
Jerry Bundler
(Originally Published in *Windsor Magazine*, 1897–98)
William Wymark ('W.W.') Jacobs (1863–1943) was born in London, England, and he is known for his deeply humorous and horrifying works. Drawing upon his childhood experiences, Jacobs wrote many works reflecting on his father's profession as a dockhand and wharf manager. His first volume of stories, *Many Cargoes*, was a great success and gave Jacobs the courage to publish other stories such as 'The Monkey's Paw' and 'The Toll-House'. Jacobs used realistic experiences as well as a combination of superstition, terror, exotic adventure and humour in each one of his famous tales.

Henry James
The Turn of the Screw
(Originally Published in *Collier's Weekly*, 1898)
Henry James (1843–1916) was born in New York City, though spent a lot of time in England, with the dynamic between Europe and America playing a key role in his novels. Writing a massive amount of literary works throughout his lifetime, he published over a hundred tales, twenty novels, sixteen plays and various other autobiographies and literary criticisms. Each work is filled with characters of great social complexity as most of his works reflect his own complicated perspectives and satirical personality. James's works include *Daisy Miller*, *The Ambassadors*, *The Golden Bowl* and *The Portrait of a Lady*. James strongly believed novels had to be a recognizable representation of the realistic truth as well as filled with imaginative action.

M.R. James
Oh, Whistle, and I'll Come to You, My Lad
(Originally Published in *Ghost Stories of an Antiquary*, 1904)
The Ash Tree
(Originally Published in *Ghost Stories of an Antiquary*, 1904)
Montague Rhodes James (1862–1936), whose works are regarded as being at the forefront of the ghost story genre, was born in Kent, England. James dispensed with the traditional,

predictable techniques of ghost story construction, instead using realistic contemporary settings for his works. He was also a British medieval scholar, so his stories tended to incorporate antiquarian elements. His stories often reflect his childhood in Suffolk and his talented acting career, which both seem to have assisted in the build-up of tension and horror in his works.

O.R. Kennett
A Soap Opera for One
(First Publication)
O.R. Kennett is an English horror and fantasy writer. His work has been compared with that of Iain Banks, Kurt Vonnegut Jr. and Roald Dahl. Oliver regularly does live readings of his darkly humorous short stories and is highly active in the creative scene of his home town of Bristol. Oliver is working on a short story collection as well as his first novel. Discover more at ORKennett.com, or find him on Twitter @OliverKennett, talking writing, blindness, frustrations with technology and other such nonsense.

John Kiste
An Inverted Haunting
(First Publication)
John Kiste is a horror writer who was previously the president of the Stark County Convention & Visitors' Bureau and a Massillon Museum board member. He is a McKinley Museum planetarian and an Edgar Allan Poe impersonator who has been published in *Third Flatiron*, *With Painted Words*, *A Shadow of Autumn*, *Modern Grimoire*, *Dark Fire Fiction*, *Six Guns Straight from Hell 3*, *Theme of Absence*, *The Dark Sire*, Jolly Horror Press's *Coffin Blossoms* anthology. His work was also included in Unnerving Press's *Haunted Are These Houses*, and Camden Press's anthology *Quoth the Raven*.

Spencer Koelle
On Bricks and Bronze
(First Publication)
Spencer Koelle worships Pagan Idols in a Philadelphia row house with a classic murder-basement. He looks up to Garth Nix, M.R. James, Stephen King, Neil Gaiman, and various Doctor Who creators. His other work can be found in *Coppice & Brake*, *Night Terrors Volume 3*, *Dark Moon Digest 27*, and *Monsters Out of the Closet Episode 34*. He tries to create the representation he would like to see in speculative fiction. His website is spencerkoelle.com, his Twitter handle is @KoelleSpencer, and his neuroses are multifarious.

Jessica Landry
Floating Ghosts
(Originally Published in *Fantasmagoriana: Volume Two*, 2019)
Bram Stoker Award winner Jessica Landry's fiction has appeared in several anthologies, including *Tales of the Lost*, *Twice-Told: A Collection of Doubles*, *Monsters of Any Kind*, *Lost Highways*, and *Fantastic Tales of Terror*, among others. Her debut collection, *The Mother Wound*, is set for release in 2021. Jessica's debut feature, *My Only Sunshine*, was accepted into Whistler Film Festival's Screenwriters Lab for the 2020 season and is currently in development. She has several produced scripts, including four Movies of the Week. She's currently writing for a sitcom and has other projects in various stages of development.

Joseph Sheridan Le Fanu

Schalken the Painter

(Originally Published in *Dublin University Magazine*, 1839, revised 1851)

The remarkable father of Victorian ghost stories Joseph Thomas Sheridan Le Fanu (1814–73) was born in Dublin, Ireland. His gothic tales and mystery novels led to him become a leading ghost story writer of the nineteenth century. Three oft-cited works of his are *Uncle Silas*, *Carmilla* and *The House by the Churchyard*, which all are assumed to have influenced Bram Stoker's *Dracula*. Le Fanu wrote his most successful and productive works after his wife's tragic death and he remained a relatively strong writer up until his own death.

Fiona Macleod

Green Branches

(Originally Published in *The Sin-Eater and Other Tales*, 1895)

William Sharp (1855–1905), the author behind the pen name Fiona Macleod, was born in prosaic Paisley and worked mundanely as a London bank clerk before he fell in with the poet-painter Dante Gabriel Rossetti (1828–82), the poet Algernon Charles Swinburne (1837–1909) and their decadent circle. So 'Fiona Macleod' wasn't so much a pseudonym as a separate persona through which he could lead a second more romantic, more aesthetic life. It was to be expected that she would join W.B. Yeats (1865–1939) in starting up his Celtic Revival in the 1890s. Sadly, Fiona went down much better with fellow-poets than William did.

J.A.W. McCarthy

We Were Supposed to Be Happy

(Originally Published in *She's Lost Control*, 2019)

J.A.W. McCarthy's short fiction has appeared or is forthcoming in numerous publications, including *LampLight*, *Apparition Lit*, *Places We Fear to Tread* (Cemetery Gates Media), *Tales to Terrify*, and *Nightscript V*. She lives with her husband and assistant cats in the Pacific Northwest, where she gets all her ideas late at night, while she's trying to sleep. You can call her Jen on Twitter and Instagram @JAWMcCarthy, and find out more at jawmccarthy.com.

Marshall J. Moore

Fudakaeshi

(First Publication)

Marshall J. Moore is a writer, filmmaker, and martial artist who was born and raised in Kwajalein, a tiny Pacific Island. He has travelled to thirty countries, sold a thousand dollars' worth of teapots to Jackie Chan, and was once tracked down by a bounty hunter for owing $300 in late fees to the Los Angeles Public Library. He lives in Atlanta, Georgia, with his wife Megan and their two cats.

Joe Nazare

Theater Crowd

(First Publication)

Joe Nazare's fiction, poetry, and nonfiction has appeared in such places as Flame Tree's *American Gothic Short Stories*, *Pseudopod*, *Clowns: The Unlikely Coulrophobia Remix*, *Dark Discoveries*, *The Lovecraft eZine*, *The Zombie Feed: Vol. 1*, *Star*Line*, *Grievous Angel*, and *Butcher Knives & Body Counts: Essays on the Formula, Frights, & Fun of the Slasher Film*. He is also the author of the collection *Autumn Lauds: Poems for the Halloween*

Season and *The Legend of Sleepy Hollow: Ultimate Annotated Edition*. Dispatches from the Macabre Republic, his blog devoted to American Gothic in literature and culture, is posted at joenazare.com.

Edith Nesbit
The Portent of the Shadow
(Originally Published in *Black and White*, 1905)
Edith Nesbit (1858–1924) was born in Kennington, England. Nesbit established herself as a successful author and poet, writing a variety of literature ranging from children's books to adult horror stories. She co-founded the Fabian Society and was also a strong political activist. Marrying young and frequently moving home, Nesbit made many friendships with other writers including H.G. Wells and George Bernard Shaw. Although she gained most of her success from her children's books, like the ever-popular *The Railway Children* (1906), she was also a well-known horror writer. Nesbit wrote four collections of ghost stories: *Something Wrong* (1893), *Grim Tales* (1893), *Tales Told in the Twilight* (1897), and *Fear* (1910).

Michael Nethercott
They Walk and Weep
(First Publication)
Michael Nethercott is the author of two suspense novels, *The Séance Society* and *The Haunting Ballad* (St. Martin's Press) He is the winner of several prose and playwriting awards, and his short fiction has appeared in numerous periodicals and anthologies including *Alfred Hitchcock Mystery Magazine*, *Best Crime and Mystery Stories of the Year*, and *The Magazine of Fantasy and Science Fiction*. He hails from an extensive Irish-American family rich with true ghost stories. He lives in Vermont.

Adam L.G. Nevill
Enlivened
(Originally Published *in Wyrd and Other Derelictions*, 2020)
Adam L.G. Nevill was born in Birmingham, England, in 1969 and grew up in England and New Zealand. He is the author of nine horror novels. Of these *The Ritual*, *Last Days* and *No One Gets Out Alive* were the winners of The August Derleth Award for Best Horror Novel and in 2016 Imaginarium adapted *The Ritual* into a feature film. He has also published three collections of short stories, with *Some Will Not Sleep* winning the British Fantasy Award for Best Collection, 2017. The author lives in Devon. More information about his books is available at adamlgnevill.com.

Fitz-James O'Brien
What Was It? A Mystery
(Originally Published in *Harper's Magazine*, 1859)
Born in County Cork in Ireland, Fitz-James O'Brien (*c.* 1828–62) was an Irish-American poet and writer deeply involved in the genre of Gothic fiction and an early writer in the science fiction movement. He was the son of a lawyer and first worked in London as a journalist before moving to New York City to begin writing. Amongst his most famous short stories are 'The Wondersmith' and 'The Diamond Lens'. O'Brien died after being wounded in the American Civil War, and H.P. Lovecraft said that O'Brien's tragically young death 'undoubtedly deprived us of some masterful tales of strangeness and terror'.

Edgar Allan Poe
Metzengerstein: A Tale in Imitation of the German
(Originally Published in *Philadelphia's Saturday Courier*, 1832)
The versatile writer Edgar Allan Poe (1809–49) was born in Boston, Massachusetts. He is well known as an influential author, poet, editor and literary critic who wrote during the American Romantic Movement. Poe is generally considered the inventor of the detective fiction genre, and his works are famously filled with terror, mystery, death and hauntings. Some of his better-known works include his poems 'The Raven' and 'Annabel Lee', and the short stories 'The Tell Tale Heart' and 'The Fall of the House of Usher'. The dark, mystifying characters of his tales have captured the public's imagination and reflect the struggling, poverty-stricken lifestyle he lived his whole life.

May Sinclair
The Victim
(Originally Published in *The Criterion*, 1922)
May Sinclair's (1863–1946) first fame was as a 'bluestocking': a literary critic and novelist of note, she was also prominent in the fight for women's suffrage. But her place among the intellectual aristocracy was hard-won. Born in Rock Ferry, Wirral, the daughter of a Liverpool shipowner, she had to move south with her family when his business failed. He fell into alcoholism and died soon after, leaving May struggling to support her sickly family, despite the fragility of her own health. Her writings on the supernatural show her working out atavistic anxieties against the unsettling insights of modern psychology and science.

Michelle Tang
The Sounds of a Bamboo Forest
(First Publication)
Michelle Tang was born in the Philippines and now writes speculative fiction from Canada, where she lives with her partner and two children. Her short stories have been published in several anthologies, including *Night Terrors*, and *Once Upon an Enchanted Forest*. 'The Sounds of a Bamboo Forest' was inspired by photos of her mother's trip to Japan. When Michelle isn't writing or working as an oncology nurse, she spends her time reading movie spoilers, watching horror movies from between her fingers, and lurking on Twitter (@a_girl_Michelle).

Jeffrey Thomas
Praying That You Feel Better Soon
(Originally Published in *Frontiers of Terror*, 2002)
Jeffrey Thomas is the author of such novels as *The American* (JournalStone), *Deadstock* (Solaris Books), and *Blue War* (Solaris Books), and short story collections such as *Punktown* (Prime Books), *The Unnamed Country* (Word Horde), and *Haunted Worlds* (Hippocampus Press). His stories have been reprinted in *The Year's Best Horror Stories XXII* (editor, Karl Edward Wagner), *The Year's Best Fantasy and Horror #14* (editors, Ellen Datlow and Terri Windling), and *Year's Best Weird Fiction #1* (editors, Laird Barron and Michael Kelly). Thomas lives in Massachusetts.

Hugh Walpole
Mrs. Lunt
(Originally Published in *The Ghost Book: Sixteen New Stories of the Uncanny*, 1926)
Sir Hugh Walpole (1884–1941) was born in Auckland, New Zealand. He was incredibly popular and successful during his lifetime. As well as writing many novel and short stories, Walpole also

conducted lecture tours of North America, and was invited to Hollywood to write scenarios for *David Copperfield* and *Little Lord Fauntleroy*. Walpole's reputation and popularity suffered after his death. Recently there has been a re-emergence in interest for the author.

H.G. Wells
The Moth
(Originally Published in *Pall Mall Gazette*, 1895)
Herbert George Wells (1866–1946) was born in Kent, England. Novelist, journalist, social reformer and historian, Wells is one of the greatest ever science fiction writers and, along with Jules Verne, is sometimes referred to as a 'founding father' of the genre. With Aldous Huxley and, later, George Orwell, he defined the adventurous, social concern of early speculative fiction where the human condition was played out on a greater stage. Wells created over fifty novels, including his famous works *The Time Machine*, *The Invisible Man*, *The Island of Dr. Moreau* and *The War of the Worlds*, as well as a fantastic array of gothic short stories.

Edith Wharton
Pomegranate Seed
(Originally Published in *Saturday Evening Post*, 1931)
Edith Wharton (1862–1937), the Pulitzer Prize-winning writer of *The Age of Innocence*, was born in New York. As well as her talent as an American novelist, Wharton was also known for her short stories and designer career. Wharton was born into a controlled New York society where women were discouraged from achieving anything beyond a proper marriage. Defeating the norms, Wharton grew to become one of America's greatest writers. Writing numerous ghost stories and murderous tales such as 'Kerfol', 'Mr. Jones' and 'Afterward', Wharton is widely known for the ghost tours that now take place at her old home, The Mount.

FLAME TREE PUBLISHING
Short Story Series

New & Classic Writing

Flame Tree's Gothic Fantasy books offer a carefully curated series of new titles, each with combinations of original and classic writing:

Chilling Horror • Chilling Ghost • Science Fiction • Murder Mayhem
Crime & Mystery • Swords & Steam • Dystopia Utopia • Supernatural Horror
Lost Worlds • Time Travel • Heroic Fantasy • Pirates & Ghosts • Agents & Spies
Endless Apocalypse • Alien Invasion • Robots & AI • Lost Souls • Haunted House
Cosy Crime • American Gothic • Urban Crime • Detective Mysteries
Epic Fantasy • Detective Thrillers • A Dying Planet • Footsteps in the Dark
Bodies in the Library • Strange Lands • Lovecraft Mythos • Black Sci-Fi

Also, new companion titles offer rich collections of classic fiction, myths and tales in the gothic fantasy tradition:

George Orwell: Visions of Dystopia • H.G. Wells • Lovecraft
Sherlock Holmes • Edgar Allan Poe • Bram Stoker • Mary Shelley
African Myths & Tales • Celtic Myths & Tales • Greek Myths & Tales
Norse Myths & Tales Chinese Myths & Tales • Japanese Myths & Tales
Irish Fairy Tales • Native American Myths & Tales • Heroes & Heroines Myths & Tales
Witches, Wizards, Seers & Healers Myths & Tales • Gods & Monsters Myths & Tales
Alice's Adventures in Wonderland • King Arthur & The Knights of the Round Table
The Divine Comedy • Hans Christian Andersen Fairy Tales • Brothers Grimm
The Wonderful Wizard of Oz • The Age of Queen Victoria

Available from all good bookstores, worldwide, and online at
flametreepublishing.com

See our new fiction imprint
FLAME TREE PRESS | FICTION WITHOUT FRONTIERS
New and original writing in Horror, Crime, SF and Fantasy

And join our monthly newsletter with offers and more stories:
FLAME TREE FICTION NEWSLETTER
flametreepress.com

GOTHIC FANTASY